J.K. ROWLING

1

英汉对照版

Harry Potter

哈利·波特与魔法石

〔英〕J.K. 罗琳 / 著

苏农 / 译

WIZARDING WORLD

人民文学出版社
PEOPLE'S LITERATURE PUBLISHING HOUSE

著作权合同登记号　图字　01-2024-1017

Harry Potter and the Philosopher's Stone
First published in Great Britain in 1997 by Bloomsbury Publishing Plc.
Text © 1997 by J.K. Rowling
Interior illustrations by Mary GrandPré © 1998 by Warner Bros.
Wizarding World, Publishing and Theatrical Rights © J.K.Rowling
Wizarding World characters, names and related indicia are TM and © Warner Bros.Entertainment Inc.
Wizarding World TM & © Warner Bros.Entertainment Inc.
Cover illustrations by Mary GrandPré © 1998 by Warner Bros.

图书在版编目（CIP）数据

哈利·波特与魔法石：英汉对照版/（英）J.K.罗琳著；苏农译．—北京：人民文学出版社，2018（2025.8重印）
ISBN 978-7-02-014352-8

Ⅰ.①哈…　Ⅱ.①J…②苏…　Ⅲ.①儿童小说—长篇小说—英国—现代—英、汉　Ⅳ.①I561.84

中国版本图书馆CIP数据核字（2018）第246411号

责任编辑	翟　灿
美术编辑	刘　静
责任印制	苏文强

出版发行	人民文学出版社
社　　址	北京市朝内大街166号
邮政编码	100705

印　刷	三河市龙林印务有限公司
经　销	全国新华书店等

字　数	692千字
开　本	640毫米×960毫米　1/16
印　张	28.75　插页3
印　数	485001—505000
版　次	2019年1月北京第1版
印　次	2025年8月第35次印刷

书　号	978-7-02-014352-8
定　价	55.00元

如有印装质量问题，请与本社图书销售中心调换。电话：010-59905336

For Jessica, who loves stories,
for Anne, who loved them too,
and for Di, who heard this one first.

谨以此书献给
杰西卡,她喜欢这故事
安妮,她也喜欢这故事
戴,她是故事的第一位听众

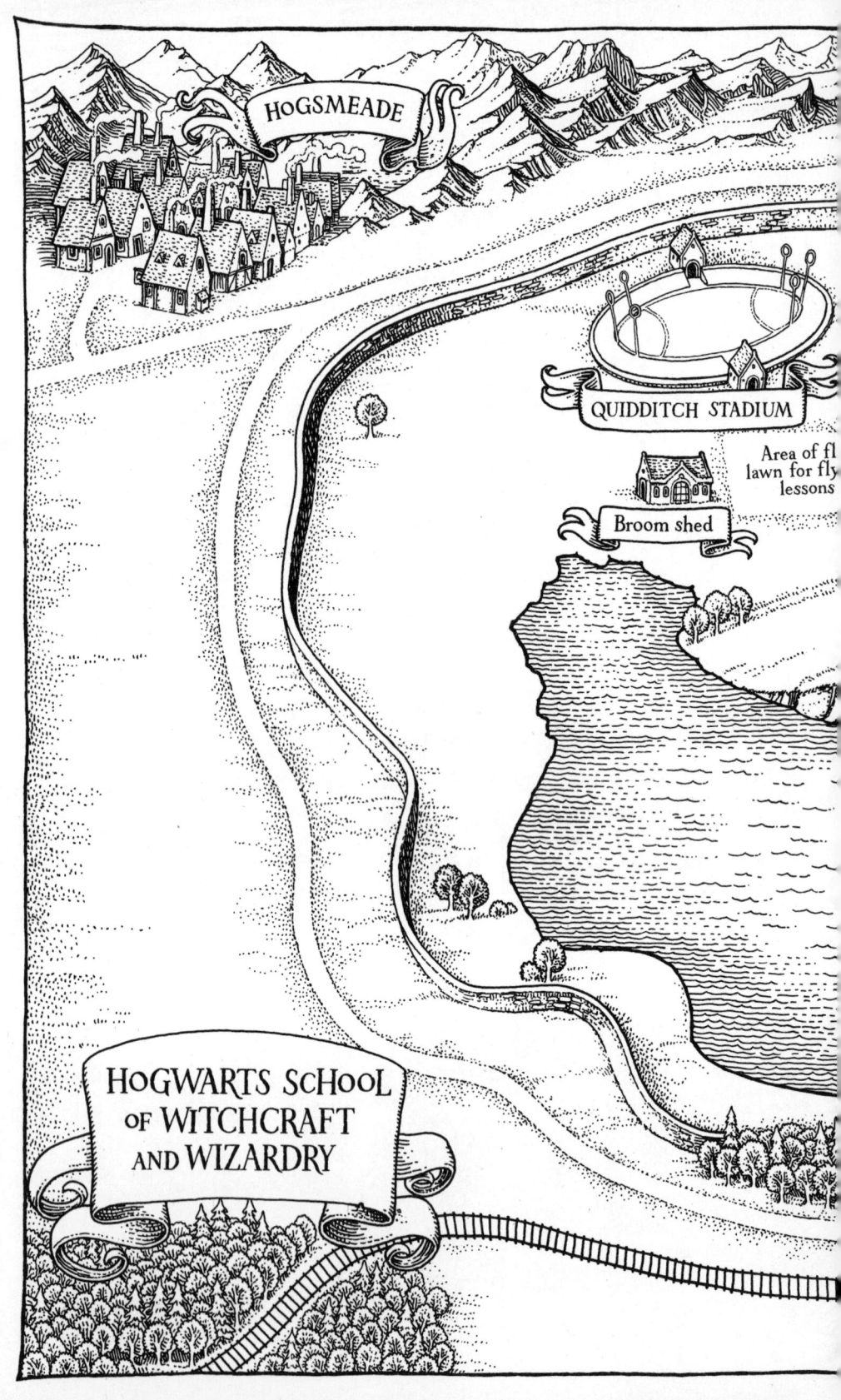

CONTENTS

CHAPTER ONE	The Boy Who Lived	006
CHAPTER TWO	The Vanishing Glass	030
CHAPTER THREE	The Letters from No One	048
CHAPTER FOUR	The Keeper of the Keys	070
CHAPTER FIVE	Diagon Alley	092
CHAPTER SIX	The Journey from Platform Nine and Three-Quarters	132
CHAPTER SEVEN	The Sorting Hat	168
CHAPTER EIGHT	The Potions Master	194
CHAPTER NINE	The Midnight Duel	212
CHAPTER TEN	Hallowe'en	242
CHAPTER ELEVEN	Quidditch	266
CHAPTER TWELVE	The Mirror of Erised	286
CHAPTER THIRTEEN	Nicolas Flamel	318
CHAPTER FOURTEEN	Norbert the Norwegian Ridgeback	338
CHAPTER FIFTEEN	The Forbidden Forest	358
CHAPTER SIXTEEN	Through the Trapdoor	386
CHAPTER SEVENTEEN	The Man with Two Faces	424

目 录

第 1 章	大难不死的男孩	007
第 2 章	悄悄消失的玻璃	031
第 3 章	猫头鹰传书	049
第 4 章	钥匙保管员	071
第 5 章	对角巷	093
第 6 章	从 $9\frac{3}{4}$ 站台开始的旅程	133
第 7 章	分院帽	169
第 8 章	魔药课老师	195
第 9 章	午夜决斗	213
第 10 章	万圣节前夕	243
第 11 章	魁地奇比赛	267
第 12 章	厄里斯魔镜	287
第 13 章	尼可·勒梅	319
第 14 章	挪威脊背龙——诺伯	339
第 15 章	禁林	359
第 16 章	穿越活板门	387
第 17 章	双面人	425

CHAPTER ONE

The Boy Who Lived

Mr and Mrs Dursley, of number four, Privet Drive, were proud to say that they were perfectly normal, thank you very much. They were the last people you'd expect to be involved in anything strange or mysterious, because they just didn't hold with such nonsense.

Mr Dursley was the director of a firm called Grunnings, which made drills. He was a big, beefy man with hardly any neck, although he did have a very large moustache. Mrs Dursley was thin and blonde and had nearly twice the usual amount of neck, which came in very useful as she spent so much of her time craning over garden fences, spying on the neighbours. The Dursleys had a small son called Dudley and in their opinion there was no finer boy anywhere.

The Dursleys had everything they wanted, but they also had a secret, and their greatest fear was that somebody would discover it. They didn't think they could bear it if anyone found out about the Potters. Mrs Potter was Mrs Dursley's sister, but they hadn't met for several years; in fact, Mrs Dursley pretended she didn't have a sister, because her sister and her good-for-nothing husband were as unDursleyish as it was possible to be. The Dursleys shuddered to think what the neighbours would say if the Potters arrived in the street. The Dursleys knew that the Potters had a small son, too, but they had never even seen him. This boy was another good reason for keeping the Potters away; they didn't want Dudley mixing with a child like that.

When Mr and Mrs Dursley woke up on the dull, grey Tuesday our story starts, there was nothing about the cloudy sky outside to suggest that strange and mysterious things would soon be happening all over the country. Mr Dursley hummed as he picked out his most boring tie for work and Mrs Dursley gossiped away happily as she wrestled a screaming Dudley into his

第 1 章

大难不死的男孩

家住女贞路 4 号的德思礼夫妇总是得意地说他们是非常规矩的人家,拜托,拜托了。他们跟神秘古怪的事从来不沾边,因为他们根本不相信那些邪门歪道。

弗农·德思礼先生在一家名叫格朗宁的公司做主管,公司生产钻机。他高大魁梧,胖得几乎连脖子都没有了,却蓄着一脸大胡子。德思礼太太是一个瘦削的金发女人。她的脖子几乎比正常人长一倍。这样每当她花许多时间隔着篱墙引颈而望、窥探左邻右舍时,她的长脖子可就派上了大用场。德思礼夫妇有一个小儿子,名叫达力。在他们看来,人世间没有比达力更好的孩子了。

德思礼一家什么都不缺,但他们拥有一个秘密,他们最害怕的就是这秘密会被人发现。他们想,一旦有人发现波特一家的事,他们会承受不住的。波特太太是德思礼太太的妹妹,不过姐妹俩已经有好几年不见面了。实际上,德思礼太太佯装自己根本没有这么个妹妹,因为她妹妹和她那一无是处的妹夫与德思礼一家的为人处世完全不一样。一想到邻居们会说波特夫妇来了,德思礼夫妇就会吓得胆战心惊。他们知道波特夫妇也有个儿子,只是他们从来没有见过。这孩子也是他们不与波特夫妇来往的一个很好的借口,他们不愿让达力跟这种孩子厮混。

我们的故事开始于一个晦暗、阴沉的星期二,德思礼夫妇一早醒来,窗外浓云低垂的天空并没有丝毫迹象预示全国各地都将发生神秘古怪的事情。德思礼先生哼着小曲,挑出一条最不讨人喜欢的领带戴着上班,德思礼太太高高兴兴,一直絮絮叨叨,把唧哇乱叫的达力塞到了儿童椅里。

CHAPTER ONE The Boy Who Lived

high chair.

None of them noticed a large tawny owl flutter past the window.

At half past eight, Mr Dursley picked up his briefcase, pecked Mrs Dursley on the cheek and tried to kiss Dudley goodbye but missed, because Dudley was now having a tantrum and throwing his cereal at the walls. 'Little tyke,' chortled Mr Dursley as he left the house. He got into his car and backed out of number four's drive.

It was on the corner of the street that he noticed the first sign of something peculiar – a cat reading a map. For a second, Mr Dursley didn't realise what he had seen – then he jerked his head around to look again. There was a tabby cat standing on the corner of Privet Drive, but there wasn't a map in sight. What could he have been thinking of? It must have been a trick of the light. Mr Dursley blinked and stared at the cat. It stared back. As Mr Dursley drove around the corner and up the road, he watched the cat in his mirror. It was now reading the sign that said *Privet Drive* – no, *looking* at the sign; cats couldn't read maps *or* signs. Mr Dursley gave himself a little shake and put the cat out of his mind. As he drove towards town he thought of nothing except a large order of drills he was hoping to get that day.

But on the edge of town, drills were driven out of his mind by something else. As he sat in the usual morning traffic jam, he couldn't help noticing that there seemed to be a lot of strangely dressed people about. People in cloaks. Mr Dursley couldn't bear people who dressed in funny clothes – the get-ups you saw on young people! He supposed this was some stupid new fashion. He drummed his fingers on the steering wheel and his eyes fell on a huddle of these weirdos standing quite close by. They were whispering excitedly together. Mr Dursley was enraged to see that a couple of them weren't young at all; why, that man had to be older than he was, and wearing an emerald-green cloak! The nerve of him! But then it struck Mr Dursley that this was probably some silly stunt – these people were obviously collecting for something ... Yes, that would be it. The traffic moved on, and a few minutes later, Mr Dursley arrived in the Grunnings car park, his mind back on drills.

Mr Dursley always sat with his back to the window in his office on the ninth floor. If he hadn't, he might have found it harder to concentrate on drills that morning. *He* didn't see the owls swooping past in broad daylight, though people down in the street did; they pointed and gazed open-mouthed

第 1 章 大难不死的男孩

他们谁也没留意一只黄褐色的猫头鹰扑扇着翅膀从窗前飞过。

八点半,德思礼先生拿起公文包,在德思礼太太面颊上亲了一下,正要亲达力,跟这个小家伙道别,可是没有亲成,小家伙正在发脾气,把麦片往墙上摔。"臭小子。"德思礼先生嘟哝了一句,咯咯笑着走出家门,坐进汽车,倒出4号车道。

在街角上,他看到了第一个异常的信号——一只猫正在看地图。一开始,德思礼先生没明白他看到了什么,于是又回过头去。只见一只花斑猫正站在女贞路街角,但是并没有看见地图。他到底在想些什么?很可能是光线使他产生了错觉吧。德思礼先生眨了眨眼,盯着猫看,猫也回瞪着他。当德思礼先生拐过街角继续上路的时候,他从后视镜里看了看那只猫。猫这时正在读女贞路的标牌,不,是在看标牌;猫是不会看地图或是读标牌的。德思礼先生定了定神,把猫从脑海里赶走了。他开车进城,一路上想的是希望今天能得到一大批钻机的订单。

但快进城时,另一件事又把钻机从他脑海里赶走了。当他的车汇入清晨拥堵的车流时,他不禁注意到路边有一群穿着奇装异服的人。他们都披着斗篷。德思礼先生最看不惯别人穿得怪模怪样,瞧年轻人的那身打扮!他猜想这大概又是一种无聊的新时尚吧。他用手指敲击着方向盘,目光落到了离他最近的一大群怪物身上。他们正兴致勃勃,交头接耳。德思礼先生很生气,因为他发现他们中间有一对根本不是年轻人了,那个男的显得比他年龄还大,竟然还披着一件翡翠绿的斗篷!真不知羞耻!接着,德思礼先生突然想到这些人大概是在为什么事募捐吧,不错,就是这么回事。车流再次开始移动了,几分钟后,德思礼先生来到格朗宁公司的停车场,他的思绪又回到了钻机上。

德思礼先生在他十楼的办公室里,总是习惯背窗而坐。如果不是这样,他可能会发现这一天早上更难把思想集中到钻机的事情上了。他没有看见成群的猫头鹰在光天化日之下从天上飞过,可街上的人都看到了;他们目瞪口呆,指指点点,盯着猫头鹰一只接一只从头顶上掠过。他们大多数人甚至在夜里都从没见过猫头鹰。不过,德思礼先

CHAPTER ONE   The Boy Who Lived

as owl after owl sped overhead. Most of them had never seen an owl even at night-time. Mr Dursley, however, had a perfectly normal, owl-free morning. He yelled at five different people. He made several important telephone calls and shouted a bit more. He was in a very good mood until lunchtime, when he thought he'd stretch his legs and walk across the road to buy himself a bun from the baker's opposite.

He'd forgotten all about the people in cloaks until he passed a group of them next to the baker's. He eyed them angrily as he passed. He didn't know why, but they made him uneasy. This lot were whispering excitedly, too, and he couldn't see a single collecting tin. It was on his way back past them, clutching a large doughnut in a bag, that he caught a few words of what they were saying.

'The Potters, that's right, that's what I heard –'

'– yes, their son, Harry –'

Mr Dursley stopped dead. Fear flooded him. He looked back at the whisperers as if he wanted to say something to them, but thought better of it.

He dashed back across the road, hurried up to his office, snapped at his secretary not to disturb him, seized his telephone and had almost finished dialling his home number when he changed his mind. He put the receiver back down and stroked his moustache, thinking ... no, he was being stupid. Potter wasn't such an unusual name. He was sure there were lots of people called Potter who had a son called Harry. Come to think of it, he wasn't even sure his nephew *was* called Harry. He'd never even seen the boy. It might have been Harvey. Or Harold. There was no point in worrying Mrs Dursley, she always got so upset at any mention of her sister. He didn't blame her – if *he'd* had a sister like that ... but all the same, those people in cloaks ...

He found it a lot harder to concentrate on drills that afternoon, and when he left the building at five o'clock, he was still so worried that he walked straight into someone just outside the door.

'Sorry,' he grunted, as the tiny old man stumbled and almost fell. It was a few seconds before Mr Dursley realised that the man was wearing a violet cloak. He didn't seem at all upset at being almost knocked to the ground. On the contrary, his face split into a wide smile and he said in a squeaky voice that made passers-by stare: 'Don't be sorry, my dear sir, for nothing could upset me today! Rejoice, for You-Know-Who has gone at last! Even Muggles

生这一天上午过得很正常,没有受到猫头鹰的干扰。他先后对五个人大喊大叫,又打了几个重要的电话,喊的声音更响。他的情绪很好,到吃午饭的时候,他想舒展一下筋骨,便到马路对角的面包房去买一只小甜圆面包。

若不是他在面包房附近又碰到那群披斗篷的人,他早就把他们忘了。他经过他们身边时,狠狠地瞪了他们一眼。他说不清这是为什么,只是觉得这些人让他心里别扭。这些人正喊喊喳喳,讲得起劲,但他连一只募捐箱也没有看见。当他拎着装在袋里的一只炸面圈往回走,经过他们身边时,他们的话断断续续飘入他的耳鼓:

"波特夫妇,不错,我正是听说——"

"——没错,他们的儿子,哈利——"

他突然停下脚步,恐惧万分。他回头朝窃窃私语的人群看了一眼,似乎想对他们说点什么,后来又改变了主意。

他冲到马路对面,回到办公室,厉声吩咐秘书不要打扰他,然后抓起话筒,刚要拨通家里的电话,临时又变了卦。他放下话筒,摸着胡须,琢磨起来……不,他太愚蠢了。波特并不是一个稀有的姓,肯定有许多人姓波特,而且有儿子叫哈利。想到这里,他甚至连自己的外甥是不是叫哈利都拿不准了。这孩子他甚至连见都没见过。说不定叫哈维,或者叫哈罗德。没有必要让太太烦心,只要一提起她妹妹,她总是心烦意乱。他并不责怪她——要是他自己有一个那样的妹妹呢……可不管怎么说,这群披斗篷的人……

那天下午,他发现自己很难集中注意力去考虑钻机的事。五点钟,他走出办公室大楼时,依旧心事重重,与站在门口的一个人撞了个满怀。

这个小老头打了个趔趄,差一点儿摔倒。"对不起。"德思礼先生咕哝说。过了几秒钟,他才发现这人披了一件紫罗兰色斗篷。他几乎被撞倒在地,可似乎一点儿也不生气,脸上反而绽出灿烂的笑容。"您不用道歉,尊贵的先生,因为今天没有事会惹我生气!太高兴了,因为'神秘人'总算走了!就连像你这种麻瓜,也应该好好庆贺这大喜大庆的日子!"他说话的声音尖细刺耳,令过往的人侧目。

CHAPTER ONE The Boy Who Lived

like yourself should be celebrating, this happy, happy day!'

And the old man hugged Mr Dursley around the middle and walked off.

Mr Dursley stood rooted to the spot. He had been hugged by a complete stranger. He also thought he had been called a Muggle, whatever that was. He was rattled. He hurried to his car and set off home, hoping he was imagining things, which he had never hoped before, because he didn't approve of imagination.

As he pulled into the driveway of number four, the first thing he saw – and it didn't improve his mood – was the tabby cat he'd spotted that morning. It was now sitting on his garden wall. He was sure it was the same one; it had the same markings around its eyes.

'Shoo!' said Mr Dursley loudly.

The cat didn't move. It just gave him a stern look. Was this normal cat behaviour, Mr Dursley wondered. Trying to pull himself together, he let himself into the house. He was still determined not to mention anything to his wife.

Mrs Dursley had had a nice, normal day. She told him over dinner all about Mrs Next Door's problems with her daughter and how Dudley had learnt a new word ('Shan't!'). Mr Dursley tried to act normally. When Dudley had been put to bed, he went into the living-room in time to catch the last report on the evening news:

'And finally, bird-watchers everywhere have reported that the nation's owls have been behaving very unusually today. Although owls normally hunt at night and are hardly ever seen in daylight, there have been hundreds of sightings of these birds flying in every direction since sunrise. Experts are unable to explain why the owls have suddenly changed their sleeping pattern.' The news reader allowed himself a grin. 'Most mysterious. And now, over to Jim McGuffin with the weather. Going to be any more showers of owls tonight, Jim?'

'Well, Ted,' said the weatherman, 'I don't know about that, but it's not only the owls that have been acting oddly today. Viewers as far apart as Kent, Yorkshire and Dundee have been phoning in to tell me that instead of the rain I promised yesterday, they've had a downpour of shooting stars! Perhaps people have been celebrating Bonfire Night early – it's not until next week, folks! But I can promise a wet night tonight.'

第1章 大难不死的男孩

老头说完，搂了搂德思礼先生的腰，就走开了。

德思礼先生站在原地一动不动，仿佛生了根。他刚刚被一个完全陌生的人搂过。他还想到自己被称作"麻瓜"，不知是什么意思。他心乱如麻，连忙朝自己的汽车跑过去，开车回家。他希望这一切只是幻想出来的景象，尽管他从来没有幻想过什么，因为他根本不赞同这种行为。

当他驶入4号车道时，第一个映入眼帘的就是早上他见过的那只花斑猫，这并没有使他的心情有任何好转。这时猫正坐在他家花园的院墙上。他敢肯定这只猫和早上的是同一只：眼睛周围的纹路一模一样。

"去……去！"德思礼先生大声喝道。

猫纹丝不动，只是狠狠地瞪了他一眼。这难道是一只正常的猫的行为吗？德思礼先生感到怀疑。他先让自己镇定下来，随后就进屋去了。他仍决定对太太只字不提。

德思礼太太这一天过得很好，一切正常。晚饭桌上，德思礼太太向丈夫讲述了邻居家的母女矛盾，还说达力又学会了一个新词（"决不"），德思礼先生也尽量表现得正常。安顿达力睡下之后，他来到起居室，听到晚间新闻的最后一段报道：

"最后，据各地鸟类观察者反映，今天全国猫头鹰表现反常。通常情况下，它们都是在夜间捕食，白天很少露面，可是今天，日出时猫头鹰就四处纷飞。专家们也无法解释猫头鹰为什么改变了它们的睡眠习惯。"新闻播音员说到这里，咧嘴一笑，"真是太奇妙了。现在我把话筒交给吉姆·麦古，问问他天气情况如何。吉姆，今天夜里还会下猫头鹰雨吗？"

"噢，泰德，"气象播音员说，"这我可不知道，今天不仅猫头鹰表现反常。全国各地，远至肯特郡、约克郡、丹地等地的目击者都纷纷打来电话说，我们原来预报昨天有雨，结果下的不是雨而是流星！也许人们把本该一星期后举行的庆祝篝火之夜晚会提前举行了，朋友们！不过我向你们保证，今晚一定有雨。"

德思礼先生坐在扶手椅上惊呆了。英国普遍下流星雨？猫头鹰光天

CHAPTER ONE The Boy Who Lived

Mr Dursley sat frozen in his armchair. Shooting stars all over Britain? Owls flying by daylight? Mysterious people in cloaks all over the place? And a whisper, a whisper about the Potters ...

Mrs Dursley came into the living-room carrying two cups of tea. It was no good. He'd have to say something to her. He cleared his throat nervously. 'Er – Petunia, dear – you haven't heard from your sister lately, have you?'

As he had expected, Mrs Dursley looked shocked and angry. After all, they normally pretended she didn't have a sister.

'No,' she said sharply. 'Why?'

'Funny stuff on the news,' Mr Dursley mumbled. 'Owls ... shooting stars ... and there were a lot of funny-looking people in town today ...'

'*So?*' snapped Mrs Dursley.

'Well, I just thought ... maybe ... it was something to do with ... you know ... *her lot.*'

Mrs Dursley sipped her tea through pursed lips. Mr Dursley wondered whether he dared tell her he'd heard the name 'Potter'. He decided he didn't dare. Instead he said, as casually as he could, 'Their son – he'd be about Dudley's age now, wouldn't he?'

'I suppose so,' said Mrs Dursley stiffly.

'What's his name again? Howard, isn't it?'

'Harry. Nasty, common name, if you ask me.'

'Oh, yes,' said Mr Dursley, his heart sinking horribly. 'Yes, I quite agree.'

He didn't say another word on the subject as they went upstairs to bed. While Mrs Dursley was in the bathroom, Mr Dursley crept to the bedroom window and peered down into the front garden. The cat was still there. It was staring down Privet Drive as though it was waiting for something.

Was he imagining things? Could all this have anything to do with the Potters? If it did ... if it got out that they were related to a pair of – well, he didn't think he could bear it.

The Dursleys got into bed. Mrs Dursley fell asleep quickly but Mr Dursley lay awake, turning it all over in his mind. His last, comforting thought before he fell asleep was that even if the Potters *were* involved, there was no reason for them to come near him and Mrs Dursley. The Potters knew very well what he and Petunia thought about them and their kind ... He couldn't see how he and Petunia could get mixed up in anything that might be going on.

化日之下四处纷飞？到处都是披着斗篷的怪人？还有一些传闻，关于波特一家的传闻……

德思礼太太端着两杯茶来到起居室。情况不妙。他应该向妻子透露一些。他心神不定，清了清嗓子。"唔——佩妮，亲爱的——最近有你妹妹的消息吗？"

不出所料，德思礼太太大为吃惊，也很生气。不管怎么说，他们通常都说自己没有这么个妹妹。

"没有，"她厉声说，"怎么了？"

"今天的新闻有点奇怪，"德思礼先生嘟哝说，"成群的猫头鹰……流星雨……今天城里又有那么多怪模怪样的人……"

"那又怎么样？"德思礼太太急赤白脸地说。

"哦，我是想……说不定……这跟……你知道……她那一伙人有关系……"

德思礼太太噘起嘴唇呷了一口茶。德思礼先生不知道自己是不是该大胆地把听到"波特"名字的事告诉她。他决定还是不要太冒失。于是他尽量漫不经心地改口说："他们的儿子——现在该有达力这么大了吧？"

"我想是吧。"德思礼太太干巴巴地说。

"他叫什么来着？是叫霍华德吧？"

"叫哈利，要我说，这是一个不讨人喜欢的普通名字。"

"哦，是的。"德思礼先生说着，感到心突然往下一沉，"不错，我也这么想。"

他们上楼睡觉时，他就再也没有提到这个话题了。德思礼太太进浴室以后，德思礼先生就轻手轻脚来到卧室窗前，看着前面的花园。那只猫还在原地，正目不转睛地盯着女贞路的街角，好像在等待什么。

他是在想入非非吗？这一切会与波特一家有关吗？如果真有关系——如果最后真跟他们夫妇有关——那么，他认为他是承受不住的。

德思礼夫妇睡下了。德思礼太太很快就睡着了，德思礼先生却思绪万千，怎么也睡不着觉。不过在他入睡前，最后一个想法使他感到安慰：即使波特一家真的被卷了进去，也没有理由牵连他和他太太。波特夫妇

CHAPTER ONE The Boy Who Lived

He yawned and turned over. It couldn't affect *them* ...

How very wrong he was.

Mr Dursley might have been drifting into an uneasy sleep, but the cat on the wall outside was showing no sign of sleepiness. It was sitting as still as a statue, its eyes fixed unblinkingly on the far corner of Privet Drive. It didn't so much as quiver when a car door slammed in the next street, nor when two owls swooped overhead. In fact, it was nearly midnight before the cat moved at all.

A man appeared on the corner the cat had been watching, appeared so suddenly and silently you'd have thought he'd just popped out of the ground. The cat's tail twitched and its eyes narrowed.

Nothing like this man had ever been seen in Privet Drive. He was tall, thin and very old, judging by the silver of his hair and beard, which were both long enough to tuck into his belt. He was wearing long robes, a purple cloak which swept the ground and high-heeled, buckled boots. His blue eyes were light, bright and sparkling behind half-moon spectacles and his nose was very long and crooked, as though it had been broken at least twice. This man's name was Albus Dumbledore.

Albus Dumbledore didn't seem to realise that he had just arrived in a street where everything from his name to his boots was unwelcome. He was busy rummaging in his cloak, looking for something. But he did seem to realise he was being watched, because he looked up suddenly at the cat, which was still staring at him from the other end of the street. For some reason, the sight of the cat seemed to amuse him. He chuckled and muttered, 'I should have known.'

He had found what he was looking for in his inside pocket. It seemed to be a silver cigarette lighter. He flicked it open, held it up in the air and clicked it. The nearest street lamp went out with a little pop. He clicked it again – the next lamp flickered into darkness. Twelve times he clicked the Put-Outer, until the only lights left in the whole street were two tiny pinpricks in the distance, which were the eyes of the cat watching him. If anyone looked out of their window now, even beady-eyed Mrs Dursley, they wouldn't be able to see anything that was happening down on the pavement. Dumbledore slipped the Put-Outer back inside his cloak and set off down the street towards number four, where he sat down on the wall next to the cat. He

很清楚德思礼夫妇对他们和他们那伙人的看法。他不觉得他和佩妮和任何可能正在发生的事有什么关系。他打了个哈欠，翻过身去。不会影响到他们的……

他可是大错特错了。

德思礼先生迷迷糊糊地陷入了并不安稳的梦乡，可花园墙头上那只猫却没有丝毫睡意。它卧在墙头上，宛如一座雕像，纹丝不动，目不转睛地盯着女贞路远处的街角。邻街的一辆汽车砰的一声关上车门，两只猫头鹰扑扇着从头顶上飞过，它也一动不动。实际上，快到午夜时，它才开始动了动。

猫一直眺望着的那个街角出现了一个男人，他来得那样突然，悄无声息，简直像是从地里冒出来的。猫尾巴抖动了一下，眼睛眯成了一条缝。

女贞路上从来没有出现过这个男人。他个子瘦高，银发和银须长到都能够塞到腰带里了，凭这一点就可以断定他年纪已经很大了。他穿着一件长袍，披着一件拖到地的紫色斗篷，蹬一双带搭扣的高跟靴子。半月形的眼镜后边一双湛蓝湛蓝的眼睛炯炯有神。他的鼻子很长，但是歪歪扭扭的，看起来至少断过两次。他的名字叫阿不思·邓布利多。

阿不思·邓布利多似乎并没有意识到从他的名字到他的靴子，在他来到的这条街上都不受欢迎。他忙着在斗篷口袋里翻寻，好像找什么东西。但是他似乎确实发现有人在监视他，因为他突然抬头看见一直在街那头注视着他的那只猫，出于某种原因，他觉得这只猫的样子很好笑。他咯咯笑着，咕哝说："我早就该想到了。"

他在里边衣袋里找出了他要找的东西，看起来像一只银质打火机。他把它轻轻弹开，高举起来，咔嗒一声，离得最近的一盏路灯噗的一声熄灭了。他又咔嗒了一下——第二盏灯也熄灭了。他用熄灯器咔嗒了十二次，整条街上只剩下远处两个小小的光点，那是监视他的那只猫的两只眼睛。如果这时有人向窗外看，即使是眼尖的德思礼太太，也不会看到马路上发生的一切。邓布利多把熄灯器放回斗篷里边的口袋里，顺着街道向4号走去。他在墙头猫的身边坐了下来。他没有看它，但过了一会儿便跟它说起话来。

"真没想到会在这里见到您，麦格教授。"

CHAPTER ONE   The Boy Who Lived

didn't look at it, but after a moment he spoke to it.

'Fancy seeing you here, Professor McGonagall.'

He turned to smile at the tabby, but it had gone. Instead he was smiling at a rather severe-looking woman who was wearing square glasses exactly the shape of the markings the cat had had around its eyes. She, too, was wearing a cloak, an emerald one. Her black hair was drawn into a tight bun. She looked distinctly ruffled.

'How did you know it was me?' she asked.

'My dear Professor, I've never seen a cat sit so stiffly.'

'You'd be stiff if you'd been sitting on a brick wall all day,' said Professor McGonagall.

'All day? When you could have been celebrating? I must have passed a dozen feasts and parties on my way here.'

Professor McGonagall sniffed angrily.

'Oh yes, everyone's celebrating, all right,' she said impatiently. 'You'd think they'd be a bit more careful, but no – even the Muggles have noticed something's going on. It was on their news.' She jerked her head back at the Dursleys' dark living-room window. 'I heard it. Flocks of owls ... shooting stars ... Well, they're not completely stupid. They were bound to notice something. Shooting stars down in Kent – I'll bet that was Dedalus Diggle. He never had much sense.'

'You can't blame them,' said Dumbledore gently. 'We've had precious little to celebrate for eleven years.'

'I know that,' said Professor McGonagall irritably. 'But that's no reason to lose our heads. People are being downright careless, out on the streets in broad daylight, not even dressed in Muggle clothes, swapping rumours.'

She threw a sharp, sideways glance at Dumbledore here, as though hoping he was going to tell her something, but he didn't, so she went on: 'A fine thing it would be if, on the very day You-Know-Who seems to have disappeared at last, the Muggles found out about us all. I suppose he really *has* gone, Dumbledore?'

'It certainly seems so,' said Dumbledore. 'We have much to be thankful for. Would you care for a sherbet lemon?'

'A *what?*'

'A sherbet lemon. They're a kind of Muggle sweet I'm rather fond of.'

第 1 章 大难不死的男孩

他回头朝花斑猫微微一笑。花斑猫不见了,换成一个神情严肃的女人,戴一副方形眼镜,看起来跟猫眼睛周围的纹路一模一样。她也披了一件翠绿色斗篷,乌黑的头发绾成一个很紧的发髻。她显得非常激动。

"您怎么认出那是我?"她问。

"我亲爱的教授,我从来没有见过一只猫会这样僵硬地待着。"

"您要是在砖墙上坐一整天,您也会变僵硬的。"麦格教授说。

"一整天?您本来应当参加庆祝会的呀?我一路来到这里,至少遇上了十二场欢快的聚会和庆祝活动。"

麦格教授气呼呼地哼了一声。

"哦,不错,人人都在庆贺,很好!"她恼火地说,"您以为他们会小心谨慎一些,其实不然,连麻瓜们都注意到发生了什么事情,都上他们的电视新闻了。"她猛地把头转向德思礼家漆黑的起居室窗口,"我都听见了。成群的猫头鹰……流星雨……好了,他们也不是十足的傻瓜,有些事也会引起他们的注意。肯特郡下的那场流星雨——我敢说准是德达洛·迪歌干的。他本来就没多少头脑。"

"您不能责怪他们,"邓布利多心平气和地说,"十一年来值得我们庆贺的事太少了。"

"这我知道,"麦格教授气呼呼地说,"但这些不是冒险胡来的理由。他们也太不小心了,大白天跑到街上,也不穿上麻瓜们的衣服,还在那里传递消息。"

说到这里,她机敏地朝邓布利多斜瞟了一眼,似乎希望他能告诉她些什么,但邓布利多没有吱声,于是她接着说:"如果正好在神秘人终于失踪的那一天,麻瓜们发现了我们的一切,那可真太奇妙了。我想他真的走了吧,邓布利多?"

"好像是这样,"邓布利多说,"我们应该感到欣慰。您来一块柠檬雪宝糖好吗?"

"一块什么?"

"一块柠檬雪宝糖。这是麻瓜们的一种甜点。我很喜欢。"

"不了,谢谢。"麦格教授冷冷地说,看来她认为现在不是吃柠檬雪宝糖的时候,"像我说的,即使神秘人真的走了——"

'No, thank you,' said Professor McGonagall coldly, as though she didn't think this was the moment for sherbet lemons. 'As I say, even if You-Know-Who *has* gone –'

'My dear Professor, surely a sensible person like yourself can call him by his name? All this "You-Know-Who" nonsense – for eleven years I have been trying to persuade people to call him by his proper name: *Voldemort*.' Professor McGonagall flinched, but Dumbledore, who was unsticking two sherbet lemons, seemed not to notice. 'It all gets so confusing if we keep saying "You-Know-Who". I have never seen any reason to be frightened of saying Voldemort's name.'

'I know you haven't,' said Professor McGonagall, sounding half-exasperated, half-admiring. 'But you're different. Everyone knows you're the only one You-Know – oh, all right, *Voldemort* – was frightened of.'

'You flatter me,' said Dumbledore calmly. 'Voldemort had powers I will never have.'

'Only because you're too – well – *noble* to use them.'

'It's lucky it's dark. I haven't blushed so much since Madam Pomfrey told me she liked my new earmuffs.'

Professor McGonagall shot a sharp look at Dumbledore and said, 'The owls are nothing to the *rumours* that are flying around. You know what everyone's saying? About why he's disappeared? About what finally stopped him?'

It seemed that Professor McGonagall had reached the point she was most anxious to discuss, the real reason she had been waiting on a cold hard wall all day, for neither as a cat nor as a woman had she fixed Dumbledore with such a piercing stare as she did now. It was plain that whatever 'everyone' was saying, she was not going to believe it until Dumbledore told her it was true. Dumbledore, however, was choosing another sherbet lemon and did not answer.

'What they're *saying*,' she pressed on, 'is that last night Voldemort turned up in Godric's Hollow. He went to find the Potters. The rumour is that Lily and James Potter are – are – that they're – *dead*.'

Dumbledore bowed his head. Professor McGonagall gasped.

'Lily and James ... I can't believe it ... I didn't want to believe it ... Oh, Albus ...'

Dumbledore reached out and patted her on the shoulder. 'I know ... I know ...' he said heavily.

第1章 大难不死的男孩

"我亲爱的教授,像您这样的明白人,总该可以直呼他的大名吧?什么'神秘人'不'神秘人'的,全都是瞎扯淡——十一年了,我一直想方设法说服大家,直呼他的本名:伏地魔,"麦格教授打了个寒战,可邓布利多在掰两块粘在一起的雪宝糖,似乎没有留意,"要是我们还继续叫神秘人神秘人的,一切就都乱套了。我看直呼伏地魔的大名也没有任何理由害怕。"

"我知道您不害怕,"麦格教授半是恼怒,半是夸赞地说,"尽人皆知,您与众不同。神秘人——哦,好吧,伏地魔——他唯一害怕的就是您。"

"您太抬举我了。"邓布利多平静地说,"伏地魔拥有我永远也不会有的功力。"

"那是因为您太——哦——太高尚了,不愿意运用它。"

"幸亏这里很黑,自打庞弗雷女士说她喜欢我的新耳套以后,我还没有像现在这样脸红过呢。"

麦格教授狠狠地瞪了邓布利多一眼,说:"跟沸沸扬扬的谣言比起来,猫头鹰已经不算什么了。您知道大伙都在说什么吗?说他为什么失踪。说最终是什么制止了他。"

这一来,麦格教授似乎点到了她急于想讨论的问题核心,这也正是她在冰冷的砖墙上守候了一整天的原因。不管她是一只猫,或是一个女人,她从来都不曾用现在这样锐利的眼光看过邓布利多。显然,不管大家怎么说,只有从邓布利多口中得到证实,她才会相信。邓布利多却挑了另一块柠檬雪宝糖,没有答话。

"他们说,"麦格教授不依不饶地说,"昨天夜里伏地魔绕到戈德里克山谷。他是去找波特夫妇的,谣传莉莉和詹姆·波特都——都——他们都已经——死了。"

邓布利多低下头。麦格教授倒抽了一口气。

"莉莉和詹姆……我不相信……我也不愿相信……哦,阿不思……"

邓布利多伸手拍了拍她的肩膀。"我知道……我知道……"他心情沉重地说。

麦格教授接着往下说,她的声音颤抖了:"还不止这些。他们说,

CHAPTER ONE   The Boy Who Lived

Professor McGonagall's voice trembled as she went on. 'That's not all. They're saying he tried to kill the Potters' son, Harry. But – he couldn't. He couldn't kill that little boy. No one knows why, or how, but they're saying that when he couldn't kill Harry Potter, Voldemort's power somehow broke – and that's why he's gone.'

Dumbledore nodded glumly.

'It's – it's *true*?' faltered Professor McGonagall. 'After all he's done ... all the people he's killed ... he couldn't kill a little boy? It's just astounding ... of all the things to stop him ... but how in the name of heaven did Harry survive?'

'We can only guess,' said Dumbledore. 'We may never know.'

Professor McGonagall pulled out a lace handkerchief and dabbed at her eyes beneath her spectacles. Dumbledore gave a great sniff as he took a golden watch from his pocket and examined it. It was a very odd watch. It had twelve hands but no numbers; instead, little planets were moving around the edge. It must have made sense to Dumbledore, though, because he put it back in his pocket and said, 'Hagrid's late. I suppose it was he who told you I'd be here, by the way?'

'Yes,' said Professor McGonagall. 'And I don't suppose you're going to tell me *why* you're here, of all places?'

'I've come to bring Harry to his aunt and uncle. They're the only family he has left now.'

'You don't mean – you *can't* mean the people who live *here*?' cried Professor McGonagall, jumping to her feet and pointing at number four. 'Dumbledore – you can't. I've been watching them all day. You couldn't find two people who are less like us. And they've got this son – I saw him kicking his mother all the way up the street, screaming for sweets. Harry Potter come and live here!'

'It's the best place for him,' said Dumbledore firmly. 'His aunt and uncle will be able to explain everything to him when he's older. I've written them a letter.'

'A letter?' repeated Professor McGonagall faintly, sitting back down on the wall. 'Really, Dumbledore, you think you can explain all this in a letter? These people will never understand him! He'll be famous – a legend – I wouldn't be surprised if today was known as Harry Potter Day in future – there will be books written about Harry – every child in our world will know his name!'

他还想杀波特夫妇的儿子哈利，可是没有成功。他杀不死那个孩子。没有人知道为什么，也没有人知道怎么会杀不死。不过他们说，当伏地魔杀不死哈利的时候，他的法力就不知怎的失灵了——所以他才走掉了。"

邓布利多愁眉不展地点了点头。

"这——这是真的吗？"麦格教授用颤巍巍的声音问，"他做了这么多坏事……杀了这么多人……可竟然杀不了一个孩子？这简直令人震惊……我们想了那么多办法去阻止他……可苍天在上，哈利究竟是怎么幸免于难的呢？"

"我们只能猜测，"邓布利多说，"可能永远也不会知道。"

麦格教授掏出一块花边手帕轻轻拭了拭镜片后边的眼睛。邓布利多深深地吸了一口气，从衣袋里掏出一块金表，认真看起来。那块表的样子很奇怪，有十二根指针，却没有数字，还有一些小星星在沿着表盘边缘转动。邓布利多显然看明白了，他把表放回衣袋，说："海格肯定迟到了。顺便问一句，我想大概是他告诉您我要到这里来的吧？"

"是的，"麦格教授说，"可去的地方多了，您为什么偏偏要到这里来呢？我想，您大概不会告诉我吧？"

"我是来接哈利，把他送到他姨妈姨父家的。现在他们是他唯一的亲人了。"

"您不会是指——您不可能是指住在这里的那家人吧？"她噌地跳了起来，指着4号那一家，"邓布利多——您可不能这么做。我观察他们一整天了。您找不到比他们更不像你我这样的人了。他们还有一个儿子——我看见他在大街上一路用脚踢他母亲，吵着要糖吃。要哈利·波特住在这里？！"

"这对他是最合适的地方了。"邓布利多坚定地说，"等他长大一些，他的姨妈姨父会向他说明一切的。我给他们写了一封信。"

"一封信？"麦格教授有气无力地重复说，又坐回到墙头上，"邓布利多，您当真认为用一封信您就能把一切都解释清楚吗？这些人永远也不会理解他的！他会成名的——一个传奇人物——如果将来有一天把今天定为哈利·波特日，我一点儿也不会觉得奇怪——会有许多写哈利的

CHAPTER ONE The Boy Who Lived

'Exactly,' said Dumbledore, looking very seriously over the top of his half-moon glasses. 'It would be enough to turn any boy's head. Famous before he can walk and talk! Famous for something he won't even remember! Can't you see how much better off he'll be, growing up away from all that until he's ready to take it?'

Professor McGonagall opened her mouth, changed her mind, swallowed and then said, 'Yes – yes, you're right, of course. But how is the boy getting here, Dumbledore?' She eyed his cloak suddenly as though she thought he might be hiding Harry underneath it.

'Hagrid's bringing him.'

'You think it – *wise* – to trust Hagrid with something as important as this?'

'I would trust Hagrid with my life,' said Dumbledore.

'I'm not saying his heart isn't in the right place,' said Professor McGonagall grudgingly, 'but you can't pretend he's not careless. He does tend to – what was that?'

A low rumbling sound had broken the silence around them. It grew steadily louder as they looked up and down the street for some sign of a headlight; it swelled to a roar as they both looked up at the sky – and a huge motorbike fell out of the air and landed on the road in front of them.

If the motorbike was huge, it was nothing to the man sitting astride it. He was almost twice as tall as a normal man and at least five times as wide. He looked simply too big to be allowed, and so *wild* – long tangles of bushy black hair and beard hid most of his face, he had hands the size of dustbin lids and his feet in their leather boots were like baby dolphins. In his vast, muscular arms he was holding a bundle of blankets.

'Hagrid,' said Dumbledore, sounding relieved. 'At last. And where did you get that motorbike?'

'Borrowed it, Professor Dumbledore, sir,' said the giant, climbing carefully off the motorbike as he spoke. 'Young Sirius Black lent it me. I've got him, sir.'

'No problems, were there?'

'No, sir – house was almost destroyed but I got him out all right before the Muggles started swarmin' around. He fell asleep as we was flyin' over Bristol.'

Dumbledore and Professor McGonagall bent forward over the bundle of blankets. Inside, just visible, was a baby boy, fast asleep. Under a tuft of jet-black hair over his forehead they could see a curiously shaped cut, like a bolt

第1章 大难不死的男孩

书——我们世界里的每一个孩子都会知道他的名字！"

"说得对极了，"邓布利多说，他那半月形眼镜上方的目光显得非常严肃，"这足以使任何一个孩子头脑发昏。在还不会走路、不会说话的时候就一举成名！甚至为他自己根本不记得的事情而成名！让他在远离过去的地方成长，直到他能接受这一切时再让他知道，不是更好吗？"

麦格教授张开嘴，改变了她的看法。她咽了口唾沫，接着说："是啊——是啊，当然您是对的。可该怎么把孩子弄到这里来呢，邓布利多？"她突然朝他的斗篷看了一眼，好像以为他会把哈利藏在斗篷里。

"海格会把他带到这里来的。"

"把这么重要的事情托付给海格去办——您觉得——明智吗？"

"我可以把我的身家性命托付给他。"邓布利多说。

"我不是说他心术不正，"麦格教授勉强地说，"可是您不能不看到他很粗心。他总是——那是什么声音？"

一阵低沉的隆隆声划破了周围的寂静。他们来回搜索街道上是否有汽车前灯的灯光，响声越来越大，最后变成了一阵吼叫。他们抬眼望着天空，只见一辆巨型摩托自天而降，停在他们面前的街道上。

如果说摩托是一辆巨型摩托，那么骑车人就更不在话下了。那人比普通人高一倍，宽度至少有五倍，显得出奇地高大，而且粗野——纠结在一起的乱蓬蓬的黑色长发和胡须几乎遮住了大部分脸庞，那双手有垃圾桶盖那么大，一双穿着皮靴的脚像两只小海豚。他那肌肉发达的粗壮双臂抱着一卷毛毯。

"海格，"邓布利多说，听起来像松了一口气，"你总算来了。这辆摩托你是从哪里弄来的？"

"借来的，邓布利多教授，"巨人一边小心翼翼地跨下摩托，一边说，"是小天狼星布莱克借给我的。我把他带来了，先生。"

"没有遇到麻烦吧？"

"没有，先生——房子几乎全毁了。我赶在麻瓜们汇拢来之前把他抱了出来。我们飞越布里斯托尔上空的时候，他睡着了……"

邓布利多和麦格教授朝那卷毛毯俯下身。他们看见毛毯里裹着一个

of lightning.

'Is that where –?' whispered Professor McGonagall.

'Yes,' said Dumbledore. 'He'll have that scar for ever.'

'Couldn't you do something about it, Dumbledore?'

'Even if I could, I wouldn't. Scars can come in useful. I have one myself above my left knee which is a perfect map of the London Underground. Well – give him here, Hagrid – we'd better get this over with.'

Dumbledore took Harry in his arms and turned towards the Dursleys' house.

'Could I – could I say goodbye to him, sir?' asked Hagrid.

He bent his great, shaggy head over Harry and gave him what must have been a very scratchy, whiskery kiss. Then, suddenly, Hagrid let out a howl like a wounded dog.

'Shhh!' hissed Professor McGonagall. 'You'll wake the Muggles!'

'S-s-sorry,' sobbed Hagrid, taking out a large spotted handkerchief and burying his face in it. 'But I c-c-can't stand it – Lily an' James dead – an' poor little Harry off ter live with Muggles –'

'Yes, yes, it's all very sad, but get a grip on yourself, Hagrid, or we'll be found,' Professor McGonagall whispered, patting Hagrid gingerly on the arm as Dumbledore stepped over the low garden wall and walked to the front door. He laid Harry gently on the doorstep, took a letter out of his cloak, tucked it inside Harry's blankets and then came back to the other two. For a full minute the three of them stood and looked at the little bundle; Hagrid's shoulders shook, Professor McGonagall blinked furiously and the twinkling light that usually shone from Dumbledore's eyes seemed to have gone out.

'Well,' said Dumbledore finally, 'that's that. We've no business staying here. We may as well go and join the celebrations.'

'Yeah,' said Hagrid in a very muffled voice. 'I'd best get this bike away. G'night, Professor McGonagall – Professor Dumbledore, sir.'

Wiping his streaming eyes on his jacket sleeve, Hagrid swung himself on to the motorbike and kicked the engine into life; with a roar it rose into the air and off into the night.

'I shall see you soon, I expect, Professor McGonagall,' said Dumbledore, nodding to her. Professor McGonagall blew her nose in reply.

Dumbledore turned and walked back down the street. On the corner he

男婴,睡得正香。孩子前额上一绺乌黑的头发下边有一处伤口,形状很奇怪,像一道闪电。

"这地方就是——"麦格教授低声说。

"是的,"邓布利多说,"他一辈子都要带着这道伤疤了。"

"你不能想想办法吗,邓布利多?"

"即使有办法,我也不会去做。伤疤今后可能会有用处。我左边膝盖上就有一个疤,是一幅完整的伦敦地铁图。好了——把他给我吧,海格——咱们最好还是把事情办妥。"

邓布利多把哈利抱在怀里,朝德思礼家走去。

"我能——我能跟他告别一下吗,先生?"海格问。

他把毛发蓬乱的大脑袋凑到哈利脸上,给了他一个胡子拉碴、痒乎乎的吻。接着海格突然像一只受伤的狗号叫了一声。

"嘘!"麦格教授嘘了他一声,"你会把麻瓜们吵醒的!"

"对—对—对不起,"海格抽抽搭搭地说,掏出一块圆点花纹的大手帕,把脸埋在手帕里,"我—我实在受—受不了——莉莉和詹姆死了——可怜的小哈利又要住在麻瓜们家里——"

"是啊,是啊,是令人难过,可你得把握住自己,不然我们会被发现的。"麦格教授小声说,轻轻拍了一下海格的臂膀。这时邓布利多正跨过花园低矮的院墙,朝大门走去。他轻轻把哈利放到大门口的台阶上,从斗篷里掏出一封信,塞到哈利的毛毯里,然后回到另外两个人身边。他们三人站在那里,对小小的毯子注视了足有一分钟。海格的肩膀在抖动,麦格教授拼命眨眼,邓布利多一向炯炯有神的眼睛也暗淡无光了。

"好了,"邓布利多终于说,"到此结束。我们没有必要继续待在这里。还是去参加庆祝会吧。"

"是啊,"海格嘟哝说,"我最好把车弄走。晚安,麦格教授——晚安,邓布利多教授。"

海格用外衣衣袖擦了擦流泪的眼睛,跨上摩托,踩着了发动机。随着一声吼叫,摩托腾空而起,消失在夜色里。

"希望很快和您见面,麦格教授。"邓布利多朝麦格教授点头说。麦

CHAPTER ONE The Boy Who Lived

stopped and took out the silver Put-Outer. He clicked it once and twelve balls of light sped back to their street lamps so that Privet Drive glowed suddenly orange and he could make out a tabby cat slinking around the corner at the other end of the street. He could just see the bundle of blankets on the step of number four.

'Good luck, Harry,' he murmured. He turned on his heel and with a swish of his cloak he was gone.

A breeze ruffled the neat hedges of Privet Drive, which lay silent and tidy under the inky sky, the very last place you would expect astonishing things to happen. Harry Potter rolled over inside his blankets without waking up. One small hand closed on the letter beside him and he slept on, not knowing he was special, not knowing he was famous, not knowing he would be woken in a few hours' time by Mrs Dursley's scream as she opened the front door to put out the milk bottles, nor that he would spend the next few weeks being prodded and pinched by his cousin Dudley ... He couldn't know that at this very moment, people meeting in secret all over the country were holding up their glasses and saying in hushed voices: 'To Harry Potter – the boy who lived!'

格教授擤了擤鼻子作为回答。

邓布利多转身顺着女贞路走了。他在街角上掏出银质熄灯器，咔嗒一声，只见十二个光球又回到各自的路灯上，女贞路顿时映照出一片橙黄，他看见一只花斑猫正悄悄从女贞路那头的拐角溜掉。他恰好可以看见4号台阶上放着的那个用毯子裹着的小包。

"祝你好运，哈利。"他喃喃地说，噔地用脚跟一转身，只听斗篷嗖的一声，他已经消失得无影无踪了。

微风拂动着女贞路两旁整洁的树篱，街道在漆黑的天空下寂静而规整，谁也不会想到这里会发生骇人听闻的事情。哈利·波特在毯子包里翻了个身，但他并没有醒。他的一只小手正好放在那封信旁边。他还在继续沉睡，一点也不知道他很特殊，不知道他名气很大，不知道再过几小时，等德思礼太太打开大门放奶瓶时，他会被她的尖叫声吵醒；更不会知道，在未来的几个星期，他表哥达力会对他连捅带戳，连掐带拧……他也不可能知道，就在此刻，全国的人都在秘密聚会，人们高举酒杯悄声说："祝福大难不死的孩子——哈利·波特！"

CHAPTER TWO

The Vanishing Glass

Nearly ten years had passed since the Dursleys had woken up to find their nephew on the front step, but Privet Drive had hardly changed at all. The sun rose on the same tidy front gardens and lit up the brass number four on the Dursleys' front door; it crept into their living-room, which was almost exactly the same as it had been on the night when Mr Dursley had seen that fateful news report about the owls. Only the photographs on the mantelpiece really showed how much time had passed. Ten years ago, there had been lots of pictures of what looked like a large pink beach ball wearing different-coloured bobble hats – but Dudley Dursley was no longer a baby, and now the photographs showed a large, blond boy riding his first bicycle, on a roundabout at the fair, playing a computer game with his father, being hugged and kissed by his mother. The room held no sign at all that another boy lived in the house, too.

Yet Harry Potter was still there, asleep at the moment, but not for long. His Aunt Petunia was awake and it was her shrill voice which made the first noise of the day.

'Up! Get up! Now!'

Harry woke with a start. His aunt rapped on the door again.

'Up!' she screeched. Harry heard her walking towards the kitchen and then the sound of the frying pan being put on the cooker. He rolled on to his back and tried to remember the dream he had been having. It had been a good one. There had been a flying motorbike in it. He had a funny feeling he'd had the same dream before.

His aunt was back outside the door.

'Are you up yet?' she demanded.

'Nearly,' said Harry.

第 2 章
悄悄消失的玻璃

自从德思礼夫妇一觉醒来在大门口台阶上发现他们的外甥以来,快十年过去了,女贞路却几乎没有变化。太阳依旧升到屋前整洁的花园上空,照亮德思礼家大门上的 4 号铜牌;阳光悄悄爬进他们的起居室,这里和德思礼先生当年收看关于猫头鹰的重大新闻的那个晚上几乎一模一样。只有壁炉台上的照片显示出流逝了多少时光。十年前,这里摆放着许多照片,上面像是一个戴着五颜六色婴儿帽的粉红色海滩大气球——但达力·德思礼已不再是婴儿了,照片上是一个体型巨大的金发男孩骑着他的第一辆自行车,在市集上乘坐旋转木马,跟父亲玩电脑游戏,被母亲拥着亲吻。这个房间里没有任何迹象表明这栋房子里还住着另一个男孩。

哈利·波特还住在这里,此刻他正在睡觉,但不会太久。他的佩妮姨妈已经醒了,今天这里发出的第一声噪音就是她的尖叫声。

"起来!起床了!赶快!"

哈利被惊醒了。姨妈又在拍打他的房门。

"起来!"她尖叫道。哈利听见她朝着厨房走过去,接着就是煎锅放到炉子上的声音。他翻身仰卧着,尽力回忆刚才做过的梦。那是一个好梦。梦里有一辆会飞的摩托车。他感到很有趣,似乎以前也做过同样的梦。

姨妈又来到门外。

"你起来了吗?"她追问。

"快了。"哈利说。

"快了,那就赶紧,我要你看着熏咸肉。你敢把它煎煳了试试。我

CHAPTER TWO   The Vanishing Glass

'Well, get a move on, I want you to look after the bacon. And don't you dare let it burn, I want everything perfect on Duddy's birthday.'

Harry groaned.

'What did you say?' his aunt snapped through the door.

'Nothing, nothing ...'

Dudley's birthday – how could he have forgotten? Harry got slowly out of bed and started looking for socks. He found a pair under his bed and, after pulling a spider off one of them, put them on. Harry was used to spiders, because the cupboard under the stairs was full of them, and that was where he slept.

When he was dressed he went down the hall into the kitchen. The table was almost hidden beneath all Dudley's birthday presents. It looked as though Dudley had got the new computer he wanted, not to mention the second television and the racing bike. Exactly why Dudley wanted a racing bike was a mystery to Harry, as Dudley was very fat and hated exercise – unless of course it involved punching somebody. Dudley's favourite punch-bag was Harry, but he couldn't often catch him. Harry didn't look it, but he was very fast.

Perhaps it had something to do with living in a dark cupboard, but Harry had always been small and skinny for his age. He looked even smaller and skinnier than he really was because all he had to wear were old clothes of Dudley's and Dudley was about four times bigger than he was. Harry had a thin face, knobbly knees, black hair and bright green eyes. He wore round glasses held together with a lot of Sellotape because of all the times Dudley had punched him on the nose. The only thing Harry liked about his own appearance was a very thin scar on his forehead which was shaped like a bolt of lightning. He had had it as long as he could remember and the first question he could ever remember asking his Aunt Petunia was how he had got it.

'In the car crash when your parents died,' she had said. 'And don't ask questions.'

Don't ask questions – that was the first rule for a quiet life with the Dursleys.

Uncle Vernon entered the kitchen as Harry was turning over the bacon.

'Comb your hair!' he barked, by way of a morning greeting.

About once a week, Uncle Vernon looked over the top of his newspaper

要达力生日这天一切都顺顺当当。"

哈利咕哝了一声。

"你说什么？"姨妈又在厉声问。

"没什么，没什么……"

达力的生日——他怎么会忘记呢？哈利慢慢吞吞地从床上爬起来，开始找袜子。他从床底下找到一双袜子，从其中一只袜子上抓下一只蜘蛛，然后把袜子穿上。哈利对蜘蛛早就习惯了，因为楼梯下边的储物间里到处是蜘蛛，而他就睡在那里。

他穿好衣服，顺着走廊来到厨房。餐桌几乎被达力的生日礼物堆得看不见了。看来达力收到了他想要的新电脑，至于第二台电视机还有竞速自行车就更不在话下了。达力为什么想要一辆竞速自行车，这对哈利来说是一个谜，因为达力胖乎乎的，而且讨厌锻炼——当然，除非这种锻炼包括拳脚相加。他最喜欢的拳击吊球就是哈利，可他并不是经常能抓住哈利。哈利看起来很单薄，但动作机敏。

也许和长年住在黑洞洞的储物间里有些关系，哈利显得比同龄人瘦小。他看上去甚至比他实际的身材还要瘦小，因为他只能穿达力的旧衣服，而达力要比他宽大三四倍。哈利有一张消瘦的面孔、膝盖骨突出的膝盖、乌黑的头发和一对翠绿的眼睛。他戴着一副用许多透明胶带粘在一起的圆框眼镜，因为达力总用拳头揍他的鼻子。对于自己的外表，哈利最喜欢的就是额头上那道像闪电似的淡淡疤痕。这道疤痕从他记事起就有了，他记得他问佩妮姨妈的第一个问题就是这道伤疤是怎么落下的。

"是在你父母被撞死的那场车祸中落下的。"姨妈这么说，"不许问问题。"

不许问问题——要想与德思礼一家相安无事，这就是规章的第一条。

弗农姨父来到厨房时，哈利正在翻熏咸肉。

"把你的头发梳一梳！"姨父咆哮着，这是他早晨见面打招呼的方式。

几乎每周一次，弗农姨父从他的报纸上方看看哈利，对哈利大喊大

and shouted that Harry needed a haircut. Harry must have had more haircuts than the rest of the boys in his class put together, but it made no difference, his hair simply grew that way – all over the place.

Harry was frying eggs by the time Dudley arrived in the kitchen with his mother. Dudley looked a lot like Uncle Vernon. He had a large, pink face, not much neck, small, watery blue eyes and thick, blond hair that lay smoothly on his thick, fat head. Aunt Petunia often said that Dudley looked like a baby angel – Harry often said that Dudley looked like a pig in a wig.

Harry put the plates of egg and bacon on the table, which was difficult as there wasn't much room. Dudley, meanwhile, was counting his presents. His face fell.

'Thirty-six,' he said, looking up at his mother and father. 'That's two less than last year.'

'Darling, you haven't counted Auntie Marge's present, see, it's here under this big one from Mummy and Daddy.'

'All right, thirty-seven then,' said Dudley, going red in the face. Harry, who could see a huge Dudley tantrum coming on, began wolfing down his bacon as fast as possible in case Dudley turned the table over.

Aunt Petunia obviously scented danger too, because she said quickly, 'And we'll buy you another *two* presents while we're out today. How's that, popkin? *Two* more presents. Is that all right?'

Dudley thought for a moment. It looked like hard work. Finally he said slowly, 'So I'll have thirty ... thirty ...'

'Thirty-nine, sweetums,' said Aunt Petunia.

'Oh.' Dudley sat down heavily and grabbed the nearest parcel. 'All right then.'

Uncle Vernon chuckled.

'Little tyke wants his money's worth, just like his father. Atta boy, Dudley!' He ruffled Dudley's hair.

At that moment the telephone rang and Aunt Petunia went to answer it while Harry and Uncle Vernon watched Dudley unwrap the racing bike, a cine-camera, a remote-control aeroplane, sixteen new computer games and a video recorder. He was ripping the paper off a gold wristwatch when Aunt Petunia came back from the telephone, looking both angry and worried.

'Bad news, Vernon,' she said. 'Mrs Figg's broken her leg. She can't take

第 2 章 悄悄消失的玻璃

叫说他该去理发了。哈利理发的次数要比他班上所有的同学理发次数加起来还要多,可这一点也不起作用,他的头发照旧疯长。

哈利正在煎蛋的时候,达力和他母亲一起来到厨房。达力更像弗农姨父:一张粉红色的大脸,脖子很短,一对水汪汪的蓝眼睛,浓密的金发平整地贴在他那厚实的胖乎乎的脑袋上。佩妮姨妈常说达力长得像小天使——可哈利却说他像一头戴假发的猪。

哈利把一盘盘煎蛋和熏咸肉放到餐桌上,这可不怎么容易,因为桌上已经没有多余的地方了。这时达力正在清点他的礼品。他的脸沉了下来。

"三十六,"他抬头看着父母说,"比去年少两件。"

"亲爱的,你还没算上玛姬姑妈送给你的礼物呢。你看,在你妈妈爸爸送给你的大包下边呢。"

"好吧,那就三十七件。"达力说,他的脸涨得通红。哈利看得出达力就要大发雷霆了,于是趁达力还没有把餐桌掀翻,连忙狼吞虎咽,把自己的一份熏咸肉一扫而光。

佩妮姨妈显然也嗅出了危险的信号,连忙说:"今天我们上街的时候,再给你买两件礼物。怎么样,宝贝?再买两件礼物,这样好了吧?"

达力想了一会儿,这似乎是一件很难的工作。最后他总算慢慢吞吞地说:"那我就有三十……三十……"

"三十九件,我的心肝宝贝。"佩妮姨妈说。

"哦,"达力重重地坐下来,抓起离他最近的一只礼包,"那好吧。"

弗农姨父咯咯地笑了。

"这臭小子是在算他的进账呢,这一点跟他爸爸一模一样。有你的,好小子,达力!"他揉了揉达力的头发。

这时电话铃响了,佩妮姨妈跑去接电话。哈利和弗农姨父看着达力拆包,一辆竞速自行车、一台摄像机、一架遥控飞机、十六张新出的电脑游戏光盘和一台磁带录像机。他正在撕开一块金表的包装纸时,佩妮姨妈接完电话回来了,显得又生气,又着急。

"坏消息,弗农,"她说,"费格太太把腿摔断了,不能来接他了。"她朝哈利那边点了一下头。

CHAPTER TWO   The Vanishing Glass

him.' She jerked her head in Harry's direction.

Dudley's mouth fell open in horror but Harry's heart gave a leap. Every year on Dudley's birthday his parents took him and a friend out for the day, to adventure parks, hamburger bars or the cinema. Every year, Harry was left behind with Mrs Figg, a mad old lady who lived two streets away. Harry hated it there. The whole house smelled of cabbage and Mrs Figg made him look at photographs of all the cats she'd ever owned.

'Now what?' said Aunt Petunia, looking furiously at Harry as though he'd planned this. Harry knew he ought to feel sorry that Mrs Figg had broken her leg, but it wasn't easy when he reminded himself it would be a whole year before he had to look at Tibbles, Snowy, Mr Paws and Tufty again.

'We could phone Marge,' Uncle Vernon suggested.

'Don't be silly, Vernon, she hates the boy.'

The Dursleys often spoke about Harry like this, as though he wasn't there – or rather, as though he was something very nasty that couldn't understand them, like a slug.

'What about what's-her-name, your friend – Yvonne?'

'On holiday in Majorca,' snapped Aunt Petunia.

'You could just leave me here,' Harry put in hopefully (he'd be able to watch what he wanted on television for a change and maybe even have a go on Dudley's computer).

Aunt Petunia looked as though she'd just swallowed a lemon.

'And come back and find the house in ruins?' she snarled.

'I won't blow up the house,' said Harry, but they weren't listening.

'I suppose we could take him to the zoo,' said Aunt Petunia slowly, '… and leave him in the car …'

'That car's new, he's not sitting in it alone …'

Dudley began to cry loudly. In fact, he wasn't really crying, it had been years since he'd really cried, but he knew that if he screwed up his face and wailed, his mother would give him anything he wanted.

'Dinky Duddydums, don't cry, Mummy won't let him spoil your special day!' she cried, flinging her arms around him.

'I … don't … want … him … t-t-to come!' Dudley yelled between huge pretend sobs. 'He always sp-spoils everything!' He shot Harry a nasty grin through the gap in his mother's arms.

第 2 章 悄悄消失的玻璃

达力吓得张口结舌，哈利却高兴得心脏怦怦直跳。每年达力生日这一天，他的父母总带着他和另一位朋友出去玩一天，上游乐园，吃汉堡包或是看电影，却把哈利留给费格太太，一个住得离这里有两条街的疯老婆子。哈利讨厌费格太太住的地方，满屋子都是卷心菜味；费格太太还非要他看她过去养过的几只猫的照片。

"现在怎么办？"佩妮姨妈气急败坏地看着哈利，仿佛这一切都是哈利一手策划的。哈利知道他应当为费格太太摔断腿感到难过，但是当想到要整整一年之后才会再见到踢踢、雪儿、爪子先生和毛毛（都是猫的名字），又觉得难过不起来了。

"咱们给玛姬挂个电话吧。"弗农姨父建议说。

"别犯傻了，弗农，她讨厌这孩子。"

德思礼夫妇经常这样当面谈论哈利，仿佛哈利根本不在场，甚至认为他是一个听不懂他们讲话的讨厌鬼，就像一条鼻涕虫。

"她叫什么来着，你的那位朋友——伊芬，怎么样？"

"上马约卡岛度假去了。"她厉声说。

"你们可以把我留在家里。"哈利满怀希望地插嘴说。（这样他就可以看他想看的电视节目，换换口味，说不定还能试着玩一把达力的电脑。）

佩妮姨妈看起来像刚刚吞下了一个柠檬。

"好让我们回来看到整个房子都给毁了？"她大吼道。

"我不会把房子炸掉的。"哈利说。可他们根本不听。

"我想我们可以带他到动物园去，"佩妮姨妈慢吞吞地说，"……然后把他留在车上……"

"那是辆新车，不能让他一个人待在车上……"

达力大哭起来。其实，他并没有真哭，他已经好多年没有真的哭过了。他知道只要他一哭丧着脸，嗷嗷号叫，母亲就会满足他的任何要求。

"我的好心肝宝贝，别哭，妈妈不会让他搅乱你的好日子的！"佩妮喊着，一下子把他搂到怀里。

"我……不……想让……他……去……去！"达力一边抽抽搭搭地假哭，一边断断续续地大喊大叫，"他总是把什么都弄坏了！"他躲在母亲臂弯里不怀好意地朝哈利撇嘴一笑。

CHAPTER TWO The Vanishing Glass

Just then, the doorbell rang – 'Oh, Good Lord, they're here!' said Aunt Petunia frantically – and a moment later, Dudley's best friend, Piers Polkiss, walked in with his mother. Piers was a scrawny boy with a face like a rat. He was usually the one who held people's arms behind their backs while Dudley hit them. Dudley stopped pretending to cry at once.

Half an hour later, Harry, who couldn't believe his luck, was sitting in the back of the Dursleys' car with Piers and Dudley, on the way to the zoo for the first time in his life. His aunt and uncle hadn't been able to think of anything else to do with him, but before they'd left, Uncle Vernon had taken Harry aside.

'I'm warning you,' he had said, putting his large purple face right up close to Harry's, 'I'm warning you now, boy – any funny business, anything at all – and you'll be in that cupboard from now until Christmas.'

'I'm not going to do anything,' said Harry, 'honestly ...'

But Uncle Vernon didn't believe him. No one ever did.

The problem was, strange things often happened around Harry and it was just no good telling the Dursleys he didn't make them happen.

Once, Aunt Petunia, tired of Harry coming back from the barber's looking as though he hadn't been at all, had taken a pair of kitchen scissors and cut his hair so short he was almost bald except for his fringe, which she left 'to hide that horrible scar'. Dudley had laughed himself silly at Harry, who spent a sleepless night imagining school the next day, where he was already laughed at for his baggy clothes and Sellotaped glasses. Next morning, however, he had got up to find his hair exactly as it had been before Aunt Petunia had sheared it off. He had been given a week in his cupboard for this, even though he had tried to explain that he *couldn't* explain how it had grown back so quickly.

Another time, Aunt Petunia had been trying to force him into a revolting old jumper of Dudley's (brown with orange bobbles). The harder she tried to pull it over his head, the smaller it seemed to become, until finally it might have fitted a glove puppet, but certainly wouldn't fit Harry. Aunt Petunia had decided it must have shrunk in the wash and, to his great relief, Harry wasn't punished.

On the other hand, he'd got into terrible trouble for being found on the roof of the school kitchens. Dudley's gang had been chasing him as usual

第2章 悄悄消失的玻璃

正在这时，门铃响了——

"哎呀，天哪，他们来了！"佩妮姨妈慌慌张张地说。过了一会儿，达力最要好的朋友皮尔·波奇斯和他的母亲一起进来了。皮尔瘦骨嶙峋，脸像老鼠脸。达力打人的时候，皮尔总是把挨打人的双手反剪在背后，牢牢抓住。达力立刻不装哭了。

哈利简直不敢相信自己这么走运。半小时后，他和皮尔、达力坐在德思礼的私家车后座，生平第一次向通往动物园的路上驶去。他姨父姨妈想不出别的办法安置他，不过在动身前，弗农姨父把哈利叫到了一旁。

"我警告你，"他把红得发紫的大脸凑到哈利跟前说，"我现在警告你，小子，只要你干出一点点蠢事——干出任何事——那你就在储物间里待着，等圣诞节再出来吧。"

"我什么事也不会做的，"哈利说，"真的……"

但弗农姨父不相信他。从来没有人相信他的话。

问题是哈利周围常常会发生一些怪事，即使他磨破嘴皮对德思礼夫妇说那些事与自己无关，也是白费唇舌。

每次哈利理发回来总像根本没有理过一样，有一次佩妮姨妈实在按捺不住，就从厨房里拿出一把剪刀，几乎把他的头发剪光了，只留下前面一绺头发"盖住他那道可怕的伤疤"。达力笑得前仰后合，可哈利整夜睡不着，思前想后，不知明天该怎么去上学，同学们本来就拿他那身松松垮垮的衣服和用胶带粘牢的眼镜当笑话。可到了第二天一早他起床的时候，竟发现自己的头发又恢复到了佩妮姨妈剪它以前的样子。尽管他拼命辩白，自己也弄不清头发为什么这么快就长出来了，可是为这件事他们还是把他在储物间里关了一个星期。

还有一次，佩妮姨妈硬要哈利穿一件达力穿过的旧套头毛衣（这件毛衣很难看，是棕色的，缀有橙色的小毛球）。她越是往哈利头上套，毛衣就缩得越小，最后缩得只能给掌上木偶穿，哈利穿当然是不合适了。佩妮姨妈断定是洗的时候缩水了，才没有处罚哈利，哈利大大地松了一口气。

然而另一次，哈利在学校伙房的屋顶上被发现了，这可给他惹出了很大的麻烦。达力和他的一伙跟往常一样追着哈利跑，结果哈利竟坐到

CHAPTER TWO The Vanishing Glass

when, as much to Harry's surprise as anyone else's, there he was sitting on the chimney. The Dursleys had received a very angry letter from Harry's headmistress telling them Harry had been climbing school buildings. But all he'd tried to do (as he shouted at Uncle Vernon through the locked door of his cupboard) was jump behind the big bins outside the kitchen doors. Harry supposed that the wind must have caught him in mid-jump.

But today, nothing was going to go wrong. It was even worth being with Dudley and Piers to be spending the day somewhere that wasn't school, his cupboard or Mrs Figg's cabbage-smelling living-room.

While he drove, Uncle Vernon complained to Aunt Petunia. He liked to complain about things: people at work, Harry, the council, Harry, the bank and Harry were just a few of his favourite subjects. This morning, it was motorbikes.

'... roaring along like maniacs, the young hoodlums,' he said, as a motorbike overtook them.

'I had a dream about a motorbike,' said Harry, remembering suddenly. 'It was flying.'

Uncle Vernon nearly crashed into the car in front. He turned right around in his seat and yelled at Harry, his face like a gigantic beetroot with a moustache, 'MOTORBIKES DON'T FLY!'

Dudley and Piers sniggered.

'I know they don't,' said Harry. 'It was only a dream.'

But he wished he hadn't said anything. If there was one thing the Dursleys hated even more than his asking questions, it was his talking about anything acting in a way it shouldn't, no matter if it was in a dream or even a cartoon – they seemed to think he might get dangerous ideas.

It was a very sunny Saturday and the zoo was crowded with families. The Dursleys bought Dudley and Piers large chocolate ice-creams at the entrance and then, because the smiling lady in the van had asked Harry what he wanted before they could hurry him away, they bought him a cheap lemon ice lolly. It wasn't bad either, Harry thought, licking it as they watched a gorilla scratching its head and looking remarkably like Dudley, except that it wasn't blond.

Harry had the best morning he'd had in a long time. He was careful to walk a little way apart from the Dursleys so that Dudley and Piers, who were starting

第 2 章 悄悄消失的玻璃

了伙房的烟囱上,这使他受到的惊吓并不比别人小。德思礼夫妇收到女校长的一封信,女校长很生气,告诉他们哈利爬到学校楼顶上去了。其实哈利当时只是在往伙房外边的大垃圾箱后面跳(他在上了锁的储物间里朝姨父大喊大叫时是这么解释的)。哈利猜想大概是风把他半路上托上去了。

今天不会出什么差错的。他觉得只要不待在学校,不待在他的储物间里或是费格太太满溢着卷心菜味的起居室里,即使跟达力或皮尔一起在什么地方消磨一天也是值得的。

弗农姨父一边开车,一边对佩妮姨妈抱怨。他喜欢怨天尤人,工作中遇到的人、哈利,开会、哈利,银行、哈利,这是他喜欢抱怨的少数几个话题。今天早上他抱怨的是摩托车。

"……疯子一样,一路轰隆隆个没完,这些小兔崽子。"当一辆摩托车超车时,他说。

"我梦见过一辆摩托车,"哈利突然想起自己的梦,说,"那车还会飞呢。"

弗农姨父差点撞到前面的车上。他从座位上转过身,脸活像一个留着大胡子的大甜菜头。他朝哈利大吼了一声:"**摩托车不会飞!**"

达力和皮尔哧哧地笑起来。

"我知道摩托车不会飞,"哈利说,"那只是一个梦。"

他想,要是什么也没有说就好了。比问问题更让德思礼夫妇恼火的就是哈利总说一些违反常理的事情,不管是做梦梦到的,还是从动画片里看来的——他们认为他总有可能产生危险的想法。

这是一个阳光灿烂的周六,动物园里挤满了举家出游的游客。在入口的地方,德思礼夫妇给达力和皮尔各买了一支大巧克力冰淇淋;他们还没来得及把哈利带走,冰淇淋车上一位笑盈盈的小姐就已经在问哈利想吃点什么,他们只好给哈利买了一支便宜的柠檬冰棍。其实冰棍也不坏,哈利心里想。他一边舔冰棍,一边观赏一只正在搔头的大猩猩,这只大猩猩跟达力长得像极了,只不过它的毛发不是金色的。

这是哈利好长时间以来过得最开心的一个早晨了。他特地小心翼翼地和德思礼一家人保持着一小段距离,以防备达力和皮尔到吃午饭的时

CHAPTER TWO   The Vanishing Glass

to get bored with the animals by lunchtime, wouldn't fall back on their favourite hobby of hitting him. They ate in the zoo restaurant and when Dudley had a tantrum because his knickerbocker glory wasn't big enough, Uncle Vernon bought him another one and Harry was allowed to finish the first.

Harry felt, afterwards, that he should have known it was all too good to last.

After lunch they went to the reptile house. It was cool and dark in here, with lit windows all along the walls. Behind the glass, all sorts of lizards and snakes were crawling and slithering over bits of wood and stone. Dudley and Piers wanted to see huge, poisonous cobras and thick, man-crushing pythons. Dudley quickly found the largest snake in the place. It could have wrapped its body twice around Uncle Vernon's car and crushed it into a dustbin – but at the moment it didn't look in the mood. In fact, it was fast asleep.

Dudley stood with his nose pressed against the glass, staring at the glistening brown coils.

'Make it move,' he whined at his father. Uncle Vernon tapped on the glass, but the snake didn't budge.

'Do it again,' Dudley ordered. Uncle Vernon rapped the glass smartly with his knuckles, but the snake just snoozed on.

'This is boring,' Dudley moaned. He shuffled away.

Harry moved in front of the tank and looked intently at the snake. He wouldn't have been surprised if it had died of boredom itself – no company except stupid people drumming their fingers on the glass trying to disturb it all day long. It was worse than having a cupboard as a bedroom, where the only visitor was Aunt Petunia hammering on the door to wake you up – at least he got to visit the rest of the house.

The snake suddenly opened its beady eyes. Slowly, very slowly, it raised its head until its eyes were on a level with Harry's.

It winked.

Harry stared. Then he looked quickly around to see if anyone was watching. They weren't. He looked back at the snake and winked, too.

The snake jerked its head towards Uncle Vernon and Dudley, then raised its eyes to the ceiling. It gave Harry a look that said quite plainly: '*I get that all the time.*'

'I know,' Harry murmured through the glass, though he wasn't sure the snake could hear him. 'It must be really annoying.'

第 2 章 悄悄消失的玻璃

候,看动物看烦了,回过头来玩他们的拿手好戏——追打他。他们在动物园餐厅吃午饭时,达力嫌给他买的那一份彩宝圣代不够大,又大发脾气。弗农姨父赶紧给他点了一份大的,把原先那份让哈利吃掉了。

哈利事后想想,觉得自己应当明白好事不会持续太久的。

吃过午饭,他们来到爬虫馆。馆里阴冷、晦暗,沿四面墙都是明亮的玻璃窗。隔着玻璃只见各色蜥蜴和蛇在木块或石块上爬来爬去,溜溜达达。达力和皮尔想看看剧毒的大眼镜蛇和攻击性很强的巨蟒。达力很快就找到了馆里最大的一条巨蟒。它能用身体缠绕弗农姨父的汽车两圈,然后把车挤压成一堆废铁……不过这时看来它并没有这种心思,它睡得正香呢。

达力用鼻子紧贴着玻璃,盯着这盘亮闪闪的棕色巨蟒。

"让它动呀。"达力哼哼唧唧地央求他父亲。弗农姨父敲了敲玻璃,巨蟒却纹丝不动。

"再敲一遍。"达力命令说。弗农姨父用指节狠狠地敲玻璃,可大蟒继续打盹。

"真烦人。"达力抱怨了一句,拖着脚慢慢吞吞地走开了。

哈利在巨蟒待的大柜子前边挪动着脚步,仔细打量着这条巨蟒。如果它快快不乐最终在这里死去,哈利不会觉得奇怪。因为它没有伙伴,只有一些愚蠢的家伙整天用手指敲玻璃想把它弄醒。这比拿储物间当卧室更糟糕,尽管每天来光顾他的只有佩妮姨妈,捶门要他起床,可至少他还能在整栋房子里到处走走。

巨蟒突然睁开亮晶晶的小眼睛,慢慢地、慢慢地抬起头,直到与哈利的眼睛一般高。

它眨了眨眼。

哈利大为惊骇。他立刻飞快地四下里扫了一眼,看是否有人在注意他们。没有人注意。他回过头看着巨蟒,也对它眨了眨眼。

巨蟒猛地把头转向弗农姨父和达力那边,然后又抬眼看着天花板。它的眼神显然在对哈利说:"我总是碰到像他们这样的人。"

"我知道。"哈利隔着玻璃小声说,尽管他不能肯定巨蟒能否听到他说话,"那一定让你很烦。"

CHAPTER TWO The Vanishing Glass

The snake nodded vigorously.

'Where do you come from, anyway?' Harry asked.

The snake jabbed its tail at a little sign next to the glass. Harry peered at it.

Boa Constrictor, Brazil.

'Was it nice there?'

The boa constrictor jabbed its tail at the sign again and Harry read on: *This specimen was bred in the zoo.* 'Oh, I see – so you've never been to Brazil?'

As the snake shook its head, a deafening shout behind Harry made both of them jump. 'DUDLEY! MR DURSLEY! COME AND LOOK AT THIS SNAKE! YOU WON'T *BELIEVE* WHAT IT'S DOING!'

Dudley came waddling towards them as fast as he could.

'Out of the way, you,' he said, punching Harry in the ribs. Caught by surprise, Harry fell hard on the concrete floor. What came next happened so fast no one saw how it happened – one second, Piers and Dudley were leaning right up close to the glass, the next, they had leapt back with howls of horror.

Harry sat up and gasped; the glass front of the boa constrictor's tank had vanished. The great snake was uncoiling itself rapidly, slithering out on to the floor – people throughout the reptile house screamed and started running for the exits.

As the snake slid swiftly past him, Harry could have sworn a low, hissing voice said, 'Brazil, here I come … Thanksss, amigo.'

The keeper of the reptile house was in shock.

'But the glass,' he kept saying, 'where did the glass go?'

The zoo director himself made Aunt Petunia a cup of strong sweet tea while he apologised over and over again. Piers and Dudley could only gibber. As far as Harry had seen, the snake hadn't done anything except snap playfully at their heels as it passed, but by the time they were all back in Uncle Vernon's car, Dudley was telling them how it had nearly bitten off his leg, while Piers was swearing it had tried to squeeze him to death. But worst of all, for Harry at least, was Piers calming down enough to say, 'Harry was talking to it, weren't you, Harry?'

Uncle Vernon waited until Piers was safely out of the house before starting on Harry. He was so angry he could hardly speak. He managed to say, 'Go – cupboard – stay – no meals,' before he collapsed into a chair and Aunt

第2章 悄悄消失的玻璃

巨蟒用力点点头。

"那么，你是从哪里来的？"哈利问。

巨蟒甩着尾巴猛地拍了下玻璃窗上的小牌子。哈利仔细看了一下。

蟒蛇，巴西。

"那边不错吧？"

巨蟒又甩着尾巴猛地拍了一下那块牌子，哈利继续读道：这是本动物园内繁殖的样品。

"哦，我明白了——这么说你从来没有去过巴西？"

巨蟒正在摇头回答，哈利背后突然传来震耳欲聋的喊叫，哈利和巨蟒都吓了一跳。"达力！**德思礼先生！快来看这条蛇！你们绝不会相信它在做什么！**"

达力摇摇摆摆地赶紧朝他们走过来。

"别挡道。"他说，朝哈利胸口就是一拳。哈利大吃一惊，重重地摔在水泥地上。随后发生的事来得太突然，谁也说不清是怎么回事。只见皮尔和达力一下子贴在玻璃上，马上又惊恐万状，大喊大叫，连蹦带跳往后退去。

哈利坐了起来，大口喘气；蟒蛇柜前的玻璃不见了。巨蟒迅速地伸展开盘着的身体，溜到地板上——整个爬虫馆的人都尖叫着向出口跑去。

当巨蟒溜过哈利身旁时，哈利清清楚楚地听到一个嗞嗞的声音轻轻地说："巴西，我来了……多谢，我的朋友。"

爬虫馆的管理员深感震惊。

"可这玻璃，"他不停地叨叨，"这玻璃到哪里去了？"

动物园园长再三道歉，并亲自给佩妮姨妈泡了一杯加糖的浓茶。皮尔和达力只在一旁东拉西扯。其实就哈利所看到的，除了巨蟒从他们身边溜过时，跟他们闹着玩，拍打了一下他们的脚后跟，别的什么也没有做。可当他们坐上弗农姨父的汽车后，达力说他的腿如何如何差一点儿被巨蟒咬断，皮尔则赌咒说这条巨蟒想把他缠死。而且，对哈利来说最糟糕的是，当皮尔镇静下来以后，他突然说："哈利还跟它说话呢，是不是，哈利？"

弗农姨父一直等到皮尔安全离开他们家之后才开始跟哈利算账。他气得几乎连话都说不出来。他勉强说了一句："去——储物间——待

CHAPTER TWO   The Vanishing Glass

Petunia had to run and get him a large brandy.

Harry lay in his dark cupboard much later, wishing he had a watch. He didn't know what time it was and he couldn't be sure the Dursleys were asleep yet. Until they were, he couldn't risk sneaking to the kitchen for some food.

He'd lived with the Dursleys almost ten years, ten miserable years, as long as he could remember, ever since he'd been a baby and his parents had died in that car crash. He couldn't remember being in the car when his parents had died. Sometimes, when he strained his memory during long hours in his cupboard, he came up with a strange vision: a blinding flash of green light and a burning pain on his forehead. This, he supposed, was the crash, though he couldn't imagine where all the green light came from. He couldn't remember his parents at all. His aunt and uncle never spoke about them, and of course he was forbidden to ask questions. There were no photographs of them in the house.

When he had been younger, Harry had dreamed and dreamed of some unknown relation coming to take him away, but it had never happened; the Dursleys were his only family. Yet sometimes he thought (or maybe hoped) that strangers in the street seemed to know him. Very strange strangers they were, too. A tiny man in a violet top hat had bowed to him once while out shopping with Aunt Petunia and Dudley. After asking Harry furiously if he knew the man, Aunt Petunia had rushed them out of the shop without buying anything. A wild-looking old woman dressed all in green had waved merrily at him once on a bus. A bald man in a very long purple coat had actually shaken his hand in the street the other day and then walked away without a word. The weirdest thing about all these people was the way they seemed to vanish the second Harry tried to get a closer look.

At school, Harry had no one. Everybody knew that Dudley's gang hated that odd Harry Potter in his baggy old clothes and broken glasses, and nobody liked to disagree with Dudley's gang.

第2章 悄悄消失的玻璃

着——不准吃饭。"就倒在扶手椅上了,佩妮姨妈连忙跑去给他端来一大杯白兰地。

哈利在黑洞洞的储物间里躺了好久,一直盼望能有一块手表。他不知道现在是几点钟,而且也不能肯定德思礼一家是不是睡了。等他们睡了,他就可以冒险偷偷溜到厨房去找点东西吃。

他还是个婴儿时,他的父母死于车祸。他记得,从那时起到现在,他已经在弗农姨父家生活近十年了,那是十年苦难的生活。他已经不记得父母身亡时,他自己也在车上。他有时躺在储物间里长时间拼命回忆,然后就会出现一种奇妙的幻象:一道耀眼的闪电般的绿光,前额上一阵火辣辣的疼痛。他猜想,这就是那场车祸,但他不知道那道绿光是从哪里来的。他一点也不记得他的父母了。姨父姨妈从来不提他们,当然,也不准他问。家里也没有他们的照片。

哈利年纪还小的时候经常做梦,梦见某一位亲戚突然来把他接走,可是他的梦从来没有实现过。德思礼一家是他唯一的亲戚。可有时候他觉得(也许是盼望)街上的陌生人似乎认识他。而且,他们都是一些非常奇怪的陌生人。一次他跟佩妮姨妈和达力上街买东西,就有一个戴紫罗兰色大礼帽的小个子男人向他鞠躬行礼。佩妮姨妈怒冲冲地追问哈利是否认识那人,之后就把他和达力赶出了商店,什么东西也没有买。另外一次在公共汽车上,一个放荡不羁、穿一身绿衣服的老太婆笑眯眯地向他招手。还有一次,一个穿紫色拖地长大衣的秃头男子在大街上竟然跑过来跟他握手,之后一句话没说就走开了。而最令人感到不可思议的是,当哈利想更仔细地看他们的时候,他们便消失得无影无踪了。

在学校里,哈利没有一个朋友。大家都知道,达力一伙最恨的就是穿松松垮垮的旧衣服、戴一副破碎眼镜的怪人哈利·波特。谁也不愿意去跟达力一伙作对。

CHAPTER THREE

The Letters from No One

The escape of the Brazilian boa constrictor earned Harry his longest-ever punishment. By the time he was allowed out of his cupboard again, the summer holidays had started and Dudley had already broken his new cine-camera, crashed his remote-control aeroplane and, first time on his racing bike, knocked down old Mrs Figg as she crossed Privet Drive on her crutches.

Harry was glad school was over, but there was no escaping Dudley's gang, who visited the house every single day. Piers, Dennis, Malcolm and Gordon were all big and stupid, but as Dudley was the biggest and stupidest of the lot, he was the leader. The rest of them were all quite happy to join in Dudley's favourite sport: Harry-hunting.

This was why Harry spent as much time as possible out of the house, wandering around and thinking about the end of the holidays, where he could see a tiny ray of hope. When September came he would be going off to secondary school and, for the first time in his life, he wouldn't be with Dudley. Dudley had a place at Uncle Vernon's old school, Smeltings. Piers Polkiss was going there, too. Harry, on the other hand, was going to Stonewall High, the local comprehensive. Dudley thought this was very funny.

'They stuff people's heads down the toilet first day at Stonewall,' he told Harry. 'Want to come upstairs and practise?'

'No thanks,' said Harry. 'The poor toilet's never had anything as horrible as your head down it – it might be sick.' Then he ran, before Dudley could work out what he'd said.

One day in July, Aunt Petunia took Dudley to London to buy his Smeltings uniform, leaving Harry at Mrs Figg's. Mrs Figg wasn't as bad as usual. It turned out she'd broken her leg tripping over one of her cats and she didn't seem quite as fond of them as before. She let Harry watch television and gave

第 3 章
猫头鹰传书

巴西巨蟒的脱逃使哈利受到了平生时间最长的一次惩罚。当他获准走出储物间时，暑假已经开始了。达力已经打坏了他的新摄像机，摔毁了遥控飞机，他的竞速自行车也在他第一次骑着上街时，把拄着拐杖过女贞路的费格太太撞倒了。

学期结束了，哈利很开心，但他无法回避达力一伙，他们每天都要到达力家来。皮尔、丹尼、莫肯、戈登都是傻大个，而且很蠢，而达力是他们中间块头最大、最蠢的，也就成了他们的头儿。达力的同伙都乐意加入达力最热衷的游戏——追打哈利。

这就是哈利尽量长时间待在外边的原因。他四处游逛，盘算着假期的结束，由此获得对生活的一线希望。到九月他就要上中学了，这将是他平生第一次跟达力分开。达力获准在弗农姨父的母校斯梅廷中学上学。皮尔·波奇斯也要上这所学校。哈利则要去当地的一所综合制中学——石墙中学。达力觉得很好笑。

"石墙中学开学的第一天，会把新生的头浸到抽水马桶里。"他对哈利说，"要不要上楼去试一试？"

"不用了，多谢。"哈利说，"可怜的马桶从来没有泡过像你脑袋这样叫人倒胃口的东西——它可能会吐呢。"不等达力弄明白这句话的意思，哈利早已经跑掉了。

七月的一天，佩妮姨妈带达力上伦敦，去给他买斯梅廷中学的校服，把哈利放在了费格太太家。这一回费格太太不像平时那么坏。原来费格太太是被自己养的猫绊倒才摔断了腿，现在她看起来没有以前那么喜欢它们了。她让哈利看电视，还给了他一小块巧克力蛋糕，可这块蛋糕吃

CHAPTER THREE The Letters from No One

him a bit of chocolate cake that tasted as though she'd had it for several years.

That evening, Dudley paraded around the living-room for the family in his brand-new uniform. Smeltings boys wore maroon tailcoats, orange knickerbockers and flat straw hats called boaters. They also carried knobbly sticks, used for hitting each other while the teachers weren't looking. This was supposed to be good training for later life.

As he looked at Dudley in his new knickerbockers, Uncle Vernon said gruffly that it was the proudest moment of his life. Aunt Petunia burst into tears and said she couldn't believe it was her Ickle Dudleykins, he looked so handsome and grown-up. Harry didn't trust himself to speak. He thought two of his ribs might already have cracked from trying not to laugh.

There was a horrible smell in the kitchen next morning when Harry went in for breakfast. It seemed to be coming from a large metal tub in the sink. He went to have a look. The tub was full of what looked like dirty rags swimming in grey water.

'What's this?' he asked Aunt Petunia. Her lips tightened as they always did if he dared to ask a question.

'Your new school uniform,' she said.

Harry looked in the bowl again.

'Oh,' he said. 'I didn't realise it had to be so wet.'

'Don't be stupid,' snapped Aunt Petunia. 'I'm dyeing some of Dudley's old things grey for you. It'll look just like everyone else's when I've finished.'

Harry seriously doubted this, but thought it best not to argue. He sat down at the table and tried not to think about how he was going to look on his first day at Stonewall High – like he was wearing bits of old elephant skin, probably.

Dudley and Uncle Vernon came in, both with wrinkled noses because of the smell from Harry's new uniform. Uncle Vernon opened his newspaper as usual and Dudley banged his Smeltings stick, which he carried everywhere, on the table.

They heard the click of the letter-box and flop of letters on the doormat.

'Get the post, Dudley,' said Uncle Vernon from behind his paper.

'Make Harry get it.'

'Get the post, Harry.'

'Make Dudley get it.'

起来像已经放了很多年似的。

那天晚上达力神气活现地在起居室里走来走去,向家人展示他那套新校服。斯梅廷中学的男生制服是棕红色燕尾服、橙色短灯笼裤和一顶叫硬草帽的扁平草帽。他们还配了一支多节的手杖,趁老师不注意时用来互相打斗,这也许是对未来生活的一种有益训练吧。

弗农姨父看着身穿崭新灯笼裤的达力,激动得声音都沙哑了,说这是他平生感到最自豪的一刻。佩妮姨妈突然哭起来,说她的宝贝疙瘩已经长大了,长得这么帅,简直让她不能相信。哈利却不敢开口。为了强忍住不笑,他的两条肋骨都快折断了。

第二天早上哈利来吃早饭时,发现厨房里有一股难闻的味儿。这气味似乎是从水池里的一只大铁盆里散发出来的。他走过去看了一眼,发现一盆灰黑色的水里泡着像破抹布似的东西。

"这是什么?"他问佩妮姨妈。她抿紧了嘴唇,每当哈利大胆问问题时,她总是这样。

"你的新校服呀。"她说。

哈利又朝盆里扫了一眼。

"哦,"他说,"我不知道还要泡得这么湿。"

"别冒傻气,"佩妮姨妈斥责说,"我把达力的旧衣服染好给你用。等我染好以后,你穿起来就会跟别人的一模一样了。"

哈利对此非常怀疑,但觉得最好不要跟她争论。他坐下来吃早饭时,竭力不去想自己第一天去石墙中学上学会是什么模样,八成像披着老象皮吧。

达力和弗农姨父进来时,都因为哈利那套新校服散发的味道皱起了鼻子。弗农姨父像通常一样打开报纸,达力则把他从不离身的斯梅廷手杖啪的一声放到桌上。

他们听到信箱咔嗒响了一声,一些信落到大门口的擦脚垫上。

"去拿信,达力。"弗农姨父从报纸后边说。

"叫哈利去捡。"

"哈利去捡。"

"达力去捡。"

CHAPTER THREE   The Letters from No One

'Poke him with your Smeltings stick, Dudley.'

Harry dodged the Smeltings stick and went to get the post. Three things lay on the doormat: a postcard from Uncle Vernon's sister Marge, who was holidaying on the Isle of Wight, a brown envelope that looked like a bill and – *a letter for Harry.*

Harry picked it up and stared at it, his heart twanging like a giant elastic band. No one, ever, in his whole life, had written to him. Who would? He had no friends, no other relatives – he didn't belong to the library so he'd never even got rude notes asking for books back. Yet here it was, a letter, addressed so plainly there could be no mistake:

> Mr H. Potter
> The Cupboard under the Stairs
> 4 Privet Drive
> Little Whinging
> Surrey

The envelope was thick and heavy, made of yellowish parchment, and the address was written in emerald-green ink. There was no stamp.

Turning the envelope over, his hand trembling, Harry saw a purple wax seal bearing a coat of arms; a lion, an eagle, a badger and a snake surrounding a large letter 'H'.

'Hurry up, boy!' shouted Uncle Vernon from the kitchen. 'What are you doing, checking for letter-bombs?' He chuckled at his own joke.

Harry went back to the kitchen, still staring at his letter. He handed Uncle Vernon the bill and the postcard, sat down and slowly began to open the yellow envelope.

Uncle Vernon ripped open the bill, snorted in disgust and flipped over the postcard.

'Marge's ill,' he informed Aunt Petunia. 'Ate a funny whelk ...'

'Dad!' said Dudley suddenly. 'Dad, Harry's got something!'

Harry was on the point of unfolding his letter, which was written on the same heavy parchment as the envelope, when it was jerked sharply out of his hand by Uncle Vernon.

'That's *mine*!' said Harry, trying to snatch it back.

"用你的斯梅廷手杖赶他去捡,达力。"

哈利躲闪着斯梅廷手杖,去捡信。擦脚垫上有三样邮件:一封是弗农姨父的姐姐玛姬姑妈寄来的明信片,她现在在怀特岛上度假;另一封是看来像账单的棕色信封;还有——一封寄给哈利的信。

哈利把信捡了起来,目不转睛地盯着看,心里像有一根很粗的橡皮筋嘣的一声弹了起来,嗡嗡直响。他活到现在,从来没有人给他写过信。这封信可能是谁写的呢?他没有朋友,没有别的亲戚;他也没有借书证,因此不会收到图书馆催还图书的通知单。可现在确实有一封信,地址清清楚楚,不会有错:

萨里郡
小惠金区
女贞路4号
楼梯下的储物间
哈利·波特先生收

信封是用厚重的羊皮纸做的,地址是用翡翠绿的墨水写的。没有贴邮票。

哈利用颤抖的手把信封翻过来,只见上面有一块紫色的蜡封,图案是一个盾牌饰章,大写"H"字母的周围圈着一头狮子、一只鹰、一只獾和一条蛇。

"小子,快拿过来!"弗农姨父在厨房里喊叫起来,"你在干什么,在检查邮包有没有炸弹吗?"他开了个玩笑,自己也咯咯地笑开了。

哈利回到厨房,目光一直盯着他的那封信。他把账单和明信片递给弗农姨父,然后坐了下来,慢慢拆开他那个黄色的信封。

弗农姨父拆开有账单的信封,厌恶地哼了一声,又把明信片轻轻翻转过来。

"玛姬病倒了,"他对佩妮姨妈说,"吃了有问题的蛾螺……"

"爸爸!"达力突然说,"爸爸,哈利收到什么东西了!"

哈利刚要打开他那封写在厚重羊皮纸上的信,信就被弗农姨父一把

CHAPTER THREE The Letters from No One

'Who'd be writing to you?' sneered Uncle Vernon, shaking the letter open with one hand and glancing at it. His face went from red to green faster than a set of traffic lights. And it didn't stop there. Within seconds it was the greyish white of old porridge.

'P-P-Petunia!' he gasped.

Dudley tried to grab the letter to read it, but Uncle Vernon held it high out of his reach. Aunt Petunia took it curiously and read the first line. For a moment it looked as though she might faint. She clutched her throat and made a choking noise.

'Vernon! Oh my goodness – Vernon!'

They stared at each other, seeming to have forgotten that Harry and Dudley were still in the room. Dudley wasn't used to being ignored. He gave his father a sharp tap on the head with his Smeltings stick.

'I want to read that letter,' he said loudly.

'*I* want to read it,' said Harry furiously, 'as it's *mine*.'

'Get out, both of you,' croaked Uncle Vernon, stuffing the letter back inside its envelope.

Harry didn't move.

'I WANT MY LETTER!' he shouted.

'Let *me* see it!' demanded Dudley.

'OUT!' roared Uncle Vernon, and he took both Harry and Dudley by the scruffs of their necks and threw them into the hall, slamming the kitchen door behind them. Harry and Dudley promptly had a furious but silent fight over who would listen at the keyhole; Dudley won, so Harry, his glasses dangling from one ear, lay flat on his stomach to listen at the crack between door and floor.

'Vernon,' Aunt Petunia was saying in a quivering voice, 'look at the address – how could they possibly know where he sleeps? You don't think they're watching the house?'

'Watching – spying – might be following us,' muttered Uncle Vernon wildly.

'But what should we do, Vernon? Should we write back? Tell them we don't want –'

Harry could see Uncle Vernon's shiny black shoes pacing up and down the kitchen.

抢过去了。

"那是写给我的！"哈利说，想把信夺回来。

"谁会给你写信？"弗农姨父讥讽地说，用一只手把信纸抖开，朝它瞥了一眼。他的脸一下子由红变青了，比红绿灯变得还快。事情到这里并没结束。几秒钟之内，他的脸就变得像灰色的麦片粥一样灰白了。

"佩——佩——佩妮！"他气喘吁吁地说。

达力想把信抢过去看，可是弗农姨父把信举得老高，他够不着。佩妮姨妈好奇地把信拿过去，刚看了第一行，她就好像要晕倒了。她抓住喉咙，噎了一下，好像要背过气去。

"弗农！哎呀！我的天哪——弗农！"

他们俩你看我，我看你，都不说话，似乎忘了哈利和达力还在屋里。达力是不习惯被人冷落的。他用斯梅廷手杖朝他父亲的头上狠狠地敲了一下。

"我要看那封信。"他大声说。

"我要看。"哈利气呼呼地说，"因为那封信是写给我的。"

"你们俩，统统给我出去。"弗农姨父用低沉而沙哑的声音说，把信重新塞到信封里。

哈利没有动。

"**我要我的信！**"他大叫着说。

"让我看！"达力命令说。

"**出去！**"弗农姨父吼了起来，揪住哈利和达力的脖领，把他们俩扔到了走廊里，砰的一声关上厨房门。哈利和达力两人为争夺从锁孔偷听的权利，激烈而无声地争斗起来。达力胜利了。哈利一只耳朵上挂着他那副破眼镜，只好趴在地板上，贴着门和地板之间的缝隙窥探动静。

"弗农，"佩妮姨妈用颤抖的声音说，"你看看这地址——他们怎么会知道他睡在什么地方？他们该不会监视我们这栋房子吧？"

"监视——暗中窥探——说不定还会跟踪咱们呢。"弗农姨父愤愤地抱怨说。

"可我们怎么办哪，弗农？要不要回信？告诉他们我们不想让——"

哈利能看见弗农姨父锃亮的黑皮鞋在厨房里走来走去。

CHAPTER THREE — The Letters from No One

'No,' he said finally. 'No, we'll ignore it. If they don't get an answer ... yes, that's best ... we won't do anything ...'

'But –'

'I'm not having one in the house, Petunia! Didn't we swear when we took him in we'd stamp out that dangerous nonsense?'

That evening when he got back from work, Uncle Vernon did something he'd never done before; he visited Harry in his cupboard.

'Where's my letter?' said Harry, the moment Uncle Vernon had squeezed through the door. 'Who's writing to me?'

'No one. It was addressed to you by mistake,' said Uncle Vernon shortly. 'I have burned it.'

'It was *not* a mistake,' said Harry angrily. 'It had my cupboard on it.'

'SILENCE!' yelled Uncle Vernon, and a couple of spiders fell from the ceiling. He took a few deep breaths and then forced his face into a smile, which looked quite painful.

'Er – yes, Harry – about this cupboard. Your aunt and I have been thinking ... you're really getting a bit big for it ... we think it might be nice if you moved into Dudley's second bedroom.'

'Why?' said Harry.

'Don't ask questions!' snapped his uncle. 'Take this stuff upstairs, now.'

The Dursleys' house had four bedrooms: one for Uncle Vernon and Aunt Petunia, one for visitors (usually Uncle Vernon's sister, Marge), one where Dudley slept and one where Dudley kept all the toys and things that wouldn't fit into his first bedroom. It only took Harry one trip upstairs to move everything he owned from the cupboard to this room. He sat down on the bed and stared around him. Nearly everything in here was broken. The month-old cine-camera was lying on top of a small, working tank Dudley had once driven over next door's dog; in the corner was Dudley's first-ever television set, which he'd put his foot through when his favourite programme had been cancelled; there was a large bird-cage which had once held a parrot that Dudley had swapped at school for a real air-rifle, which was up on a shelf with the end all bent because Dudley had sat on it. Other shelves were full of books. They were the only things in the room that looked as though they'd never been touched.

"不，"他终于说，"不，我们给他来个置之不理。如果他们收不到回信……对，这是最好的办法……我们按兵不动……"

"可是——"

"佩妮，我决不允许家里出这样的人。我们抱他进来的时候，不是发过誓，要制止这种耸人听闻的荒唐事吗？"

那天傍晚，弗农姨父下班回来，做了一件他从来没有做过的事，他竟然到储物间来看望哈利了。

"我的信呢？"弗农姨父刚刚挤进门，哈利就问，"是谁写给我的？"

"没有人。因为地址写错了才寄给你的。"弗农姨父直截了当说，"我已经把信烧掉了。"

"根本没有写错，"哈利生气地说，"上面还写着我住在储物间里呢。"

"**住嘴**！"弗农姨父咆哮起来，两只蜘蛛从储物间的顶上被震了下来。他做了几次深呼吸，勉强挤出一个笑脸，但看起来像苦笑。

"唔——不错，哈利——说起这个储物间，你姨妈和我都考虑到……你已经长大了，这地方确实小了点……我们想，你不如搬到达力的另外一间卧室比较好。"

"为什么？"哈利说。

"不准问问题！"姨父吼道，"把你的东西搬到楼上去，现在就搬。"

德思礼家总共有四间卧室：一间是供弗农姨父和佩妮姨妈用的；一间是客房（通常是给弗农姨父的姐姐玛姬准备的）；一间是达力的睡房；还有一间用来堆放达力卧室里放不下的玩具和什物。哈利只走了一趟就把他的全部家当从储物间搬到了楼上这个房间。他端坐在床上，朝房间里四下打量着。这里所有的东西几乎都是坏的。只用了一个月的摄像机放在一辆小手推车顶上，达力有一次还用这辆手推车去轧过邻居家的小狗；屋角放着达力的第一台电视机，当他心爱的节目被取消时，他给了电视机一脚；这里还有一只大鸟笼，达力用它养过一只鹦鹉，后来他把鹦鹉带到学校换回了一支真正的气枪——这支气枪现在扔在架子上，枪管的一头被达力坐弯了。另外的一些架子上摆满了书。这些书看上去大概是这个房间里唯一没有翻动过的东西。

CHAPTER THREE   The Letters from No One

From downstairs came the sound of Dudley bawling at his mother: 'I don't *want* him in there ... I *need* that room ... make him get out ...'

Harry sighed and stretched out on the bed. Yesterday he'd have given anything to be up here. Today he'd rather be back in his cupboard with that letter than up here without it.

Next morning at breakfast, everyone was rather quiet. Dudley was in shock. He'd screamed, whacked his father with his Smeltings stick, been sick on purpose, kicked his mother and thrown his tortoise through the greenhouse roof and he still didn't have his room back. Harry was thinking about this time yesterday and bitterly wishing he'd opened the letter in the hall. Uncle Vernon and Aunt Petunia kept looking at each other darkly.

When the post arrived, Uncle Vernon, who seemed to be trying to be nice to Harry, made Dudley go and get it. They heard him banging things with his Smeltings stick all the way down the hall. Then he shouted, 'There's another one! *Mr H. Potter, The Smallest Bedroom, 4 Privet Drive –*'

With a strangled cry, Uncle Vernon leapt from his seat and ran down the hall, Harry right behind him. Uncle Vernon had to wrestle Dudley to the ground to get the letter from him, which was made difficult by the fact that Harry had grabbed Uncle Vernon around the neck from behind. After a minute of confused fighting, in which everyone got hit a lot by the Smeltings stick, Uncle Vernon straightened up, gasping for breath, with Harry's letter clutched in his hand.

'Go to your cupboard – I mean, your bedroom,' he wheezed at Harry. 'Dudley – go – just go.'

Harry walked round and round his new room. Someone knew he had moved out of his cupboard and they seemed to know he hadn't received his first letter. Surely that meant they'd try again? And this time he'd make sure they didn't fail. He had a plan.

The repaired alarm clock rang at six o'clock the next morning. Harry turned it off quickly and dressed silently. He mustn't wake the Dursleys. He stole downstairs without turning on any of the lights.

He was going to wait for the postman on the corner of Privet Drive and get the letters for number four first. His heart hammered as he crept across the dark hall towards the front door –

楼下传来达力缠着他母亲哭闹的声音："我不要他住那个房间……那个房间我要用……让他搬出去……"

哈利叹了口气，伸开四肢躺到床上。如果是昨天，要他搬上来，他会不惜任何代价。可是今天他宁愿拿着那封信搬回他的储物间，也不愿搬到这里来却拿不到那封信。

第二天吃早饭时，大家都觉得最好还是不说话。达力歇斯底里大发作，用斯梅廷手杖使劲敲打他父亲，故意装吐，拼命踢他母亲，用他的乌龟把温室的屋顶砸了个窟窿，可他还是没能把自己的房间要回去。哈利回想着昨天的这个时候，非常后悔没有在走廊里就把信打开。弗农姨父和佩妮姨妈一直沉着脸面面相觑。

今天来信的时候，弗农姨父似乎要对哈利示好，便让达力去拿信。他们听见达力穿过走廊时用斯梅廷手杖敲敲打打。之后，达力大喊大叫起来："又有一封信！女贞路4号最小的一间卧室　哈利·波特先生收——"

弗农姨父像被掐住了脖子，喊了一声，从椅子上一跃而起，朝走廊跑去。哈利紧跟在他背后。弗农姨父只有把达力摔倒在地，才能把信拿到手，可哈利从背后搂住了他的脖子，这就增加了他的难度。经过片刻的混战，弗农姨父和哈利都挨了达力不少棍子。最后，弗农姨父直起腰大口喘着气，手里捏着哈利的信。

"上你的储物间去——我是说，上你的卧室去。"他呼哧带喘地对哈利说，"达力——走开——快走开！"

哈利在他新搬来的房间里来回兜着圈子。有人知道他已经搬出了储物间，好像还知道他没有收到写给他的第一封信。这足以说明他们还会再试一次。这回他可要保证让他们获得成功。他设计了一个方案。

第二天一早，修好的闹钟在六点钟时响了。哈利连忙把闹钟铃关掉，悄没声息地穿好衣服。他不能吵醒德思礼一家。他一盏灯也没有开就悄悄溜下楼去。

他要去女贞路街口等邮差来，抢先把4号的邮件取到手。当他穿过漆黑的走廊朝大门口走去时，他的心怦怦直跳——

CHAPTER THREE — The Letters from No One

'AAAAARRRGH!'

Harry leapt into the air – he'd trodden on something big and squashy on the doormat – something *alive*!

Lights clicked on upstairs and to his horror Harry realised that the big squashy something had been his uncle's face. Uncle Vernon had been lying at the foot of the front door in a sleeping bag, clearly making sure that Harry didn't do exactly what he'd been trying to do. He shouted at Harry for about half an hour and then told him to go and make a cup of tea. Harry shuffled miserably off into the kitchen, and by the time he got back, the post had arrived, right into Uncle Vernon's lap. Harry could see three letters addressed in green ink.

'I want –' he began, but Uncle Vernon was tearing the letters into pieces before his eyes.

Uncle Vernon didn't go to work that day. He stayed at home and nailed up the letter-box.

'See,' he explained to Aunt Petunia through a mouthful of nails, 'if they can't *deliver* them they'll just give up.'

'I'm not sure that'll work, Vernon.'

'Oh, these people's minds work in strange ways, Petunia, they're not like you and me,' said Uncle Vernon, trying to knock in a nail with the piece of fruit cake Aunt Petunia had just brought him.

On Friday, no fewer than twelve letters arrived for Harry. As they couldn't go through the letter-box they had been pushed under the door, slotted through the sides and a few even forced through the small window in the downstairs toilet.

Uncle Vernon stayed at home again. After burning all the letters, he got out a hammer and nails and boarded up the cracks around the front and back doors so no one could go out. He hummed 'Tiptoe through the Tulips' as he worked, and jumped at small noises.

On Saturday, things began to get out of hand. Twenty-four letters to Harry found their way into the house, rolled up and hidden inside each of the two dozen eggs that their very confused milkman had handed Aunt Petunia through the living-room window. While Uncle Vernon made furious telephone calls to the post office and the dairy trying to find someone to complain to, Aunt Petunia shredded the letters in her food mixer.

第 3 章 猫头鹰传书

"哎哟哟——！"

哈利一蹦老高——他一脚踩到了擦鞋垫上一个软绵绵的大东西，还是一个活物！

楼上的灯都亮了，哈利踩着的那个软绵绵的大东西竟是他姨父的脸，这使他大为惊骇。弗农姨父裹着睡袋躺在大门口是为了不让哈利做他想做的事。他朝哈利大喊大叫，嚷嚷了有半个钟头，才让哈利去泡杯热茶。哈利难过地拖着脚步，慢慢吞吞地来到厨房。等他转回来的时候，信件已经到了，刚好掉在弗农姨父的膝盖上。哈利看见了三封信，地址是用翠绿色墨水写的。

"我想——"他刚要开口，弗农姨父已经当着他的面把三封信撕得粉碎。

那天弗农姨父没去上班。他待在家里，把信箱钉死了。

"你看，"他嘴里含着一把钉子，对佩妮姨妈解释说，"如果他们没法投送，自然也就放弃了。"

"这是不是真能起作用，我不敢说，弗农。"

"哦，那些人的头脑想问题都古里古怪的，佩妮，跟你我不一样。"弗农姨父说，用佩妮姨妈刚给他端来的水果蛋糕捶起了钉子。

星期五，寄给哈利的信至少有十二封。既然不能往信箱里插，只好往门底下的缝里塞，从门边的缝里塞，有几封信甚至从楼下盥洗室的小窗口塞了进来。

弗农姨父又待在家里。他把信全部烧光之后，就找来锤子、钉子，把前门后门的门缝全都用木板钉死，这样谁也出不去了。他一边干，一边哼着《从郁金香花园中悄悄走过》，一有点动静就吓一跳。

星期六，事态开始失控。二十四封写给哈利的信设法进入了德思礼家中。这些信是卷成小卷藏在两打鸡蛋里边，由深感困惑的送奶员从起居室窗口递给佩妮姨妈的。弗农姨父怒冲冲地给邮局、奶厂打电话找人说理。佩妮姨妈把二十四封信都塞到食品粉碎机里搅得粉碎。

"究竟什么人这么急着要找你联系？"达力吃惊地问哈利。

CHAPTER THREE   The Letters from No One

'Who on earth wants to talk to *you* this badly?' Dudley asked Harry in amazement.

On Sunday morning, Uncle Vernon sat down at the breakfast table looking tired and rather ill, but happy.

'No post on Sundays,' he reminded them happily as he spread marmalade on his newspapers, 'no damn letters today –'

Something came whizzing down the kitchen chimney as he spoke and caught him sharply on the back of the head. Next moment, thirty or forty letters came pelting out of the fireplace like bullets. The Dursleys ducked, but Harry leapt into the air trying to catch one –

'Out! OUT!'

Uncle Vernon seized Harry around the waist and threw him into the hall. When Aunt Petunia and Dudley had run out with their arms over their faces, Uncle Vernon slammed the door shut. They could hear the letters still streaming into the room, bouncing off the walls and floor.

'That does it,' said Uncle Vernon, trying to speak calmly but pulling great tufts out of his moustache at the same time. 'I want you all back here in five minutes, ready to leave. We're going away. Just pack some clothes. No arguments!'

He looked so dangerous with half his moustache missing that no one dared argue. Ten minutes later they had wrenched their way through the boarded-up doors and were in the car, speeding towards the motorway. Dudley was sniffling in the back seat; his father had hit him round the head for holding them up while he tried to pack his television, video and computer in his sports bag.

They drove. And they drove. Even Aunt Petunia didn't dare ask where they were going. Every now and then Uncle Vernon would take a sharp turning and drive in the opposite direction for a while.

'Shake 'em off … shake 'em off,' he would mutter whenever he did this.

They didn't stop to eat or drink all day. By nightfall Dudley was howling. He'd never had such a bad day in his life. He was hungry, he'd missed five television programmes he'd wanted to see and he'd never gone so long without blowing up an alien on his computer.

Uncle Vernon stopped at last outside a gloomy-looking hotel on the

第3章 猫头鹰传书

星期天早上，弗农姨父坐下来吃早饭时，显得很疲惫，气色也不太好，不过很开心。

"星期天没有邮差，"他一边把果酱抹在报纸上，一边高兴地提醒大家，"今天不会有该死的信来了……"

就在他正说着的时候，突然有东西嗖嗖地从厨房烟囱里掉了下来，狠狠地砸到了他的后脑勺上。接着，又有三四十封信像子弹一样从壁炉里射出来。德思礼一家忙着躲避，哈利却一蹿老高，伸出手想抓住一封——

"出去！**出去！**"

弗农姨父伸手抱住哈利的腰，把他扔到了走廊里。佩妮姨妈和达力双手抱头逃出屋去，弗农姨父砰的一声把门关上。他们能听见信件源源不断地向厨房里涌，弹到地板上和墙上。

"我受够了！"弗农姨父尽量保持镇静，但又大把大把地把胡子从脸上揪了下来，"我要你们五分钟之内都回到这里，准备走。我们要离开这里。赶紧去收拾几件衣服。没有商量！"

他揪掉了自己一半的胡子，看起来可怕极了，谁也不敢顶撞他。十分钟后，他们奋力拆开用木条钉死的大门，冲出来，坐上汽车朝公路疾驰而去。达力坐在后座上哭鼻子，因为他刚才要把电视机、录像机和电脑都塞到他的运动背包里，耽误了大家的时间，父亲打了他的头好几下。

他们一个劲往前开。连佩妮姨妈也不敢问这是要去哪里。弗农姨父会不时打个紧急掉头，往回开一小段路。

"甩掉他们……甩掉他们……"每次他往回开的时候，总这么喃喃自语。

他们一整天都没有停下来吃东西或喝水。夜幕降临时，达力哇哇大哭起来。他平生从没遇到过像今天这么糟糕的事情。他饿极了；五个他想看的电视节目也错过了；他还从没遇到过今天这种情况，一整天都没坐到电脑前炸外星人。

汽车来到一座大城市的郊区，弗农姨父终于在一家显得幽暗阴沉的旅馆门口停了车。达力和哈利合住一个有两张床位的房间，潮湿的床单

CHAPTER THREE The Letters from No One

outskirts of a big city. Dudley and Harry shared a room with twin beds and damp, musty sheets. Dudley snored but Harry stayed awake, sitting on the window-sill, staring down at the lights of passing cars and wondering ...

They ate stale cornflakes and cold tinned tomatoes on toast for breakfast next day. They had just finished when the owner of the hotel came over to their table.

''Scuse me, but is one of you Mr H. Potter? Only I got about an 'undred of these at the front desk.'

She held up a letter so they could read the green ink address:

> Mr H. Potter
> Room 17
> Railview Hotel
> Cokeworth

Harry made a grab for the letter but Uncle Vernon knocked his hand out of the way. The woman stared.

'I'll take them,' said Uncle Vernon, standing up quickly and following her from the dining-room.

'Wouldn't it be better just to go home, dear?' Aunt Petunia suggested timidly, hours later, but Uncle Vernon didn't seem to hear her. Exactly what he was looking for, none of them knew. He drove them into the middle of a forest, got out, looked around, shook his head, got back in the car and off they went again. The same thing happened in the middle of a ploughed field, halfway across a suspension bridge and at the top of a multi-storey car park.

'Daddy's gone mad, hasn't he?' Dudley asked Aunt Petunia dully late that afternoon. Uncle Vernon had parked at the coast, locked them all inside the car and disappeared.

It started to rain. Great drops beat on the roof of the car. Dudley snivelled.

'It's Monday,' he told his mother. 'The Great Humberto's on tonight. I want to stay somewhere with a *television*.'

Monday. This reminded Harry of something. If it *was* Monday – and

第3章 猫头鹰传书

散发着一股霉味。达力打着呼噜,哈利却睡不着,只好坐在窗台上看着下边过往的汽车灯光,感到纳闷……

第二天早餐,他们吃的是走味的玉米片和罐头冷番茄加烤面包。刚吃完,旅馆的老板娘就过来了。

"对不起,你们当中有位哈利·波特先生吗?前边服务台大概收到了一百封像这样的信。"

她举起一封信好让他们看清用绿墨水写的地址:

科克沃斯
铁路风景旅馆
17号房间
哈利·波特先生收

哈利伸手去抓信,可是他的手被弗农姨父挡了回去。老板娘瞪大眼睛看着他。

"我去拿信。"弗农姨父说着,立刻站起来跟随老板娘走出餐厅。

"我们还是回家比较好吧,亲爱的。"几小时过后,佩妮姨妈胆怯地建议说。弗农姨父好像根本没有听到她说话。他究竟在寻找什么,他们谁也不知道。他开车把他们带到了一处森林中间。他下车四下里看了看,摇摇头,又回到车上,继续往前开。后来在一片新耕的田地里、在一座吊桥的中央和立体停车场的顶层又发生了同样的事。

"爸爸是不是疯了?"这时天色已经相当晚了,达力无精打采地问佩妮姨妈。弗农姨父把车停在海边,把他们锁在车里就不见了。

开始下雨了。豆大的雨点落到车顶上。达力又抽抽噎噎地哭鼻子了。

"今天是星期一,"他对母亲说,"晚上演《伟大的亨伯托》,我真想待在能看电视的地方。"

星期一。这使哈利想起一件事。他通常总是靠达力来推算每天是星期几,因为达力要看电视。如果今天是星期一,那么明天,星期二,将

CHAPTER THREE The Letters from No One

you could usually count on Dudley to know the days of the week, because of television – then tomorrow, Tuesday, was Harry's eleventh birthday. Of course, his birthdays were never exactly fun – last year, the Dursleys had given him a coat-hanger and a pair of Uncle Vernon's old socks. Still, you weren't eleven every day.

Uncle Vernon was back and he was smiling. He was also carrying a long, thin package and didn't answer Aunt Petunia when she asked what he'd bought.

'Found the perfect place!' he said. 'Come on! Everyone out!'

It was very cold outside the car. Uncle Vernon was pointing at what looked like a large rock way out to sea. Perched on top of the rock was the most miserable little shack you could imagine. One thing was certain, there was no television in there.

'Storm forecast for tonight!' said Uncle Vernon gleefully, clapping his hands together. 'And this gentleman's kindly agreed to lend us his boat!'

A toothless old man came ambling up to them, pointing, with a rather wicked grin, at an old rowing boat bobbing in the iron-grey water below them.

'I've already got us some rations,' said Uncle Vernon, 'so all aboard!'

It was freezing in the boat. Icy sea spray and rain crept down their necks and a chilly wind whipped their faces. After what seemed like hours they reached the rock, where Uncle Vernon, slipping and sliding, led the way to the broken-down house.

The inside was horrible; it smelled strongly of seaweed, the wind whistled through the gaps in the wooden walls and the fireplace was damp and empty. There were only two rooms.

Uncle Vernon's rations turned out to be a packet of crisps each and four bananas. He tried to start a fire but the empty crisp packets just smoked and shrivelled up.

'Could do with some of those letters now, eh?' he said cheerfully.

He was in a very good mood. Obviously he thought nobody stood a chance of reaching them here in a storm to deliver post. Harry privately agreed, though the thought didn't cheer him up at all.

As night fell, the promised storm blew up around them. Spray from the high waves splattered the walls of the hut and a fierce wind rattled the filthy

第3章 猫头鹰传书

是哈利十一岁的生日。当然,他的生日从来都没有一点儿意思。去年德思礼夫妇送给他一个挂上衣的挂衣钩和一双弗农姨父的旧袜子。但是,他毕竟不是天天过十一岁的生日呀。

弗农姨父回来了,而且面带微笑。他还拎着一个细长的包裹,佩妮姨妈问他买的是什么,他没有回答。

"我找到了一个特别理想的地方!"他说,"走吧!都下车!"

车外边很冷。弗农姨父指着海上一块巨大的礁石。礁石上有一间可以想象的最寒酸的破烂小木屋。有一点可以肯定,那就是小屋里绝对不会有电视。

"天气预报说今天夜里有暴风雨!"弗农姨父高兴地拍着手说,"而这位先生好心地同意把船借给我们!"

一个牙齿掉光的老汉慢慢吞吞地朝他们走来,脸上挂着不怀好意的奸笑,指着在铁灰色海面上漂荡的一只破旧的划艇。

"我已经给大家弄到了一些吃的!"弗农姨父说,"我们就都上船吧!"

船上寒气逼人。冰冷的海水掀起的浪花夹着雨水顺着他们的脖子往下流淌,刺骨的寒风拍打着他们的面孔。大概过了好几个小时,他们来到了那块礁石边,弗农姨父连滚带爬地领着他们朝东倒西歪的小屋走去。

小屋里更显得可怕,有一股浓重的海藻腥味,寒风透过木墙的缝隙飕飕地往里灌,壁炉里湿漉漉的,什么也没有。屋里总共只有两个房间。

弗农姨父弄来的吃的东西也只是每人一包薯片和四根香蕉。他想把火生起来,但薯片的空包装袋只冒了一股烟,就卷缩成了一堆灰烬。

"现在要是有信,可就有用处了,是吧?"他开心地说。

他的心情很好。看得出他认为在这样暴风雨的天气,是不会有人冒雨来送信的。哈利心里当然也同意,但这种想法让他一点儿也高兴不起来。

夜幕降临,意料之中的暴风雨果然从四面八方向他们袭来。滔滔翻滚的海浪,拍打着小木屋的四壁,肆虐的狂风吹得几扇污秽不堪的窗户

CHAPTER THREE — The Letters from No One

windows. Aunt Petunia found a few mouldy blankets in the second room and made up a bed for Dudley on the moth-eaten sofa. She and Uncle Vernon went off to the lumpy bed next door and Harry was left to find the softest bit of floor he could and to curl up under the thinnest, most ragged blanket.

The storm raged more and more ferociously as the night went on. Harry couldn't sleep. He shivered and turned over, trying to get comfortable, his stomach rumbling with hunger. Dudley's snores were drowned by the low rolls of thunder that started near midnight. The lighted dial of Dudley's watch, which was dangling over the edge of the sofa on his fat wrist, told Harry he'd be eleven in ten minutes' time. He lay and watched his birthday tick nearer, wondering if the Dursleys would remember at all, wondering where the letter-writer was now.

Five minutes to go. Harry heard something creak outside. He hoped the roof wasn't going to fall in, although he might be warmer if it did. Four minutes to go. Maybe the house in Privet Drive would be so full of letters when they got back that he'd be able to steal one somehow.

Three minutes to go. Was that the sea, slapping hard on the rock like that? And (two minutes to go) what was that funny crunching noise? Was the rock crumbling into the sea?

One minute to go and he'd be eleven. Thirty seconds ... twenty ... ten – nine – maybe he'd wake Dudley up, just to annoy him – three – two – one –

BOOM.

The whole shack shivered and Harry sat bolt upright, staring at the door. Someone was outside, knocking to come in.

咔嗒咔嗒直响。佩妮姨妈从另一间屋里找来几床发霉的被子，在虫蛀的沙发上给达力铺了一张床。她和弗农姨父到隔壁一张坑坑洼洼、高低不平的床上睡了。哈利勉强找到一块不太硌人的地板，把身子蜷缩在一条薄而又薄的破被子下面。

深夜，雨暴风狂，暴风雨越发肆无忌惮。哈利不能入眠，他瑟瑟发抖，辗转反侧，总想睡得舒服些，肚子又饿得咕咕直叫。临近午夜，一阵沉闷的隆隆雷声淹没了达力的鼾声。达力的一只胳膊耷拉在沙发边上，胖乎乎的手腕上戴着手表，夜光的表盘告诉哈利再过十分钟他就满十一岁了。他躺在那里期待着他的生日在滴答声中一分一秒地临近。他心里想，不知德思礼夫妇会不会记得他的生日，不知那个写信的人此刻会在什么地方。

还有五分钟。哈利听见屋外不知什么嘎吱响了一声。但愿屋顶不会塌下来，尽管塌下来也许反倒会暖和些。还有四分钟。说不定等他回到女贞路时，那幢房子已经堆满了信，没准儿他还能想办法偷到一封呢。

还有三分钟。那是海浪汹涌澎湃，冲击着礁石吗？还有两分钟。那个嘎吱嘎吱的奇怪声音又是什么呢？是礁石碎裂滚入大海的声音吗？

再过一分钟他就十一岁了。三十秒——二十秒——十——九——也许应该把达力叫醒，故意气气他——三——二——一——

轰！

整个小屋被震得摇摇晃晃，哈利坐了起来，盯着房门。门外有人捶门要进来。

CHAPTER FOUR

The Keeper of the Keys

B OOM. They knocked again. Dudley jerked awake.
'Where's the cannon?' He said stupidly.

There was a crash behind them and Uncle Vernon came skidding into the room. He was holding a rifle in his hands – now they knew what had been in the long, thin package he had brought with them.

'Who's there?' He shouted. 'I warn you – I'm armed!'

There was a pause. Then –

SMASH!

The door was hit with such force that it swung clean off its hinges and with a deafening crash landed flat on the floor.

A giant of a man was standing in the doorway. His face was almost completely hidden by a long, shaggy mane of hair and a wild, tangled beard, but you could make out his eyes, glinting like black beetles under all the hair.

The giant squeezed his way into the hut, stooping so that his head just brushed the ceiling. He bent down, picked up the door and fitted it easily back into its frame. The noise of the storm outside dropped a little. He turned to look at them all.

'Couldn't make us a cup o' tea, could yeh? It's not been an easy journey …'

He strode over to the sofa where Dudley sat frozen with fear.

'Budge up, yeh great lump,' said the stranger.

Dudley squeaked and ran to hide behind his mother, who was crouching, terrified, behind Uncle Vernon.

'An' here's Harry!' said the giant.

Harry looked up into the fierce, wild, shadowy face and saw that the beetle eyes were crinkled in a smile.

第4章

钥匙保管员

轰！又是捶门声。达力惊醒了。

"什么地方打炮？"达力迷迷糊糊地说。

他们背后又是哗啦一声响。弗农姨父抱着一支来复枪连滚带爬地跑进屋，这时他们才明白他那细长的包裹里原来是什么东西。

"门外是什么人？"他喊道，"我警告你——我有枪！"

外面静了一会儿。然后——

咔嚓！

门从合页上脱落下来，随着震耳欲聋的哗啦一声，门板摔在地上。

门口站着一个彪形大汉。他的脸几乎完全被蓬乱的长发和纠结的浓密胡须掩盖了，但你仍能看见他那双眼睛在头发下像黑甲虫似的闪闪发光。

巨人好不容易才挤进屋来，他弓着腰，这样他的头刚刚擦着天花板。他弯腰捡起门板，轻轻松松地就把门装到了门框上。外面的风暴声减弱了。他转身看着大家。

"能给我来杯热茶吗？走这么一趟可真不容易……"

他大步走到沙发跟前，达力坐在那里吓傻了。

"喂，让一点儿地方吧，你这个傻大个儿。"巨人说。

达力尖叫着跑过去躲到母亲身后，他母亲吓得蹲在弗农姨父背后。

"这就是哈利了！"巨人说。

哈利抬头看着他那张凶狠、粗野、面貌不清的脸，他那对甲壳虫似的眼睛眯起来，露出一丝笑容。

CHAPTER FOUR The Keeper of the Keys

'Las' time I saw you, you was only a baby,' said the giant. 'Yeh look a lot like yer dad, but yeh've got yer mum's eyes.'

Uncle Vernon made a funny rasping noise.

'I demand that you leave at once, sir!' he said. 'You are breaking and entering!'

'Ah, shut up, Dursley, yeh great prune,' said the giant. He reached over the back of the sofa, jerked the gun out of Uncle Vernon's hands, bent it into a knot as easily as if it had been made of rubber, and threw it into a corner of the room.

Uncle Vernon made another funny noise, like a mouse being trodden on.

'Anyway – Harry,' said the giant, turning his back on the Dursleys, 'a very happy birthday to yeh. Got summat fer yeh here – I mighta sat on it at some point, but it'll taste all right.'

From an inside pocket of his black overcoat he pulled a slightly squashed box. Harry opened it with trembling fingers. Inside was a large, sticky chocolate cake with *Happy Birthday Harry* written on it in green icing.

Harry looked up at the giant. He meant to say thank you, but the words got lost on the way to his mouth, and what he said instead was, 'Who are you?'

The giant chuckled.

'True, I haven't introduced meself. Rubeus Hagrid, Keeper of Keys and Grounds at Hogwarts.'

He held out an enormous hand and shook Harry's whole arm.

'What about that tea then, eh?' he said, rubbing his hands together. 'I'd not say no ter summat stronger if yeh've got it, mind.'

His eyes fell on the empty grate with the shrivelled crisp packets in it and he snorted. He bent down over the fireplace; they couldn't see what he was doing but when he drew back a second later, there was a roaring fire there. It filled the whole damp hut with flickering light and Harry felt the warmth wash over him as though he'd sunk into a hot bath.

The giant sat back down on the sofa, which sagged under his weight, and began taking all sorts of things out of the pockets of his coat: a copper kettle, a squashy package of sausages, a poker, a teapot, several chipped mugs and a bottle of some amber liquid which he took a swig from before starting to make tea. Soon the hut was full of the sound and smell of sizzling

第4章 钥匙保管员

"上次见到你,你还是个小娃娃。"巨人说,"你很像你爸爸,可眼睛像你妈妈。"

弗农姨父发出一声刺耳的怪叫。

"我要你马上离开,先生!"他说,"你这是私闯民宅!"

"哦,住嘴,德思礼,你这个大傻瓜。"巨人说。他隔着沙发把枪从弗农姨父手里抢过来,轻轻一撅,绾了一个结,把它扔到屋角,仿佛这支枪是用橡皮做的。

弗农姨父又发出一声怪叫,好像一只老鼠被人踩了。

"不管怎么说——哈利,"巨人转过身来,背对着弗农夫妇,"祝你生日非常愉快。我这里有一件东西要送给你——有的地方我可能压坏了,不过味道还是一样。"

他从黑外衣内袋里取出一只稍稍有些压扁的盒子。哈利用颤抖的手将它打开,只见盒子里是一个黏糊糊的巧克力大蛋糕,上边用绿色糖汁写着:祝哈利生日快乐。

哈利抬眼看着这个巨人。他本来想向他致谢,可是话到嘴边却不见了,他脱口说出:"你是谁?"

巨人咯咯地笑起来。

"说真的,我还没向你做自我介绍呢。鲁伯·海格,霍格沃茨的钥匙保管员和猎场看守。"

他伸出一只巨手握了握哈利的整只胳膊。

"哦,茶怎么样了?"他搓着手说,"要知道,如果有比茶更烈的东西我也不会拒绝的。"

他的目光落到空空的炉箅子上,那上边只有缩成一团的包装袋。他哼了一声,朝壁炉弯下腰,谁也没看见他做什么,但是当他随即退回来的时候,那里已是炉火熊熊。潮湿的木屋里火光摇曳,哈利感到周身暖和起来,仿佛跳进了热水池。

巨人又坐回到沙发上,沉重的身躯把沙发压得直往下塌。他开始从外衣口袋里掏出各式各样的东西:一把铜壶、一包压扁的香肠、一只拨火钳、一把茶壶、几只缺口的大杯子和一瓶琥珀色的液体。他先喝了一大口那种液体,然后开始泡茶。小屋里随即充满了烤香肠的香味和嘶嘶

CHAPTER FOUR   The Keeper of the Keys

sausage. Nobody said a thing while the giant was working, but as he slid the first six fat, juicy, slightly burnt sausages from the poker, Dudley fidgeted a little. Uncle Vernon said sharply, 'don't touch anything he gives you, Dudley.'

The giant chuckled darkly.

'Yer great puddin' of a son don' need fattenin' any more, Dursley, don' worry.'

He passed the sausages to Harry, who was so hungry he had never tasted anything so wonderful, but he still couldn't take his eyes off the giant. Finally, as nobody seemed about to explain anything, he said, 'I'm sorry, but I still don't really know who you are.'

The giant took a gulp of tea and wiped his mouth with the back of his hand.

'Call me Hagrid,' he said, 'everyone does. An' like I told yeh, I'm Keeper of Keys at Hogwarts – yeh'll know all about Hogwarts, o' course.'

'Er – no,' said Harry.

Hagrid looked shocked.

'Sorry,' Harry said quickly.

'*Sorry?*' Barked Hagrid, turning to stare at the Dursleys, who shrank back into the shadows. 'It's them as should be sorry! I knew yeh weren't gettin' yer letters but I never thought yeh wouldn't even know abou' Hogwarts, fer cryin' out loud! Did yeh never wonder where yer parents learnt it all?'

'All what?' Asked Harry.

'ALL WHAT?' Hagrid thundered. 'Now wait jus' one second!'

He had leapt to his feet. In his anger he seemed to fill the whole hut. The Dursleys were cowering against the wall.

'Do you mean ter tell me,' he growled at the Dursleys, 'that this boy – this boy! –knows nothin' abou' – about ANYTHING?'

Harry thought this was going a bit far. He had been to school, after all, and his marks weren't bad.

'I know *some* things,' he said. 'I can, you know, do maths and stuff.'

But Hagrid simply waved his hand and said, 'About *our* world, I mean. *Your* world. *My* world. *Yer parents' world.*'

'What world?'

的声音。在巨人忙活的时候，谁也没有吱声。但是当他把第一批烤好的六根粗粗的、油汪汪的、稍稍有点焦的香肠从拨火钳上拿下来时，达力有些坐不住了。弗农姨父厉声说："达力，不准碰他给你的任何东西。"

巨人拉下脸轻蔑地一笑。

"你这个呆瓜儿子用不着再长膘了，德思礼，你放心吧。"

他把香肠递给哈利，哈利早就饿极了。他这辈子也没吃过这么好吃的东西，但他始终无法将目光从巨人身上移开。最后，他看不会有人出来做任何解释，于是问："对不起，可我真的还是不知道您是谁？"

巨人喝下一大口茶，用手背擦了擦嘴。

"就叫我海格吧，"他说，"大伙都这么叫我。我刚才对你说过，我是霍格沃茨的钥匙保管员——当然，霍格沃茨你总该知道吧？"

"唔——我不知道。"哈利说。

海格显得很吃惊。

"对不起。"哈利连忙说。

"对不起？"海格吼叫起来，调过头瞪着德思礼夫妇，他们俩吓得躲到暗处去了，"说对不起的应该是他们！我知道你没有收到那些信，但是我万万没有想到你竟然不知道霍格沃茨。我的天哪！难道你从来没想过你父母是在哪里学会那一切的吗？"

"一切什么？"

"**一切什么**？"海格大喝道，"你等等！"

他一跃而起，火冒三丈，似乎整个小屋都被他庞大的身躯填满了。德思礼夫妇吓得贴着墙瑟瑟发抖。

"你们的意思是要告诉我，"他朝德思礼夫妇咆哮道，"这孩子——这孩子！——对——**什么都不知道吗**？"

哈利觉得他这么说也未免太过分了。他毕竟还上过学，而且成绩也不坏。

"我知道一些事情，"哈利说，"比如，我会做算术之类的功课。"

可是海格朝他一摆手说："我是说，知道我们的世界。你的世界。我的世界。你父母的世界。"

"什么世界？"

CHAPTER FOUR The Keeper of the Keys

Hagrid looked as if he was about to explode.

'DURSLEY!' he boomed.

Uncle Vernon, who had gone very pale, whispered something that sounded like 'Mimblewimble'. Hagrid stared wildly at Harry.

'But yeh must know about yer mum and dad,' he said. 'I mean, they're *famous. You're* famous.'

'What? My – my mum and dad weren't famous, were they?'

'Yeh don' know ... yeh don' know ...' Hagrid ran his fingers through his hair, fixing Harry with a bewildered stare.

'Yeh don' know what yeh *are?*' He said finally.

Uncle Vernon suddenly found his voice.

'Stop!' he commanded. 'Stop right there, sir! I forbid you to tell the boy anything!'

A braver man than Vernon Dursley would have quailed under the furious look Hagrid now gave him; when Hagrid spoke, his every syllable trembled with rage.

'You never told him? Never told him what was in the letter Dumbledore left fer him? I was there! I saw Dumbledore leave it, Dursley! An' you've kept it from him all these years?'

'Kept *what* from me?' Said Harry eagerly.

'STOP! I FORBID YOU!' yelled Uncle Vernon in panic.

Aunt Petunia gave a gasp of horror.

'Ah, go boil yer heads, both of yeh,' said Hagrid. 'Harry – yer a wizard.'

There was silence inside the hut. Only the sea and the whistling wind could be heard.

'I'm a *what?*' gasped Harry.

'A wizard, o' course,' said Hagrid, sitting back down on the sofa, which groaned and sank even lower, 'an' a thumpin' good'un, I'd say, once yeh've been trained up a bit. With a mum an' dad like yours, what else would yeh be? An' I reckon it's abou' time yeh read yer letter.'

Harry stretched out his hand at last to take the yellowish envelope, addressed in emerald green to *Mr H. Potter, The Floor, Hut-on-the-Rock, The Sea.* He pulled out the letter and read:

第4章 钥匙保管员

海格看起来简直要爆炸了。

"**德思礼！**"他大吼一声。

弗农姨父面色煞白，嘀嘀咕咕不知小声说着什么。海格怒冲冲地瞪着哈利。

"你总该知道你父母的事吧，"他说，"我是说，他们很有名气，你也很有名气。"

"什么？我的——我爸妈没有什么名气吧？"

"哦，你不知道……你不知道……"他用手指拢了拢头发，用困惑不解的目光盯着哈利。

"你不知道你是什么人吗？"他终于问。

弗农姨父突然能开口说话了。

"住嘴！"他命令说，"不要再说了，先生！我不准你对这孩子讲任何事！"

即使比弗农姨父更勇敢的人，在海格暴跳如雷、对他怒目而视的时候也会不寒而栗。海格说话时，每一个字都因愤怒而颤抖。

"你就从来没有告诉过他？没有告诉他邓布利多留给他的那封信的内容？我当时在场！我亲眼看见他留下了那封信。德思礼！这么多年你就一直瞒着不告诉他？"

"瞒着什么不让我知道？"哈利急不可耐地问。

"**住嘴！我不准你说！**"弗农姨父惊慌失措，大喊大叫起来。

佩妮姨妈吓得上气不接下气。

"哦，气死你们，把你们两个统统活活气死。"海格说，"哈利，你是一个**巫师**。"

小屋里鸦雀无声，只听见滚滚的涛声和狂风呼号。

"我是什么？"哈利喘着气说。

"一个巫师，当然。"海格说着，坐回到沙发上，沙发嘎吱嘎吱响得更厉害了，"我相信，只要经过一段时间培训，你一定会成为一名优秀的巫师。你有那样的父母，怎么可能不是巫师呢？我想现在该是你看这封信的时候了。"

哈利终于伸手接过一个淡黄色的信封，上边用翡翠绿色墨水写着：大海，礁石上的小屋，地板上，哈利·波特先生收。他抽出信读了起来：

CHAPTER FOUR The Keeper of the Keys

HOGWARTS SCHOOL OF
WITCHCRAFT AND WIZARDRY

Headmaster: Albus Dumbledore
(Order of Merlin, First Class, Grand Sorc., Chf. Warlock,
Supreme Mugwump, International Confed. Of Wizards)

Dear Mr Potter,
We are pleased to inform you that you have a place at
Hogwarts School of Witchcraft and Wizardry. Please find
enclosed a list of all necessary books and equipment.
Term begins on 1 September. We await your owl by no later
than 31 July.

Yours sincerely,

Minerva McGonagall
Deputy Headmistress

Questions exploded inside Harry's head like fireworks and he couldn't decide which to ask first. After a few minutes he stammered, 'What does it mean, they await my owl?'

'Gallopin' Gorgons, that reminds me,' said Hagrid, clapping a hand to his forehead with enough force to knock over a cart horse, and from yet another pocket inside his overcoat he pulled an owl – a real, live, rather ruffled-looking owl – a long quill and a roll of parchment. With his tongue between his teeth he scribbled a note which Harry could read upside-down:

DEAR MR DUMBLEDORE,
GIVEN HARRY HIS LETTER.
TAKING HIM TO BUY HIS THINGS TOMORROW.
WEATHER'S HORRIBLE. HOPE YOU'RE WELL.
HAGRID

Hagrid rolled up the note, gave it to the owl, which clamped it in its beak, went to the door and threw the owl out into the storm. Then he came back

第4章 钥匙保管员

霍格沃茨魔法学校

校长：阿不思·邓布利多

（国际巫师联合会会长、梅林爵士团一级勋章获得者、大魔法师、威森加摩首席魔法师）

亲爱的波特先生：

我们愉快地通知您，您已获准在霍格沃茨魔法学校就读。随信附上所需书籍及装备一览表。

学期定于九月一日开始。我们将于七月三十一日前静候您的猫头鹰带来您的回信。

副校长
米勒娃·麦格 谨上

哈利的问题像烟花一样在头脑里纷纷爆裂，他一时拿不定该先问什么。过了一会儿，他才结结巴巴地说："他们静候我的猫头鹰是什么意思？"

"狂奔的戈耳工啊，哟，我想起来了。"海格用足以推倒一匹壮马的力量拍了拍他的脑门，又从外衣的另一个内袋里掏出一只猫头鹰——一只真的、活蹦乱跳、参着毛的猫头鹰——还掏出一支长长的羽毛笔和一卷羊皮纸。他用牙齿咬着舌尖匆匆写了一张字条，哈利倒着看见字条上写道：

亲爱的邓布利多先生：

已将信交给哈利。明天带他去购买他要用的东西。天气糟透了。祝您安好。

海 格

海格将字条卷起来，让猫头鹰衔在嘴里，走到门口，把猫头鹰放飞到暴风雨中。随后他又回来坐下，仿佛这一切像打了个电话一样平常。

CHAPTER FOUR The Keeper of the Keys

and sat down as though this was as normal as talking on the telephone.

Harry realised his mouth was open and closed it quickly.

'Where was I?' said Hagrid, but at that moment, Uncle Vernon, still ashen-faced but looking very angry, moved into the firelight.

'He's not going,' he said.

Hagrid grunted.

'I'd like ter see a great Muggle like you stop him,' he said.

'A what?' Said Harry, interested.

'A Muggle,' said Hagrid. 'It's what we call non-magic folk like them. An' it's your bad luck you grew up in a family o' the biggest Muggles I ever laid eyes on.'

'We swore when we took him in we'd put a stop to that rubbish,' said Uncle Vernon, 'swore we'd stamp it out of him! Wizard, indeed!'

'You *knew*?' Said Harry. 'You *knew* I'm a – a wizard?'

'Knew!' Shrieked Aunt Petunia suddenly. '*Knew*! Of course we knew! How could you not be, my dratted sister being what she was? Oh, she got a letter just like that and disappeared off to that – that *school* – and came home every holiday with her pockets full of frog-spawn, turning teacups into rats. I was the only one who saw her for what she was – a freak! But for my mother and father, oh no, it was Lily this and Lily that, they were proud of having a witch in the family!'

She stopped to draw a deep breath and then went ranting on. It seemed she had been wanting to say all this for years.

'Then she met that Potter at school and they left and got married and had you, and of course I knew you'd be just the same, just as strange, just as – as – *abnormal* – and then, if you please, she went and got herself blown up and we got landed with you!'

Harry had gone very white. As soon as he found his voice he said, 'Blown up? You told me they died in a car crash!'

'CAR CRASH!' roared Hagrid, jumping up so angrily that the Dursleys scuttled back to their corner. 'How could a car crash kill Lily an' James Potter? It's an outrage! A scandal! Harry Potter not knowin' his own story when every kid in our world knows his name!'

'But why? What happened?' Harry asked urgently.

哈利发现自己一直张着嘴,连忙把嘴闭上。

"我说到哪儿了?"海格说。这时弗农姨父突然移到火光照亮的地方,脸色依旧惨白,但看上去很生气。

"他不会去的。"他说。

海格哼了一声。

"我倒要看看,像你这样的大麻瓜用什么办法阻拦他。"他说。

"你这样的什么?"哈利好奇地问。

"麻瓜,"海格说,"这是我们对像他们这类没有魔法的人的称呼。不幸的是,你竟然在这么一个不相信魔法的家庭里长大。"

"我们收养他的时候就发过誓,要制止这类荒唐事,"弗农姨父说,"发誓要让他与这一切一刀两断!什么巫师,哼!"

"您早就知道了?"哈利说,"您早就知道我是一个——一个巫师?"

"老早就知道,"佩妮姨妈突然尖着嗓子喊了起来,"老早就知道!我们当然老早就知道!我那个该死的妹妹既然是,你怎么可能不是?哦,她就是收到这样的一封信,然后就不见了——进了那所学校——每次放假回来,口袋里装满了癞蛤蟆蛋,把茶杯都变成老鼠。只有我一个人,算是把她看透了——十足一个怪物!可是我的父母却看不清,整天莉莉长、莉莉短,家里有个巫婆他们还美滋滋的!"

她停下来喘了一大口气,接着又喋喋不休地讲起来。看来这些话她已经憋在心里很多年,一直想一吐为快呢。

"然后她就在学校里遇到了那个波特,毕业后他们结了婚,有了你。当然,我也知道你会跟他们一样,一样古怪,一样——一样——不正常——后来,对不起,她走了,自我爆炸了,我们只好收养你!"

哈利的脸色变得煞白。等到能说出话来时,他立刻说:"爆炸?您对我说过,他们是遇到车祸丧生的!"

"**车祸**!"海格咆哮起来,他一跃而起,火冒三丈,吓得德思礼夫妇又躲到他们的角落里去了,"车祸怎么会伤害莉莉和詹姆·波特?这是诬蔑!是诽谤!我们世界里的每个孩子都知道哈利的名字,而他却不知道自己的身世!"

"可是为什么?怎么回事?"哈利急不可耐地问。

CHAPTER FOUR   The Keeper of the Keys

The anger faded from Hagrid's face. He looked suddenly anxious.

'I never expected this,' he said, in a low, worried voice. 'I had no idea, when Dumbledore told me there might be trouble gettin' hold of yeh, how much yeh didn't know. Ah, Harry, I don' know if I'm the right person ter tell yeh – but someone's gotta – yeh can't go off ter Hogwarts not knowin'.'

He threw a dirty look at the Dursleys.

'Well, it's best yeh know as much as I can tell yeh – mind, I can't tell yeh everythin', it's a great myst'ry, parts of it …'

He sat down, stared into the fire for a few seconds and then said, 'It begins, I suppose, with – with a person called – but it's incredible yeh don't know his name, everyone in our world knows –'

'Who?'

'Well – I don' like sayin' the name if I can help it. No one does.'

'Why not?'

'Gulpin' gargoyles, Harry, people are still scared. Blimey, this is difficult. See, there was this wizard who went … bad. As bad as you could go. Worse. Worse than worse. His name was …'

Hagrid gulped, but no words came out.

'Could you write it down?' Harry suggested.

'Nah – can't spell it. All right – *Voldemort*.' Hagrid shuddered. 'Don' make me say it again. Anyway, this – this wizard, about twenty years ago now, started lookin' fer followers. Got 'em, too – some were afraid, some just wanted a bit o' his power, 'cause he was gettin' himself power, all right. Dark days, harry. Didn't know who ter trust, didn't dare get friendly with strange wizards or witches … Terrible things happened. He was takin' over. 'course, some stood up to him – an' he killed 'em. Horribly. One o' the only safe places left was Hogwarts. Reckon Dumbledore's the only one you-know-who was afraid of. Didn't dare try takin' the school, not jus' then, anyway.

'Now, yer mum an' dad were as good a witch an' wizard as I ever knew. Head Boy an' Girl at Hogwarts in their day! Suppose the myst'ry is why you-know-who never tried to get 'em on his side before … probably knew they were too close ter Dumbledore ter want anythin' ter do with the Dark Side.

第4章 钥匙保管员

海格脸上的怒气消了,他突然显得焦虑不安起来。

"我从来没有料到会是这样。"他用低沉而焦虑的声调说,"邓布利多对我说过找你可能会遇到麻烦,因为有许多事你不知道。哦,哈利,我不知道由我来告诉你是不是合适——不过总得有人告诉你——你不能一无所知就去霍格沃茨上学呀。"

他鄙夷地朝德思礼夫妇扫了一眼。

"好,我来把我所知道的一切都告诉你——不过,我不能告诉你事情的全部,因为很多事情还是一个谜……"

他坐下来,朝炉火看了一会儿,然后说:"我想,我从一个叫——不过你不知道他的名字,真叫人不能相信,我们的世界里人人都知道——"

"谁?"

"好,除非万不得已,我不想提他的名字。没有人愿意提。"

"为什么不愿意提?"

"贪吃的滴水嘴石兽啊,哈利,人们到现在还心有余悸呢。哎呀,难哪。当时有一个巫师,他后来……变坏了。坏透了。坏得不能再坏了。他的名字叫……"

海格咽了一口唾沫,可还是说不出一个字来。

"你能写出来吗?"哈利提醒说。

"不行——这个字我不会拼。好吧——他叫伏地魔。"海格打了个寒战,"别逼我重复他的名字了。总之,这个……这个巫师,大概二十年前,开始为自己找门徒。他也找到了一些人……他们有些是因为怕他,有些是想从他那里学到法力,因为他的法力在一天天变强。好了,那段日子可真是黑暗啊,哈利。你不知道该相信谁,也不敢跟陌生巫师交朋友……还发生了许多可怕的事情。他接管了我们这个世界。当然有人反对他,他就把他们都杀掉了。太可怕了。当时唯一安全的地方就是霍格沃茨。那个神秘人唯一害怕的就是邓布利多。他不敢动那所学校,至少当时是这样。

"现在来说说你的父母吧,他们是我知道的最优秀的巫师。当年在霍格沃茨还分别担任男女学生会的主席呢!叫人弄不明白的是当初那个神秘人为什么没有把他们拉到他那边去……也许他知道他们和邓布利多很接近,不想与黑魔势力有关系吧。

CHAPTER FOUR   The Keeper of the Keys

'Maybe he thought he could persuade 'em ... maybe he just wanted 'em outta the way. All anyone knows is, he turned up in the village where you was all living, on Hallowe'en ten years ago. You was just a year old. He came ter yer house an' – an' –'

Hagrid suddenly pulled out a very dirty, spotted handkerchief and blew his nose with a sound like a foghorn.

'Sorry,' he said. 'But it's that sad – knew yer mum an' dad, an' nicer people yeh couldn't find – anyway –

'You-Know-Who killed 'em. An' then – an' this is the real myst'ry of the thing – he tried to kill you, too. Wanted ter make a clean job of it, I suppose, or maybe he just liked killin' by then. But he couldn't do it. Never wondered how you got that mark on yer forehead? That was no ordinary cut. That's what yeh get when a powerful, evil curse touches yeh – took care of yer mum an' dad an' yer house, even – but it didn't work on you, an' that's why yer famous, Harry. No one ever lived after he decided ter kill 'em, no one except you, an' he'd killed some o' the best witches an' wizards of the age – the McKinnons, the Bones, the Prewetts – an' you was only a baby, an' you lived.'

Something very painful was going on in Harry's mind. As Hagrid's story came to a close, he saw again the blinding flash of green light, more clearly than he had ever remembered it before – and he remembered something else, for the first time in his life – a high, cold, cruel laugh.

Hagrid was watching him sadly.

'Took yeh from the ruined house myself, on Dumbledore's orders. Brought yeh ter this lot ...'

'Load of old tosh,' said Uncle Vernon. Harry jumped, he had almost forgotten that the Dursleys were there. Uncle Vernon certainly seemed to have got back his courage. He was glaring at Hagrid and his fists were clenched.

'Now, you listen here, boy,' he snarled. 'I accept there's something strange about you, probably nothing a good beating wouldn't have cured – and as for all this about your parents, well, they were weirdos, no denying it, and the world's better off without them in my opinion – asked for all they got, getting mixed up with these wizarding types – just what I expected, always knew they'd come to a sticky end –'

But at that moment, Hagrid leapt from the sofa and drew a battered pink umbrella from inside his coat. Pointing this at Uncle Vernon like a sword, he said, 'I'm warning you, Dursley – I'm warning you – one more word ...'

第4章 钥匙保管员

"也许他认为他可以说服他们……也许想干脆把他们干掉。大家都知道,十年前的万圣节前夕,他来到你们住的村庄,当时你只有一岁。他来到你们家就——就——"

海格突然掏出一块脏得要命的圆点花纹手帕擤了擤鼻涕,那声音响得像在吹雾角。

"对不起,"他说,"这是一个不幸的消息。我认识你的父母,再也找不到比他们更好的人了,不管怎么说——

"神秘人把他们杀了,他也要杀你,也许是想斩尽杀绝吧。可是叫人弄不明白的是他没有杀成。你就从来没有想过你脑门上那道伤疤是怎么来的吗?那不是一般的伤疤。那是一道很厉害的魔咒留下的。那道魔咒杀了你的父母,毁了你的家,可是碰到你身上却没有起作用。于是你也就因为这个出名了,哈利。凡是他决定要杀的人,没有一个能躲过劫难,只有你大难不死。他杀掉了当时一些优秀的巫师,比如麦金农夫妇、博恩斯夫妇、普威特兄弟俩。你是唯一大难不死,活下来的人。"

哈利的脑海里出现了一些非常悲惨的景象。当海格的故事就要讲完的时候,那道耀眼的绿光突然闪现,比他记忆中的任何一次都更加清晰。他又想起另外一些事,平生第一次听到一阵响亮、阴冷、凶残的笑声。

海格难过地看着他。

"我奉邓布利多之命亲自把你从那栋被毁的房子里抱了出来,送到这伙人这里……"

"胡说八道。"弗农姨父说。哈利跳了起来,他差一点儿忘了德思礼夫妇还在这里。弗农姨父显然恢复了勇气,他紧握双拳,对海格怒目而视。

"小子,现在听我说,"他咆哮起来,"我承认你身上是有些奇怪的地方,但是可能揍你一顿就好了。至于你父母,我只能说,他们都是怪物,这不可否认。我是说,这世界没有他们会更好,看看他们都干了什么,整天跟巫师混在一起,我早就知道他们迟早要吃苦头——"

弗农姨父正说着,海格突然从沙发上跳起来,从外衣内袋里掏出一把粉红色的破伞。他像拿着一把剑那样用伞指着弗农姨父说:"我警告你,德思礼,我警告你……敢再说一个字……"

CHAPTER FOUR The Keeper of the Keys

In danger of being speared on the end of an umbrella by a bearded giant, Uncle Vernon's courage failed again; he flattened himself against the wall and fell silent.

'That's better,' said Hagrid, breathing heavily and sitting back down on the sofa, which this time sagged right down to the floor.

Harry, meanwhile, still had questions to ask, hundreds of them.

'But what happened to Vol – sorry – I mean, You-Know-Who?'

'Good question, Harry. Disappeared. Vanished. Same night he tried ter kill you. Makes yeh even more famous. That's the biggest myst'ry, see ... He was gettin' more an' more powerful – why'd he go?

'Some say he died. Codswallop, in my opinion. Dunno if he had enough human left in him to die. Some say he's still out there, bidin' his time, like, but I don' believe it. People who was on his side came back ter ours. Some of 'em came outta kinda trances. Don' reckon they could've done if he was comin' back.

'Most of us reckon he's still out there somewhere but lost his powers. Too weak to carry on. 'cause somethin' about you finished him, Harry. There was somethin' goin' on that night he hadn't counted on – *I* dunno what it was, no one does – but somethin' about you stumped him, all right.'

Hagrid looked at Harry with warmth and respect blazing in his eyes, but Harry, instead of feeling pleased and proud, felt quite sure there had been a horrible mistake. A wizard? Him? How could he possibly be? He'd spent his life being clouted by Dudley and bullied by Aunt Petunia and Uncle Vernon; if he was really a wizard, why hadn't they been turned into warty toads every time they'd tried to lock him in his cupboard? If he'd once defeated the greatest sorcerer in the world, how come Dudley had always been able to kick him around like a football?

'Hagrid,' he said quietly, 'I think you must have made a mistake. I don't think I can be a wizard.'

To his surprise, Hagrid chuckled.

'Not a wizard, eh? Never made things happen when you was scared, or angry?'

Harry looked into the fire. Now he came to think about it ... Every odd thing that had ever made his aunt and uncle furious with him had happened when he, Harry, had been upset or angry ... Chased by Dudley's gang, he

弗农姨父怕被这个大胡子巨人的伞头戳伤，又泄气了，紧贴着墙不再说话。

"这样才好。"海格说着，大口喘着气坐到沙发上，这回沙发整个塌到地板上了。

哈利还有许多问题，成百上千的问题要问。

"可是伏——对不起，我是说，那个神秘人后来怎么样了？"

"问得好，哈利。他不见了。失踪了。就在要杀你的那天夜里。这一来就让你的名气更大了。这也是最让人弄不明白的地方，你看……他的法力越来越强，为什么要走掉呢？

"有人说他死了。我认为纯粹是胡说八道。他身上恐怕已经没有多少人性，所以也就不可能死去。有人说他还在这一带，等待时机，可能吧，但我不相信。原来支持他的人都回到我们这边来了。有些人已经从噩梦中清醒。如果他还会卷土重来，他们是不可能这么做的。

"我们大多数人都认为他还在这一带，不过已经失去了法力，已经虚弱得成不了气候了。因为你身上具有的某种力量把他毁了，哈利。那天晚上肯定发生了一件他没有预料到的事——我不知道那是什么事，没有人知道——不过你身上具有的某种力量使他受挫了，就是这样。"

海格用热切而崇敬的目光注视着哈利，但哈利并没有感觉到高兴和自豪；相反，他认为这肯定是一个可怕的错误。一个巫师？他？他怎么可能是巫师呢？他一直在达力的殴打和佩妮姨妈、弗农姨父的凌辱下偷生；如果他真是巫师，当他们要把他锁进储物间的时候，他们为什么没有变成疙疙瘩瘩的癫蛤蟆呢？如果他曾经打败过世界上最强大的魔法师，达力为什么能像踢足球那样把他踢得到处乱跑呢？

"海格，"他轻声说，"我想您一定搞错了，我想，我不可能是一个巫师。"

哈利很吃惊，海格居然咯咯地笑了起来。

"不是巫师，你害怕或生气的时候就从来没有事情发生过吗？"

哈利看着炉火，开始思索——每件惹得他姨父姨妈对他大发雷霆的怪事都发生在他——哈利——情绪不好或生气的时候……被达力一伙追打的时候，他总有办法让他们追不着……他正为剪成可笑的发型上学发

CHAPTER FOUR The Keeper of the Keys

had somehow found himself out of their reach ... Dreading going to school with that ridiculous haircut, he'd managed to make it grow back ... And the very last time Dudley had hit him, hadn't he got his revenge, without even realising he was doing it? Hadn't he set a boa constrictor on him?

Harry looked back at Hagrid, smiling, and saw that Hagrid was positively beaming at him.

'See?' said Hagrid. 'Harry Potter, not a wizard – you wait, you'll be right famous at Hogwarts.'

But Uncle Vernon wasn't going to give in without a fight.

'Haven't I told you he's not going?' he hissed. 'He's going to stonewall high and he'll be grateful for it. I've read those letters and he needs all sorts of rubbish – spell books and wands and –'

'If he wants ter go, a great Muggle like you won't stop him,' growled Hagrid. 'Stop Lily an' James Potter's son goin' ter Hogwarts! Yer mad. His name's been down ever since he was born. He's off ter the finest school of witchcraft and wizardry in the world. Seven years there and he won't know himself. He'll be with youngsters of his own sort, fer a change, an' he'll be under the greatest Headmaster Hogwarts ever had, Albus Dumbled–'

'I AM NOT PAYING FOR SOME CRACKPOT OLD FOOL TO TEACH HIM MAGIC TRICKS!' yelled Uncle Vernon.

But he had finally gone too far. Hagrid seized his umbrella and whirled it over his head. 'NEVER –' he thundered, '– INSULT – ALBUS – DUMBELDORE – IN – FRONT – OF – ME!'

He brought the umbrella swishing down through the air to point at Dudley – there was a flash of violet light, a sound like a firecracker, a sharp squeal and next second, Dudley was dancing on the spot with his hands clasped over his fat bottom, howling in pain. When he turned his back on them, Harry saw a curly pig's tail poking through a hole in his trousers.

Uncle Vernon roared. Pulling Aunt Petunia and Dudley into the other room, he cast one last terrified look at Hagrid and slammed the door behind them.

Hagrid looked down at his umbrella and stroked his beard.

'Shouldn'ta lost me temper,' he said ruefully, 'but it didn't work anyway. Meant ter turn him into a pig, but I suppose he was so much like a pig anyway there wasn't much left ter do.'

He cast a sideways look at Harry under his bushy eyebrows.

第4章 钥匙保管员

怵，可他又让头发恢复了原样……而最近一次达力追打他的时候，他不是在不知不觉中就对他进行了报复吗？他不是放出一条巨蟒去吓唬达力了吗？

哈利回过头来对海格报以一笑，发现海格也朝他露出了笑容。

"明白了吧？"海格说，"哈利·波特，不是巫师——你等着瞧吧，你会在霍格沃茨名声大噪的。"

但弗农姨父也不甘心就此罢休。

"难道我没有对你说过他不去吗？"他尖着嗓子说，"他要去上石墙中学，他会感激我的。我看过那些信，要他准备一大堆无用的东西——像咒语书，还有魔杖什么的——"

"如果他真想去，像你这样不信魔法的大傻瓜是拦不住他的，"海格咆哮道，"阻止莉莉和詹姆·波特的儿子上霍格沃茨，你这是疯了！他一生下来，他的名字就入了霍格沃茨的名册。他要进的是世界上最优秀的魔法学校。七年之后，他会面貌一新。他要和跟他一样的孩子在一起，换换环境，还要在霍格沃茨有史以来最伟大的校长阿不思·邓布利多的教导下——"

"我决不花钱让一个疯老头子，一个大傻瓜去教他变戏法！"弗农姨父大吼起来。

这次他确实太过分了。海格抓起他的伞在头顶上绕了几圈，怒喝道："永远——不准——在——我——面前——侮辱——阿不思——邓布利多！"

他用伞嗖地在空中挥了一下，然后直指达力，忽地一道紫罗兰色的闪光、一声鞭炮似的响声、一声尖叫，接着达力就用双手捂着肥胖的屁股，疼得直蹦，哇哇乱叫。当他把身子转过去、背朝他们时，哈利看见一根卷曲的猪尾巴从裤子的破洞里伸了出来。

弗农姨父一边吼叫，一边把佩妮姨妈和达力朝另一间屋拖去。他最后惊恐地望了海格一眼，砰的一声把门带上了。

海格低头看了看伞，捋了捋胡须。

"我不该发火，"他懊恼地说，"不过，还是没有成功。我本来想把他变成一只猪，也许他已经太像猪了，所以用不着再去变什么了。"

他从浓密的眉毛下斜瞟了哈利一眼。

CHAPTER FOUR The Keeper of the Keys

'Be grateful if yeh didn't mention that ter anyone at Hogwarts,' he said. 'I'm – er – not supposed ter do magic, strictly speakin'. I was allowed ter do a bit ter follow yeh an' get yer letters to yeh an' stuff – one o' the reasons I was so keen ter take on the job –'

'Why aren't you supposed to do magic?' asked Harry.

'Oh, well – I was at Hogwarts meself but I – er – got expelled, ter tell yeh the truth. In me third year. They snapped me wand in half an' everything. But Dumbledore let me stay on as gamekeeper. Great man, Dumbledore.'

'Why were you expelled?'

'It's gettin' late and we've got lots ter do tomorrow,' said Hagrid loudly. 'Gotta get up ter town, get all yer books an' that.'

He took off his thick black coat and threw it to Harry.

'You can kip under that,' he said. 'Don' mind if it wriggles a bit, I think I still got a couple o' dormice in one o' the pockets.'

第4章 钥匙保管员

"要是你对霍格沃茨的任何人都不提起这件事，我就谢谢你了。"他说，"我——哦——严格地讲，我不能施用魔法。只有在找你或给你送信的时候才准许我用一点儿——这也是我热心接下这个工作的原因之一。"

"为什么不准许您施用魔法呢？"哈利问。

"哦，是这样，我自己也在霍格沃茨上过学，但是，实话对你说，我——哦——被开除了。我当时上三年级。他们撅断了我的魔杖，其他东西都没收了。可邓布利多让我留下看管猎场。他可真是个了不起的人哪。"

"你为什么被开除？"

"时间太晚了，明天我们还有许多事情要做，"海格大声说，"明天一早还要进城给你买书什么的。"

他脱下黑色的厚呢外衣，扔给哈利。

"你就盖着这个睡吧。"他说，"要是有什么东西乱动，不用理会，有个衣袋里好像还装着两只睡鼠。"

CHAPTER FIVE
Diagon Alley

Harry woke early the next morning. Although he could tell it was daylight, he kept his eyes shut tight.

'It was a dream,' he told himself firmly. 'I dreamed a giant called Hagrid came to tell me I was going to a school for wizards. When I open my eyes I'll be at home in my cupboard.'

There was suddenly a loud tapping noise.

'And there's Aunt Petunia knocking on the door,' Harry thought, his heart sinking. But he still didn't open his eyes. It had been such a good dream.

Tap. Tap. Tap.

'All right,' Harry mumbled, 'I'm getting up.'

He sat up and Hagrid's heavy coat fell off him. The hut was full of sunlight, the storm was over, Hagrid himself was asleep on the collapsed sofa and there was an owl rapping its claw on the window, a newspaper held in its beak.

Harry scrambled to his feet, so happy he felt as though a large balloon was swelling inside him. He went straight to the window and jerked it open. The owl swooped in and dropped the newspaper on top of Hagrid, who didn't wake up. The owl then fluttered on to the floor and began to attack Hagrid's coat.

'Don't do that.'

Harry tried to wave the owl out of the way, but it snapped its beak fiercely at him and carried on savaging the coat.

'Hagrid!' said Harry loudly. 'There's an owl –'

'Pay him,' Hagrid grunted into the sofa.

'What?'

'He wants payin' fer deliverin' the paper. Look in the pockets.'

第 5 章
对 角 巷

第二天一大早哈利就醒了。他明明知道天已经亮了，可还是把眼睛闭得紧紧的。

"这是一个梦，"他确定地对自己说，"我梦见一个叫海格的巨人，他来对我说，我要进一所魔法学校。等我一睁眼，我准在家里的储物间里。"

突然传来一阵啪啪的响声。

"又是佩妮姨妈在捶门了。"哈利想，他的心一沉。可他没有睁开眼，因为那个梦实在太好了。

啪。啪。啪。

"好了，"哈利咕哝说，"我这就起来。"

他坐起来，海格的厚外衣从身上滑了下去。小屋里充满了阳光，暴风雨已经过去了。海格睡在坍塌的沙发上。一只猫头鹰正用爪子敲打着窗户，嘴里衔着一份报纸。

哈利感到特别高兴，仿佛胸中揣着的一个气球渐渐鼓了起来，使他飘飘欲仙了。他径直走到窗前，用力推开窗户。猫头鹰飞了进来，把报纸扔到海格身上，但他还是没有醒。猫头鹰扑腾着翅膀飞到地上，开始抓海格的外衣。

"别抓。"

哈利挥挥手想让猫头鹰走开，可是猫头鹰用它的利喙朝哈利猛啄过来，之后又去抓海格的外衣。

"海格！"哈利大声喊道，"这里有一只猫头鹰——"

"把钱付给它。"海格在沙发上哼哼唧唧地说。

"什么？"

CHAPTER FIVE   Diagon Alley

Hagrid's coat seemed to be made of nothing *but* pockets – bunches of keys, slug pellets, balls of string, mint humbugs, tea-bags ... finally, Harry pulled out a handful of strange-looking coins.

'Give him five Knuts,' said Hagrid sleepily.

'Knuts?'

'The little bronze ones.'

Harry counted out five little bronze coins and the owl held out its leg so he could put the money into a small leather pouch tied to it. Then it flew off through the open window.

Hagrid yawned loudly, sat up and stretched.

'Best be off, Harry, lots ter do today, gotta get up ter London an' buy all yer stuff fer school.'

Harry was turning over the wizard coins and looking at them. He had just thought of something which made him feel as though the happy balloon inside him had got a puncture.

'Um – Hagrid?'

'Mm?' said Hagrid, who was pulling on his huge boots.

'I haven't got any money – and you heard Uncle Vernon last night – he won't pay for me to go and learn magic.'

'Don't worry about that,' said Hagrid, standing up and scratching his head. 'D'yeh think yer parents didn't leave yeh anything?'

'But if their house was destroyed –'

'They didn' keep their gold in the house, boy! Nah, first stop fer us is Gringotts. Wizards' bank. Have a sausage, they're not bad cold – an' I wouldn' say no teh a bit o' yer birthday cake, neither.'

'Wizards have *banks*?'

'Just the one. Gringotts. Run by goblins.'

Harry dropped the bit of sausage he was holding.

'*Goblins?*'

'Yeah – so yeh'd be mad ter try an' rob it, I'll tell yeh that. Never mess with goblins, Harry. Gringotts is the safest place in the world fer anything yeh want ter keep safe – 'cept maybe Hogwarts. As a matter o' fact, I gotta visit Gringotts anyway. Fer Dumbledore. Hogwarts business.' Hagrid drew himself up proudly. 'He usually gets me ter do important

第 5 章　对角巷

"它要你付送报费。你在外衣袋里找找。"

海格的外衣上似乎除了口袋还是口袋——口袋里装着成串的钥匙、除鼻涕虫药、线团、薄荷硬糖、茶袋……最后，哈利终于掏出了一把稀奇古怪的硬币。

"给它五个纳特。"海格睡意蒙眬地说。

"'纳特'？"

"那些小铜板。"

哈利数出五个铜板，猫头鹰伸出一只腿，要他把硬币放进绑在腿上的一只小皮囊里。随后它从敞开的窗口飞了出去。

海格打了个大哈欠，坐起来伸了伸懒腰。

"咱们最好还是早点走吧，哈利，今天还有好多事要做呢，要去伦敦给你买上学需要的所有东西。"

哈利摆弄着巫师的钱币，沉思起来。他不知想起了什么，觉得胸中那只快乐的气球被戳破了。

"唔，海格？"

"怎么？"海格说，正在套他的大靴子。

"我一个钱也没有，昨天晚上你已经听弗农姨父说过了，他不会花钱让我去学魔法的。"

"这个你不用担心，"海格说，站起来搔了搔头，"你以为你父母什么也没有给你留下吗？"

"可要是连他们的房子全都毁了——"

"他们不会把黄金放在家里的，孩子！我们第一站去古灵阁。巫师银行。来根香肠吧，冷的也不难吃——加上一块你的生日蛋糕更不错。"

"巫师还有银行？"

"只有一家。古灵阁。是妖精们开的。"

哈利手里的香肠掉到了地上。

"妖精？"

"是的，所以，听我说，你要是想抢银行，那你就是发疯了。绝对不能把妖精们惹恼了，哈利。如果你想找一个安全可靠的地方存放东西，那么，我想除了霍格沃茨之外就是古灵阁了。其实，不管怎样我都要去

stuff fer him. Fetchin' you – gettin' things from Gringotts – knows he can trust me, see.'

'Got everythin'? Come on, then.'

Harry followed Hagrid out on to the rock. The sky was quite clear now and the sea gleamed in the sunlight. The boat Uncle Vernon had hired was still there, with a lot of water in the bottom after the storm.

'How did you get here?' Harry asked, looking around for another boat.

'Flew,' said Hagrid.

'*Flew?*'

'Yeah – but we'll go back in this. Not s'pposed ter use magic now I've got yeh.'

They settled down in the boat, Harry still staring at Hagrid, trying to imagine him flying.

'Seems a shame ter row, though,' said Hagrid, giving Harry another of his sideways looks. 'If I was ter – er – speed things up a bit, would yeh mind not mentionin' it at Hogwarts?'

'Of course not,' said Harry, eager to see more magic. Hagrid pulled out the pink umbrella again, tapped it twice on the side of the boat and they sped off towards land.

'Why would you be mad to try and rob Gringotts?' Harry asked.

'Spells – enchantments,' said Hagrid, unfolding his news-paper as he spoke. 'They say there's dragons guardin' the high-security vaults. And then yeh gotta find yer way – Gringotts is hundreds of miles under London, see. Deep under the Underground. Yeh'd die of hunger tryin' ter get out, even if yeh did manage ter get yer hands on summat.'

Harry sat and thought about this while Hagrid read his newspaper, the *Daily Prophet*. Harry had learnt from Uncle Vernon that people liked to be left alone while they did this, but it was very difficult, he'd never had so many questions in his life.

'Ministry o' Magic messin' things up as usual,' Hagrid muttered, turning the page.

'There's a Ministry of Magic?' Harry asked, before he could stop himself.

''Course,' said Hagrid. 'They wanted Dumbledore fer Minister, o' course,

第5章 对角巷

一趟古灵阁，去替邓布利多办一件霍格沃茨的公事。"海格很得意地挺起胸来，"重要的事情他总是交给我办，比如来接你，去古灵阁取东西，都要我办，他知道他可以信任我，明白吗？

"东西都带好了吗？那就走吧。"

哈利跟着海格来到外面的礁石上。这时天晴气爽，海水闪烁着阳光。弗农姨父租的那条船还停泊在原处，暴风雨过后，船舱里积了许多水。

"您是怎么到这里来的？"哈利问，四下里搜寻另外一条船。

"飞过来的。"海格说。

"飞过来的？"

"是的——不过我们得坐这条船回去。找到你以后，我就不能用魔法了。"

他们在船上坐定，哈利还在目不转睛地盯着海格，竭力想象他飞行的样子。

"可惜得划船，不过，"海格说着，又朝哈利斜瞟了一眼，"我要是让——让——船开快一点，你能在霍格沃茨不提这件事吗？"

"当然可以。"哈利说，他心急火燎地想看到更多的魔法。海格抽出他那把粉红色的伞，敲了两下船帮，船就飞快地向岸边驶去了。

"您为什么说疯子才会去抢古灵阁呢？"哈利问。

"因为他们会咒语——会施妖术。"海格一边说，一边翻开报纸，"据说那些防范最严密的金库都由火龙把守着。要到那里还得先找到路——古灵阁在伦敦地下好几百英里的地方呢，明白吗？比地铁还要深。如果你真有办法偷到了一点东西，恐怕在找到出来的路之前，你早就饿死了。"

海格开始看他的《预言家日报》，哈利还坐在那里思前想后。哈利从弗农姨父那里知道人读报的时候总喜欢清静，可这实在太难了，他平生从来没有像现在这样有这么多问题想问。

"魔法部总是把事情搞得一团糟。"海格翻过报纸，抱怨说。

"还有魔法部？"哈利忍不住问。

"当然了，"海格说，"他们当然希望邓布利多当部长，可是邓布利

but he'd never leave Hogwarts, so old Cornelius Fudge got the job. Bungler if ever there was one. So he pelts Dumbledore with owls every morning, askin' fer advice.'

'But what does a Ministry of Magic *do*?'

'Well, their main job is to keep it from the Muggles that there's still witches an' wizards up an' down the country.'

'Why?'

'*Why*? Blimey, Harry, everyone'd be wantin' magic solutions to their problems. Nah, we're best left alone.'

At this moment the boat bumped gently into the harbour wall. Hagrid folded up his newspaper and they clambered up the stone steps on to the street.

Passers-by stared a lot at Hagrid as they walked through the little town to the station. Harry couldn't blame them. Not only was Hagrid twice as tall as anyone else, he kept pointing at perfectly ordinary things like parking meters and saying loudly, 'See that, Harry? Things these Muggles dream up, eh?'

'Hagrid,' said Harry, panting a bit as he ran to keep up, 'did you say there are *dragons* at Gringotts?'

'Well, so they say,' said Hagrid. 'Crikey, I'd like a dragon.'

'You'd *like* one?'

'Wanted one ever since I was a kid – here we go.'

They had reached the station. There was a train to London in five minutes' time. Hagrid, who didn't understand 'Muggle money', as he called it, gave the notes to Harry so he could buy their tickets.

People stared more than ever on the train. Hagrid took up two seats and sat knitting what looked like a canary-yellow circus tent.

'Still got yer letter, Harry?' he asked as he counted stitches.

Harry took the parchment envelope out of his pocket.

'Good,' said Hagrid. 'There's a list there of everything yeh need.'

Harry unfolded a second piece of paper he hadn't noticed the night before and read:

第 5 章 对角巷

多坚决不肯离开霍格沃茨。这么一来,老康奈利·福吉就担任了这一职务。他是天下最没头脑的人了,总是砸锅。所以他每天早晨总派出许多猫头鹰到邓布利多那里去要邓布利多出点子。"

"可这个魔法部做些什么呢?"

"哦,他们的主要工作是不让麻瓜们发现这个国家还有那么多巫师。"

"为什么?"

"为什么?我的天哪,哈利,那样一来,人人都会希望用魔法来解决难题了。我们最好还是别去惹麻烦。"

这时船轻轻地碰到了码头。海格卷起报纸,两人踏上石阶向大街走去。

当他们俩穿过小城向车站走去时,一路上过往的人都目不转睛地盯着海格。哈利并不怪他们,这不仅因为海格比普通人要高大一倍,而且他还不停地对一些诸如汽车停车计费器之类很平常的东西指指点点,大声说:"看见那玩意儿了吗,哈利?这又是麻瓜们搞出来的什么名堂,嗯?"

"海格,"哈利说,为了追上海格的脚步,他已经有些气喘吁吁了,"您是说古灵阁有火龙吗?"

"是的,他们这么说。"海格说,"哟,我也想要一条火龙呢。"

"您也想要一条火龙?"

"我从小就想要了——走这边。"

他们来到了车站,再过五分钟有一趟开往伦敦的列车。海格说他不会用麻瓜的钱,就把钞票塞到了哈利手中,让他去买车票。

在火车上,人们就更盯着他们看了。海格占据了两个座位。落座之后还编织起一顶淡黄色的、像马戏团帐篷一样的东西。

"给你的信带了吗?"他一边数针,一边问。

哈利从衣袋里掏出一个羊皮纸信封。

"好,"海格说,"里边有一张必备用品的单子。"

哈利打开昨天夜里没有留意的第二页信纸,读道:

HOGWARTS SCHOOL OF
WITCHCRAFT AND WIZARDRY

UNIFORM

First-year students will require:
1. Three sets of plain work robes (black)
2. One plain pointed hat (black) for day wear
3. One pair of protective gloves (dragon hide or similar)
4. One winter cloak (black, silver fastenings)

Please note that all pupils' clothes should carry name tags

SET BOOKS

All students should have a copy of each of the following:

The Standard Book of Spells (Grade 1) by Miranda Goshawk
A History of Magic by Bathilda Bagshot
Magical Theory by Adalbert Waffling
A Beginner's Guide to Transfiguration by Emeric Switch
One Thousand Magical Herbs and Fungi by Phyllida Spore
Magical Drafts and Potions by Arsenius Jigger
Fantastic Beasts and Where to Find Them by Newt Scamander
The Dark Forces: A Guide to Self-Protection by Quentin Trimble

OTHER EQUIPMENT

1 wand
1 cauldron (pewter, standard size 2)
1 set glass or crystal phials
1 telescope
1 set brass scales

Students may also bring an owl OR a cat OR a toad

霍格沃茨魔法学校

〔制服〕

一年级新生需要:

　　1. 三套素面工作袍（黑色）

　　2. 一顶日间戴的素面尖顶帽（黑色）

　　3. 一双防护手套（龙皮或同类材料制作）

　　4. 一件冬用斗篷（黑色，银扣）

请注意：学生全部服装均须缀有姓名标牌

〔课本〕

全部学生均须准备下列图书：

　　《标准咒语，初级》，米兰达·戈沙克著

　　《魔法史》，巴希达·巴沙特著

　　《魔法理论》，阿德贝·沃夫林著

　　《初学变形指南》，埃默瑞·斯威奇著

　　《千种神奇药草及蕈类》，菲利达·斯波尔著

　　《魔法药剂与药水》，阿森尼·吉格著

　　《神奇动物在哪里》，纽特·斯卡曼德著

　　《黑魔法：自卫指南》，昆丁·特林布著

〔其他装备〕

　　一支魔杖

　　一口坩埚（锡镴质，标准尺寸2号）

　　一套玻璃或水晶小药瓶

　　一架望远镜

　　一台黄铜天平

学生可携带一只猫头鹰或一只猫或一只蟾蜍

CHAPTER FIVE   Diagon Alley

PARENTS ARE REMINDED THAT FIRST-YEARS ARE NOT ALLOWED THEIR OWN BROOMSTICKS

'Can we buy all this in London?' Harry wondered aloud.

'If yeh know where to go,' said Hagrid.

Harry had never been to London before. Although Hagrid seemed to know where he was going, he was obviously not used to getting there in an ordinary way. He got stuck in the ticket barrier on the Underground and complained loudly that the seats were too small and the trains too slow.

'I don't know how the Muggles manage without magic,' he said, as they climbed a broken-down escalator which led up to a bustling road lined with shops.

Hagrid was so huge that he parted the crowd easily; all Harry had to do was keep close behind him. They passed book shops and music stores, hamburger bars and cinemas, but nowhere that looked as if it could sell you a magic wand. This was just an ordinary street full of ordinary people. Could there really be piles of wizard gold buried miles beneath them? Were there really shops that sold spell books and broomsticks? Might this not all be some huge joke that the Dursleys had cooked up? If Harry hadn't known that the Dursleys had no sense of humour, he might have thought so; yet somehow, even though everything Hagrid had told him so far was unbelievable, Harry couldn't help trusting him.

'This is it,' said Hagrid, coming to a halt, 'the Leaky Cauldron. It's a famous place.'

It was a tiny, grubby-looking pub. If Hagrid hadn't pointed it out, Harry wouldn't have noticed it was there. The people hurrying by didn't glance at it. Their eyes slid from the big book shop on one side to the record shop on the other as if they couldn't see the Leaky Cauldron at all. In fact, Harry had the most peculiar feeling that only he and Hagrid could see it. Before he could mention this, Hagrid had steered him inside.

For a famous place, it was very dark and shabby. A few old women were sitting in a corner, drinking tiny glasses of sherry. One of them was smoking a long pipe. A little man in a top hat was talking to the old barman, who was quite bald and looked like a gummy walnut. The low buzz of chatter

第5章 对角巷

在此特别提请家长注意，一年级新生不准自带飞天扫帚

"这些东西我们在伦敦都能买到吗？"哈利大声问。
"只要你知道门径就行。"海格说。

哈利以前从没有来过伦敦。海格尽管知道路，但他过去显然不是以常人的方法来的。他在地铁验票口被卡住了，接着又大声抱怨座位太窄，车速太慢。

"我真不知道这些麻瓜们不用魔法怎么办事。"当他们顺着出了故障的自动扶梯来到店铺林立、人群熙攘的大街上时，海格又说。

海格人高马大，毫不费事就从人群中挤了过去，哈利只消紧跟在他背后就可以了。他们经过书店、唱片店、汉堡专卖店、电影院，就是没有一家看上去像是卖魔杖的商店。这只是一条普普通通的街道，挤满了普通人。当真会有成堆的巫师金币埋藏在他们脚下吗？真会有出售咒语书和飞天扫帚的商店吗？这一切可不可能是德思礼夫妇开的一个大玩笑呢？要不是哈利知道德思礼夫妇毫无幽默感，他也许就会这么想；可是到目前为止，海格所讲的一切都太离奇了，令人难以置信，可哈利还是不能不相信他。

"就是这里了，"海格停下来说，"破釜酒吧。这是一个很有名的地方。"

这是一家肮脏的狭小酒吧。要不是海格指出来，哈利很可能都不会注意到它。匆忙过往的人们连看也不看它一眼，目光只落在它一边的一家大书店和另一边的一家唱片店上。他们好像根本看不见破釜酒吧。哈利有一种很奇怪的感觉，似乎只有他和海格能看见这家酒吧。他还没来得及说话，海格就已经把他推到店里去了。

作为一个出名的地方，这里实在是太黑太脏了。几个老太婆坐在屋角拿着小杯喝雪利酒，其中一个正在抽一杆长烟袋。一个戴大礼帽的小男人正在跟那个头发几乎脱光、长得像瘪胡桃似的酒吧老板聊天。他们刚一进门，叽叽喳喳的说话声就突然停了下来。这里好像人人都认识海格，他们向他微笑、招手。酒吧老板拿起一只杯子说："照老规矩，

stopped when they walked in. Everyone seemed to know Hagrid; they waved and smiled at him, and the barman reached for a glass, saying, 'The usual, Hagrid?'

'Can't, Tom, I'm on Hogwarts business,' said Hagrid, clapping his great hand on Harry's shoulder and making Harry's knees buckle.

'Good Lord,' said the barman, peering at Harry, 'is this – can this be –?'

The Leaky Cauldron had suddenly gone completely still and silent.

'Bless my soul,' whispered the old barman. 'Harry Potter ... what an honour.'

He hurried out from behind the bar, rushed towards Harry and seized his hand, tears in his eyes.

'Welcome back, Mr Potter, welcome back.'

Harry didn't know what to say. Everyone was looking at him. The old woman with the pipe was puffing on it without realising it had gone out. Hagrid was beaming.

Then there was a great scraping of chairs and, next moment, Harry found himself shaking hands with everyone in the Leaky Cauldron.

'Doris Crockford, Mr Potter, can't believe I'm meeting you at last.'

'So proud, Mr Potter, I'm just so proud.'

'Always wanted to shake your hand – I'm all of a flutter.'

'Delighted, Mr Potter, just can't tell you. Diggle's the name, Dedalus Diggle.'

'I've seen you before!' said Harry, as Dedalus Diggle's top hat fell off in his excitement. 'You bowed to me once in a shop.'

'He remembers!' cried Dedalus Diggle, looking around at everyone. 'Did you hear that? He remembers me!'

Harry shook hands again and again – Doris Crockford kept coming back for more.

A pale young man made his way forward, very nervously. One of his eyes was twitching.

'Professor Quirrell!' said Hagrid. 'Harry, Professor Quirrell will be one of your teachers at Hogwarts.'

'P-P-Potter,' stammered Professor Quirrell, grasping Harry's hand, 'c-can't t-tell you how p-pleased I am to meet you.'

海格？"

"不了,汤姆,我正在给霍格沃茨办事呢。"海格用他的巨掌拍了拍哈利的肩膀,差一点儿把他压趴下。

"我的天哪,"酒吧老板仔细端详着哈利,说道,"这位是——这位莫非是——"

破釜酒吧里顿时悄然无声。

"哎呀!"酒吧老板小声说,"哈利·波特——荣幸之至。"

他连忙从吧台后边出来,朝哈利跑来,抓起他的手,激动得热泪盈眶。"欢迎回来,波特先生,欢迎你回来。"

哈利不知说什么好。大家都在看他。那个抽长烟袋的老太婆一个劲地抽,根本没发现烟袋已经熄灭了。海格一直在笑。

接着椅子噼噼啪啪地响了起来,哈利突然发现自己竟跟破釜酒吧的人——一握起手来。

"我是科多利,波特先生,真是不敢相信,总算见到您了。"

"太荣幸了,波特先生,太荣幸了。"

"早就盼着跟您握手了——我的心怦怦直跳。"

"太高兴了,波特先生,简直没法说明我的心情,我叫迪歌,德达洛·迪歌。"

"我以前见过您,"当德达洛·迪歌过分激动而把礼帽弄掉时,哈利大声喊道,"有一次在商店里,您朝我鞠躬。"

"他居然还记得!"迪歌看着在场的每一个人喊道,"你们听见没有?他还记得我呢!"

于是哈利就一遍又一遍地握手——科多利总跑过来要求再跟他握一次。

一个面色苍白的年轻人走了过来,神情显得非常紧张,他的一只眼睛在抽动。

"奇洛教授!"海格说,"哈利,奇洛教授是在霍格沃茨教你的老师之一呢。"

"波—波—波特,"奇洛教授结结巴巴地说,抓起哈利的手,"见到你有说—说不出的—高—高兴。"

CHAPTER FIVE   Diagon Alley

'What sort of magic do you teach, Professor Quirrell?'

'D-Defence Against the D-D-Dark Arts,' muttered Professor Quirrell, as though he'd rather not think about it. 'N-not that you n-need it, eh, P-P-Potter?' He laughed nervously. 'You'll be g-getting all your equipment, I suppose? I've g-got to p-pick up a new b-book on vampires, m-myself.' He looked terrified at the very thought.

But the others wouldn't let Professor Quirrell keep Harry to himself. It took almost ten minutes to get away from them all. At last, Hagrid managed to make himself heard over the babble.

'Must get on – lots ter buy. Come on, Harry.'

Doris Crockford shook Harry's hand one last time and Hagrid led them through the bar and out into a small, walled courtyard, where there was nothing but a dustbin and a few weeds.

Hagrid grinned at Harry.

'Told yeh, didn't I? Told yeh you was famous. Even Professor Quirrell was tremblin' ter meet yeh – mind you, he's usually tremblin'.'

'Is he always that nervous?'

'Oh, yeah. Poor bloke. Brilliant mind. He was fine while he was studyin' outta books but then he took a year off ter get some first-hand experience ... They say he met vampires in the Black Forest and there was a nasty bit o' trouble with a hag – never been the same since. Scared of the students, scared of his own subject – now, where's me umbrella?'

Vampires? Hags? Harry's head was swimming. Hagrid, meanwhile, was counting bricks in the wall above the dustbin.

'Three up ... two across ...' he muttered. 'Right, stand back, Harry.'

He tapped the wall three times with the point of his umbrella.

The brick he had touched quivered – it wriggled – in the middle, a small hole appeared – it grew wider and wider – a second later they were facing an archway large enough even for Hagrid, an archway on to a cobbled street which twisted and turned out of sight.

'Welcome,' said Hagrid, 'to Diagon alley.'

He grinned at Harry's amazement. They stepped through the archway. Harry looked quickly over his shoulder and saw the archway shrink instantly back into solid wall.

第5章 对角巷

"您教哪一类魔法，奇洛教授？"

"黑—黑—黑魔法防—防御术。"奇洛教授含糊不清地说，似乎他觉得还是不提为好，"这你已经用—用不—不着学了，是吧，波—波—波特先生？"他神经质地笑了笑。"你这是准—准备去买你需要的东西吧？我也要—要去买—买一本关于吸血鬼的新—新书。"似乎他想起这件事就把自己吓坏了。

可是其余的人不会让奇洛教授跟哈利说个没完的。哈利花了大概快十分钟的时间才把他们摆脱掉。在一片喋喋不休的说话声中，海格提高嗓门叫哈利道：

"该走了，还有好多东西要买呢。走吧，哈利。"

科多利最后一次跟哈利握过手，海格就领着哈利穿过吧台，来到四面有围墙的小天井里。这里除了一只垃圾桶和一些杂草，什么也没有。

海格朝哈利咧嘴一笑。

"我不是对你说过吗，是不是？对你说过你很有名气。连奇洛教授在你面前都要发抖——不过，我要提醒你，他经常发抖。"

"他总是这么神经质吗？"

"哦，是的。倒霉的家伙。头脑聪明极了，书本知识学得很好。可后来他请了一年假出去游历，为了获得第一手的实践经验……据说，他在黑森林里遇到了吸血鬼，一个女妖又使他遭到了麻烦，从那以后，他就变成了另外一个人。害怕学生，害怕自己教的科目……哦，我的伞呢？"

吸血鬼？女妖？哈利听得晕头转向。这时海格正在数垃圾箱上边的墙砖。

"往上数三块——再往横里数两块——"他小声念叨，"好了，往后站，哈利。"

他用伞头在墙上轻轻敲了三下。

他敲过的那块砖抖动起来，开始移动，中间的地方出现了一个小洞，洞口越变越大。不多时，他们面前就出现了一条足以让海格通过的宽阔的拱道，通向一条蜿蜒曲折、看不见尽头的鹅卵石铺砌的街道。

"欢迎，"海格说，"欢迎来到对角巷。"

见哈利惊讶不已，海格朝他咧嘴一笑。他们沿拱道走去，哈利忙侧身回头看，只见拱道一下子变窄了，然后又变成了原来坚实的墙壁。

CHAPTER FIVE Diagon Alley

The sun shone brightly on a stack of cauldrons outside the nearest shop. *Cauldrons – All Sizes – Copper, Brass, Pewter, Silver – Self-Stirring – Collapsible* said a sign hanging over them.

'Yeah, you'll be needin' one,' said Hagrid, 'but we gotta get yer money first.'

Harry wished he had about eight more eyes. He turned his head in every direction as they walked up the street, trying to look at everything at once: the shops, the things outside them, the people doing their shopping. A plump woman outside an apothecary's was shaking her head as they passed, saying, 'Dragon liver, sixteen Sickles an ounce, they're mad ...'

A low, soft hooting came from a dark shop with a sign saying *Eeylops Owl Emporium – Tawny, Screech, Barn, Brown and Snowy*. Several boys of about Harry's age had their noses pressed against a window with broomsticks in it. 'Look,' Harry heard one of them say, 'the new Nimbus Two Thousand – fastest ever –' There were shops selling robes, shops selling telescopes and strange silver instruments Harry had never seen before, windows stacked with barrels of bat spleens and eels' eyes, tottering piles of spell books, quills and rolls of parchment, potion bottles, globes of the moon ...

'Gringotts,' said Hagrid.

They had reached a snowy-white building which towered over the other little shops. Standing beside its burnished bronze doors, wearing a uniform of scarlet and gold, was –

'Yeah, that's a goblin,' said Hagrid quietly as they walked up the white stone steps towards him. The goblin was about a head shorter than Harry. He had a swarthy, clever face, a pointed beard and, Harry noticed, very long fingers and feet. He bowed as they walked inside. Now they were facing a second pair of doors, silver this time, with words engraved upon them:

ENTER, STRANGER, BUT TAKE HEED
OF WHAT AWAITS THE SIN OF GREED,
FOR THOSE WHO TAKE, BUT DO NOT EARN,
MUST PAY MOST DEARLY IN THEIR TURN,

第 5 章 对角巷

耀眼的阳光投射在最近一家商店门外的一摞坩埚上。坩埚的上方悬挂着一块牌子，上边写着：

> 铜质——黄铜质——锡镴质——银质坩埚，型号齐全，自动搅拌——可折叠。

"哦，你需要买一个，"海格说，"不过我们先得去取钱。"

哈利恨不能再多长八只眼睛。他们走在街上，他一路东张西望，希望把一切都看个通通透透：所有的店铺、店铺前的物件、购物的人。一个胖女人站在药店外边，当他们经过时，她摇着头说："龙肝，十六西可一盎司，他们疯了……"

从一家晦暗的商店里传出一阵低沉轻柔的呜呜声，门前的招牌上写着：咿啦猫头鹰商店——灰林鸮、鸣角鸮、仓鸮、褐鸮、雪鸮。几个与哈利年龄相仿的男孩鼻尖紧贴着橱窗玻璃，橱窗里摆着飞天扫帚。"看哪，"哈利听见一个男孩说，"那是新型的光轮2000——最高速——"还有的商店出售长袍，有的出售望远镜和哈利从没有见过的稀奇古怪的银器。还有的橱窗里摆满了一篓篓蝙蝠脾脏和鳗鱼眼珠，堆满了咒语书、羽毛笔、一卷卷羊皮纸、药瓶、月球仪……

"古灵阁到了。"海格说。

他们来到一幢高高耸立在周围店铺之上的雪白楼房前，亮闪闪的青铜大门旁，站着一个穿一身猩红镶金制服的身影，那不就是——

"不错，那就是一个妖精。"当他们沿着白色石阶朝那人走去时，海格镇定地小声说。这个妖精大约比哈利矮一头，生着一张透着聪明的黝黑面孔，尖尖的胡子，哈利发现他的手和脚都特别长。他们进门时，那妖精向他们鞠躬行礼。之后他们面前出现了第二道门，是银色的，两扇门上镌刻着如下的文字：

> 请进，陌生人，不过你要当心
> 贪得无厌会是什么下场，
> 一味索取，不劳而获，
> 必将受到最严厉的惩罚，

> SO IF YOU SEEK BENEATH OUR FLOORS
> A TREASURE THAT WAS NEVER YOURS,
> THIEF, YOU HAVE BEEN WARNED, BEWARE
> OF FINDING MORE THAN TREASURE THERE.

'Like I said, yeh'd be mad ter try an' rob it,' said Hagrid.

A pair of goblins bowed them through the silver doors and they were in a vast marble hall. About a hundred more goblins were sitting on high stools behind a long counter, scribbling in large ledgers, weighing coins on brass scales, examining precious stones through eyeglasses. There were too many doors to count leading off the hall, and yet more goblins were showing people in and out of these. Hagrid and Harry made for the counter.

'Morning,' said Hagrid to a free goblin. 'We've come ter take some money outta Mr Harry Potter's safe.'

'You have his key, sir?'

'Got it here somewhere,' said Hagrid and he started emptying his pockets on to the counter, scattering a handful of mouldy dog-biscuits over the goblin's book of numbers. The goblin wrinkled his nose. Harry watched the goblin on their right weighing a pile of rubies as big as glowing coals.

'Got it,' said Hagrid at last, holding up a tiny golden key.

The goblin looked at it closely.

'That seems to be in order.'

'An' I've also got a letter here from Professor Dumbledore,' said Hagrid importantly, throwing out his chest. 'It's about the You-Know-What in vault seven hundred and thirteen.'

The goblin read the letter carefully.

'Very well,' he said, handing it back to Hagrid, 'I will have someone take you down to both vaults. Griphook!'

Griphook was yet another goblin. Once Hagrid had crammed all the dog-biscuits back inside his pockets, he and Harry followed Griphook towards one of the doors leading off the hall.

'What's the You-Know-What in vault seven hundred and thirteen?' Harry asked.

'Can't tell yeh that,' said Hagrid mysteriously. 'Very secret. Hogwarts

第5章 对角巷

因此如果你想从我们的地下金库取走
一份从来不属于你的财富，
窃贼啊，你已经受到警告，
当心招来的不是宝藏，而是恶报。

"就像我说的，你要是想抢这个银行，那你就是疯了。"海格说。

两个妖精向他们鞠躬，把他们引进一间高大的大理石大厅。大约有百十来个妖精坐在一排长柜台后边的高凳上，他们有的在用铜天平称钱币，有的在用目镜检验宝石，一边往大账本上草草地登记。大厅里有数不清的门，分别通往不同的地方，许多妖精正指引着来来往往的人出入这些门。海格和哈利朝柜台走去。

"早，"海格对一个闲着的妖精说，"我们要从哈利·波特先生的保险库里取一些钱。"

"您有他的钥匙吗，先生？"

"带来了。"海格说着，把衣袋里所有的东西都掏出来放到柜台上，不小心将一把发霉的狗饼干撒在了妖精的账本上。妖精皱了皱鼻子。哈利看着右边那个妖精正在称一堆跟烧红的煤块一般大小的红宝石。

"找到了。"海格终于说，举起一把小金钥匙。

妖精认真仔细地查看了一番。

"应当没有问题。"

"我这里还有一封邓布利多教授写的信，"海格郑重其事地说着，挺起胸来，"是关于713号地下金库里的'那件东西'的。"

妖精仔细看了信。

"很好，"他说着，把信交还给海格，"我找人带你们去这两个地下金库。拉环！"

拉环是另外一个妖精。海格把狗饼干全装回口袋里之后，就和哈利跟随拉环从其中一扇门走出了大厅。

"713号地下金库里的'那件东西'是什么？"哈利问。

"这我不能告诉你。"海格神神秘秘地说，"这是绝对机密。是关于霍格沃茨的事。邓布利多信任我。这是我的工作，不能讲给你听。"

business. Dumbledore's trusted me. More'n my job's worth ter tell yeh that.'

Griphook held the door open for them. Harry, who had expected more marble, was surprised. They were in a narrow stone passageway lit with flaming torches. It sloped steeply downwards and there were little railway tracks on the floor. Griphook whistled and a small cart came hurtling up the tracks towards them. They climbed in – Hagrid with some difficulty – and were off.

At first they just hurtled through a maze of twisting passages. Harry tried to remember, left, right, right, left, middle fork, right, left, but it was impossible. The rattling cart seemed to know its own way, because Griphook wasn't steering.

Harry's eyes stung as the cold air rushed past them, but he kept them wide open. Once, he thought he saw a burst of fire at the end of a passage and twisted around to see if it was a dragon, but too late – they plunged even deeper, passing an underground lake where huge stalactites and stalagmites grew from the ceiling and floor.

'I never know,' Harry called to Hagrid over the noise of the cart, 'what's the difference between a stalagmite and a stalactite?'

'Stalagmite's got an "m" in it,' said Hagrid. 'An' don' ask me questions just now, I think I'm gonna be sick.'

He did look very green and when the cart stopped at last beside a small door in the passage wall, Hagrid got out and had to lean against the wall to stop his knees trembling.

Griphook unlocked the door. A lot of green smoke came billowing out, and as it cleared, Harry gasped. Inside were mounds of gold coins. Columns of silver. Heaps of little bronze Knuts.

'All yours,' smiled Hagrid.

All Harry's – it was incredible. The Dursleys couldn't have known about this or they'd have had it from him faster than blinking. How often had they complained how much Harry cost them to keep? And all the time there had been a small fortune belonging to him, buried deep under London.

Hagrid helped Harry pile some of it into a bag.

'The gold ones are Galleons,' he explained. 'Seventeen silver Sickles to a Galleon and twenty-nine Knuts to a Sickle, it's easy enough. Right, that should be enough fer a couple o' terms, we'll keep the rest safe for yeh.' He

第 5 章 对角巷

拉环为他们俩打开门。哈利本以为又会看到许多大理石，但他吃了一惊。眼前是一道狭窄的石廊，燃烧的火把将它照得通明。石廊是一道陡峭的下坡，下边有一条小铁路。拉环吹了一声口哨，一辆小推车沿着铁道朝他们猛冲过来。他们爬上车——海格可费了不少劲——就出发了。

起初，他们沿着迷宫似的蜿蜒曲折的通道疾驰，哈利想记住走过的路，左拐，右拐，右拐，左拐，中间的岔路口，再右拐，左拐，根本记不住。咔嗒咔嗒响的小推车似乎认识路，根本不用拉环去驾车。

冰冷的空气呼啸而过，把哈利的眼睛都吹痛了，但是他还是竭力睁大双眼。一次，他似乎看到通道尽头有一团火，便转过身去，想看看那里是不是有一条火龙。但是，已经来不及了，他们已经冲到地底下更深的地方，经过一片地下湖，巨大的钟乳石和石笋分别从头顶和湖底生长出来。

"我一直弄不清，"哈利在咔嗒咔嗒的车声中，对海格喊道，"石笋和钟乳石有什么区别？"

"石笋这个字中间有字母 m。"海格说，"现在别向我提问题，我觉得要吐了。"

海格脸色铁青，当小推车终于在通道的一扇小门前停下来时，他爬下车就紧靠在通道墙上，这样才使双膝不至于发抖。

拉环打开门锁。一股浓浓的绿烟从门里冒了出来，浓烟散尽之后，哈利倒抽了一口气。里边是成堆的金币、银币和堆积如山的青铜币。

"这全都是你的。"海格笑着说。

全都是哈利的，真令人难以置信。德思礼夫妇对此肯定一无所知，否则用不了一眨眼的工夫，他们就会把这一切全部据为己有。他们不是经常抱怨收养哈利要花费许多钱吗？可哈利一直拥有一笔属于他的小小财富，深埋在伦敦地下呢。

海格帮哈利把钱装进袋子里。

"金币是加隆，"海格解释说，"十七个银西可合一个加隆，二十九个纳特合一个西可，够简单的吧。好了，足够两学期用的了，剩下的替你保管着。"他转身对拉环说："现在带我们去 713 号地下金库吧，不过能不能麻烦你让车开得慢一些？"

turned to Griphook. 'Vault seven hundred and thirteen now, please, and can we go more slowly?'

'One speed only,' said Griphook.

They were going even deeper now and gathering speed. The air became colder and colder as they hurtled round tight corners. They went rattling over an underground ravine and Harry leant over the side to try and see what was down at the dark bottom but Hagrid groaned and pulled him back by the scruff of his neck.

Vault seven hundred and thirteen had no keyhole.

'Stand back,' said Griphook importantly. He stroked the door gently with one of his long fingers and it simply melted away.

'If anyone but a Gringotts goblin tried that, they'd be sucked through the door and trapped in there,' said Griphook.

'How often do you check to see if anyone's inside?' Harry asked.

'About once every ten years,' said Griphook, with a rather nasty grin.

Something really extraordinary had to be inside this top-security vault, Harry was sure, and he leant forward eagerly, expecting to see fabulous jewels at the very least – but at first he thought it was empty. Then he noticed a grubby little package wrapped up in brown paper lying on the floor. Hagrid picked it up and tucked it deep inside his coat. Harry longed to know what it was, but knew better than to ask.

'Come on, back in this infernal cart, and don't talk to me on the way back, it's best if I keep me mouth shut,' said Hagrid.

One wild cart-ride later they stood blinking in the sunlight outside Gringotts. Harry didn't know where to run first now that he had a bag full of money. He didn't have to know how many Galleons there were to a pound to know that he was holding more money than he'd had in his whole life – more money than even Dudley had ever had.

'Might as well get yer uniform,' said Hagrid, nodding towards *Madam Malkin's Robes for All Occasions*. 'Listen, Harry, would yeh mind if I slipped off fer a pick-me-up in the Leaky Cauldron? I hate them Gringotts carts.' He did still look a bit sick, so Harry entered Madam Malkin's shop alone, feeling nervous.

第 5 章 对角巷

"车速只有一个。"拉环说。

他们下到更深的地方,速度越来越快。在急转弯的地方,空气变得更加寒冷刺骨。小推车咔嗒咔嗒响着来到一处山涧之上。哈利将身子探出车外,想看看黑洞洞的山涧里究竟有什么东西。海格哼了一声,揪住哈利的脖领,把他拽了回来。

713 号地下金库没有钥匙孔。

"往后站。"拉环郑重其事地说。他伸出一根长长的手指轻轻敲门,那门竟轻轻地一点一点地消失了。

"除了古灵阁的妖精之外,其他任何人要这么做,都会被门吸进去,陷在门里出不来。"拉环说。

"你多长时间才来查看一次,看里边是否有人?"

"大概十年一次吧。"拉环说,不怀好意地咧嘴一笑。

在这个超级保险的地下金库里,毫无疑问会存放着非同一般的东西,这一点哈利很肯定。于是他凑过去急于想看看,至少里边会有神奇的珠宝吧,可是他最初的感觉是里边什么也没有。之后,他发现地上有一个用棕色纸包着的脏兮兮的小包。海格把它捡了起来,深深地塞到外衣里边的口袋里。哈利很想知道纸包里究竟是什么,但他明白问了也没用。

"走,回去上那辆该死的车吧,回去的路上别跟我说话,不过我最好还是把嘴闭上。"海格说。

又乘小车狂奔了一通之后,他们终于站在了古灵阁外面阳光耀眼的街上。哈利背着满满一口袋钱,不知道先去哪里好。他用不着计算一英镑合多少加隆,就知道他一辈子也没有过这么多钱,甚至达力也从来没有过。

"还是去买制服吧。"海格冲着摩金夫人长袍专卖店点点头,说,"哈利,我想去破釜酒吧喝一杯提神饮料,你不介意吧?古灵阁那小推车太可恨了。"他看上去脸色确实还不好,所以哈利独自踏进了摩金夫人的长袍店,觉得很紧张。

摩金夫人是一个矮矮胖胖的女巫,笑容可掬,穿一身紫衣。

"是要买霍格沃茨学校的制服吗,亲爱的?"不等哈利开口说话,

CHAPTER FIVE Diagon Alley

Madam Malkin was a squat, smiling witch dressed all in mauve.

'Hogwarts, dear?' she said, when Harry started to speak. 'Got the lot here – another young man being fitted up just now, in fact.'

In the back of the shop, a boy with a pale, pointed face was standing on a footstool while a second witch pinned up his long black robes. Madam Malkin stood Harry on a stool next to him, slipped a long robe over his head and began to pin it to the right length.

'Hullo,' said the boy, 'Hogwarts too?'

'Yes,' said Harry.

'My father's next door buying my books and Mother's up the street looking at wands,' said the boy. He had a bored, drawling voice. 'Then I'm going to drag them off to look at racing brooms. I don't see why first-years can't have their own. I think I'll bully Father into getting me one and I'll smuggle it in somehow.'

Harry was strongly reminded of Dudley.

'Have *you* got your own broom?' the boy went on.

'No,' said Harry.

'Play Quidditch at all?'

'No,' Harry said again, wondering what on earth Quidditch could be.

'*I* do – Father says it's a crime if I'm not picked to play for my house, and I must say, I agree. Know what house you'll be in yet?'

'No,' said Harry, feeling more stupid by the minute.

'Well, no one really knows until they get there, do they, but I know I'll be in Slytherin, all our family have been – imagine being in Hufflepuff, I think I'd leave, wouldn't you?'

'Mmm,' said Harry, wishing he could say something a bit more interesting.

'I say, look at that man!' said the boy suddenly, nodding towards the front window. Hagrid was standing there, grinning at Harry and pointing at two large ice-creams to show he couldn't come in.

'That's Hagrid,' said Harry, pleased to know something the boy didn't. 'He works at Hogwarts.'

'Oh,' said the boy, 'I've heard of him. He's a sort of servant, isn't he?'

'He's the gamekeeper,' said Harry. He was liking the boy less and less every second.

第5章 对角巷

她就说了,"都在这儿呢,说实在的,现在就有一个年轻人在里边试衣服呢。"

在店堂后边,有一个面色苍白、身体瘦削的男孩站在脚凳上,一个女巫正用别针别起他的黑袍。摩金夫人让哈利站到男孩旁边的另一张脚凳上,给他套上一件长袍,用别针别出适合他的身长。

"喂,"男孩说,"也是去上霍格沃茨吗?"

"是的。"哈利说。

"我爸爸在隔壁帮我买书,妈妈到街上找魔杖去了。"他说话慢慢吞吞,拖着长腔,叫人讨厌,"然后我要拖他们去看飞天扫帚,我搞不懂为什么一年级新生就不能有自己的飞天扫帚。我想,我要逼着爸爸给我买一把,然后想办法偷偷带进去。"

哈利立刻想起了达力。

"你有自己的飞天扫帚吗?"男孩继续说。

"没有。"哈利说。

"打过魁地奇吗?"

"没有。"哈利又说,弄不清魁地奇到底是什么。

"我打过。爸爸说,要是我不能入选我们学院的代表队,那就太丢人了。我同意这种看法。你知道你会被分到哪个学院吗?"

"不知道。"哈利说,越来越觉得自己太笨了。

"当然,在没有到校之前没有人真正知道会被分到哪个学院。不过,我知道我会被分到斯莱特林,因为我们全家都是从那里毕业的——如果被分到赫奇帕奇,我想我会退学,你说呢?"

哈利嗯了一声,希望他能说点更有趣的话题。

"喂,你瞧那个人!"男孩突然朝前面的窗户点头说。海格正好站在窗口,朝哈利咧嘴笑着并指指两个大冰淇淋,说明他不能进店。

"那是海格。"哈利说,能知道一些男孩不知道的事,觉得很开心,"他在霍格沃茨工作。"

"哦,"男孩说,"我听说过他。他是做仆人的,是吧?"

"他是猎场看守。"哈利说。他越来越不喜欢这个男孩了。

'Yes, exactly. I heard he's a sort of *savage* – lives in a hut in the school grounds and every now and then he gets drunk, tries to do magic and ends up setting fire to his bed.'

'I think he's brilliant,' said Harry coldly.

'*Do* you?' said the boy, with a slight sneer. 'Why is he with you? Where are your parents?'

'They're dead,' said Harry shortly. He didn't feel much like going into the matter with this boy.

'Oh, sorry,' said the other, not sounding sorry at all. 'But they were *our* kind, weren't they?'

'They were a witch and wizard, if that's what you mean.'

'I really don't think they should let the other sort in, do you? They're just not the same, they've never been brought up to know our ways. Some of them have never even heard of Hogwarts until they get the letter, imagine. I think they should keep it in the old wizarding families. What's your surname, anyway?'

But before Harry could answer, Madam Malkin said, 'That's you done, my dear,' and Harry, not sorry for an excuse to stop talking to the boy, hopped down from the footstool.

'Well, I'll see you at Hogwarts, I suppose,' said the drawling boy.

Harry was rather quiet as he ate the ice-cream Hagrid had bought him (chocolate and raspberry with chopped nuts).

'What's up?' said Hagrid.

'Nothing,' Harry lied. They stopped to buy parchment and quills. Harry cheered up a bit when he found a bottle of ink that changed colour as you wrote. When they had left the shop, he said, 'Hagrid, what's Quidditch?'

'Blimey, Harry, I keep forgettin' how little yeh know – not knowin' about Quidditch!'

'Don't make me feel worse,' said Harry. He told Hagrid about the pale boy in Madam Malkin's.

'– and he said people from Muggle families shouldn't even be allowed in –'

'Yer not *from* a Muggle family. If he'd known who yeh *were* – he's grown up knowin' yer name if his parents are wizardin' folk – you saw 'em in the Leaky Cauldron. Anyway, what does he know about it, some o' the best I ever saw

第 5 章 对角巷

"对，一点不错。我听说，这个人很粗野，住在学校场地上的一间小木屋里，时不时地喝醉酒，玩弄些魔法，结果把自己的床也烧了。"

"我认为他很聪明。"哈利冷冷地说。

"是吗？"男孩略带嘲弄地说，"为什么是他来陪你？你的父母呢？"

"他们都去世了。"哈利简单地说，不想跟这个男孩谈论这件事。

"哦，对不起。"男孩说，可他的话里听不出丝毫歉意，"他们也是跟我们一类的人，是吧？"

"他们是巫师，我想你大概是指这个吧。"

"我确实认为不应该让另类入学，你说呢？他们不一样，从小就没有接受过我们这样的教育，不了解我们的世界。想想看，他们当中有些人在没有接到信之前甚至没听说过霍格沃茨这个学校。我想学校应当只限于招收古老巫师家族出身的学生。对了，你姓什么？"

哈利还没来得及回答，只听摩金夫人说："已经试好了，亲爱的。"哈利庆幸自己能找到借口不再跟那男孩聊下去，便从脚凳上跳了下来。

"好，那么我们就到霍格沃茨再见了。"男孩拖长声调说。

哈利在吃海格给他买的冰淇淋（巧克力加覆盆子和碎果仁冰淇淋）时一直不吭声。

"怎么了？"海格问。

"没什么。"哈利撒谎了。他们停下来买羊皮纸和羽毛笔。哈利发现了一瓶写字时会变色的墨水，心情便好了起来。当他们走出店铺时，哈利问："海格，什么是魁地奇？"

"哎呀，我的天哪，哈利，我忘记你知道得太少了，竟然连魁地奇都不知道。"

"劳驾，别让我的情绪变得更坏好不好？"他向海格说起在摩金夫人店里碰到的那个面色苍白的男孩。

"——他还说甚至不应该准许麻瓜家庭出身的人入学——"

"你又不是麻瓜家庭出来的。如果他父母是巫师——你在破釜酒吧已经看到了——那么他就该是听着你的名字长大的。其实，他又知道多少，我见过许多最优秀的巫师都是麻瓜家庭里唯一懂魔法的人——看看

were the only ones with magic in 'em in a long line o' Muggles – look at yer mum! Look what she had fer a sister!'

'So what *is* Quidditch?'

'It's our sport. Wizard sport. It's like – like football in the Muggle world – everyone follows Quidditch – played up in the air on broomsticks and there's four balls – sorta hard ter explain the rules.'

'And what are Slytherin and Hufflepuff?'

'School houses. There's four. Everyone says Hufflepuff are a lot o' duffers, but –'

'I bet I'm in Hufflepuff,' said Harry gloomily.

'Better Hufflepuff than Slytherin,' said Hagrid darkly. 'There's not a single witch or wizard who went bad who wasn't in Slytherin. You-Know-Who was one.'

'Vol– sorry – You-Know-Who was at Hogwarts?'

'Years an' years ago,' said Hagrid.

They bought Harry's school books in a shop called Flourish and Blotts where the shelves were stacked to the ceiling with books as large as paving stones bound in leather; books the size of postage stamps in covers of silk; books full of peculiar symbols and a few books with nothing in them at all. Even Dudley, who never read anything, would have been wild to get his hands on some of these. Hagrid almost had to drag Harry away from *Curses and Counter-Curses (Bewitch your Friends and Befuddle your Enemies with the Latest Revenges: Hair Loss, Jelly-Legs, Tongue-Tying and much, much more)* by Professor Vindictus Viridian.

'I was trying to find out how to curse Dudley.'

'I'm not sayin' that's not a good idea, but yer not ter use magic in the Muggle world except in very special circumstances,' said Hagrid. 'An' anyway, yeh couldn' work any of them curses yet, yeh'll need a lot more study before yeh get ter that level.'

Hagrid wouldn't let Harry buy a solid gold cauldron, either ('it says pewter on yer list'), but they got a nice set of scales for weighing potion ingredients and a collapsible brass telescope. Then they visited the apothecary's, which was fascinating enough to make up for its horrible smell, a mixture of bad eggs and rotted cabbages. Barrels of slimy stuff stood on the floor, jars of

第5章 对角巷

你母亲！看看她有一个什么样的姐姐！"

"那魁地奇到底是什么呢？"

"那是我们的一种运动。一种巫师们玩的球类运动。它像——麻瓜世界的足球——人人都喜欢玩魁地奇——骑飞天扫帚在空中打，有四个球——至于玩球的规则嘛，解释起来还真有点儿困难。"

"那么斯莱特林和赫奇帕奇又是什么呢？"

"那是学院名字。学校共有四个学院。都说赫奇帕奇有许多饭桶，不过——"

"我想，我一定会被分到赫奇帕奇了。"哈利快快不乐地说。

"宁愿进赫奇帕奇，也不要进斯莱特林。"海格脸色阴沉地说，"没有一个后来变坏的巫师不是从斯莱特林出来的，神秘人就是其中的一个。"

"伏——对不起——神秘人也在霍格沃茨上过学？"

"很多很多年以前了。"海格说。

他们在一家名叫丽痕的书店里买了哈利上学要用的课本。这里的书架上摆满了书，一直到天花板上，有大到像铺路石板的皮面精装书，也有邮票大小的绢面书；有的书里写满了各种奇特的符号，还有少数则是无字书。即使从来不读书的达力，要是有幸能得到其中的一两本，也一定会欣喜若狂的。哈利拿起一本温迪克教授著的《魔咒与破解魔咒》（用最新的复仇术捉弄你的朋友，蛊惑你的敌人：脱发、打折腿、绑舌头及其他许许多多手法），海格好不容易才把哈利从这本书前拖开。

"我想找出办法来给达力施魔咒。"

"我说这主意不坏，但你不能在麻瓜世界使用魔法，除非在很特殊的情况下。"海格说，"不过，你现在用不了那些魔咒，你还需要学习很多东西，才能达到那个水平。"

海格也不让哈利买一只纯金坩埚（购物单上开的是锡镴坩埚），不过他们买了一台计量药品的质量很好的天平和一架可折叠的黄铜望远镜。随后他们光顾了一家药店，那里散发出一股臭鸡蛋和烂卷心菜叶的刺鼻气味。但药店十分神奇，地上摆放着一桶桶黏糊糊的东西，顺墙摆着一罐罐药草、干草根和各种颜色鲜亮的粉末，天花板上挂着成捆的羽

herbs, dried roots and bright powders lined the walls, bundles of feathers, strings of fangs and snarled claws hung from the ceiling. While Hagrid asked the man behind the counter for a supply of some basic potion ingredients for Harry, Harry himself examined silver unicorn horns at twenty-one Galleons each and minuscule, glittery black beetle eyes (five Knuts a scoop).

Outside the apothecary's, Hagrid checked Harry's list again.

'Just yer wand left – oh yeah, an' I still haven't got yeh a birthday present.'

Harry felt himself go red.

'You don't have to –'

'I know I don't have to. Tell yeh what, I'll get yer animal. Not a toad, toads went outta fashion years ago, yeh'd be laughed at – an' I don' like cats, they make me sneeze. I'll get yer an owl. All the kids want owls, they're dead useful, carry yer post an' everythin'.'

Twenty minutes later, they left Eeylops Owl Emporium, which had been dark and full of rustling and flickering, jewel-bright eyes. Harry now carried a large cage which held a beautiful snowy owl, fast asleep with her head under her wing. He couldn't stop stammering his thanks, sounding just like Professor Quirrell.

'Don' mention it,' said Hagrid gruffly. 'Don' expect you've had a lotta presents from them Dursleys. Just Ollivanders left now – only place fer wands, Ollivanders, and yeh gotta have the best wand.'

A magic wand ... this was what Harry had been really looking forward to.

The last shop was narrow and shabby. Peeling gold letters over the door read *Ollivanders: Makers of Fine Wands since 382 BC.* A single wand lay on a faded purple cushion in the dusty window.

A tinkling bell rang somewhere in the depths of the shop as they stepped inside. It was a tiny place, empty except for a single spindly chair which Hagrid sat on to wait. Harry felt strangely as though he had entered a very strict library; he swallowed a lot of new questions which had just occurred to him and looked instead at the thousands of narrow boxes piled neatly right up to the ceiling. For some reason, the back of his neck prickled. The very dust and silence in here seemed to tingle with some secret magic.

'Good afternoon,' said a soft voice. Harry jumped. Hagrid must have jumped, too, because there was a loud crunching noise and he got quickly off

第5章 对角巷

毛、成串的尖牙和毛爹爹的爪子。当海格向柜台后边的营业员买各种标准剂量的药粉时，哈利正在细细察看独角兽的银角，每个价值二十一加隆，以及乌黑、亮闪闪的甲虫小眼珠（五纳特一勺）。

他们走出药店，海格又核对了一遍哈利的购物单。

"就剩下你的魔杖了——哦，对了，我还没给你买一份生日礼物呢。"

哈利觉得自己脸红了。

"您不必了——"

"我知道不用买。是这样，我要送你一只动物，不是蟾蜍，蟾蜍好多年前就不时兴了，人家会笑话你的。我也不喜欢猫，猫总惹我打喷嚏。我给你弄一只猫头鹰。孩子们都喜欢猫头鹰，它能替你送信，送包裹。"

二十分钟后，他们离开了黑洞洞的咿啦猫头鹰商店，离开了窸窸窣窣的拍翅声和宝石般闪光的眼睛，哈利手里提着一只大鸟笼，里边装着一只漂亮的雪鸮，头埋在翅膀底下睡得正香。哈利忍不住结结巴巴地一再道谢，听起来像奇洛教授在说话。

"不用谢，"海格声音沙哑地说，"德思礼夫妇是不会送给你礼物的。现在就剩下奥利凡德没去了，只有奥利凡德一家卖魔杖，到那里你一定能买到一根最好的魔杖。"

魔杖——这正是哈利梦寐以求的。

最后一家商店又小又破，门上的金字招牌已经剥落，上边写着：奥利凡德：自公元前382年即制作精良魔杖。尘封的橱窗里，褪色的紫色软垫上孤零零地摆着一根魔杖。

他们进店时，店堂后边的什么地方传来了阵阵叮叮当当的铃声。店堂很小，除了一张长椅，别的什么也没有。海格坐到长椅上等候，哈利有一种奇怪的感觉，仿佛来到了一家管理严格的图书馆；他强压住脑海里刚刚产生的许许多多新问题，开始看几乎码到天花板的几千个狭长的匣子。不知为什么，他突然感到心里发毛。这里的尘埃和肃静似乎使人感到暗藏着神秘的魔法。

"下午好。"一个轻柔的声音说，把哈利吓了一跳。海格也吓得不轻，因为这时突然传来一阵响亮的咔嚓咔嚓的声音，他连忙从长椅上站了起来。

CHAPTER FIVE Diagon Alley

the spindly chair.

An old man was standing before them, his wide, pale eyes shining like moons through the gloom of the shop.

'Hello,' said Harry awkwardly.

'Ah yes,' said the man. 'Yes, yes. I thought I'd be seeing you soon. Harry Potter.' It wasn't a question. 'You have your mother's eyes. It seems only yesterday she was in here herself, buying her first wand. Ten and a quarter inches long, swishy, made of willow. Nice wand for charm work.'

Mr Ollivander moved closer to Harry. Harry wished he would blink. Those silvery eyes were a bit creepy.

'Your father, on the other hand, favoured a mahogany wand. Eleven inches. Pliable. A little more power and excellent for transfiguration. Well, I say your father favoured it – it's really the wand that chooses the wizard, of course.'

Mr Ollivander had come so close that he and Harry were almost nose to nose. Harry could see himself reflected in those misty eyes.

'And that's where ...'

Mr Ollivander touched the lightning scar on Harry's forehead with a long, white finger.

'I'm sorry to say I sold the wand that did it,' he said softly. 'Thirteen and a half inches. Yew. Powerful wand, very powerful, and in the wrong hands ... Well, if I'd known what that wand was going out into the world to do ...'

He shook his head and then, to Harry's relief, spotted Hagrid.

'Rubeus! Rubeus Hagrid! How nice to see you again ... Oak, sixteen inches, rather bendy, wasn't it?'

'It was, sir, yes,' said Hagrid.

'Good wand, that one. But I suppose they snapped it in half when you got expelled?' said Mr Ollivander, suddenly stern.

'Er – yes, they did, yes,' said Hagrid, shuffling his feet. 'I've still got the pieces, though,' he added brightly.

'But you don't use them?' said Mr Ollivander sharply.

'Oh, no, sir,' said Hagrid quickly. Harry noticed he gripped his pink umbrella very tightly as he spoke.

'Hmmm,' said Mr Ollivander, giving Hagrid a piercing look. 'Well, now –

一个老头站在他们面前，他那对颜色很浅的大眼睛在暗淡的店铺里像两轮闪亮的月亮。

"你好。"哈利拘谨地说。

"哦，是的，"老头说，"是的，是的，我知道我很快就会见到你，哈利·波特。"他肯定地说道，"你的眼睛跟你母亲的一样。当年她到这里来买走她的第一根魔杖，这简直像昨天的事。十又四分之一英寸长，柳条做的，挥起来嗖嗖响，是一根施魔法的好魔杖。"

奥利凡德先生走到哈利跟前，哈利希望他能眨眨眼，他那对银白色的眼睛使哈利汗毛直竖。

"你父亲就不一样了，他喜欢桃花心木魔杖。十一英寸长，柔韧，力量更强些，用于变形术是最好不过了。我说你父亲喜欢它——实际上，当然是魔杖在选择它的巫师。"

奥利凡德先生凑得离哈利越来越近，鼻子都要贴到哈利脸上了。哈利已经看到老头浑浊的眼睛里映出了自己的影子。

"哦，这就是……"

奥利凡德先生用苍白的长手指抚摸着哈利额上那道闪电形的伤疤。

"很对不起，这是我卖出的一根魔杖干的。"他柔声细语地说，"十三英寸半长。紫杉木的。力量很强，强极了，却落到了坏人手里……要是早知道这根魔杖做成后，会做出这样的事……"

他摇摇头，接着一眼认出了海格，这使哈利松了一口气。

"鲁伯！鲁伯·海格！又见到你了，真是太高兴啦……橡木的，十六英寸长，很容易弯曲，对吧？"

"不错，先生。"海格说。

"那可是一根好魔杖啊。可我想，在他们开除你的时候，准被他们撅折了吧？"奥利凡德先生说，突然变得严肃起来。

"啊，不错，是被他们撅折了，是的。"海格慢慢地移动着脚步说道，"撅折的魔杖我还留着呢。"他又高兴地说。

"可你不用它了吧？"奥利凡德先生敏锐地问道。

"哦，不用了，先生。"海格忙回答。哈利注意到海格在回答时紧紧抓住了那把粉红色的伞。

CHAPTER FIVE Diagon Alley

Mr Potter. Let me see.' He pulled a long tape measure with silver markings out of his pocket. 'Which is your wand arm?'

'Er – well, I'm right-handed,' said Harry.

'Hold out your arm. That's it.' He measured Harry from shoulder to finger, then wrist to elbow, shoulder to floor, knee to armpit and round his head. As he measured, he said, 'Every Ollivander wand has a core of a powerful magical substance, Mr Potter. We use unicorn hairs, phoenix tail feathers and the heartstrings of dragons. No two Ollivander wands are the same, just as no two unicorns, dragons or phoenixes are quite the same. And of course, you will never get such good results with another wizard's wand.'

Harry suddenly realised that the tape measure, which was measuring between his nostrils, was doing this on its own. Mr Ollivander was flitting around the shelves, taking down boxes.

'That will do,' he said, and the tape measure crumpled into a heap on the floor. 'Right then, Mr Potter. Try this one. Beechwood and dragon heartstring. Nine inches. Nice and flexible. Just take it and give it a wave.'

Harry took the wand and (feeling foolish) waved it around a bit, but Mr Ollivander snatched it out of his hand almost at once.

'Maple and phoenix feather. Seven inches. Quite whippy. Try –'

Harry tried – but he had hardly raised the wand when it, too, was snatched back by Mr Ollivander.

'No, no – here, ebony and unicorn hair, eight and a half inches, springy. Go on, go on, try it out.'

Harry tried. And tried. He had no idea what Mr Ollivander was waiting for. The pile of tried wands was mounting higher and higher on the spindly chair, but the more wands Mr Ollivander pulled from the shelves, the happier he seemed to become.

'Tricky customer, eh? Not to worry, we'll find the perfect match here somewhere – I wonder, now – yes, why not – unusual combination – holly and phoenix feather, eleven inches, nice and supple.'

Harry took the wand. He felt a sudden warmth in his fingers. He raised the wand above his head, brought it swishing down through the dusty air and a stream of red and gold sparks shot from the end like a firework, throwing dancing spots of light on to the walls. Hagrid whooped and clapped and Mr

"唔。"奥利凡德先生说着,用锐利的目光扫了他一眼。"好了,波特先生,来吧。让我看看。"他从衣袋里掏出一长条印有银色刻度的卷尺,"你用哪只胳膊使魔杖?"

"呃——呃,我习惯用右手。"哈利说。

"把胳膊抬起来。好。"他为哈利量尺寸,先从肩头到指尖,之后,从腕到肘,肩到地板,膝到腋下,最后量头围。他一边量,一边说:"每一根奥利凡德魔杖的杖芯都由超强的魔法物质制成,波特先生。我们用的是独角兽毛、凤凰尾羽和火龙的心脏神经。每一根奥利凡德魔杖都是独一无二的,因为没有两只完全相同的独角兽、火龙或凤凰。当然,你如果用了本应属于其他巫师的魔杖,就绝不会有这样好的效果了。"

当量到两鼻孔间的距离时,哈利突然发现竟是卷尺在自动操作。奥利凡德先生正在货架间穿梭,忙着选出一些长匣子往下搬。

"好了。"他说,卷尺滑落到地上卷成一团,"那么,波特先生,试试这一根。山毛榉木和火龙的心脏神经做的。九英寸长。不错,很柔韧。你挥一下试试。"

哈利接过魔杖(心里觉得有点冒傻气),刚挥了一下,奥利凡德先生就立刻把魔杖从他手里夺了过去。

"槭木的,凤凰羽毛。七英寸长。弹性不错,试试看——"

可哈利刚一试,还没来得及举起来,魔杖就又被奥利凡德先生夺走了。

"不,不——试试这根,用黑檀木和独角兽毛做的。八英寸半长。弹性很强。来吧,来吧,试试这根。"

哈利试了一根又一根。他一点不明白奥利凡德先生认为什么样的才合适。试过的魔杖都堆放在长椅上,越堆越高。但奥利凡德先生从货架上抽出的魔杖越多,似乎显得越高兴。

"一位挑剔的顾客吧,嗯?不要紧,我想,这里总能找到一款最理想,最完美,最适合你的——让我想想看——哦,有了,为何不试试呢——非凡的组合,冬青木,凤凰羽毛,十一英寸长。不错,也柔韧。"

哈利接过魔杖,突然感到指尖一热。他把魔杖高举过头,嗖的一声向下一挥,划过尘土飞扬的空气,只见一道红光,魔杖头上像烟花一样金星四射,跳动的光斑投到四壁上。海格拍手喝彩,奥利凡德先生大声

CHAPTER FIVE Diagon Alley

Ollivander cried, 'Oh, bravo! Yes, indeed, oh, very good. Well, well, well ... how curious ... how very curious ...'

He put Harry's wand back into its box and wrapped it in brown paper, still muttering, 'Curious ... curious ...'

'Sorry,' said Harry, 'but *what's* curious?'

Mr Ollivander fixed Harry with his pale stare.

'I remember every wand I've ever sold, Mr Potter. Every single wand. It so happens that the phoenix whose tail feather is in your wand, gave another feather – just one other. It is very curious indeed that you should be destined for this wand when its brother – why, its brother gave you that scar.'

Harry swallowed.

'Yes, thirteen and a half inches. Yew. Curious indeed how these things happen. The wand chooses the wizard, remember ... I think we must expect great things from you, Mr Potter ... After all, He Who Must Not Be Named did great things – terrible, yes, but great.'

Harry shivered. He wasn't sure he liked Mr Ollivander too much. He paid seven gold Galleons for his wand and Mr Ollivander bowed them from his shop.

The late-afternoon sun hung low in the sky as Harry and Hagrid made their way back down Diagon alley, back through the wall, back through the Leaky Cauldron, now empty. Harry didn't speak at all as they walked down the road; he didn't even notice how much people were gawping at them on the Underground, laden as they were with all their funny-shaped packages, with the sleeping snowy owl on Harry's lap. Up another escalator, out into Paddington station; Harry only realised where they were when Hagrid tapped him on the shoulder.

'Got time fer a bite to eat before yer train leaves,' he said.

He bought Harry a hamburger and they sat down on plastic seats to eat them. Harry kept looking around. Everything looked so strange, somehow.

'You all right, Harry? Yer very quiet,' said Hagrid.

Harry wasn't sure he could explain. He'd just had the best birthday of his life – and yet – he chewed his hamburger, trying to find the words.

'Everyone thinks I'm special,' he said at last. 'All those people in the Leaky

第5章 对角巷

喊起来:"哦,好极了,哦,真的,太好了。哎呀,哎呀,哎呀……太奇妙了……真是太奇妙了……"

他把哈利的魔杖装到匣子里,用棕色纸包好,嘴里还不停地说:"奇妙……奇妙……"

"对不起,"哈利说,"什么地方让您觉得奇妙?"

奥利凡德先生用苍白无色的眼睛注视着哈利。

"我卖出的每一根魔杖我都记得,波特先生。每一根魔杖我都记得。是这样,同一只凤凰的两根尾羽,一根做了这根魔杖,另一根做了另外一根魔杖。你注定要用这根魔杖,而它的兄弟——咳,正是它的兄弟给你落下了那道伤疤。"

哈利倒抽了一口气。

"不错,十三英寸半长。紫杉木的。怎么会有这样的事,真是太奇妙了。记住,是魔杖选择巫师……我想,你会成就一番大事业的,波特先生……不管怎么说,那个神秘的连名字都不能提的人就做了大事——尽管可怕,但还是大事。"

哈利浑身一激灵。他不敢肯定自己是否喜欢这位奥利凡德先生。他花了七个加隆买下了魔杖,奥利凡德先生鞠躬把他们送出店门。

傍晚,哈利和海格沿着对角巷往回走时,太阳已快下山了。他们穿过墙,经过已空无一人的破釜酒吧,走上大路。一路上,哈利一言不发。在地铁里他甚至没有留意那么多人正张大了嘴凝视着他们提着大大小小、奇形怪状的包裹,而他怀里还抱着一只熟睡的雪鸮。他们又乘了一段自动扶梯,来到帕丁顿车站。海格拍拍哈利的肩膀,哈利这才猛地意识到他们在什么地方。

"开车前,我们还有时间吃一点儿东西。"海格说。

他给哈利买了一个汉堡,他们就坐在塑料椅上吃了起来。哈利一直在东张西望。不知怎的,他总觉得周围的一切都很奇怪。

"你没什么吧,哈利?你一句话也不说。"海格说。

哈利不知道自己能不能讲清楚。他刚刚过了一个生平最好的生日——可是——他嚼着汉堡,一边寻思着该怎么说。

Cauldron, Professor Quirrell, Mr Ollivander ... but I don't know anything about magic at all. How can they expect great things? I'm famous and I can't even remember what I'm famous for. I don't know what happened when Vol– sorry – I mean, the night my parents died.'

Hagrid leant across the table. Behind the wild beard and eyebrows he wore a very kind smile.

'Don' you worry, Harry. You'll learn fast enough. Everyone starts at the beginning at Hogwarts, you'll be just fine. Just be yerself. I know it's hard. Yeh've been singled out, an' that's always hard. But yeh'll have a great time at Hogwarts – I did – still do, 'smatter of fact.'

Hagrid helped Harry on to the train that would take him back to the Dursleys, then handed him an envelope.

'Yer ticket fer Hogwarts,' he said. 'First o' September – King's Cross – it's all on yer ticket. Any problems with the Dursleys, send me a letter with yer owl, she'll know where to find me ... See yeh soon, Harry.'

The train pulled out of the station. Harry wanted to watch Hagrid until he was out of sight; he rose in his seat and pressed his nose against the window, but he blinked and Hagrid had gone.

第5章 对角巷

"人人都觉得我很特别，"他终于说，"破釜酒吧的那些人、奇洛教授、奥利凡德先生……可我对魔法一窍不通。他们怎么能期望我成就大事呢？我有名气，可那些让我出名的事，我甚至一点儿也不记得。在伏——对不起——我是说，我父母去世的那天夜里，我根本不知道发生了什么事。"

海格隔着桌子探过身来。他那蓬乱的胡须和眉毛下边露出慈祥的微笑。

"别担心，哈利。你很快就会学会的。在霍格沃茨，人人都是从基础开始学的。你会很好的。打起精神来。我知道这对于你很难。你一直孤零零一个人，总是很难过的。不过你在霍格沃茨一定会很愉快，像我——说实话——过去和现在都很愉快。"

海格把哈利送上可以回德思礼家的火车，然后递给他一封信。

"这是你去霍格沃茨的车票。"他说，"九月一日——国王十字车站——票上都有。德思礼夫妇要是欺负你，就写封信让猫头鹰给我送来，它知道到什么地方去找我……下次再见了，哈利。"

火车驶出了车站。哈利想目送海格离去，他跪到座位上，鼻子紧贴着车窗，可一眨眼的工夫，海格就不见了。

CHAPTER SIX
The Journey from Platform Nine and Three-Quarters

Harry's last month with the Dursleys wasn't fun. True, Dudley was now so scared of Harry he wouldn't stay in the same room, while Aunt Petunia and Uncle Vernon didn't shut Harry in his cupboard, force him to do anything or shout at him – in fact, they didn't speak to him at all. Half-terrified, half-furious, they acted as though any chair with Harry in it was empty. Although this was an improvement in many ways, it did become a bit depressing after a while.

Harry kept to his room, with his new owl for company. He had decided to call her Hedwig, a name he had found in *A History of Magic*. His school books were very interesting. He lay on his bed reading late into the night, Hedwig swooping in and out of the open window as she pleased. It was lucky that Aunt Petunia didn't come in to hoover any more, because Hedwig kept bringing back dead mice. Every night before he went to sleep, Harry ticked off another day on the piece of paper he had pinned to the wall, counting down to September the first.

On the last day of August he thought he'd better speak to his aunt and uncle about getting to King's Cross station next day, so he went down to the living-room, where they were watching a quiz show on television. He cleared his throat to let them know he was there, and Dudley screamed and ran from the room.

'Er – Uncle Vernon?'

Uncle Vernon grunted to show he was listening.

'Er – I need to be at King's Cross tomorrow to – to go to Hogwarts.'

Uncle Vernon grunted again.

'Would it be all right if you gave me a lift?'

Grunt. Harry supposed that meant yes.

第6章
从 $9\frac{3}{4}$ 站台开始的旅程

　　哈利与德思礼一家相处的最后一个月并不愉快。说真的，达力着实被哈利吓坏了，他不敢跟哈利待在同一个房间里，佩妮姨妈和弗农姨父也不敢再把哈利关在储物间里，也不强迫他干活儿了，也不再朝他大喊大叫了——事实上，他们根本不跟他讲话。一半出于恐惧，一半出于恼怒，他们对哈利的存在视而不见。尽管这在许多方面是一个进步，但时间一久就使人感到有些没趣。

　　哈利大多时间都待在他的房间里，有他新买的猫头鹰做伴。他决定管它叫海德薇，这是他从《魔法史》这本书里找到的名字。他的学校课本都很有趣。他躺在床上，一读就到深夜，海德薇从打开的窗口尽情地飞进飞出。幸运的是佩妮姨妈不再到房间里来吸尘了，因为海德薇总是叼回来死老鼠。哈利把九月一日以前的每个日期一天一天写在一张纸上，钉在墙上，每天临睡前就在第二天的日期上打一个钩。

　　八月的最后一天，哈利觉得最好还是跟姨父姨妈谈谈明天去国王十字车站的事，于是他下楼来到起居室。姨父姨妈正在看竞猜电视节目。他清了一下嗓子，好让他们知道他来了；达力尖叫着跑出屋去。

　　"哦——弗农姨父？"

　　弗农姨父哼了一声，表示他在听。

　　"哦——我明天得去国王十字车站——去霍格沃茨。"

　　弗农姨父又哼了一声。

　　"请问您用车送我一下行吗？"

　　"哼。"哈利认为这就是表示可以。

CHAPTER SIX   The Journey from Platform Nine and Three-Quarters

'Thank you.'

He was about to go back upstairs when Uncle Vernon actually spoke.

'Funny way to get to a wizards' school, the train. Magic carpets all got punctures, have they?'

Harry didn't say anything.

'Where is this school, anyway?'

'I don't know,' said Harry, realising this for the first time. He pulled the ticket Hagrid had given him out of his pocket.

'I just take the train from platform nine and three-quarters at eleven o'clock,' he read.

His aunt and uncle stared.

'Platform what?'

'Nine and three-quarters.'

'Don't talk rubbish,' said Uncle Vernon, 'there is no platform nine and three-quarters.'

'It's on my ticket.'

'Barking,' said Uncle Vernon, 'howling mad, the lot of them. You'll see. You just wait. All right, we'll take you to King's Cross. We're going up to London tomorrow anyway, or I wouldn't bother.'

'Why are you going to London?' Harry asked, trying to keep things friendly.

'Taking Dudley to hospital,' growled Uncle Vernon. 'Got to have that ruddy tail removed before he goes to Smeltings.'

Harry woke at five o'clock the next morning and was too excited and nervous to go back to sleep. He got up and pulled on his jeans because he didn't want to walk into the station in his wizard's robes – he'd change on the train. He checked his Hogwarts list yet again to make sure he had everything he needed, saw that Hedwig was shut safely in her cage and then paced the room, waiting for the Dursleys to get up. Two hours later, Harry's huge, heavy trunk had been loaded into the Dursleys' car, Aunt Petunia had talked Dudley into sitting next to Harry and they had set off.

They reached King's Cross at half past ten. Uncle Vernon dumped Harry's trunk on to a trolley and wheeled it into the station for him. Harry thought this was strangely kind until Uncle Vernon stopped dead, facing the

* 第6章 从 $9\frac{3}{4}$ 站台开始的旅程 *

"谢谢您。"

他刚要回到楼上去，弗农姨父却真的开口说话了。

"坐火车去巫师学校未免太可笑了吧。他们的魔毯全都破光了吗？"

哈利没吭声。

"这所学校到底在什么地方？你说。"

"我不知道。"哈利说，这才想到这一点。他从衣袋里掏出海格给他的火车票。

"我应该坐十一点钟从 $9\frac{3}{4}$ 站台开出的火车。"他读道。

姨父姨妈瞪大了眼睛。

"第几站台？"

"$9\frac{3}{4}$ 站台。"

"别胡说八道了，"弗农姨父说，"根本就没有 $9\frac{3}{4}$ 站台。"

"我的火车票上就是这么写的。"

"胡说，"弗农姨父说，"他们好多人都疯了，到处乱咋呼。你会明白的。你等着瞧吧。好了，我们送你去国王十字车站。反正我们明天要去伦敦，要不然我才不去找麻烦呢。"

"您上伦敦做什么？"哈利问，希望保持友好气氛。

"带达力上医院，"弗农姨父咆哮起来，"在他上斯梅廷之前把那条可恶的尾巴割掉。"

第二天，哈利早上五点就醒了。他又兴奋又紧张，再也睡不着了。他从床上爬起来，穿上牛仔裤，因为他不愿穿巫师长袍进火车站——准备上车再换。他又核对了一遍霍格沃茨的购物单，看需要的东西是否都买齐了，再看看海德薇是不是好好地关在笼子里，之后就在房间里踱起步来，等候德思礼夫妇起床。两小时后，哈利沉重的大箱子终于被抬上了德思礼家的汽车，佩妮姨妈说服达力坐到哈利身边，他们就上路了。

他们十点半来到国王十字车站。弗农姨父把哈利的皮箱放到手推车上，帮他推进站。哈利正在琢磨弗农姨父为什么一下子变得出奇地好，弗农姨父突然面对站台停下来不走了，心怀鬼胎地咧嘴一笑。

CHAPTER SIX   The Journey from Platform Nine and Three-Quarters

platforms with a nasty grin on his face.

'Well, there you are, boy. Platform nine – platform ten. Your platform should be somewhere in the middle, but they don't seem to have built it yet, do they?'

He was quite right, of course. There was a big plastic number nine over one platform and a big plastic number ten over the one next to it, and in the middle, nothing at all.

'Have a good term,' said Uncle Vernon with an even nastier smile. He left without another word. Harry turned and saw the Dursleys drive away. All three of them were laughing. Harry's mouth went rather dry. What on earth was he going to do? He was starting to attract a lot of funny looks, because of Hedwig. He'd have to ask someone.

He stopped a passing guard, but didn't dare mention platform nine and three-quarters. The guard had never heard of Hogwarts and when Harry couldn't even tell him what part of the country it was in, he started to get annoyed, as though Harry was being stupid on purpose. Getting desperate, Harry asked for the train that left at eleven o'clock, but the guard said there wasn't one. In the end the guard strode away, muttering about time-wasters. Harry was now trying hard not to panic. According to the large clock over the arrivals board, he had ten minutes left to get on the train to Hogwarts and he had no idea how to do it; he was stranded in the middle of a station with a trunk he could hardly lift, a pocket full of wizard money and a large owl.

Hagrid must have forgotten to tell him something you had to do, like tapping the third brick on the left to get into Diagon Alley. He wondered if he should get out his wand and start tapping the ticket box between platforms nine and ten.

At that moment a group of people passed just behind him and he caught a few words of what they were saying.

'– packed with Muggles, of course –'

Harry swung round. The speaker was a plump woman who was talking to four boys, all with flaming red hair. Each of them was pushing a trunk like Harry's in front of him – and they had an *owl*.

Heart hammering, Harry pushed his trolley after them. They stopped and so did he, just near enough to hear what they were saying.

'Now, what's the platform number?' said the boys' mother.

第6章 从 $9\frac{3}{4}$ 站台开始的旅程

"好了,你到了,小子。第9站台——第10站台。你的站台应该是在这两个站台之间吧,可看起来好像还没来得及修建呢,是吧?"

当然,他说得不错。一个站台上挂着一块大大的9字塑料牌,另一个站台上挂着大大的10字塑料牌,而两者中间什么也没有。

"祝你学期顺利。"弗农姨父说着又咧嘴一笑,显得更没怀好心。他没再说什么就走开了。哈利转身眼看着弗农一家开车离去。他们三个人都在哈哈大笑。哈利觉得嘴有一点儿发干。他究竟该怎么办呢?因为海德薇,他已经招来许多好奇的目光。他得找人问问。

他拦住一个过路的警卫,但不敢提 $9\frac{3}{4}$ 站台。警卫从来没听说过霍格沃茨。当他发现哈利甚至说不清霍格沃茨具体在英国什么地方时,开始生气了,认为哈利是在故意装傻愚弄他。哈利实在没辙了,只好问十一点发出的列车有几班,警卫说一班也没有。最后警卫迈着大步走开了,一路抱怨有些人专门浪费别人的时间。哈利告诫自己尽量不要惊慌失措。到达列车时刻表上方的大钟显示,再过十分钟他就该登上开往霍格沃茨的列车了,可他一点也不知道该怎么办。他身边是一个他简直提不动的大箱子,满满一口袋魔币和一只大猫头鹰,他站在站台中央,一筹莫展。

一定是海格忘记告诉他什么秘诀了,诸如敲左边第三块砖就可以到达对角巷之类的。他在想要不要拿出魔杖来敲第9和第10站台之间的隔墙。

正在这时,一群人从他背后经过,一两句话飘进了他的耳朵里。

"——当然挤满了麻瓜们——"

哈利连忙转身,只见说话的是一个矮矮胖胖的女人,正在跟四个红头发的男孩说话。他们每人都推着像哈利那样的皮箱——他们也有一只猫头鹰。

哈利的心怦怦直跳,连忙推着车紧跟着他们。他们停下来,他也跟着停在离他们不远的地方,以便能听见他们说话。

"好了,是几号站台?"孩子们的母亲问。

"$9\frac{3}{4}$!"一个红头发的小姑娘牵着妈妈的手,尖着嗓子大声说,"妈妈,我能去吗……?"

CHAPTER SIX The Journey from Platform Nine and Three-Quarters

'Nine and three-quarters!' piped a small girl, also red-headed, who was holding her hand. 'Mum, can't I go ...'

'You're not old enough, Ginny, now be quiet. All right, Percy, you go first.'

What looked like the oldest boy marched towards platforms nine and ten. Harry watched, careful not to blink in case he missed it – but just as the boy reached the divide between the two platforms, a large crowd of tourists came swarming in front of him, and by the time the last rucksack had cleared away, the boy had vanished.

'Fred, you next,' the plump woman said.

'I'm not Fred, I'm George,' said the boy. 'Honestly, woman, call yourself our mother? Can't you *tell* I'm George?'

'Sorry, George, dear.'

'Only joking, I am Fred,' said the boy, and off he went. His twin called after him to hurry up, and he must have done, because a second later, he had gone – but how had he done it?

Now the third brother was walking briskly towards the ticket barrier – he was almost there – and then, quite suddenly, he wasn't anywhere.

There was nothing else for it.

'Excuse me,' Harry said to the plump woman.

'Hullo, dear,' she said. 'First time at Hogwarts? Ron's new, too.'

She pointed at the last and youngest of her sons. He was tall, thin and gangling, with freckles, big hands and feet and a long nose.

'Yes,' said Harry. 'The thing is – the thing is, I don't know how to –'

'How to get on to the platform?' she said kindly, and Harry nodded.

'Not to worry,' she said. 'All you have to do is walk straight at the barrier between platforms nine and ten. Don't stop and don't be scared you'll crash into it, that's very important. Best do it at a bit of a run if you're nervous. Go on, go now before Ron.'

'Er – OK,' said Harry.

He pushed his trolley round and stared at the barrier. It looked very solid.

He started to walk towards it. People jostled him on their way to platforms nine and ten. Harry walked more quickly. He was going to smash right into that ticket box and then he'd be in trouble – leaning forward on his trolley he broke into a heavy run – the barrier was coming nearer and nearer – he wouldn't be able to stop – the trolley was out of control – he was a foot away –

第6章　从 9$\frac{3}{4}$ 站台开始的旅程

"你还太小，金妮，现在，别说话了。珀西，你走在最前头。"

看上去年龄最大的那个男孩朝第9和第10站台中间走去。哈利目不转睛地盯着他，连眼也不敢眨，生怕漏掉了什么——但正当那孩子走到第9和第10站台分界的地方时，一大群旅客突然拥到哈利前面，等最后一只大帆布背包挪开时，那孩子竟然不见了。

"弗雷德，该你了。"胖女人说。

"我不是弗雷德，我是乔治。"一个男孩说，"说实在的，您说您是我们的母亲，可为什么您认不出我是乔治呢？"

"对不起，乔治，亲爱的。"

"开个玩笑，我是弗雷德。"这孩子说完就朝前走了。他的孪生兄弟在背后催他快点。他想必听了兄弟的话，因为他一转眼就不见了——可他是怎么做的呢？

这时第三个兄弟迈着轻快的步子朝隔墙走去——他刚要走到——突然，也不见了。

没有别的办法。

"对不起。"哈利对胖女人说。

"喂，亲爱的，"她说，"头一回上霍格沃茨吧？罗恩也是新生。"

她指着最后、也是她最小的儿子说。这孩子又瘦又高，显得笨手笨脚，满脸雀斑，大手、大脚、长鼻子。

"是的，"哈利说，"问题是——问题是我不知道该怎么去——"

"该怎么去站台是吗？"她善解人意地说，哈利点点头。

"别担心，"她说，"你只要照直朝第9和第10站台之间的隔墙走就是了。别停下来，别害怕，照直往里冲，这很重要。你要是心里紧张，就一溜小跑。走吧，你先走，罗恩跟着你。"

"哦——好吧。"哈利说。

他把小车掉过头来，眼睛拼命盯着隔墙，它看起来还很结实呢。

他开始向隔墙走去，一路上被拥向第9和第10站台的旅客推来搡去。哈利加快脚步。他肯定会直接撞上隔墙，那样可就麻烦了——他弯腰趴在手推车上，向前猛冲——眼看隔墙越来越近——仅一步之遥——他已无法停步——手推车也失去了控制——他闭着眼睛准备撞上去——

he closed his eyes ready for the crash –

It didn't come ... he kept on running ... he opened his eyes.

A scarlet steam engine was waiting next to a platform packed with people. A sign overhead said *Hogwarts Express, 11 o'clock*. Harry looked behind him and saw a wrought-iron archway where the ticket box had been, with the words *Platform Nine and Three-Quarters* on it. He had done it.

Smoke from the engine drifted over the heads of the chattering crowd, while cats of every colour wound here and there between their legs. Owls hooted to each other in a disgruntled sort of way over the babble and the scraping of heavy trunks.

The first few carriages were already packed with students, some hanging out of the window to talk to their families, some fighting over seats. Harry pushed his trolley off down the platform in search of an empty seat. He passed a round-faced boy who was saying, 'Gran, I've lost my toad again.'

'Oh, *Neville*,' he heard the old woman sigh.

A boy with dreadlocks was surrounded by a small crowd.

'Give us a look, Lee, go on.'

The boy lifted the lid of a box in his arms and the people around him shrieked and yelled as something inside poked out a long, hairy leg.

Harry pressed on through the crowd until he found an empty compartment near the end of the train. He put Hedwig inside first and then started to shove and heave his trunk towards the train door. He tried to lift it up the steps but could hardly raise one end and twice he dropped it painfully on his foot.

'Want a hand?' It was one of the red-haired twins he'd followed through the ticket box.

'Yes, please,' Harry panted.

'Oy, Fred! C'mere and help!'

With the twins' help, Harry's trunk was at last tucked away in a corner of the compartment.

'Thanks,' said Harry, pushing his sweaty hair out of his eyes.

'What's that?' said one of the twins suddenly, pointing at Harry's lightning scar.

'Blimey,' said the other twin. 'Are you –?'

'He *is*,' said the first twin. 'Aren't you?' he added to Harry.

'What?' said Harry.

第6章 从 $9\frac{3}{4}$ 站台开始的旅程

但什么事也没有发生……他继续朝前跑着……他睁开了眼睛。

一辆深红色蒸汽机车停靠在挤满旅客的站台旁。列车上挂的标牌写着：霍格沃茨特快列车，十一点。哈利回头一看，原来是隔墙的地方现在竟成了一条锻铁拱道，上边写着：$9\frac{3}{4}$ 站台。他成功了。

蒸汽机车的浓烟在叽叽喳喳的人群上空缭绕，各种花色的猫在人们脚下穿来穿去。在人群嗡嗡的说话声和拖拉笨重行李的嘈杂声中，猫头鹰也刺耳地鸣叫着，你呼我应。

头几节车厢已经挤满了学生，他们有的从车窗探出身来和家人说话，有的在座位上打闹。哈利在站台上推着小车朝前走，准备找一个空位子。他走过时，一个圆脸男孩说："奶奶，我又把蟾蜍弄丢了。"

"唉，纳威呀。"他听见一个老太婆叹气说。

一个留着脏辫的男孩被一些孩子围着。

"让咱们也见识见识，李，快点。"

那个孩子把抱着的盒子打开，里边露出一只毛茸茸的长腿，吓得周围的孩子们叽哇乱叫，直往后退。

哈利从人群中挤过去，在靠近车尾处找到了一个没人的包厢。他先把海德薇放上去，然后连拖带拉地把皮箱朝车门口搬。他想把皮箱搬上踏板，可是根本抬不起来。他试了两次，箱子都重重地砸在他的脚上。

"要帮忙吗？"说话的正是他在检票口碰到的那对红头发孪生兄弟中的一个。

"是的，劳驾搭把手吧。"哈利气喘吁吁地说。

"喂，弗雷德，快过来帮忙！"

有孪生兄弟帮忙，哈利总算把箱子推到了包厢角落里。

"多谢了。"哈利说，一边把汗湿的头发从眼前掠开。

"那是什么？"孪生兄弟中的一个突然指着哈利那道闪电形伤疤说。

"哎呀，我的天哪，"孪生兄弟中的另一个说，"莫非你是——？"

"他是……"孪生兄弟中第一个说话的说，"你是不是？"他又问哈利。

"是什么？"哈利问。

CHAPTER SIX The Journey from Platform Nine and Three-Quarters

'*Harry Potter*,' chorused the twins.

'Oh, him,' said Harry. 'I mean, yes, I am.'

The two boys gawped at him and Harry felt himself going red. Then, to his relief, a voice came floating in through the train's open door.

'Fred? George? Are you there?'

'Coming, Mum.'

With a last look at Harry, the twins hopped off the train.

Harry sat down next to the window where, half-hidden, he could watch the red-haired family on the platform and hear what they were saying. Their mother had just taken out her handkerchief.

'Ron, you've got something on your nose.'

The youngest boy tried to jerk out of the way, but she grabbed him and began rubbing the end of his nose.

'*Mum* – geroff.' He wriggled free.

'Aaah, has ickle Ronnie got somefink on his nosie?' said one of the twins.

'Shut up,' said Ron.

'Where's Percy?' said their mother.

'He's coming now.'

The oldest boy came striding into sight. He had already changed into his billowing black Hogwarts robes and Harry noticed a shiny red and gold badge on his chest with the letter *P* on it.

'Can't stay long, Mother,' he said. 'I'm up front, the Prefects have got two compartments to themselves –'

'Oh, are you a *Prefect*, Percy?' said one of the twins, with an air of great surprise. 'You should have said something, we had no idea.'

'Hang on, I think I remember him saying something about it,' said the other twin. 'Once –'

'Or twice –'

'A minute –'

'All summer –'

'Oh, shut up,' said Percy the Prefect.

'How come Percy gets new robes, anyway?' said one of the twins.

'Because he's a *Prefect*,' said their mother fondly. 'All right, dear, well, have a good term – send me an owl when you get there.'

"哈利·波特。"孪生兄弟异口同声地说。

"哦，他呀。"哈利说，"我是说，不错，我就是。"

兄弟俩呆呆地盯着他看，哈利觉得脸都红了。这时从开着的车门口传来一阵喊声，使哈利如释重负。

"弗雷德？乔治？你们在车上吗？"

"就来了，妈妈。"

孪生兄弟最后看了一眼哈利，就跳下车去了。

哈利靠窗口坐下，半遮半掩。他能看到站台上红头发的一家人，也能听见他们在说些什么，孩子们的母亲正掏出一块手帕。

"罗恩，你鼻子上有脏东西。"

最小的一个正要躲闪，却被母亲一把抓住，替他擦了擦鼻子尖。

"妈妈——放开我。"他挣脱了。

"好哇，罗恩，你这个小鬼头，鼻子又碰灰啦？"孪生兄弟中的一个说。

"住嘴。"罗恩说。

"珀西呢？"他们的母亲问。

"他来了。"

他们的哥哥大步朝这边走来，已经换上了他那件飘飘摆摆的霍格沃茨黑色长袍。哈利发现他胸前别着一枚金红色的徽章，上面有一个字母P。

"我不能待太久，妈妈，"他说，"我在前边，那里专门给级长划出了两个包厢——"

"哎呀，珀西，你原来是级长呀？"孪生兄弟中的一个用非常吃惊的口吻说，"你早该告诉我们嘛，我一点儿都不知道呢。"

"慢着，我想，我记得他说过，"孪生兄弟中的另一个说，"说过一次——"

"说不定是两次——"

"等一会儿——"

"说了整整一个夏天呢——"

"喂，住嘴。"级长珀西说。

"你说，珀西是怎么弄到新长袍的？"孪生兄弟中的一个问。

"因为他是级长呀。"母亲怜爱地说，"好了，亲爱的，祝你学期顺利，到学校以后让猫头鹰给我带封信来。"

CHAPTER SIX The Journey from Platform Nine and Three-Quarters

She kissed Percy on the cheek and he left. Then she turned to the twins.

'Now, you two – this year, you behave yourselves. If I get one more owl telling me you've – you've blown up a toilet or –'

'Blown up a toilet? We've never blown up a toilet.'

'Great idea though, thanks, Mum.'

'It's *not funny*. And look after Ron.'

'Don't worry, ickle Ronniekins is safe with us.'

'Shut up,' said Ron again. He was almost as tall as the twins already and his nose was still pink where his mother had rubbed it.

'Hey, Mum, guess what? Guess who we just met on the train?'

Harry leant back quickly so they couldn't see him looking.

'You know that black-haired boy who was near us in the station? Know who he is?'

'Who?'

'*Harry Potter!*'

Harry heard the little girl's voice.

'Oh, Mum, can I go on the train and see him, Mum, oh please …'

'You've already seen him, Ginny, and the poor boy isn't something you goggle at in a zoo. Is he really, Fred? How do you know?'

'Asked him. Saw his scar. It's really there – like lightning.'

'Poor *dear* – no wonder he was alone. I wondered. He was ever so polite when he asked how to get on to the platform.'

'Never mind that, do you think he remembers what You-Know-Who looks like?'

Their mother suddenly became very stern.

'I forbid you to ask him, Fred. No, don't you dare. As though he needs reminding of that on his first day at school.'

'All right, keep your hair on.'

A whistle sounded.

'Hurry up!' their mother said, and the three boys clambered on to the train. They leant out of the window for her to kiss them goodbye and their younger sister began to cry.

'Don't, Ginny, we'll send you loads of owls.'

'We'll send you a Hogwarts toilet seat.'

她亲过珀西的面颊，珀西就走开了。之后，她转身对孪生兄弟说：

"现在轮到你俩了——这一年你们俩要放规矩点。如果猫头鹰给我报信，说你们——你们炸了一只抽水马桶，或是——"

"炸了一只马桶？我们从来没炸过马桶。"

"这倒是好主意，多谢了，妈妈。"

"这可不是闹着玩的。好好照顾罗恩。"

"放心吧，罗恩小鬼头跟着我们不会有事的。"

"住嘴。"罗恩说。他的个子差不多跟孪生兄弟一般高，只是鼻尖上他妈妈擦过的地方还红着呢。

"嘿，妈妈，您猜怎么着？猜猜我刚才在火车上碰见谁了？"

哈利连忙往后闪，免得被他们发现他在偷看。

"你知道刚才在车站上，站在我们旁边的那个黑头发的男孩吗？知道他是谁吗？"

"谁？"

"哈利·波特！"

哈利听到了一个小女孩的声音：

"哎呀，妈妈，我能上车去看看他吗？求求您了，妈妈……"

"你已经见过他了，金妮。这个可怜的孩子又不是动物园里的动物，让你看来看去的。他真是哈利吗，弗雷德？你怎么知道的？"

"我问过他了。我看见他那道伤疤了。真的就在那地方，像一道闪电。"

"可怜的孩子……难怪他孤零零一个人。我还纳闷呢。你看他打听去站台怎么走的时候，多有礼貌啊。"

"这些不用去管了，你想他会记得神秘人的长相吗？"

他们的母亲突然沉下脸来。

"不许你们去问他，弗雷德。不许问，你敢去问！你们是想让他在到校的第一天就想起那件事呀！"

"好了，别发火嘛。"

一阵汽笛声响起。

"快！"他们的母亲说，三个孩子匆忙爬上火车。他们从车窗中探出身来，让母亲吻别。他们的小妹妹又哭了起来。

"别哭，金妮，我们会派好多好多猫头鹰去找你。"

CHAPTER SIX   The Journey from Platform Nine and Three-Quarters

'*George!*'

'Only joking, Mum.'

The train began to move. Harry saw the boys' mother waving and their sister, half laughing, half crying, running to keep up with the train until it gathered too much speed; then she fell back and waved.

Harry watched the girl and her mother disappear as the train rounded the corner. Houses flashed past the window. Harry felt a great leap of excitement. He didn't know what he was going to – but it had to be better than what he was leaving behind.

The door of the compartment slid open and the youngest red-headed boy came in.

'Anyone sitting there?' he asked, pointing at the seat opposite Harry. 'Everywhere else is full.'

Harry shook his head and the boy sat down. He glanced at Harry and then looked quickly out of the window, pretending he hadn't looked. Harry saw he still had a black mark on his nose.

'Hey, Ron.'

The twins were back.

'Listen, we're going down the middle of the train – Lee Jordan's got a giant tarantula down there.'

'Right,' mumbled Ron.

'Harry,' said the other twin, 'did we introduce ourselves? Fred and George Weasley. And this is Ron, our brother. See you later, then.'

'Bye,' said Harry and Ron. The twins slid the compartment door shut behind them.

'Are you really Harry Potter?' Ron blurted out.

Harry nodded.

'Oh – well, I thought it might be one of Fred and George's jokes,' said Ron. 'And have you really got – you know ...'

He pointed at Harry's forehead.

Harry pulled back his fringe to show the lightning scar. Ron stared.

'So that's where You-Know-Who –?'

'Yes,' said Harry, 'but I can't remember it.'

'Nothing?' said Ron eagerly.

'Well – I remember a lot of green light, but nothing else.'

"好了，我们会送给你一个霍格沃茨的马桶圈。"

"乔治！"

"开个玩笑嘛，妈妈。"

火车启动了。哈利看到孩子们的母亲在挥手，他们的小妹妹又哭又笑，跟着火车跑，直到火车加速，她被抛在后面，还在不停地挥手。

哈利一直注视着母女俩，直到火车拐过弯去，看不见她们了。一栋栋房屋从车窗前闪过。哈利感到兴奋极了。他不知道前面会怎么样，但至少要比抛在后面的过去好。

包厢的推拉门开了，最小的那个红头发的男孩走了进来。

"这里有人吗？"他指着哈利对面的座位问，"别的地方都满了。"

哈利摇摇头。男孩坐了下来。他瞟了哈利一眼，立刻把目光转向车窗外，装作没看哈利的样子。哈利见他鼻尖上还有一块脏东西。

"嘿，罗恩。"

那对孪生兄弟也来了。

"听着，我们现在要到中间车厢走走——李·乔丹弄到了一只很大的袋蜘蛛呢。"

"哦。"罗恩咕哝了一声。

"哈利，"孪生兄弟中的另一个说，"我们还没向你做自我介绍吧？弗雷德和乔治·韦斯莱。这是罗恩，我们的小弟弟。一会儿见。"

"再见。"哈利和罗恩说。孪生兄弟随手把包厢门拉上了。

"你真是哈利·波特吗？"罗恩脱口而出。

哈利点点头。

"哦，那好，我还以为弗雷德和乔治跟我开玩笑呢。"罗恩说，"那你当真——你知道……"

他指了指哈利的额头。

哈利掠开前额上的一绺头发，露出闪电形伤疤。罗恩瞪大了眼睛。

"这就是神秘人干的？"

"是的，"哈利说，"可我已经不记得了。"

"一点都不记得了？"罗恩急切地问。

"唔——我只记得有许多绿光，别的什么也不记得了。"

CHAPTER SIX The Journey from Platform Nine and Three-Quarters

'Wow,' said Ron. He sat and stared at Harry for a few moments, then, as though he had suddenly realised what he was doing, he looked quickly out of the window again.

'Are all your family wizards?' asked Harry, who found Ron just as interesting as Ron found him.

'Er – yes, I think so,' said Ron. 'I think Mum's got a second cousin who's an accountant, but we never talk about him.'

'So you must know loads of magic already.'

The Weasleys were clearly one of those old wizarding families the pale boy in Diagon alley had talked about.

'I heard you went to live with Muggles,' said Ron. 'What are they like?'

'Horrible – well, not all of them. My aunt and uncle and cousin are, though. Wish I'd had three wizard brothers.'

'Five,' said Ron. For some reason, he was looking gloomy. 'I'm the sixth in our family to go to Hogwarts. You could say I've got a lot to live up to. Bill and Charlie have already left – Bill was Head Boy and Charlie was captain of Quidditch. Now Percy's a Prefect. Fred and George mess around a lot, but they still get really good marks and everyone thinks they're really funny. Everyone expects me to do as well as the others, but if I do, it's no big deal, because they did it first. You never get anything new, either, with five brothers. I've got Bill's old robes, Charlie's old wand and Percy's old rat.'

Ron reached inside his jacket and pulled out a fat grey rat, which was asleep.

'His name's Scabbers and he's useless, he hardly ever wakes up. Percy got an owl from my dad for being made a Prefect, but they couldn't aff– I mean, I got Scabbers instead.'

Ron's ears went pink. He seemed to think he'd said too much, because he went back to staring out of the window.

Harry didn't think there was anything wrong with not being able to afford an owl. After all, he'd never had any money in his life until a month ago, and he told Ron so, all about having to wear Dudley's old clothes and never getting proper birthday presents. This seemed to cheer Ron up.

'... and until Hagrid told me, I didn't know anything about being a wizard or about my parents or Voldemort –'

Ron gasped.

第6章 从 9¾ 站台开始的旅程

"哎呀。"罗恩说。他坐在那里盯着哈利看了好一会儿,似乎才突然意识到自己在做什么,就连忙把视线转向窗外。

"你全家都是巫师吗?"哈利问,发现自己和罗恩都对彼此感兴趣。

"哦,是的,我想是这样。"罗恩说,"好像我妈妈有一个远房表兄是一个会计师,不过我们从来不谈他。"

"那么你一定学会许多魔法了?"

这个韦斯莱家族显然就是对角巷那个面色苍白的男孩说过的古老的巫师家族之一了。

"我听说你后来跟麻瓜们住在一起。"罗恩说,"他们怎么样?"

"太差劲了,当然不是所有的人都这样。不过我的姨父姨妈和表哥都太差劲了。我要是有三个巫师兄弟就好了。"

"五个。"罗恩说,不知为什么他显得有些不高兴,"我是我们家去霍格沃茨上学的第六个了。你可以说,我应当以他们为榜样。比尔和查理已经毕业了。比尔是男生学生会主席,查理是魁地奇球队队长。现在珀西当上了级长。弗雷德和乔治尽管调皮捣蛋,但他们的成绩都是顶呱呱的,大家都觉得他们很有意思。所有人都盼望我能跟哥哥们一样,可话又说回来,即使我能做到,也没什么了不起的了,因为他们在我之前就做到了。你要是有五个哥哥,你就永远用不上新东西。我穿比尔的旧长袍,用查理的旧魔杖,还有珀西扔了不要的老鼠。"

罗恩说着,伸手从上衣内袋里掏出一只肥肥的灰老鼠,它正在睡觉。

"它叫斑斑,已经毫无用处了,整天睡不醒。珀西当上了级长,我爸送给他一只猫头鹰,他们买不起——我是说,就把老鼠给我了。"

罗恩的耳朵涨红了。他似乎觉得自己话太多,就又开始看着窗外。

哈利觉得买不起猫头鹰也没有什么不好,他自己一个月前不也一直是身无分文吗?他对罗恩讲了实情,说他总是穿达力的旧衣服,从来没有收到过一份像样的生日礼物。这似乎使罗恩的心情好多了。

"……在海格告诉我这些之前,我一点也不知道巫师或者我父母的情况,以及伏地魔的事——"

罗恩吓得喘不上气来。

CHAPTER SIX   The Journey from Platform Nine and Three-Quarters

'What?' said Harry.

'*You said You-Know-Who's name!*' said Ron, sounding both shocked and impressed. 'I'd have thought you, of all people –'

'I'm not trying to be *brave* or anything, saying the name,' said Harry. 'I just never knew you shouldn't. See what I mean? I've got loads to learn ... I bet,' he added, voicing for the first time something that had been worrying him a lot lately, 'I bet I'm the worst in the class.'

'You won't be. There's loads of people who come from Muggle families and they learn quick enough.'

While they had been talking, the train had carried them out of London. Now they were speeding past fields full of cows and sheep. They were quiet for a time, watching the fields and lanes flick past.

Around half past twelve there was a great clattering outside in the corridor and a smiling, dimpled woman slid back their door and said, 'Anything off the trolley, dears?'

Harry, who hadn't had any breakfast, leapt to his feet, but Ron's ears went pink again and he muttered that he'd brought sandwiches. Harry went out into the corridor.

He had never had any money for sweets with the Dursleys and now that he had pockets rattling with gold and silver he was ready to buy as many Mars Bars as he could carry – but the woman didn't have Mars Bars. What she did have were Bertie Bott's Every-Flavour Beans, Drooble's Best Blowing Gum, Chocolate Frogs, Pumpkin Pasties, Cauldron Cakes, Liquorice Wands and a number of other strange things Harry had never seen in his life. Not wanting to miss anything, he got some of everything and paid the woman eleven silver Sickles and seven bronze Knuts.

Ron stared as Harry brought it all back into the compartment and tipped it on to an empty seat.

'Hungry, are you?'

'Starving,' said Harry, taking a large bite out of a pumpkin pasty.

Ron had taken out a lumpy package and unwrapped it. There were four sandwiches in there. He pulled one of them apart and said, 'She always forgets I don't like corned beef.'

'Swap you for one of these,' said Harry, holding up a pasty. 'Go on –'

'You don't want this, it's all dry,' said Ron. 'She hasn't got much time,' he

"怎么了?"哈利问。

"你说出神秘人的名字了!"罗恩说,显得又震惊,又佩服,"我早就想到,所有的人当中只有你——"

"说出他的名字,并不是因为我勇敢什么的,"哈利说,"而是因为我一直不知道那个名字不能说。明白我的意思吗?我相信,我有许多东西需要学……"他又说,听得出他最近正为此感到忧心忡忡,"我敢说,我一定会是班上最差的学生。"

"不会的。有很多学生都来自麻瓜家庭,可他们也学得很快。"

在他们谈话的时候,列车已驶出伦敦,正沿着遍地牛羊的田野飞驰。他们沉默了片刻,望着田野和草场从眼前掠过。

大约十二点半左右,过道上咔嚓咔嚓传来一阵响亮的嘈杂声,一个笑容可掬、面带酒窝的女人推开包厢门问:"亲爱的,要不要买车上的什么食品?"

哈利早上一点东西也没吃,于是一下子跳了起来。罗恩的耳朵又涨红了,嘟哝说他带着三明治。哈利来到过道里。

在德思礼家时,他从来没有一分零用钱买糖吃,现在他口袋里装满了哗哗响的金币、银币。只要拿得下,他要买一大堆火星棒,可惜车上没有。只有比比多味豆、吹宝超级泡泡糖、巧克力蛙、南瓜馅饼、坩埚形蛋糕、甘草魔杖,还有一些哈利从未见过的稀奇古怪的食品。哈利一样不落,每种都买了一些,付给那个女售货员十一个银西可和七枚青铜纳特。

罗恩直勾勾地看着哈利把买来的食品抱进包厢,一下子都倒在空位子上。

"你饿了?"

"饿坏了。"哈利咬了一大口南瓜馅饼说。

罗恩拿出一个鼓鼓囊囊的纸盒打开,里面装有四块三明治。他拿出一块,说:"她总不记得我不爱吃腌牛肉。"

"跟你换一块吧,"哈利拿起一个馅饼说,"来吧……"

"你不会喜欢吃这个的,太干。"罗恩说,"她没有时间,"他连忙又

added quickly, 'you know, with five of us.'

'Go on, have a pasty,' said Harry, who had never had anything to share before or, indeed, anyone to share it with. It was a nice feeling, sitting there with Ron, eating their way through all Harry's pasties and cakes (the sandwiches lay forgotten).

'What are these?' Harry asked Ron, holding up a pack of Chocolate Frogs. 'They're not *really* frogs, are they?' He was starting to feel that nothing would surprise him.

'No,' said Ron. 'But see what the card is, I'm missing Agrippa.'

'What?'

'Oh, of course, you wouldn't know – Chocolate Frogs have cards inside them, you know, to collect – Famous Witches and Wizards. I've got about five hundred, but I haven't got Agrippa or Ptolemy.'

Harry unwrapped his Chocolate Frog and picked up the card. It showed a man's face. He wore half-moon glasses, had a long crooked nose and flowing silver hair, beard and moustache. Underneath the picture was the name *Albus Dumbledore*.

'So *this* is Dumbledore!' said Harry.

'Don't tell me you'd never heard of Dumbledore!' said Ron. 'Can I have a frog? I might get Agrippa – thanks –'

Harry turned over his card and read:

ALBUS DUMBLEDORE,

currently Headmaster of Hogwarts. Considered by many the greatest wizard of modern times, Professor Dumbledore is particularly famous for his defeat of the Dark wizard Grindelwald in 1945, for the discovery of the twelve uses of dragon's blood and his work on alchemy with his partner, Nicolas Flamel. Professor Dumbledore enjoys chamber music and tenpin bowling.

说,"你看,她要同时照顾我们五个。"

"来吧,来一个馅饼。"哈利说。在这之前他没有和别人分享过任何东西,其实也没有人跟他分享。现在跟罗恩坐在一起大嚼自己买来的馅饼和蛋糕(三明治早已放在一边被冷落了),边吃边聊,哈利感觉好极了。

"这些是什么?"哈利拿起一包巧克力蛙问罗恩,"它们不会是真青蛙吧?"他开始觉得什么也不会让自己吃惊了。

"不是。"罗恩说,"你看看里边的画片,我少一张阿格丽芭。"

"什么?"

"哦,我忘了你不知道,巧克力蛙里都附有画片,可以收集起来,都是些有名的巫师。我差不多攒了五百张,就缺阿格丽芭和波托勒米了。"

哈利打开巧克力蛙,取出画片。画片上是一张男人的脸,戴一副半月形眼镜,长着一个歪扭的长鼻子,银发和胡须披垂着。画片下边的名字是:阿不思·邓布利多。

"原来他就是邓布利多!"哈利说。

"你可别说你从来没听说过邓布利多!"罗恩说,"给我一块巧克力蛙好吗?说不定我能拿到阿格丽芭呢——谢谢——"

哈利把画片翻了过来,读着背面的文字:

> 阿不思·邓布利多,
> 现任霍格沃茨校长,
> 被公认为当代最伟大的巫师,
> 邓布利多广为人知的贡献包括:
> 一九四五年击败黑巫师格林德沃,
> 发现火龙血的十二种用途,
> 与合作伙伴尼可·勒梅在炼金术方面卓有成效,
> 邓布利多教授爱好室内乐及十柱滚木球戏。

哈利重新把画片翻到正面,吃惊地发现邓布利多的脸竟然不见了。

CHAPTER SIX The Journey from Platform Nine and Three-Quarters

Harry turned the card back over and saw, to his astonishment, that Dumbledore's face had disappeared.

'He's gone!'

'Well, you can't expect him to hang around all day,' said Ron. 'He'll be back. No, I've got Morgana again and I've got about six of her ... do you want it? You can start collecting.'

Ron's eyes strayed to the pile of Chocolate Frogs waiting to be unwrapped.

'Help yourself,' said Harry. 'But in, you know, the Muggle world, people just stay put in photos.'

'Do they? What, they don't move at all?' Ron sounded amazed. '*Weird*!'

Harry stared as Dumbledore sidled back into the picture on his card and gave him a small smile. Ron was more interested in eating the frogs than looking at the Famous Witches and Wizards cards, but Harry couldn't keep his eyes off them. Soon he had not only Dumbledore and Morgana, but Hengist of Woodcroft, Alberic Grunnion, Circe, Paracelsus and Merlin. He finally tore his eyes away from the druidess Cliodna, who was scratching her nose, to open a bag of Bertie Bott's Every-Flavour Beans.

'You want to be careful with those,' Ron warned Harry. 'When they say every flavour, they *mean* every flavour – you know, you get all the ordinary ones like chocolate and peppermint and marmalade, but then you can get spinach and liver and tripe. George reckons he had a bogey-flavoured one once.'

Ron picked up a green bean, looked at it carefully and bit into a corner.

'Bleaaargh – see? Sprouts.'

They had a good time eating the Every-Flavour Beans. Harry got toast, coconut, baked bean, strawberry, curry, grass, coffee, sardine and was even brave enough to nibble the end off a funny grey one Ron wouldn't touch, which turned out to be pepper.

The countryside now flying past the window was becoming wilder. The neat fields had gone. Now there were woods, twisting rivers and dark green hills.

There was a knock on the door of their compartment and the round-faced boy Harry had passed on platform nine and three-quarters came in. He looked tearful.

'Sorry,' he said, 'but have you seen a toad at all?'

When they shook their heads, he wailed, 'I've lost him! He keeps getting away from me!'

"他不见了!"

"你当然不能指望他整天待在这里。"罗恩说,"他会回来的。不过我又拿到了一张莫佳娜。我已经有六张她的画片了……给你吧?你也可以开始收集了。"

罗恩眼睛盯着一堆没有拆包的巧克力蛙。

"你自己拿吧。"哈利说,"可你知道,在麻瓜世界里,人们一旦被拍成照片就永远保留在照片上不变了。"

"是吗?什么,他们一动不动吗?"罗恩显得很惊讶,"太奇怪了!"

哈利眼看着邓布利多又溜回到画片上,还朝他微微一笑。罗恩的兴趣在于吃巧克力蛙,而不是看那些著名巫师的画片。可哈利却怎么也不能把目光从那些画片上移开。他一下子不仅有了邓布利多和莫佳娜,而且还有了汉吉斯、阿博瑞克、瑟斯、帕拉瑟和梅林。最后他总算强迫自己不再去看挠鼻子的女德鲁伊克丽奥娜,打开了一袋比比多味豆。

"吃这个你要当心,"罗恩警告哈利说,"他们所说的多味,你知道,意思是各种味道一应俱全,吃起来不仅有巧克力、薄荷糖、橘子酱等一般的味道,而且还会有菠菜、肝和肚的味道。乔治说,有一次他还吃到一粒干鼻屎味的豆子呢。"

罗恩捡起一粒绿色的豆子,仔细看了看,咬下一点。

"哎呀呀,明白了吧?芽豆。"

这包多味豆让他们俩都好好地享受了一番。哈利吃到了吐司、椰子、烘豆、草莓、咖喱、青草、咖啡、沙丁鱼等各种口味的,甚至还勇敢地舔了一下罗恩连碰都不敢碰的一粒奇怪的灰豆,原来那是胡椒口味的。

这时,在车窗外飞驰而过的田野显得更加荒芜,整齐的农田已经消逝了。随之而来的是一片树林、弯弯曲曲的河流和暗绿色的山丘。

又有人敲他们的包厢门。与哈利在 $9\frac{3}{4}$ 站台擦肩而过的圆脸男孩走了进来,满眼含泪。

"对不起,"他说,"我想问问,你们看见我的蟾蜍了吗?"

哈利和罗恩都摇摇头,他就大哭起来。"我又把它弄丢了!它总想从我身边跑掉!"

'He'll turn up,' said Harry.

'Yes,' said the boy miserably. 'Well, if you see him ...'

He left.

'Don't know why he's so bothered,' said Ron. 'If I'd brought a toad I'd lose it as quick as I could. Mind you, I brought Scabbers, so I can't talk.'

The rat was still snoozing on Ron's lap.

'He might have died and you wouldn't know the difference,' said Ron in disgust. 'I tried to turn him yellow yesterday to make him more interesting, but the spell didn't work. I'll show you, look ...'

He rummaged around in his trunk and pulled out a very battered-looking wand. It was chipped in places and something white was glinting at the end.

'Unicorn hair's nearly poking out. Anyway –'

He had just raised his wand when the compartment door slid open again. The toadless boy was back, but this time he had a girl with him. She was already wearing her new Hogwarts robes.

'Has anyone seen a toad? Neville's lost one,' she said. She had a bossy sort of voice, lots of bushy brown hair and rather large front teeth.

'We've already told him we haven't seen it,' said Ron, but the girl wasn't listening, she was looking at the wand in his hand.

'Oh, are you doing magic? Let's see it, then.'

She sat down. Ron looked taken aback.

'Er – all right.'

He cleared his throat.

'Sunshine, daisies, butter mellow,
Turn this stupid, fat rat yellow.'

He waved his wand, but nothing happened. Scabbers stayed grey and fast asleep.

'Are you sure that's a real spell?' said the girl. 'Well, it's not very good, is it? I've tried a few simple spells just for practice and it's all worked for me. Nobody in my family's magic at all, it was ever such a surprise when I got my letter, but I was ever so pleased, of course, I mean, it's the very best school

"它会回来的。"哈利说。

"是啊,"男孩伤心地说,"那么,要是你们看见……"

他走了。

"我不明白,他为什么这么着急。"罗恩说,"我要是买了一只蟾蜍,我会想办法尽快把它弄丢,越快越好。不过我既然带了斑斑,也就没话可说了。"

老鼠还在罗恩的腿上打盹。

"它说不定早死了,反正死活都一样。"罗恩厌烦地说,"我昨天试着想把它变成黄色的,变得好玩一些,可是我的咒语不灵。我现在来做给你看看,注意了……"

他在皮箱里摸索了半天,拽出一根很破旧的魔杖,有些地方都剥落了,一头还闪着白色亮光。

"独角兽毛都要露出来了。不过……"

他刚举起魔杖,包厢门又开了。那个丢蟾蜍的男孩再次来到他们面前,但这回是一个小姑娘陪他来的。小姑娘已经换上了霍格沃茨的新长袍。

"你们有人看到一只蟾蜍了吗?纳威丢了一只蟾蜍。"她说,语气显得自高自大,目中无人。她有一头浓密的棕色头发和一对大门牙。

"我们已经对他说过了,我们没有看见。"罗恩说,可小姑娘根本不理会,只看着他手里的魔杖。

"哦,你是在施魔法吗?那就让我们开开眼吧。"

她坐了下来。罗恩显然吃了一惊,有些不知所措。

"哦——好吧。"

他清了清嗓子。

雏菊、甜奶油和阳光,
把这只傻乎乎的肥老鼠变黄。

他挥动魔杖,但什么也没有发生。斑斑还是灰色的,睡得正香呢。

"你肯定这真是一道咒语吗?"小姑娘问,"看来不怎么样,是吧?我在家里试过几道简单的咒语,只是为了练习,结果都起作用了。我家没有一个人懂魔法,所以当我收到入学通知书时,我吃惊极了,但又特别高兴,因为,我的意思是说,据我所知,这是一所最优秀的魔法学校——

CHAPTER SIX   The Journey from Platform Nine and Three-Quarters

of witchcraft there is, I've heard – I've learnt all our set books off by heart, of course, I just hope it will be enough – I'm Hermione Granger, by the way, who are you?'

She said all this very fast.

Harry looked at Ron and was relieved to see by his stunned face that he hadn't learnt all the set books off by heart either.

'I'm Ron Weasley,' Ron muttered.

'Harry Potter,' said Harry.

'Are you really?' said Hermione. 'I know all about you, of course – I got a few extra books for background reading, and you're in *Modern Magical History* and *The Rise and Fall of the Dark Arts* and *Great Wizarding Events of the Twentieth Century*.'

'Am I?' said Harry, feeling dazed.

'Goodness, didn't you know, I'd have found out everything I could if it was me,' said Hermione. 'Do either of you know what house you'll be in? I've been asking around and I hope I'm in Gryffindor, it sounds by far the best, I hear Dumbledore himself was one, but I suppose Ravenclaw wouldn't be too bad ... Anyway, we'd better go and look for Neville's toad. You two had better change, you know, I expect we'll be there soon.'

And she left, taking the toadless boy with her.

'Whatever house I'm in, I hope she's not in it,' said Ron. He threw his wand back into his trunk. 'Stupid spell – George gave it to me, bet he knew it was a dud.'

'What house are your brothers in?' asked Harry.

'Gryffindor,' said Ron. Gloom seemed to be settling on him again. 'Mum and Dad were in it, too. I don't know what they'll say if I'm not. I don't suppose Ravenclaw *would* be too bad, but imagine if they put me in Slytherin.'

'That's the house Vol– I mean, You-Know-Who was in?'

'Yeah,' said Ron. He flopped back into his seat, looking depressed.

'You know, I think the ends of Scabbers's whiskers are a bit lighter,' said Harry, trying to take Ron's mind off houses. 'So what do your oldest brothers do now they've left, anyway?'

Harry was wondering what a wizard did once he'd finished school.

所有的课本我都背会了,当然,但愿这能够用——我叫赫敏·格兰杰,顺便问一句,你们叫什么名字?"

她连珠炮似的一气说完。

哈利看看罗恩,从罗恩吃惊的表情看出他也没把书全部背会,不觉松了一口气。

"我叫罗恩·韦斯莱。"罗恩咕哝说。

"哈利·波特。"哈利说。

"真的是你吗?"赫敏问,"你的事我全都知道,当然——我额外多买了几本参考书,《现代魔法史》《黑魔法的兴衰》《二十世纪重要魔法事件》,这几本书里都提到了你。"

"提到我?"哈利说,突然感到一阵头晕目眩。

"天哪,你居然会不知道。要是我,我一定想办法把所有提到我的书都找来。"赫敏说,"你们俩知不知道自己会被分到哪个学院?我已经到处打听过了,我希望能分到格兰芬多,都说那是最好的,我听说邓布利多自己就是从那里毕业的,不过我想拉文克劳也不算太坏……不管怎么说,我们最好还是先去找纳威的蟾蜍吧。你们俩最好赶快把衣服换上,要知道,我们大概很快就要到了。"

于是她领着那个丢蟾蜍的男孩一道走了。

"不管分到哪个学院,我都不希望跟她分在一起。"罗恩说,他把魔杖扔到了旅行箱里,"这个咒语没用,是乔治告诉我的。我敢说,他准早就知道这是一发瞎炮。"

"你的两个哥哥都在哪个学院?"哈利问。

"格兰芬多。"罗恩说,他似乎又显得不开心了,"妈妈和爸爸以前也是这个学院的。如果我不去这里,不知道他们会怎么说。我想去拉文克劳也没有什么特别不好的,可想想看,千万别把我分到斯莱特林学院。"

"那是伏——对不起,我是说,那是神秘人待过的吗?"

"不错。"罗恩说着,倒在座位上,显得很沮丧。

"你看,我觉得斑斑胡子尖的颜色变淡了。"哈利说,想把罗恩的注意力从学院的事情上转移开来,"你的两个哥哥既然毕业了,现在他们都在做什么呢?"

哈利想知道巫师从学校毕业后会去做什么。

CHAPTER SIX The Journey from Platform Nine and Three-Quarters

'Charlie's in Romania studying dragons and Bill's in Africa doing something for Gringotts,' said Ron. 'Did you hear about Gringotts? It's been all over the *Daily Prophet*, but I don't suppose you get that with the Muggles – someone tried to rob a high-security vault.'

Harry stared.

'Really? What happened to them?'

'Nothing, that's why it's such big news. They haven't been caught. My dad says it must've been a powerful Dark wizard to get round Gringotts, but they don't think they took anything, that's what's odd. 'Course, everyone gets scared when something like this happens in case You-Know-Who's behind it.'

Harry turned this news over in his mind. He was starting to get a prickle of fear every time You-Know-Who was mentioned. He supposed this was all part of entering the magical world, but it had been a lot more comfortable saying 'Voldemort' without worrying.

'What's your Quidditch team?' Ron asked.

'Er – I don't know any,' Harry confessed.

'What!' Ron looked dumbfounded. 'Oh, you wait, it's the best game in the world –' and he was off, explaining all about the four balls and the positions of the seven players, describing famous games he'd been to with his brothers and the broomstick he'd like to get if he had the money. He was just taking Harry through the finer points of the game when the compartment door slid open yet again, but it wasn't Neville the toadless boy or Hermione Granger this time.

Three boys entered and Harry recognised the middle one at once: it was the pale boy from Madam Malkin's robe shop. He was looking at Harry with a lot more interest than he'd shown back in Diagon alley.

'Is it true?' he said. 'They're saying all down the train that Harry Potter's in this compartment. So it's you, is it?'

'Yes,' said Harry. He was looking at the other boys. Both of them were thickset and looked extremely mean. Standing either side of the pale boy they looked like bodyguards.

'Oh, this is Crabbe and this is Goyle,' said the pale boy carelessly, noticing where Harry was looking. 'And my name's Malfoy, Draco Malfoy.'

Ron gave a slight cough, which might have been hiding a snigger. Draco Malfoy looked at him.

'Think my name's funny, do you? No need to ask who you are. My father

第6章 从9¾站台开始的旅程

"查理在罗马尼亚研究火龙,比尔在非洲替古灵阁做事。"罗恩说,"你听说古灵阁的事了吗?《预言家日报》上都登满了,不过你跟麻瓜住在一起,我想你是看不到的——有人试图抢劫防范高度严密的地下金库呢。"

哈利瞪大了眼睛。

"真的吗?后来怎么样了?"

"什么事也没有,正因为这样才爆出一件大新闻。他们没有被抓住。我爸爸说,显然只有法力最高强的黑巫师才能设法摆脱古灵阁的追捕。不过他们什么也没有拿走,怪就怪在这里。当然,每当这类事情发生时,就人人自危,人们担心事情背后有神秘人指使。"

哈利在脑子里反复琢磨着这件新闻。每当提到神秘人,他都有一种隐隐的惧意。他认为这也许是初入魔法世界的必然感受吧,但是先前能毫无顾忌地直呼伏地魔的名字,那感觉比现在好受多了。

"你喜欢哪一支魁地奇球队?"罗恩问。

"哦——我全都不了解。"哈利承认说。

"什么!"罗恩似乎惊呆了,"哦,你等等,这是世界上最好的娱乐——"接着他开始滔滔不绝地讲解四只球,七名队员的位置,绘声绘色地讲他跟几个哥哥去看的几场有名的球赛,并说等他有了钱,要买一把他喜欢的飞天扫帚。他正好讲到球赛最精彩的地方时,包厢门又被推开了,不过这回进来的不是丢失蟾蜍的男孩纳威,也不是赫敏·格兰杰。

进来的是三个男孩,哈利立刻认出中间那个正是他在摩金夫人长袍店遇到的面色苍白的男孩。他怀着比在对角巷时大得多的兴趣看着哈利。

"是真的吗?"他问,"整列火车上的人都在纷纷议论,说哈利·波特在这个包厢里。这么说,就是你了,对吧?"

"是的。"哈利说,看着另外两个男孩,他们俩都长得粗粗壮壮,而且长相特别难看,站在小白脸两边,一边一个,简直像他的一对保镖。

"哦,这是克拉布,这是高尔。"面色苍白的男孩发现哈利在看他们,就随随便便地说,"我叫马尔福,德拉科·马尔福。"

罗恩轻轻咳了一声,免得笑出声来。德拉科·马尔福看着他。

"你觉得我的名字太可笑,是吗?不用问你是谁。我父亲告诉我,韦斯莱家的人都是红头发,满脸雀斑,而且孩子多得养不起。"

CHAPTER SIX The Journey from Platform Nine and Three-Quarters

told me all the Weasleys have red hair, freckles and more children than they can afford.'

He turned back to Harry.

'You'll soon find out some wizarding families are much better than others, Potter. You don't want to go making friends with the wrong sort. I can help you there.'

He held out his hand to shake Harry's, but Harry didn't take it.

'I think I can tell who the wrong sort are for myself, thanks,' he said coolly.

Draco Malfoy didn't go red, but a pink tinge appeared in his pale cheeks.

'I'd be careful if I were you, Potter,' he said slowly. 'Unless you're a bit politer you'll go the same way as your parents. They didn't know what was good for them, either. You hang around with riff-raff like the Weasleys and that Hagrid and it'll rub off on you.'

Both Harry and Ron stood up. Ron's face was as red as his hair.

'Say that again,' he said.

'Oh, you're going to fight us, are you?' Malfoy sneered.

'Unless you get out now,' said Harry, more bravely than he felt, because Crabbe and Goyle were a lot bigger than him or Ron.

'But we don't feel like leaving, do we, boys? We've eaten all our food and you still seem to have some.'

Goyle reached towards the Chocolate Frogs next to Ron – Ron leapt forward, but before he'd so much as touched Goyle, Goyle let out a horrible yell.

Scabbers the rat was hanging off his finger, sharp little teeth sunk deep into Goyle's knuckle – Crabbe and Malfoy backed away as Goyle swung Scabbers round and round, howling, and when Scabbers finally flew off and hit the window, all three of them disappeared at once. Perhaps they thought there were more rats lurking among the sweets, or perhaps they'd heard footsteps, because a second later, Hermione Granger had come in.

'What *has* been going on?' she said, looking at the sweets all over the floor and Ron picking up Scabbers by his tail.

'I think he's been knocked out,' Ron said to Harry. He looked closer at Scabbers. 'No – I don't believe it – he's gone back to sleep.'

And so he had.

'You've met Malfoy before?'

Harry explained about their meeting in Diagon Alley.

第6章 从9$\frac{3}{4}$站台开始的旅程

他转身对哈利说：

"你很快就会发现，有些巫师家庭要比其他家庭好许多，波特。你不会想跟另类的人交朋友吧。在这一点上我能帮你。"

他伸出手要跟哈利握手，可哈利没有搭理他。

"我想我自己能分辨出谁是另类，多谢了。"哈利冷冷地说。

德拉科·马尔福苍白的面颊没有涨红，只是泛出淡淡的红晕。

"我要是你呀，波特，我会特别小心。"他慢吞吞地说，"你应当放客气点，否则你会同样走上你父母的那条路。他们也不知好歹。你如果跟韦斯莱家或海格这样不三不四的人混在一起，你会受到影响的。"

哈利和罗恩腾地站了起来。罗恩脸红得跟他的红头发一样。

"你再说一遍。"他说。

"哦，想打架，是不是？"马尔福冷笑说。

"除非你们现在就给我出去。"哈利说，实际上他内心并不像外表这么勇敢，因为克拉布和高尔的块头要比他和罗恩大得多。

"可是我们并没有想走的意思，是不是啊，小伙子们？我们吃的东西都吃光了，你们这里好像还有。"

高尔伸手去拿罗恩旁边的巧克力蛙……罗恩朝前一扑，根本还没碰到高尔，就听高尔一声惨叫。

老鼠斑斑吊在高尔的手指上，尖利的小牙深深地咬进了他的肉里——高尔一边大叫，一边不停地挥手想把斑斑甩掉，克拉布和马尔福直往后退。最后斑斑终于被甩掉了，撞到车窗上，他们三人也立刻趁机溜掉了。也许他们以为糖果里还埋伏着更多的老鼠，也许他们已经听到了脚步声，因为跟着赫敏·格兰杰就进来了。

"出什么事了？"她看着撒满一地的糖果问。

罗恩提着斑斑的尾巴，把它从地上捡起来。

"我想，它肯定摔晕了。"罗恩对哈利说，他凑到斑斑跟前仔细查看，"哎呀，我简直不敢相信，它又睡着了。"

它真的睡着了。

"你以前碰到过马尔福吗？"

哈利向罗恩讲述了他在对角巷与马尔福相遇的事。

CHAPTER SIX The Journey from Platform Nine and Three-Quarters

'I've heard of his family,' said Ron darkly. 'They were some of the first to come back to our side after You-Know-Who disappeared. Said they'd been bewitched. My dad doesn't believe it. He says Malfoy's father didn't need an excuse to go over to the Dark Side.' He turned to Hermione. 'Can we help you with something?'

'You'd better hurry up and put your robes on, I've just been up the front to ask the driver and he says we're nearly there. You haven't been fighting, have you? You'll be in trouble before we even get there!'

'Scabbers has been fighting, not us,' said Ron, scowling at her. 'Would you mind leaving while we change?'

'All right – I only came in here because people outside are behaving very childishly, racing up and down the corridors,' said Hermione in a sniffy voice. 'And you've got dirt on your nose, by the way, did you know?'

Ron glared at her as she left. Harry peered out of the window. It was getting dark. He could see mountains and forests under a deep-purple sky. The train did seem to be slowing down.

He and Ron took off their jackets and pulled on their long black robes. Ron's were a bit short for him, you could see his trainers underneath them.

A voice echoed through the train: 'We will be reaching Hogwarts in five minutes' time. Please leave your luggage on the train, it will be taken to the school separately.'

Harry's stomach lurched with nerves and Ron, he saw, looked pale under his freckles. They crammed their pockets with the last of the sweets and joined the crowd thronging the corridor.

The train slowed right down and finally stopped. People pushed their way towards the door and out on to a tiny, dark platform. Harry shivered in the cold night air. Then a lamp came bobbing over the heads of the students and Harry heard a familiar voice: 'Firs'-years! Firs'-years over here! All right there, Harry?'

Hagrid's big hairy face beamed over the sea of heads.

'C'mon, follow me – any more firs'-years? Mind yer step, now! Firs'-years follow me!'

Slipping and stumbling, they followed Hagrid down what seemed to be a steep, narrow path. It was so dark either side of them that Harry thought there must be thick trees there. Nobody spoke much. Neville, the boy who kept losing his toad, sniffed once or twice.

* 第6章 从9$\frac{3}{4}$站台开始的旅程 *

"我听说过他家的事。"罗恩阴郁地说,"神秘人失踪以后,他们是第一批回到我们这边的人。说他们走火入魔了,我爸爸不相信。他说马尔福的父亲不用找任何借口就倒到黑魔势力那边去了。"他又转过身来对赫敏说:"需要我们帮什么忙吗?"

"你们最好还是赶快换上长袍,我刚到车头上问过司机,他说我们就要到了。你们没有打架吧?还没到地方,你们就要惹出麻烦来!"

"斑斑干了一架,我们没有。"罗恩绷着脸瞪着她说,"我们要换衣服了,请你出去一下好吗?"

"好吧——我来这里是因为外面那些人太淘气了,在走道上跑来跑去的。"赫敏不屑地说,"哦,顺便说一句,你鼻子上有块脏东西,你知道吗?"

她出去时,罗恩瞪了瞪她。哈利朝车窗外瞥了一眼。天已经黑下来了。他看见深紫色的天空下一片山峦和树林。火车似乎减慢了速度。

哈利和罗恩脱下外衣,换上黑长袍。罗恩的长袍短了一点儿,下边露出了他那双球鞋。

"再过五分钟列车就要到达霍格沃茨了,请将行李留在车上,我们会替你们送到学校去的。"这声音在列车上回荡。

哈利紧张得胃里的东西直往上翻,他看见罗恩雀斑下的脸也发白了。他们把剩下的糖果塞进衣袋,就随着过道上的人流朝前拥去。

列车速度越来越慢,最后终于停了下来。旅客们推推搡搡,纷纷拥向车门,下到一个又黑又小的站台上。夜里的寒气使哈利打了个寒战。接着一盏灯在学生们头顶上晃动着,哈利听见一个熟悉的声音在高喊:"一年级新生!一年级新生到这边来!哈利,到这边来,你好吗?"

在万头攒动的一片人海之上,海格蓄着大胡子的脸露着微笑。

"来吧,跟我来,还有一年级新生吗?当心你们的脚底下,好了!一年级新生跟我来!"

他们跟随海格连滑带溜,磕磕绊绊,似乎沿着一条陡峭狭窄的小路走下坡去。小路两旁一片漆黑,哈利心想两边应该是茂密的树林。没有人说话。只有丢失蟾蜍的那个男孩偶尔吸一两下鼻子。

'Yeh'll get yer firs' sight o' Hogwarts in a sec,' Hagrid called over his shoulder, 'jus' round this bend here.'

There was a loud 'Oooooh!'.

The narrow path had opened suddenly on to the edge of a great black lake. Perched atop a high mountain on the other side, its windows sparkling in the starry sky, was a vast castle with many turrets and towers.

'No more'n four to a boat!' Hagrid called, pointing to a fleet of little boats sitting in the water by the shore. Harry and Ron were followed into their boat by Neville and Hermione.

'Everyone in?' shouted Hagrid, who had a boat to himself, 'Right then – FORWARD!'

And the fleet of little boats moved off all at once, gliding across the lake, which was as smooth as glass. Everyone was silent, staring up at the great castle overhead. It towered over them as they sailed nearer and nearer to the cliff on which it stood.

'Heads down!' yelled Hagrid as the first boats reached the cliff; they all bent their heads and the little boats carried them through a curtain of ivy which hid a wide opening in the cliff face. They were carried along a dark tunnel, which seemed to be taking them right underneath the castle, until they reached a kind of underground harbour, where they clambered out on to rocks and pebbles.

'Oy, you there! Is this your toad?' said Hagrid, who was checking the boats as people climbed out of them.

'Trevor!' cried Neville blissfully, holding out his hands. Then they clambered up a passageway in the rock after Hagrid's lamp, coming out at last on to smooth, damp grass right in the shadow of the castle.

They walked up a flight of stone steps and crowded around the huge, oak front door.

'Everyone here? You there, still got yer toad?'

Hagrid raised a gigantic fist and knocked three times on the castle door.

第6章 从 $9\frac{3}{4}$ 站台开始的旅程

"拐过这个弯,你们马上就要第一次看到霍格沃茨了。"海格回头喊道。

接着是一阵嘹亮的"噢——!"

狭窄的小路尽头突然展开了一片黑色的湖泊。湖对岸高高的山坡上耸立着一座巍峨的城堡,城堡上塔尖林立,一扇扇窗口在星空下闪烁。

"每条船上不能超过四个人!"海格指着泊在岸边的一队小船大声说。哈利和罗恩上了小船,纳威和赫敏也跟着上来了。

"都上船了吗?"海格喊道,他自己一人乘一条船,"那好……**前进啰!**"

一队小船即刻划过波平如镜的湖面向前驶去。大家都沉默无语,凝视着高入云天的巨大城堡。当他们临近城堡所在的悬崖时,那城堡仿佛耸立在他们头顶上空。

"低头!"第一批小船驶近峭壁时,海格大声喊道。大家都低下头去,小船载着他们穿过覆盖着山崖正面的常春藤帐幔,来到隐秘的开阔入口。他们沿着一条漆黑的隧道似乎来到了城堡地下,最后到达了一个类似地下码头的地方,然后又攀上一片碎石和小鹅卵石的地面。

"喂,你看看!这是你的蟾蜍吗?"学生们纷纷下船,海格在清查空船时说。

"莱福!"纳威伸出双臂欣喜若狂地喊道。之后他们在海格提灯的灯光映照下攀上山岩中的一条隧道,终于到达了城堡阴影下的一处平坦潮湿的草地。

大家攀上一段石阶,聚在一扇巨大的橡木门前。

"都到齐了吗?你看看,你的蟾蜍还在吧?"

海格举起一只硕大的拳头,往城堡大门上敲了三下。

CHAPTER SEVEN

The Sorting Hat

The door swung open at once. A tall, black-haired witch in emerald-green robes stood there. She had a very stern face and Harry's first thought was that this was not someone to cross.

'The firs'-years, Professor McGonagall,' said Hagrid.

'Thank you, Hagrid. I will take them from here.'

She pulled the door wide. The Entrance Hall was so big you could have fitted the whole of the Dursleys' house in it. The stone walls were lit with flaming torches like the ones at Gringotts, the ceiling was too high to make out, and a magnificent marble staircase facing them led to the upper floors.

They followed Professor McGonagall across the flagged stone floor. Harry could hear the drone of hundreds of voices from a doorway to the right – the rest of the school must already be here – but Professor McGonagall showed the first-years into a small empty chamber off the hall. They crowded in, standing rather closer together than they would usually have done, peering about nervously.

'Welcome to Hogwarts,' said Professor McGonagall. 'The start-of-term banquet will begin shortly, but before you take your seats in the Great Hall, you will be sorted into your houses. The Sorting is a very important ceremony because, while you are here, your house will be something like your family within Hogwarts. You will have classes with the rest of your house, sleep in your house dormitory and spend free time in your house common room.

'The four houses are called Gryffindor, Hufflepuff, Ravenclaw and Slytherin. Each house has its own noble history and each has produced outstanding witches and wizards. While you are at Hogwarts, your triumphs will earn your house points, while any rule-breaking will lose house points. At the end of the year, the house with the most points is awarded the House Cup, a great honour. I hope each of you will be a credit to whichever house

第 7 章

分 院 帽

大门立时洞开。一个身穿翠绿色长袍的高个儿黑发女巫站在大门前。她神情严肃,哈利首先想到的是这个人可不好对付。

"一年级新生到了,麦格教授。"海格说。

"谢谢你,海格。到这里就交给我来接走。"

她把门拉得大开。门厅大得能把德思礼家整栋房子搬进去。像古灵阁一样,石墙周围都是熊熊燃烧的火把。天花板高得几乎看不到顶。正面是一段豪华的大理石楼梯,直通楼上。

他们跟随麦格教授沿石铺地板走去。哈利听见右边门里传来几百人嗡嗡的说话声,学校其他年级的同学想必已经到了——但是麦格教授却把一年级新生带到了大厅另一头一间很小的空屋里。大家一拥而入,摩肩擦背地挤在一起,紧张地仔细凝望着周围的一切。

"欢迎你们来到霍格沃茨。"麦格教授说,"开学宴就要开始了,不过在你们到礼堂入座之前,首先要确定一下你们各自进入哪一所学院。分院是一项很重要的仪式,因为你们在校期间,学院就像你们在霍格沃茨的家。你们要与学院里的其他同学一起上课,一起在学院的宿舍住宿,一起在学院的公共休息室里度过课余时间。

"四所学院的名称分别是:格兰芬多、赫奇帕奇、拉文克劳和斯莱特林。每所学院都拥有自己的光荣历史,都培育了杰出的巫师。在霍格沃茨就读期间,你们的出色表现会使你们所在的学院加分,而任何违规行为则会使你们所在的学院减分。年终时,获最高分的学院可获得学院杯,这是很高的荣誉。我希望你们不论分到哪所学院都能为学院争光。

CHAPTER SEVEN The Sorting Hat

becomes yours.

'The Sorting Ceremony will take place in a few minutes in front of the rest of the school. I suggest you all smarten yourselves up as much as you can while you are waiting.'

Her eyes lingered for a moment on Neville's cloak, which was fastened under his left ear, and on Ron's smudged nose. Harry nervously tried to flatten his hair.

'I shall return when we are ready for you,' said Professor McGonagall. 'Please wait quietly.'

She left the chamber. Harry swallowed.

'How exactly do they sort us into houses?' he asked Ron.

'Some sort of test, I think. Fred said it hurts a lot, but I think he was joking.'

Harry's heart gave a horrible jolt. A test? In front of the whole school? But he didn't know any magic yet – what on earth would he have to do? He hadn't expected something like this the moment they arrived. He looked around anxiously and saw that everyone else looked terrified too. No one was talking much except Hermione Granger, who was whispering very fast about all the spells she'd learnt and wondering which one she'd need. Harry tried hard not to listen to her. He'd never been more nervous, never, not even when he'd had to take a school report home to the Dursleys saying that he'd somehow turned his teacher's wig blue. He kept his eyes fixed on the door. Any second now, Professor McGonagall would come back and lead him to his doom.

Then something happened which made him jump about a foot in the air – several people behind him screamed.

'What the –?'

He gasped. So did the people around him. About twenty ghosts had just streamed through the back wall. Pearly-white and slightly transparent, they glided across the room talking to each other and hardly glancing at the first-years. They seemed to be arguing. What looked like a fat little monk was saying, 'Forgive and forget, I say, we ought to give him a second chance –'

'My dear Friar, haven't we given Peeves all the chances he deserves? He gives us all a bad name and you know, he's not really even a ghost – I say, what are you all doing here?'

A ghost wearing a ruff and tights had suddenly noticed the first-years.

Nobody answered.

第7章 分院帽

"过几分钟，分院仪式就要在全校师生面前举行。我建议你们在等候时，好好把自己整理一下，显得精神一些。"

她的目光在纳威的斗篷（斗篷带系在左耳下边）和罗恩鼻子那块脏东西上游移了一下。哈利紧张地拼命把头发抚平。

"等那边准备好了，我就来接你们。"麦格教授说，"等候时，请保持安静。"

她离开了房间。哈利这才吐了一口气。

"他们怎么能准确地把我们分到哪所学院去呢？"他问罗恩。

"我想，总要通过一种测验吧。弗雷德说很疼，可我想他是在开玩笑。"

哈利心里猛地一颤。做测验？在全校师生面前？可他直到现在连一点儿魔法也不会——究竟该怎么办呢？来到这里时，他根本没想到还会来这一招。他焦急地看看周围，所有的人也都惶恐不安。没有人说话。只有赫敏口中念念有词，在飞快地背诵她学过的咒语，拿不准该用哪一道。哈利尽量不去听她背诵。他从来没有像现在这样紧张过，从来没有，即使他把学校报告书带回家交给德思礼夫妇：报告书上说他把老师的假发套变成了蓝色。他目不转睛地盯着房门，麦格教授随时都可能回来带他去面对毁灭。

这时发生了一件怪事，吓得他一蹦三丈高——他背后有几个人还高声尖叫起来。

"那是——"

他吓得透不过气来，周围的人也是一样。从他们背后的墙上突然蹿出二十来个幽灵。这些珍珠白、半透明的幽灵，一边滑过整个房间，一边交头接耳，但很少留意这些一年级新生。他们好像在争论什么。一个胖乎乎的小修士模样的幽灵说："应当原谅，应当忘掉，我说，我们应当再给他一次机会——"

"我的好修士，难道我们给皮皮鬼的机会还不够多吗？可他令我们都背上了坏名声。你知道，他甚至连一个起码的幽灵都够不上——我说，你们在这里干什么？"

一个穿轮状皱领紧身衣的幽灵突然发现了一年级新生。

没有人答话。

CHAPTER SEVEN   The Sorting Hat

'New students!' said the Fat Friar, smiling around at them. 'About to be sorted, I suppose?'

A few people nodded mutely.

'Hope to see you in Hufflepuff!' said the Friar. 'My old house, you know.'

'Move along now,' said a sharp voice. 'The Sorting Ceremony's about to start.'

Professor McGonagall had returned. One by one, the ghosts floated away through the opposite wall.

'Now, form a line,' Professor McGonagall told the first-years, 'and follow me.'

Feeling oddly as though his legs had turned to lead, Harry got into line behind a boy with sandy hair, with Ron behind him, and they walked out of the chamber, back across the hall and through a pair of double doors into the Great Hall.

Harry had never even imagined such a strange and splendid place. It was lit by thousands and thousands of candles which were floating in mid-air over four long tables, where the rest of the students were sitting. These tables were laid with glittering golden plates and goblets. At the top of the Hall was another long table where the teachers were sitting. Professor McGonagall led the first-years up here, so that they came to a halt in a line facing the other students, with the teachers behind them. The hundreds of faces staring at them looked like pale lanterns in the flickering candlelight. Dotted here and there among the students, the ghosts shone misty silver. Mainly to avoid all the staring eyes, Harry looked upwards and saw a velvety black ceiling dotted with stars. He heard Hermione whisper, 'It's bewitched to look like the sky outside, I read about it in *Hogwarts: A History.*'

It was hard to believe there was a ceiling there at all, and that the Great Hall didn't simply open on to the heavens.

Harry quickly looked down again as Professor McGonagall silently placed a four-legged stool in front of the first-years. On top of the stool she put a pointed wizard's hat. This hat was patched and frayed and extremely dirty. Aunt Petunia wouldn't have let it in the house.

Maybe they had to try and get a rabbit out of it, Harry thought wildly, that seemed the sort of thing – noticing that everyone in the Hall was now staring at the hat, he stared at it too. For a few seconds, there was complete silence. Then the hat twitched. A rip near the brim opened wide like a mouth – and the hat began to sing:

第 7 章 分院帽

"新生哟！"那个胖修士朝他们微笑着说，"我想，大概是准备接受分院吧？"

有些学生默默地点点头。

"希望你们能分到赫奇帕奇！"修士说，"我以前就在那个学院。"

"现在朝前动动，"一个尖厉的声音说，"分院仪式马上就要开始了。"

麦格教授回来了。幽灵们飘飘荡荡，鱼贯穿过对面的墙壁不见了。

"现在，排成单行，"麦格教授对一年级新生说，"跟我走。"

哈利觉得两腿像灌了铅一样难受，可他还是站到了队列里，在一个淡茶色头发男孩背后，而他的背后是罗恩。他们走出房间，穿过门厅，再经过一道双扇门，进入豪华的礼堂。

哈利从未想到过竟会有如此神奇美妙、富丽堂皇的地方。学校其他年级的同学都已围坐在四张长桌旁，桌子上方成千上万只飘荡在半空的蜡烛把礼堂照得透亮。四张桌子上摆着熠熠闪光的金盘和高脚酒杯。礼堂上首的台子上另摆着一张长桌，那是教师们的席位。麦格教授把一年级新生带到那边，让他们面对全体高年级学生排成一排，教师们在他们背后。烛光摇曳，几百张注视着他们的面孔像一盏盏苍白的灯笼。幽灵们也夹杂在学生们当中闪着朦胧的银光。哈利为避开他们的目光，便抬头朝上看，只见天鹅绒般漆黑的天花板上闪烁着点点星光。他听见赫敏在小声说："这里施过魔法，看起来跟外边的天空一样，我在《霍格沃茨：一段校史》里读到过。"

很难相信那上边真有天花板，也很难相信礼堂不是露天的。

麦格教授在一年级新生面前轻轻放了一个四脚凳，哈利连忙收回了目光。麦格教授又往凳子上放了一顶尖顶巫师帽。帽子打着补丁，磨得很旧，而且脏极了。佩妮姨妈决不会让这样的东西进家门。

说不定他们要用这顶帽子变出一只兔子吧，哈利想入非非，大概就是这类事吧——他发现礼堂里的人都在盯着这顶帽子，于是他也盯着它。有那么几秒钟，礼堂里鸦雀无声。接着，帽子扭动了，裂开了一道宽宽的缝，像一张嘴——帽子开始唱了起来：

CHAPTER SEVEN The Sorting Hat

'Oh, you may not think I'm pretty,
But don't judge on what you see,
I'll eat myself if you can find
A smarter hat than me.
You can keep your bowlers black,
Your top hats sleek and tall,
For I'm the Hogwarts Sorting Hat
And I can cap them all.
There's nothing hidden in your head
The Sorting Hat can't see,
So try me on and I will tell you
Where you ought to be.
You might belong in Gryffindor,
Where dwell the brave at heart,
Their daring, nerve and chivalry
Set Gryffindors apart;
You might belong in Hufflepuff,
Where they are just and loyal,
Those patient Hufflepuffs are true
And unafraid of toil;
Or yet in wise old Ravenclaw,
If you've a ready mind,
Where those of wit and learning,
Will always find their kind;
Or perhaps in Slytherin
You'll make your real friends,
Those cunning folk use any means
To achieve their ends.
So put me on! Don't be afraid!
And don't get in a flap!
You're in safe hands (though I have none)
For I'm a Thinking Cap!'

第 7 章 分院帽

你们也许觉得我不算漂亮,
但千万不要以貌取人,
如果你们能找到比我更聪明的帽子,
我可以把自己吃掉。
你们可以让你们的圆顶礼帽乌黑油亮,
让你们的高顶丝帽光滑挺括,
我可是霍格沃茨的分院帽,
自然比你们的帽子高超出众。
你们头脑里隐藏的任何念头,
都躲不过分院帽的金睛火眼,
戴上它试一下吧,我会告诉你们
应该分到哪一所学院。
你也许属于格兰芬多,
那里有埋藏在心底的勇敢,
他们的胆识、气魄和侠义,
使格兰芬多出类拔萃;
你也许属于赫奇帕奇,
那里的人正直忠诚,
赫奇帕奇的学子们坚忍诚实,
不畏惧艰辛的劳动;
如果你头脑精明,
或许会进智慧的老拉文克劳,
那些睿智博学的人,
总会在那里遇见他们的同道;
也许你会进斯莱特林,
在这里交上真正的朋友,
那些狡黠的人会不惜一切手段,
去达到他们的目的。
来戴上我吧!不必害怕!
千万不要惊慌失措!

CHAPTER SEVEN The Sorting Hat

The whole Hall burst into applause as the hat finished its song. It bowed to each of the four tables and then became quite still again.

'So we've just got to try on the hat!' Ron whispered to Harry. 'I'll kill Fred, he was going on about wrestling a troll.'

Harry smiled weakly. Yes, trying on the hat was a lot better than having to do a spell, but he did wish they could have tried it on without everyone watching. The hat seemed to be asking rather a lot; Harry didn't feel brave or quick-witted or any of it at the moment. If only the hat had mentioned a house for people who felt a bit queasy, that would have been the one for him.

Professor McGonagall now stepped forward holding a long roll of parchment.

'When I call your name, you will put on the hat and sit on the stool to be sorted,' she said. 'Abbott, Hannah!'

A pink-faced girl with blonde pigtails stumbled out of line, put on the hat, which fell right down over her eyes, and sat down. A moment's pause –

'HUFFLEPUFF!' shouted the hat.

The table on the right cheered and clapped as Hannah went to sit down at the Hufflepuff table. Harry saw the ghost of the Fat Friar waving merrily at her.

'Bones, Susan!'

'HUFFLEPUFF!' shouted the hat again, and Susan scuttled off to sit next to Hannah.

'Boot, Terry!'

'RAVENCLAW!'

The table second from the left clapped this time; several Ravenclaws stood up to shake hands with Terry as he joined them.

'Brocklehurst, Mandy' went to Ravenclaw too, but 'Brown, Lavender' became the first new Gryffindor and the table on the far left exploded with cheers; Harry could see Ron's twin brothers catcalling.

'Bulstrode, Millicent' then became a Slytherin. Perhaps it was Harry's imagination, after all he'd heard about Slytherin, but he thought they looked an unpleasant lot.

He was starting to feel definitely sick now. He remembered being picked for teams during sports lessons at his old school. He had always been last to

第7章 分院帽

在我的手里（尽管我一只手也没有）
你绝对安全
因为我是一顶会思想的魔帽！

帽子唱完歌后，全场掌声雷动。帽子向四张餐桌一一鞠躬行礼，随后就静止不动了。

"看来，我们只要戴上这顶帽子就可以了。"罗恩悄悄对哈利说，"我要把弗雷德杀掉，听他说得像是要跟巨怪搏斗似的。"

哈利淡淡地一笑。当然，戴帽子要比来一段咒语好多了，但他还是不希望在众目睽睽之下去戴。看来这顶帽子的要求高了一些。哈利觉得自己没有那份勇气和机灵劲或其他任何优点。如果帽子提出有一所专门让优柔寡断的人进的学院，那倒是对他最合适的地方。

这时麦格教授朝前走了几步，手里拿着一卷羊皮纸。

"我现在叫到谁的名字，谁就戴上帽子，坐到凳子上，听候分院。"她说，"汉娜·艾博！"

一个面色红润、梳着两条金色发辫的小姑娘跌跌撞撞地走出队列，戴上帽子，帽子刚好遮住她的眼睛。她坐了下来。片刻停顿之后——

"**赫奇帕奇**！"帽子喊道。

右边一桌的人向汉娜鼓掌欢呼，欢迎她在他们那一桌就座。哈利看见胖修士幽灵也高兴地向她挥手致意。

"苏珊·博恩斯！"

"**赫奇帕奇**！"帽子又喊道。苏珊飞快地跑到汉娜身边坐下。

"泰瑞·布特！"

"**拉文克劳**！"

这次左边第二桌拍手鼓掌。当泰瑞加入到他们的行列时，有几名拉文克劳的学生站起来和他握手。

曼蒂·布洛贺也分到了拉文克劳，拉文德·布朗则成了格兰芬多的第一位新生，左边最远的一张餐桌立刻爆发出一阵欢呼，哈利看见罗恩的一对孪生哥哥发出了嘘声。

接着米里森·伯斯德成为斯莱特林的新生。也许哈利听多了关于斯

CHAPTER SEVEN The Sorting Hat

be chosen, not because he was no good, but because no one wanted Dudley to think they liked him.

'Finch-Fletchley, Justin!'

'HUFFLEPUFF!'

Sometimes, Harry noticed, the hat shouted out the house at once, but at others it took a little while to decide. 'Finnigan, Seamus', the sandy-haired boy next to Harry in the line, sat on the stool for almost a whole minute before the hat declared him a Gryffindor.

'Granger, Hermione!'

Hermione almost ran to the stool and jammed the hat eagerly on her head.

'GRYFFINDOR!' shouted the hat. Ron groaned.

A horrible thought struck Harry, as horrible thoughts always do when you're very nervous. What if he wasn't chosen at all? What if he just sat there with the hat over his eyes for ages, until Professor McGonagall jerked it off his head and said there had obviously been a mistake and he'd better get back on the train?

When Neville Longbottom, the boy who kept losing his toad, was called, he fell over on his way to the stool. The hat took a long time to decide with Neville. When it finally shouted 'GRYFFINDOR', Neville ran off still wearing it, and had to jog back amid gales of laughter to give it to 'MacDougal, Morag'.

Malfoy swaggered forward when his name was called and got his wish at once: the hat had barely touched his head when it screamed, 'SLYTHERIN!'

Malfoy went to join his friends Crabbe and Goyle, looking pleased with himself.

There weren't many people left now.

'Moon' ... 'Nott' ... 'Parkinson' ... then a pair of twin girls, 'Patil' and 'Patil' ... then 'Perks, Sally-Anne' ... and then, at last –

'Potter, Harry!'

As Harry stepped forward, whispers suddenly broke out like little hissing fires all over the hall.

'*Pott*er, did she say?'

'*The* Harry Potter?'

第7章 分院帽

莱特林的议论，总觉得这些人看起来不讨人喜欢，但这可能是他的错觉吧。

他现在开始感到特别不舒服。他回想起在小学上体育课时分组的事，总是挑到最后剩他一个人，这并不是因为他不够好，而是因为谁也不想让达力认为他们喜欢他。

"贾斯廷·芬列里！"

"**赫奇帕奇！**"

哈利发现有时帽子立刻就会喊出学院的名字，但另一些时候会花一些时间才做出决定。比如排在哈利旁边的那个浅茶色头发的男孩西莫·斐尼甘就在凳子上几乎坐了整整一分钟，帽子才宣布他被分到格兰芬多。

"赫敏·格兰杰！"

赫敏几乎是跑着奔到凳子跟前，急急忙忙把帽子扣到头上。

"**格兰芬多！**"帽子喊道。罗恩哼了一声。

当你非常紧张的时候，就会生出许多可怕的想法，哈利也是一样。他突然想到万一帽子根本就不挑选他会怎么样呢？如果帽子扣在头上盖住他的眼睛好长时间，最后还是麦格教授把帽子从他头上拽下来，然后说，明摆着是搞错了，要他最好还是坐火车回去，那又会怎么样呢？

叫到那个总丢失蟾蜍的男孩纳威·隆巴顿的名字时，他在朝凳子跑的路上摔了一跤。帽子用了好长时间才对纳威做出决定。当帽子最后喊出"**格兰芬多**"时，纳威戴着帽子就跑掉了，最后不得不在一片哄笑声中又一溜小跑回来，把帽子还给了莫拉格·麦克道格。

叫到马尔福的名字时，马尔福大模大样地走了过去，而且立刻如愿以偿，帽子几乎刚碰到他的头就尖叫道："**斯莱特林！**"

马尔福前去和他的朋友克拉布与高尔会合，露出对自己很满意的样子。

这时，剩下的人已经不多了。

莫恩……诺特……帕金森……之后是佩蒂尔孪生姐妹……然后是莎莉安·波克斯……最后，总算轮到——

"哈利·波特！"

当哈利朝前走去时，餐厅里突然发出一阵嗡嗡低语，像小火苗的嘶嘶响声。

CHAPTER SEVEN The Sorting Hat

The last thing Harry saw before the hat dropped over his eyes was the Hall full of people craning to get a good look at him. Next second he was looking at the black inside of the hat. He waited.

'Hmm,' said a small voice in his ear. 'Difficult. Very difficult. Plenty of courage, I see. Not a bad mind, either. There's talent, oh my goodness, yes – and a nice thirst to prove yourself, now that's interesting ... So where shall I put you?'

Harry gripped the edges of the stool and thought, 'Not Slytherin, not Slytherin.'

'Not Slytherin, eh?' said the small voice. 'Are you sure? You could be great, you know, it's all here in your head, and Slytherin will help you on the way to greatness, no doubt about that – no? Well, if you're sure – better be GRYFFINDOR!'

Harry heard the hat shout the last word to the whole Hall. He took off the hat and walked shakily towards the Gryffindor table. He was so relieved to have been chosen and not put in Slytherin, he hardly noticed that he was getting the loudest cheer yet. Percy the Prefect got up and shook his hand vigorously, while the Weasley twins yelled, 'We got Potter! We got Potter!' Harry sat down opposite the ghost in the ruff he'd seen earlier. The ghost patted his arm, giving Harry the sudden, horrible feeling he'd just plunged it into a bucket of ice-cold water.

He could see the High Table properly now. At the end nearest him sat Hagrid, who caught his eye and gave him the thumbs-up. Harry grinned back. And there, in the centre of the High Table, in a large gold chair, sat Albus Dumbledore. Harry recognised him at once from the card he'd got out of the Chocolate Frog on the train. Dumbledore's silver hair was the only thing in the whole Hall that shone as brightly as the ghosts. Harry spotted Professor Quirrell, too, the nervous young man from the Leaky Cauldron. He was looking very peculiar in a large purple turban.

And now there were only three people left to be sorted. 'Turpin, Lisa' became a Ravenclaw and then it was Ron's turn. He was pale green by now. Harry crossed his fingers under the table and a second later the hat had shouted, 'GRYFFINDOR!'

Harry clapped loudly with the rest as Ron collapsed into the chair next to him.

第7章 分院帽

"波特,她是在叫波特吗?"

"是那个哈利·波特吗?"

在帽子就要扣到头上遮住视线时,哈利看到餐厅里人头攒动,人人引颈而望,希望看清他的模样。接着就是帽子里的黑暗世界和等待。

"嗯,"他听到耳边一个细微的声音说,"难。非常难。看得出很有勇气。心地也不坏。有天分,哦,我的天哪,不错——你有急于证明自己的强烈愿望,那么,很有意思……我该把你分到哪里去呢?"

哈利紧紧抓住凳子边,心里想:"不去斯莱特林,不去斯莱特林。"

"不去斯莱特林,对吧?"那个细微的声音问,"拿定主意了吗?你会成大器的,你知道,在你一念之间,斯莱特林会帮助你走向辉煌,这毫无疑问——不乐意?那好,既然你已经拿定主意——那就最好去**格兰芬多吧!**"

哈利听见帽子向整个礼堂喊出了最后那个名字。他摘下帽子,两腿微微颤抖着走向格兰芬多那一桌。他入选了,而且没有被分到斯莱特林,这使他大大松了一口气,也使他几乎没有注意到自己竟获得了最响亮的欢呼喝彩。级长珀西站起来紧紧地跟他握手。韦斯莱家的孪生兄弟大声喊道:"我们有波特了!我们有波特了!"哈利坐到他先前碰到的那个穿轮状皱领的幽灵对面。幽灵拍了拍他的手臂,使他突然产生了一种刚刚跳进一桶冰水的可怕感觉。

现在哈利总算可以好好看看高台上的主宾席了。海格坐在离他最近的角落。他捕捉到了哈利的目光,向他竖起大拇指。哈利咧嘴报以一笑。主宾席的中央,一把大金椅上坐着阿不思·邓布利多。哈利一眼就认出了他的面孔,因为火车上在巧克力蛙的巫师画片上见过。整个餐厅里只有邓布利多的银发和幽灵们一样闪闪发光。哈利也同样认出了奇洛教授,那个他在破釜酒吧遇到的神经质的年轻人。他头上裹着一条很大的紫色围巾,显得很古怪。

现在听候分配的只剩下三个人了。莉莎·杜平成了拉文克劳的新生。接着就轮到了罗恩。他这时脸色发青。哈利手指交叉放在桌下。一眨眼工夫帽子就高喊道:"**格兰芬多!**"

当罗恩一下子瘫倒在哈利旁边的座位上时,哈利跟其他人一起大声

CHAPTER SEVEN The Sorting Hat

'Well done, Ron, excellent,' said Percy Weasley pompously across Harry as 'Zabini, Blaise' was made a Slytherin. Professor McGonagall rolled up her scroll and took the Sorting Hat away.

Harry looked down at his empty gold plate. He had only just realised how hungry he was. The pumpkin pasties seemed ages ago.

Albus Dumbledore had got to his feet. He was beaming at the students, his arms opened wide, as if nothing could have pleased him more than to see them all there.

'Welcome!' he said. 'Welcome to a new year at Hogwarts! Before we begin our banquet, I would like to say a few words. And here they are: Nitwit! Blubber! Oddment! Tweak!

'Thank you!'

He sat back down. Everybody clapped and cheered. Harry didn't know whether to laugh or not.

'Is he – a bit mad?' he asked Percy uncertainly.

'Mad?' said Percy airily. 'He's a genius! Best wizard in the world! But he is a bit mad, yes. Potatoes, Harry?'

Harry's mouth fell open. The dishes in front of him were now piled with food. He had never seen so many things he liked to eat on one table: roast beef, roast chicken, pork chops and lamb chops, sausages, bacon and steak, boiled potatoes, roast potatoes, chips, Yorkshire pudding, peas, carrots, gravy, ketchup and, for some strange reason, mint humbugs.

The Dursleys had never exactly starved Harry, but he'd never been allowed to eat as much as he liked. Dudley had always taken anything that Harry really wanted, even if it made him sick. Harry piled his plate with a bit of everything except the humbugs and began to eat. It was all delicious.

'That does look good,' said the ghost in the ruff sadly, watching Harry cut up his steak.

'Can't you –?'

'I haven't eaten for nearly five hundred years,' said the ghost. 'I don't need to, of course, but one does miss it. I don't think I've introduced myself? Sir Nicholas de Mimsy-Porpington at your service. Resident ghost of Gryffindor Tower.'

'I know who you are!' said Ron suddenly. 'My brothers told me about you –

第7章 分院帽

鼓掌。

"很好，罗恩，太好了！"珀西·韦斯莱越过哈利，用夸张的口吻说。这时剩下的最后一名新生布雷司·沙比尼被分到了斯莱特林。麦格教授卷起羊皮纸，拿起分院帽离去了。

哈利低头看着面前空空的金盘子，这才感觉到早已饥肠辘辘。吃南瓜馅饼似乎是很久以前的事了。

阿不思·邓布利多站了起来。他笑容满面地看着学生们，向他们伸开双臂，似乎没有什么比看到学生们济济一堂更使他高兴的了。

"欢迎啊！"他说，"欢迎大家来霍格沃茨开始新的学年！在宴会开始前，我想讲几句话。那就是：笨蛋！哭鼻子！残渣！拧！

"谢谢大家！"

他重新坐下来。大家鼓掌欢呼。哈利不知道是否该一笑置之。

"他是不是——有点疯疯癫癫？"他迟疑地问珀西。

"疯疯癫癫？"珀西小声说，"他是一位天才！世界上最优秀的巫师！不过你说得也对，他是有点疯疯癫癫。要不要来点马铃薯，哈利？"

哈利目瞪口呆。这时他面前的餐盘里放满了吃的。他从来没见过桌上一下子摆出这么多他喜欢吃的东西：烤牛肉、烤仔鸡、猪排、羊羔排、腊肠、熏咸肉、牛排、煮马铃薯、烤马铃薯、炸薯条、约克夏布丁、豌豆、胡萝卜、肉汁、番茄酱，而且不知出于什么古怪的原因，还有薄荷硬糖。

说实在的，德思礼夫妇并没让哈利饿着，可也没有真正让他放开肚皮吃过。达力总是把哈利想吃的东西抢走，尽管这些东西有时候让达力想吐。除了薄荷硬糖之外，哈利每样都往餐盘里拿了一点儿，开始大嚼起来。样样都很好吃。

"看起来真不错呀。"穿轮状皱领的幽灵睁睁地看着哈利切牛排，难过地说。

"你不来上一点儿吗？"

"我已经将近五百年没有吃东西了。"那个幽灵说，"当然啦，我不需要吃，但很怀念食物的美味。我想，我还没有做自我介绍吧？我是尼古拉斯·德·敏西-波平顿爵士，格兰芬多塔楼的常驻幽灵。"

"我知道你是谁了！"罗恩突然说，"我的哥哥们对我讲起过你——

you're Nearly Headless Nick!'

'I would *prefer* you to call me Sir Nicholas de Mimsy –' the ghost began stiffly, but sandy-haired Seamus Finnigan interrupted.

'*Nearly* Headless? How can you be *nearly* headless?'

Sir Nicholas looked extremely miffed, as if their little chat wasn't going at all the way he wanted.

'Like *this*,' he said irritably. He seized his left ear and pulled. His whole head swung off his neck and fell on to his shoulder as if it was on a hinge. Someone had obviously tried to behead him, but not done it properly. Looking pleased at the stunned looks on their faces, Nearly Headless Nick flipped his head back on to his neck, coughed and said, 'So – new Gryffindors! I hope you're going to help us win the House Championship this year? Gryffindor have never gone so long without winning. Slytherin have got the cup six years in a row! The Bloody Baron's becoming almost unbearable – he's the Slytherin ghost.'

Harry looked over at the Slytherin table and saw a horrible ghost sitting there, with blank staring eyes, a gaunt face and robes stained with silver blood. He was right next to Malfoy who, Harry was pleased to see, didn't look too pleased with the seating arrangements.

'How did he get covered in blood?' asked Seamus with great interest.

'I've never asked,' said Nearly Headless Nick delicately.

When everyone had eaten as much as they could, the remains of the food faded from the plates, leaving them sparkling clean as before. A moment later the puddings appeared. Blocks of ice-cream in every flavour you could think of, apple pies, treacle tarts, chocolate éclairs and jam doughnuts, trifle, strawberries, jelly, rice pudding ...

As Harry helped himself to a treacle tart, the talk turned to their families.

'I'm half and half,' said Seamus. 'Me dad's a Muggle. Mam didn't tell him she was a witch 'til after they were married. Bit of a nasty shock for him.'

The others laughed.

'What about you, Neville?' said Ron.

'Well, my gran brought me up and she's a witch,' said Neville, 'but the family thought I was all Muggle for ages. My great-uncle Algie kept trying to catch me off my guard and force some magic out of me – he pushed me off the end of Blackpool pier once, I nearly drowned – but nothing happened

第7章 分院帽

你是那个'差点没头的尼克'!"

"我想,我比较喜欢你们叫我尼古拉斯·德·敏西-波平顿爵士——"幽灵显得有些局促不安,但是淡茶色头发的西莫·斐尼甘插话说:

"差点没头?你怎么会差点没头呢?"

尼古拉斯爵士显得很生气,看来他不想谈这个话题。

"就像这样。"他不耐烦地说。他抓住左耳朵往下拽。他的头摇摇晃晃从脖子上滑了下来,掉到肩上,仿佛头是用铰链连接的。看来有人砍他的头,没有砍彻底。差点没头的尼克眼看他们一个个目瞪口呆的表情,很开心。他把头轻轻弹回到脖子上,清了清嗓子,说:"好了,格兰芬多的新同学们!我希望你们能帮助我们赢得本学年的学院杯冠军,好吗?格兰芬多从来没有这么长时间没赢过奖了。斯莱特林来了个六连冠!血人巴罗实在让人忍无可忍了——他是斯莱特林的幽灵。"

哈利朝斯莱特林那一桌看过去,看见桌旁坐着一个幽灵,十分可怕,瞪着呆滞的眼睛,形容枯槁,长袍上沾满银色的血斑。血人巴罗正好坐在马尔福旁边,马尔福对这样的座位安排不太满意,哈利看了心里觉得乐滋滋的。

"他怎么弄得浑身都是血?"西莫特别感兴趣。

"我从来没问过。"差点没头的尼克谨慎地说。

等到每人都敞开肚皮吃饱以后,剩下的食物就一股脑儿地从餐盘里消失了。餐盘又都变得光洁如初。过了一会儿,布丁上来了。各种口味的冰淇淋应有尽有,苹果饼、糖浆水果馅饼、巧克力松糕、炸果酱甜圈、酒浸果酱布丁、草莓、果冻、米布丁……

哈利取过一块糖浆水果馅饼,这时话题又转到了各自的家庭。

"我是一半一半。"西莫说,"爸爸是一个麻瓜,妈妈直到结婚以后才告诉爸爸自己是个巫师。可把他吓得不轻。"

大家都哈哈大笑。

"那你呢,纳威?"罗恩问。

"哦,我是由奶奶带大的,她是巫师。"纳威说,"不过这么多年来我们家一直以为我是麻瓜。我的阿尔吉叔爷总想趁人不备,想方设法逼我露一手魔法——有一次他把我从布莱克浦码头推了下去,差一点儿把

CHAPTER SEVEN   The Sorting Hat

until I was eight. Great-uncle Algie came round for tea and he was hanging me out of an upstairs window by the ankles when my great-auntie Enid offered him a meringue and he accidentally let go. But I bounced – all the way down the garden and into the road. They were all really pleased. Gran was crying, she was so happy. And you should have seen their faces when I got in here – they thought I might not be magic enough to come, you see. Great-uncle Algie was so pleased he bought me my toad.'

On Harry's other side, Percy Weasley and Hermione were talking about lessons ('I *do* hope they start straight away, there's so much to learn, I'm particularly interested in Transfiguration, you know, turning something into something else, of course, it's supposed to be very difficult –'; 'You'll be starting small, just matches into needles and that sort of thing –').

Harry, who was starting to feel warm and sleepy, looked up at the High Table again. Hagrid was drinking deeply from his goblet. Professor McGonagall was talking to Professor Dumbledore. Professor Quirrell, in his absurd turban, was talking to a teacher with greasy black hair, a hooked nose and sallow skin.

It happened very suddenly. The hook-nosed teacher looked past Quirrell's turban straight into Harry's eyes – and a sharp, hot pain shot across the scar on Harry's forehead.

'Ouch!' Harry clapped a hand to his head.

'What is it?' asked Percy.

'N-nothing.'

The pain had gone as quickly as it had come. Harder to shake off was the feeling Harry had got from the teacher's look – a feeling that he didn't like Harry at all.

'Who's that teacher talking to Professor Quirrell?' he asked Percy.

'Oh, you know Quirrell already, do you? No wonder he's looking so nervous, that's Professor Snape. He teaches Potions, but he doesn't want to – everyone knows he's after Quirrell's job. Knows an awful lot about the Dark Arts, Snape.'

Harry watched Snape for a while but Snape didn't look at him again.

At last, the puddings too disappeared and Professor Dumbledore got to his feet again. The Hall fell silent.

'Ahem – just a few more words now we are all fed and watered. I have a

第7章 分院帽

我淹死——结果什么事也没有发生。直到我八岁那年,有一天我阿尔吉叔爷过来喝茶,他把我脚脖子朝上从楼上窗口向下吊着,正好我的艾妮叔婆递给他一块蛋白蛋糕。他一失手,没有抓稳我。我自己弹了起来——飞过整个花园,摔到马路上。他们都高兴极了。奶奶甚至高兴得哭了起来。你要是能看看我接到入学通知书时他们脸上的表情就好了,你看,他们原以为我的魔法功力不够,不能进这所学校呢。我的阿尔吉叔爷一时高兴,还买了一只蟾蜍送给我呢。"

哈利的另一边,珀西·韦斯莱和赫敏正在谈论功课("我真希望马上开始,要学的东西太多了,我对变形术特别感兴趣。你知道,把一样东西变成另一样东西,当然应该是非常困难——";"你应当从小的东西变起,比如把火柴变成针什么的——")。

哈利浑身热起来,想睡觉,但他又抬头看了看主宾席。海格正举杯狂饮。麦格教授在跟邓布利多教授说着什么。头上裹着可笑的围巾的奇洛教授正在跟一位一头油腻黑发、鹰钩鼻、皮肤蜡黄的老师说话。

事情发生在一瞬间。鹰钩鼻老师的视线越过奇洛教授的围巾直视哈利的眼睛——哈利顿感他前额上的那道伤疤一阵灼痛。

"哎呀!"哈利用一只手捂住前额。

"怎么了?"珀西问。

"没—没什么。"

灼痛像来时一样,刹那间就消失了。挥之不去的是哈利从那位老师目光中得到的感受,他觉得那位老师对他没有一点儿好感。

"跟奇洛教授讲话的那位老师是谁?"他问珀西。

"哦,奇洛教授你已经认识了,他看上去那么紧张并不奇怪。那位是斯内普教授,教魔药学,但他不愿意教这门课——大家都知道他眼馋奇洛教授的工作。斯内普对黑魔法可是大大在行。"

哈利注视了斯内普片刻,但斯内普没有再看他。

最后,布丁也消失了,邓布利多教授又站了起来。礼堂里也复归肃静。

"哦,现在大家都吃饱了,喝足了,我要再对大家说几句话。在学期开始的时候,我要向大家提出几点注意事项。

CHAPTER SEVEN   The Sorting Hat

few start-of-term notices to give you.

'First-years should note that the forest in the grounds is forbidden to all pupils. And a few of our older students would do well to remember that as well.'

Dumbledore's twinkling eyes flashed in the direction of the Weasley twins.

'I have also been asked by Mr Filch, the caretaker, to remind you all that no magic should be used between classes in the corridors.

'Quidditch trials will be held in the second week of term. Anyone interested in playing for their house teams should contact Madam Hooch.

'And finally, I must tell you that this year, the third-floor corridor on the right-hand side is out of bounds to everyone who does not wish to die a very painful death.'

Harry laughed, but he was one of the few who did.

'He's not serious?' he muttered to Percy.

'Must be,' said Percy, frowning at Dumbledore. 'It's odd, because he usually gives us a reason why we're not allowed to go somewhere – the forest's full of dangerous beasts, everyone knows that. I do think he might have told us Prefects, at least.'

'And now, before we go to bed, let us sing the school song!' cried Dumbledore. Harry noticed that the other teachers' smiles had become rather fixed.

Dumbledore gave his wand a little flick as if he was trying to get a fly off the end and a long golden ribbon flew out of it, which rose high above the tables and twisted itself snake-like into words.

'Everyone pick their favourite tune,' said Dumbledore, 'and off we go!'

And the school bellowed:

> *'Hogwarts, Hogwarts, Hoggy Warty Hogwarts,*
> *Teach us something please,*
> *Whether we be old and bald*
> *Or young with scabby knees,*
> *Our heads could do with filling*
> *With some interesting stuff,*
> *For now they're bare and full of air,*
> *Dead flies and bits of fluff,*
> *So teach us things worth knowing,*
> *Bring back what we've forgot,*

第7章 分院帽

"一年级新生注意,学校场地上的那片林区禁止任何学生进入。我们有些高年级的同学也要好好记住这一点。"

邓布利多那双闪亮的眼睛朝韦斯莱孪生兄弟那边扫了一下。

"再有,管理员费尔奇先生要我提醒大家,课间不要在走廊施魔法。

"魁地奇球员的审核工作将在本学期的第二周举行。凡有志参加学院代表队的同学请与霍琦女士联系。

"最后,我必须告诉大家,凡不愿遭遇意外、痛苦惨死的人,请不要进入四楼靠右边的走廊。"

哈利哈哈大笑,但笑的人只有少数几个。

"他不是认真的吧?"哈利悄声问珀西。

"不可能,"珀西朝邓布利多皱起眉头说,"可奇怪的是,凡不准许我们去的地方,他通常都说明原因,比如,那片林区里有许多危险的野兽,这一点大家都知道。我想他至少该对我们级长讲清楚的。"

"现在,在大家就寝之前,让我们一起来唱校歌!"邓布利多大声说。哈利发现其他老师的笑容似乎都僵住了。

邓布利多将魔杖轻轻一弹,魔杖中就飘飞出一条长长的金色彩带,在餐桌的上空像蛇一样高高地扭动盘绕出一行行文字。

"每人选择自己喜欢的曲调。"邓布利多说,"预备,唱!"

于是全体师生放声高唱起来:

霍格沃茨,霍格沃茨,霍格沃茨,霍格沃茨,
请教给我们知识,
不论我们是谢顶的老人
还是跌伤膝盖的孩子,
我们的头脑可以接纳
一些有趣的事物。
因为现在我们大脑空空,充满空气、
死苍蝇和鸡毛蒜皮,
教给我们一些有价值的知识,
把被我们遗忘的,还给我们,

CHAPTER SEVEN   The Sorting Hat

Just do your best, we'll do the rest,
And learn until our brains all rot.'

Everybody finished the song at different times. At last, only the Weasley twins were left singing along to a very slow funeral march. Dumbledore conducted their last few lines with his wand, and when they had finished, he was one of those who clapped loudest.

'Ah, music,' he said, wiping his eyes. 'A magic beyond all we do here! And now, bedtime. Off you trot!'

The Gryffindor first-years followed Percy through the chattering crowds, out of the Great Hall and up the marble staircase. Harry's legs were like lead again, but only because he was so tired and full of food. He was too sleepy even to be surprised that the people in the portraits along the corridors whispered and pointed as they passed, or that twice Percy led them through doorways hidden behind sliding panels and hanging tapestries. They climbed more staircases, yawning and dragging their feet, and Harry was just wondering how much further they had to go when they came to a sudden halt.

A bundle of walking sticks was floating in mid-air ahead of them and as Percy took a step towards them they started throwing themselves at him.

'Peeves,' Percy whispered to the first-years. 'A poltergeist.' He raised his voice, 'Peeves – show yourself.'

A loud, rude sound, like the air being let out of a balloon, answered.

'Do you want me to go to the Bloody Baron?'

There was a *pop* and a little man with wicked dark eyes and a wide mouth appeared, floating cross-legged in the air, clutching the walking sticks.

'Oooooooh!' he said, with an evil cackle. 'Ickle firsties! What fun!'

He swooped suddenly at them. They all ducked.

'Go away, Peeves, or the Baron'll hear about this, I mean it!' barked Percy.

Peeves stuck out his tongue and vanished, dropping the walking sticks on Neville's head. They heard him zooming away, rattling coats of armour as he passed.

'You want to watch out for Peeves,' said Percy, as they set off again. 'The Bloody Baron's the only one who can control him, he won't even listen to us

第7章 分院帽

你们只要尽全力，其他的交给我们自己，
我们将努力学习，直到化为尘土。

大家七零八落地唱完了这首校歌。只有韦斯莱家的孪生兄弟仍随着《葬礼进行曲》徐缓的旋律在继续歌唱。邓布利多用魔杖为他们俩指挥了最后几个小节，等他们唱完，他的掌声最响亮。

"音乐啊，"他擦了擦眼睛说，"比我们在这里所做的一切都更富魅力！现在是就寝的时间了。大家回宿舍去吧。"

格兰芬多的一年级新生跟着珀西，穿过嘈杂的人群，走出礼堂，登上大理石楼梯。哈利的两腿又像灌了铅似的，不过这次是因为他太累，而且吃得太饱。他实在太困了，因此当走廊肖像上的人在他们经过时喁喁私语，指指点点，当珀西两次带领他们穿过暗藏在滑动挡板和垂挂的帷幔后边的门时，他甚至一点儿也没有感到吃惊。他们哈欠连天，拖着沉重的脚步又爬了许多楼梯。哈利正在纳闷，不知还要走多久，这时，前边的人突然停了下来。

在他们前边，一捆手杖在半空中飘荡着，珀西向前迈了一步，于是那些手杖纷纷朝他飞来。

"是皮皮鬼，"珀西小声对一年级新生说，"一个恶作剧精灵。"他又抬高嗓门说："皮皮鬼——显形吧。"

回答他的是响亮、刺耳、像气球泄气似的噗噗响声。

"你是要我去找血人巴罗吗？"

噗的一声，突然冒出一个小矮人，一对邪恶的黑眼睛，一张大嘴，盘腿在半空中飘荡着，双手牢牢抓着那捆手杖。

"嘀嘀嘀！"他咯咯地奸笑着，"原来是讨厌的一年级小鬼头啊！太好玩了！"

他突然朝他们猛扑过来。学生们一下子惊呆了。

"走开，皮皮鬼，不然我去告诉血人巴罗，我可不是开玩笑！"珀西大吼道。

皮皮鬼伸出舌头，不见了。手杖正好砸在纳威头上。他们听见皮皮鬼腾空而去，飞过时盔甲铿锵作响。

CHAPTER SEVEN The Sorting Hat

Prefects. Here we are.'

At the very end of the corridor hung a portrait of a very fat woman in a pink silk dress.

'Password?' she said.

'*Caput Draconis*,' said Percy, and the portrait swung forward to reveal a round hole in the wall. They all scrambled through it – Neville needed a leg up – and found themselves in the Gryffindor common room, a cosy, round room full of squashy armchairs.

Percy directed the girls through one door to their dormitory and the boys through another. At the top of a spiral staircase – they were obviously in one of the towers – they found their beds at last: five four-posters hung with deep-red velvet curtains. Their trunks had already been brought up. Too tired to talk much, they pulled on their pyjamas and fell into bed.

'Great food, isn't it?' Ron muttered to Harry through the hangings. 'Get *off*, Scabbers! He's chewing my sheets.'

Harry was going to ask Ron if he'd had any of the treacle tart, but he fell asleep almost at once.

Perhaps Harry had eaten a bit too much, because he had a very strange dream. He was wearing Professor Quirrell's turban, which kept talking to him, telling him he must transfer to Slytherin at once, because it was his destiny. Harry told the turban he didn't want to be in Slytherin; it got heavier and heavier; he tried to pull it off but it tightened painfully – and there was Malfoy, laughing at him as he struggled with it – then Malfoy turned into the hook-nosed teacher, Snape, whose laugh became high and cold – there was a burst of green light and Harry woke, sweating and shaking.

He rolled over and fell asleep again, and when he woke next day, he didn't remember the dream at all.

第7章 分院帽

"你们应当对皮皮鬼有所防备。"珀西说,领着大家继续朝前走,"血人巴罗是唯一能降住他的,他甚至连我们这些级长的话都听不进去。我们到了。"

走廊尽头挂着一幅肖像,肖像上是一个非常富态的穿着一身粉色衣服的女人。

"口令?"她问。

"龙首。"珀西说。只见这幅画摇摇晃晃地朝前移去,露出墙上的一个圆形洞口。他们都从墙洞里爬了过去——纳威还得有人拉他一把——然后他们就发现已经来到格兰芬多的公共休息室了。这是一个舒适的圆形房间,摆满了软绵绵的扶手椅。

珀西指引女生们进一扇门,去往她们的寝室,然后再带男生们走进另一道门。在一部螺旋形的楼梯顶上——他们显然是在一座塔楼里——他们终于找到了自己的铺位:五张带四根帷柱的床,垂挂着深红色天鹅绒帷帐。行李箱子早已送了上来。他们已精疲力竭,不想再多说话,一个个换上睡衣就倒下睡了。

"今天的伙食太丰盛了,是吧?"罗恩隔着帷帐对哈利小声说,"走开,斑斑!它在啃我的床单呢。"

哈利本想问罗恩吃没吃糖浆水果馅饼,可没等开口就睡着了。

也许是哈利吃得过饱的缘故,他做了一个非常奇怪的梦。他头上顶着奇洛教授的大围巾,那围巾一个劲地絮絮叨叨,对他说,应当立刻转到斯莱特林去,因为那是命中注定的。哈利告诉围巾他不想去斯莱特林;围巾变得越来越重,他想把它扯掉,但它却箍得他头痛——他在挣扎的时候,马尔福在一旁看着他,哈哈大笑;接着马尔福变成了鹰钩鼻老师斯内普;斯内普的笑声更响,也更冷了——只见一道绿光突然一闪,哈利惊醒了,一身冷汗,不停地发抖。

他翻过身去,又睡着了。第二天醒来时,他一点儿也不记得这个梦了。

CHAPTER EIGHT

The Potions Master

'There, look.'
'Where?'
'Next to the tall kid with the red hair.'
'Wearing the glasses?'
'Did you see his face?'
'Did you see his scar?'

Whispers followed Harry from the moment he left his dormitory next day. People queuing outside classrooms stood on tiptoe to get a look at him, or doubled back to pass him in the corridors again, staring. Harry wished they wouldn't, because he was trying to concentrate on finding his way to classes.

There were a hundred and forty-two staircases at Hogwarts: wide, sweeping ones; narrow, rickety ones; some that led somewhere different on a Friday; some with a vanishing step halfway up that you had to remember to jump. Then there were doors that wouldn't open unless you asked politely, or tickled them in exactly the right place, and doors that weren't really doors at all, but solid walls just pretending. It was also very hard to remember where anything was, because it all seemed to move around a lot. The people in the portraits kept going to visit each other and Harry was sure the coats of armour could walk.

The ghosts didn't help, either. It was always a nasty shock when one of them glided suddenly through a door you were trying to open. Nearly Headless Nick was always happy to point new Gryffindors in the right direction, but Peeves the poltergeist was worth two locked doors and a trick staircase if you met him when you were late for class. He would drop wastepaper baskets on your head, pull rugs from under your feet, pelt you with bits of chalk or sneak up behind you, invisible, grab your nose and screech, 'GOT

第8章

魔药课老师

"就在那边,快看。"
"哪边?"
"在那个高个红头发男生旁边。"
"那个戴眼镜的?"
"你看见他的脸了吗?"
"看见他那道伤疤了吗?"

第二天,哈利走出寝室,这些窃窃私语就一直紧追着他。学生们在教室外边排着长队,个个踮着脚尖,想一睹他的真面目。在走廊里,他们从他身边走过去,又折回来,死死地盯着他看。哈利希望他们不要这样,因为他要集中注意力寻找去教室的路。

霍格沃茨的楼梯总共有一百四十二处之多。它们有的又宽又大;有的又窄又小,而且摇摇晃晃;有的每逢星期五就通到不同的地方;有些上到半截,一个台阶会突然消失,你得记住在什么地方应当跳过去。另外,这里还有许多门,如果你不客客气气地请它们打开,或者确切地捅对地方,它们是不会为你开门的;还有些门根本不是真正的门,只是一堵堵貌似是门的坚固的墙壁。想要记住哪些东西在什么地方很不容易,因为一切似乎都在不停地移动。肖像上的人也不断地互访,而且哈利可以肯定,连甲胄都会行走。

你拿幽灵们也没有办法。常常是当你正要开一扇门时,一个幽灵突然从门后蹿出来,吓你一大跳。差点没头的尼克当然乐意为格兰芬多的新生们指路;可如果你上课已经要迟到,偏偏又碰上恶作剧精灵皮皮鬼,那就比碰到上了锁的两道门外加一道机关重重的楼梯更加难办了。他会

CHAPTER EIGHT   The Potions Master

YOUR CONK!'

Even worse than Peeves, if that was possible, was the caretaker, Argus Filch. Harry and Ron managed to get on the wrong side of him on their very first morning. Filch found them trying to force their way through a door which unluckily turned out to be the entrance to the out-of-bounds corridor on the third floor. He wouldn't believe they were lost, was sure they were trying to break into it on purpose and was threatening to lock them in the dungeons when they were rescued by Professor Quirrell, who was passing.

Filch owned a cat called Mrs Norris, a scrawny, dust-coloured creature with bulging, lamp-like eyes just like Filch's. She patrolled the corridors alone. Break a rule in front of her, put just one toe out of line, and she'd whisk off for Filch, who'd appear, wheezing, two seconds later. Filch knew the secret passageways of the school better than anyone (except perhaps the Weasley twins) and could pop up as suddenly as any of the ghosts. The students all hated him and it was the dearest ambition of many to give Mrs Norris a good kick.

And then, once you had managed to find them, there were the lessons themselves. There was a lot more to magic, as Harry quickly found out, than waving your wand and saying a few funny words.

They had to study the night skies through their telescopes every Wednesday at midnight and learn the names of different stars and the movements of the planets. Three times a week they went out to the greenhouses behind the castle to study Herbology, with a dumpy little witch called Professor Sprout, where they learnt how to take care of all the strange plants and fungi and found out what they were used for.

Easily the most boring lesson was History of Magic, which was the only class taught by a ghost. Professor Binns had been very old indeed when he had fallen asleep in front of the staff-room fire and got up next morning to teach, leaving his body behind him. Binns droned on and on while they scribbled down names and dates and got Emeric the Evil and Uric the Oddball mixed up.

Professor Flitwick, the Charms teacher, was a tiny little wizard who had to stand on a pile of books to see over his desk. At the start of their first lesson he took the register, and when he reached Harry's name he gave an excited squeak and toppled out of sight.

第8章 魔药课老师

把废纸篓扣到你头上,抽掉你脚下的地毯,朝你扔粉笔头,或是偷偷跟在你背后,趁你看不见的时候,抓住你的鼻子大声尖叫:"揪住你的鼻子喽!"

如果还有什么比皮皮鬼更糟糕的,那就要数管理员阿格斯·费尔奇了。开学的第一天早上,罗恩和哈利就跟费尔奇之间产生了芥蒂。费尔奇发现他们硬要闯一道门,而那道门正好是通往四楼禁区走廊的入口。费尔奇不相信他们是迷了路,认为他们故意要闯,便威胁着要把他们锁进地牢,幸亏奇洛教授刚好经过这里,帮他们解了围。

费尔奇养了一只猫,名叫洛丽丝夫人。这只骨瘦如柴、毛色暗灰的活物长着像费尔奇那样灯泡似的鼓眼睛。它经常独自在走廊里巡逻。如果谁当它的面犯规,即使一个脚趾尖出线,它也会飞快地跑去找费尔奇。两分钟后,费尔奇就会吭哧吭哧、连吁带喘地跑过来。费尔奇比谁都清楚校园里的秘密通道(也许韦斯莱家的孪生兄弟除外),而且会像幽灵一样冷不丁蹿出来。同学们对他恨之入骨,许多人都恨不得照他的洛丽丝夫人狠狠地踹上一脚。

然后,一旦你找到教室,那就要面对课程本身了。哈利很快发现除了挥动魔杖、念几句好玩的咒语之外,魔法还有许多很高深的学问呢。

每星期三晚上,他们都要用望远镜观测星空,学习不同星星的名称和行星运行的轨迹。一星期三次,他们都要由一个叫斯普劳特的矮胖女巫带着到城堡后边的温室去上草药课,学习如何培育这些奇异的植物和菌类并了解它们的用途。

最令人厌烦的课程大概要算魔法史了,这也是唯一由幽灵教授的课程。想当年宾斯教授在教工休息室的壁炉前睡着了,第二天早上去上课时竟忘记带上自己的身体,足见宾斯教授生前确实已经很老了。上课时宾斯教授用单调乏味的声音不停地讲,学生们则潦潦草草地记下人名和日期,把恶人默瑞克和怪人尤里克也搞混了。

教授魔咒的是一位身材小得出奇的男巫弗立维教授,上课时他必须站在一摞书上,才够得着讲桌。开始上第一堂课时,他拿出名册点名,念到哈利的名字时,激动得尖叫了一声,就倒在地上不见了。

麦格教授跟他们都不一样。哈利没有看错。他一眼就看出这位教授

CHAPTER EIGHT   The Potions Master

Professor McGonagall was again different. Harry had been quite right to think she wasn't a teacher to cross. Strict and clever, she gave them a talking-to the moment they had sat down in her first class.

'Transfiguration is some of the most complex and dangerous magic you will learn at Hogwarts,' she said. 'Anyone messing around in my class will leave and not come back. You have been warned.'

Then she changed her desk into a pig and back again. They were all very impressed and couldn't wait to get started, but soon realised they weren't going to be changing the furniture into animals for a long time. After making a lot of complicated notes, they were each given a match and started trying to turn it into a needle. By the end of the lesson, only Hermione Granger had made any difference to her match; Professor McGonagall showed the class how it had gone all silver and pointy and gave Hermione a rare smile.

The class everyone had really been looking forward to was Defence Against the Dark Arts, but Quirrell's lessons turned out to be a bit of a joke. His classroom smelled strongly of garlic, which everyone said was to ward off a vampire he'd met in Romania and was afraid would be coming back to get him one of these days. His turban, he told them, had been given to him by an African prince as a thank-you for getting rid of a troublesome zombie, but they weren't sure they believed this story. For one thing, when Seamus Finnigan asked eagerly to hear how Quirrell had fought off the zombie, Quirrell went pink and started talking about the weather; for another, they had noticed that a funny smell hung around the turban, and the Weasley twins insisted that it was stuffed full of garlic as well, so that Quirrell was protected wherever he went.

Harry was very relieved to find out that he wasn't miles behind everyone else. Lots of people had come from Muggle families and, like him, hadn't had any idea that they were witches and wizards. There was so much to learn that even people like Ron didn't have much of a head start.

Friday was an important day for Harry and Ron. They finally managed to find their way down to the Great Hall for breakfast without getting lost once.

'What have we got today?' Harry asked Ron as he poured sugar on his porridge.

'Double Potions with the Slytherins,' said Ron. 'Snape's Head of Slytherin house. They say he always favours them – we'll be able to see if it's true.'

不好对付。她严格、聪明，学生们刚坐下来上第一堂课她就给他们来了个下马威。

"变形术是你们在霍格沃茨所学的课程中最复杂也最危险的魔法。"她说，"任何人要是在我的课堂上调皮捣蛋，我就请他出去，永远不准再进来。我可是警告过你们了。"

然后，她把她的讲桌变成了一头猪，然后又变了回来。学生们个个都被吸引了，恨不能马上开始学，可他们很快就明白，要把家具变成动物，还需要好长一段时间呢。他们记下了一大堆复杂艰深的笔记之后，她发给他们每人一根火柴，开始让他们试着变成一根针。到下课的时候，只有赫敏·格兰杰让她的火柴起了些变化；麦格教授让全班看那根火柴是怎么变成银亮亮的针的，而且一头还很尖，又向赫敏露出了难得的微笑。

全班真正期待的课程是黑魔法防御术。可奇洛教授的这一课几乎成了一场笑话。他上课的教室里充满了一股大蒜味，大家都说这是为了驱走他在罗马尼亚遇到的一个吸血鬼，怕那个吸血鬼会回过头来抓他。他告诉他们，他的大围巾是一位非洲王子送给他的礼物，那位王子是为了答谢他帮忙摆脱了僵尸的纠缠，不过谁也说不上是不是真的相信他说的这个故事。首先，当西莫·斐尼甘急不可耐地问奇洛教授是怎么打败僵尸的时候，教授满脸涨得通红，含含糊糊，说起了天气；其次，他们发现他那块大围巾也散发出一股怪味，韦斯莱家的孪生兄弟坚持说那里面肯定也塞满了大蒜，这样无论奇洛教授走到哪里，他都有了防护。

哈利发现自己和大家也不过五十步与百步之差，于是大大地松了一口气。这里许多人像他一样，来自麻瓜家庭，根本没有想到自己会是巫师。他们需要学习的东西太多了，就连像罗恩这样巫师世家出身的人也不见得领先多少。

星期五对哈利和罗恩来说是一个关键的日子。他们终于找到了去礼堂吃早饭的路，中途没有迷失方向。

"今天我们都有哪些课？"哈利一边往麦片粥里放糖，一边问罗恩。

"跟斯莱特林的学生一起上两节魔药课。"罗恩说，"斯内普是斯莱特林学院的院长，都说他偏向自己的学生，现在倒可以看看是不是真的这样。"

CHAPTER EIGHT   The Potions Master

'Wish McGonagall favoured us,' said Harry. Professor McGonagall was Head of Gryffindor house, but it hadn't stopped her giving them a huge pile of homework the day before.

Just then, the post arrived. Harry had got used to this by now, but it had given him a bit of a shock on the first morning, when about a hundred owls had suddenly streamed into the Great Hall during breakfast, circling the tables until they saw their owners and dropping letters and packages on to their laps.

Hedwig hadn't brought Harry anything so far. She sometimes flew in to nibble his ear and have a bit of toast before going off to sleep in the owlery with the other school owls. This morning, however, she fluttered down between the marmalade and the sugar bowl and dropped a note on to Harry's plate. Harry tore it open at once.

> **DEAR HARRY,** (it said, in a very untidy scrawl)
> I KNOW YOU GET FRIDAY AFTERNOONS OFF, SO WOULD YOU LIKE TO COME AND HAVE A CUP OF TEA WITH ME AROUND THREE? I WANT TO HEAR ALL ABOUT YOUR FIRST WEEK. SEND US AN ANSWER BACK WITH HEDWIG.
> HAGRID

Harry borrowed Ron's quill, scribbled '*Yes, please, see you later*' on the back of the note and sent Hedwig off again.

It was lucky that Harry had tea with Hagrid to look forward to, because the Potions lesson turned out to be the worst thing that had happened to him so far.

At the start-of-term banquet, Harry had got the idea that Professor Snape disliked him. By the end of the first Potions lesson, he knew he'd been wrong. Snape didn't dislike Harry – he *hated* him.

Potions lessons took place down in one of the dungeons. It was colder here than up in the main castle and would have been quite creepy enough without the pickled animals floating in glass jars all around the walls.

Snape, like Flitwick, started the class by taking the register, and like

第8章 魔药课老师

"但愿麦格教授也能偏向我们。"哈利说。麦格教授是格兰芬多学院的院长,但她昨天照样给他们留了一大堆作业。

就在这时,邮件到了。现在哈利已经习惯了。可是在第一天吃早饭的时候,百十来只猫头鹰突然飞进礼堂,着实把他吓了一跳。这些猫头鹰围着餐桌飞来飞去,直到找到各自的主人,把信件或包裹扔到他们腿上。

到目前为止,海德薇还没有给哈利带来过任何东西。它有时飞进来啄一下哈利的耳朵,讨上一小口吐司,然后就飞回猫头鹰屋,和校园里的其他猫头鹰一起睡觉去了。但是今天早上,它却扑棱着翅膀落到果酱盘和糖罐之间,将一张字条放到了哈利的餐盘上。哈利即刻把字条打开。

亲爱的哈利:(字迹非常潦草零乱)

  我知道你星期五下午没有课,不知能否在午后三时前后过来和我一起喝茶?我很想知道你第一周的情况。请让海德薇给我一个回音。

海　格

哈利向罗恩借来羽毛笔在字条背面匆匆写道:好的,我很乐意,下午见。然后就让海德薇飞走了。

幸好哈利还有跟海格一起喝茶这么个盼头,因为魔药课是哈利进霍格沃茨之后最厌烦的一门课程。

在开学宴会上,哈利就感到斯内普教授不喜欢他。第一节魔药课结束的时候,他才知道自己想错了。斯内普教授不是不喜欢他,而是恨他。

魔药课是在一间地下教室里上课。这里比上边城堡主楼阴冷,沿墙摆放着玻璃罐,里面浸泡的动物标本更令你瑟瑟发抖。

斯内普和弗立维一样,一上课就拿起名册,而且也像弗立维一样,点到哈利的名字时总是停下来。

"哦,是的,"他小声说,"哈利·波特,这是我们新来的——鼎鼎

CHAPTER EIGHT The Potions Master

Flitwick, he paused at Harry's name.

'Ah, yes,' he said softly, 'Harry Potter. Our new – *celebrity*.'

Draco Malfoy and his friends Crabbe and Goyle sniggered behind their hands. Snape finished calling the names and looked up at the class. His eyes were black like Hagrid's, but they had none of Hagrid's warmth. They were cold and empty and made you think of dark tunnels.

'You are here to learn the subtle science and exact art of potion-making,' he began. He spoke in barely more than a whisper, but they caught every word – like Professor McGonagall, Snape had the gift of keeping a class silent without effort. 'As there is little foolish wand-waving here, many of you will hardly believe this is magic. I don't expect you will really understand the beauty of the softly simmering cauldron with its shimmering fumes, the delicate power of liquids that creep through human veins, bewitching the mind, ensnaring the senses ... I can teach you how to bottle fame, brew glory, even stopper death – if you aren't as big a bunch of dunderheads as I usually have to teach.'

More silence followed this little speech. Harry and Ron exchanged looks with raised eyebrows. Hermione Granger was on the edge of her seat and looked desperate to start proving that she wasn't a dunderhead.

'Potter!' said Snape suddenly. 'What would I get if I added powdered root of asphodel to an infusion of wormwood?'

Powdered root of what to an infusion of what? Harry glanced at Ron, who looked as stumped as he was; Hermione's hand had shot into the air.

'I don't know, sir,' said Harry.

Snape's lips curled into a sneer.

'Tut, tut – fame clearly isn't everything.'

He ignored Hermione's hand.

'Let's try again. Potter, where would you look if I told you to find me a bezoar?'

Hermione stretched her hand as high into the air as it would go without her leaving her seat, but Harry didn't have the faintest idea what a bezoar was. He tried not to look at Malfoy, Crabbe and Goyle, who were shaking with laughter.

'I don't know, sir.'

'Thought you wouldn't open a book before coming, eh, Potter?'

第8章 魔药课老师

大名的人物啊。"

德拉科·马尔福和他的朋友克拉布和高尔用手捂着嘴咻咻地笑起来。斯内普点完名,便抬眼看着全班同学,他的眼睛像海格的一样乌黑,却没有海格的那股暖意。他的眼睛冷漠、空洞,使你想到两条漆黑的隧道。

"你们到这里来为的是学习配制魔药这门精密科学和严格工艺。"他开口道,说话的声音几乎只比耳语略高一些,但人人都听清了他说的每一个字。像麦格教授一样,斯内普教授也有不费吹灰之力就让教室秩序井然的威慑力量。"由于这里不用傻乎乎地挥动魔杖,所以你们中间有许多人不会相信这是魔法。我并不指望你们能真正领会那文火慢煨的坩埚冒着白烟、飘出阵阵清香的美妙所在,你们不会真正懂得流入人们血管的液体,令人心荡神驰、意志迷离的那种神妙魔力……我可以教会你们怎样提高声望,酿造荣耀,甚至阻止死亡——但必须有一条,那就是你们不是我经常遇到的那种笨蛋傻瓜才行。"

他讲完短短的开场白之后,全班哑然无声。哈利和罗恩扬了扬眉,交换了一下眼色。赫敏·格兰杰几乎挪到椅子边上,朝前探着身子,似乎急于证明自己不是笨蛋傻瓜。

"波特!"斯内普突然说,"如果我把水仙根粉末加入艾草浸液会得到什么?"

什么草根粉末放到什么浸液里?哈利看了罗恩一眼,罗恩跟他一样也怔住了;赫敏的手臂高高地举到空中。

"我不知道,先生。"哈利说。

斯内普轻蔑地撇了撇嘴。

"啧,啧——看来名气并不能代表一切。"

斯内普有意不去理会赫敏高举的手臂。

"我们再试一次。波特,如果我要你去找一块粪石,你会去哪里找?"

赫敏尽量在不离开座位的情况下,把手举得老高,哈利却根本不知道粪石是什么。他尽量不去看马尔福、克拉布和高尔,他们三人笑得浑身发颤。

"我不知道,先生。"

"我想,你在开学前一本书也没有翻过,是吧,波特?"

CHAPTER EIGHT   The Potions Master

Harry forced himself to keep looking straight into those cold eyes. He *had* looked through his books at the Dursleys', but did Snape expect him to remember everything in *One Thousand Magical Herbs and Fungi?*

Snape was still ignoring Hermione's quivering hand.

'What is the difference, Potter, between monkshood and wolfsbane?'

At this, Hermione stood up, her hand stretching towards the dungeon ceiling.

'I don't know,' said Harry quietly. 'I think Hermione does, though, why don't you try her?'

A few people laughed; Harry caught Seamus's eye and Seamus winked. Snape, however, was not pleased.

'Sit down,' he snapped at Hermione. 'For your information, Potter, asphodel and wormwood make a sleeping potion so powerful it is known as the Draught of Living Death. A bezoar is a stone taken from the stomach of a goat and it will save you from most poisons. As for monkshood and wolfsbane, they are the same plant, which also goes by the name of aconite. Well? Why aren't you all copying that down?'

There was a sudden rummaging for quills and parchment. Over the noise, Snape said, 'And a point will be taken from Gryffindor house for your cheek, Potter.'

Things didn't improve for the Gryffindors as the Potions lesson continued. Snape put them all into pairs and set them to mixing up a simple potion to cure boils. He swept around in his long black cloak, watching them weigh dried nettles and crush snake fangs, criticising almost everyone except Malfoy, whom he seemed to like. He was just telling everyone to look at the perfect way Malfoy had stewed his horned slugs when clouds of acid green smoke and a loud hissing filled the dungeon. Neville had somehow managed to melt Seamus's cauldron into a twisted blob and their potion was seeping across the stone floor, burning holes in people's shoes. Within seconds, the whole class were standing on their stools while Neville, who had been drenched in the potion when the cauldron collapsed, moaned in pain as angry red boils sprang up all over his arms and legs.

'Idiot boy!' snarled Snape, clearing the spilled potion away with one wave of his wand. 'I suppose you added the porcupine quills before taking the cauldron off the fire?'

第8章 魔药课老师

哈利强迫自己直勾勾地盯着他那对冷漠的眼睛。在德思礼家时，他真的把所有的书都翻过了，但是难道斯内普要求他把《千种神奇药草及蕈类》的内容都背下来吗？

斯内普仍旧没有理会赫敏颤抖的手臂。

"波特，那你说说，舟形乌头和狼毒乌头有什么区别？"

这时，赫敏站了起来，她的手笔直伸向地下教室的天花板。

"我不知道，"哈利小声说，"不过，我想，赫敏知道答案，您为什么不问问她呢？"

有几个学生笑出声来。哈利碰到了西莫的目光，西莫朝他使了个眼色。斯内普当然很不高兴。

"坐下。"他对赫敏怒喝道，"让我来告诉你吧，波特，水仙根粉和艾草加在一起可以配制成一种效力很强的安眠药，就是一服生死水。粪石是从山羊的胃里取出来的一种石头，有极强的解毒作用。至于舟形乌头和狼毒乌头则是同一种植物，统称乌头。明白了吗？你们为什么不把这些都记下来？"

教室里突然响起一阵摸索羽毛笔和羊皮纸的沙沙声。在一片嘈杂声中，斯内普说："波特，由于你顶撞老师，格兰芬多会为此被扣掉一分。"

魔药课继续上了下去，但格兰芬多的学生们的处境并没有改善。斯内普把他们分成两人一组，指导他们混合调制一种治疗疖子的简单药水。斯内普拖着他那件很长的黑斗篷在教室里走来走去，看他们称干荨麻，粉碎蛇的毒牙。几乎所有的学生都挨过批评，只有马尔福幸免，看来马尔福是斯内普偏爱的学生。正当斯内普让大家看马尔福蒸煮带触角的鼻涕虫的方法多么完美时，地下教室里突然冒出一股酸性的绿色浓烟，传来一阵很响的嘶嘶声。纳威不知怎的把西莫的坩埚烧成了歪歪扭扭的一块东西，坩埚里的药水泼到了石板地上，把同学们的鞋都烧出了洞。几秒钟内，全班同学都站到了凳子上，坩埚被打翻时，纳威浑身浸透了药水，这时他胳膊和腿上到处是红肿的疖子，痛得哇哇乱叫。

"白痴！"斯内普咆哮起来，挥起魔杖将泼在地上的药水一扫而光。"我想你大概是没有把坩埚从火上端开就把豪猪刺放进去了，是不是？"

CHAPTER EIGHT   The Potions Master

Neville whimpered as boils started to pop up all over his nose.

'Take him up to the hospital wing,' Snape spat at Seamus. Then he rounded on Harry and Ron, who had been working next to Neville.

'You – Potter – why didn't you tell him not to add the quills? Thought he'd make you look good if he got it wrong, did you? That's another point you've lost for Gryffindor.'

This was so unfair that Harry opened his mouth to argue, but Ron kicked him behind their cauldron.

'Don't push it,' he muttered. 'I've heard Snape can turn very nasty.'

As they climbed the steps out of the dungeon an hour later, Harry's mind was racing and his spirits were low. He'd lost two points for Gryffindor in his very first week – *why* did Snape hate him so much?

'Cheer up,' said Ron. 'Snape's always taking points off Fred and George. Can I come and meet Hagrid with you?'

At five to three they left the castle and made their way across the grounds. Hagrid lived in a small wooden house on the edge of the Forbidden Forest. A crossbow and a pair of galoshes were outside the front door.

When Harry knocked they heard a frantic scrabbling from inside and several booming barks. Then Hagrid's voice rang out, saying, '*Back*, Fang – *back*.'

Hagrid's big hairy face appeared in the crack as he pulled the door open.

'Hang on,' he said. '*Back*, Fang.'

He let them in, struggling to keep a hold on the collar of an enormous black boarhound.

There was only one room inside. Hams and pheasants were hanging from the ceiling, a copper kettle was boiling on the open fire and in a corner stood a massive bed with a patchwork quilt over it.

'Make yerselves at home,' said Hagrid, letting go of Fang, who bounded straight at Ron and started licking his ears. Like Hagrid, Fang was clearly not as fierce as he looked.

'This is Ron,' Harry told Hagrid, who was pouring boiling water into a large teapot and putting rock cakes on to a plate.

'Another Weasley, eh?' said Hagrid, glancing at Ron's freckles. 'I spent half me life chasin' yer twin brothers away from the Forest.'

The rock cakes almost broke their teeth, but Harry and Ron pretended to

纳威抽抽搭搭地哭起来，连鼻子上都突然冒出了许多疖子。

"把他送到上面的医院去。"斯内普对西莫厉声说。接着他在哈利和罗恩身边转来转去，他们俩正好挨着纳威操作。

"波特，你为什么不告诉他不要加进豪猪刺呢？你以为他出了错就显出你高明吗？格兰芬多又因为你丢了一分。"

这也太不公平了。哈利正要开口辩解，罗恩在坩埚后边踢了他一脚。

"别胡来，"他小声说，"听说斯内普特别不讲理。"

一小时后，他们顺着台阶爬出地下教室，哈利头脑里思绪翻滚，情绪低落。开学第一周格兰芬多就因为他被扣掉了两分，他不知道斯内普为什么这么恨他。

"打起精神来，"罗恩说，"斯内普经常扣弗雷德和乔治的分。我能跟你一起去见海格吗？"

三点差五分，他们离开城堡穿过场地向海格的住处走去。海格住在禁林边缘的一间小木屋里，大门前有一张弩和一双橡胶套鞋。

哈利敲门时，他们听见屋里传来一阵紧张的挣扎声和几声低沉的犬吠。接着传来海格的说话声："往后退，牙牙，往后退。"

海格把门开了一道缝，露出他满是胡须的大脸。

"等一等。"他说，"往后退，牙牙。"

海格把他们俩让了进去，一边拼命抓住一只庞大的黑色猎狗的项圈。

小木屋只有一个房间。天花板上挂着火腿、野鸡，火盆里用铜壶烧着开水，墙角放着一张大床，床上是用碎布拼接的被褥。

"不要客气。"海格说着，把牙牙放开了。牙牙立刻纵身朝罗恩扑过去舔他的耳朵。像海格一样，牙牙显然也不像它的外表那样凶猛。

"这是罗恩。"哈利对海格说。海格正忙着把开水倒进一只大茶壶里，一边把岩皮饼往餐盘里放。

"又是韦斯莱家的一个小兄弟吧？"海格说，朝罗恩的满脸雀斑瞟了一眼，"为了把你家那对孪生兄弟赶出禁林，我几乎耗费了大半辈子的精力。"

岩皮饼差点把他们的牙都硌掉了。可哈利和罗恩一边装出很爱吃的样子，一边把这几天上课的情景讲给海格听。牙牙把头枕在哈利膝头上，

CHAPTER EIGHT   The Potions Master

be enjoying them as they told Hagrid all about their first lessons. Fang rested his head on Harry's knee and drooled all over his robes.

Harry and Ron were delighted to hear Hagrid call Filch 'that old git'.

'An' as fer that cat, Mrs Norris, I'd like ter introduce her to Fang some time. D'yeh know, every time I go up ter the school, she follows me everywhere? Can't get rid of her – Filch puts her up to it.'

Harry told Hagrid about Snape's lesson. Hagrid, like Ron, told Harry not to worry about it, that Snape liked hardly any of the students.

'But he seemed to really *hate* me.'

'Rubbish!' said Hagrid. 'Why should he?'

Yet Harry couldn't help thinking that Hagrid didn't quite meet his eyes when he said that.

'How's yer brother Charlie?' Hagrid asked Ron. 'I liked him a lot – great with animals.'

Harry wondered if Hagrid had changed the subject on purpose. While Ron told Hagrid all about Charlie's work with dragons, Harry picked up a piece of paper that was lying on the table under the tea cosy. It was a cutting from the *Daily Prophet*:

GRINGOTTS BREAK-IN LATEST

Investigations continue into the break-in at Gringotts on 31 July, widely believed to be the work of Dark wizards or witches unknown.

Gringotts' goblins today insisted that nothing had been taken. The vault that was searched had in fact been emptied the same day.

'But we're not telling you what was in there, so keep your noses out if you know what's good for you,' said a Gringotts spokesgoblin this afternoon.

Harry remembered Ron telling him on the train that someone had tried to rob Gringotts, but Ron hadn't mentioned the date.

'Hagrid!' said Harry. 'That Gringotts break-in happened on my birthday! It might've been happening while we were there!'

There was no doubt about it, Hagrid definitely didn't meet Harry's eyes this time. He grunted and offered him another rock cake. Harry read the story again. *The vault that was searched had in fact been emptied earlier that same day.* Hagrid had emptied vault seven hundred and thirteen, if you could call it

口水把他的长袍都洇湿了一大片。

听海格管费尔奇叫"那个老饭桶",哈利和罗恩很高兴。

"至于那只猫,那个洛丽丝夫人,有朝一日我真想把它介绍给我的牙牙认识认识。你们知道吗,每次我去学校,无论到哪儿它都跟着我,甩也甩不掉,准是费尔奇让它这么干的。"

哈利对海格讲了斯内普课上的事。海格跟罗恩一样,要哈利不要担心,因为斯内普几乎没有喜欢过任何学生。

"可他好像真的很恨我。"

"瞎说!"海格说,"他为什么要恨你?"

可哈利总觉得海格在说这话时有些故意回避他的目光。

"你哥哥查理怎么样?"海格问罗恩,"我很喜欢他——他对动物很有办法。"

哈利怀疑海格有意转移话题。罗恩向海格讲查理研究火龙的情况时,哈利发现茶壶暖罩下压着一张小纸片,那是从《预言家日报》上剪下来的一段报道。

古灵阁非法闯入事件最新报道

有关七月三十一日古灵阁非法闯入事件的调查仍在进行。普遍认为这是不知姓名的黑巫师所为。

古灵阁的妖精们今日再度强调未被盗走任何物品。被闯入者搜索过的地下金库事实上已于当日早些时候提取一空。

一位古灵阁妖精发言人今日午后表示:金库中究竟存放何物,无可奉告,请勿干预此事为好。

哈利想起罗恩在火车上对他说过有人试图抢劫古灵阁,不过罗恩没有告诉他具体日期。

"海格!"哈利说,"古灵阁闯入事件发生的那一天正好是我的生日。很可能事情发生的时候我们正好也在那里!"

毫无疑问,海格这次确实不敢正视哈利的眼睛。他只哼了一声,又递给哈利一块岩皮饼。哈利把这篇报道又看了一遍。被闯入者搜索过的

emptying, taking out that grubby little package. Had that been what the thieves were looking for?

As Harry and Ron walked back to the castle for dinner, their pockets weighed down with rock cakes they'd been too polite to refuse, Harry thought that none of the lessons he'd had so far had given him as much to think about as tea with Hagrid. Had Hagrid collected that package just in time? Where was it now? And did Hagrid know something about Snape that he didn't want to tell Harry?

第8章 魔药课老师

地下金库事实上已于当日早些时候提取一空。如果拿走那个脏兮兮的小包就意味着提取一空的话，那么海格就已经把713号地下金库提取一空了。那个脏兮兮的小包难道就是闯入者要找的东西吗？

哈利和罗恩步行回城堡吃晚饭时，他们的衣袋里沉甸甸地装满了岩皮饼，出于礼貌，他们不好意思拒绝。哈利觉得与海格喝了一下午茶后，需要思考的问题比这几天上课时需要思考的多得多：海格及时拿到了那个小包吗？小包现在在什么地方？海格是不是知道一些关于斯内普的事情，但又不愿意告诉他呢？

CHAPTER NINE

The Midnight Duel

Harry had never believed he would meet a boy he hated more than Dudley, but that was before he met Draco Malfoy. Still, first-year Gryffindors only had Potions with the Slytherins, so they didn't have to put up with Malfoy much. Or at least, they didn't until they spotted a notice pinned up in the Gryffindor common room which made them all groan. Flying lessons would be starting on Thursday – and Gryffindor and Slytherin would be learning together.

'Typical,' said Harry darkly. 'Just what I always wanted. To make a fool of myself on a broomstick in front of Malfoy.'

He had been looking forward to learning to fly more than anything else.

'You don't know you'll make a fool of yourself,' said Ron reasonably. 'Anyway, I know Malfoy's always going on about how good he is at Quidditch, but I bet that's all talk.'

Malfoy certainly did talk about flying a lot. He complained loudly about first-years never getting in the house Quidditch teams and told long, boastful stories which always seemed to end with him narrowly escaping Muggles in helicopters. He wasn't the only one, though: the way Seamus Finnigan told it, he'd spent most of his childhood zooming around the countryside on his broomstick. Even Ron would tell anyone who'd listen about the time he'd almost hit a hang-glider on Charlie's old broom. Everyone from wizarding families talked about Quidditch constantly. Ron had already had a big argument with Dean Thomas, who shared their dormitory, about football. Ron couldn't see what was exciting about a game with only one ball where no one was allowed to fly. Harry had caught Ron prodding Dean's poster of West Ham football team, trying to make the players move.

Neville had never been on a broomstick in his life, because his

第 9 章

午夜决斗

哈利以前一直不相信，他竟然会认识一个男孩，他恨这家伙比恨达力还厉害，他是在遇到德拉科·马尔福之后才相信这一点的。不过，一年级的格兰芬多学生只有魔药课是和斯莱特林的学生一起上的，所以要忍受马尔福还不算困难。至少起初是这样的。后来有一天，他们发现格兰芬多的公共休息室里贴出了一张启事，看了之后全都唉声叹气。星期四就要开始上飞行课了——格兰芬多的学生要和斯莱特林的学生一起上课。

"真倒霉，"哈利沮丧地说，"果然不出我的所料。骑着一把飞天扫帚在马尔福面前出洋相。"

他一直在盼望学习飞行，这愿望比什么都强烈。

"你是不是会出洋相还不一定呢。"罗恩理智地说，"我知道马尔福总是吹嘘，说他玩魁地奇玩得特棒，但我敢打赌他只是在说大话。"

马尔福整天大谈特谈飞行。他大声抱怨说一年级新生没有资格参加学院魁地奇球队，他还讲了许多冗长的、自吹自擂的故事，最后总是以他惊险地躲过一架麻瓜的直升机为结束。不过，说这种大话的并不止他一个：听西莫·斐尼甘的口气，似乎他童年的大部分时间都是骑着飞天扫帚在旷野里飞来飞去。就连罗恩，只要有人愿意听，也会说起他有一次骑着查理的破扫帚，差点儿撞上了一架悬挂式滑翔机。每个来自巫师家庭的人都喋喋不休地谈论着魁地奇。罗恩为了足球，已经与同宿舍的迪安·托马斯大吵了一架。罗恩不明白，全场只有一只球，而且谁也不许飞，这种比赛有什么令人激动的。哈利无意中看见罗恩用手在迪安那张西汉姆足球队的海报上捅来捅去，想让队员们都动起来。

CHAPTER NINE The Midnight Duel

grandmother had never let him near one. Privately, Harry felt she'd had good reason, because Neville managed to have an extraordinary number of accidents even with both feet on the ground.

Hermione Granger was almost as nervous about flying as Neville was. This was something you couldn't learn by heart out of a book – not that she hadn't tried. At breakfast on Thursday she bored them all stupid with flying tips she'd got out of a library book called *Quidditch Through the Ages*. Neville was hanging on to her every word, desperate for anything that might help him hang on to his broomstick later, but everybody else was very pleased when Hermione's lecture was interrupted by the arrival of the post.

Harry hadn't had a single letter since Hagrid's note, something that Malfoy had been quick to notice, of course. Malfoy's eagle owl was always bringing him packages of sweets from home, which he opened gloatingly at the Slytherin table.

A barn owl brought Neville a small package from his grandmother. He opened it excitedly and showed them a glass ball the size of a large marble, which seemed to be full of white smoke.

'It's a Remembrall!' he explained. 'Gran knows I forget things – this tells you if there's something you've forgotten to do. Look, you hold it tight like this and if it turns red – oh ...' His face fell, because the Remembrall had suddenly glowed scarlet, '... you've forgotten something ...'

Neville was trying to remember what he'd forgotten when Draco Malfoy, who was passing the Gryffindor table, snatched the Remembrall out of his hand.

Harry and Ron jumped to their feet. They were half hoping for a reason to fight Malfoy, but Professor McGonagall, who could spot trouble quicker than any teacher in the school, was there in a flash.

'What's going on?'

'Malfoy's got my Remembrall, Professor.'

Scowling, Malfoy quickly dropped the Remembrall back on the table.

'Just looking,' he said, and he sloped away with Crabbe and Goyle behind him.

* * *

At three-thirty that afternoon, Harry, Ron and the other Gryffindors

第9章 午夜决斗

纳威这辈子还没有骑过扫帚呢，因为他奶奶从来不让他接近飞天扫帚。哈利私下里觉得他奶奶很有道理，纳威即使两只脚都老老实实地踩在地面上，还总能制造层出不穷的事故呢。

对于飞行，赫敏·格兰杰差不多和纳威一样紧张。这种本领你是不可能从书上看到并用心记住的——她不是没有试过。星期四早晨吃早饭的时候，她不停地对他们念叨她从一本名叫《神奇的魁地奇球》的图书馆藏书中看来的一些飞行指导，把他们烦得够呛。纳威则全神贯注地听着她说的每一个字，眼巴巴地希望听到一些有用的知识，待会儿可以帮助他牢牢地坐在飞天扫帚上。不过，当邮差到来打断了赫敏的演讲时，其他人还是感到非常高兴的。

自从上次海格的那封短信之后，哈利一直没有收到信，不用说，这一点马尔福早已注意到了。马尔福的雕鸮倒是经常给他从家里捎来大包小包的糖果，他总是在斯莱特林的饭桌上得意扬扬地把它们拆开。

一只猫头鹰从纳威的奶奶那里给他带来了一个小包裹。纳威激动地打开，给大家看一个大弹子那么大的玻璃球，里面仿佛充满了白色的烟雾。

"这是记忆球！"他解释说，"奶奶知道我总是没记性——它会告诉你是不是有什么事情忘记做了。瞧，你把它紧紧捏住，像这样，如果它变红了——哦……"他顿时拉长了脸，因为记忆球突然红得发亮，"……你就是忘记什么事情了……"

纳威拼命回忆他忘记了什么，就在这时，德拉科·马尔福经过格兰芬多的餐桌，猛地将记忆球从他手里夺了过去。

哈利和罗恩一跃而起。出于某种原因，他们多少有些希望跟马尔福干上一架。可是，麦格教授总能比别的老师更敏锐地察觉到出了乱子，一眨眼的工夫她就出现了。

"怎么回事？"

"马尔福抢了我的记忆球，教授。"

马尔福阴沉着脸，迅速地把记忆球扔回到桌上。

"等着瞧。"他说完便匆匆溜走了，克拉布和高尔紧随其后。

那天下午三点半，哈利、罗恩和格兰芬多的其他学生匆匆走下台阶，

CHAPTER NINE   The Midnight Duel

hurried down the front steps into the grounds for their first flying lesson. It was a clear, breezy day and the grass rippled under their feet as they marched down the sloping lawns towards a smooth lawn on the opposite side of the grounds to the Forbidden Forest, whose trees were swaying darkly in the distance.

The Slytherins were already there, and so were twenty broomsticks lying in neat lines on the ground. Harry had heard Fred and George Weasley complain about the school brooms, saying that some of them started to vibrate if you flew too high, or always flew slightly to the left.

Their teacher, Madam Hooch, arrived. She had short, grey hair and yellow eyes like a hawk.

'Well, what are you all waiting for?' she barked. 'Everyone stand by a broomstick. Come on, hurry up.'

Harry glanced down at his broom. It was old and some of the twigs stuck out at odd angles.

'Stick out your right hand over your broom,' called Madam Hooch at the front, 'and say, "Up!"'

'UP!' everyone shouted.

Harry's broom jumped into his hand at once, but it was one of the few that did. Hermione Granger's had simply rolled over on the ground and Neville's hadn't moved at all. Perhaps brooms, like horses, could tell when you were afraid, thought Harry; there was a quaver in Neville's voice that said only too clearly that he wanted to keep his feet on the ground.

Madam Hooch then showed them how to mount their brooms without sliding off the end, and walked up and down the rows, correcting their grips. Harry and Ron were delighted when she told Malfoy he'd been doing it wrong for years.

'Now, when I blow my whistle, you kick off from the ground, hard,' said Madam Hooch. 'Keep your brooms steady, rise a few feet and then come straight back down by leaning forwards slightly. On my whistle – three – two –'

But Neville, nervous and jumpy and frightened of being left on the ground, pushed off hard before the whistle had touched Madam Hooch's lips.

'Come back, boy!' she shouted, but Neville was rising straight up like a

来到门前的场地上,准备上他们的第一堂飞行课。这是一个晴朗的、有微风的日子,当他们快步走下倾斜的草地,向场地对面一处平坦的草坪走去时,小草在他们脚下微微起着波浪。草坪那边就是禁林,远处黑魆魆的树木在风中摇曳。

斯莱特林的学生已经在那里了,还有二十把飞天扫帚整整齐齐地排放在地上。哈利曾经听弗雷德和乔治·韦斯莱抱怨过学校里的飞天扫帚,说有的扫帚在你飞得太高时会簌簌发抖,还有的呢,总是微微地偏向左边。

他们的老师霍琦女士来了。她一头短短的灰发,两只眼睛是黄色的,像老鹰的眼睛一样。

"好了,你们大家还等什么?"她厉声说道,"每个人都站到一把飞天扫帚旁边。快,快,抓紧时间。"

哈利低头看了一眼他的飞天扫帚,它又破又旧,一些枝子横七竖八地戳了出来。

"伸出右手,放在扫帚上方,"霍琦女士在前面喊道,"然后说:'起来!'"

"起来!"每个人都喊道。

哈利的扫帚立刻就跳到了他手里,但这样听话的扫帚只有少数几把。赫敏·格兰杰的扫帚只是在地上打了个滚,而纳威的扫帚根本纹丝不动。哈利心想,也许扫帚也像马一样,能够看出你内心的胆怯。纳威的声音微微发颤,再明显不过地说明他希望稳稳地站在地面上。

接着,霍琦女士向他们示范怎样骑上扫帚而不从头上滑下来。她在队伍里走来走去,给他们纠正手的握法。哈利和罗恩听见她批评马尔福一直做得不对,心里不由得暗暗高兴。

"好了,我一吹口哨,你们就两腿一蹬,离开地面,要用力蹬。"霍琦女士说,"把扫帚拿稳,上升几英尺,然后身体微微前倾,垂直落回地面。听我的口哨——三——二——"

然而,纳威太紧张了,生怕被留在地面上,于是他不等哨子碰到霍琦女士的嘴唇,就使劲一蹬,飞了上去。

"回来,孩子!"霍琦女士喊道,可是纳威径直往上升,就像瓶塞从瓶口喷出去一样——十二英尺——二十英尺。哈利看见他惊恐、煞白

cork shot out of a bottle – twelve feet – twenty feet. Harry saw his scared white face look down at the ground falling away, saw him gasp, slip sideways off the broom and –

WHAM – a thud and a nasty crack and Neville lay, face down, on the grass in a heap. His broomstick was still rising higher and higher and started to drift lazily towards the Forbidden Forest and out of sight.

Madam Hooch was bending over Neville, her face as white as his.

'Broken wrist,' Harry heard her mutter. 'Come on, boy – it's all right, up you get.'

She turned to the rest of the class.

'None of you is to move while I take this boy to the hospital wing! You leave those brooms where they are or you'll be out of Hogwarts before you can say "Quidditch". Come on, dear.'

Neville, his face tear-streaked, clutching his wrist, hobbled off with Madam Hooch, who had her arm around him.

No sooner were they out of earshot than Malfoy burst into laughter.

'Did you see his face, the great lump?'

The other Slytherins joined in.

'Shut up, Malfoy,' snapped Parvati Patil.

'Ooh, sticking up for Longbottom?' said Pansy Parkinson, a hard-faced Slytherin girl. 'Never thought *you'd* like fat little cry babies, Parvati.'

'Look!' said Malfoy, darting forward and snatching something out of the grass. 'It's that stupid thing Longbottom's gran sent him.'

The Remembrall glittered in the sun as he held it up.

'Give that here, Malfoy,' said Harry quietly. Everyone stopped talking to watch.

Malfoy smiled nastily.

'I think I'll leave it somewhere for Longbottom to collect – how about – up a tree?'

'Give it *here*!' Harry yelled, but Malfoy had leapt on to his broomstick and taken off. He hadn't been lying, he *could* fly well – hovering level with the topmost branches of an oak he called, 'Come and get it, Potter!'

Harry grabbed his broom.

'*No!*' shouted Hermione Granger. 'Madam Hooch told us not to move –

第9章 午夜决斗

的脸望着下面飞速远去的地面，看见他张着大嘴喘气，从扫帚把的一边滑下来，然后——

砰——一声坠落，一声猛烈的撞击，纳威面朝下躺在地上的草丛中，缩成一团。他的飞天扫帚还在越升越高，然后开始缓缓地朝禁林方向飘去，消失不见了。

霍琦女士俯身看着纳威，她的脸和纳威的一样惨白。

"手腕断了。"哈利听见她小声说，"好了，孩子——没事，你起来吧。"她转身望着班上其他同学。

"我送这孩子去医院，你们谁都不许动！把飞天扫帚放回原处，不然的话，不等你们来得及说一句'魁地奇'，就被赶出霍格沃茨大门了。走吧，亲爱的。"

纳威脸上挂着一条条泪痕，他抓着手腕，一瘸一拐地和霍琦女士一同离去了。霍琦女士用胳膊搂着他。

他们刚走得听不见了，马尔福就放声大笑起来。

"你们看见他那副面孔了吗，那个傻大个？"

其他斯莱特林的学生也随声附和。

"闭嘴，马尔福。"帕瓦蒂·佩蒂尔厉声说。

"嚍，护着隆巴顿？"潘西·帕金森说，她是一个长相丑陋的斯莱特林女生，"没想到你居然会喜欢胖乎乎的小泪包，帕瓦蒂。"

"瞧！"马尔福说着，冲过去抓起草地上的什么东西，"是那个大傻瓜隆巴顿的奶奶捎给他的。"

他举起记忆球，球在阳光下闪闪发光。

"拿过来，马尔福。"哈利低声说。大家都停止了说话，注视着。

马尔福露出丑恶的狞笑。

"我想把它放在一个什么地方，让隆巴顿去捡——放在一棵树上——怎么样？"

"拿过来！"哈利大喊，可是马尔福已经跳上他的扫帚，起飞了。他以前的话并不是吹牛——他确实飞得好——悬浮在与一棵橡树的树梢平行的高度，大声叫道："过来拿吧，波特！"

哈利抓起他的扫帚。

CHAPTER NINE The Midnight Duel

you'll get us all into trouble.'

Harry ignored her. Blood was pounding in his ears. He mounted the broom and kicked hard against the ground and up, up he soared, air rushed through his hair and his robes whipped out behind him – and in a rush of fierce joy he realised he'd found something he could do without being taught – this was easy, this was *wonderful*. He pulled his broomstick up a little to take it even higher and heard screams and gasps of girls back on the ground and an admiring whoop from Ron.

He turned his broomstick sharply to face Malfoy in mid-air. Malfoy looked stunned.

'Give it here,' Harry called, 'or I'll knock you off that broom!'

'Oh, yeah?' said Malfoy, trying to sneer, but looking worried.

Harry knew, somehow, what to do. He leant forward and grasped the broom tightly in both hands and it shot towards Malfoy like a javelin. Malfoy only just got out of the way in time; Harry made a sharp about turn and held the broom steady. A few people below were clapping.

'No Crabbe and Goyle up here to save your neck, Malfoy,' Harry called.

The same thought seemed to have struck Malfoy.

'Catch it if you can, then!' he shouted, and he threw the glass ball high into the air and streaked back towards the ground.

Harry saw, as though in slow motion, the ball rise up in the air and then start to fall. He leant forward and pointed his broom handle down – next second he was gathering speed in a steep dive, racing the ball – wind whistled in his ears, mingled with the screams of people watching – he stretched out his hand – a foot from the ground he caught it, just in time to pull his broom straight, and he toppled gently on to the grass with the Remembrall clutched safely in his fist.

'HARRY POTTER!'

His heart sank faster than he'd just dived. Professor McGonagall was running towards them. He got to his feet, trembling.

'*Never* – in all my time at Hogwarts –'

Professor McGonagall was almost speechless with shock, and her glasses flashed furiously, '– how *dare* you – might have broken your neck –'

'It wasn't his fault, Professor –'

第9章 午夜决斗

"不行!"赫敏·格兰杰喊道,"霍琦女士叫我们不要动——你会给我们大家带来麻烦的。"

哈利没有理她,血撞得他的耳膜轰轰直响。他骑上飞天扫帚,用力蹬了一下地面,于是他升了上去,空气呼呼地刮过他的头发,长袍在身后呼啦啦地飘扬——他心头陡然一阵狂喜,意识到自己发现了一种他可以无师自通的技能——这么容易,这么美妙。他把飞天扫帚又抬起了一些,让它飞得更高。他听见地面上传来女孩子们的尖叫声和大喘气声,还听到罗恩发出的敬佩的喊叫。

他猛地把扫帚掉转过来,对着空中的马尔福。马尔福显然大吃一惊。

"拿过来,"哈利喊道,"不然我就把你从扫帚上撞下去。"

"哦,是吗?"马尔福说。他想发出嘲笑,但脸上的表情却很紧张。

哈利好像天生就知道该怎么做。他将身体前倾,用双手紧紧抓住扫帚,于是扫帚就像标枪一样朝马尔福射去。马尔福勉强闪身躲过;哈利又猛地掉转回身,稳稳地抓住扫帚。下面有几个人在鼓掌。

"这里可没有克拉布和高尔为你保驾,马尔福。"哈利喊道。

马尔福似乎也产生了同样的想法。

"给,看你能不能接住!"他大叫一声,把玻璃球高高地扔向空中,然后迅速朝地面降落。

哈利看见球仿佛是以慢动作升上了天空,随即开始坠落。他前倾着身体,使飞天扫帚指向下面——一眨眼的工夫,他就加速俯冲下去,追赶玻璃球——风在他耳边呼啸,混杂着下面同学们的尖叫声——他伸出手去,在离地面一英尺的高度接住了球。他及时把扫帚把扳直,然后轻轻倒在草地上,手心里稳稳地攥着那只记忆球。

"**哈利·波特!**"

他的心突然往下一沉,比他刚才俯冲的速度还快。麦格教授正向他们跑来。哈利从地上站起来,浑身发抖。

"我在霍格沃茨这么多年——从来没有——"

麦格教授简直惊讶得说不出话来,她的眼镜片闪烁着愤怒的光芒,"——你怎么敢——你会摔断脖子的——"

"不是他的错,教授——"

CHAPTER NINE The Midnight Duel

'Be quiet, Miss Patil –'

'But Malfoy –'

'That's *enough*, Mr Weasley. Potter, follow me, now.'

Harry caught sight of Malfoy, Crabbe and Goyle's triumphant faces as he left, walking numbly in Professor McGonagall's wake as she strode towards the castle. He was going to be expelled, he just knew it. He wanted to say something to defend himself, but there seemed to be something wrong with his voice. Professor McGonagall was sweeping along without even looking at him; he had to jog to keep up. Now he'd done it. He hadn't even lasted two weeks. He'd be packing his bags in ten minutes. What would the Dursleys say when he turned up on the doorstep?

Up the front steps, up the marble staircase inside, and still Professor McGonagall didn't say a word to him. She wrenched open doors and marched along corridors with Harry trotting miserably behind her. Maybe she was taking him to Dumbledore. He thought of Hagrid, expelled but allowed to stay on as gamekeeper. Perhaps he could be Hagrid's assistant. His stomach twisted as he imagined it, watching Ron and the others becoming wizards while he stumped around the grounds, carrying Hagrid's bag.

Professor McGonagall stopped outside a classroom. She opened the door and poked her head inside.

'Excuse me, Professor Flitwick, could I borrow Wood for a moment?'

Wood? Thought Harry, bewildered; was Wood a cane she was going to use on him?

But Wood turned out to be a person, a burly fifth-year boy who came out of Flitwick's class looking confused.

'Follow me, you two,' said Professor McGonagall, and they marched on up the corridor, Wood looking curiously at Harry.

'In here.'

Professor McGonagall pointed them into a classroom which was empty except for Peeves, who was busy writing rude words on the blackboard.

'Out, Peeves!' she barked. Peeves threw the chalk into a bin, which clanged loudly, and he swooped out cursing. Professor McGonagall slammed the door behind him and turned to face the two boys.

'Potter, this is Oliver Wood. Wood – I've found you a Seeker.'

第9章 午夜决斗

"住嘴，佩蒂尔小姐——"

"可是马尔福——"

"别说了，韦斯莱先生。好了，波特，跟我来。"

麦格教授大步朝城堡走去，哈利机械地跟在后面。他离开时发觉马尔福、克拉布和高尔脸上露出了得意的神情。他只知道自己要被开除了，想说几句话为自己辩护，但嗓子似乎出了毛病。麦格教授大步流星地朝前走着，看也不看他一眼；他必须小跑着才能跟得上。现在完了。他来了还不到两个星期，再过十分钟，就要收拾东西滚蛋了。达力一家看见他出现在大门口，会说什么呢？

两人登上大门前的台阶，登上里面的大理石楼梯，麦格教授还是一言不发。她拧开一扇扇门，大步穿过一道道走廊，哈利可怜兮兮地跟在后面。教授大概是要带他去见邓布利多吧。他想起了海格，虽然被开除了，但还是获准作为猎场看守继续留在学校里。也许他可以给海格当个助手。他仿佛看见自己拎着海格的口袋，拖着沉重的脚步在场地周围走来走去，眼巴巴地看着罗恩和其他人成为巫师。他一想起这些，就觉得胃拧成了一团。

麦格教授在一间教室外面停住脚步。她推开门，把头伸了进去。

"对不起，弗立维教授，可以让伍德出来一会儿吗？"

伍德？哈利迷惑地想，难道是木头拐杖，麦格教授要用它来教训他？

谁知，伍德原来是一个人，一个高大结实的五年级男生，他一脸茫然地走出弗立维的教室。

"你们两个，跟我走。"麦格教授说。三个人一起在走廊里大步前进，伍德好奇地打量着哈利。

"进去。"

麦格教授指着一间教室叫他们进去，里面只有皮皮鬼，正忙着在黑板上写骂人的话。

"出去，皮皮鬼！"她大吼一声。皮皮鬼把粉笔当啷一声扔进垃圾箱，骂骂咧咧地冲出教室。麦格教授把门重重地关上，转过身来，面对两个男孩。

"波特，这是奥利弗·伍德。伍德——我替你发现了一个找球手。"

CHAPTER NINE   The Midnight Duel

Wood's expression changed from puzzlement to delight.

'Are you serious, Professor?'

'Absolutely,' said Professor McGonagall crisply. 'The boy's a natural. I've never seen anything like it. Was that your first time on a broomstick, Potter?'

Harry nodded silently. He didn't have a clue what was going on, but he didn't seem to be being expelled, and some of the feeling started coming back to his legs.

'He caught that thing in his hand after a fifty-foot dive,' Professor McGonagall told Wood. 'Didn't even scratch himself. Charlie Weasley couldn't have done it.'

Wood was now looking as though all his dreams had come true at once.

'Ever seen a game of Quidditch, Potter?' he asked excitedly.

'Wood's captain of the Gryffindor team,' Professor McGonagall explained.

'He's just the build for a Seeker, too,' said Wood, now walking around Harry and staring at him. 'Light – speedy – we'll have to get him a decent broom, Professor – a Nimbus Two Thousand or a Cleansweep Seven, I'd say.'

'I shall speak to Professor Dumbledore and see if we can't bend the first-year rule. Heaven knows, we need a better team than last year. *Flattened* in that last match by Slytherin, I couldn't look Severus Snape in the face for weeks ...'

Professor McGonagall peered sternly over her glasses at Harry.

'I want to hear you're training hard, Potter, or I may change my mind about punishing you.'

Then she suddenly smiled.

'Your father would have been proud,' she said. 'He was an excellent Quidditch player himself.'

*

'You're *joking*.'

It was dinner time. Harry had just finished telling Ron what had happened when he'd left the grounds with Professor McGonagall. Ron had a piece of steak-and-kidney pie halfway to his mouth, but he'd forgotten all about it.

'*Seeker?*' he said. 'But first-years *never* – you must be the youngest house player in about –'

'– a century,' said Harry, shovelling pie into his mouth. He felt particularly hungry after the excitement of the afternoon. 'Wood told me.'

第9章 午夜决斗

伍德脸上的表情从困惑转为喜悦。

"你当真吗，教授？"

"绝对当真。"麦格教授干脆地说，"这孩子是个天才。我从来没见过这样的事情。波特，你是第一次骑飞天扫帚吗？"

哈利默默地点点头，完全不明白是怎么回事，但看来他不会被开除了，他的双腿又开始慢慢恢复了知觉。

"他俯冲五十英尺，伸手抓住了那东西，"麦格教授对伍德说，"一点儿皮肉擦伤都没有。查理·韦斯莱也做不到这点。"

伍德现在的表情，就好像他所有的梦想一下子全变成了现实。

"看过魁地奇比赛吗，波特？"他激动地问。

"伍德是格兰芬多魁地奇球队的队长。"麦格教授解释说。

"他的体型正适合当一个找球手，"伍德说，在哈利周围绕着圈子打量他，"轻盈——敏捷——我们必须给他弄一把像样的扫帚，教授——我看，就来一把光轮2000或横扫七星吧。"

"我要去跟邓布利多教授谈谈，看能不能破格使用一年级新生。确实，我们需要一支比去年更棒的魁地奇球队。上次比赛被斯莱特林队打得惨败，我几个星期都不敢和西弗勒斯·斯内普照面……"

麦格教授从眼镜上方严厉地瞅着哈利。

"我希望听到你在刻苦训练，波特，不然我就改变主意，要惩罚你了。"

接着，她又突然绽开笑容。

"你父亲会为你骄傲的，"她说，"他以前就是一个出色的魁地奇球员。"

"你在开玩笑吧。"

这是吃晚饭的时间，哈利对罗恩讲了他和麦格教授离开场地后发生的事情。罗恩正要把一块牛排腰子馅饼往嘴里送，送到一半忘记了。

"找球手？"他说，"可是一年级学生从不——你一定是许多年来年龄最小的院队选手了。"

"是一个世纪以来。"哈利说着，用手撮起馅饼塞进嘴里，经过下午这场惊心动魄的遭遇，他觉得特别饿，"伍德告诉我的。"

CHAPTER NINE The Midnight Duel

Ron was so amazed, so impressed, he just sat and gaped at Harry.

'I start training next week,' said Harry. 'Only don't tell anyone, Wood wants to keep it a secret.'

Fred and George Weasley now came into the hall, spotted Harry and hurried over.

'Well done,' said George in a low voice. 'Wood told us. We're on the team too – Beaters.'

'I tell you, we're going to win that Quidditch Cup for sure this year,' said Fred. 'We haven't won since Charlie left, but this year's team is going to be brilliant. You must be good, Harry, Wood was almost skipping when he told us.'

'Anyway, we've got to go, Lee Jordan reckons he's found a new secret passageway out of the school.'

'Bet it's that one behind the statue of Gregory the Smarmy that we found in our first week. See you.'

Fred and George had hardly disappeared when someone far less welcome turned up: Malfoy, flanked by Crabbe and Goyle.

'Having a last meal, Potter? When are you getting the train back to the Muggles?'

'You're a lot braver now you're back on the ground and you've got your little friends with you,' said Harry coolly. There was of course nothing at all little about Crabbe and Goyle, but as the High Table was full of teachers, neither of them could do more than crack their knuckles and scowl.

'I'd take you on any time on my own,' said Malfoy. 'Tonight, if you want. Wizard's duel. Wands only – no contact. What's the matter? Never heard of a wizard's duel before, I suppose?'

'Of course he has,' said Ron, wheeling round. 'I'm his second, who's yours?'

Malfoy looked at Crabbe and Goyle, sizing them up.

'Crabbe,' he said. 'Midnight all right? We'll meet you in the trophy room, that's always unlocked.'

When Malfoy had gone, Ron and Harry looked at each other.

'What *is* a wizard's duel?' said Harry. 'And what do you mean, you're my second?'

第9章 午夜决斗

罗恩太诧异、太震惊了。他只是坐在那里，呆呆地望着哈利。

"我下星期开始训练。"哈利说，"千万别跟任何人说，伍德想保密呢。"

这时，弗雷德和乔治·韦斯莱走进饭厅。他们一眼看见哈利，快步走了过来。

"好样的，"乔治低声说，"伍德告诉我们了。我们也是学院队的——是击球手。"

"告诉你们，我们今年一定能拿下魁地奇杯。"弗雷德说，"自从查理走后就没有赢过，不过今年，我们球队一定会大放异彩的。你肯定很棒，哈利，伍德跟我们说这件事时，激动得简直语无伦次了。"

"不过，我们得走了，李·乔丹认为他发现了一条新的秘密通道，可以通到学校外面。"

"我猜就是马屁精格雷戈里雕像后面的那条通道，我们进校的第一个星期就发现了。再见。"

弗雷德和乔治刚刚离去，某个很不受欢迎的人就露面了：马尔福。克拉布和高尔跟在他两旁。

"在吃最后一顿饭吗，波特？你什么时候乘火车返回麻瓜那里？"

"现在你回到地面上，又有你的小不点儿朋友陪伴左右，胆子就大多了。"哈利冷冷地说。当然啦，克拉布和高尔根本不能算小不点儿，但由于主宾席上坐满了老师，他们俩不敢造次，只好阴沉着脸，把手指捏得叭叭响。

"我随时愿意跟你单挑，"马尔福说，"如果你没意见，就在今晚。巫师之间的决斗。只用魔杖——不许肢体接触。怎么啦？我猜，你还没听说过巫师决斗吧？"

"他当然听说过。"罗恩说着，突然转过身，"我是他的助手，你的助手是谁？"

马尔福看着克拉布和高尔，把他们俩挨个儿掂量了一番。

"克拉布。"他说，"就在午夜，怎么样？我们在奖品陈列室和你们见面，那里从来不锁门。"

马尔福走后，罗恩和哈利面面相觑。

"巫师决斗是怎么回事？"哈利问，"你说做我的助手，这又是什么意思？"

CHAPTER NINE The Midnight Duel

'Well, a second's there to take over if you die,' said Ron casually, getting started at last on his cold pie. Catching the look on Harry's face, he added quickly, 'but people only die in proper duels, you know, with real wizards. The most you and Malfoy'll be able to do is send sparks at each other. Neither of you knows enough magic to do any real damage. I bet he expected you to refuse, anyway.'

'And what if I wave my wand and nothing happens?'

'Throw it away and punch him on the nose,' Ron suggested.

'Excuse me.'

They both looked up. It was Hermione Granger.

'Can't a person eat in peace in this place?' said Ron.

Hermione ignored him and spoke to Harry.

'I couldn't help overhearing what you and Malfoy were saying –'

'Bet you could,' Ron muttered.

'– and you *mustn't* go wandering around the school at night, think of the points you'll lose Gryffindor if you're caught, and you're bound to be. It's really very selfish of you.'

'And it's really none of your business,' said Harry.

'Goodbye,' said Ron.

All the same, it wasn't what you'd call the perfect end to the day, Harry thought, as he lay awake much later listening to Dean and Seamus falling asleep (Neville wasn't back from the hospital wing). Ron had spent all evening giving him advice such as 'If he tries to curse you, you'd better dodge it, because I can't remember how to block them'. There was a very good chance they were going to get caught by Filch or Mrs Norris, and Harry felt he was pushing his luck, breaking another school rule today. On the other hand, Malfoy's sneering face kept looming up out of the darkness – this was his big chance to beat Malfoy, face to face. He couldn't miss it.

'Half past eleven,' Ron muttered at last. 'We'd better go.'

They pulled on their dressing-gowns, picked up their wands and crept across the tower room, down the spiral staircase and into the Gryffindor common room. A few embers were still glowing in the fireplace, turning all the armchairs into hunched black shadows. They had almost reached the

第9章 午夜决斗

"噢,如果你死了,助手就接着上。"罗恩轻描淡写地说,终于又开始吃他那已经冷却的馅饼。他捕捉到哈利脸上的神情,便又急忙补充道:"不过你知道,只有跟真正的巫师进行正规决斗时才会死。你和马尔福充其量只能向对方发射点儿火花。你们俩懂的魔法太少,不会真正伤着对方的。不过,我敢说他还以为你会拒绝呢。"

"如果我挥动魔杖,一点儿反应也没有,怎么办呢?"

"那就扔掉魔杖,对准他的鼻子揍一拳。"罗恩建议道。

"对不起,打扰一下。"

他们俩抬头一看,原来是赫敏·格兰杰。

"能不能让人在这里消消停停地吃饭呢?"罗恩说。

赫敏没有理他,却对哈利说:

"我忍不住偷听了你和马尔福说的——"

"我就知道你会这样。"罗恩咕哝道。

"——夜里你绝对不能在学校乱逛,想想吧,如果被抓住,会给格兰芬多丢多少分啊,而且你肯定会被抓住的。你真的太自私了。"

"这事真的与你无关。"哈利说。

"再见。"罗恩说。

以决斗来结束一天,这无论如何也不能算是美妙圆满,哈利躺在床上想道。他早就听见迪安和西莫进入了梦乡(纳威还没有从医院回来)。罗恩一晚上都在给他出谋划策,例如:"如果他想给你念咒语,你最好躲开,因为我不记得怎样挡住咒语。"他们很可能会被费尔奇或洛丽丝夫人抓住,哈利觉得自己是在与命运作对,今天又要违反一条校规了。另一方面,马尔福讥讽的脸不时在黑暗里显现——这是哈利面对面打败马尔福的一个大好机会,他不能放过。

"十一点半了,"终于,罗恩低声说道,"我们得走了。"

他们穿上晨衣,拿起魔杖,蹑手蹑脚地穿过房间,走下旋转楼梯,进入格兰芬多的公共休息室。壁炉里还有一些余火在闪烁着微光,扶手椅仿佛都变成了一团团黑乎乎的影子。他们刚要走到肖像洞口,就听见离得最近的一把椅子上有人说话:"我不敢相信你竟然这么做,哈利。"

CHAPTER NINE   The Midnight Duel

portrait hole when a voice spoke from the chair nearest them: 'I can't believe you're going to do this, Harry.'

A lamp flickered on. It was Hermione Granger, wearing a pink dressing-gown and a frown.

'*You*!' said Ron furiously. 'Go back to bed!'

'I almost told your brother,' Hermione snapped. 'Percy – he's a Prefect, he'd put a stop to this.'

Harry couldn't believe anyone could be so interfering.

'Come on,' he said to Ron. He pushed open the portrait of the Fat Lady and climbed through the hole.

Hermione wasn't going to give up that easily. She followed Ron through the portrait hole, hissing at them like an angry goose.

'Don't you *care* about Gryffindor, do you *only* care about yourselves, *I* don't want Slytherin to win the House Cup and you'll lose all the points I got from Professor McGonagall for knowing about Switching Spells.'

'Go away.'

'All right, but I warned you, you just remember what I said when you're on the train home tomorrow, you're so –'

But what they were, they didn't find out. Hermione had turned to the portrait of the Fat Lady to get back inside and found herself facing an empty painting. The Fat Lady had gone on a night-time visit and Hermione was locked out of Gryffindor Tower.

'Now what am I going to do?' she asked shrilly.

'That's your problem,' said Ron. 'We've got to go, we're going to be late.'

They hadn't even reached the end of the corridor when Hermione caught up with them.

'I'm coming with you,' she said.

'You are *not*.'

'D'you think I'm going to stand out here and wait for Filch to catch me? If he finds all three of us I'll tell him the truth, that I was trying to stop you and you can back me up.'

'You've got some nerve –' said Ron loudly.

'Shut up, both of you!' said Harry sharply. 'I heard something.'

It was a sort of snuffling.

第9章 午夜决斗

一盏灯噗地闪亮，是赫敏·格兰杰。她穿着粉红色的晨衣，皱着眉头。

"你！"罗恩恼怒地说，"回去睡觉！"

"我差一点儿就告诉你哥哥了，"赫敏不客气地回敬，"珀西——他是级长，他会阻止这一切的。"

哈利无法相信居然有这样好管闲事的人。

"走吧。"他对罗恩说。他推开胖夫人的肖像，从洞口爬了出去。

赫敏可不会这么轻易让步。她跟着罗恩爬出洞口，像一只发怒的母鹅压低声音朝他们嚷嚷。

"你难道不关心格兰芬多，只关心你自己吗？我不想让斯莱特林再赢得学院杯，不想让你把我用转换咒从麦格教授那里弄来的分数全丢光。"

"走开。"

"好吧，不过我警告你，等你明天坐火车回家时，别忘了我说的话，你真是太——"

至于太怎么样，他们就不知道了。赫敏转向胖夫人的肖像，想重新钻回去，却发现面对的画上已空空如也。胖夫人深夜出去串门儿了，赫敏被关在了格兰芬多塔楼外面。

"哎呀，现在我怎么办呢？"她扯着嗓子问。

"那是你的问题。"罗恩说，"我们得走了，快迟到了。"

没等他们走到走廊尽头，赫敏就赶了上来。

"我和你们一起去。"她说。

"你不许去。"

"你们难道以为我会站在这外面，等费尔奇来把我抓住吗？如果他发现了我们三个人，我就把实情告诉他，就说我在试图劝阻你们，到时候，你们可以为我的话作证。"

"你胆子倒不小——"罗恩大声说。

"闭嘴，你们两个！"哈利严厉地说，"我听见有声音。"

是一种呼哧呼哧的声音。

"是洛丽丝夫人吗？"罗恩屏住呼吸问道，眯起眼睛看着暗处。

CHAPTER NINE   The Midnight Duel

'Mrs Norris?' breathed Ron, squinting through the dark.

It wasn't Mrs Norris. It was Neville. He was curled up on the floor, fast asleep, but jerked suddenly awake as they crept nearer.

'Thank goodness you found me! I've been out here for hours. I couldn't remember the new password to get in to bed.'

'Keep your voice down, Neville. The password's "Pig snout" but it won't help you now, the Fat Lady's gone off somewhere.'

'How's your arm?' said Harry.

'Fine,' said Neville, showing them. 'Madam Pomfrey mended it in about a minute.'

'Good – well, look, Neville, we've got to be somewhere, we'll see you later –'

'Don't leave me!' said Neville, scrambling to his feet. 'I don't want to stay here alone, the Bloody Baron's been past twice already.'

Ron looked at his watch and then glared furiously at Hermione and Neville.

'If either of you get us caught, I'll never rest until I've learnt that Curse of the Bogies Quirrell told us about and used it on you.'

Hermione opened her mouth, perhaps to tell Ron exactly how to use the Curse of the Bogies, but Harry hissed at her to be quiet and beckoned them all forward.

They flitted along corridors striped with bars of moonlight from the high windows. At every turn Harry expected to run into Filch or Mrs Norris, but they were lucky. They sped up a staircase to the third floor and tiptoed towards the trophy room.

Malfoy and Crabbe weren't there yet. The crystal trophy cases glimmered where the moonlight caught them. Cups, shields, plates and statues winked silver and gold in the darkness. They edged along the walls, keeping their eyes on the doors at either end of the room. Harry took out his wand in case Malfoy leapt in and started at once. The minutes crept by.

'He's late, maybe he's chickened out,' Ron whispered.

Then a noise in the next room made them jump. Harry had only just raised his wand when they heard someone speak – and it wasn't Malfoy.

'Sniff around, my sweet, they might be lurking in a corner.'

It was Filch speaking to Mrs Norris. Horror-struck, Harry waved madly

第9章 午夜决斗

不是洛丽丝夫人，是纳威。他蜷缩在地板上，睡得正香，但他们一走近，他就猛地惊醒了。

"谢天谢地，你们找到我了！我在这外面待了好几个小时。我记不得新口令了，没法回去睡觉。"

"小声点儿，纳威。口令是'猪鼻子'，可现在对你也没有用了。胖夫人不知跑到什么地方去了。"

"你的胳膊怎么样了？"哈利问道。

"没事儿，"纳威说着，举起胳膊给他们看，"庞弗雷女士一眨眼就把它治好了。"

"不错——好了，纳威，你听着，我们要去一个地方，待会儿见——"

"别撇下我！"纳威说着，从地上爬了起来，"我不想一个人待在这里，血人巴罗已经两次从这里经过了。"

罗恩看了看表，又愤怒地瞪着赫敏和纳威。

"如果你们两个有谁害得我们被抓住，我一定要学会奇洛提到的那种鼻涕咒，用在你们身上。"

赫敏张了张嘴，大概是想告诉罗恩到底怎样使用鼻涕咒，可是哈利朝她嘘了一声，叫她安静，然后招呼大家快走。

他们沿着走廊轻快地走着，月光从高高的窗口洒进来，一道道地横在地上。每一次拐弯，哈利都以为要撞上费尔奇或洛丽丝夫人，不过还好，他们运气不错。几个人匆匆登上楼梯，来到四楼，蹑手蹑脚地朝奖品陈列室走去。

马尔福和克拉布不在。陈列奖品的水晶玻璃柜在月光下熠熠闪亮。黑暗中，奖杯、盾牌、奖牌和雕像闪着金光和银光。四个人贴着墙向前移动，眼睛紧盯着房间两头的门，哈利拿出魔杖，以防马尔福突然冲进来和他决斗。时间一分一秒地过去了。

"他迟到了，也许他因为害怕，不敢来了。"罗恩悄声说。

这时，隔壁房间传来一个声音，吓得他们跳了起来。哈利刚举起魔杖，就听见有人说话了——不是马尔福。

"到处闻闻，我亲爱的，他们可能躲在哪个角落里。"

是费尔奇在对洛丽丝夫人说话。哈利吓坏了，使劲朝另外三个人挥

CHAPTER NINE   The Midnight Duel

at the other three to follow him as quickly as possible; they scurried silently towards the door away from Filch's voice. Neville's robes had barely whipped round the corner when they heard Filch enter the trophy room.

'They're in here somewhere,' they heard him mutter, 'probably hiding.'

'This way!' Harry mouthed to the others and, petrified, they began to creep down a long gallery full of suits of armour. They could hear Filch getting nearer. Neville suddenly let out a frightened squeak and broke into a run – he tripped, grabbed Ron around the waist and the pair of them toppled right into a suit of armour.

The clanging and crashing were enough to wake the whole castle.

'RUN!' Harry yelled and the four of them sprinted down the gallery, not looking back to see whether Filch was following – they swung around the doorpost and galloped down one corridor then another, Harry in the lead without any idea where they were or where they were going. They ripped through a tapestry and found themselves in a hidden passageway, hurtled along it and came out near their Charms classroom, which they knew was miles from the trophy room.

'I think we've lost him,' Harry panted, leaning against the cold wall and wiping his forehead. Neville was bent double, wheezing and spluttering.

'I – *told* – you,' Hermione gasped, clutching at the stitch in her chest. 'I – told – you.'

'We've got to get back to Gryffindor Tower,' said Ron, 'quickly as possible.'

'Malfoy tricked you,' Hermione said to Harry. 'You realise that, don't you? He was never going to meet you – Filch knew someone was going to be in the trophy room, Malfoy must have tipped him off.'

Harry thought she was probably right, but he wasn't going to tell her that.

'Let's go.'

It wasn't going to be that simple. They hadn't gone more than a dozen paces when a doorknob rattled and something came shooting out of a classroom in front of them.

It was Peeves. He caught sight of them and gave a squeal of delight.

'Shut up, Peeves – please – you'll get us thrown out.'

Peeves cackled.

'Wandering around at midnight, ickle firsties? Tut, tut, tut. Naughty,

手,叫他们尽快跟着他;他们悄没声儿地走向那扇远离费尔奇声音的门。纳威的长袍刚掠过拐角,他们就听见费尔奇走进了奖品陈列室。

"他们就在这里的什么地方,"他们听见他低声嘟哝,"大概躲起来了。"

"这边走!"哈利不出声地对大家说。他们都吓傻了,悄悄地沿着摆满盔甲的走廊往前走,可以听见费尔奇离他们越来越近了。突然,纳威忍不住发出一声恐怖的尖叫,撒腿就跑——他被绊了一下,赶紧一把搂住罗恩的腰,两人一起跌倒在一套盔甲上。

顿时,哐啷啷,哗啦啦,那声音足以吵醒整个城堡。

"快跑!"哈利大喊一声,四个人顺着走廊全速跑去,不敢回头看费尔奇是不是跟上来了——他们绕过门柱,跑过一道又一道走廊。哈利跑在最前面,他不知道他们在哪里,也不知道正往哪里跑。他们穿过一条挂毯,发现自己置身于一条密道;他们沿着密道急奔,出来后到达了魔咒课的教室附近。他们知道,这里离奖品陈列室有好几英里呢。

"我想,我们已经把他甩掉了。"哈利喘着粗气说。他靠在冰冷的墙上,擦着额头上的汗。纳威弯着身子,呼哧呼哧地喘气,连话都说不利索了。

"我——告诉过——你们,"赫敏气喘吁吁地说,用手抓住胸前的衣服,"我——告诉过——你们。"

"我们必须返回格兰芬多塔楼,"罗恩说,"越快越好。"

"马尔福骗了你,"赫敏对哈利说,"你明白了吧?他根本没打算上那儿和你会面——费尔奇知道有人要去奖品陈列室,准是马尔福向他透露了消息。"

哈利认为赫敏可能是对的,但他不想对她这么说。

"我们走吧。"

然而事情没那么简单。刚走了十来步,就听见一扇门的球形把手嘎啦啦一响,什么东西从他们面前的一间教室里蹿了出来。

是皮皮鬼。他一看见他们,就开心地尖声怪叫起来。

"闭嘴,皮皮鬼——求求你——你会害得我们被开除的。"

皮皮鬼咯咯地笑着。

"讨厌的一年级小鬼头,半夜三更到处乱逛。啧,啧,啧,淘气,淘气,

CHAPTER NINE The Midnight Duel

naughty, you'll get caughty.'

'Not if you don't give us away, Peeves, please.'

'Should tell Filch, I should,' said Peeves in a saintly voice, but his eyes glittered wickedly. 'It's for your own good, you know.'

'Get out of the way,' snapped Ron, taking a swipe at Peeves – this was a big mistake.

'STUDENTS OUT OF BED!' Peeves bellowed. 'STUDENTS OUT OF BED DOWN THE CHARMS CORRIDOR!'

Ducking under Peeves they ran for their lives, right to the end of the corridor, where they slammed into a door – and it was locked.

'This is it!' Ron moaned, as they pushed helplessly at the door. 'We're done for! This is the end!'

They could hear footsteps, Filch running as fast as he could towards Peeves's shouts.

'Oh, move over,' Hermione snarled. She grabbed Harry's wand, tapped the lock and whispered, '*Alohomora!*'

The lock clicked and the door swung open – they piled through it, shut it quickly and pressed their ears against it, listening.

'Which way did they go, Peeves?' Filch was saying. 'Quick, tell me.'

'Say "please".'

'Don't mess me about, Peeves, now *where did they go?*'

'Shan't say nothing if you don't say please,' said Peeves in his annoying sing-song voice.

'All right – *please.*'

'NOTHING! Ha haaa! Told you I wouldn't say nothing if you didn't say please! Ha ha! Haaaaaa!' And they heard the sound of Peeves whooshing away and Filch cursing in rage.

'He thinks this door is locked,' Harry whispered. 'I think we'll be OK – get *off*, Neville!' For Neville had been tugging on the sleeve of Harry's dressing-gown for the last minute. '*What?*'

Harry turned around – and saw, quite clearly, what. For a moment, he was sure he'd walked into a nightmare – this was too much, on top of everything that had happened so far.

They weren't in a room, as he had supposed. They were in a corridor.

第9章 午夜决斗

你们会被抓起来的。"

"不会的,只要你不出卖我们,皮皮鬼,求求你。"

"应该告诉费尔奇,应该。"皮皮鬼一本正经地说,但他眼睛里闪烁着调皮的光芒,"这是为你们好,知道吗?"

"滚开。"罗恩凶狠地说,使劲打了皮皮鬼一下——这就酿成了大错。

"**学生不睡觉!**"皮皮鬼吼了起来,"**学生不睡觉,在魔咒课教室的走廊里!**"

他们一低头闪过皮皮鬼,没命地逃着,一直逃到走廊尽头,重重地撞在一扇门上——门是锁着的。

"完了!"罗恩呜咽着说。他们绝望地推那扇门。"我们完蛋了!死到临头了!"

他们听见了脚步声,费尔奇正循着皮皮鬼的声音尽快赶来。

"哦,快过来。"赫敏粗暴地说。她夺过哈利的魔杖,敲了敲门锁,低声说道:"阿拉霍洞开!"

锁咔嗒一响,门突然开了——他们一拥而入,赶紧把门关上,将耳朵贴在上面,听着。

"他们往哪边跑了,皮皮鬼?"只听费尔奇说,"快,告诉我。"

"说'请'。"

"别跟我捣乱,皮皮鬼,快说,他们去哪儿了?"

"如果你不说'请',我就什么也不说。"皮皮鬼用他那恼人的连哼带唱的声调说。

"好吧——请你告诉我。"

"**什么都不知道!**哈哈!即使你说了'请',我也什么都不知道!哈哈!哈哈哈哈!"他们听见皮皮鬼飞快地离去,费尔奇恼羞成怒地咒骂着。

"他以为这扇门是锁着的,"哈利低声说,"我想我们不会有事了——走吧,纳威!"纳威一直在拉扯哈利晨衣的袖子。"怎么啦?"

哈利一转身——看见了,清清楚楚地看见了。一时间,他相信自己一定是走进了一场噩梦——在已经发生了这么多事情之后,这简直太过分了。

他们以为自己是在一个房间里,其实不然。他们是在一条走廊

CHAPTER NINE The Midnight Duel

The forbidden corridor on the third floor. And now they knew why it was forbidden.

They were looking straight into the eyes of a monstrous dog, a dog which filled the whole space between ceiling and floor. It had three heads. Three pairs of rolling, mad eyes; three noses, twitching and quivering in their direction; three drooling mouths, saliva hanging in slippery ropes from yellowish fangs.

It was standing quite still, all six eyes staring at them, and Harry knew that the only reason they weren't already dead was that their sudden appearance had taken it by surprise, but it was quickly getting over that, there was no mistaking what those thunderous growls meant.

Harry groped for the doorknob – between Filch and death, he'd take Filch.

They fell backwards – Harry slammed the door shut, and they ran, they almost flew, back down the corridor. Filch must have hurried off to look for them somewhere else because they didn't see him anywhere, but they hardly cared – all they wanted to do was put as much space as possible between them and that monster. They didn't stop running until they reached the portrait of the Fat Lady on the seventh floor.

'Where on earth have you all been?' she asked, looking at their dressing-gowns hanging off their shoulders and their flushed, sweaty faces.

'Never mind that – pig snout, pig snout,' panted Harry, and the portrait swung forward. They scrambled into the common room and collapsed, trembling, into armchairs.

It was a while before any of them said anything. Neville, indeed, looked as if he'd never speak again.

'What do they think they're doing, keeping a thing like that locked up in a school?' said Ron finally. 'If any dog needs exercise, that one does.'

Hermione had got both her breath and her bad temper back again.

'You don't use your eyes, any of you, do you?' she snapped. 'Didn't you see what it was standing on?'

'The floor?' Harry suggested. 'I wasn't looking at its feet, I was too busy with its heads.'

'No, *not* the floor. It was standing on a trapdoor. It's obviously guarding something.'

She stood up, glaring at them.

第9章 午夜决斗

里。是四楼那条禁止入内的走廊。现在他们知道这里为什么禁止入内了。

他们正面对着一条怪物般的大狗的眼睛,这条狗大得填满了从天花板到地板的所有空间。它有三个脑袋,三双滴溜溜转的凶恶的眼睛,三个鼻子——正朝他们这边抽搐、颤抖着,还有三张流着口水的嘴巴,口水像黏糊糊的绳子,从泛黄的狗牙上挂落下来。

它一动不动地站在那里,六只眼睛都盯着他们。哈利知道,他们之所以还没有死,唯一的原因就是他们的突然出现使它大吃了一惊。但它正在迅速回过神来,那一声声震耳欲聋的咆哮意味着什么,是再清楚不过的了。

哈利摸索着去拧门把手——在费尔奇和死亡之间,他宁愿选择费尔奇。

他们一步步后退——哈利砰地把门关上。他们回到走廊里,撒腿就跑,简直是在飞奔。费尔奇一定忙着到别处去寻找他们了,他们没有看见他的踪影,何况也根本顾不上了——只想尽可能远地逃离那个怪物。他们一直跑到八楼胖夫人的肖像前才停住脚步。

"你们都上哪儿去了?"胖夫人问道,看着他们从肩膀上耷拉下来的晨衣,以及大汗淋漓的通红脸庞。

"别问啦——'猪鼻子,猪鼻子'。"哈利喘着气说,肖像向前旋转着开了。他们跌跌撞撞地爬进公共休息室,浑身发抖地瘫倒在扶手椅上。

有好一会儿,谁都没有说话。纳威呢,看上去似乎永远也不会说话了。

"他们到底想干什么?把那么一个玩意儿关在学校里!"最后,罗恩说道,"如果有哪条狗需要运动,就是那条了。"

赫敏的气喘匀了,但她的坏脾气也回来了。

"你们,你们几个,长着眼睛是干什么用的?"她气冲冲地说,"你们没看见那狗站在什么上面吗?"

"地板上?"哈利猜测,"我没有看它的脚,光顾看它的脑袋了。"

"不,不是地板。它站在一个活板门上。显然是在看守什么东西。"

她站起身,愤怒地瞪着他们。

'I hope you're pleased with yourselves. We could all have been killed – or worse, expelled. Now, if you don't mind, I'm going to bed.'

Ron stared after her, his mouth open.

'No, we don't mind,' he said. 'You'd think we dragged her along, wouldn't you?'

But Hermione had given Harry something else to think about as he climbed back into bed. The dog was guarding something ... What had Hagrid said? Gringotts was the safest place in the world for something you wanted to hide – except perhaps Hogwarts.

It looked as though Harry had found out where the grubby little package from vault seven hundred and thirteen was.

第9章 午夜决斗

"但愿你们为自己感到得意。我们都差点被咬死——或者更糟,被学校开除。好了,如果你们没意见的话,我要去睡觉了。"

罗恩盯着她的背影,吃惊地张大了嘴巴。

"去睡吧,我们没意见。"他说,"这叫什么事儿?就好像我们把她硬拉去似的。"

可是,赫敏的话使哈利回到床上后又陷入了沉思。那只狗在看守着什么东西……海格是怎么说的?如果你想藏什么东西,古灵阁是世界上最安全的地方——大概除了霍格沃茨吧。

看来,哈利似乎已经弄清了713号地下金库那只脏兮兮的小包的下落。

CHAPTER TEN

Hallowe'en

Malfoy couldn't believe his eyes when he saw that Harry and Ron were still at Hogwarts next day, looking tired but perfectly cheerful. Indeed, by next morning Harry and Ron thought that meeting the three-headed dog had been an excellent adventure and they were quite keen to have another one. In the meantime, Harry filled Ron in about the package that seemed to have been moved from Gringotts to Hogwarts, and they spent a lot of time wondering what could possibly need such heavy protection.

'It's either really valuable or really dangerous,' said Ron.

'Or both,' said Harry.

But as all they knew for sure about the mysterious object was that it was about two inches long, they didn't have much chance of guessing what it was without further clues.

Neither Neville or Hermione showed the slightest interest in what lay underneath the dog and the trapdoor. All Neville cared about was never going near the dog again.

Hermione was now refusing to speak to Harry and Ron, but she was such a bossy know-it-all that they saw this as an added bonus. All they really wanted now was a way of getting back at Malfoy, and to their great delight, just such a thing arrived with the post about a week later.

As the owls flooded into the Great Hall as usual, everyone's attention was caught at once by a long thin package carried by six large screech owls. Harry was just as interested as everyone else to see what was in this large parcel and was amazed when the owls soared down and dropped it right in front of him, knocking his bacon to the floor. They had hardly fluttered out of the way when another owl dropped a letter on top of the parcel.

Harry ripped open the letter first, which was lucky, because it said:

第 10 章

万圣节前夕

第二天,马尔福简直不敢相信自己的眼睛,他看见哈利和罗恩居然还在霍格沃茨,虽然显得有些疲倦,但非常开心。确实,哈利和罗恩第二天一早醒来,都觉得看见那条三个脑袋的大狗是一次十分精彩的奇遇,巴不得再经历一次。而且,哈利原原本本地对罗恩讲了那个似乎已从古灵阁转移到霍格沃茨的小包,于是他们花了许多时间猜测,是什么东西需要这样严加看守。

"它要么特别宝贵,要么特别危险。"罗恩说。

"或者两项全占了。"哈利说。

但是,关于那个神秘物件,他们唯一能够确定的只是它的长度有两英寸。如果没有更多的线索,是不可能猜到它是什么东西的。

纳威和赫敏对于大狗和活板门下面藏着什么,似乎一点儿也不感兴趣。纳威只想着千万别再走近那条大狗。

赫敏现在不答理哈利和罗恩了。她一向自以为是,喜欢发号施令,所以他们倒觉得这是一件意外的好事。他们现在最希望的就是对马尔福进行报复。令人高兴的是,大约一个星期后,这样的机会就随着邮差一起到来了。

当猫头鹰像往常一样拥进礼堂时,每个人的注意力都被六只长耳猫头鹰驮着的那个细长包裹吸引住了。哈利和别人一样渴望知道这个包裹里是什么。没想到,几只猫头鹰盘旋而下,正好落在他面前,把他的熏咸肉碰落到了地板上。他惊讶极了。它们扑扇着翅膀刚刚飞走,又有一只猫头鹰携来一封信,扔在包裹上面。

哈利先把信撕开——幸亏他这么做了——只见信上写着:

CHAPTER TEN   Hallowe'en

DO NOT OPEN THE PARCEL AT THE TABLE.
It contains your new Nimbus Two Thousand,
but I don't want everybody knowing you've
got a broomstick or they'll all want one.
Oliver Wood will meet you tonight on the
Quidditch pitch at seven o'clock for your
first training session.

Prof. M. McGonagall

Harry had difficulty hiding his glee as he handed the note to Ron to read.

'A Nimbus Two Thousand!' Ron moaned enviously. 'I've never even *touched* one.'

They left the Hall quickly, wanting to unwrap the broomstick in private before their first lesson, but halfway across the Entrance Hall they found the way upstairs barred by Crabbe and Goyle. Malfoy seized the package from Harry and felt it.

'That's a broomstick,' he said, throwing it back to Harry with a mixture of jealousy and spite on his face. 'You'll be for it this time, Potter, first-years aren't allowed them.'

Ron couldn't resist it.

'It's not any old broomstick,' he said, 'it's a Nimbus Two Thousand. What did you say you've got at home, Malfoy, a Comet Two Sixty?' Ron grinned at Harry. 'Comets look flashy, but they're not in the same league as the Nimbus.'

'What would you know about it, Weasley, you couldn't afford half the handle,' Malfoy snapped back. 'I suppose you and your brothers have to save up, twig by twig.'

Before Ron could answer, Professor Flitwick appeared at Malfoy's elbow.

'Not arguing, I hope, boys?' he squeaked.

'Potter's been sent a broomstick, Professor,' said Malfoy quickly.

'Yes, yes, that's right,' said Professor Flitwick, beaming at Harry. 'Professor McGonagall told me all about the special circumstances, Potter. And what model is it?'

'A Nimbus Two Thousand, sir,' said Harry, fighting not to laugh at the look of horror on Malfoy's face. 'And it's really thanks to Malfoy here that I've

第 10 章 万圣节前夕

不要打开桌上的包裹。

里面装着你新的飞天扫帚光轮 2000,
我不想让大家知道你有了新扫帚,
免得他们都想要。
奥利弗·伍德今晚七点
在魁地奇球场等你,
给你上第一堂训练课。

米·麦格教授

哈利掩饰不住内心的喜悦,把短信递给了罗恩。

"光轮 2000!"罗恩羡慕地感叹道,"我连碰都没有碰过。"

他们匆匆离开礼堂,想赶在第一节课之前,找个没人的地方拆开包裹,拿出飞天扫帚。可是,就在穿过门厅时,他们发现上楼的路被克拉布和高尔挡住了。马尔福把包裹从哈利手里夺过去,摸了摸。

"是一把飞天扫帚。"他一边说,一边把包裹扔还给哈利,脸上混杂着嫉妒和怨恨的表情,"你等着挨罚吧,波特,一年级学生是不许玩这个的。"

罗恩按捺不住了。

"这不是什么旧型扫帚,"他说,"这是光轮 2000。你说你在家里有一把什么来着,马尔福?彗星 260 吧?"罗恩对哈利咧着嘴大笑,"彗星是挺耀眼的,但它们和光轮根本不是一个档次。"

"你怎么知道?韦斯莱,你连半个扫帚把都买不起。"马尔福凶巴巴地回敬道,"我猜你和你那些兄弟不得不一根枝子一根枝子地攒吧。"

罗恩还没来得及回答,弗立维教授在马尔福胳膊肘边出现了。

"我希望不是在吵架吧,孩子们?"他尖着嗓子问。

"有人给波特捎来了一把飞天扫帚,教授。"马尔福忙不迭地说。

"是啊,是啊,是这样的。"弗立维教授说着,朝哈利绽开了笑容,"麦格教授把情况的特殊性都跟我说了,波特。是什么型号的?"

"光轮 2000,先生。"哈利说。看到马尔福脸上惊恐的表情,他拼命忍着笑。"我能得到它,还多亏了这位马尔福呢。"他补充道。

CHAPTER TEN Hallowe'en

got it,' he added.

Harry and Ron headed upstairs, smothering their laughter at Malfoy's obvious rage and confusion.

'Well, it's true,' Harry chortled as they reached the top of the marble staircase. 'If he hadn't stolen Neville's Remembrall I wouldn't be in the team …'

'So I suppose you think that's a reward for breaking rules?' came an angry voice from just behind them. Hermione was stomping up the stairs looking disapprovingly at the package in Harry's hand.

'I thought you weren't speaking to us?' said Harry.

'Yes, don't stop now,' said Ron, 'it's doing us so much good.'

Hermione marched away with her nose in the air.

Harry had a lot of trouble keeping his mind on his lessons that day. It kept wandering up to the dormitory, where his new broomstick was lying under his bed, or straying off to the Quidditch pitch where he'd be learning to play that night. He bolted his dinner that evening without noticing what he was eating and then rushed upstairs with Ron to unwrap the Nimbus Two Thousand at last.

'Wow,' Ron sighed, as the broomstick rolled on to Harry's bedspread.

Even Harry, who knew nothing about the different brooms, thought it looked wonderful. Sleek and shiny, with a mahogany handle, it had a long tail of neat, straight twigs and *Nimbus Two Thousand* written in gold near the top.

As seven o'clock drew nearer, Harry left the castle and set off towards the Quidditch pitch in the dusk. He'd never been inside the stadium before. Hundreds of seats were raised in stands around the pitch so that the spectators were high enough to see what was going on. At either end of the pitch were three golden poles with hoops on the end. They reminded Harry of the little plastic sticks Muggle children blew bubbles through, except that they were fifty feet high.

Too eager to fly again to wait for Wood, Harry mounted his broomstick and kicked off from the ground. What a feeling – he swooped in and out of the goalposts and then sped up and down the pitch. The Nimbus Two Thousand turned wherever he wanted at his lightest touch.

'Hey, Potter, come down!'

Oliver Wood had arrived. He was carrying a large wooden crate under his arm. Harry landed next to him.

第10章 万圣节前夕

哈利和罗恩往楼上走去。他们看到马尔福那明显愤怒和迷惑的样子，不得不使劲把笑忍住。

"真的，我说的是实话，"来到大理石楼梯顶上时，哈利咯咯地笑着说，"如果不是他抢了纳威的玻璃球，我就进不了球队……"

"所以你认为这是对你违反校规的奖励？"他们俩身后传来一个愤怒的声音。赫敏噔噔地走上楼来，不满地看着哈利手里的包裹。

"我还以为你不跟我们说话了呢。"哈利说。

"是啊，现在也别说，"罗恩说，"这使我们感到很舒服。"

赫敏大踏步地走开了，鼻子扬得高高的。

那天，哈利很难定下心来认真听课。他的思绪不住地飞向宿舍，那把新的飞天扫帚就躺在他的床底下。他还不时地想到今晚就要去训练的魁地奇球场。晚饭时他三口两口咽下食物，根本没有注意吃的是什么，然后就和罗恩一起迅速奔上了楼梯，终于可以打开光轮2000了。

"哇！"当扫帚滚落在哈利的床单上时，罗恩惊叹道。

就连对飞天扫帚的种类一无所知的哈利，也认为这把扫帚简直太棒了：线条优美，富有光泽，把是红木的，长长的尾巴用整齐、笔直的枝子扎成，光轮2000几个字金灿灿地印在扫帚把的顶端。

七点钟越来越近了，哈利离开城堡，朝暮色中的魁地奇球场走去。几百把椅子高高地排放在周围的看台上，每一位观众都能看见球场上的情况。球场两端各有三根金色的杆子，顶上带着圆环。它们使哈利想起麻瓜小孩子们吹肥皂泡用的小塑料棍，只是这些杆子每根都有五十英尺高。

哈利太想再飞上天去了。他等不及伍德，便骑上扫帚，双脚一蹬离开地面。多么美妙的滋味——他快速地在球门柱间穿梭，又在球场上空忽上忽下地飞翔。他只需轻轻一碰，光轮2000就转向他需要的方向。

"喂，波特，下来！"

是奥利弗·伍德来了。他胳膊底下夹着一个很大的板条箱。哈利降落在他旁边。

CHAPTER TEN — Hallowe'en

'Very nice,' said Wood, his eyes glinting. 'I see what McGonagall meant ... you really are a natural. I'm just going to teach you the rules this evening, then you'll be joining team practice three times a week.'

He opened the crate. Inside were four different-sized balls.

'Right,' said Wood. 'Now, Quidditch is easy enough to understand, even if it's not too easy to play. There are seven players on each side. Three of them are called Chasers.'

'Three Chasers,' Harry repeated, as Wood took out a bright red ball about the size of a football.

'This ball's called the Quaffle,' said Wood. 'The Chasers throw the Quaffle to each other and try and get it through one of the hoops to score a goal. Ten points every time the Quaffle goes through one of the hoops. Follow me?'

'The Chasers throw the Quaffle and put it through the hoops to score,' Harry recited. 'So – that's sort of like basketball on broomsticks with six hoops, isn't it?'

'What's basketball?' said Wood curiously.

'Never mind,' said Harry quickly.

'Now, there's another player on each side who's called the Keeper – I'm Keeper for Gryffindor. I have to fly around our hoops and stop the other team from scoring.'

'Three Chasers, one Keeper,' said Harry, who was determined to remember it all. 'And they play with the Quaffle. OK, got that. So what are they for?' He pointed at the three balls left inside the box.

'I'll show you now,' said Wood. 'Take this.'

He handed Harry a small club, a bit like a rounders bat.

'I'm going to show you what the Bludgers do,' Wood said. 'These two are the Bludgers.'

He showed Harry two identical balls, jet black and slightly smaller than the red Quaffle. Harry noticed that they seemed to be straining to escape the straps holding them inside the box.

'Stand back,' Wood warned Harry. He bent down and freed one of the Bludgers.

At once, the black ball rose high in the air and then pelted straight at Harry's face. Harry swung at it with the bat to stop it breaking his nose and sent it zigzagging away into the air – it zoomed around their heads and then

第 10 章　万圣节前夕

"非常精彩。"伍德说,眼睛闪闪发亮,"我明白麦格教授的意思了……你确实是个天才。我今晚把规则教给你,然后你就可以参加队里每周三次的训练了。"

他打开板条箱,里面是四个大小不等的球。

"好,"伍德说,"是这样,魁地奇球的规则很容易理解,不过玩起来可不容易。每边七个人,其中三个是追球手。"

"三个追球手。"哈利重复道,这时伍德拿出一个足球那么大的鲜红的球。

"这个球叫鬼飞球。"伍德说,"追球手互相传递鬼飞球,争取让它通过其中一个圆环,这样便能得分。鬼飞球每次通过一个圆环,就可以得十分。明白了吗?"

"追球手把鬼飞球投出去,让它穿过圆环,便能得分了。"哈利复述道,"这么说——这是一种用飞天扫帚和六个圆环玩的篮球,是吗?"

"篮球是什么?"伍德好奇地问。

"没什么。"哈利赶紧说。

"好吧,每边还有另一个队员,叫守门员——我就是格兰芬多队的守门员。我必须在我们的圆环周围飞来飞去,不让对方得分。"

"三个追球手,一个守门员。"哈利说,决心把这些都记在心里,"他们打的是鬼飞球。行,明白了。那么这些是做什么用的?"他指着留在箱子里的另外三个球问。

"我现在就演示给你看。"伍德说,"你拿着这个。"

他递给哈利一根小木棒,有点像跑柱式棒球的球棒。

"我来让你看看游走球是做什么用的。"伍德说,"这两个就是游走球。"

他拿出两个一模一样的球给哈利看,它们黑得发亮,比刚才的红色鬼飞球略小一些。哈利注意到,它们似乎在拼命挣扎,想摆脱把它们束缚在箱子里的皮带。

"往后站。"伍德提醒哈利。他弯下腰,松开了一个游走球。

顿时,那个黑球嗖地蹿上半空,然后径直朝哈利脸上打来。哈利眼看它要撞碎自己的鼻子,赶紧用短棒拦截,打得它重新左拐右拐地蹿向

shot at Wood, who dived on top of it and managed to pin it to the ground.

'See?' Wood panted, forcing the struggling Bludger back into the crate and strapping it down safely. 'The Bludgers rocket around trying to knock players off their brooms. That's why you have two Beaters on each team. The Weasley twins are ours – it's their job to protect their side from the Bludgers and try and knock them towards the other team. So – think you've got all that?'

'Three Chasers try and score with the Quaffle; the Keeper guards the goalposts; the Beaters keep the Bludgers away from their team,' Harry reeled off.

'Very good,' said Wood.

'Er – have the Bludgers ever killed anyone?' Harry asked, hoping he sounded offhand.

'Never at Hogwarts. We've had a couple of broken jaws but nothing worse than that. Now, the last member of the team is the Seeker. That's you. And you don't have to worry about the Quaffle or the Bludgers –'

'– unless they crack my head open.'

'Don't worry, the Weasleys are more than a match for the Bludgers – I mean, they're like a pair of human Bludgers themselves.'

Wood reached into the crate and took out the fourth and last ball. Compared with the Quaffle and the Bludgers, it was tiny, about the size of a large walnut. It was bright gold and had little fluttering silver wings.

'*This*,' said Wood, 'is the Golden Snitch, and it's the most important ball of the lot. It's very hard to catch because it's so fast and difficult to see. It's the Seeker's job to catch it. You've got to weave in and out of the Chasers, Beaters, Bludgers and Quaffle to get it before the other team's Seeker, because whichever Seeker catches the Snitch wins his team an extra hundred and fifty points, so they nearly always win. That's why Seekers get fouled so much. A game of Quidditch only ends when the Snitch is caught, so it can go on for ages – I think the record is three months, they had to keep bringing on substitutes so the players could get some sleep.

'Well, that's it – any questions?'

Harry shook his head. He understood what he had to do all right, it was doing it that was going to be the problem.

'We won't practise with the Snitch yet,' said Wood, carefully shutting it

第 10 章 万圣节前夕

空中——在他们头顶上呼呼盘旋,又突然朝伍德冲来。伍德猛地伸手罩住它,把它牢牢按在地面上。

"看到了吧?"伍德喘着气说,一边使劲把游走球塞进板条箱,用皮带结结实实地拴好,"游走球飞来蹿去,想把球员们从飞天扫帚上打落。所以,每一边还有两个击球手。韦斯莱孪生兄弟就是我们队的击球手——他们的工作是保护我方球员不被游走球打中,并把游走球击向对方球员。所以——你都听明白了吧?"

"三个追球手争取用鬼飞球得分;守门员看守球门柱;击球手不让游走球撞伤自己的队员。"哈利一口气说道。

"很好。"伍德说。

"嗯——游走球有没有打死过人?"哈利问,希望他的口气显得随便。

"在霍格沃茨从来没有。有一两个人被撞碎了下巴,仅此而已。好了,球队里的最后一名球员是找球手。那就是你。你不用去管鬼飞球和游走球——"

"——除非它们把我的脑袋撞开了花。"

"不用担心,韦斯莱兄弟对付游走球绰绰有余——说实在的,他们自己就像两个游走球。"

伍德又把手伸进板条箱,拿出第四个也是最后一个球。这个球与鬼飞球和游走球相比,显得很小,约莫只有一个胡桃那么大。它金灿灿的,还有不断扇动着的银色小翅膀。

"这个,"伍德说,"就是金色飞贼,是所有球当中最重要的。你很难抓住它,它飞得像闪电一般快,根本看不清。找球手的工作就是要把它抓住。你必须在追球手、击球手、游走球和鬼飞球之间来回穿梭,赶在对方找球手之前把它抓住。如果哪个队的找球手抓住了金色飞贼,他的队就能额外赢得一百五十分,差不多就是稳操胜券了。只有当金色飞贼被抓住时,魁地奇比赛才算结束,所以有时候一场比赛会持续好多日子——我想最高纪录大概是三个月吧,他们不得不找替补队员上场,把球员换下来睡一会儿觉。

"行了,就是这样——还有问题吗?"

哈利摇了摇头。他明白自己该做什么了,但究竟能不能做好还是问题。

"我们先不拿飞贼来训练,"伍德说着,小心地把金色飞贼放进箱子

CHAPTER TEN Hallowe'en

back inside the crate. 'It's too dark, we might lose it. Let's try you out with a few of these.'

He pulled a bag of ordinary golf balls out of his pocket, and a few minutes later, he and Harry were up in the air, Wood throwing the golf balls as hard as he could in every direction for Harry to catch.

Harry didn't miss a single one, and Wood was delighted. After half an hour, night had really fallen and they couldn't carry on.

'That Quidditch Cup'll have our name on it this year,' said Wood happily as they trudged back up to the castle. 'I wouldn't be surprised if you turn out better than Charlie Weasley, and he could have played for England if he hadn't gone off chasing dragons.'

* * *

Perhaps it was because he was now so busy, what with Quidditch practice three evenings a week on top of all his homework, but Harry could hardly believe it when he realised that he'd already been at Hogwarts two months. The castle felt more like home than Privet Drive had ever done. His lessons, too, were becoming more and more interesting now that they had mastered the basics.

On Hallowe'en morning they woke to the delicious smell of baking pumpkin wafting through the corridors. Even better, Professor Flitwick announced in Charms that he thought they were ready to start making objects fly, something they had all been dying to try since they'd seen him make Neville's toad zoom around the classroom. Professor Flitwick put the class into pairs to practise. Harry's partner was Seamus Finnigan (which was a relief, because Neville had been trying to catch his eye). Ron, however, was to be working with Hermione Granger. It was hard to tell whether Ron or Hermione was angrier about this. She hadn't spoken to either of them since the day Harry's broomstick had arrived.

'Now, don't forget that nice wrist movement we've been practising!' squeaked Professor Flitwick, perched on top of his pile of books as usual. 'Swish and flick, remember, swish and flick. And saying the magic words properly is very important, too – never forget Wizard Baruffio, who said "s" instead of "f" and found himself on the floor with a buffalo on his chest.'

It was very difficult. Harry and Seamus swished and flicked, but the feather they were supposed to be sending skywards just lay on the desktop.

第10章 万圣节前夕

里关了起来,"天太黑了,会把它弄丢的。就用几个这样的球让你训练吧。"

他从口袋里掏出一袋普通的高尔夫球,几分钟后,他和哈利就到了空中。伍德使出吃奶的力气,把高尔夫球掷往各个方向,让哈利去接。

哈利百发百中,一个球都没有漏过,伍德非常高兴。过了半小时,天完全黑透了,他们无法再训练了。

"今年的魁地奇杯上将刻上我们的名字。"当他们疲倦地走回城堡时,伍德兴高采烈地说,"如果你表现得比查理·韦斯莱还要出色,我一点儿也不会吃惊。他要是没去研究火龙,肯定会代表英格兰队参赛的。"

也许是因为现在太忙了——除了各门功课的家庭作业,还有每周三个晚上的魁地奇训练——哈利突然意识到自己在霍格沃茨已经整整待了两个月,感到简直难以置信。城堡一天比一天更像家了,而他在女贞路时从来没有过这样的感觉。当掌握了一些基础知识之后,功课也变得越来越有趣了。

万圣节前夕,他们一早醒来,就闻到走廊里飘着一股香甜诱人的烤南瓜的气味。更妙的是,弗立维教授在魔咒课上宣布,他认为他们可以开始使物体飞起来了。同学们自从看见弗立维教授把纳威的蟾蜍弄得在教室里到处乱飞之后,就一直眼巴巴地希望尝试一下这种技能。弗立维教授把全班同学分成两个人一组开始训练。哈利的搭档是西莫·斐尼甘(谢天谢地,因为纳威一直想引起哈利的注意)。而罗恩呢,要和赫敏·格兰杰一起合作。关于这件事,很难说清罗恩和赫敏谁更加恼火一点儿。赫敏自从哈利的飞天扫帚送到的那天起,就一直不跟他们俩说话。

"好了,千万不要忘记我们一直在训练的那个微妙的手腕动作!"弗立维教授像往常一样站在他的那堆书上,尖声说道,"一挥一抖,记住,一挥一抖。念准咒语也非常重要——千万别忘了巴鲁费奥巫师,他把'f'说成了's',结果发现自己躺在地板上,胸口上站着一头水牛。"

做起来很不容易。哈利和西莫一挥一抖,一挥一抖,做了一遍又一遍,但应该被他们送上空中的羽毛还是一动不动地躺在地板上。西莫一气之下,用魔杖朝羽毛一捅,羽毛着火了——哈利不得不用他的帽子将

CHAPTER TEN   Hallowe'en

Seamus got so impatient that he prodded it with his wand and set fire to it – Harry had to put it out with his hat.

Ron, at the next table, wasn't having much more luck.

'*Wingardium Leviosa*!' he shouted, waving his long arms like a windmill.

'You're saying it wrong,' Harry heard Hermione snap. 'It's Wing-*gar*-dium Levi-*o*-sa, make the "gar" nice and long.'

'You do it, then, if you're so clever,' Ron snarled.

Hermione rolled up the sleeves of her gown, flicked her wand and said, '*Wingardium Leviosa*!'

Their feather rose off the desk and hovered about four feet above their heads.

'Oh, well done!' cried Professor Flitwick, clapping. 'Everyone see here, Miss Granger's done it!'

Ron was in a very bad temper by the end of the class.

'It's no wonder no one can stand her,' he said to Harry as they pushed their way into the crowded corridor. 'She's a nightmare, honestly.'

Someone knocked into Harry as they hurried past him. It was Hermione. Harry caught a glimpse of her face – and was startled to see that she was in tears.

'I think she heard you.'

'So?' said Ron, but he looked a bit uncomfortable. 'She must've noticed she's got no friends.'

Hermione didn't turn up for the next class and wasn't seen all afternoon. On their way down to the Great Hall for the Hallowe'en feast, Harry and Ron overheard Parvati Patil telling her friend Lavender that Hermione was crying in the girls' toilets and wanted to be left alone. Ron looked still more awkward at this, but a moment later they had entered the Great Hall, where the Hallowe'en decorations put Hermione out of their minds.

A thousand live bats fluttered from the walls and ceiling while a thousand more swooped over the tables in low black clouds, making the candles in the pumpkins stutter. The feast appeared suddenly on the golden plates, as it had at the start-of-term banquet.

Harry was just helping himself to a jacket potato when Professor Quirrell came sprinting into the Hall, his turban askew and terror on his face. Everyone stared as he reached Professor Dumbledore's chair, slumped

火扑灭。

在另一个桌子上的罗恩,运气似乎也好不到哪里去。

"羽加迪姆 勒维奥萨!"他大声喊道,一边像风车一样挥动着两条长长的手臂。

"你说错了,"哈利听见赫敏毫不客气地说,"是羽加——迪姆 勒维——奥——萨,那个'加'字要说得又长又清楚。"

"既然你这么机灵,你倒来试试看。"罗恩咆哮着说。

赫敏卷起衣袖,挥动着魔杖,说道:"羽加迪姆 勒维奥萨!"

他们的那根羽毛从桌上升了起来,飘悬在头顶上方四英尺的地方。

"哦,做得好!"弗立维教授拍着手喊道,"大家快看,格兰杰小姐已经成功了!"

到了快下课时,罗恩的情绪坏到了极点。

"怪不得大家都受不了她,"他对哈利说,这时他们正在拥挤的走廊里费力地穿行,"说实在的,她简直就像一个噩梦。"

有人撞了哈利一下,又匆匆地从他们身边走了过去。是赫敏。哈利瞥见了她的脸——惊讶地发现她在掉眼泪。

"我想她听见你的话了。"

"那又怎么样?"罗恩说,但也显出了一丝不安,"她一定已经注意到了,她一个朋友也没有。"

下一节课赫敏没有露面,而且整个下午都不见人影。哈利和罗恩下楼走向礼堂,去参加万圣节前夕的宴会,无意间听见帕瓦蒂·佩蒂尔对她的朋友拉文德说,赫敏在女盥洗室里伤心地哭泣,还不让别人安慰她。罗恩听了这话,显得更不自在了。然而片刻之后,当他们走进礼堂、看见五光十色的万圣节装饰品时,立刻就把赫敏忘到了脑后。

一千只蝙蝠在墙壁和天花板上扑棱棱地飞翔,另外还有一千只蝙蝠像一团团低矮的乌云,在餐桌上方盘旋飞舞,使南瓜肚里的蜡烛火苗一阵阵扑闪。美味佳肴突然出现在金色的盘子里,就跟那次开学时的宴会上一样。

哈利正在吃一个带皮的土豆,奇洛教授突然一头冲进了礼堂,他的大围巾歪戴在头上,脸上满是惊恐。大家都盯着他,只见他走到邓布利多教授的椅子旁,一歪身倚在桌上,喘着气说:"巨怪——在地下教室

CHAPTER TEN   Hallowe'en

against the table and gasped, 'Troll – in the dungeons – thought you ought to know.'

He then sank to the floor in a dead faint.

There was uproar. It took several purple firecrackers exploding from the end of Professor Dumbledore's wand to bring silence.

'Prefects,' he rumbled, 'lead your houses back to the dormitories immediately!'

Percy was in his element.

'Follow me! Stick together, first-years! No need to fear the troll if you follow my orders! Stay close behind me, now. Make way, first-years coming through! Excuse me, I'm a Prefect!'

'How could a troll get in?' Harry asked as they climbed the stairs.

'Don't ask me, they're supposed to be really stupid,' said Ron. 'Maybe Peeves let it in for a Hallowe'en joke.'

They passed different groups of people hurrying in different directions. As they jostled their way through a crowd of confused Hufflepuffs, Harry suddenly grabbed Ron's arm.

'I've just thought – Hermione.'

'What about her?'

'She doesn't know about the troll.'

Ron bit his lip.

'Oh, all right,' he snapped. 'But Percy'd better not see us.'

Ducking down, they joined the Hufflepuffs going the other way, slipped down a deserted side corridor and hurried off towards the girls' toilets. They had just turned the corner when they heard quick footsteps behind them.

'Percy!' hissed Ron, pulling Harry behind a large stone griffin.

Peering around it, however, they saw not Percy but Snape. He crossed the corridor and disappeared from view.

'What's he doing?' Harry whispered. 'Why isn't he down in the dungeons with the rest of the teachers?'

'Search me.'

Quietly as possible, they crept along the next corridor after Snape's fading footsteps.

里——以为你应该知道的。"

说完，他一头栽倒在地板上，昏了过去。

礼堂里顿时乱成一团。邓布利多教授不得不让他的魔杖头上爆出几次紫色的烟火，大家才安静下来。

"级长，"他声音低沉地说，"立刻把各学院的学生领到宿舍去！"

珀西自然是驾轻就熟。

"跟我来！不要走散，一年级学生！只要你们听我的吩咐，就不用害怕什么巨怪！好了，紧紧跟在我后面。让一让，一年级学生要过去！请原谅，我是级长！"

"巨怪怎么能钻进来呢？"他们上楼梯时，哈利问道。

"不要问我，巨怪应该都傻得出奇，"罗恩说，"也许是皮皮鬼把它放进来的，为了给万圣节前夕增加一点儿乐子。"

路上，他们遇到了一些匆匆赶往不同方向的人群。当他们费力挤过一堆神情困惑的赫奇帕奇学院的学生时，哈利猛地抓住了罗恩的手臂。

"我刚想起来——赫敏。"

"她怎么啦？"

"她还不知道巨怪的事。"

罗恩咬着嘴唇。

"噢，好吧，"他果断地说，"但最好别让珀西看见我们。"

他们埋下身子，混在赫奇帕奇的人群里，朝另一个方向走去。他们悄悄溜过一条空荡荡的侧廊，急匆匆地赶往女盥洗室。刚转过拐角，就听见身后传来了急促的脚步声。

"珀西！"罗恩压低声音说，拉着哈利躲到一个很大的狮身鹰首兽的石雕后面。

他们从石雕后面望过去，却发现不是珀西，而是斯内普。他穿过走廊，从他们的视线中消失了。

"他在做什么？"哈利低声问道，"为什么不和其他老师一起，待在下面的地下教室里？"

"我怎么知道！"

他们跟着斯内普渐渐远去的脚步声，悄悄顺着另一道走廊向前走，尽量不发出声音。

CHAPTER TEN Hallowe'en

'He's heading for the third floor,' Harry said, but Ron held up his hand.

'Can you smell something?'

Harry sniffed and a foul stench reached his nostrils, a mixture of old socks and the kind of public toilet no one seems to clean.

And then they heard it – a low grunting and the shuffling footfalls of gigantic feet. Ron pointed: at the end of a passage to the left, something huge was moving towards them. They shrank into the shadows and watched as it emerged into a patch of moonlight.

It was a horrible sight. Twelve feet tall, its skin was a dull, granite grey, its great lumpy body like a boulder with its small bald head perched on top like a coconut. It had short legs thick as tree trunks with flat, horny feet. The smell coming from it was incredible. It was holding a huge wooden club, which dragged along the floor because its arms were so long.

The troll stopped next to a doorway and peered inside. It waggled its long ears, making up its tiny mind, then slouched slowly into the room.

'The key's in the lock,' Harry muttered. 'We could lock it in.'

'Good idea,' said Ron nervously.

They edged towards the open door, mouths dry, praying the troll wasn't about to come out of it. With one great leap, Harry managed to grab the key, slam the door and lock it.

'*Yes!*'

Flushed with their victory they started to run back up the passage, but as they reached the corner they heard something that made their hearts stop – a high, petrified scream – and it was coming from the chamber they'd just locked up.

'Oh, no,' said Ron, pale as the Bloody Baron.

'It's the girls' toilets!' Harry gasped.

'*Hermione!*' they said together.

It was the last thing they wanted to do, but what choice did they have? Wheeling around they sprinted back to the door and turned the key, fumbling in their panic – Harry pulled the door open – they ran inside.

Hermione Granger was shrinking against the wall opposite, looking as if she was about to faint. The troll was advancing on her, knocking the sinks off the walls as it went.

'Confuse it!' Harry said desperately to Ron, and seizing a tap he threw it

第 10 章 万圣节前夕

"他在朝四楼走呢。"哈利说,但是罗恩举起了手。

"你能闻到什么吗?"

哈利吸了吸鼻子,一股恶臭钻进了他的鼻孔,那是一种臭袜子和从来无人打扫的公共盥洗室混合在一起的气味。

接着他们听见了——一阵低沉的嘟哝声和巨大的脚掌拖在地上走路的声音。罗恩注意到,在左边一条通道的尽头,一个庞然大物正在向这边移动。他们赶紧退缩到暗处,注视着它慢慢走进一片月光。

那景象十分恐怖。巨怪有十二英尺高,皮肤暗淡无光,像花岗岩一般灰乎乎的,庞大而蠢笨的身体如同一块巨大的岩石,上面顶着一个椰子般光秃秃的小脑袋。它的短腿粗壮得像树桩,下面是扁平的、粗硬起茧的大脚。它身上散发出的那股臭味令人作呕。巨怪手里抓着一根粗大的木棒,由于它的手臂很长,木棒在地上拖着。

巨怪停在一个门边,朝里面窥视。它摆动着长耳朵,用它的小脑袋做出了决定,然后垂下头,慢慢钻进了房间。

"钥匙在锁眼里呢,"哈利喃喃地低语,"我们可以把它锁在里面。"

"好主意。"罗恩紧张地说。

他们侧着身子走向敞开的门,觉得嘴里发干,一心只希望巨怪不要突然跑出来。哈利大步一跳,把钥匙抓在手里,猛地撞上门,牢牢锁住。

"成了!"

他们因为得手而兴奋得满脸通红,开始顺着通道往回跑,可是,刚跑到拐弯处,就听见了一个几乎使他们心脏停止跳动的声音——一个凄厉的、惊恐万状的声音——是从他们刚刚锁上的房间里传出来的。

"哦,糟糕。"罗恩说,脸色苍白得像是血人巴罗。

"那是女盥洗室!"哈利连气都透不过来了。

"赫敏!"两人同时说道。

他们真不愿再回去,可还有什么别的选择呢?他们猛一转身,奔回那扇门,拧动钥匙,因为紧张而笨手笨脚——哈利拉开门——两人冲了进去。

赫敏·格兰杰缩在对面的墙边,似乎随时都有可能晕倒。巨怪正在朝她逼近,它一边走,一边把水池撞得与墙脱开了。

"把它搞糊涂!"哈利孤注一掷地对罗恩说,一边抓起一个水龙头,

CHAPTER TEN Hallowe'en

as hard as he could against the wall.

The troll stopped a few feet from Hermione. It lumbered around, blinking stupidly, to see what had made the noise. Its mean little eyes saw Harry. It hesitated, then made for him instead, lifting its club as it went.

'Oy, pea-brain!' yelled Ron from the other side of the chamber, and he threw a metal pipe at it. The troll didn't even seem to notice the pipe hitting its shoulder, but it heard the yell and paused again, turning its ugly snout towards Ron instead, giving Harry time to run around it.

'Come on, run, *run*!' Harry yelled at Hermione, trying to pull her towards the door, but she couldn't move, she was still flat against the wall, her mouth open with terror.

The shouting and the echoes seemed to be driving the troll berserk. It roared again and started towards Ron, who was nearest and had no way to escape.

Harry then did something that was both very brave and very stupid: he took a great running jump and managed to fasten his arms around the troll's neck from behind. The troll couldn't feel Harry hanging there, but even a troll will notice if you stick a long bit of wood up its nose, and Harry's wand had still been in his hand when he'd jumped – it had gone straight up one of the troll's nostrils.

Howling with pain, the troll twisted and flailed its club, with Harry clinging on for dear life; any second, the troll was going to rip him off or catch him a terrible blow with the club.

Hermione had sunk to the floor in fright; Ron pulled out his own wand – not knowing what he was going to do he heard himself cry the first spell that came into his head: '*Wingardium Leviosa!*'

The club flew suddenly out of the troll's hand, rose high, high up into the air, turned slowly over – and dropped, with a sickening crack, on to its owner's head. The troll swayed on the spot and then fell flat on its face, with a thud that made the whole room tremble.

Harry got to his feet. He was shaking and out of breath. Ron was standing there with his wand still raised, staring at what he had done.

It was Hermione who spoke first.

'Is it – dead?'

'I don't think so,' said Harry. 'I think it's just been knocked out.'

使劲朝墙上扔去。

巨怪在离赫敏几步远的地方停住了。它笨拙地转过身,愚蠢地眨巴着眼睛,想看清声音是什么东西发出来的。那双丑陋的小眼睛看见了哈利。它迟疑了一下,然后便朝哈利走来,一边举起手里的木棒。

"嘿,大笨蛋!"罗恩从房间的另一边喊道,同时把一根金属管朝巨怪扔去。巨怪似乎根本没注意金属管打中了它的肩膀,但它听见了喊声,便又停住脚步,把丑陋的大鼻子转向了罗恩,哈利趁此机会绕到它的身后。

"过来,快跑,快跑!"哈利朝赫敏喊道,想把她拉向门口,但是赫敏动弹不得,仍然紧紧贴在墙上,嘴巴惊恐地张得老大。

喊声和回音似乎把巨怪逼得发狂了。它又咆哮了一声,开始向罗恩逼近。罗恩离巨怪最近,而且没有退路。

这时,哈利做了一件非常勇敢但又十分愚蠢的事:他猛地向前一跳,用双臂从后面搂住了巨怪的脖子。巨怪是不会感觉到哈利吊在它身上的,但如果你把一根长长的木头插进巨怪的鼻子,它就不可能毫无感觉了。哈利在跳起时手里拿着魔杖——它径直插进了巨怪的一个鼻孔。

巨怪痛苦地吼叫起来,扭动着身子,连连挥舞手里的木棒,哈利死死地搂住巨怪不放;巨怪随时都会把哈利甩下来,然后抓住他,用木棒给他可怕的一击。

赫敏吓呆了,扑通一声瘫倒在地板上;罗恩抽出自己的魔杖——他正不知道该怎么办呢,却听见自己喊出了脑子里想到的第一句咒语:"羽加迪姆 勒维奥萨!"

木棒突然从巨怪手里飞出,高高地、高高地升向空中,又慢慢地转了个身——落下来,敲在它主人的头上,发出惊天动地的一声爆响。巨怪原地摇摆了一下,面朝下倒在地板上,轰隆一声,把整个房间都震得发抖。

哈利爬起身。他浑身颤抖,气喘吁吁。罗恩站在那里,瞪眼看着自己所做的事情,魔杖还高高地举在手里。

最后是赫敏先开口说话了。

"它——死了吗?"

"我认为没有,"哈利说,"大概只是被打昏了。"

CHAPTER TEN   Hallowe'en

He bent down and pulled his wand out of the troll's nose. It was covered in what looked like lumpy grey glue.

'Urgh – troll bogies.'

He wiped it on the troll's trousers.

A sudden slamming and loud footsteps made the three of them look up. They hadn't realised what a racket they had been making, but of course, someone downstairs must have heard the crashes and the troll's roars. A moment later, Professor McGonagall had come bursting into the room, closely followed by Snape, with Quirrell bringing up the rear. Quirrell took one look at the troll, let out a faint whimper and sat quickly down on a toilet, clutching his heart.

Snape bent over the troll. Professor McGonagall was looking at Ron and Harry. Harry had never seen her look so angry. Her lips were white. Hopes of winning fifty points for Gryffindor faded quickly from Harry's mind.

'What on earth were you thinking of?' said Professor McGonagall, with cold fury in her voice. Harry looked at Ron, who was still standing with his wand in the air. 'You're lucky you weren't killed. Why aren't you in your dormitory?'

Snape gave Harry a swift, piercing look. Harry looked at the floor. He wished Ron would put his wand down.

Then a small voice came out of the shadows.

'Please, Professor McGonagall – they were looking for me.'

'Miss Granger!'

Hermione had managed to get to her feet at last.

'I went looking for the troll because I – I thought I could deal with it on my own – you know, because I've read all about them.'

Ron dropped his wand. Hermione Granger, telling a downright lie to a teacher?

'If they hadn't found me, I'd be dead now. Harry stuck his wand up its nose and Ron knocked it out with its own club. They didn't have time to come and fetch anyone. It was about to finish me off when they arrived.'

Harry and Ron tried to look as though this story wasn't new to them.

'Well – in that case ...' said Professor McGonagall, staring at the three of them. 'Miss Granger, you foolish girl, how could you think of tackling a mountain troll on your own?'

第 10 章 万圣节前夕

他弯下腰,从巨怪的鼻子里拔出自己的魔杖,那上面沾着一大块一大块灰色的胶状物质。

"呸——巨怪的鼻屎。"

他把魔杖在巨怪的裤子上擦了擦。

突然传来一阵猛烈的撞门声和响亮的脚步声,房间里的三个人都抬起头来。他们没有意识到刚才闹出了多么大的动静,一定是楼下的人听见了剧烈的碰撞和巨怪的吼叫。片刻之后,麦格教授冲进了盥洗室,后面紧跟着斯内普,奇洛在最后。奇洛只朝巨怪看了一眼,就发出一阵无力的抽泣,坐在一个抽水马桶上,紧紧地攥住了自己的胸口。

斯内普弯腰去看巨怪。麦格教授看着罗恩和哈利。哈利从没有见过她这么生气的样子。她嘴唇煞白。为格兰芬多赢得五十分的希望迅速从哈利脑海中消失了。

"你们到底在玩什么鬼把戏?"麦格教授说,声音里带着冷冰冰的愤怒。哈利看着罗恩,只见他仍然高举着魔杖站在那里。"算你们走运,没有被它弄死。你们为什么不老老实实待在宿舍里?"

斯内普用逼人的目光迅速剜了哈利一眼。哈利看着地上,他希望罗恩赶紧把魔杖放下来。

这时,阴影里传来一个低低的声音。

"请别这样,麦格教授——他们是在找我。"

"格兰杰小姐!"

赫敏终于挣扎着站了起来。

"我来找巨怪,因为我——我以为我能独自对付它——你知道,因为我在书里读到过它们,对它们很了解。"

罗恩放下了魔杖。赫敏·格兰杰对一位老师撒下了弥天大谎?

"如果他们没有找到我,我现在肯定已经死了。哈利把他的魔杖插进了巨怪的鼻孔,罗恩用巨怪自己的木棒把它打昏了过去。他们来不及去找人。他们赶来的时候,巨怪正要把我一口吞掉。"

哈利和罗恩竭力装出一副早已熟悉这个故事的样子。

"噢——如果是这样……"麦格教授注视着他们,沉吟道,"格兰杰小姐,你这个傻姑娘,怎么能认为你独自就能对付一个大山般的巨怪呢?"

CHAPTER TEN Hallowe'en

Hermione hung her head. Harry was speechless. Hermione was the last person to do anything against the rules, and here she was, pretending she had, to get them out of trouble. It was as if Snape had started handing out sweets.

'Miss Granger, five points will be taken from Gryffindor for this,' said Professor McGonagall. 'I'm very disappointed in you. If you're not hurt at all, you'd better get off to Gryffindor Tower. Students are finishing the feast in their houses.'

Hermione left.

Professor McGonagall turned to Harry and Ron.

'Well, I still say you were lucky, but not many first-years could have taken on a full-grown mountain troll. You each win Gryffindor five points. Professor Dumbledore will be informed of this. You may go.'

They hurried out of the chamber and didn't speak at all until they had climbed two floors up. It was a relief to be away from the smell of the troll, quite apart from anything else.

'We should have got more than ten points,' Ron grumbled.

'Five, you mean, once she's taken off Hermione's.'

'Good of her to get us out of trouble like that,' Ron admitted. 'Mind you, we *did* save her.'

'She might not have needed saving if we hadn't locked the thing in with her,' Harry reminded him.

They had reached the portrait of the Fat Lady.

'Pig snout,' they said and entered.

The common room was packed and noisy. Everyone was eating the food that had been sent up. Hermione, however, stood alone by the door, waiting for them. There was a very embarrassed pause. Then, none of them looking at each other, they all said 'Thanks', and hurried off to get plates.

But from that moment on, Hermione Granger became their friend. There are some things you can't share without ending up liking each other, and knocking out a twelve-foot mountain troll is one of them.

第10章 万圣节前夕

赫敏垂下了头。哈利一句话也说不出来。赫敏是最不可能违反校规的人，而现在，她为了使他们摆脱麻烦，居然撒谎说自己违反了校规。这简直就像斯内普开始给大家发糖一样，令人难以置信。

"格兰杰小姐，因为这件事，格兰芬多要被扣去五分，"麦格教授说，"我对你感到很失望。如果你一点儿也没有受伤，最好赶紧回格兰芬多塔楼去。学生们都在自己的学院里享用万圣节晚宴呢。"

赫敏离去了。

麦格教授转向哈利和罗恩。

"好吧，我仍然要说算你们走运，没有几个一年级学生能跟一个成年巨怪展开较量的。你们每人为格兰芬多赢得了五分。我会把这件事通知邓布利多教授。你们可以走了。"

他们急忙走出盥洗室，一言不发地上了两层楼梯。总算闻不到巨怪身上的恶臭了，他们松了一口气。

"我们应该赢得不止十分。"罗恩嘟嘟囔囔地抱怨。

"只有五分，算上她在赫敏身上扣掉的分数。"

"赫敏真好，挺身而出，使我们摆脱了麻烦。"罗恩承认说，"不过你别忘了，我们确实救了她。"

"如果我们没有把她和那东西关在一起，她也许根本用不着别人去救。"哈利提醒他。

他们来到了胖夫人的肖像前。

"猪鼻子。"他们说完口令，钻了进去。

公共休息室里挤满了人，吵吵闹闹的。每个人都在吃着送上来的食物。只有赫敏独自站在门口，等着他们。一时间，三个人都很尴尬。接着，他们谁也没看谁，只同时说了一句"谢谢你"，就匆匆奔向自己的盘子。

然而就从那一刻起，赫敏·格兰杰成了他们的朋友。当你和某人共同经历了某件事之后，你们之间不能不产生好感，而打昏一个十二英尺高的巨怪就是这样一件事。

CHAPTER ELEVEN

Quidditch

As they entered November, the weather turned very cold. The mountains around the school became icy grey and the lake like chilled steel. Every morning the ground was covered in frost. Hagrid could be seen from the upstairs windows, defrosting broomsticks on the Quidditch pitch, bundled up in a long moleskin overcoat, rabbit-fur gloves and enormous beaverskin boots.

The Quidditch season had begun. On Saturday, Harry would be playing in his first match after weeks of training: Gryffindor versus Slytherin. If Gryffindor won, they would move up into second place in the House Championship.

Hardly anyone had seen Harry play because Wood had decided that, as their secret weapon, Harry should be kept, well, secret. But the news that he was playing Seeker had leaked out somehow, and Harry didn't know which was worse – people telling him he'd be brilliant or people telling him they'd be running around underneath him, holding a mattress.

It was really lucky that Harry now had Hermione as a friend. He didn't know how he'd have got through all his homework without her, what with all the last-minute Quidditch practice Wood was making them do. She had also lent him *Quidditch Through the Ages*, which turned out to be a very interesting read.

Harry learnt that there were seven hundred ways of committing a Quidditch foul and that all of them had happened during a World Cup match in 1473; that Seekers were usually the smallest and fastest players and that most serious Quidditch accidents seemed to happen to them; that although people rarely died playing Quidditch, referees had been known to vanish and turn up months later in the Sahara Desert.

第 11 章

魁地奇比赛

进入十一月后，天气变得非常寒冷。学校周围的大山上灰蒙蒙的，覆盖着冰雪，湖面像淬火钢一样又冷又硬。每天早晨，地面都有霜冻。从楼上的窗口可以看见海格，他全身裹在长长的鼹鼠皮大衣里，戴着兔毛皮手套，穿着巨大的海狸毛皮靴子，在魁地奇球场上给飞天扫帚除霜。

魁地奇赛季开始了。哈利经过几个星期的训练，星期六就要参加他有生以来的第一场比赛了，是格兰芬多队对斯莱特林队。如果格兰芬多队赢了，他们在学院杯冠军赛的名次就会升到第二名。

几乎没有人看见过哈利打魁地奇，因为伍德决定对哈利参赛的事严加保密，要把他作为他们队的一个秘密武器。但是哈利要担当找球手的消息还是泄漏了出去。结果，有人对他说他会打得很棒，也有人对他说到时候他们要举着床垫，在下面跟着他跑，防止他摔下来——哈利不知道哪种说法更糟糕。

说起来真是幸运，哈利现在有了赫敏这样一位朋友。如果没有赫敏，他真不知道怎么完成那么多家庭作业，因为伍德强迫他们抓紧每分钟训练魁地奇。赫敏还借给他一本《神奇的魁地奇球》，他发现这本书读起来非常有趣。

哈利得知，魁地奇比赛有七百种犯规的行为，而它们都出现在一四七三年的一场世界杯比赛中；找球手通常是个头最小、速度最快的选手，最严重的魁地奇事故似乎都发生在他们身上；尽管魁地奇比赛时很少有人死亡，但据说曾有裁判消失得无影无踪，几个月后才出现在撒哈拉沙漠。

CHAPTER ELEVEN   Quidditch

Hermione had become a bit more relaxed about breaking rules since Harry and Ron had saved her from the mountain troll and she was much nicer for it. The day before Harry's first Quidditch match the three of them were out in the freezing courtyard during break, and she had conjured them up a bright blue fire which could be carried around in a jam jar. They were standing with their backs to it, getting warm, when Snape crossed the yard. Harry noticed at once that Snape was limping. Harry, Ron and Hermione moved closer together to block the fire from view; they were sure it wouldn't be allowed. Unfortunately, something about their guilty faces caught Snape's eye. He limped over. He hadn't seen the fire, but he seemed to be looking for a reason to tell them off anyway.

'What's that you've got there, Potter?'

It was *Quidditch Through the Ages*. Harry showed him.

'Library books are not to be taken outside the school,' said Snape. 'Give it to me. Five points from Gryffindor.'

'He's just made that rule up,' Harry muttered angrily as Snape limped away. 'Wonder what's wrong with his leg?'

'Dunno, but I hope it's really hurting him,' said Ron bitterly.

The Gryffindor common room was very noisy that evening. Harry, Ron and Hermione sat together next to a window. Hermione was checking Harry and Ron's Charms homework for them. She would never let them copy ('How will you learn?'), but by asking her to read it through, they got the right answers anyway.

Harry felt restless. He wanted *Quidditch Through the Ages* back, to take his mind off his nerves about tomorrow. Why should he be afraid of Snape? Getting up, he told Ron and Hermione he was going to ask Snape if he could have it.

'Rather you than me,' they said together, but Harry had an idea that Snape wouldn't refuse if there were other teachers listening.

He made his way down to the staff room and knocked. There was no answer. He knocked again. Nothing.

Perhaps Snape had left the book in there? It was worth a try. He pushed the door ajar and peered inside – and a horrible scene met his eyes.

Snape and Filch were inside, alone. Snape was holding his robes above his

第11章 魁地奇比赛

自从哈利和罗恩把赫敏从庞大的巨怪手里救出来后，她对于违反校规便不那么在意了，这就使她变得可爱多了。哈利参加魁地奇比赛的前一天，他们三人趁课间休息的时候来到外面寒冷的院子里。赫敏用魔法为他们变出了一捧明亮的蓝色火焰，可以放在一只果酱罐里随身携带。他们站在那里，背对火焰取暖。这时，斯内普从院子里穿过。哈利一眼就注意到斯内普走路一瘸一拐的。哈利、罗恩和赫敏靠得更拢一些，想挡住火焰，不让斯内普看见；他们知道这肯定是不被允许的。不幸的是，他们脸上那种心虚的表情吸引了斯内普的视线。他一瘸一拐地走过来。他没有看见火焰，但似乎在寻找一个理由，不管怎么说都要训他们一顿。

"你手里拿的是什么，波特？"

是《神奇的魁地奇球》。哈利给他看。

"图书馆的书是不许带出学校的，"斯内普说，"把它给我。格兰芬多被扣五分。"

"他临时编了个规定。"哈利看着斯内普一瘸一拐地走远，愤愤不平地咕哝道，"不知道他的腿怎么了？"

"不知道，但我希望他疼得够呛。"罗恩幸灾乐祸地说。

那天晚上，格兰芬多公共休息室里闹哄哄的。哈利、罗恩和赫敏一起坐在一扇窗户旁边。赫敏正在检查哈利和罗恩的魔咒课作业。她坚决不让他们抄她的作业（"那样你们能学到什么呢？"），但是请她检查一遍之后，他们总能得到正确的答案。

哈利感到不安。他想把《神奇的魁地奇球》要回来，使自己的神经放松一下，不要老想着明天的比赛。他为什么要害怕斯内普呢？于是，他站起来对罗恩和赫敏说，他要去问问斯内普能不能把书还给他。

"换了我才不去呢。"他们俩异口同声地说。但是哈利有了一个主意，如果旁边有其他老师听着，斯内普便不会拒绝他。

他下楼来到教工休息室，敲了敲门。没人回答。他又敲了敲，还是没动静。

没准斯内普把书留在里面了？值得试一试。他把门推开一道缝，朝里面望去——眼前出现了一副可怕的景象。

房间里只有斯内普和费尔奇两个人。斯内普把他的长袍撩到了膝盖

knees. One of his legs was bloody and mangled. Filch was handing Snape bandages.

'Blasted thing,' Snape was saying. 'How are you supposed to keep your eyes on all three heads at once?'

Harry tried to shut the door quietly, but –

'POTTER!'

Snape's face was twisted with fury as he dropped his robes quickly to hide his leg. Harry gulped.

'I just wondered if I could have my book back.'

'GET OUT! *OUT!*'

Harry left, before Snape could take any more points from Gryffindor. He sprinted back upstairs.

'Did you get it?' Ron asked as Harry joined them. 'What's the matter?'

In a low whisper, Harry told them what he'd seen.

'You know what this means?' he finished breathlessly. 'He tried to get past that three-headed dog at Hallowe'en! That's where he was going when we saw him – he's after whatever it's guarding! And I'd bet my broomstick *he* let that troll in, to create a diversion!'

Hermione's eyes were wide.

'No – he wouldn't,' she said. 'I know he's not very nice, but he wouldn't try and steal something Dumbledore was keeping safe.'

'Honestly, Hermione, you think all teachers are saints or something,' snapped Ron. 'I'm with Harry. I wouldn't put anything past Snape. But what's he after? What's that dog guarding?'

Harry went to bed with his head buzzing with the same question. Neville was snoring loudly, but Harry couldn't sleep. He tried to empty his mind – he needed to sleep, he had to, he had his first Quidditch match in a few hours – but the expression on Snape's face when Harry had seen his leg wasn't easy to forget.

The next morning dawned very bright and cold. The Great Hall was full of the delicious smell of fried sausages and the cheerful chatter of everyone looking forward to a good Quidditch match.

'You've got to eat some breakfast.'

'I don't want anything.'

以上。他的一条腿鲜血淋漓，血肉模糊。费尔奇正在把绷带递给他。

"该死的东西，"只听斯内普说，"你怎么可能同时盯住三个脑袋呢？"

哈利正要轻轻把门关上，可是——

"波特！"

斯内普赶紧放下长袍挡住伤腿。他气得脸都歪了。哈利喘不过气来。

"我想知道能不能拿回我的书。"

"滚出去！出去！"

哈利不等斯内普给格兰芬多扣分就赶紧离开了。他一路狂奔着上了楼。

"书拿到了吗？"哈利回到罗恩和赫敏身边时，罗恩问道，"怎么回事？"

哈利压低声音，把刚才看到的一切都告诉了他们。

"你知道这意味着什么吗？"最后，他屏住呼吸说道，"万圣节前夕，他想从那条三个脑袋的大狗身边通过！当时我们看见他时，他正要往那里去——他在寻找大狗看守的那件东西！我敢用我的飞天扫帚打赌，是他放那头巨怪进来的，为了转移人们的注意力！"

赫敏的眼睛睁得圆圆的。

"不——他不会的，"她说，"我知道他不太好，但他绝不会去偷邓布利多严加保管的东西。"

"说老实话，赫敏，你总认为所有的老师都是圣人。"罗恩很不客气地说，"我同意哈利的话。我认为斯内普什么事都做得出来。可是他在寻找什么呢？那条大狗在看守什么呢？"

哈利上床时，脑子里还嗡嗡地响着这个问题。纳威发出了响亮的鼾声，哈利却久久无法入睡。他想排除杂念——他需要睡觉，必须睡觉，再过几个小时，就要参加他的第一场魁地奇比赛了——但是，刚才他看见斯内普的腿时，斯内普脸上的表情总令他难以忘记。

第二天一早，天气晴朗而寒冷。餐厅里弥漫着烤香肠的诱人气味，每个人都在期待一场精彩的魁地奇比赛，兴高采烈地聊个不停。

"你必须吃几口早饭。"

"我什么也不想吃。"

'Just a bit of toast,' wheedled Hermione.

'I'm not hungry.'

Harry felt terrible. In an hour's time he'd be walking on to the pitch.

'Harry, you need your strength,' said Seamus Finnigan. 'Seekers are always the ones who get nobbled by the other team.'

'Thanks, Seamus,' said Harry, watching Seamus pile ketchup on his sausages.

By eleven o'clock the whole school seemed to be out in the stands around the Quidditch pitch. Many students had binoculars. The seats might be raised high in the air but it was still difficult to see what was going on sometimes.

Ron and Hermione joined Neville, Seamus and Dean the West Ham fan up in the top row. As a surprise for Harry, they had painted a large banner on one of the sheets Scabbers had ruined. It said *Potter for President* and Dean, who was good at drawing, had done a large Gryffindor lion underneath. Then Hermione had performed a tricky little charm so that the paint flashed different colours.

Meanwhile, in the changing rooms, Harry and the rest of the team were changing into their scarlet Quidditch robes (Slytherin would be playing in green).

Wood cleared his throat for silence.

'OK, men,' he said.

'And women,' said Chaser Angelina Johnson.

'And women,' Wood agreed. 'This is it.'

'The big one,' said Fred Weasley.

'The one we've all been waiting for,' said George.

'We know Oliver's speech by heart,' Fred told Harry. 'We were in the team last year.'

'Shut up, you two,' said Wood. 'This is the best team Gryffindor's had in years. We're going to win. I know it.'

He glared at them all as if to say, 'Or else.'

'Right. It's time. Good luck, all of you.'

Harry followed Fred and George out of the changing room and,

"吃一点儿烤面包吧。"赫敏哄劝道。

"我不饿。"

哈利的感觉糟透了。再过一个小时,他就要走向赛场了。

"哈利,你需要保持旺盛的体力。"西莫·斐尼甘说,"找球手总是对方重点防范的人。"

"谢谢你,西莫。"哈利说,看着西莫往香肠上涂抹厚厚的番茄酱。

到了十一点钟,似乎全校师生都来到了魁地奇球场周围的看台上。许多学生还带了双筒望远镜。座位简直被升到了半空,但有时仍然难以看清比赛情况。

罗恩和赫敏来到最高一排,加入纳威、西莫和西汉姆足球队球迷迪安的行列。为了给哈利一个惊喜,他们用一条被小老鼠斑斑弄脏的床单绘制了一条巨大的横幅,上面写着波特必胜。擅长绘画的迪安还在下面画了一头很大的格兰芬多狮子。然后,赫敏施了一个巧妙的魔法,让横幅上的颜料闪烁不同的色彩。

与此同时,在更衣室里,哈利和其他队员正在换上深红色的魁地奇队袍(斯莱特林队穿的是绿色衣服)。

伍德清了清嗓子让大家安静下来。

"好了,小伙子们。"他说。

"还有姑娘们。"追球手安吉利娜·约翰逊说。

"还有姑娘们。"伍德赞同道,"是时候了。"

"这个重要的时刻。"弗雷德·韦斯莱说。

"我们大家一直在等待的时刻。"乔治说。

"奥利弗的讲话我们已经记得烂熟,"弗雷德对哈利说,"我们去年就在队里。"

"闭嘴,你们两个。"伍德说,"这是格兰芬多这么多年来最好的一支队伍;我们会赢的。我知道。"

他狠狠地瞪着大家,似乎在说:"要不够你们受的。"

"好了,时间到了。祝大家好运。"

哈利跟着弗雷德和乔治走出更衣室,然后走向欢呼鼎沸的球场,他

hoping his knees weren't going to give way, walked on to the pitch to loud cheers.

Madam Hooch was refereeing. She stood in the middle of the pitch, waiting for the two teams, her broom in her hand.

'Now, I want a nice fair game, all of you,' she said, once they were all gathered around her. Harry noticed that she seemed to be speaking particularly to the Slytherin captain, Marcus Flint, a fifth-year. Harry thought Flint looked as if he had some troll blood in him. Out of the corner of his eye he saw the fluttering banner high above, flashing *Potter for President* over the crowd. His heart skipped. He felt braver.

'Mount your brooms, please.'

Harry clambered on to his Nimbus Two Thousand.

Madam Hooch gave a loud blast on her silver whistle.

Fifteen brooms rose up, high, high into the air. They were off.

'And the Quaffle is taken immediately by Angelina Johnson of Gryffindor – what an excellent Chaser that girl is, and rather attractive, too –'

'JORDAN!'

'Sorry, Professor.'

The Weasley twins' friend, Lee Jordan, was doing the commentary for the match, closely watched by Professor McGonagall.

'And she's really belting along up there, a neat pass to Alicia Spinnet, a good find of Oliver Wood's, last year only a reserve – back to Johnson and – no, Slytherin have taken the Quaffle, Slytherin captain Marcus Flint gains the Quaffle and off he goes – Flint flying like an eagle up there – he's going to sc– no, stopped by an excellent move by Gryffindor Keeper Wood and Gryffindor take the Quaffle – that's Chaser Katie Bell of Gryffindor there, nice dive around Flint, off up the field and – OUCH – that must have hurt, hit in the back of the head by a Bludger – Quaffle taken by Slytherin – that's Adrian Pucey speeding off towards the goalposts, but he's blocked by a second Bludger – sent his way by Fred or George Weasley, can't tell which – nice play by the Gryffindor Beater, anyway, and Johnson back in possession of the Quaffle, a clear field ahead and off she goes – she's really flying – dodges a speeding Bludger – the goalposts are ahead – come on, now, Angelina – Keeper Bletchley dives – misses –

希望自己的膝盖不要发软。

霍琦女士做裁判。她站在球场中央，手里拿着飞天扫帚，等着双方队员。

"听着，我希望大家都公平、诚实地参加比赛。"队员们一聚拢到她身边，她就说道。哈利注意到，她的这句话，似乎是专门针对斯莱特林队的队长、五年级学生马库斯·弗林特说的。哈利觉得马库斯看上去似乎有几分巨怪的血统。哈利从眼角看见了那条高高飘扬的横幅，在人群上方闪耀着波特必胜的字样。他的心顿时欢跳起来。他觉得有了勇气。

"请大家骑上飞天扫帚。"

哈利跨上他的光轮2000。

霍琦女士使劲吹响了她的银哨。

十五把飞天扫帚腾空而起，高高地升上天空。比赛开始了。

"鬼飞球立刻被格兰芬多的安吉利娜·约翰逊抢到了——那姑娘是一个多么出色的追球手，而且长得也很迷人——"

"**乔丹**！"

"对不起，教授。"

李·乔丹是韦斯莱孪生兄弟的朋友。他正在麦格教授的密切监视下，担任比赛的解说员。

"她在上面真是一路飞奔，一个漂亮的传球，给了艾丽娅·斯平内特，她是奥利弗·伍德慧眼发现的人才，去年还只是个替补队员——球又传给了约翰逊，然后——糟糕，斯莱特林队把鬼飞球抢去了，斯莱特林队的队长马库斯·弗林特得到了鬼飞球，飞奔而去——弗林特在上面像鹰一样飞翔——他要得分了——没有，格兰芬多队的守门员伍德一个漂亮的动作，把球断掉了，现在是格兰芬多队拿球——那是格兰芬多队的追球手凯蒂·贝尔，在球场上空，在弗林特周围敏捷地冲来冲去——哎哟——那一定很疼，被一只游走球击中了后脑勺——鬼飞球被斯莱特林队抢断——那是德里安·普塞飞快地朝球门柱冲去，但是他被另一只游走球打倒了——游走球被弗雷德或者乔治·韦斯莱拨到一边，那两个双胞胎实在难以分清——格兰芬多队的击球手干得真漂亮，约翰逊又夺回了鬼飞球，前面没有阻力，她拼命飞奔——真像是飞一样——躲开一只游走球——球门柱就在前面——加油，安吉利娜——守门员布莱奇俯

GRYFFINDOR SCORE!'

Gryffindor cheers filled the cold air, with howls and moans from the Slytherins.

'Budge up there, move along.'

'Hagrid!'

Ron and Hermione squeezed together to give Hagrid enough space to join them.

'Bin watchin' from me hut,' said Hagrid, patting a large pair of binoculars round his neck, 'But it isn't the same as bein' in the crowd. No sign of the Snitch yet, eh?'

'Nope,' said Ron. 'Harry hasn't had much to do yet.'

'Kept outta trouble, though, that's somethin',' said Hagrid, raising his binoculars and peering skywards at the speck that was Harry.

Way up above them, Harry was gliding over the game, squinting about for some sign of the Snitch. This was part of his and Wood's game plan.

'Keep out of the way until you catch sight of the Snitch,' Wood had said. 'We don't want you attacked before you have to be.'

When Angelina had scored, Harry had done a couple of loop-the-loops to let out his feelings. Now he was back to staring around for the Snitch. Once he caught sight of a flash of gold but it was just a reflection from one of the Weasleys' wristwatches, and once a Bludger decided to come pelting his way, more like a cannon ball than anything, but Harry dodged it and Fred Weasley came chasing after it.

'All right there, Harry?' he had time to yell, as he beat the Bludger furiously towards Marcus Flint.

'Slytherin in possession,' Lee Jordan was saying. 'Chaser Pucey ducks two Bludgers, two Weasleys and Chaser Bell and speeds towards the – wait a moment – was that the Snitch?'

A murmur ran through the crowd as Adrian Pucey dropped the Quaffle, too busy looking over his shoulder at the flash of gold that had passed his left ear.

Harry saw it. In a great rush of excitement he dived downwards after the streak of gold. Slytherin Seeker Terence Higgs had seen it, too. Neck and neck they hurtled towards the Snitch – all the Chasers seemed to have forgotten what they were supposed to be doing as they hung in mid-air to watch.

冲过来——漏过了——**格兰芬多队得分！**"

格兰芬多们的欢呼声在寒冷的空气中回荡，其中还夹杂着斯莱特林们的怒吼和呻吟。

"借光，借光，让一让。"

"海格！"

罗恩和赫敏互相挤了挤，腾出地方让海格坐进来。

"刚才一直在我那小屋里看呢，"海格拍着他挂在脖子上的那只大望远镜说道，"可那和在人群里看比赛气氛不一样。飞贼还不见踪影，是吗？"

"没看见，"罗恩说，"哈利还没什么要做的。"

"只要没出麻烦，就算走运。"海格说着，举起望远镜，费力地看着空中的一个小点——那就是哈利。

哈利在很高的空中，在赛场上方轻盈地滑来滑去，眯着眼睛搜寻飞贼的影子。这是他和伍德制订的比赛计划的一部分。

"你先躲在一边，等看见飞贼再说。"伍德这样说，"我们不想让你早早地就遭到袭击。"

安吉利娜得分后，哈利翻了几个跟头，表达自己喜悦的情绪。现在他又回去寻找飞贼了。有一次，他突然看见金光一闪，但这只是韦斯莱孪生兄弟中某一个的手表的反光；还有一次，一只游走球决定朝他这边冲来，那样子就像一颗炮弹，但是哈利躲开了，弗雷德追着球赶来。

"没事儿吧，哈利？"弗雷德只喊了一声，就狠狠地把球打向了马库斯·弗林特那边。

"斯莱特林队得球，"李·乔丹解说道，"追球手普塞低头躲过两只游走球，又躲过韦斯莱双胞胎和追球手贝尔，奔向——等等——那是飞贼吗？"

德里安·普塞只顾扭头看从他左耳边飞过的一道金光，把鬼飞球漏掉了，人群中传出一片窃窃私语。

哈利看见飞贼了。他一阵激动，俯冲下去，追逐着那道金色的流光。斯莱特林队的找球手特伦斯·希格斯也看见了。两人并排朝飞贼飞过去——追球手们似乎都忘记了他们自己该做的事，一个个停在空中，注视着。

Harry was faster than Higgs – he could see the little round ball, wings fluttering, darting up ahead – he put on an extra spurt of speed –

WHAM! A roar of rage echoed from the Gryffindors below – Marcus Flint had blocked Harry on purpose and Harry's broom spun off course, Harry holding on for dear life.

'Foul!' screamed the Gryffindors.

Madam Hooch spoke angrily to Flint and then ordered a free shot at the goalposts for Gryffindor. But in all the confusion, of course, the Golden Snitch had disappeared from sight again.

Down in the stands, Dean Thomas was yelling, 'Send him off, ref! Red card!'

'This isn't football, Dean,' Ron reminded him. 'You can't send people off in Quidditch – and what's a red card?'

But Hagrid was on Dean's side.

'They oughta change the rules, Flint coulda knocked Harry outta the air.'

Lee Jordan was finding it difficult not to take sides.

'So – after that obvious and disgusting bit of cheating –'

'Jordan!' growled Professor McGonagall.

'I mean, after that open and revolting foul –'

'*Jordan, I'm warning you –*'

'All right, all right. Flint nearly kills the Gryffindor Seeker, which could happen to anyone, I'm sure, so a penalty to Gryffindor, taken by Spinnet, who puts it away, no trouble, and we continue play, Gryffindor still in possession.'

It was as Harry dodged another Bludger which went spinning dangerously past his head that it happened. His broom gave a sudden, frightening lurch. For a split second, he thought he was going to fall. He gripped the broom tightly with both his hands and knees. He'd never felt anything like that.

It happened again. It was as though the broom was trying to buck him off. But Nimbus Two Thousands did not suddenly decide to buck their riders off. Harry tried to turn back towards the Gryffindor goalposts; he had half a mind to ask Wood to call time out – and then he realised that his broom was completely out of his control. He couldn't turn it. He couldn't direct it at all. It was zigzagging through the air and every now and then making violent swishing movements which almost unseated him.

Lee was still commentating.

第11章 魁地奇比赛

哈利的速度比希格斯快——他能看见那只小小的圆球，扑扇着翅膀，在前面飞蹿——他又猛地加快了速度——

嘭！下面的格兰芬多们传出一阵愤怒的吼叫声——马库斯·弗林特故意冲撞哈利，哈利的飞天扫帚猛地偏离方向，但哈利死死地抓住了它。

"犯规！"格兰芬多们大声叫道。

霍奇女士怒气冲冲地责备了弗林特，然后命令格兰芬多队在球门柱前罚任意球。但是，当然啦，在一片混乱中，金色飞贼又从视线中消失了。

看台上，迪安·托马斯大声嚷道："把他罚下场，裁判！红牌！"

"这不是足球，迪安。"罗恩提醒他道，"在魁地奇比赛里，你不能把人罚下场——还有，什么是红牌？"

可是海格赞成迪安的意见。

"他们应该改变一下比赛规则，弗林特在空中差点把哈利撞了下来。"

李·乔丹觉得很难做到不偏不倚。

"这样——经过刚才那个明显而卑鄙的作弊行为——"

"乔丹！"麦格教授低声吼道。

"我是说，经过刚才那个公开的、令人反感的犯规行为——"

"乔丹，我提醒你——"

"好吧，好吧。弗林特差一点儿使格兰芬多队的找球手丧命，我相信这种事情谁都会遇到，所以格兰芬多队罚任意球。球被斯平内特拿到了，她把球传了出去，很顺利。比赛继续进行，格兰芬多队仍然控制着球。"

就在哈利躲过另一只嗖嗖旋转、擦着他头皮飞过的游走球时，事情发生了。他的飞天扫帚突然很吓人地抖了一下。一时间，他以为自己要掉下去了。他两只手紧紧地抓住扫帚把，并用膝盖死死夹住。他从没有过这样害怕的感觉。

又来了。就好像飞天扫帚拼命想把他摔下去似的。可是，照理说光轮2000是不会突然决定把主人摔下去的。哈利试着转向格兰芬多队的球门柱；他隐约打算叫伍德暂停比赛——接着发现他的飞天扫帚完全不受控制了。他无法让它调头。他根本无法指挥它。飞天扫帚左拐右拐地在空中穿梭，不时嗖嗖地剧烈晃动着，差点把他从上面摔下来。

李还在滔滔不绝地解说。

'Slytherin in possession – Flint with the Quaffle – passes Spinnet – passes Bell – hit hard in the face by a Bludger, hope it broke his nose – only joking, Professor – Slytherin score – oh no ...'

The Slytherins were cheering. No one seemed to have noticed that Harry's broom was behaving strangely. It was carrying him slowly higher, away from the game, jerking and twitching as it went.

'Dunno what Harry thinks he's doing,' Hagrid mumbled. He stared through his binoculars. 'if I didn' know better, I'd say he'd lost control of his broom ... but he can't have ...'

Suddenly, people were pointing up at Harry all over the stands. His broom had started to roll over and over, with him only just managing to hold on. Then the whole crowd gasped. Harry's broom had given a wild jerk and Harry swung off it. He was now dangling from it, holding on with only one hand.

'Did something happen to it when Flint blocked him?' Seamus whispered.

'Can't have,' Hagrid said, his voice shaking. 'Can't nothing interfere with a broomstick except powerful Dark Magic – no kid could do that to a Nimbus Two Thousand.'

At these words, Hermione seized Hagrid's binoculars, but instead of looking up at Harry, she started looking frantically at the crowd.

'What are you doing?' moaned Ron, grey-faced.

'I knew it,' Hermione gasped. 'Snape – look.'

Ron grabbed the binoculars. Snape was in the middle of the stands opposite them. He had his eyes fixed on Harry and was muttering non-stop under his breath.

'He's doing something – jinxing the broom,' said Hermione.

'What should we do?'

'Leave it to me.'

Before Ron could say another word, Hermione had disappeared. Ron turned the binoculars back on Harry. His broom was vibrating so hard, it was almost impossible for him to hang on much longer. The whole crowd were on their feet, watching, terrified, as the Weasleys flew up to try and pull Harry safely on to one of their brooms, but it was no good – every time they got near him, the broom would jump higher still. They dropped lower and circled beneath him, obviously hoping to catch him if he fell. Marcus Flint seized the Quaffle and scored five times without anyone noticing.

第 11 章 魁地奇比赛

"斯莱特林队得球——弗林特拿到鬼飞球——绕过斯平内特——绕过贝尔——被一只游走球狠狠打中面孔,希望把他的鼻子打断——开个玩笑,教授——斯莱特林队得分——哦,糟糕……"

斯莱特林们欢呼雀跃。似乎谁也没有注意到哈利的飞天扫帚表现异常。扫帚一路疯狂地抽搐、扭动,慢慢地、越来越高地使哈利远离了赛场。

"真不知道哈利想做什么。"海格嘟哝着。他通过望远镜仔细看着。"如果我不是这么了解他,就会以为他无法控制他的扫帚了——但是他不可能……"

突然,看台上的人们全部向上指着哈利。他的飞天扫帚开始不停地翻腾打滚,哈利只能勉强支撑着不掉下来。这时,飞天扫帚又是一阵疯狂的扭动,哈利被它甩了下来。他现在仅用一只手抓住扫帚把,悬在空中。

"刚才弗林特冲撞他时,扫帚是不是出了问题?"西莫小声说。

"不可能,"海格说,他的声音微微发颤,"除了厉害的黑魔法,没什么能干扰一把飞天扫帚——小孩子是不可能对光轮 2000 施这种魔法的。"

听了这话,赫敏一把抓住海格的望远镜,她没有抬头去看哈利,而是开始焦急地眺望人群。

"你在做什么?"罗恩呻吟着说,脸色死灰一般。

"我早就猜到了,"赫敏喘着气说,"是斯内普——看。"

罗恩抓过望远镜。斯内普站在他们对面的看台中间。他眼睛紧盯着哈利,嘴里不出声地念念有词。

"他在使坏——给飞天扫帚念恶咒。"赫敏说。

"我们怎么办?"

"看我的。"

不等罗恩再说一个字,赫敏就消失了。罗恩把望远镜的镜头又对准了哈利。飞天扫帚震动得太厉害了,哈利不可能再悬很长时间。观众们全部站了起来,惊恐地注视着。韦斯莱孪生兄弟飞了上去,想把哈利安全地拉到他们的一把扫帚上,然而不行——每当他们接近他时,飞天扫帚就噌地一下蹿得更高。于是,他们落下来一些,在他下边打着转,显然是想在他坠落时接住他。马库斯·弗林特抓住鬼飞球,投中了五次,却没有一个人注意他。

CHAPTER ELEVEN Quidditch

'Come on, Hermione,' Ron muttered desperately.

Hermione had fought her way across to the stand where Snape stood and was now racing along the row behind him; she didn't even stop to say sorry as she knocked Professor Quirrell headfirst into the row in front. Reaching Snape, she crouched down, pulled out her wand and whispered a few, well chosen words. Bright blue flames shot from her wand on to the hem of Snape's robes.

It took perhaps thirty seconds for Snape to realise that he was on fire. A sudden yelp told her she had done her job. Scooping the fire off him into a little jar in her pocket she scrambled back along the row – Snape would never know what had happened.

It was enough. Up in the air, Harry was suddenly able to clamber back on to his broom.

'Neville, you can look!' Ron said. Neville had been sobbing into Hagrid's jacket for the last five minutes.

Harry was speeding towards the ground when the crowd saw him clap his hand to his mouth as though he was about to be sick – he hit the pitch on all fours – coughed – and something gold fell into his hand.

'I've got the Snitch!' he shouted, waving it above his head, and the game ended in complete confusion.

'He didn't *catch* it, he nearly *swallowed* it,' Flint was still howling twenty minutes later, but it made no difference – Harry hadn't broken any rules and Lee Jordan was still happily shouting the result – Gryffindor had won by one hundred and seventy points to sixty. Harry heard none of this, though. He was being made a cup of strong tea back in Hagrid's hut, with Ron and Hermione.

'It was Snape,' Ron was explaining. 'Hermione and I saw him. He was cursing your broomstick, muttering, he wouldn't take his eyes off you.'

'Rubbish,' said Hagrid, who hadn't heard a word of what had gone on next to him in the stands. 'Why would Snape do somethin' like that?'

Harry, Ron and Hermione looked at each other, wondering what to tell him. Harry decided on the truth.

'I found out something about him,' he told Hagrid. 'He tried to get past that three-headed dog at Hallowe'en. It bit him. We think he was trying to steal whatever it's guarding.'

"快点儿，赫敏。"罗恩绝望地低声说。

赫敏艰难地穿过人群，来到斯内普所在的看台。她沿着他身后的那排座位飞快地走着，撞得奇洛教授一头摔向前排座位都没有停下来说一声对不起。总算到了斯内普身边，她蹲下去，抽出魔杖，低声说了几句经过推敲的话。明亮的蓝色火苗从魔杖里蹿出来，扑向斯内普长袍的下摆。

过了大约三十秒钟，斯内普才意识到自己身上着了火。听到一声惊叫，赫敏知道她的工作完成了。她迅速把火从他身上收拢，收进自己的口袋，然后顺着那排座位匆匆返回——斯内普永远不会知道是怎么回事。

这就够了。高空中，哈利突然能够爬回到他的扫帚上了。

"纳威，你可以看了！"罗恩说。在刚才的五分钟里，纳威一直把脸埋在海格的夹克衫里哭泣。

哈利飞快地朝地面俯冲，人们看见他用手捂住嘴巴，好像要呕吐似的——他四肢着地落在地上——咳嗽——一个金色的东西落进了他的手掌。

"我抓住了飞贼！"他大喊道，把球高高举过头顶挥舞着，比赛在一片混乱中结束了。

"他没有抓住飞贼，他差点把它吞了下去。"二十分钟后，弗林特还在愤愤不平地吼叫，但是完全不起作用——哈利并没有违犯任何规则，李·乔丹还在喜悦地大喊比赛结果——格兰芬多队以一百七十分比六十分获胜。不过，哈利没有听到这些。他和罗恩、赫敏一起来到海格的小屋，主人正在为他沏一杯浓茶。

"是斯内普干的，"罗恩在向大家解释，"赫敏和我都看见了。他在给你的飞天扫帚念咒，嘴里嘀嘀咕咕的，眼睛一直死盯着你。"

"胡说，"海格说，他对看台上发生在自己身边的事一无所知，"斯内普为什么要做这样的事？"

哈利、罗恩和赫敏交换了一下目光，不知道该怎么告诉他。哈利决定实话实说。

"我发现了他的一些事情，"他对海格说，"万圣节前夕，他想通过那条三个脑袋的大狗。狗咬了他。我们认为他是想偷大狗看守的东西。"

Hagrid dropped the teapot.

'How do you know about Fluffy?' he said.

'*Fluffy?*'

'Yeah – he's mine – bought him off a Greek chappie I met in the pub las' year – I lent him to Dumbledore to guard the –'

'Yes?' said Harry eagerly.

'Now, don't ask me any more,' said Hagrid gruffly. 'That's top secret, that is.'

'But Snape's trying to *steal* it.'

'Rubbish,' said Hagrid again. 'Snape's a Hogwarts teacher, he'd do nothin' of the sort.'

'So why did he just try and kill Harry?' cried Hermione.

The afternoon's events certainly seemed to have changed her mind about Snape.

'I know a jinx when I see one, Hagrid, I've read all about them! You've got to keep eye contact, and Snape wasn't blinking at all, I saw him!'

'I'm tellin' yeh, yer wrong!' said Hagrid hotly. 'I don' know why Harry's broom acted like that, but Snape wouldn' try an' kill a student! Now, listen to me, all three of yeh – yer meddlin' in things that don' concern yeh. It's dangerous. You forget that dog, an' you forget what it's guardin', that's between Professor Dumbledore an' Nicolas Flamel –'

'Aha!' said Harry. 'So there's someone called Nicolas Flamel involved, is there?'

Hagrid looked furious with himself.

海格重重地放下茶壶。

"你们怎么会知道路威?"他问。

"路威?"

"是啊——它是我的——是从我去年在酒店认识的一个希腊佬儿手里买的——我把它借给邓布利多去看守——"

"什么?"哈利急切地问。

"行了,不要再问了,"海格粗暴地说,"那是一号机密,懂吗?"

"可是斯内普想去偷它。"

"胡说,"海格又说,"斯内普是霍格沃茨的教师,绝不会做那样的事。"

"那他为什么想害死哈利?"赫敏大声问道。

这个下午发生的事件,似乎使她对斯内普的看法发生了很大转变。

"我如果看见有人施恶咒,是能够认出来的,海格。我在书上读到过关于它们的所有介绍!你必须用眼睛保持对视。斯内普的眼睛一眨也不眨,我看见的!"

"我告诉你,你错了!"海格暴躁地说,"我不知道哈利的飞天扫帚为什么会有那样的表现,但是斯内普绝不可能想害死一个学生!现在,你们三个都听我说——你们在插手跟你们无关的事情。这是很危险的。忘记那条大狗,忘记它在看守的东西,这是邓布利多教授和尼可·勒梅之间的——"

"啊哈!"哈利说,"这么说还牵涉一个叫尼可·勒梅的人,是吗?"

海格大怒,他在生自己的气。

CHAPTER TWELVE

The Mirror of Erised

Christmas was coming. One morning in mid-December, Hogwarts woke to find itself covered in several feet of snow. The lake froze solid and the Weasley twins were punished for bewitching several snowballs so that they followed Quirrell around, bouncing off the back of his turban. The few owls that managed to battle their way through the stormy sky to deliver post had to be nursed back to health by Hagrid before they could fly off again.

No one could wait for the holidays to start. While the Gryffindor common room and the Great Hall had roaring fires, the draughty corridors had become icy and a bitter wind rattled the windows in the classrooms. Worst of all were Professor Snape's classes down in the dungeons, where their breath rose in a mist before them and they kept as close as possible to their hot cauldrons.

'I do feel so sorry,' said Draco Malfoy, one Potions class, 'for all those people who have to stay at Hogwarts for Christmas because they're not wanted at home.'

He was looking over at Harry as he spoke. Crabbe and Goyle chuckled. Harry, who was measuring out powdered spine of lionfish, ignored them. Malfoy had been even more unpleasant than usual since the Quidditch match. Disgusted that Slytherin had lost, he had tried to get everyone laughing at how a wide-mouthed tree frog would be replacing Harry as Seeker next. Then he'd realised that nobody found this funny, because they were all so impressed at the way Harry had managed to stay on his bucking broomstick. So Malfoy, jealous and angry, had gone back to taunting Harry about having no proper family.

It was true that Harry wasn't going back to Privet Drive for Christmas.

第 12 章

厄里斯魔镜

圣诞节即将来临。十二月中旬的一天早晨，霍格沃茨学校从梦中醒来，发现四下里覆盖着好几尺厚的积雪，湖面结着硬邦邦的冰。韦斯莱孪生兄弟受到了惩罚，因为他们给几只雪球施了魔法，让它们追着奇洛到处跑，最后砸在他的缠头巾后面。几只猫头鹰飞过风雪交加的天空递送邮件，经历了千辛万苦；它们必须在海格的照料下恢复体力，才能继续起飞。

大家都迫不及待地盼着放假。虽然格兰芬多公共休息室和礼堂里燃着熊熊旺火，但刮着穿堂风的走廊里还是寒冷刺骨，教室的窗户玻璃也被凛冽的寒风吹得咔嗒作响。最糟糕的是，斯内普教授的课都是在地下教室上的，学生们一哈气面前就形成一团白雾，只好尽量靠近热腾腾的坩埚。

"我真的很替那些人感到难过，"在一次魔药课上，德拉科·马尔福说道，"他们不得不留在霍格沃茨过圣诞节，因为家里人不要他们。"

他说话的时候眼睛看着哈利。克拉布和高尔在一旁窃笑。哈利正在称研成粉末的狮子鱼脊椎骨，没有理睬他们。自从魁地奇比赛之后，马尔福比以前更加阴沉了。他为斯莱特林队的失败而愤慨，说下次比赛将由一只大嘴巴树蛙代替哈利充当找球手。他本想把大家逗得哈哈大笑，却发现并没有人觉得他的话可笑，因为大家都很佩服哈利居然能够牢牢地待在他那把横冲直撞的飞天扫帚上。马尔福又嫉妒又气愤，只好转过来嘲笑哈利没有一个像样的家庭。

确实，哈利不想回女贞路过圣诞节。上个星期，麦格教授过来登记留校过节的学生名单，哈利立刻就在上面签了名。他一点儿也不为自己

CHAPTER TWELVE   The Mirror of Erised

Professor McGonagall had come round the week before, making a list of students who would be staying for the holidays, and Harry had signed up at once. He didn't feel sorry for himself at all; this would probably be the best Christmas he'd ever had. Ron and his brothers were staying too, because Mr and Mrs Weasley were going to Romania to visit Charlie.

When they left the dungeons at the end of Potions, they found a large fir tree blocking the corridor ahead. Two enormous feet sticking out at the bottom and a loud puffing sound told them that Hagrid was behind it.

'Hi, Hagrid, want any help?' Ron asked, sticking his head through the branches.

'Nah, I'm all right, thanks, Ron.'

'Would you mind moving out of the way?' came Malfoy's cold drawl from behind them. 'Are you trying to earn some extra money, Weasley? Hoping to be gamekeeper yourself when you leave Hogwarts, I suppose – that hut of Hagrid's must seem like a palace compared to what your family's used to.'

Ron dived at Malfoy just as Snape came up the stairs.

'WEASLEY!'

Ron let go of the front of Malfoy's robes.

'He was provoked, Professor Snape,' said Hagrid, sticking his huge hairy face out from behind the tree. 'Malfoy was insultin' his family.'

'Be that as it may, fighting is against Hogwarts rules, Hagrid,' said Snape silkily. 'Five points from Gryffindor, Weasley, and be grateful it isn't more. Move along, all of you.'

Malfoy, Crabbe and Goyle pushed roughly past the tree, scattering needles everywhere and smirking.

'I'll get him,' said Ron, grinding his teeth at Malfoy's back, 'one of these days, I'll get him –'

'I hate them both,' said Harry, 'Malfoy and Snape.'

'Come on, cheer up, it's nearly Christmas,' said Hagrid. 'Tell yeh what, come with me an' see the Great Hall, looks a treat.'

So Harry, Ron and Hermione followed Hagrid and his tree off to the Great Hall, where Professor McGonagall and Professor Flitwick were busy with the Christmas decorations.

'Ah, Hagrid, the last tree – put it in the far corner, would you?'

第12章 厄里斯魔镜

感到难过。这很可能是他这辈子度过的最好的圣诞节了。罗恩和他的两个孪生哥哥也准备留下来，因为韦斯莱夫妇要到罗马尼亚去看望查理。

他们上完魔药课离开地下教室时，发现前面的走廊被一棵很大的冷杉树挡得严严实实。看见树底下伸出来的那两只大脚，又听见那响亮的呼哧呼哧声，他们知道树后面的一定是海格。

"嘿，海格，需要帮忙吗？"罗恩问道，把头从那些枝枝丫丫间伸了过去。

"不用，我能行，谢谢你，罗恩。"

"你能不能闪开，别挡着道？"他们身后传来马尔福冷冰冰的、拖着长腔的声音，"你是不是想挣几个零花钱哪，韦斯莱？我猜想，你大概希望自己从霍格沃茨毕业后也去看守猎场吧？——海格的小屋和你原先那个家比起来，一定是像个宫殿吧！"

罗恩一头朝马尔福冲去，恰恰就在这时，斯内普在楼梯上出现了。

"**韦斯莱！**"

罗恩松开马尔福胸前的衣服。

"是有人先惹他的，斯内普教授。"海格从树后面探出毛发蓬乱的大脑袋，说道，"马尔福刚才侮辱他的家庭。"

"不管怎么样，动手打人都是违反霍格沃茨校规的，海格。"斯内普用圆滑的声音说，"格兰芬多被扣去五分。韦斯莱，你应该感到庆幸没有扣得更多。好了，快走吧，你们大家。"

马尔福、克拉布和高尔粗鲁地从树旁边挤过，把针叶碰落得到处都是，一边还得意地笑着。

"我要教训他，"罗恩看着马尔福的背影，咬牙切齿地说，"总有一天，我要狠狠地教训——"

"我真讨厌他们两个人，"哈利说，"马尔福和斯内普。"

"好了，高兴一点儿吧，快要过圣诞节了。"海格说，"你们猜怎么着，快跟我到礼堂去看看吧，真是妙不可言。"

于是，哈利、罗恩和赫敏跟着海格和他的冷杉树，一起来到礼堂里，麦格教授和弗立维教授都在那里，忙着布置圣诞节的装饰品。

"啊，海格，最后一棵树也拿进来了——放在那边的角落里，行吗？"

CHAPTER TWELVE The Mirror of Erised

The Hall looked spectacular. Festoons of holly and mistletoe hung all around the walls and no fewer than twelve towering Christmas trees stood around the room, some sparkling with tiny icicles, some glittering with hundreds of candles.

'How many days you got left until yer holidays?' Hagrid asked.

'Just one,' said Hermione. 'And that reminds me – Harry, Ron, we've got half an hour before lunch, we should be in the library.'

'Oh yeah, you're right,' said Ron, tearing his eyes away from Professor Flitwick, who had golden bubbles blossoming out of his wand and was trailing them over the branches of the new tree.

'The library?' said Hagrid, following them out of the Hall. 'Just before the holidays? Bit keen, aren't yeh?'

'Oh, we're not working,' Harry told him brightly. 'Ever since you mentioned Nicolas Flamel we've been trying to find out who he is.'

'You *what?*' Hagrid looked shocked. 'Listen here – I've told yeh – drop it. It's nothin' to you what that dog's guardin'.'

'We just want to know who Nicolas Flamel is, that's all,' said Hermione.

'Unless you'd like to tell us and save us the trouble?' Harry added. 'We must've been through hundreds of books already and we can't find him anywhere – just give us a hint – I know I've read his name somewhere.'

'I'm sayin' nothin',' said Hagrid flatly.

'Just have to find out for ourselves, then,' said Ron, and they left Hagrid looking disgruntled and hurried off to the library.

They had indeed been searching books for Flamel's name ever since Hagrid had let it slip, because how else were they going to find out what Snape was trying to steal? The trouble was, it was very hard to know where to begin, not knowing what Flamel might have done to get himself into a book. He wasn't in *Great Wizards of the Twentieth Century*, or *Notable Magical Names of Our Time*; he was missing, too, from *Important Modern Magical Discoveries*, and *A Study of Recent Developments in Wizardry*. And then, of course, there was the sheer size of the library; tens of thousands of books; thousands of shelves; hundreds of narrow rows.

Hermione took out a list of subjects and titles she had decided to search while Ron strode off down a row of books and started pulling them off

第12章 厄里斯魔镜

礼堂看上去美丽壮观。墙上挂满了冬青和槲寄生组成的垂花彩带，四下里竖着整整十二棵高耸的圣诞树，有些树上挂着亮晶晶的小冰柱，有些树上闪烁着几百支蜡烛。

"还有几天才放假啊？"海格问。

"只有一天啦。"赫敏说，"噢，这倒提醒了我——哈利、罗恩，还有半个小时才吃饭呢，我们应该到图书馆去。"

"噢，是啊，你说得对。"罗恩说着，恋恋不舍地把目光从弗立维教授身上移开。教授正在用他的魔杖喷出一串串金色的泡泡，并把它们挂在新搬来的那棵树的枝子上。

"图书馆？"海格一边说，一边跟着他们走出礼堂，"要放假了还看书？未免太用功了吧，啊？"

"噢，我们不是复习功课。"哈利愉快地对他说，"自从你提到尼可·勒梅之后，我们就一直在设法弄清他是谁。"

"什么？"海格显得很惊恐，"听我说——我告诉过你们——罢手吧。那条大狗看守的东西，与你们毫无关系。"

"我们只想知道尼可·勒梅是谁，没别的。"赫敏说。

"除非你愿意告诉我们，省得我们那么费事。"哈利又说道，"我们翻了至少有一百本书了，却连他的影子也没有发现——你就给我们一点儿提示吧——我知道我曾在什么地方看到过他的名字。"

"我什么也不会说的。"海格干巴巴地说。

"那么我们只好自己去找了。"罗恩说。他们匆匆往图书馆赶去，留下海格一个人站在那里，一脸怒气。

确实，自从海格说漏了嘴以后，他们一直在书里寻找勒梅的名字，除此之外，还有什么办法可以弄清斯内普想偷的是什么东西呢？麻烦的是，他们并不清楚勒梅有什么突出成就能够被写进书里，所以很难知道从何处入手，他不在《二十世纪的伟大巫师》里，也不在《当代著名魔法家名录》里。另外，《现代魔法的重大发现》和《近代巫术发展研究》中也找不到他的名字。还有，当然啦，单是馆内藏书的规模就令人望而却步，那里有成千上万本书，几千个书架，几百条狭窄的通道。

赫敏从口袋里掏出一张清单，上面列着她决定要查找的主题和书名。

CHAPTER TWELVE   The Mirror of Erised

the shelves at random. Harry wandered over to the Restricted Section. He had been wondering for a while if Flamel wasn't somewhere in there. Unfortunately, you needed a specially signed note from one of the teachers to look in any of the restricted books and he knew he'd never get one. These were the books containing powerful Dark Magic never taught at Hogwarts and only read by older students studying advanced Defence Against the Dark Arts.

'What are you looking for, boy?'

'Nothing,' said Harry.

Madam Pince the librarian brandished a feather duster at him.

'You'd better get out, then. Go on – out!'

Wishing he'd been a bit quicker at thinking up some story, Harry left the library. He, Ron and Hermione had already agreed they'd better not ask Madam Pince where they could find Flamel. They were sure she'd be able to tell them, but they couldn't risk Snape hearing what they were up to.

Harry waited outside in the corridor to see if the other two had found anything, but he wasn't very hopeful. They had been looking for a fortnight, after all, but as they only had odd moments between lessons it wasn't surprising they'd found nothing. What they really needed was a nice long search without Madam Pince breathing down their necks.

Five minutes later, Ron and Hermione joined him, shaking their heads. They went off to lunch.

'You will keep looking while I'm away, won't you?' said Hermione. 'And send me an owl if you find anything.'

'And you could ask your parents if they know who Flamel is,' said Ron. 'It'd be safe to ask them.'

'Very safe, as they're both dentists,' said Hermione.

Once the holidays had started, Ron and Harry were having too good a time to think much about Flamel. They had the dormitory to themselves and the common room was far emptier than usual, so they were able to get the good armchairs by the fire. They sat by the hour eating anything they could spear on a toasting fork – bread, crumpets, marshmallows – and plotting ways of getting Malfoy expelled, which were fun to talk about even if they wouldn't work.

第12章 厄里斯魔镜

与此同时，罗恩在一排图书前溜达着，漫无目标地把一些书从书架上抽出来。哈利不知不觉来到禁书区。他已经想了一阵子，尼可·勒梅会不会在那里。不幸的是，要查找任何一本禁书都必须有老师亲笔签名的纸条，哈利知道他是不可能弄到的。这些书里包含着霍格沃茨课堂上从来不讲的很厉害的黑魔法，只有高年级学生在研究高深的黑魔法防御术时才能读到。

"你想找什么，孩子？"

"没什么。"哈利回答。

图书馆管理员平斯女士朝他挥舞着一把鸡毛掸。

"那么你最好出去。走吧——出去！"

哈利离开了图书馆，后悔刚才应该脑子灵活一点儿，信口编出几句谎话。他和罗恩、赫敏一致认为，最好别向平斯女士打听在什么地方能找到勒梅。他们知道她肯定能告诉他们，但他们不能冒险让斯内普探听到他们想做什么。

哈利在外面的走廊里等着，看另外两个人是否能有所发现，但并不抱很大的希望。他们已经找了两个星期，但只是利用了课余的时间，所以一无所获也并不奇怪。现在最需要的是痛痛快快地好好搜寻一番，别让平斯女士在后面盯着，把呼吸喷在他们的后脖颈上。

五分钟后，罗恩和赫敏回到他身边，失望地摇了摇头。他们一起去吃午饭。

"我不在的时候，你们还要继续查找，好吗？"赫敏说，"一旦有什么发现，就派一只猫头鹰告诉我。"

"你也可以问问你的父母，他们是不是知道勒梅这个人。"罗恩说，"问问他们是很安全的。"

"非常安全，因为他们俩都是牙医。"赫敏说。

放假后，罗恩和哈利玩得太开心了，没有多少时间去想勒梅的事。宿舍完全归他们支配，公共休息室里的人也比平常少了许多，他们能够占领炉火边那几把更舒服的扶手椅了。这会儿，他们就坐在那里，一边吃着所有能用烤叉戳起的食物——面包、面饼、棉花糖，一边设计着能使马尔福被开除的方案。尽管这些方案都不可能付诸实施，但是谈谈总是令人开心的。

CHAPTER TWELVE The Mirror of Erised

Ron also started teaching Harry wizard chess. This was exactly like Muggle chess except that the figures were alive, which made it a lot like directing troops in battle. Ron's set was very old and battered. Like everything else he owned, it had once belonged to someone else in his family – in this case, his grandfather. However, old chessmen weren't a drawback at all. Ron knew them so well he never had trouble getting them to do what he wanted.

Harry played with chessmen Seamus Finnigan had lent him and they didn't trust him at all. He wasn't a very good player yet and they kept shouting different bits of advice at him, which was confusing: 'Don't send me there, can't you see his knight? Send *him*, we can afford to lose *him*.'

On Christmas Eve, Harry went to bed looking forward to the next day for the food and the fun, but not expecting any presents at all. When he woke early next morning, however, the first thing he saw was a small pile of packages at the foot of his bed.

'Happy Christmas,' said Ron sleepily as Harry scrambled out of bed and pulled on his dressing-gown.

'You too,' said Harry. 'Will you look at this? I've got some presents!'

'What did you expect, turnips?' said Ron, turning to his own pile, which was a lot bigger than Harry's.

Harry picked up the top parcel. It was wrapped in thick brown paper and scrawled across it was *To Harry, from Hagrid*. Inside was a roughly cut wooden flute. Hagrid had obviously whittled it himself. Harry blew it – it sounded a bit like an owl.

A second, very small parcel contained a note.

We received your message and enclose your Christmas present. From Uncle Vernon and Aunt Petunia. Sellotaped to the note was a fifty-pence piece.

'That's friendly,' said Harry.

Ron was fascinated by the fifty pence.

'*Weird!*' he said. 'What a shape! This is *money?*'

'You can keep it,' said Harry, laughing at how pleased Ron was. 'Hagrid and my aunt and uncle – so who sent these?'

'I think I know who that one's from,' said Ron, going a bit pink and pointing to a very lumpy parcel. 'My mum. I told her you didn't expect any presents and – oh, no,' he groaned, 'she's made you a Weasley jumper.'

第 12 章　厄里斯魔镜

罗恩还开始教哈利下巫师棋。巫师棋和麻瓜象棋一模一样，但它的棋子都是活的，所以使人感觉更像是在指挥军队作战。罗恩的那副棋已经很旧了，破破烂烂的。罗恩所有的东西原先都属于家里的其他人，这副棋是他爷爷的。不过，棋子旧一些丝毫没有妨碍。罗恩对它们非常熟悉，毫不费力就能让它们听从他的调遣。

哈利用的是西莫·斐尼甘留给他的那套棋子，它们根本不信任他。他的水平还不很高，棋子们东一句西一句地对他指手画脚，把他的脑袋都吵昏了："不要把我派到那里，你没看见他的马吗？派他去吧，他牺牲了没关系。"

圣诞节前夕，哈利上床睡觉的时候，只盼着第二天可以大吃一顿，开开心心地玩一场，根本没有想到会收到礼物。然而，第二天一早醒来，第一眼看见的就是他床脚边放着的一小堆包裹。

"圣诞快乐。"哈利摸索着下了床，套上晨衣，这时罗恩睡眼惺忪地说。

"也祝你快乐。"哈利说，"你快来看看，我收到了几件礼物！"

"你以为会收到什么？卷心菜吗？"罗恩说，转向他自己的那堆包裹，它比哈利的那堆大得多。

哈利拿起最顶上的那个纸包。它外面包着厚厚的牛皮纸，上面龙飞凤舞地写着海格致哈利。里面是一只做工很粗糙的笛子，显然是海格自己动手做的。哈利吹了一下——声音有点像猫头鹰叫。

第二个很小的纸包里有一张纸条。

我们收到了你的信，附上给你的圣诞礼物。弗农姨父和佩妮姨妈。用透明胶带粘在纸条上的是一枚五十便士的硬币。

"还算友好。"哈利说。

罗恩被那枚硬币迷住了。

"真古怪！"他说，"这样的形状！这也是钱吗？"

"你留着吧。"哈利说，看到罗恩欣喜若狂的样子，不由得大笑起来，"海格送的，姨妈姨父送的——那么这些是谁送的呢？"

"我想我知道这份是谁送的。"罗恩说，微微地红了脸，指着一个鼓鼓囊囊的大纸包，"是我妈妈。我对她说，你以为自己不会收到礼物——哦，糟糕，"他呻吟了一声，"她给你织了一件韦斯莱家特有的那种毛衣。"

CHAPTER TWELVE The Mirror of Erised

Harry had torn open the parcel to find a thick, hand-knitted sweater in emerald green and a large box of home-made fudge.

'Every year she makes us a jumper,' said Ron, unwrapping his own, 'and mine's *always* maroon.'

'That's really nice of her,' said Harry, trying the fudge, which was very tasty.

His next present also contained sweets – a large box of Chocolate Frogs from Hermione.

This left only one parcel. Harry picked it up and felt it. It was very light. He unwrapped it.

Something fluid and silvery grey went slithering to the floor, where it lay in gleaming folds. Ron gasped.

'I've heard of those,' he said in a hushed voice, dropping the box of Every-Flavour Beans he'd got from Hermione. 'If that's what I think it is – they're really rare, and *really* valuable.'

'What is it?'

Harry picked the shining, silvery cloth off the floor. It was strange to the touch, like water woven into material.

'It's an Invisibility Cloak,' said Ron, a look of awe on his face. 'I'm sure it is – try it on.'

Harry threw the Cloak around his shoulders and Ron gave a yell.

'It *is*! Look down!'

Harry looked down at his feet, but they had gone. He dashed to the mirror. Sure enough, his reflection looked back at him, just his head suspended in mid-air, his body completely invisible. He pulled the Cloak over his head and his reflection vanished completely.

'There's a note!' said Ron suddenly. 'A note fell out of it!'

Harry pulled off the Cloak and seized the letter. Written in narrow, loopy writing he had never seen before were the following words:

Your father left this in my possession before he died.
It is time it was returned to you.
Use it well.
A Very Merry Christmas to you.

第12章 厄里斯魔镜

哈利扯开纸包，看见一件厚厚的鲜绿色的手编毛衣，还有一大盒自制的乳脂软糖。

"她每年都给我们织一件毛衣，"罗恩说着，打开他自己的那个纸包，"我的总是暗紫红色的。"

"她真是太好了。"哈利说着，尝了一块乳脂软糖，觉得味道非常甜美。

接下来的一份礼物也是糖——是赫敏送的一大盒巧克力蛙。

还剩最后一个纸包。哈利把它拿起来摸了摸，分量很轻。他拆开纸包。

一种像液体一样的、银灰色的东西簌簌地滑落到地板上，聚成一堆，闪闪发亮。罗恩倒抽了一口冷气。

"我听说过这东西。"他压低声音说，把赫敏送给他的那盒比比多味豆扔到了一边，"如果我想得不错——这东西是非常稀罕、非常宝贵的。"

"是什么？"

哈利从地板上捡起那件银光闪闪的织物。它摸在手里怪怪的，仿佛是用水编织而成。

"是一件隐形衣。"罗恩说，脸上透着敬畏的神色，"我可以肯定——把它穿上试试。"

哈利把隐形衣披在肩头，罗恩发出一声高喊。

"果然是！你往下看！"

哈利低头看自己的脚，真奇怪，它们消失了。他三步两步冲到镜子前面。没错，镜子里的他只有脑袋悬在半空中，身体完全看不见了。他把隐形衣拉到头顶上，镜子里的他便完全隐去了。

"有一张纸条！"罗恩突然说道，"一张纸条从它里面掉出来了！"

哈利脱掉隐形衣，一把抓过那封信。上面用一种他从没有见过的细长的、圈圈套圈圈的字体，写着下面几行字：

> 你父亲死前留下这件东西给我。
> 现在应该归还给你。
> 好好使用。
> 衷心祝你圣诞快乐。

CHAPTER TWELVE The Mirror of Erised

There was no signature. Harry stared at the note. Ron was admiring the Cloak.

'I'd give *anything* for one of these,' he said. '*Anything*. What's the matter?'

'Nothing,' said Harry. He felt very strange. Who had sent the Cloak? Had it really once belonged to his father?

Before he could say or think anything else, the dormitory door was flung open and Fred and George Weasley bounded in. Harry stuffed the Cloak quickly out of sight. He didn't feel like sharing it with anyone else yet.

'Merry Christmas!'

'Hey, look – Harry's got a Weasley jumper, too!'

Fred and George were wearing blue jumpers, one with a large yellow F on it, the other with a large yellow G.

'Harry's is better than ours, though,' said Fred, holding up Harry's jumper. 'She obviously makes more of an effort if you're not family.'

'Why aren't you wearing yours, Ron?' George demanded. 'Come on, get it on, they're lovely and warm.'

'I hate maroon,' Ron moaned half-heartedly as he pulled it over his head.

'You haven't got a letter on yours,' George observed. 'I suppose she thinks you don't forget your name. But we're not stupid – we know we're called Gred and Forge.'

'What's all this noise?'

Percy Weasley stuck his head through the door, looking disapproving. He had clearly come halfway through unwrapping his presents as he, too, carried a lumpy jumper over his arm, which Fred seized.

'P for prefect! Get it on, Percy, come on, we're all wearing ours, even Harry got one.'

'I – don't – want –' said Percy thickly, as the twins forced the jumper over his head, knocking his glasses askew.

'And you're not sitting with the Prefects today, either,' said George. 'Christmas is a time for family.'

They frog-marched Percy from the room, his arms pinned to his sides by his jumper.

Harry had never in all his life had such a Christmas dinner. A hundred fat, roast turkeys, mountains of roast and boiled potatoes, platters of fat

第12章　厄里斯魔镜

没有署名。哈利瞪着纸条发呆，罗恩则对着隐形衣赞叹不已。

"如果能得到这样一件东西，我什么都可以不要，"他说，"什么都可以不要。你怎么啦？"

"没什么。"哈利说。他觉得这件事非常蹊跷。隐形衣是谁送来的呢？它以前真的属于他父亲吗？

没等他再说什么或再想什么，宿舍的门猛地被推开了，弗雷德和乔治·韦斯莱冲了进来。哈利赶紧把隐形衣藏了起来。他还不想让别人知道。

"圣诞快乐！"

"嘿，瞧——哈利也得到了一件韦斯莱毛衣！"

弗雷德和乔治都穿着蓝色毛衣，一件上面有个大大的、黄色的"F"，另一件上面有个大大的、黄色的"G"。

"哈利的比我们俩的好，"弗雷德说着，举起了哈利的毛衣，"显然，妈妈对不是自家的人更上心一些。"

"你为什么不穿上你的呢，罗恩？"乔治问道，"来吧，穿上吧，这毛衣可是又漂亮又暖和啊。"

"我不喜欢暗紫红色。"罗恩半真半假地抱怨着，把毛衣套上了脑袋。

"你的毛衣上没有字母，"乔治说，"她大概认为你不会忘记自己的名字。我们也不傻，知道自己叫乔雷德和弗治。"

"这里吵吵什么呢？"

珀西·韦斯莱从门缝里探进头来，一脸不满的神情。显然他也正在拆他的圣诞礼物，胳膊上搭着一件鼓鼓囊囊的毛衣，弗雷德一把抓了过去。

"'P'是级长的意思！快穿上吧，珀西，快点儿，我们都穿上了，就连哈利也得到了一件呢。"

"我——不想——穿——"珀西含糊不清地说，但双胞胎不管三七二十一，硬是把毛衣套进珀西的脑袋，把他的眼镜都撞歪了。

"而且你今天不许和级长们坐在一起，"乔治说，"圣诞节是全家团圆的日子。"

他们将珀西抬着推出房间，珀西的手臂被毛衣束缚着，动弹不得。

哈利有生以来从未参加过这样的圣诞宴会。一百只胖墩墩的烤火鸡、

CHAPTER TWELVE   The Mirror of Erised

chipolatas, tureens of buttered peas, silver boats of thick, rich gravy and cranberry sauce – and stacks of wizard crackers every few feet along the table. These fantastic crackers were nothing like the feeble Muggle ones the Dursleys usually bought, with their little plastic toys and their flimsy paper hats. Harry pulled a wizard cracker with Fred and it didn't just bang, it went off with a blast like a cannon and engulfed them all in a cloud of blue smoke, while from the inside exploded a rear-admiral's hat and several live, white mice. Up on the High Table, Dumbledore had swapped his pointed wizard's hat for a flowered bonnet and was chuckling merrily at a joke Professor Flitwick had just read him.

Flaming Christmas puddings followed the turkey. Percy nearly broke his teeth on a silver Sickle embedded in his slice. Harry watched Hagrid getting redder and redder in the face as he called for more wine, finally kissing Professor McGonagall on the cheek, who, to Harry's amazement, giggled and blushed, her top hat lop-sided.

When Harry finally left the table, he was laden down with a stack of things out of the crackers, including a pack of non-explodable, luminous balloons, a grow-your-own-warts kit and his own new wizard chess set. The white mice had disappeared and Harry had a nasty feeling they were going to end up as Mrs Norris' Christmas dinner.

Harry and the Weasleys spent a happy afternoon having a furious snowball fight in the grounds. Then, cold, wet and gasping for breath, they returned to the fire in the Gryffindor common room, where Harry broke in his new chess set by losing spectacularly to Ron. He suspected he wouldn't have lost so badly if Percy hadn't tried to help him so much.

After a tea of turkey sandwiches, crumpets, trifle, and Christmas cake, everyone felt too full and sleepy to do much before bed except sit and watch Percy chase Fred and George all over Gryffindor Tower because they'd stolen his prefect badge.

It had been Harry's best Christmas day ever. Yet something had been nagging at the back of his mind all day. Not until he climbed into bed was he free to think about it: the Invisibility Cloak and whoever had sent it.

Ron, full of turkey and cake and with nothing mysterious to bother him, fell asleep almost as soon as he'd drawn the curtains of his four-poster. Harry leant over the side of his own bed and pulled the Cloak out from under it.

第12章 厄里斯魔镜

堆成小山似的烤肉和煮土豆、一大盘一大盘的美味小香肠、一碗碗拌了黄油的豌豆、一碟碟又浓又稠的肉卤和越橘酱——顺着餐桌每走几步，就有大堆大堆的巫师彩包爆竹在等着你。这些奇妙的彩包爆竹可不像德思礼家通常买的那些寒酸的麻瓜爆竹，里面只有一些小塑料玩具和很不结实的纸帽子。哈利和弗雷德一起抽了一个彩包爆竹，它不是嘭的一声闷响，而是发出了像大炮轰炸那样的爆响，把他们都吞没在一股蓝色的烟雾中，同时从里面炸出一顶海军少将的帽子，以及几只活蹦乱跳的小白鼠。在主宾席上，邓布利多将他尖尖的巫师帽换成了一顶装点着鲜花的女帽。弗立维教授刚给他说了一段笑话，他开心地呵呵笑着。

火鸡之后是火焰圣诞布丁。珀西的那块布丁里裹着一个银西可，差点硌碎了他的牙齿。哈利看着海格一杯接一杯地要酒喝，脸膛越来越红，最后竟然在麦格教授的面颊上亲了一口。令哈利惊讶的是，麦格教授竟咯咯地笑着，羞红了脸，她的高顶黑色大礼帽歪到了一边。

哈利离开餐桌时，怀里抱着一大堆从彩包爆竹里炸出来的东西，包括一袋不会爆炸的闪光气球、一个模仿肉瘤的小设备，还有一套属于他自己的巫师棋。那几只小白鼠不见了。哈利有一种很不舒服的感觉，怀疑它们最后都成了洛丽丝夫人的圣诞大餐。

哈利和韦斯莱兄弟几个在操场上打雪仗，疯玩了一下午，过得非常愉快。然后，他们实在冷得不行了，衣服湿漉漉的，气喘吁吁地回到公共休息室的炉火旁。哈利试了试他的新棋子，结果很惨地输给了罗恩。哈利心里嘀咕，如果没有珀西在一旁不停地瞎出主意，他还不会输得这样惨。

吃过由火鸡三明治、烤面饼、酒浸果酱布丁和圣诞蛋糕组成的茶点，大家都感到肚子太饱，有点犯困了。他们睡觉前不想再做别的，只是看着珀西追着弗雷德和乔治在格兰芬多塔楼里跑来跑去，因为双胞胎抢走了珀西的级长徽章。

这是哈利有生以来最愉快的一个圣诞节。然而，一整天来，总有一件事情萦绕在他的脑海里。直到上床以后，他才有了空闲去想它：那件隐形衣，以及把隐形衣送给他的那个人。

罗恩肚子里塞满了火鸡和蛋糕，又没有什么奇怪的事情困扰他，几乎一放下床帷就睡着了。哈利从自己床边探出身去，从床底下抽出隐形衣。

CHAPTER TWELVE The Mirror of Erised

His father's ... this had been his father's. He let the material flow over his hands, smoother than silk, light as air. *Use it well*, the note had said.

He had to try it, now. He slipped out of bed and wrapped the Cloak around himself. Looking down at his legs, he saw only moonlight and shadows. It was a very funny feeling.

Use it well.

Suddenly, Harry felt wide awake. The whole of Hogwarts was open to him in this Cloak. Excitement flooded through him as he stood there in the dark and silence. He could go anywhere in this, anywhere, and Filch would never know.

Ron grunted in his sleep. Should Harry wake him? Something held him back – his father's Cloak – he felt that this time – the first time – he wanted to use it alone.

He crept out of the dormitory, down the stairs, across the common room and climbed through the portrait hole.

'Who's there?' squawked the Fat Lady. Harry said nothing. He walked quickly down the corridor.

Where should he go? He stopped, his heart racing, and thought. And then it came to him. The Restricted Section in the library. He'd be able to read as long as he liked, as long as it took to find out who Flamel was. He set off, drawing the Invisibility Cloak tight around him as he walked.

The library was pitch black and very eerie. Harry lit a lamp to see his way along the rows of books. The lamp looked as if it was floating along in mid-air, and even though Harry could feel his arm supporting it, the sight gave him the creeps.

The Restricted Section was right at the back of the library. Stepping carefully over the rope which separated these books from the rest of the library, he held up his lamp to read the titles.

They didn't tell him much. Their peeling, faded gold letters spelled words in languages Harry couldn't understand. Some had no title at all. One book had a dark stain on it that looked horribly like blood. The hairs on the back of Harry's neck prickled. Maybe he was imagining it, maybe not, but he thought a faint whispering was coming from the books, as though they knew someone was there who shouldn't be.

He had to start somewhere. Setting the lamp down carefully on the

第12章　厄里斯魔镜

他父亲的……它以前曾是他父亲的。他让织物从手上流过，感觉比丝还要光滑，比光还要轻盈。好好使用，那张纸条上这么说。

他现在必须试一试了。他悄悄从床上滑下来，把隐形衣裹在身上。他低头看自己的腿，却只看见月光和黑影。这真是一种十分奇怪的感觉。

好好使用。

突然，哈利一下子清醒了。有了这件隐形衣，整个霍格沃茨就对他完全敞开了。他站在黑暗和寂静中，内心感到一阵兴奋。穿着这件隐形衣，他可以去任何地方。任何地方啊，费尔奇永远也不会知道。

罗恩在睡梦中嘟哝了几声。哈利想，要不要叫醒他呢？出于某种原因，哈利没有这么做——他父亲的隐形衣——他觉得这一次——这是第一次——他想独自使用。

他蹑手蹑脚地出了宿舍，走下楼梯，穿过公共休息室，爬过那个肖像洞口。

"是谁呀？"胖夫人声音粗哑地问。哈利没有吭声。他飞快地在走廊里走着。

去哪儿呢？他停下脚步，想着，心怦怦乱跳。突然，他想起来了。图书馆的禁书区。他可以尽情地阅读，直到弄清勒梅是何许人。他把隐形衣紧紧地裹在身上，向前走去。

图书馆内漆黑一片，阴森可怖。哈利点亮一盏灯，端着它走过一排排书架。那灯看上去就像悬浮在半空中，哈利虽然感觉到自己用手端着它，但这景象仍然使他毛骨悚然。

禁书区在图书馆的后部。哈利小心翼翼地跨过把这些书与其他藏书隔开的绳子，举起灯照着，读着书名。

然而，从书名上看不出什么头绪。那些剥落的、褪了色的烫金字母，拼出的都是哈利无法理解的单词。有些书根本没有书名。有一本书上沾着一块暗色的印渍，很像血迹，看上去非常可怕。哈利脖子后面的汗毛都竖了起来。他觉得从书里传出了一阵阵若有若无的低语，似乎那些书知道有一个不该待在那里的人待在那里——这也许是他的幻觉，也许不是。

他必须从什么地方入手。他把灯小心地放在地板上，顺着书架底部

CHAPTER TWELVE   The Mirror of Erised

floor, he looked along the bottom shelf for an interesting-looking book. A large black and silver volume caught his eye. He pulled it out with difficulty, because it was very heavy, and, balancing it on his knee, let it fall open.

A piercing, blood-curdling shriek split the silence – the book was screaming! Harry snapped it shut, but the shriek went on and on, one high, unbroken, ear-splitting note. He stumbled backwards and knocked over his lamp, which went out at once. Panicking, he heard footsteps coming down the corridor outside – stuffing the shrieking book back on the shelf, he ran for it. He passed Filch almost in the doorway; Filch's pale, wild eyes looked straight through him and Harry slipped under Filch's outstretched arm and streaked off up the corridor, the book's shrieks still ringing in his ears.

He came to a sudden halt in front of a tall suit of armour. He had been so busy getting away from the library, he hadn't paid attention to where he was going. Perhaps because it was dark, he didn't recognise where he was at all. There was a suit of armour near the kitchens, he knew, but he must be five floors above there.

'You asked me to come directly to you, Professor, if anyone was wandering around at night, and somebody's been in the library – Restricted Section.'

Harry felt the blood drain out of his face. Wherever he was, Filch must know a short cut, because his soft, greasy voice was getting nearer, and to his horror, it was Snape who replied.

'The Restricted Section? Well, they can't be far, we'll catch them.'

Harry stood rooted to the spot as Filch and Snape came around the corner ahead. They couldn't see him, of course, but it was a narrow corridor and if they came much nearer they'd knock right into him – the Cloak didn't stop him being solid.

He backed away as quietly as he could. A door stood ajar to his left. It was his only hope. He squeezed through it, holding his breath, trying not to move it, and to his relief he managed to get inside the room without their noticing anything. They walked straight past and Harry leant against the wall, breathing deeply, listening to their footsteps dying away. That had been close, very close. It was a few seconds before he noticed anything about the room he had hidden in.

It looked like a disused classroom. The dark shapes of desks and chairs were piled against the walls and there was an upturned waste-paper basket –

第12章 厄里斯魔镜

望过去,想找一本看上去有点意思的书。他突然看见一本黑色和银色相间的大书。书很沉,他费力地把它抽了出来,放在膝盖上,让它自己打开来。

一阵凄厉的、令人毛骨悚然的尖叫划破了寂静——那本书在惨叫!哈利猛地把它合上,但是尖叫声没有停止,那是一种高亢的、持续不断的、震耳欲聋的声调。他跟跄着后退了几步,灯被撞翻,立刻就熄灭了。在惊慌失措中,他听见外面的走廊里传来了脚步声——他赶紧把那本尖叫的书插回书架,撒腿就跑。几乎就在门口,他与费尔奇擦肩而过,费尔奇那双狂怒的浅色眼睛径直透过他的身体望出去。哈利从费尔奇张开的臂膀下溜过,沿着走廊狂奔,那本书的尖叫声仍然在他耳畔回荡。

他在一套高高的盔甲前突然刹住了脚步。他刚才急于逃离图书馆,根本没有注意在往哪儿走。也许是因为四下里太黑了,他辨不清自己身在何处。他知道厨房附近有一套盔甲,但是他现在肯定要比厨房高出五层。

"教授,你说过的,如果有人夜里到处乱逛,就立刻来向你汇报,刚才有人在图书馆,在禁书区。"

哈利觉得自己脸上顿时失去了血色。不管他在哪里,费尔奇肯定知道一条捷径,因为他那黏糊糊的、发腻的声音离他越来越近了,而且令他大为惊恐的是,他听见了斯内普的声音在回答。

"禁书区?那么他们不可能走远,我们一定能抓住他们。"

哈利像脚底生了根似的待在原地,费尔奇和斯内普从前面的墙角拐过来了。他们看不见他,但这道走廊很窄,如果他们再走近一些,就会撞到他身上——隐形衣并没有使他的实体也消失啊。

他一步步后退,尽量不发出声音。左边有一扇门开了一条缝。这是他唯一的希望。他侧身挤了进去,小心翼翼地不把门碰动。谢天谢地,总算进了房间。他们什么也没有注意到,径直走了进去。哈利靠在墙上,深深地吸气,听着他们的脚步声渐渐远去。刚才真惊险呀,太惊险了。几秒钟后,他才开始留意他借以藏身的这个房间里的情景。

它看上去像是一间废弃不用的教室。许多桌椅堆放在墙边,呈现出大团黑乎乎的影子,另外还有一只倒扣着的废纸篓——但是,在正对着

CHAPTER TWELVE   The Mirror of Erised

but propped against the wall facing him was something that didn't look as if it belonged there, something that looked as if someone had just put it there to keep it out of the way.

It was a magnificent mirror, as high as the ceiling, with an ornate gold frame, standing on two clawed feet. There was an inscription carved around the top: *Erised stra ehru oyt ube cafru oyt on wohsi.*

His panic fading now that there was no sound of Filch and Snape, Harry moved nearer to the mirror, wanting to look at himself but see no reflection again. He stepped in front of it.

He had to clap his hands to his mouth to stop himself screaming. He whirled around. His heart was pounding far more furiously than when the book had screamed – for he had seen not only himself in the mirror, but a whole crowd of people standing right behind him.

But the room was empty. Breathing very fast, he turned slowly back to the mirror.

There he was, reflected in it, white and scared-looking, and there, reflected behind him, were at least ten others. Harry looked over his shoulder – but, still, no one was there. Or were they all invisible, too? Was he in fact in a room full of invisible people and this mirror's trick was that it reflected them, invisible or not?

He looked in the mirror again. A woman standing right behind his reflection was smiling at him and waving. He reached out a hand and felt the air behind him. If she was really there, he'd touch her, their reflections were so close together, but he felt only air – she and the others existed only in the mirror.

She was a very pretty woman. She had dark red hair and her eyes – her eyes are just like mine, Harry thought, edging a little closer to the glass. Bright green – exactly the same shape, but then he noticed that she was crying; smiling, but crying at the same time. The tall, thin, black-haired man standing next to her put his arm around her. He wore glasses, and his hair was very untidy. It stuck up at the back, just like Harry's did.

Harry was so close to the mirror now that his nose was nearly touching that of his reflection.

'Mum?' he whispered. 'Dad?'

They just looked at him, smiling. and slowly, Harry looked into the faces

第12章 厄里斯魔镜

他的那面墙边上，却搁着一件似乎不属于这里的东西，仿佛是有人因为没有地方放，临时把它搁在这里的。

这是一面非常气派的镜子，高度直达天花板，华丽的金色镜框，底下是两只爪子形的脚支撑着。顶部刻着一行字：厄里斯　斯特拉　厄赫鲁　阿伊特乌比　卡弗鲁　阿伊特昂　沃赫斯

现在，费尔奇和斯内普的声音听不见了，哈利紧张的心情松弛下来。他慢慢走近镜子，想看一眼自己的形象，但镜子里空空如也。他又跨近几步，站到镜子前面。

他不得不用手捂住嘴巴，才没有失声尖叫起来。他猛地转过身，心跳得比刚才那本书尖叫时还要疯狂——因为他在镜子里不仅看见了他自己，还看见一大堆人站在他身后。

但是房间里没有人啊。他急促地喘息着，慢慢地转身看着镜子。

没错，镜子里有他，脸色煞白，惊恐万分，同时镜子里还有至少十来个人，站在他的身后。哈利又扭头朝后看去——还是一个人也没有。难道他们也都隐形了？难道他实际上是在一间有许多隐形人的房间里，而这面镜子的魔力就是把他们都照出来，不管隐形的还是没有隐形的？

他又仔细看着镜子。在镜子里，一个站在他身后的女人正在对他微笑和招手。他伸出手去，在身后摸索着。如果那女人真的存在，哈利应该能碰到她，他们两人在镜子里挨得多么近啊，可是哈利触摸到的只有空气——那女人和其他人只存在于镜子里。

这是一个非常美丽的女人，有着深红色的头发，她的眼睛——她的眼睛长得和我一模一样，哈利想道。他往前又走了一步。翠绿色的双眼——形状也一样。但这时他发现女人在哭泣，她面带微笑，同时又在哭泣。站在她身边的那个黑头发的高大、消瘦的男人用手搂住她。男人戴着眼镜，头发乱蓬蓬的，后脑勺儿上的一撮头发很不听话地竖着，正和哈利的一样。

哈利现在离镜子很近很近了，鼻子几乎碰到了镜子中自己的鼻子。

"妈妈？"他低声唤道，"爸爸？"

他们都看着他，亲切地微笑着。哈利慢慢地挨个儿打量镜子里其他

CHAPTER TWELVE The Mirror of Erised

of the other people in the mirror and saw other pairs of green eyes like his, other noses like his, even a little old man who looked as though he had Harry's knobbly knees – Harry was looking at his family, for the first time in his life.

The Potters smiled and waved at Harry and he stared hungrily back at them, his hands pressed flat against the glass as though he was hoping to fall right through it and reach them. He had a powerful kind of ache inside him, half joy, half terrible sadness.

How long he stood there, he didn't know. The reflections did not fade and he looked and looked until a distant noise brought him back to his senses. He couldn't stay here, he had to find his way back to bed. He tore his eyes away from his mother's face, whispered, 'I'll come back,' and hurried from the room.

'You could have woken me up,' said Ron, crossly.

'You can come tonight, I'm going back, I want to show you the mirror.'

'I'd like to see your mum and dad,' Ron said eagerly.

'And I want to see all your family, all the Weasleys, you'll be able to show me your other brothers and everyone.'

'You can see them any old time,' said Ron. 'Just come round my house this summer. Anyway, maybe it only shows dead people. Shame about not finding Flamel, though. Have some bacon or something, why aren't you eating anything?'

Harry couldn't eat. He had seen his parents and would be seeing them again tonight. He had almost forgotten about Flamel. It didn't seem very important any more. Who cared what the three-headed dog was guarding? What did it matter if Snape stole it, really?

'Are you all right?' said Ron. 'You look odd.'

What Harry feared most was that he might not be able to find the mirror room again. With Ron covered in the Cloak too, they had to walk much more slowly next night. They tried retracing Harry's route from the library, wandering around the dark passageways for nearly an hour.

'I'm freezing,' said Ron. 'Let's forget it and go back.'

'*No!*' Harry hissed. 'I know it's here somewhere.'

人的脸，发现他们都有着和他一模一样的绿眼睛、一模一样的鼻子，一个小老头儿甚至还有着和哈利一模一样的凹凸不平的膝盖——哈利正在望着他的家人，这是他有生以来的第一次。

波特一家人笑眯眯地朝哈利挥手。他如饥似渴地凝视着他们，双手紧紧按在镜子玻璃上，就好像他希望能够扑进去和他们待在一起。他内心感到一阵强烈的剧痛，一半是因为喜悦，一半是因为深切的忧伤。

他在那里站了多久，他不知道。镜子里的形象始终没有隐去，他看呀看呀，怎么也看不够，直到远处传来一些声音，才使他恢复了理智。他不能待在这里，必须回去睡觉。他恋恋不舍地把目光从他母亲脸上挪开，低声说道："我还会再来的。"便匆匆离开了房间。

"你应该把我叫醒的。"罗恩生气地说。

"今晚你可以去，我还要去的，我想让你看看那面镜子。"

"我想看看你的爸爸妈妈。"罗恩急切地说。

"我也想看看你的全家，看看韦斯莱的一大家人，你可以把你另外的几个兄弟和所有的亲戚都指给我看。"

"你随时都能看到他们的，"罗恩说，"今年暑假到我们家来吧。不过，镜子里或许只能出现死人。唉，真惭愧，我们还没有找到勒梅的资料。你吃点熏咸肉或别的什么吧，你怎么什么也不吃？"

哈利吃不下去。他见到了他的父母，而且今晚还要与他们相见。他差不多把勒梅忘到了脑后。这件事似乎已经不再那么重要了。谁管那条三个脑袋的大狗在看守什么呢？就算斯内普把那东西偷走，又有什么关系呢？

"你没事吧？"罗恩说，"你看上去挺怪的。"

哈利最担心的是他找不到那个放镜子的房间。第二天，因为罗恩也罩在隐形衣里，他们走得就慢多了。他们想找到哈利从图书馆出来的那条路线，在昏暗的过道里漫无目的地转了将近一个小时。

"我冻坏了，"罗恩说，"我们不找了，回去吧。"

"不行！"哈利嘶哑着声音说，"我知道就在附近的什么地方。"

CHAPTER TWELVE   The Mirror of Erised

They passed the ghost of a tall witch gliding in the opposite direction, but saw no one else. Just as Ron started moaning that his feet were dead with cold, Harry spotted the suit of armour.

'It's here – just here – yes!'

They pushed the door open. Harry dropped the Cloak from round his shoulders and ran to the mirror.

There they were. His mother and father beamed at the sight of him.

'See?' Harry whispered.

'I can't see anything.'

'Look! Look at them all ... there are loads of them ...'

'I can only see you.'

'Look in it properly, go on, stand where I am.'

Harry stepped aside, but with Ron in front of the mirror, he couldn't see his family any more, just Ron in his paisley pyjamas.

Ron, though, was staring transfixed at his image.

'Look at me!' he said.

'Can you see all your family standing around you?'

'No – I'm alone – but I'm different – I look older – and I'm Head Boy!'

'*What?*'

'I am – I'm wearing the badge like Bill used to – and I'm holding the House Cup and the Quidditch Cup – I'm Quidditch captain, too!'

Ron tore his eyes away from this splendid sight to look excitedly at Harry.

'Do you think this mirror shows the future?'

'How can it? All my family are dead – let me have another look –'

'You had it to yourself all last night, give me a bit more time.'

'You're only holding the Quidditch Cup, what's interesting about that? I want to see my parents.'

'Don't push me –'

A sudden noise outside in the corridor put an end to their discussion. They hadn't realised how loudly they had been talking.

'Quick!'

Ron threw the Cloak back over them as the luminous eyes of Mrs Norris came round the door. Ron and Harry stood quite still, both thinking the

第12章 厄里斯魔镜

他们与一个从对面游荡过来的高个子女巫的幽灵擦肩而过,但没有看见其他人。就在罗恩开始哼叫着说他的脚都要冻僵了时,哈利看见了那套盔甲。

"是这里——就是这里——没错!"

他们推开门。哈利把隐形衣从肩头脱掉,飞奔到镜子前面。

他们还在那里。他的妈妈和爸爸一看见他,顿时喜形于色。

"看见了吗?"哈利小声问。

"我什么也看不见。"

"看呀!看呀……他们都在……有一大堆人呢……"

"我只能看见你。"

"好好看看,过来,站在我这个位置。"

哈利让到一边,然而罗恩一站到镜子前面,哈利就再也看不见他的家人了,只看见罗恩穿着螺纹花呢睡衣站在那里。

罗恩目瞪口呆地看着镜子中的自己。

"看看我!"罗恩说。

"你能看见你的家人都围在你身边吗?"

"没有——只有我一个人——但是跟现在不一样——我好像大了一些——我还是男生学生会主席呢!"

"什么?"

"我—我戴着比尔以前戴的那种徽章——手里还举着学院杯和魁地奇杯——我还是魁地奇球队的队长呢!"

罗恩好不容易才使自己的目光离开这副辉煌的景象,兴奋地看着哈利。

"你说,这面镜子是不是预示着未来?"

"怎么可能呢?我家里的人都死了——让我再看看——"

"你已经独自看了一晚上,就让给我一点儿时间吧。"

"你只是捧着魁地奇杯,这有什么好玩的?我想看看我的父母。"

"你别推我——"

外面走廊里突然响起的声音,结束了他们的争执。他们没有意识到刚才他们的说话声有多响。

"快!"

罗恩刚把隐形衣披在两人身上,洛丽丝夫人那双亮晶晶的眼睛就拐

CHAPTER TWELVE   The Mirror of Erised

same thing – did the Cloak work on cats? After what seemed an age, she turned and left.

'This isn't safe – she might have gone for Filch, I bet she heard us. Come on.'

And Ron pulled Harry out of the room.

The snow still hadn't melted next morning.

'Want to play chess, Harry?' said Ron.

'No.'

'Why don't we go down and visit Hagrid?'

'No ... you go ...'

'I know what you're thinking about, Harry, that mirror. Don't go back tonight.'

'Why not?'

'I dunno, I've just got a bad feeling about it – and anyway, you've had too many close shaves already. Filch, Snape and Mrs Norris are wandering around. So what if they can't see you? What if they walk into you? What if you knock something over?'

'You sound like Hermione.'

'I'm serious, Harry, don't go.'

But Harry only had one thought in his head, which was to get back in front of the mirror, and Ron wasn't going to stop him.

That third night he found his way more quickly than before. He was walking so fast he knew he was making more noise than was wise, but he didn't meet anyone.

And there were his mother and father smiling at him again, and one of his grandfathers nodding happily. Harry sank down to sit on the floor in front of the mirror. There was nothing to stop him staying here all night with his family. Nothing at all.

Except –

'So – back again, Harry?'

Harry felt as though his insides had turned to ice. He looked behind him. Sitting on one of the desks by the wall was none other than Albus Dumbledore. Harry must have walked straight past him, so desperate to get

第12章 厄里斯魔镜

进门来了。罗恩和哈利一动不动地站着，心里想着同样的念头——隐形衣对猫有作用吗？过了大约一个世纪，洛丽丝夫人终于转身离去了。

"还是不安全——它可能去找费尔奇了，我敢肯定它听见我们的声音了。走吧。"

罗恩拉着哈利，走出了房间。

第二天早晨，雪还没有融化。
"想下棋吗？"罗恩问。
"不想。"
"我们干吗不下去看看海格呢？"
"不去……你去吧……"
"我知道你在想什么，哈利，你在想那面镜子。今晚别再去了。"
"为什么？"
"我不知道。我只是有一种很不好的感觉——而且，这么多次你都是侥幸脱险。费尔奇、斯内普和洛丽丝夫人正在到处转悠。如果他们看见你怎么办？如果他们撞到你身上怎么办？"
"你说话的口气像赫敏。"
"我不是开玩笑，哈利，真的别去了。"

可是哈利脑海里只有一个念头，那就是回到镜子前。罗恩是怎么也拦不住他的。

第三个晚上，哈利已是轻车熟路。他一路走得飞快，虽然意识到自己发出了很响的声音，但他并没有遇到什么人。

啊，他的妈妈和爸爸又在那里对他微笑了，还有他的一个爷爷在愉快地点头。哈利一屁股坐在镜子前面的地板上。他要整晚待在这里，和自己的家人在一起，什么也不能阻拦他。什么也不能！

除非——

"这么说——你又来了，哈利？"

哈利觉得自己的五脏六腑一下子冻成了冰。他朝身后看去。坐在墙边一张桌子上的，不是别人，正是阿不思·邓布利多。哈利刚才一定是

CHAPTER TWELVE The Mirror of Erised

to the mirror he hadn't noticed him.

'I – I didn't see you, sir.'

'Strange how short-sighted being invisible can make you,' said Dumbledore, and Harry was relieved to see that he was smiling.

'So,' said Dumbledore, slipping off the desk to sit on the floor with Harry, 'you, like hundreds before you, have discovered the delights of the Mirror of Erised.'

'I didn't know it was called that, sir.'

'But I expect you've realised by now what it does?'

'It – well – it shows me my family –'

'And it showed your friend Ron himself as Head Boy.'

'How did you know –?'

'I don't need a cloak to become invisible,' said Dumbledore gently. 'Now, can you think what the Mirror of Erised shows us all?'

Harry shook his head.

'Let me explain. The happiest man on earth would be able to use the Mirror of Erised like a normal mirror, that is, he would look into it and see himself exactly as he is. Does that help?'

Harry thought. Then he said slowly, 'It shows us what we want ... whatever we want ...'

'Yes and no,' said Dumbledore quietly. 'It shows us nothing more or less than the deepest, most desperate desire of our hearts. You, who have never known your family, see them standing around you. Ronald Weasley, who has always been overshadowed by his brothers, sees himself standing alone, the best of all of them. However, this mirror will give us neither knowledge or truth. Men have wasted away before it, entranced by what they have seen, or been driven mad, not knowing if what it shows is real or even possible.

'The Mirror will be moved to a new home tomorrow, Harry, and I ask you not to go looking for it again. If you ever *do* run across it, you will now be prepared. It does not do to dwell on dreams and forget to live, remember that. Now, why don't you put that admirable Cloak back on and get off to bed?'

Harry stood up.

'Sir – Professor Dumbledore? Can I ask you something?'

径直从他身边走过的,他太急着去看镜子了,根本没有注意到他。

"我——我没有看见你,先生。"

"真奇怪,隐形以后你居然还变得近视了。"邓布利多说。哈利看到他脸上带着微笑,不由得松了口气。

"这么说,"邓布利多说着,从桌子上滑下来,和哈利一起坐到地板上,"你和你之前的千百个人一样,已经发现了厄里斯魔镜的乐趣。"

"我不知道它叫这个名字,先生。"

"不过我猜想你现在已经知道它的魔力了吧?"

"它——哦——它使我看到我的家人——"

"还使你的朋友罗恩看到自己变成了男生学生会主席。"

"你怎么知道——"

"我可不是非要隐形衣才能隐形的。"邓布利多温和地说,"那么,你能不能想一想,厄里斯魔镜使我们大家看到了什么呢?"

哈利摇了摇头。

"让我解释一下吧。世界上最幸福的人把厄里斯魔镜当成普通的镜子使用,也就是说,他在镜子里看见的就是他自己。明白点什么了吗?"

哈利在思考。然后他慢慢地说:"镜子使我们看到自己想要的东西……不管我们想要什么……"

"也对,也不对,"邓布利多轻轻地说,"它只令我们看到内心深处最迫切、最强烈的渴望。你从没见过你的家人,所以看见他们站在你的周围。罗恩·韦斯莱一直在他的哥哥面前相形见绌,所以他看见自己独自站着,是他们中最出色的。然而,这面镜子既不能教给我们知识,也不能告诉我们实情。人们在它面前虚度时日,为自己所见的东西而痴迷,甚至被逼得发疯,因为他们不知道镜子里的一切是否真实,是否能实现。

"明天镜子就要搬到一个新的地方了,哈利,我请你不要再去找它。如果你哪天碰巧再看见它,你要有心理准备。沉湎于虚幻的梦想,而忘记现实的生活,这是毫无益处的,千万记住。好了,为什么不穿上那件奇妙无比的隐形衣回去睡觉呢?"

哈利站了起来。

"先生——邓布利多教授?我可以问你一句话吗?"

CHAPTER TWELVE The Mirror of Erised

'Obviously, you've just done so,' Dumbledore smiled. 'You may ask me one more thing, however.'

'What do you see when you look in the Mirror?'

'I? I see myself holding a pair of thick, woollen socks.'

Harry stared.

'One can never have enough socks,' said Dumbledore. 'Another Christmas has come and gone and I didn't get a single pair. People will insist on giving me books.'

It was only when he was back in bed that it struck Harry that Dumbledore might not have been quite truthful. But then, he thought, as he shoved Scabbers off his pillow, it had been quite a personal question.

第 12 章　厄里斯魔镜

"那还用说,你刚才就这么做了。"邓布利多笑了,"不过,你还可以再问我一个问题。"

"你照镜子的时候,看见了什么?"

"我?我看见自己拿着一双厚厚的羊毛袜。"

哈利睁大了眼睛。

"袜子永远不够穿,"邓布利多说,"圣诞节来了又去,我一双袜子也没有收到。人们坚持要送书给我。"

哈利回到床上以后,才突然想到邓布利多也许并没有说实话。可是,当他推开枕头上的斑斑时,又想:那是一个涉及隐私的问题啊。

CHAPTER THIRTEEN

Nicolas Flamel

Dumbledore had convinced Harry not to go looking for the Mirror of Erised again and for the rest of the Christmas holidays the Invisibility Cloak stayed folded at the bottom of his trunk. Harry wished he could forget what he'd seen in the Mirror as easily, but he couldn't. He started having nightmares. Over and over again he dreamed about his parents disappearing in a flash of green light while a high voice cackled with laughter.

'You see, Dumbledore was right, that mirror could drive you mad,' said Ron, when Harry told him about these dreams.

Hermione, who came back the day before term started, took a different view of things. She was torn between horror at the idea of Harry being out of bed, roaming the school three nights in a row ('If Filch had caught you!') and disappointment that he hadn't at least found out who Nicolas Flamel was.

They had almost given up hope of ever finding Flamel in a library book, even though Harry was still sure he'd read the name somewhere. Once term had started, they were back to skimming through books for ten minutes during their breaks. Harry had even less time than the other two, because Quidditch practice had started again.

Wood was working the team harder than ever. Even the endless rain that had replaced the snow couldn't dampen his spirits. The Weasleys complained that Wood was becoming a fanatic, but Harry was on Wood's side. If they won their next match, against Hufflepuff, they would overtake Slytherin in the House Championship for the first time in seven years. Quite apart from wanting to win, Harry found that he had fewer nightmares when he was tired out after training.

Then, during one particularly wet and muddy practice session, Wood gave

第 13 章

尼可·勒梅

邓布利多说服哈利不要再去寻找厄里斯魔镜,所以在圣诞假期剩下来的日子里,那件隐形衣就一直叠得好好的,放在箱子底部。哈利希望能轻松地忘记他在魔镜里看到的东西,然而不能。他开始做噩梦。他一遍遍地梦见爸爸妈妈在突如其来的一道绿光中消失,同时还有一个很响的声音在嘎嘎怪笑。

"你看,邓布利多说得对,魔镜可能会使你发疯的。"当哈利把这些梦境告诉罗恩时,罗恩这么说。

赫敏在开学前一天回来了,她的看法有所不同。她心情十分复杂,一方面为哈利接连三个夜里从床上起来,在学校里游荡而感到惊恐("费尔奇把你抓住了怎么办!"),一方面又为哈利连尼可·勒梅是谁都没有弄清而深感失望。

他们几乎放弃了在图书馆查到勒梅的希望,尽管哈利仍然坚信自己在什么地方看到过这个名字。学期开始后,他们又恢复了利用课间休息十分钟的时间浏览图书的做法,但哈利的时间比他们俩更少,因为魁地奇训练又开始了。

伍德对队员的要求比以往任何时候都严格。即使在大雪过后连绵不断的阴雨天里,他的热情也没有半点冷却。韦斯莱孪生兄弟抱怨说伍德正在变成一个训练狂,但哈利却站在伍德一边。如果他们赢得下一场对赫奇帕奇的比赛,就能在学院杯冠军赛中战胜斯莱特林队了,这可是七年以来的第一次啊。除了希望比赛取胜以外,哈利还发现,当他训练之后精疲力竭时,噩梦就做得少了。

后来,在一次特别潮湿和泥泞的训练中,伍德告诉队员们一个坏消

the team a bit of bad news. He'd just got very angry with the Weasleys, who kept dive-bombing each other and pretending to fall off their brooms.

'Will you stop messing around!' he yelled. 'That's exactly the sort of thing that'll lose us the match! Snape's refereeing this time, and he'll be looking for any excuse to knock points off Gryffindor!'

George Weasley really did fall off his broom at these words.

'*Snape's* refereeing?' he spluttered through a mouthful of mud. 'When's he ever refereed a Quidditch match? He's not going to be fair if we might overtake Slytherin.'

The rest of the team landed next to George to complain, too.

'It's not *my* fault,' said Wood. 'We've just got to make sure we play a clean game, so Snape hasn't got an excuse to pick on us.'

Which was all very well, thought Harry, but he had another reason for not wanting Snape near him while he was playing Quidditch ...

The rest of the team hung back to talk to each other as usual at the end of practice, but Harry headed straight back to the Gryffindor common room, where he found Ron and Hermione playing chess. Chess was the only thing Hermione ever lost at, something Harry and Ron thought was very good for her.

'Don't talk to me for a moment,' said Ron when Harry sat down next to him. 'I need to concen–' He caught sight of Harry's face. 'What's the matter with you? You look terrible.'

Speaking quietly so that no one else would hear, Harry told the other two about Snape's sudden, sinister desire to be a Quidditch referee.

'Don't play,' said Hermione at once.

'Say you're ill,' said Ron.

'Pretend to break your leg,' Hermione suggested.

'*Really* break your leg,' said Ron.

'I can't,' said Harry. 'There isn't a reserve Seeker. If I back out, Gryffindor can't play at all.'

At that moment Neville toppled into the common room. How he had managed to climb through the portrait hole was anyone's guess, because his legs had been stuck together with what they recognised at once as the Leg-Locker Curse. He must have had to bunny hop all the way up to Gryffindor Tower.

息。他刚才对韦斯莱孪生兄弟发了一顿脾气,因为他们不停地彼此俯冲轰炸,假装从飞天扫帚上摔下来。

"你们能不能别再胡闹了!"伍德嚷道,"这样做肯定会使我们输掉比赛!这次是斯内普当裁判,他准会千方百计找借口给格兰芬多队扣分的!"

乔治·韦斯莱听了这话,真的从飞天扫帚上摔了下来。

"斯内普当裁判?"他一边吐着嘴里的泥土,一边问,"他什么时候当过魁地奇比赛的裁判?如果我们有可能战胜斯莱特林队,他肯定不会公正裁决的。"

其他队员也都降落在乔治旁边,连声抱怨。

"这不能怪我。"伍德说,"我们只能保证自己在比赛中遵守规则,斯内普也就没有借口找我们的碴了。"

这是非常正确的,哈利想,但他还有一个不想让斯内普在比赛时接近他的理由。

训练结束后,其他队员还在磨磨蹭蹭地聊天,哈利却直奔格兰芬多的公共休息室,他发现罗恩和赫敏正在那里下棋。赫敏只有在下棋时才会输,哈利和罗恩认为这对她很有好处。

"先别跟我说话,"哈利在罗恩身边坐下时,罗恩说道,"我需要考虑——"可他一看见哈利的脸,又说,"你怎么啦?你的脸色真可怕。"

哈利压低声音,不想让别人听见,把斯内普不怀好意地突然想当魁地奇裁判的事告诉了他们俩。

"别参加比赛了。"赫敏立刻就说。

"就说你病了。"罗恩说。

"假装把腿摔断了。"赫敏建议道。

"真的把腿摔断。"罗恩说。

"我不能这样,"哈利说,"队里没有替补的找球手。如果我退出,格兰芬多队就无法比赛了。"

就在这时,纳威一头跌进了公共休息室。大家都猜不出他是怎么从肖像洞口钻进来的,因为他的两条腿紧紧地粘在一起。哈利他们一眼就看出,这是被施了锁腿咒。纳威肯定是像兔子那样一路蹦跳着爬上格兰芬多塔楼的。

CHAPTER THIRTEEN   Nicolas Flamel

Everyone fell about laughing except Hermione, who leapt up and performed the counter-curse. Neville's legs sprang apart and he got to his feet, trembling.

'What happened?' Hermione asked him, leading him over to sit with Harry and Ron.

'Malfoy,' said Neville shakily. 'I met him outside the library. He said he'd been looking for someone to practise that on.'

'Go to Professor McGonagall!' Hermione urged Neville. 'Report him!'

Neville shook his head.

'I don't want more trouble,' he mumbled.

'You've got to stand up to him, Neville!' said Ron. 'He's used to walking all over people, but that's no reason to lie down in front of him and make it easier.'

'There's no need to tell me I'm not brave enough to be in Gryffindor, Malfoy's already done that,' Neville choked.

Harry felt in the pocket of his robes and pulled out a Chocolate Frog, the very last one from the box Hermione had given him for Christmas. He gave it to Neville, who looked as though he might cry.

'You're worth twelve of Malfoy,' Harry said. 'The Sorting Hat chose you for Gryffindor, didn't it? And where's Malfoy? In stinking Slytherin.'

Neville's lips twitched in a weak smile as he unwrapped the Frog.

'Thanks, Harry ... I think I'll go to bed ... D'you want the card, you collect them, don't you?'

As Neville walked away Harry looked at the Famous Wizard card.

'Dumbledore again,' he said. 'He was the first one I ever –'

He gasped. He stared at the back of the card. Then he looked up at Ron and Hermione.

'*I've found him!*' he whispered. 'I've found Flamel! I *told* you I'd read the name somewhere before, I read it on the train coming here – listen to this: "Professor Dumbledore is particularly famous for his defeat of the Dark wizard Grindelwald in 1945, for the discovery of the twelve uses of dragon's blood *and his work on alchemy with his partner, Nicolas Flamel*"!'

Hermione jumped to her feet. She hadn't looked so excited since they'd got back the marks for their very first piece of homework.

'Stay there!' she said, and she sprinted up the stairs to the girls'

第13章 尼可·勒梅

大伙儿都笑了起来,只有赫敏没笑。她跳上前去,给纳威施了一个破解咒,纳威的腿一下子分开了。他站起来,浑身颤抖。

"怎么回事?"赫敏把他领过来和哈利、罗恩坐在一起,问道。

"马尔福,"纳威声音颤抖地说,"我在图书馆外面碰到了他。他说他一直在找人练习练习那个咒。"

"去找麦格教授!"赫敏催促纳威,"告他一状!"

纳威摇了摇头。

"我不想再惹麻烦了。"他含糊地嘟哝。

"你必须勇敢地对付他,纳威!"罗恩说,"他一贯盛气凌人,我们没有理由在他面前屈服,让他轻易得逞。"

"你不用对我说我胆子太小,不配待在格兰芬多,马尔福已经对我说过这个话了。"纳威哽咽着说。

哈利把手伸进长袍口袋,掏出一块巧克力蛙,这是圣诞节时赫敏送给他的那盒里的最后一块。哈利把它递给纳威。纳威看上去快要哭了。

"你比十二个马尔福都强,"哈利说,"分院帽把你选进了格兰芬多,不是吗?马尔福在哪里呢?在令人讨厌的斯莱特林。"

纳威拆开巧克力蛙,嘴唇抽动着,露出一个无力的微笑。

"谢谢你,哈利……我想去睡觉了……你要画片吗?你收集画片的,是吗?"

纳威离去后,哈利看着那张著名巫师画片。

"又是邓布利多,"他说,"我第一次就是——"

他倒抽了一口冷气,瞪着画片背面,然后抬头看着罗恩和赫敏。

"我找到他了!"他小声说,"我找到勒梅了!我告诉过你们,我以前在什么地方看到过这个名字,原来,我是在来这儿的火车上看到的——听听这个:邓布利多广为人知的贡献包括:一九四五年击败黑巫师格林德沃,发现火龙血的十二种用途,与合作伙伴尼可·勒梅在炼金术方面卓有成效!"

赫敏一跃而起。自从他们第一次家庭作业的成绩下来之后,她还没有这么兴奋过。

"等着!"她说,然后飞奔上楼,到女生宿舍去了。哈利和罗恩还

CHAPTER THIRTEEN Nicolas Flamel

dormitories. Harry and Ron barely had time to exchange mystified looks before she was dashing back, an enormous old book in her arms.

'I never thought to look in here!' she whispered excitedly. 'I got this out of the library weeks ago for a bit of light reading.'

'*Light?*' said Ron, but Hermione told him to be quiet until she'd looked something up, and started flicking frantically through the pages, muttering to herself.

At last she found what she was looking for.

'I knew it! I *knew* it!'

'Are we allowed to speak yet?' said Ron grumpily. Hermione ignored him.

'Nicolas Flamel,' she whispered dramatically, 'is the *only known maker of the Philosopher's Stone!*'

This didn't have quite the effect she'd expected.

'The what?' said Harry and Ron.

'Oh, *honestly*, don't you two read? Look – read that, there.'

She pushed the book towards them, and Harry and Ron read:

> The ancient study of alchemy is concerned with making the Philosopher's Stone, a legendary substance with astonishing powers. The Stone will transform any metal into pure gold. It also produces the Elixir of Life, which will make the drinker immortal.
>
> There have been many reports of the Philosopher's Stone over the centuries, but the only Stone currently in existence belongs to Mr Nicolas Flamel, the noted alchemist and opera-lover. Mr Flamel, who celebrated his six hundred and sixty-fifth birthday last year, enjoys a quiet life in Devon with his wife, Perenelle (six hundred and fifty-eight).

'See?' said Hermione, when Harry and Ron had finished. 'The dog must be guarding Flamel's Philosopher's Stone! I bet he asked Dumbledore to keep it safe for him, because they're friends and he knew someone was after it. That's why he wanted the Stone moved out of Gringotts!'

'A stone that makes gold and stops you ever dying!' said Harry. 'No wonder Snape's after it! *Anyone* would want it.'

第13章 尼可·勒梅

没来得及交换一下困惑的目光,她就又冲了回来,怀里抱着一本巨大的旧书。

"我就没想到在这里找找!"她激动地低声说,"这是几星期前我从图书馆借出来,想读着消遣的。"

"消遣?"罗恩说,可是赫敏叫他安静,让她查找一个东西。她开始飞快地翻动书页,嘴里念念有词。

终于,她找到了。

"我知道了!我知道了!"

"我们现在可以说话了吧?"罗恩没好气地说。赫敏不理睬他。

"尼可·勒梅,"她像演戏一样压低声音说,"是人们所知的魔法石的唯一制造者!"

她的话并没有取得她预期的效果。

"什么石?"哈利和罗恩问。

"哦,怎么搞的,你们俩平常看不看书啊?瞧——读读这一段。"

她把书推给了他们,哈利和罗恩读道:

> 古代炼金术涉及魔法石的炼造,这是一种具有惊人功能的神奇物质。魔法石能把任何金属变成纯金,还能制造出长生不老药,使喝了这种药的人永远不死。
>
> 许多世纪以来,关于魔法石有过许多报道,但目前唯一仅存的一块魔法石属于著名炼金术士和歌剧爱好者尼可·勒梅先生。他去年庆祝了六百六十五岁生日,现与妻子佩雷纳尔(六百五十八岁)一起隐居于德文郡。

"明白了吗?"哈利和罗恩读完后,赫敏问道,"那条大狗一定是在看守勒梅的魔法石!我敢说是勒梅请邓布利多替他保管的,因为他们是朋友,而且他知道有人在打魔法石的主意,所以才要求把魔法石从古灵阁转移了出来。"

"一块石头能变出金子,还能让你永远不死!"哈利说,"怪不得斯内普也在打它的主意呢!谁都会想得到它的!"

CHAPTER THIRTEEN   Nicolas Flamel

'And no wonder we couldn't find Flamel in that *Study of Recent Developments in Wizardry*,' said Ron. 'He's not exactly recent if he's six hundred and sixty-five, is he?'

Next morning in Defence Against the Dark Arts, while copying down different ways of treating werewolf bites, Harry and Ron were still discussing what they'd do with a Philosopher's Stone if they had one. It wasn't until Ron said he'd buy his own Quidditch team that Harry remembered about Snape and the coming match.

'I'm going to play,' he told Ron and Hermione. 'If I don't, all the Slytherins will think I'm just too scared to face Snape. I'll show them ... it'll really wipe the smiles off their faces if we win.'

'Just as long as we're not wiping you off the pitch,' said Hermione.

As the match drew nearer, however, Harry became more and more nervous, whatever he told Ron and Hermione. The rest of the team weren't too calm, either. The idea of overtaking Slytherin in the House Championship was wonderful, no one had done it for nearly seven years, but would they be allowed to, with such a biased referee?

Harry didn't know whether he was imagining it or not, but he seemed to keep running into Snape wherever he went. At times, he even wondered whether Snape was following him, trying to catch him on his own. Potions lessons were turning into a sort of weekly torture, Snape was so horrible to Harry. Could Snape possibly know they'd found out about the Philosopher's Stone? Harry didn't see how he could – yet he sometimes had the horrible feeling that Snape could read minds.

Harry knew, when they wished him good luck outside the changing rooms next afternoon, that Ron and Hermione were wondering whether they'd ever see him alive again. This wasn't what you'd call comforting. Harry hardly heard a word of Wood's pep talk as he pulled on his Quidditch robes and picked up his Nimbus Two Thousand.

Ron and Hermione, meanwhile, had found a place in the stands next to Neville, who couldn't understand why they looked so grim and worried, or why they had both brought their wands to the match. Little did Harry know

第13章 尼可·勒梅

"怪不得我们在《近代巫术发展研究》里找不到勒梅。"罗恩说,"既然他已经六百六十五岁,就不能算是近代了,是吧?"

第二天上午在黑魔法防御术课上,哈利和罗恩一边记录被狼人咬伤后的多种医治办法,一边还在讨论如果他们弄到魔法石将怎么办。直到罗恩说他要买下一支自己的魁地奇球队时,哈利才想起斯内普和即将到来的比赛。

"我必须参加比赛,"他对罗恩和赫敏说,"如果我退出,斯莱特林们会以为我害怕了,不敢面对斯内普。我要让他们看看……如果我们赢了,就能彻底清除他们脸上得意的笑容。"

"只要我们不把你从赛场上抬下来就好。"赫敏说。

比赛临近了,不管哈利嘴上怎么跟罗恩和赫敏说,他的心情越来越紧张了,其他队员也不太平静。一想到要在学院杯冠军赛中战胜斯莱特林,大家就激动不已。在将近七年的时间里,还没有人能够打败他们。然而,有这样一个偏心的裁判,他们能成功吗?

哈利不知道是他多心呢还是事实如此,似乎他不管走到哪里都会碰到斯内普。有时,他甚至怀疑斯内普在跟踪他,想独自把他抓住。每周一次的魔药课变成了一种痛苦的折磨,斯内普对哈利的态度很恶劣。难道斯内普知道他们发现了魔法石的奥秘?哈利不明白斯内普怎么能知道——他经常有一种可怕的感觉,似乎斯内普能看透别人的思想。

第二天下午,当罗恩和赫敏在更衣室外面祝他好运时,哈利知道,他们实际上在暗暗担心再也见不到他活着回来了。这样能给他什么安慰呢?哈利穿上魁地奇球袍,拿起他的光轮2000,对伍德那番鼓舞士气的话根本没听进去。

与此同时,罗恩和赫敏在看台上找了个地方,就在纳威旁边。纳威不明白他们为什么显得这么沉重和担忧,也不明白他们为什么都把自己的魔杖带到赛场上来了。哈利不知道罗恩和赫敏一直在偷偷练习锁腿咒。

CHAPTER THIRTEEN Nicolas Flamel

that Ron and Hermione had been secretly practising the Leg-Locker Curse. They'd got the idea from Malfoy using it on Neville, and were ready to use it on Snape if he showed any sign of wanting to hurt Harry.

'Now, don't forget, it's *Locomotor Mortis*,' Hermione muttered as Ron slipped his wand up his sleeve.

'I *know*,' Ron snapped. 'Don't nag.'

Back in the changing room, Wood had taken Harry aside.

'Don't want to pressure you, Potter, but if we ever need an early capture of the Snitch it's now. Finish the game before Snape can favour Hufflepuff too much.'

'The whole school's out there!' said Fred Weasley, peering out of the door. 'Even – blimey – Dumbledore's come to watch!'

Harry's heart did a somersault.

'*Dumbledore?*' he said, dashing to the door to make sure. Fred was right. There was no mistaking that silver beard.

Harry could have laughed out loud with relief. He was safe. There was simply no way that Snape would dare to try and hurt him if Dumbledore was watching.

Perhaps that was why Snape was looking so angry as the teams marched on to the pitch, something that Ron noticed, too.

'I've never seen Snape look so mean,' he told Hermione. 'Look – they're off. Ouch!'

Someone had poked Ron in the back of the head. It was Malfoy.

'Oh, sorry, Weasley, didn't see you there.'

Malfoy grinned broadly at Crabbe and Goyle.

'Wonder how long Potter's going to stay on his broom this time? Anyone want a bet? What about you, Weasley?'

Ron didn't answer; Snape had just awarded Hufflepuff a penalty because George Weasley had hit a Bludger at him. Hermione, who had all her fingers crossed in her lap, was squinting fixedly at Harry, who was circling the game like a hawk, looking for the Snitch.

'You know how I think they choose people for the Gryffindor team?' said Malfoy loudly a few minutes later, as Snape awarded Hufflepuff another penalty for no reason at all. 'It's people they feel sorry for. See, there's Potter, who's got no parents, then there's the Weasleys, who've got no money – you

第13章 尼可·勒梅

他们从马尔福给纳威施咒这件事中获得了启发，打算一旦斯内普显示出要伤害哈利的苗头，就对他施咒。

"记住，别忘了，是腿立僵停死。"罗恩把魔杖插在袖子上时，赫敏小声说。

"我知道，"罗恩不耐烦地说，"别唠叨了。"

在更衣室里，伍德把哈利拉到一边。

"不是想给你施加压力，波特，但我们今天比任何时候都需要尽快抓住飞贼。要速战速决，不让斯内普有时间过分偏袒赫奇帕奇。"

"全校学生都出来了！"弗雷德·韦斯莱朝门外窥视，说道，"就连——天哪——邓布利多也来看比赛了！"

哈利的心猛地翻腾了一下。

"邓布利多？"他说着，快步冲到门口，想确认一下。弗雷德说得没错。那银白色的胡子绝不会有错。

哈利一下子如释重负，差点儿放声大笑起来。他没有危险了。如果邓布利多在场观看比赛，斯内普是绝对不敢伤害他的。

也许正是因为这一点，当队员们排着队走向赛场时，斯内普才显得那么恼火，这点罗恩也注意到了。

"我从没看见斯内普脸色这么阴沉。"他对赫敏说，"看——他们出发了。哎哟！"

有人捅了一下罗恩的后脑勺。是马尔福。

"哦，对不起，韦斯莱，没看见你在那儿。"

马尔福对克拉布和高尔咧嘴大笑。

"不知道波特这次能在他的飞天扫帚上待多久？有人愿意打赌吗？你怎么样，韦斯莱？"

罗恩没有回答；斯内普刚才判给赫奇帕奇队一个罚球，因为乔治把一只游走球对准他打了过来。赫敏十指交叉放在膝盖上，眯起眼睛紧紧地盯着哈利，只见哈利像老鹰一样围着赛场盘旋，寻找金色飞贼。

"你知道格兰芬多队是怎么挑选队员的吗？"几分钟后，当斯内普毫无道理地又判给赫奇帕奇队一个罚球时，马尔福大声说道，"他们挑选的是那些他们觉得可怜的人。比如波特，没爹没妈，还有韦斯莱兄弟，

should be on the team, Longbottom, you've got no brains.'

Neville went bright red but turned in his seat to face Malfoy.

'I'm worth twelve of you, Malfoy,' he stammered.

Malfoy, Crabbe and Goyle howled with laughter, but Ron, still not daring to take his eyes from the game, said, 'You tell him, Neville.'

'Longbottom, if brains were gold you'd be poorer than Weasley, and that's saying something.'

Ron's nerves were already stretched to breaking point with anxiety about Harry.

'I'm warning you, Malfoy – one more word –'

'Ron!' said Hermione suddenly. 'Harry –!'

'What? Where?'

Harry had suddenly gone into a spectacular dive, which drew gasps and cheers from the crowd. Hermione stood up, her crossed fingers in her mouth, as Harry streaked towards the ground like a bullet.

'You're in luck, Weasley, Potter's obviously spotted some money on the ground!' said Malfoy.

Ron snapped. Before Malfoy knew what was happening, Ron was on top of him, wrestling him to the ground. Neville hesitated, then clambered over the back of his seat to help.

'Come on, Harry!' Hermione screamed, leaping on to her seat to watch as Harry sped straight at Snape – she didn't even notice Malfoy and Ron rolling around under her seat, or the scuffles and yelps coming from the whirl of fists that was Neville, Crabbe and Goyle.

Up in the air, Snape turned on his broomstick just in time to see something scarlet shoot past him, missing him by inches – next second, Harry had pulled out of the dive, his arm raised in triumph, the Snitch clasped in his hand.

The stands erupted; it had to be a record, no one could ever remember the Snitch being caught so quickly.

'Ron! Ron! Where are you? The game's over! Harry's won! We've won! Gryffindor are in the lead!' shrieked Hermione, dancing up and down on her seat and hugging Parvati Patil in the row in front.

Harry jumped off his broom, a foot from the ground. He couldn't believe it. He'd done it – the game was over; it had barely lasted five minutes. as

第13章 尼可·勒梅

家里没钱——你也应该入队呀,纳威·隆巴顿,因为你没有头脑。"

纳威脸涨得通红,从椅子上转过身子,面对着马尔福。

"我比十二个你加在一起都强,马尔福。"他结结巴巴地说。

马尔福、克拉布和高尔怪声怪气地大笑起来,罗恩不敢让眼睛离开赛场,嘴里说:"给他点厉害瞧瞧,纳威。"

"隆巴顿,如果头脑是金子,你就比韦斯莱还要穷,这就很能说明问题了。"

罗恩一直为哈利揪着心,紧张得神经都要绷断了。

"我警告你,马尔福——你再敢说一句——"

"罗恩!"赫敏突然说道,"哈利——!"

"怎么啦?在哪儿?"

哈利突然来了一个漂亮的俯冲,观众们发出一片惊呼和喝彩。赫敏站了起来,交叉着的手指放在嘴里,只见哈利像一颗子弹一样射向地面。

"你很幸运,韦斯莱,波特显然看见了地上有钱!"马尔福说。

罗恩迅速行动起来。马尔福还没明白是怎么回事,罗恩就蹿到了他身上,把他摆倒在地。纳威迟疑了一下,也从座椅背上翻过来相助。

"快点儿,哈利!"赫敏尖叫着,跳上座位,看着哈利径直冲向斯内普——她甚至没有注意到马尔福和罗恩在她座位下滚成了一团,也没有注意到纳威、克拉布和高尔扭打在一起,拳脚相加,都痛得发出一声声尖叫。

在空中,斯内普刚刚在飞天扫帚上转过身,就看见一个深红色的身影嗖地从他耳边飞过,离他只差几寸——紧接着,哈利停止了俯冲。他胜利地举起手臂,飞贼被他紧紧地抓在手里。

看台上沸腾了;这将是一个新的纪录,谁都不记得在哪次比赛中飞贼这么快就被抓住了。

"罗恩,罗恩!你在哪儿?比赛结束了!哈利赢了!我们赢了!格兰芬多队领先了!"赫敏尖叫着,在椅子上跳个不停,并紧紧地拥抱了一下前排的佩蒂尔。

哈利在离地面一英尺的高度从飞天扫帚上跳了下来。他简直无法相信。他成功了——比赛结束了;只持续了不到五分钟。当格兰芬多们拥

CHAPTER THIRTEEN Nicolas Flamel

Gryffindors came spilling on to the pitch, he saw Snape land nearby, white-faced and tight-lipped – then Harry felt a hand on his shoulder and looked up into Dumbledore's smiling face.

'Well done,' said Dumbledore quietly, so that only Harry could hear. 'Nice to see you haven't been brooding about that mirror … been keeping busy … excellent …'

Snape spat bitterly on the ground.

Harry left the changing room alone some time later, to take his Nimbus Two Thousand back to the broomshed. He couldn't ever remember feeling happier. He'd really done something to be proud of now – no one could say he was just a famous name any more. The evening air had never smelled so sweet. He walked over the damp grass, reliving the last hour in his head, which was a happy blur: Gryffindors running to lift him on to their shoulders; Ron and Hermione in the distance, jumping up and down, Ron cheering through a heavy nosebleed.

Harry had reached the shed. He leant against the wooden door and looked up at Hogwarts, with its windows glowing red in the setting sun. Gryffindor in the lead. He'd done it, he'd shown Snape …

And speaking of Snape …

A hooded figure came swiftly down the front steps of the castle. Clearly not wanting to be seen, it walked as fast as possible towards the Forbidden Forest. Harry's victory faded from his mind as he watched. He recognised the figure's prowling walk. Snape, sneaking into the Forest while everyone else was at dinner – what was going on?

Harry jumped back on his Nimbus Two Thousand and took off. Gliding silently over the castle he saw Snape enter the Forest at a run. He followed.

The trees were so thick he couldn't see where Snape had gone. He flew in circles, lower and lower, brushing the top branches of trees until he heard voices. He glided towards them and landed noiselessly in a towering beech tree.

He climbed carefully along one of the branches, holding tight to his broomstick, trying to see through the leaves.

Below, in a shadowy clearing, stood Snape, but he wasn't alone. Quirrell was there, too. Harry couldn't make out the look on his face, but he was

第13章 尼可·勒梅

进赛场时,哈利看见斯内普降落在他旁边,脸色煞白,嘴唇抿得紧紧的——接着,哈利感到一只手搭在了他的肩膀上。他抬起头来,看到了邓布利多微笑的脸。

"干得好,"邓布利多的声音很轻,只有哈利一个人能听见,"很高兴看到你没有整天想着那面镜子……生活得很充实……太好了……"

斯内普愤恨地朝地上吐了口唾沫。

一小时后,哈利独自离开更衣室,准备把他的光轮2000送回扫帚棚。他的心情比任何时候都欢快。他总算做了一件真正值得自豪的事——以后再也不会有人说他不过是有一个响亮的名字而已。夜晚的空气从没有像现在这样甜蜜。他走过潮湿的草地,刚才一小时的情景又在脑海中重现,是一些模糊不清的幸福的片段:格兰芬多们跑过来把他架在他们的肩膀上;罗恩和赫敏在远处跳上跳下,罗恩一边淌着鼻血一边欢呼雀跃。

哈利已经来到了扫帚棚。他靠在木门上,抬头望着霍格沃茨,那些窗户在夕阳的辉映下闪着红光。格兰芬多队领先了。他成功了,他使斯内普看到……

说到斯内普……

一个戴着兜帽的身影迅速走下城堡的正门台阶,显然是不想让人看见,飞快地直奔禁林而去。哈利注视着,心头胜利的喜悦渐渐消失了。他认出了那个身影的鬼鬼祟祟的步态。正是斯内普。他趁别人吃晚饭的时候,偷偷溜往禁林——他想干什么?

哈利跳回到飞天扫帚上,腾地起飞了。他悄无声息地滑过城堡上空,看见斯内普奔跑着进了禁林。他跟了过去。

树木太茂密了,他看不清斯内普去了哪儿。他盘旋着,越来越低,擦着树梢飞翔,最后终于听见了有人说话的声音。他轻盈地朝他们飞去,静悄悄地落在一棵高耸的山毛榉上。

他小心地顺着一根树枝往前爬,手里紧紧抓住飞天扫帚,他想透过树叶往下看。

下面,在一片布满阴影的空地上,站着斯内普,但他并不是一个人。奇洛也在那里。哈利看不清奇洛脸上的表情,但他结巴得比任何时候都

CHAPTER THIRTEEN   Nicolas Flamel

stuttering worse than ever. Harry strained to catch what they were saying.

'... d-don't know why you wanted t-t-to meet here of all p-places, Severus ...'

'Oh, I thought we'd keep this private,' said Snape, his voice icy. 'Students aren't supposed to know about the Philosopher's Stone, after all.'

Harry leant forward. Quirrell was mumbling something. Snape interrupted him.

'Have you found out how to get past that beast of Hagrid's yet?'

'B-b-but Severus, I –'

'You don't want me as your enemy, Quirrell,' said Snape, taking a step towards him.

'I-I don't know what you –'

'You know perfectly well what I mean.'

An owl hooted loudly and Harry nearly fell out of the tree. He steadied himself in time to hear Snape say, '– your little bit of hocus-pocus. I'm waiting.'

'B-but I d-d-don't –'

'Very well,' Snape cut in. 'We'll have another little chat soon, when you've had time to think things over and decided where your loyalties lie.'

He threw his cloak over his head and strode out of the clearing. It was almost dark now, but Harry could see Quirrell, standing quite still as though he was petrified.

'Harry, where have you been?' Hermione squeaked.

'We won! You won! We won!' shouted Ron, thumping Harry on the back. 'And I gave Malfoy a black eye and Neville tried to take on Crabbe and Goyle single-handed! He's still out cold but Madam Pomfrey says he'll be all right – talk about showing Slytherin! Everyone's waiting for you in the common room, we're having a party, Fred and George stole some cakes and stuff from the kitchens.'

'Never mind that now,' said Harry breathlessly. 'Let's find an empty room, you wait 'til you hear this ...'

He made sure Peeves wasn't inside before shutting the door behind them, then he told them what he'd seen and heard.

'So we were right, it is the Philosopher's Stone, and Snape's trying to force

厉害。哈利全神贯注地听他们在说什么。

"……不—不知道你为什么要—要—要选在这里见面，西弗勒斯……"

"噢，我认为此事不宜公开，"斯内普说，声音冷冰冰的，"毕竟，学生们是不应该知道魔法石的。"

哈利探身向前。奇洛正在嘀咕着什么。斯内普打断了他。

"你有没有弄清怎样才能通过海格的那头怪兽？"

"可—可—可是，西弗勒斯，我——"

"你不希望我与你为敌吧，奇洛。"斯内普说着，朝他逼近了一步。

"我—我不知—知道你——"

"你很清楚我的意思。"

一只猫头鹰高声叫了起来，哈利差点儿从树上摔下去。他稳住自己，正好听见斯内普说："——你的秘密小花招。我等着。"

"可—可是，我不—不—不——"

"很好。"斯内普打断了他，"过不了多久，等你有时间考虑清楚，决定了为谁效忠之后，我们还会再谈一次。"

他用斗篷罩住脑袋，大步流星地走出了空地。天几乎完全黑了，但哈利仍能看见奇洛一动不动地站在那里，像是被石化了一样。

"哈利，你去哪儿了？"赫敏尖声地说。

"我们赢了！你赢了！我们赢了！"罗恩重重地拍着哈利的后背，大声喊道，"我把马尔福的眼睛打青了。纳威一个人对付克拉布和高尔！他还完全昏迷着，但庞弗雷女士说会好起来的——谈谈教训斯莱特林的经过吧！大伙儿都在公共休息室里等着你呢，我们正在搞一个庆祝会，弗雷德和乔治从厨房里偷了一些蛋糕什么的。"

"先别管那些，"哈利气喘吁吁地说，"我们找一间空屋子，你们听我告诉你们……"

哈利确信皮皮鬼不在屋里之后，才回身关上门，然后把他刚才看到和听到的情形告诉了他们。

"这么说，我们的分析是对的，那东西就是魔法石，斯内普想强迫

Quirrell to help him get it. He asked if he knew how to get past Fluffy – and he said something about Quirrell's "hocus-pocus" – I reckon there are other things guarding the stone apart from Fluffy, loads of enchantments, probably, and Quirrell would have done some anti-Dark Arts spell which Snape needs to break through –'

'So you mean the Stone's only safe as long as Quirrell stands up to Snape?' said Hermione in alarm.

'It'll be gone by next Tuesday,' said Ron.

第13章 尼可·勒梅

奇洛帮助他拿到那块石头。他问奇洛是不是知道怎样才能通过路威——并提到奇洛的'秘密小花招'——我猜想,除了路威,大概还有其他机关在守护着那块石头,很可能有一大堆魔法巫术,说不定奇洛就施了一些反黑魔法咒语,斯内普需要把它们解除——"

"你的意思是说,只有在奇洛能够抵抗斯内普时,魔法石才是安全的?"赫敏惊慌地问。

"那恐怕石头下个星期二就不在了。"罗恩说。

CHAPTER FOURTEEN

Norbert the Norwegian Ridgeback

Quirrell, however, must have been braver than they'd thought. In the weeks that followed he did seem to be getting paler and thinner, but it didn't look as though he'd cracked yet.

Every time they passed the third-floor corridor, Harry, Ron and Hermione would press their ears to the door to check that Fluffy was still growling inside. Snape was sweeping about in his usual bad temper, which surely meant that the Stone was still safe. Whenever Harry passed Quirrell these days he gave him an encouraging sort of smile, and Ron had started telling people off for laughing at Quirrell's stutter.

Hermione, however, had more on her mind than the Philosopher's Stone. She had started drawing up revision timetables and colour-coding all her notes. Harry and Ron wouldn't have minded, but she kept nagging them to do the same.

'Hermione, the exams are ages away.'

'Ten weeks,' Hermione snapped. 'That's not ages, that's like a second to Nicolas Flamel.'

'But we're not six hundred years old,' Ron reminded her. 'Anyway, what are you revising for, you already know it all.'

'What am I revising for? Are you mad? You realise we need to pass these exams to get into the second year? They're very important, I should have started studying a month ago, I don't know what's got into me …'

Unfortunately, the teachers seemed to be thinking along the same lines as Hermione. They piled so much homework on them that the Easter holidays weren't nearly as much fun as the Christmas ones. It was hard to relax with Hermione next to you reciting the twelve uses of dragon's blood or practising wand movements. Moaning and yawning, Harry and Ron spent most of

第 14 章
挪威脊背龙——诺伯

然而，奇洛肯定要比他们所想的勇敢。在之后的几星期中，他看上去确实越来越苍白、消瘦，但没有显出彻底垮掉的样子。

每次经过四楼走廊，哈利、罗恩和赫敏都要把耳朵贴在门上，听路威是不是还在里面低声咆哮。斯内普整天在学校里大步流星地走来走去，脾气和往常一样暴躁，这无疑说明魔法石还是安全的。这些日子，哈利每次在路上碰到奇洛，都要给他一个含有鼓励意味的微笑；罗恩也开始斥责那些嘲笑奇洛结巴的人。

赫敏呢，除了魔法石之外，还操心着更多的事情。她已经开始制订复习计划，并在她所有的笔记上标出不同的颜色。哈利和罗恩本来满不在乎，但她不停地对他们唠叨，叫他们也这样做。

"赫敏，考试离我们还有好几百年呢。"

"十个星期，"赫敏反驳道，"不是好几百年，对尼可·勒梅来说，只是一眨眼的工夫。"

"可是我们也没有六百岁啊。"罗恩提醒她，"而且，不管怎么说，你为什么还要复习呢？你已经什么都知道了。"

"为什么要复习？你疯了吗？你知不知道，我们要通过这些考试才能升入二年级？它们是很重要的，我应该在一个月前就开始温习的，真不知道我当时是怎么了……"

不幸的是，老师们的想法似乎和赫敏是一样的。他们布置了一大堆家庭作业，复活节假期远不像圣诞节的时候那样充满乐趣。有赫敏在旁边背诵火龙血的十二种用途，或者练习魔杖的动作，你很难轻轻松松地休息。哈利和罗恩只好大部分空余时间都陪她一起待在图书馆里，唉声

CHAPTER FOURTEEN   Norbert the Norwegian Ridgeback

their free time in the library with her, trying to get through all their extra work.

'I'll never remember this,' Ron burst out one afternoon, throwing down his quill and looking longingly out of the library window. It was the first really fine day they'd had in months. The sky was a clear, forget-me-not blue and there was a feeling in the air of summer coming.

Harry, who was looking up 'Dittany' in *One Thousand Magical Herbs and Fungi*, didn't look up until he heard Ron say, 'Hagrid! What are you doing in the library?'

Hagrid shuffled into view, hiding something behind his back. He looked very out of place in his moleskin overcoat.

'Jus' lookin',' he said, in a shifty voice that got their interest at once. 'An' what're you lot up ter?' He looked suddenly suspicious. 'Yer not still lookin' fer Nicolas Flamel, are yeh?'

'Oh, we found out who he is ages ago,' said Ron impressively. '*And* we know what that dog's guarding, it's a Philosopher's St–'

'*Shhhh!*' Hagrid looked around quickly to see if anyone was listening. 'Don' go shoutin' about it, what's the matter with yeh?'

'There are a few things we wanted to ask you, as a matter of fact,' said Harry, 'about what's guarding the Stone apart from Fluffy –'

'SHHHH!' said Hagrid again. 'Listen – come an' see me later, I'm not promisin' I'll tell yeh anythin', mind, but don' go rabbitin' about it in here, students aren' s'pposed ter know. They'll think I've told yeh –'

'See you later, then,' said Harry.

Hagrid shuffled off.

'What was he hiding behind his back?' said Hermione thoughtfully.

'Do you think it had anything to do with the Stone?'

'I'm going to see what section he was in,' said Ron, who'd had enough of working. He came back a minute later with a pile of books in his arms and slammed them down on the table.

'*Dragons!*' he whispered. 'Hagrid was looking up stuff about dragons! Look at these: *Dragon Species of Great Britain and Ireland; From Egg to Inferno, A Dragon Keeper's Guide.*'

'Hagrid's always wanted a dragon, he told me so the first time I ever met him,' said Harry.

叹气，哈欠连天，拼命完成繁重的功课。

"我永远也记不住这个。"一天下午，罗恩终于受不了了，把羽毛笔一扔，眼巴巴地看着图书馆的窗外。几个月来，他们第一次碰到这样的好天气。天空清澈明净，蓝得像勿忘我花的颜色，空气里有一种夏天即将来临的气息。

哈利只顾埋头在《千种神奇药草及蕈类》里查找"白鲜"，突然他听见罗恩说："海格！你到图书馆来做什么？"

海格踢踢踏踏地走了过来，把什么东西藏在了身后。他穿着鼹鼠皮大衣，显得很不合时宜。

"随便看看。"海格说，声音躲躲闪闪的，一下就引起了他们的兴趣。"你们在这里干吗？"他突然显得疑心起来，"还在查尼可·勒梅，是吗？"

"哦，我们几百年前就弄清他是何许人了，"罗恩得意扬扬地说，"还知道那条狗在看守什么，是魔法石——"

"嘘——"海格飞快地往四下张望了一眼，看有没有人听见，"不要大声嚷嚷，你们到底想干什么？"

"说实话，我们有几件事想问问你，"哈利说，"是关于守护魔法石的机关，除了路威——"

"**嘘**！"海格又说，"听着——过会儿来找我，记住，我可没答应要告诉你们什么，可是别在这里瞎扯呀，有些事情学生是不应该知道的。他们会以为是我告诉你们的——"

"那么，待会儿见。"哈利说。

海格踢踢踏踏地走了。

"他把什么藏在背后？"赫敏若有所思地说。

"你认为会跟魔法石有关吗？"

"我去看看他刚才在找什么书。"罗恩说，他读书早就读得不耐烦了。一分钟后，他回来了，怀里抱着一大堆书，把它们重重地扔到桌上。

"火龙！"他低声说，"海格在查找关于火龙的资料！看看这些：《不列颠和爱尔兰的火龙种类》《从火龙蛋到地狱：饲养火龙指南》。"

"海格一直想要一条火龙，我第一次见到他时，他就对我这么说过。"哈利说。

CHAPTER FOURTEEN   Norbert the Norwegian Ridgeback

'But it's against our laws,' said Ron. 'Dragon-breeding was outlawed by the Warlocks' Convention of 1709, everyone knows that. It's hard to stop Muggles noticing us if we're keeping dragons in the back garden – anyway, you can't tame dragons, it's dangerous. You should see the burns Charlie's got off wild ones in Romania.'

'But there aren't wild dragons in *Britain*?' said Harry.

'Of course there are,' said Ron. 'Common Welsh Green and Hebridean Blacks. The Ministry of Magic has a job hushing them up, I can tell you. Our lot have to keep putting spells on Muggles who've spotted them, to make them forget.'

'So what on earth's Hagrid up to?' said Hermione.

When they knocked on the door of the gamekeeper's hut an hour later, they were surprised to see that all the curtains were closed. Hagrid called, 'Who is it?' before he let them in and then shut the door quickly behind them.

It was stiflingly hot inside. Even though it was such a warm day, there was a blazing fire in the grate. Hagrid made them tea and offered them stoat sandwiches, which they refused.

'So – yeh wanted to ask me somethin'?'

'Yes,' said Harry. There was no point beating about the bush. 'We were wondering if you could tell us what's guarding the Philosopher's Stone apart from Fluffy.'

Hagrid frowned at him.

'O' course I can't,' he said. 'Number one, I don' know meself. Number two, yeh know too much already, so I wouldn' tell yeh if I could. That Stone's here fer a good reason. It was almost stolen outta Gringotts – I s'ppose yeh've worked that out an' all? Beats me how yeh even know abou' Fluffy.'

'Oh, come on, Hagrid, you might not want to tell us, but you *do* know, you know everything that goes on round here,' said Hermione in a warm, flattering voice. Hagrid's beard twitched and they could tell he was smiling. 'We only wondered who had *done* the guarding, really.' Hermione went on. 'We wondered who Dumbledore had trusted enough to help him, apart from you.'

Hagrid's chest swelled at these last words. Harry and Ron beamed at Hermione.

"但这是犯法的,"罗恩说,"在一七〇九年的巫师大会上,正式通过了禁止饲养火龙的法案,这是每个人都知道的。如果我们在后花园里饲养火龙,很难不让麻瓜注意到我们——而且,你也很难把火龙驯服,那是很危险的。你真应该看看查理身上那些被烧伤的地方,都是他在罗马尼亚驱逐野龙时留下的。"

"可是不列颠就没有野龙吗?"哈利说。

"当然有,"罗恩说,"有普通威尔士绿龙和赫布里底群岛黑龙。我可以告诉你,魔法部有项工作就是隐瞒这些野龙的存在。我们的巫师不得不经常给那些看到野龙的麻瓜念咒,让他们把这件事忘得一干二净。"

"那么海格到底想做什么呢?"赫敏说。

一小时后,他们敲响了猎场看守的小屋门。他们吃惊地发现,所有的窗帘都被拉得严严实实。海格先是喊了一句"谁呀?"才让他们进屋,接着又赶紧回身把门关上了。

小屋里热得令人窒息。尽管是这样一个温暖的晴天,壁炉里还燃着熊熊的旺火。海格给他们沏了茶,还端来了白鼬三明治,他们婉言谢绝了。

"这么说——你们有话要问我?"

"是的。"哈利说,觉得没有必要拐弯抹角,"我们不知道你能不能告诉我们,除了路威以外,守护魔法石的还有什么机关?"

海格朝他们皱起了眉头。

"我当然不能说。"他说,"第一,我自己也不知道。第二,你们已经知道得太多了,所以我即使知道也不会告诉你们。那块石头在这里是很有道理的。它在古灵阁差点被人偷走——我猜你们把这些也弄得一清二楚了吧?真不明白你们怎么连路威的事都知道。"

"哦,海格,你大概是不想告诉我们吧,你肯定是知道的。这里发生的事情,有哪一件能逃过你的眼睛啊。"赫敏用一种甜甜的、奉承的口气说。海格的胡子抖动起来,他们看出他在笑呢。"实际上,我们只想知道是谁设计了那些机关。"赫敏继续说道,"我们想知道,除了你以外,邓布利多还相信谁能够帮助他呢?"

听了最后这句话,海格挺起胸。哈利和罗恩对赫敏露出满意的微笑。

CHAPTER FOURTEEN Norbert the Norwegian Ridgeback

'Well, I don' s'pose it could hurt ter tell yeh that ... let's see ... he borrowed Fluffy from me ... then some o' the teachers did enchantments ... Professor Sprout – Professor Flitwick – Professor McGonagall –' he ticked them off on his fingers, 'Professor Quirrell – an' Dumbledore himself did somethin', o' course. Hang on, I've forgotten someone. Oh yeah, Professor Snape.'

'*Snape?*'

'Yeah – yer not still on abou' that, are yeh? Look, Snape helped *protect* the Stone, he's not about ter steal it.'

Harry knew Ron and Hermione were thinking the same as he was. If Snape had been in on protecting the Stone, it must have been easy to find out how the other teachers had guarded it. He probably knew everything – except, it seemed, Quirrell's spell and how to get past Fluffy.

'You're the only one who knows how to get past Fluffy, aren't you, Hagrid?' said Harry anxiously. 'And you wouldn't tell anyone, would you? Not even one of the teachers?'

'Not a soul knows except me an' Dumbledore,' said Hagrid proudly.

'Well, that's something,' Harry muttered to the others. 'Hagrid, can we have a window open? I'm boiling.'

'Can't, Harry, sorry,' said Hagrid. Harry noticed him glance at the fire. Harry looked at it, too.

'Hagrid – what's *that?*'

But he already knew what it was. In the very heart of the fire, underneath the kettle, was a huge, black egg.

'Ah,' said Hagrid, fiddling nervously with his beard. 'That's – er ...'

'Where did you get it, Hagrid?' said Ron, crouching over the fire to get a closer look at the egg. 'It must've cost you a fortune.'

'Won it,' said Hagrid. 'Las' night. I was down in the village havin' a few drinks an' got into a game o' cards with a stranger. Think he was quite glad ter get rid of it, ter be honest.'

'But what are you going to do with it when it's hatched?' said Hermione.

'Well, I've bin doin' some readin',' said Hagrid, pulling a large book from under his pillow. 'Got this outta the library – *Dragon-Breeding for Pleasure and Profit* – it's a bit outta date, o' course, but it's all in here. Keep the egg in the fire, 'cause their mothers breathe on 'em, see, an' when it hatches, feed it on

第14章 挪威脊背龙——诺伯

"好吧，对你们说说也无妨——让我想想——他从我这里借去了路威——然后请另外几个老师施了魔法……斯普劳特教授——弗立维教授——麦格教授——"他扳着手指数着，"奇洛教授——当然啦，邓布利多自己也施了魔法。等一下，我还忘记了一个人。哦，对了，是斯内普教授。"

"斯内普？"

"是啊——难道你们还在怀疑他，嗯？瞧，斯内普也帮着一块儿保护魔法石了，他不会去偷它的。"

哈利知道罗恩和赫敏内心的想法跟他一样。既然斯内普也参加了保护魔法石的工作，他一定很容易弄清其他老师设下了什么机关。他很可能什么都知道了——似乎只除了奇洛的魔法和怎样通过路威。

"只有你一个人知道怎样通过路威，是吗，海格？"哈利急切地问，"你不会告诉任何人的，是吗？即使是老师也不告诉，是吗？"

"除了我和邓布利多，谁也别想知道。"海格骄傲地说。

"那就好，那就好。"哈利对另外两人小声嘟哝了一句，"海格，我们能不能开一扇窗户呢？我热坏了。"

"不能，哈利，对不起。"海格说。哈利注意到他朝壁炉那儿扫了一眼。哈利便也扭头看着炉火。

"海格——那是什么？"

其实他已经知道了。在炉火正中央的水壶下面，卧着一只黑乎乎的大蛋。

"呵，"海格局促不安地捻着胡子说，"那是——哦……"

"你从哪儿弄来的，海格？"罗恩说着，蹲到火边，更仔细地端详那只大蛋，"肯定花了你一大笔钱吧！"

"赢来的。"海格说，"昨晚，我在村子里喝酒，和一个陌生人玩牌来着。说实在的，那人大概正巴不得摆脱它呢。"

"可是，等它孵出来以后，你打算怎么办呢？"赫敏问。

"噢，我一直在看书。"海格说着，从他的枕头底下抽出一本大部头的书，"从图书馆借来的——《为消遣和盈利而饲养火龙》——当然啦，已经有点过时了，但内容很全。要把蛋放在火里，因为火龙妈妈会对着蛋喷火。你们看，这里写着呢，等它孵出来后，每半个小时喂它一桶鸡

CHAPTER FOURTEEN Norbert the Norwegian Ridgeback

a bucket o' brandy mixed with chicken blood every half hour. An' see here – how ter recognise diff'rent eggs – what I got there's a Norwegian Ridgeback. They're rare, them.'

He looked very pleased with himself, but Hermione didn't.

'Hagrid, you live in a *wooden house*,' she said.

But Hagrid wasn't listening. He was humming merrily as he stoked the fire.

So now they had something else to worry about: what might happen to Hagrid if anyone found out he was hiding an illegal dragon in his hut.

'Wonder what it's like to have a peaceful life,' Ron sighed, as evening after evening they struggled through all the extra homework they were getting. Hermione had now started making revision timetables for Harry and Ron, too. It was driving them mad.

Then, one breakfast time, Hedwig brought Harry another note from Hagrid. He had written only two words: *It's hatching.*

Ron wanted to skip Herbology and go straight down to the hut. Hermione wouldn't hear of it.

'Hermione, how many times in our lives are we going to see a dragon hatching?'

'We've got lessons, we'll get into trouble, and that's nothing to what Hagrid's going to be in when someone finds out what he's doing –'

'Shut up!' Harry whispered.

Malfoy was only a few feet away and he had stopped dead to listen. How much had he heard? Harry didn't like the look on Malfoy's face at all.

Ron and Hermione argued all the way to Herbology, and in the end, Hermione agreed to run down to Hagrid's with the other two during morning break. When the bell sounded from the castle at the end of their lesson, the three of them dropped their trowels at once and hurried through the grounds to the edge of the Forest. Hagrid greeted them looking flushed and excited.

'It's nearly out.' He ushered them inside.

The egg was lying on the table. There were deep cracks in it. Something was moving inside; a funny clicking noise was coming from it.

They all drew their chairs up to the table and watched with bated breath.

All at once there was a scraping noise and the egg split open. The baby dragon flopped on to the table. It wasn't exactly pretty; Harry thought it

血白兰地酒。再看这里——怎样辨别不同的蛋——我得到的是一只挪威脊背龙。很稀罕的呢。"

他看上去很得意，赫敏却不以为然。

"海格，别忘了你住在木头房子里。"她说。

但是海格根本没有听。他一边拨弄着炉火，一边快乐地哼着小曲儿。

现在，他们又有新的事情要操心了：如果有人发现海格在他的小屋里非法饲养火龙，会把他怎么样呢？

"真想知道和平安宁的日子是什么样的。"罗恩叹着气说。一个晚上接一个晚上，他们奋力完成老师布置的一大堆家庭作业。赫敏已经开始为哈利和罗恩制订复习计划。这简直要把他们逼疯了。

然后，在一天吃早饭的时候，海德薇又给哈利捎来了一张海格的纸条。海格只在上面写了四个字：快出壳了。

罗恩不想上草药课了，想直奔海格的小屋。赫敏坚决不同意。

"赫敏，我们一辈子能看见几次小火龙出壳啊？"

"我们要上课，不然会惹麻烦的；如果有人发现了海格做的事情，他会比我们更倒霉——"

"别说了。"哈利小声警告。

马尔福就在离他们几步远的地方，停下来听他们说话。给他听去了多少？哈利真讨厌马尔福脸上的那副表情。

在去上草药课的路上，罗恩一直在和赫敏争论。最后，赫敏终于答应在上午课间休息时，和他们俩一起跑到海格的小屋里去看看。下课了，城堡里刚刚传出铃声，他们三个就扔下小铲子，匆匆跑过场地，朝禁林的边缘奔去。海格迎接了他们。他满面红光，非常兴奋。

"快要出来了。"他把他们让进小屋。

那只蛋躺在桌上，上面已经有了一条深深的裂缝。有什么东西在里面不停地动着，传出一种古怪的咔嗒咔嗒的声音。

他们都把椅子挪得更靠近桌子，屏住呼吸，密切注视着。

突然，随着一阵刺耳的擦刮声，蛋裂开了。小火龙在桌上摇摇摆摆地扑腾着。它其实并不漂亮；哈利觉得它的样子就像一把皱巴巴的黑伞。

looked like a crumpled, black umbrella. Its spiny wings were huge compared to its skinny jet body and it had a long snout with wide nostrils, stubs of horns and bulging, orange eyes.

It sneezed. A couple of sparks flew out of its snout.

'Isn't he *beautiful?*' Hagrid murmured. He reached out a hand to stroke the dragon's head. It snapped at his fingers, showing pointed fangs.

'Bless him, look, he knows his mummy!' said Hagrid.

'Hagrid,' said Hermione, 'how fast do Norwegian Ridgebacks grow, exactly?'

Hagrid was about to answer when the colour suddenly drained from his face – he leapt to his feet and ran to the window.

'What's the matter?'

'Someone was lookin' through the gap in the curtains – it's a kid – he's runnin' back up ter the school.'

Harry bolted to the door and looked out. Even at a distance there was no mistaking him.

Malfoy had seen the dragon.

Something about the smile lurking on Malfoy's face during the next week made Harry, Ron and Hermione very nervous. They spent most of their free time in Hagrid's darkened hut, trying to reason with him.

'Just let him go,' Harry urged. 'Set him free.'

'I can't,' said Hagrid. 'He's too little. He'd die.'

They looked at the dragon. It had grown three times in length in just a week. Smoke kept furling out of its nostrils. Hagrid hadn't been doing his gamekeeping duties because the dragon was keeping him so busy. There were empty brandy bottles and chicken feathers all over the floor.

'I've decided to call him Norbert,' said Hagrid, looking at the dragon with misty eyes. 'He really knows me now, watch. Norbert! Norbert! Where's Mummy?'

'He's lost his marbles,' Ron muttered in Harry's ear.

'Hagrid,' said Harry loudly, 'give it a fortnight and Norbert's going to be as long as your house. Malfoy could go to Dumbledore at any moment.'

Hagrid bit his lip.

'I – I know I can't keep him for ever, but I can't jus' dump him, I can't.'

多刺的翅膀与它瘦瘦的乌黑身体比起来，显得特别大。它还有一个长长的大鼻子，鼻孔宽宽的，脑袋上长着角疙瘩，橘红色的眼睛向外突起。

它打了个喷嚏，鼻子里喷出几点火星。

"它很漂亮，是不是？"海格喃喃地说。他伸出一只手，摸了摸小火龙的脑袋。小火龙一口咬住他的手指，露出尖尖的长牙。

"天哪，你们看，它认识它的妈妈！"海格说。

"海格，"赫敏说，"挪威脊背龙长得到底有多快？"

海格正要回答，突然脸色唰地变白了——他一跃而起，奔向窗口。

"怎么回事？"

"刚才有人透过窗帘缝偷看——是个男孩——正往学校里跑呢。"

哈利一下子蹿到门边，向外望去。即使隔着一段距离，他也绝不会认错。

马尔福看见了小火龙。

在接下来的一个星期里，马尔福脸上隐藏的不怀好意的笑容使哈利、罗恩和赫敏非常不安。他们大部分课余时间都待在海格昏暗的小屋里，对他摆事实讲道理。

"你就让它走吧，"哈利劝道，"把它放掉。"

"我不能，"海格说，"它太小了，会死的。"

他们打量着小火龙。短短一个星期，它的长度已经是原来的三倍。一团团的烟从它鼻孔里喷出来。海格把看守猎场的工作撇在了一边，因为小火龙弄得他手忙脚乱。地上扔满了空白兰地酒瓶和鸡毛。

"我决定叫它诺伯，"海格用泪水模糊的眼睛看着小火龙，说，"它现在真的认识我了，你们看着。诺伯！诺伯！妈妈在哪儿？"

"他疯了。"罗恩在哈利耳边悄悄说。

"海格，"哈利提高了嗓门，"再过两个星期，诺伯就会变得跟你的房子一样长。马尔福随时都可能去找邓布利多。"

海格咬着嘴唇。

"我——我知道不能永远养着它，可也不能就这样把它扔掉，不能啊。"

CHAPTER FOURTEEN   Norbert the Norwegian Ridgeback

Harry suddenly turned to Ron.

'Charlie,' he said.

'You're losing it, too,' said Ron. 'I'm Ron, remember?'

'No – Charlie – your brother Charlie. In Romania. Studying dragons. We could send Norbert to him. Charlie can take care of him and then put him back in the wild!'

'Brilliant!' said Ron. 'How about it, Hagrid?'

And in the end, Hagrid agreed that they could send an owl to Charlie to ask him.

The following week dragged by. Wednesday night found Hermione and Harry sitting alone in the common room, long after everyone else had gone to bed. The clock on the wall had just chimed midnight when the portrait hole burst open. Ron appeared out of nowhere as he pulled off Harry's Invisibility Cloak. He had been down at Hagrid's hut, helping him feed Norbert, who was now eating dead rats by the crate.

'It bit me!' he said, showing them his hand, which was wrapped in a bloody handkerchief. 'I'm not going to be able to hold a quill for a week. I tell you, that dragon's the most horrible animal I've ever met, but the way Hagrid goes on about it, you'd think it was a fluffy little bunny rabbit. When it bit me he told me off for frightening it. And when I left, he was singing it a lullaby.'

There was a tap on the dark window.

'It's Hedwig!' said Harry, hurrying to let her in. 'She'll have Charlie's answer!'

The three of them put their heads together to read the note.

Dear Ron,

How are you? Thanks for the letter - I'd be glad to take the Norwegian Ridgeback, but it won't be easy getting him here. I think the best thing will be to send him over with some friends of mine who are coming to visit me next week. Trouble is, they mustn't be seen carrying an illegal dragon.

Could you get the Ridgeback up the tallest tower at midnight on

第14章 挪威脊背龙——诺伯

哈利突然转向罗恩。

"查理。"他说。

"你也犯糊涂了，"罗恩说，"我是罗恩，记得吗？"

"不——查理——你的哥哥查理。在罗马尼亚，研究火龙的查理。我们不妨把诺伯送给他。查理可以照料它，然后把它放回野生环境里。"

"太棒了！"罗恩说，"怎么样，海格？"

最后，海格总算同意他们先派一只猫头鹰去问问查理。

再接下来的一个星期简直度日如年。星期三晚上，在别人都已上床睡觉之后，赫敏和哈利仍坐在公共休息室里。墙上的钟刚敲过十二点，肖像洞突然打开了。罗恩脱下哈利的隐形衣，仿佛从天而降一般。他刚才到海格的小屋去帮他喂诺伯，诺伯现在开始吃板条箱边的死老鼠了。

"它咬了我！"罗恩说，给他们看他的手，上面包着沾满血迹的手绢，"我一星期都没法拿笔了。告诉你们吧，火龙是我见过的最可怕的动物，可是看海格对待它的样子，你还以为那是一只毛茸茸的小兔子呢。它咬了我以后，海格还怪我吓着它了。我走的时候，还听见海格在给它唱摇篮曲呢。"

漆黑的窗户上传来一阵拍打声。

"是海德薇！"哈利说，赶紧过去把它放了进来，"它肯定带来了查理的回信！"

三个人脑袋凑在一起，看那张纸条。

亲爱的罗恩：

你好吗？谢谢你给我写信——我很高兴收养那只挪威脊背龙，但是要把它弄到这儿来不太容易。我认为最好的办法是让几个下周要来看我的朋友顺路把它带过来。麻烦就在于，千万不能让别人看见他们非法携带一条火龙。

你能否在星期六的午夜，把脊背龙带到最高的塔楼上？他们可

CHAPTER FOURTEEN Norbert the Norwegian Ridgeback

Saturday? They can meet you there and take him away while it's still dark.
Send me an answer as soon as possible.
Love,
Charlie

They looked at each other.

'We've got the Invisibility Cloak,' said Harry. 'It shouldn't be too difficult – I think the Cloak's big enough to cover two of us and Norbert.'

It was a mark of how bad the last week had been that the other two agreed with him. Anything to get rid of Norbert – and Malfoy.

There was a hitch. By next morning, Ron's bitten hand had swollen to twice its usual size. He didn't know whether it was safe to go to Madam Pomfrey – would she recognise a dragon bite? By the afternoon, though, he had no choice. The cut had turned a nasty shade of green. It looked as if Norbert's fangs were poisonous.

Harry and Hermione rushed up to the hospital wing at the end of the day to find Ron in a terrible state in bed.

'It's not just my hand,' he whispered, 'although that feels like it's about to fall off. Malfoy told Madam Pomfrey he wanted to borrow one of my books so he could come and have a good laugh at me. He kept threatening to tell her what really bit me – I've told her it was a dog but I don't think she believes me – I shouldn't have hit him at the Quidditch match, that's why he's doing this.'

Harry and Hermione tried to calm Ron down.

'It'll all be over at midnight on Saturday,' said Hermione, but this didn't soothe Ron at all. On the contrary, he sat bolt upright and broke into a sweat.

'Midnight on Saturday!' he said in a hoarse voice. 'Oh no – oh no – I've just remembered – Charlie's letter was in that book Malfoy took, he's going to know we're getting rid of Norbert.'

Harry and Hermione didn't get a chance to answer. Madam Pomfrey came over at that moment and made them leave, saying Ron needed sleep.

第14章 挪威脊背龙——诺伯

以在那里与你会面，趁着天黑把火龙带走。

请尽快给我回音。

爱你。

查 理

三个人面面相觑。

"我们有隐形衣呢，"哈利说，"应该不会太难——我认为隐形衣足够遮住我们两个人和诺伯。"

罗恩和赫敏立刻就同意了，这说明上个星期的日子多么难熬。怎么都行，只要能摆脱诺伯——还有马尔福。

事情出了麻烦。第二天早晨，罗恩被咬的那只手肿成了原来的两倍。他不知道去找庞弗雷女士是不是妥当——她会不会看出来这是被火龙咬的？然而到了下午，他就没有别的选择了。伤口变成了一种难看的绿颜色。看来诺伯的牙齿是有毒的。

一天的课上完之后，哈利和赫敏飞快地赶到医院，发现罗恩躺在床上，情况非常糟糕。

"不光是我的手，"他低声说，"虽然它疼得像要断了一样。更糟糕的是，马尔福对庞弗雷女士说要向我借一本书，这样他就进来了，尽情地把我嘲笑了一通。他不停地威胁说，他要告诉庞弗雷女士是什么东西咬了我——我对庞弗雷女士说是狗咬的，但我认为她并不相信——我不应该在魁地奇比赛时跟马尔福打架，他现在是报复我呢。"

哈利和赫敏竭力使罗恩平静下来。

"到了星期六午夜，就一切都结束了。"赫敏说，但这丝毫没有使罗恩得到安慰。恰恰相反，他腾地从床上坐了起来，急出了一身冷汗。

"星期六午夜！"他声音嘶哑地说，"哦，糟糕——哦，糟糕——我刚想起来——查理的信就夹在马尔福借走的那本书里，他一定知道我们要弄走诺伯了。"

哈利和赫敏还没有来得及回答，庞弗雷女士走了进来，叫他们离开，她说罗恩需要睡觉了。

CHAPTER FOURTEEN Norbert the Norwegian Ridgeback

'It's too late to change the plan now,' Harry told Hermione. 'We haven't got time to send Charlie another owl and this could be our only chance to get rid of Norbert. We'll have to risk it. And we *have* got the Invisibility Cloak, Malfoy doesn't know about that.'

They found Fang the boarhound sitting outside with a bandaged tail when they went to tell Hagrid, who opened a window to talk to them.

'I won't let you in,' he puffed. 'Norbert's at a tricky stage – nothin' I can't handle.'

When they told him about Charlie's letter, his eyes filled with tears, although that might have been because Norbert had just bitten him on the leg.

'Aargh! It's all right, he only got my boot – jus' playin' – he's only a baby, after all.'

The baby banged its tail on the wall, making the windows rattle. Harry and Hermione walked back to the castle, feeling Saturday couldn't come quickly enough.

They would have felt sorry for Hagrid when the time came for him to say goodbye to Norbert if they hadn't been so worried about what they had to do. It was a very dark, cloudy night and they were a bit late arriving at Hagrid's hut because they'd had to wait for Peeves to get out of their way in the Entrance Hall, where he'd been playing tennis against the wall.

Hagrid had Norbert packed and ready in a large crate.

'He's got lots o' rats an' some brandy fer the journey,' said Hagrid in a muffled voice. 'An' I've packed his teddy bear in case he gets lonely.'

From inside the crate came ripping noises that sounded to Harry as though teddy was having his head torn off.

'Bye-bye, Norbert!' Hagrid sobbed, as Harry and Hermione covered the crate with the Invisibility Cloak and stepped underneath it themselves. 'Mummy will never forget you!'

How they managed to get the crate back up to the castle, they never knew. Midnight ticked nearer as they heaved Norbert up the marble staircase in the Entrance Hall and along the dark corridors. Up another staircase, then another – even one of Harry's short cuts didn't make the work much easier.

'Nearly there!' Harry panted as they reached the corridor beneath the tallest tower.

第 14 章 挪威脊背龙——诺伯

"已经来不及改变计划了,"哈利对赫敏说,"我们没有时间再派一只猫头鹰去找查理,而且这大概也是我们摆脱诺伯的唯一机会。不得不冒一次险。我们有隐形衣呢,这是马尔福不知道的。"

他们去通知海格时,发现大猎狗牙牙坐在门外,尾巴上缠着绷带。海格打开窗户跟他们说话。

"我不能让你们进来,"他喘着气说,"诺伯现在很难对付——不过我都能应付。"

他们把查理来信的事对他说了,他的眼里噙满泪水,不过这也可能是因为诺伯刚刚咬了他的腿。

"呵呵!没关系,它只咬了我的靴子——是在闹着玩呢——说到底,它还是个小毛娃啊。"

小毛娃用尾巴梆梆地敲着墙,震得窗户咔咔直响。哈利和赫敏走回城堡,心里盼望着星期六早点到来。

海格要跟诺伯告别了,哈利和赫敏如果不是忧心忡忡地想着即将采取的行动,一定会为海格感到难过的。那是一个漆黑的、阴云密布的夜晚,他们来到海格的小屋时已经有点晚了,因为皮皮鬼在门厅里对着墙壁打网球,他们只好一直等到他离开。

海格已经把诺伯装进了一个大板条箱,准备就绪了。

"给它准备了许多老鼠,还有一些白兰地酒,够它一路上吃喝的了。"海格用沉闷的声音说,"我还把它的玩具熊也放了进去,免得它觉得孤单。"

板条箱里传出了撕扯的声音,哈利觉得玩具熊的脑袋似乎被扯掉了。

"再见,诺伯!"海格抽抽搭搭地说,"妈妈不会忘记你的!"哈利和赫敏用隐形衣罩住板条箱,随即自己也钻到袍子下面。

怎么把板条箱搬到塔楼上去呢,他们心里没底。随着午夜一分一秒地临近,他们抬着诺伯走上门厅的大理石台阶,走过漆黑一片的走廊。上了一层楼,又上一层楼——尽管哈利抄了近路,也一点儿不省劲。

"快到了!"他们到了最高的塔楼下边一层的走廊里,哈利喘着气说。

CHAPTER FOURTEEN   Norbert the Norwegian Ridgeback

Then a sudden movement ahead of them made them almost drop the crate. Forgetting that they were already invisible, they shrank into the shadows, staring at the dark outlines of two people grappling with each other ten feet away. A lamp flared.

Professor McGonagall, in a tartan dressing-gown and a hairnet, had Malfoy by the ear.

'Detention!' she shouted. 'And twenty points from Slytherin! Wandering around in the middle of the night, how *dare* you –'

'You don't understand, Professor, Harry Potter's coming – he's got a dragon!'

'What utter rubbish! How dare you tell such lies! Come on – I shall see Professor Snape about you, Malfoy!'

The steep spiral staircase up to the top of the tower seemed the easiest thing in the world after that. Not until they'd stepped out into the cold night air did they throw off the Cloak, glad to be able to breathe properly again. Hermione did a sort of jig.

'Malfoy's got detention! I could sing!'

'Don't,' Harry advised her.

Chuckling about Malfoy, they waited, Norbert thrashing about in his crate. About ten minutes later, four broomsticks came swooping down out of the darkness.

Charlie's friends were a cheery lot. They showed Harry and Hermione the harness they'd rigged up, so they could suspend Norbert between them. They all helped buckle Norbert safely into it and then Harry and Hermione shook hands with the others and thanked them very much.

At last, Norbert was going ... going ... *gone*.

They slipped back down the spiral staircase, their hearts as light as their hands, now that Norbert was off them. No more dragon – Malfoy in detention – what could spoil their happiness?

The answer to that was waiting at the foot of the stairs. As they stepped into the corridor, Filch's face loomed suddenly out of the darkness.

'Well, well, well,' he whispered, 'we *are* in trouble.'

They'd left the Invisibility Cloak on top of the tower.

第14章 挪威脊背龙——诺伯

前面突然有了动静,吓得他们差点扔掉了手里的箱子。他们忘了自己已经隐形,赶紧退缩到阴影里,看着离他们十来步远的地方,两个黑乎乎的人影正在互相纠缠。一盏灯在闪亮。

是麦格教授,穿着格子花纹的晨衣,戴着发网,揪着马尔福的耳朵。

"关禁闭!"她喊道,"斯莱特林扣掉二十分!半夜三更到处乱逛,你怎么敢——"

"你没有明白,教授,哈利·波特要来了——他带着一条火龙!"

"完全胡说八道!你怎么敢编出这样的谎话!走——我倒要看看斯内普教授怎么处置你,马尔福!"

摆脱了马尔福之后,通向塔楼的那道很陡的旋转楼梯似乎是世界上最轻松的一段路程了。他们一直来到寒冷的夜空下,才脱掉了隐形衣。多好啊,终于又能自如地呼吸了。赫敏还跳起了一种快步舞。

"马尔福要被关禁闭了!我真想唱歌!"

"别唱。"哈利提醒她。

他们一边等待,一边咯咯地嘲笑马尔福。诺伯在箱子里剧烈地动个不停。大约十分钟后,四把扫帚突然从黑暗中降落了。

查理的朋友都是性情快活的人。他们给哈利和赫敏看了他们拴好的几道绳索,这样就能把诺伯悬挂在他们中间了。他们七手八脚地把诺伯安全地系在绳索上,然后哈利和赫敏跟他们握了握手,又对他们说了许多感谢的话。

终于,诺伯走了……走了……不见了。

哈利和赫敏悄悄走下旋转楼梯,总算摆脱了诺伯这个沉重的负担,他们的心情和手一样轻快。火龙走了——马尔福将被关禁闭——还有什么能破坏他们的这份喜悦呢?

答案就在楼梯下面等着呢。他们一跨进走廊,费尔奇的脸就突然从黑暗里显现出来。

"啧,啧,啧,"费尔奇低声说,"我们有麻烦了。"

他们把隐形衣忘在塔楼顶上了。

CHAPTER FIFTEEN

The Forbidden Forest

Things couldn't have been worse.

Filch took them down to Professor McGonagall's study on the first floor, where they sat and waited without saying a word to each other. Hermione was trembling. Excuses, alibis and wild cover-up stories chased each other around Harry's brain, each more feeble than the last. He couldn't see how they were going to get out of trouble this time. They were cornered. How could they have been so stupid as to forget the Cloak? There was no reason on earth that Professor McGonagall would accept for their being out of bed and creeping around the school in the dead of night, let alone being up the tallest astronomy tower, which was out-of-bounds except for classes. Add Norbert and the Invisibility Cloak and they might as well be packing their bags already.

Had Harry thought that things couldn't have been worse? He was wrong. When Professor McGonagall appeared, she was leading Neville.

'Harry!' Neville burst out, the moment he saw the other two. 'I was trying to find you to warn you, I heard Malfoy saying he was going to catch you, he said you had a drag–'

Harry shook his head violently to shut Neville up, but Professor McGonagall had seen. She looked more likely to breathe fire than Norbert as she towered over the three of them.

'I would never have believed it of any of you. Mr Filch says you were up the astronomy tower. It's one o'clock in the morning. *Explain yourselves.*'

It was the first time Hermione had ever failed to answer a teacher's question. She was staring at her slippers, as still as a statue.

'I think I've got a good idea of what's been going on,' said Professor McGonagall. 'It doesn't take a genius to work it out. You fed Draco Malfoy some cock-and-bull story about a dragon, trying to get him out of bed and

第15章

禁　林

事情糟得不能再糟了。

费尔奇把他们领到二楼麦格教授的书房，他们坐在那里，一句话也不说。赫敏浑身发抖。哈利的脑海里飞快地设想出许多为自己辩解的借口和理由，还编了一些谎话想蒙混过关，但发现它们一个比一个站不住脚。他不知道这次有什么办法摆脱困境。他们走投无路了。唉，他们怎么就这么糊涂，居然把隐形衣给忘了！无论摆出什么理由，麦格教授都不会原谅他们深更半夜不睡觉，在学校里鬼鬼祟祟地游荡，而且还爬到了最高的天文塔上，那里除了平常上课是不能上去的。再加上诺伯和隐形衣，他们早就该收拾行李回家了。

哈利认为事情糟得不能再糟了吗？他错了。当麦格教授回来时，她后面跟着纳威。

"哈利！"纳威一看见他们两个，就脱口而出，"我一直在找你们，想给你们提个醒儿，我听见马尔福说他要来抓你，说你有一条火龙——"

哈利拼命摇头，不让纳威再说下去，可是被麦格教授看见了。她高高耸立在他们三个人面前，似乎比诺伯更有可能喷出火来。

"我真不该相信你们几个人。费尔奇说你们到天文塔上去了。别忘了现在是凌晨一点钟。自己解释一下吧。"

这是赫敏第一次回答不出老师的提问。她低头盯着自己的拖鞋，像雕像一样一动不动。

"我认为我完全明白这是怎么回事，"麦格教授说，"要弄清楚来龙去脉，并不需要脑筋多么灵光。你们凭空编出一套谎话告诉德拉科·马尔福，说有一条火龙什么的，想把他从床上骗出来，害他倒霉。我已经

CHAPTER FIFTEEN The Forbidden Forest

into trouble. I've already caught him. I suppose you think it's funny that Longbottom here heard the story and believed it, too?'

Harry caught Neville's eye and tried to tell him without words that this wasn't true, because Neville was looking stunned and hurt. Poor, blundering Neville – Harry knew what it must have cost him to try and find them in the dark, to warn them.

'I'm disgusted,' said Professor McGonagall. 'Four students out of bed in one night! I've never heard of such a thing before! You, Miss Granger, I thought you had more sense. As for you, Mr Potter, I thought Gryffindor meant more to you than this. All three of you will receive detentions – yes, you too, Mr Longbottom, *nothing* gives you the right to walk around school at night, especially these days, it's very dangerous – and fifty points will be taken from Gryffindor.'

'*Fifty?*' Harry gasped – they would lose the lead, the lead he'd won in the last Quidditch match.

'Fifty points *each*,' said Professor McGonagall, breathing heavily through her long pointed nose.

'Professor – please –'

'You *can't* –'

'Don't tell me what I can and can't do, Potter. Now get back to bed, all of you. I've never been more ashamed of Gryffindor students.'

A hundred and fifty points lost. That put Gryffindor in last place. In one night, they'd ruined any chance Gryffindor had had for the House Cup. Harry felt as though the bottom had dropped out of his stomach. How could they ever make up for this?

Harry didn't sleep all night. He could hear Neville sobbing into his pillow for what seemed like hours. Harry couldn't think of anything to say to comfort him. He knew Neville, like himself, was dreading the dawn. What would happen when the rest of Gryffindor found out what they'd done?

At first, Gryffindors passing the giant hourglasses that recorded the house points next day thought there'd been a mistake. How could they suddenly have a hundred and fifty points fewer than yesterday? And then the story started to spread: Harry Potter, the famous Harry Potter, their hero of two Quidditch matches, had lost them all those points, him and a couple of other stupid first-years.

第15章 禁 林

抓住他了。没想到隆巴顿也听到了这套谎话并且信以为真,我猜你们觉得这很有趣吧?"

哈利捕捉到纳威的目光,想用无声的语言告诉他不是这么回事,因为纳威显得既吃惊又委屈。可怜的、莽莽撞撞的纳威——哈利知道,纳威在黑夜里跑出来寻找他们,要给他们提个醒,这需要多大的勇气啊。

"我感到很气愤,"麦格教授说,"一晚上有四个学生不睡觉!这种事情我以前还从没听说过!你,格兰杰小姐,我原以为你头脑更清醒一些。至于你,波特先生,我原以为你是十分看重格兰芬多荣誉的。你们三个都要被关禁闭——是的,还有你,隆巴顿先生,不管是怎么回事,你都无权半夜三更在学校里乱逛,这是非常危险的——格兰芬多被扣掉五十分。"

"五十?"哈利觉得喘不过气来了——他们的领先地位保不住了,这名次还是他在上次魁地奇比赛中好不容易赢来的呢。

"每人五十分。"麦格教授说,长长的尖鼻子喷着粗气。

"教授——求求您——"

"您不能——"

"不用你告诉我说我能做什么,不能做什么,波特。好了,你们都上床去吧。我从没有像现在这样为格兰芬多的学生感到脸红。"

一下子丢掉一百五十分。这样一来,格兰芬多就落到最后一名了。仅仅一个晚上,他们就摧毁了格兰芬多赢得学院杯的所有希望。哈利觉得心里一下子空落落的。这样大的损失,他们还有没有可能弥补呢?

哈利整夜无法入睡。他能听见纳威伏在枕头上哭泣,哭了很长时间。哈利不知道说什么话来安慰他。他知道纳威像他自己一样,都很害怕黎明的到来。当格兰芬多的其他学生知道了他们做的好事,会怎么样呢?

第二天,格兰芬多的学生们经过记录学院杯比分的巨大沙漏时,还以为出了什么差错。他们怎么可能突然比昨天少了一百五十分呢?随后,事情就慢慢传开了:哈利·波特,大名鼎鼎的哈利·波特,两次魁地奇比赛的英雄,竟然害得他们丢掉这么多分数,他,还有另外两个愚蠢的一年级学生。

CHAPTER FIFTEEN The Forbidden Forest

From being one of the most popular and admired people at the school, Harry was suddenly the most hated. Even Ravenclaws and Hufflepuffs turned on him, because everyone had been longing to see Slytherin lose the House Cup. Everywhere Harry went, people pointed and didn't trouble to lower their voices as they insulted him. Slytherins, on the other hand, clapped as he walked past them, whistling and cheering, 'Thanks Potter, we owe you one!'

Only Ron stood by him.

'They'll all forget this in a few weeks. Fred and George have lost loads of points in all the time they've been here, and people still like them.'

'They've never lost a hundred and fifty points in one go, though, have they?' said Harry miserably.

'Well – no,' Ron admitted.

It was a bit late to repair the damage, but Harry swore to himself not to meddle in things that weren't his business from now on. He'd had it with sneaking around and spying. He felt so ashamed of himself that he went to Wood and offered to resign from the Quidditch team.

'*Resign?*' Wood thundered. 'What good'll that do? How are we going to get any points back if we can't win at Quidditch?'

But even Quidditch had lost its fun. The rest of the team wouldn't speak to Harry during practice, and if they had to speak about him, they called him 'the Seeker'.

Hermione and Neville were suffering, too. They didn't have as bad a time as Harry, because they weren't as well known, but nobody would speak to them either. Hermione had stopped drawing attention to herself in class, keeping her head down and working in silence.

Harry was almost glad that the exams weren't far away. All the revision he had to do kept his mind off his misery. He, Ron and Hermione kept to themselves, working late into the night, trying to remember the ingredients in complicated potions, learn charms and spells off by heart, memorise the dates of magical discoveries and goblin rebellions ...

Then, about a week before the exams were due to start, Harry's new resolution not to interfere in anything that didn't concern him was put to an unexpected test. Walking back from the library on his own one afternoon, he heard somebody whimpering from a classroom up ahead. As he drew closer, he heard Quirrell's voice.

第15章 禁林

哈利原是学校里最受欢迎、最受敬佩的人物之一，现在一下子变成了众矢之的。就连拉文克劳和赫奇帕奇的学生也没有好脸色给他，因为大家本来一直希望看到斯莱特林输掉学院杯。哈利不管走到哪儿，人们都对他指指点点，而且说一些侮辱他的话时也并不把声音放低。另一方面，每当他从斯莱特林们身边走过时，他们总是又鼓掌又吹口哨，欢呼喝彩："谢谢你，波特，你帮了我们一个大忙！"

只有罗恩和他站在一边。

"再过几个星期，他们就会把这些忘得一干二净的。弗雷德和乔治自从入学以来，就一直在丢分，人们照样很喜欢他们。"

"但他们从来没有一下子丢掉过一百五十分，是吗？"哈利忧伤地说。

"嗯——那倒没有。"罗恩承认。

损失已经造成，后悔也来不及了，哈利对自己发誓，从今往后，他再也不去多管闲事了。他就是因为偷偷摸摸地乱转、暗中监视才致此恶果的。他为自己感到非常羞愧，就去找伍德，表示要退出魁地奇球队。

"退出？"伍德大声斥责道，"那有什么用？如果我们赢不了魁地奇比赛，又怎么可能把分数挣回来呢？"

可是，对哈利来说，就连魁地奇也失去了原有的乐趣。训练时，其他队员都不跟他说话，如果不得不提到他，就管他叫"找球手"。

赫敏和纳威也很痛苦。他们的日子不像哈利那样难熬，因为没有他那么出名，但是也没有人愿意跟他们说话了。赫敏在班上不再抛头露面，总是低着头，默默地学习。

哈利简直很高兴快要考试了。他必须埋头复习，这使他暂时忘却了烦恼。他、罗恩和赫敏三个人总是单独在一起，每天复习到深夜，努力记住复杂的魔药配方，记住那些魔法和咒语，记住重大魔术发明和妖精叛乱的日期……

然而，就在考试前的一个星期，哈利不再多管闲事的决心受到了一次意外的考验。那天下午，他独自一人从图书馆出来，听见有人在前面的教室里抽抽搭搭地哭泣。他走近几步，听出是奇洛的声音。

CHAPTER FIFTEEN   The Forbidden Forest

'No – no – not again, please –'

It sounded as though someone was threatening him. Harry moved closer.

'All right – all right –' he heard Quirrell sob.

Next second, Quirrell came hurrying out of the classroom, straightening his turban. He was pale and looked as though he was about to cry. He strode out of sight; Harry didn't think Quirrell had even noticed him. He waited until Quirrell's footsteps had disappeared, then peered into the classroom. It was empty, but a door stood ajar at the other end. Harry was halfway towards it before he remembered what he'd promised himself about not meddling.

All the same, he'd have gambled twelve Philosopher's Stones that Snape had just left the room, and from what Harry had just heard, Snape would be walking with a new spring in his step – Quirrell seemed to have given in at last.

Harry went back to the library, where Hermione was testing Ron on Astronomy. Harry told them what he'd heard.

'Snape's done it, then!' said Ron. 'If Quirrell's told him how to break his Anti-Dark Force spell –'

'There's still Fluffy, though,' said Hermione.

'Maybe Snape's found out how to get past him without asking Hagrid,' said Ron, looking up at the thousands of books surrounding them. 'I bet there's a book somewhere in here, telling you how to get past a giant three-headed dog. So what do we do, Harry?'

The light of adventure was kindling again in Ron's eyes, but Hermione answered before Harry could.

'Go to Dumbledore. That's what we should have done ages ago. If we try anything ourselves we'll be thrown out for sure.'

'But we've got no *proof!*' said Harry. 'Quirrell's too scared to back us up. Snape's only got to say he doesn't know how the troll got in at Hallowe'en and that he was nowhere near the third floor – who do you think they'll believe, him or us? It's not exactly a secret we hate him, Dumbledore'll think we made it up to get him sacked. Filch wouldn't help us if his life depended on it, he's too friendly with Snape, and the more students get thrown out, the better, he'll think. And don't forget, we're not supposed to know about the Stone or Fluffy. That'll take a lot of explaining.'

Hermione looked convinced, but Ron didn't.

第15章 禁林

"不行——不行——不能再干了,求求你——"

听上去似乎有人在威胁他。哈利又走近了几步。

"好吧——好吧——"他听见奇洛在抽泣。

接着,奇洛匆匆走出教室,一边整理着他的围巾。他脸色苍白,好像快要哭出声来似的,大步地走出了哈利的视线。哈利觉得奇洛根本就没有注意到自己。他一直等到奇洛的脚步声听不见了,才朝教室里望去。里面空无一人,但另一边的那扇门开了一道缝。哈利正要走过去,突然想起他对自己的保证,再也不能多管闲事了。

不过,他愿意拿十二块魔法石打赌:刚才离开教室的是斯内普,从脚步声听,斯内普的步子陡然变得轻快了——看来奇洛终于投降了。

哈利返回图书馆,赫敏正在那里为罗恩测验天文学。哈利把他刚才听到的告诉了他们。

"这么说,斯内普终于得手了!"罗恩说,"如果奇洛告诉了他怎样解除他的反黑魔法咒语——"

"别忘了还有路威呢。"赫敏说。

"说不定斯内普已经知道了怎样通过路威,根本用不着去问海格。"罗恩说道,抬头看着他们周围的无数本书,"我敢说这里肯定藏着一本书,可以告诉你怎样通过一条三个脑袋的大狗。那么我们怎么办呢,哈利?"

渴望冒险的光芒又在罗恩眼睛里闪烁,可赫敏赶在哈利前面答话了。

"去找邓布利多。早就应该这么做了。如果我们再单独行动,肯定会被学校开除的。"

"可是我们没有证据!"哈利说,"奇洛怕得要命,肯定不会出来为我们作证。斯内普只需咬定他不知道万圣节前夕那个巨怪是怎么进来的,他根本没在四楼附近——你们说他们会相信谁,是斯内普还是我们?我们恨斯内普,这已经不是什么秘密,邓布利多会认为我们编出这套鬼话,是想害得斯内普被开除。费尔奇即使生命受到威胁也不会帮助我们的。他和斯内普的关系太密切了,而且他还会认为被开除的学生越多越好。还有,别忘了,我们是不应该知道魔法石和路威的,那要解释起来就太麻烦了。"

赫敏似乎被他说服了,可是罗恩没有。

CHAPTER FIFTEEN   The Forbidden Forest

'If we just do a bit of poking around –'

'No,' said Harry flatly, 'we've done enough poking around.'

He pulled a map of Jupiter towards him and started to learn the names of its moons.

The following morning, notes were delivered to Harry, Hermione and Neville at the breakfast table. They were all the same:

> Your detention will take place at eleven o'clock tonight. Meet Mr Filch in the Entrance Hall.
>
> *Prof. M. McGonagall*

Harry had forgotten they still had detentions to do in the furore over the points they'd lost. He half expected Hermione to complain that this was a whole night of revision lost, but she didn't say a word. Like Harry, she felt they deserved what they'd got.

At eleven o'clock that night they said goodbye to Ron in the common room and went down to the entrance hall with Neville. Filch was already there – and so was Malfoy. Harry had also forgotten that Malfoy had got a detention, too.

'Follow me,' said Filch, lighting a lamp and leading them outside. 'I bet you'll think twice about breaking a school rule again, won't you, eh?' he continued, leering at them. 'Oh yes ... hard work and pain are the best teachers if you ask me ... it's just a pity they let the old punishments die out ... hang you by your wrists from the ceiling for a few days, I've got the chains still in my office, keep 'em well oiled in case they're ever needed ... Right, off we go, and don't think of running off, now, it'll be worse for you if you do.'

They marched off across the dark grounds. Neville kept sniffing. Harry wondered what their punishment was going to be. It must be something really horrible, or Filch wouldn't be sounding so delighted.

The moon was bright, but clouds scudding across it kept throwing them into darkness. Ahead, Harry could see the lighted windows of Hagrid's hut. Then they heard a distant shout.

'Is that you, Filch? Hurry up, I want ter get started.'

Harry's heart rose; if they were going to be working with Hagrid it

第15章 禁林

"如果我们到处探听一下——"

"不行,"哈利干脆地说,"我们已经探听得够多的了。"

他把一张木星天文图拉到面前,开始复习木星卫星的名字。

第二天早晨,哈利、赫敏和纳威在早饭桌上都收到了字条。三张字条一模一样:

你的禁闭从今晚十一点开始。在门厅找费尔奇先生。

麦格教授

哈利自从丢了分数以后,就一直遭到人们的白眼和唾弃,他几乎忘记了还要被关禁闭的事。本以为赫敏会抱怨一番,说又要耽误一晚上复习时间,但她什么也没说。她和哈利一样,觉得他们理应受到这样的惩罚。

那天夜里十一点,他们在公共休息室里与罗恩告别,然后和纳威一起下楼来到门厅。费尔奇已经等在那里了——还有马尔福。哈利同样忘记了马尔福也是要关禁闭的。

"跟我来。"费尔奇说着,点亮一盏灯,领他们出去,"我认为,以后你们再想要违反校规,就要三思而行了,是不是,嗯?"他斜眼看着他们,继续说道,"哦,是啊……如果你们问我的话,我得说干活和吃苦是最好的老师……真遗憾他们废除了过去那种老派的惩罚方式……吊住你们的手腕,把你们悬挂在天花板上,一吊就是好几天。我办公室里还留着那些链条呢,经常给它们上上油,说不定哪一天就派上了用场……好了,走吧,可别想着逃跑。如果逃跑,你们更没有好果子吃。"

他们大步穿过漆黑的场地。纳威不停地抽着鼻子。哈利不知道他们将会受到什么惩罚。肯定非常可怕,不然费尔奇的口气不会这么欢快。

月光很皎洁,但不断有云飘过来遮住月亮,使他们陷入一片黑暗。哈利可以看见海格的小屋那些映着灯光的窗户。接着,听见远处传来一声喊叫。

"是你吗,费尔奇?快点儿,我要出发了。"

哈利的心欢腾起来;如果他们要和海格一起劳动,那就不算太糟。

CHAPTER FIFTEEN   The Forbidden Forest

wouldn't be so bad. His relief must have showed in his face, because Filch said, 'I suppose you think you'll be enjoying yourself with that oaf? Well, think again, boy – it's into the Forest you're going and I'm much mistaken if you'll all come out in one piece.'

At this, Neville let out a little moan and Malfoy stopped dead in his tracks.

'The Forest?' he repeated, and he didn't sound quite as cool as usual. 'We can't go in there at night – there's all sorts of things in there – werewolves, I heard.'

Neville clutched the sleeve of Harry's robe and made a choking noise.

'That's your lookout, isn't it?' said Filch, his voice cracking with glee. 'Should've thought of them werewolves before you got in trouble, shouldn't you?'

Hagrid came striding towards them out of the dark, Fang at his heel. He was carrying his large crossbow, and a quiver of arrows hung over his shoulder.

'Abou' time,' he said. 'I bin waitin' fer half an hour already. All right, Harry, Hermione?'

'I shouldn't be too friendly to them, Hagrid,' said Filch coldly, 'they're here to be punished, after all.'

'That's why yer late, is it?' said Hagrid, frowning at Filch. 'Bin lecturin' them, eh? 'Snot your place ter do that. Yeh've done yer bit, I'll take over from here.'

'I'll be back at dawn,' said Filch, 'for what's left of them,' he added nastily, and he turned and started back towards the castle, his lamp bobbing away in the darkness.

Malfoy now turned to Hagrid.

'I'm not going in that Forest,' he said, and Harry was pleased to hear the note of panic in his voice.

'Yeh are if yeh want ter stay at Hogwarts,' said Hagrid fiercely. 'Yeh've done wrong an' now yeh've got ter pay fer it.'

'But this is servant stuff, it's not for students to do. I thought we'd be writing lines or something. If my father knew I was doing this, he'd –'

'– tell yer that's how it is at Hogwarts,' Hagrid growled. 'Writin' lines! What good's that ter anyone? Yeh'll do summat useful or yeh'll get out. If yeh think yer father'd rather you were expelled, then get back off ter the castle an' pack. Go on!'

Malfoy didn't move. He looked at Hagrid furiously but then dropped his gaze.

第15章 禁 林

他一定在脸上表现出了这种宽慰的心情，只听费尔奇说："你大概以为你会和那个蠢货一起玩个痛快吧？再好好想想吧，小子——你是要去禁林！如果你能安然无恙地出来，就算我估计错了。"

听了这话，纳威忍不住哼了一声，马尔福猛地停住了脚步。

"禁林？"他跟着说了一句，声音远不像平时那样冷静了，"我们不能在半夜里进去——那里面什么都有——我听说有狼人。"

纳威紧紧抓住哈利的衣袖，发出一声哽咽。

"那只能怪你自己，是不是？"费尔奇说，声音喜滋滋的，"你在惹麻烦之前，就应该想到这些狼人的，是不是？"

海格从黑暗中大步向他们走来，牙牙跟在后面。海格带着他的巨弩，肩上挂着装得满满的箭筒。

"时间差不多了，"他说，"我已经等了半个小时。怎么样，哈利？赫敏？"

"不应该对他们这么客气，海格，"费尔奇冷冰冰地说，"毕竟，他们到这里来是接受惩罚的。"

"所以你才迟到了，是吗？"海格冲费尔奇皱着眉头，说道，"一直在教训他们，嗯？这里可不是你教训人的地方。你的任务完成了，从现在起由我负责。"

"我天亮的时候回来，"费尔奇说，"收拾他们的残骸。"他恶狠狠地说罢，转身朝城堡走去，那盏灯摇摇摆摆地消失在黑暗中。

这时马尔福转向了海格。

"我不进那个禁林。"他说。哈利高兴地听出他声音里透着一丝惊恐。

"如果你还想待在霍格沃茨，就非去不可。"海格毫不留情地说，"你做了错事，现在必须付出代价。"

"但这是仆人的差使，不是学生干的。我还以为我们最多写写检查什么的。如果我父亲知道我在干这个，他会——"

"——告诉你霍格沃茨就是这样的。"海格粗暴地说，"写写检查！这对任何人有什么好处吗？你得做点有用的事，不然就得滚蛋。如果你认为你父亲情愿让你被开除，就尽管回城堡收拾行李去吧。走吧！"

马尔福没有动弹。他愤怒地看着海格，但随即又垂下了目光。

CHAPTER FIFTEEN   The Forbidden Forest

'Right then,' said Hagrid, 'now, listen carefully, 'cause it's dangerous what we're gonna do tonight an' I don' want no one takin' risks. Follow me over here a moment.'

He led them to the very edge of the Forest. Holding his lamp up high he pointed down a narrow, winding earth track that disappeared into the thick black trees. A light breeze lifted their hair as they looked into the Forest.

'Look there,' said Hagrid, 'see that stuff shinin' on the ground? Silvery stuff? That's unicorn blood. There's a unicorn in there bin hurt badly by summat. This is the second time in a week. I found one dead last Wednesday. We're gonna try an' find the poor thing. We might have ter put it out of its misery.'

'And what if whatever hurt the unicorn finds us first?' said Malfoy, unable to keep the fear out of his voice.

'There's nothin' that lives in the Forest that'll hurt yeh if yer with me or Fang,' said Hagrid. 'An' keep ter the path. Right, now, we're gonna split inter two parties an' follow the trail in diff'rent directions. There's blood all over the place, it must've bin staggerin' around since last night at least.'

'I want Fang,' said Malfoy quickly, looking at Fang's long teeth.

'All right, but I warn yeh, he's a coward,' said Hagrid. 'So me, Harry an' Hermione'll go one way an' Draco, Neville an' Fang'll go the other. Now, if any of us finds the unicorn, we'll send up green sparks, right? Get yer wands out an' practise now – that's it – an' if anyone gets in trouble, send up red sparks, an' we'll all come an' find yeh – so, be careful – let's go.'

The Forest was black and silent. A little way into it they reached a fork in the earth path and Harry, Hermione and Hagrid took the left path while Malfoy, Neville and Fang took the right.

They walked in silence, their eyes on the ground. Every now and then a ray of moonlight through the branches above lit a spot of silver blue blood on the fallen leaves.

Harry saw that Hagrid looked very worried.

'*Could* a werewolf be killing the unicorns?' Harry asked.

'Not fast enough,' said Hagrid. 'It's not easy ter catch a unicorn, they're powerful magic creatures. I never knew one ter be hurt before.'

They walked past a mossy tree-stump. Harry could hear running water; there must be a stream somewhere close by. There were still spots of unicorn

第15章 禁　林

"好吧，"海格说，"现在仔细听着，今天晚上我们要做的事情非常危险，我不愿意让任何一个人冒险。先跟我到这边来。"

他领着他们来到禁林边缘，把灯高高举起，指着一条逐渐隐入黑色密林深处的羊肠小路。他们往禁林里望去，一阵微风吹拂着他们的头发。

"你们往那边瞧，"海格说，"看见地上那个闪光的东西了吗？银白色的？那就是独角兽的血。禁林里的一只独角兽被什么东西打伤了，伤得很重。这已经是一个星期里的第二次了。上星期三我就发现死了一只。我们要争取找到那只可怜的独角兽，使它摆脱痛苦。"

"如果那个伤害独角兽的东西先发现了我们，怎么办呢？"马尔福问，声音里含着无法抑制的恐惧。

"只要你和我或者牙牙在一起，禁林里的任何生物都不会伤害你。"海格说，"不要离开小路。好了，现在我们兵分两路，分头循着血迹寻找。到处都是血迹，显然，它至少从昨天晚上起，就一直跌跌撞撞地到处徘徊。"

"我要牙牙。"马尔福看着牙牙长长的牙齿，忙不迭地说。

"好吧，不过我提醒你，它可是个胆小鬼。"海格说，"那么，我、哈利和赫敏走一条路，马尔福、纳威和牙牙走另一条路。如果谁找到了独角兽，就发射绿色火花，明白吗？把你们的魔杖拿出来，练习一下——对了——如果有谁遇到了麻烦，就发射红色火花，我们都会过来找你——行了，大家多加小心——我们走吧。"

禁林里黑黢黢的，一片寂静。他们往里走了一段，就到了岔路口，哈利、赫敏和海格走左边的路，马尔福、纳威和牙牙走右边的路。

他们默默地走着，眼睛盯着地上。时不时地，一道月光从上面的树枝间洒下来，照亮落叶上一块银蓝色的血迹。

哈利看出海格显得很焦虑。

"会是狼人杀死了独角兽吗？"哈利问。

"不会这么快的，"海格说，"抓住一只独角兽很不容易，它们这种动物具有很强的魔法。我以前从没听说过独角兽受到伤害。"

他们走过一个布满苔藓的树桩。哈利可以听见潺潺的流水声，显然，附近什么地方有一条小溪。在蜿蜒曲折的小路上，仍然散落着斑斑点点

CHAPTER FIFTEEN The Forbidden Forest

blood here and there along the winding path.

'You all right, Hermione?' Hagrid whispered. 'Don' worry, it can't've gone far if it's this badly hurt an' then we'll be able ter – GET BEHIND THAT TREE!'

Hagrid seized Harry and Hermione and hoisted them off the path behind a towering oak. He pulled out an arrow and fitted it into his crossbow, raising it, ready to fire. The three of them listened. Something was slithering over dead leaves nearby: it sounded like a cloak trailing along the ground. Hagrid was squinting up the dark path, but after a few seconds, the sound faded away.

'I knew it,' he murmured. 'There's summat in here that shouldn' be.'

'A werewolf?' Harry suggested.

'That wasn' no werewolf an' it wasn' no unicorn, neither,' said Hagrid grimly. 'Right, follow me, but careful, now.'

They walked more slowly, ears straining for the faintest sound. Suddenly, in a clearing ahead, something definitely moved.

'Who's there?' Hagrid called. 'Show yerself – I'm armed!'

And into the clearing came – was it a man, or a horse? To the waist, a man, with red hair and beard, but below that was a horse's gleaming chestnut body with a long, reddish tail. Harry and Hermione's jaws dropped.

'Oh, it's you, Ronan,' said Hagrid in relief. 'How are yeh?'

He walked forward and shook the centaur's hand.

'Good evening to you, Hagrid,' said Ronan. He had a deep, sorrowful voice. 'Were you going to shoot me?'

'Can't be too careful, Ronan,' said Hagrid, patting his crossbow. 'There's summat bad loose in this Forest. This is Harry Potter an' Hermione Granger, by the way. Students up at the school. An' this is Ronan, you two. He's a centaur.'

'We'd noticed,' said Hermione faintly.

'Good evening,' said Ronan. 'Students, are you? And do you learn much, up at the school?'

'Erm –'

'A bit,' said Hermione timidly.

'A bit. Well, that's something.' Ronan sighed. He flung back his head and stared at the sky. 'Mars is bright tonight.'

第15章 禁　林

的独角兽血迹。

"你没事吧，赫敏？"海格低声问，"不要担心，它伤得这样重，不可能走得很远，我们很快就能——不好，**快躲到那棵树后面去！**"

海格一把抓住哈利和赫敏，拎着他们离开了小路，藏到一棵高耸的栎树后面。他抽出一支箭，装在弩上，举起来准备射击。三个人侧耳细听。什么东西正在近旁的落叶上嗖嗖地滑行：那声音就像是斗篷在地面上拖曳。海格眯眼注视着漆黑的小路，几秒钟后，声音渐渐消失了。

"我知道了，"他喃喃地说，"有一样东西，它原本是不属于这里的。"

"狼人？"哈利问道。

"不是狼人，也不是独角兽。"海格沉重地说，"好了，跟我来吧，现在可得小心了。"

他们走得比刚才更慢了，竖着耳朵，捕捉着最细微的声音。突然，在前面的空地上，他们清清楚楚地看见了一个东西在动。

"谁在那儿？"海格喊道，"快出来——我带着武器呢！"

那东西应声走进了空地——到底是人，还是马？腰部以上是人，红色的头发和胡子，但腰部以下却是棕红色的发亮的马身，后面还拖着一条长长的红尾巴。哈利和赫敏吃惊地张大了嘴巴。

"哦，原来是你，罗南。"海格松了一口气，说道，"你好吗？"

他走上前，和马人握了握手。

"晚上好，海格。"罗南说，他的声音低沉而忧伤，"你想用弓箭射我？"

"不得不提高警惕啊，罗南，"海格一边说，一边拍了拍他的箭筒，"这片森林里有个坏家伙在到处活动。噢，对了，这是哈利·波特和赫敏·格兰杰，是上边那所学校里的学生。我来给你们俩介绍一下，这位是罗南，一个马人。"

"我们已经注意到了。"赫敏小声地说。

"晚上好，"罗南说，"你们是学生？在学校里学到的东西多吗？"

"嗯——"

"学到一点儿。"赫敏腼腆地说。

"学到一点儿，好，那就很不错了。"罗南叹了口气。他仰起头，凝视着天空。"今晚的火星很明亮。"

CHAPTER FIFTEEN   The Forbidden Forest

'Yeah,' said Hagrid, glancing up too. 'Listen, I'm glad we've run inter yeh, Ronan, 'cause there's a unicorn bin hurt – you seen anythin'?'

Ronan didn't answer immediately. He stared unblinkingly upwards, then sighed again.

'Always the innocent are the first victims,' he said. 'So it has been for ages past, so it is now.'

'Yeah,' said Hagrid, 'but have yeh seen anythin', Ronan? Anythin' unusual?'

'Mars is bright tonight,' Ronan repeated while Hagrid watched him impatiently. 'Unusually bright.'

'Yeah, but I was meanin' anythin' unusual a bit nearer home,' said Hagrid. 'So yeh haven't noticed anythin' strange?'

Yet again, ronan took a while to answer. At last, he said, 'The Forest hides many secrets.'

A movement in the trees behind Ronan made Hagrid raise his bow again, but it was only a second centaur, black-haired and -bodied and wilder-looking than Ronan.

'Hullo, Bane,' said Hagrid. 'All right?'

'Good evening, Hagrid, I hope you are well?'

'Well enough. Look, I've jus' bin askin' Ronan, you seen anythin' odd in here lately? Only there's a unicorn bin injured – would yeh know anythin' about it?'

Bane walked over to stand next to Ronan. He looked skywards.

'Mars is bright tonight,' he said simply.

'We've heard,' said Hagrid grumpily. 'Well, if either of you do see anythin', let me know, won't yeh? We'll be off, then.'

Harry and Hermione followed him out of the clearing, staring over their shoulders at Ronan and Bane until the trees blocked their view.

'Never,' said Hagrid irritably, 'try an' get a straight answer out of a centaur. Ruddy star-gazers. Not interested in anythin' closer'n the moon.'

'Are there many of *them* in here?' asked Hermione.

'Oh, a fair few ... Keep themselves to themselves mostly, but they're good enough about turnin' up if ever I want a word. They're deep, mind, centaurs ... they know things ... jus' don' let on much.'

'D'you think that was a centaur we heard earlier?' said Harry.

第15章 禁 林

"是啊。"海格说着,也抬头看了一眼天空,"听我说,罗南,我很高兴我们碰见了你,因为有一只独角兽受伤了——你看见了什么没有?"

罗南没有马上回答。他眼睛一眨不眨地向上凝望着,接着又叹了口气。

"总是无辜者首先受害。"他说,"几百年来是这样,现在还是这样。"

"是啊。"海格说,"可是你有没有看见什么,罗南?看见什么异常的东西?"

"今晚的火星很明亮。"罗南又重复了一句,海格不耐烦地看着他。"异常明亮。"罗南说。

"不错,但我的意思是,离咱们这儿近一点儿的地方有没有异常情况?"海格说,"你没有注意到一些奇怪的动静吗?"

罗南还是迟迟没有回答。最后,他说:"森林里藏着许多秘密。"

罗南身后的树丛里突然有了动静,海格又举起了弩,结果那只是第二个马人,黑头发、黑身体,看上去比罗南粗野一些。

"你好,贝恩,"海格说,"近来好吗?"

"晚上好,海格,我希望你一切都好。"

"还可以吧。你瞧,我刚才正问罗南呢,你们最近在这儿有没有看见什么古怪的东西?有一只独角兽受了伤——你们知道一些情况吗?"

贝恩走过来站在罗南身边,抬头望着天空。

"今晚的火星很明亮。"他就说了这么一句。

"这句话我们已经听过了。"海格暴躁地说,"好吧,如果你们谁看见了什么,就赶紧来告诉我,好吗?那么我们走吧。"

哈利和赫敏跟在他后面走出空地,一边不住地扭头望望罗南和贝恩,直到树木挡住了视线。

"唉,从马人那里总是得不到直截了当的回答。"海格恼火地说,"总是仰头看着星星,真讨厌。他们对任何比月亮离得近的事情都不感兴趣。"

"这里的马人多吗?"赫敏问。

"哦,有那么几个……他们大部分都跟自己的同类待在一起,不过心眼不错,每当我想跟他们说说话的时候,他们总能及时出现。这些马人深奥莫测……知道许多事情……却总是守口如瓶。"

"你说,我们先前听见的动静会不会也是一个马人?"哈利问。

CHAPTER FIFTEEN   The Forbidden Forest

'Did that sound like hooves to you? Nah, if yeh ask me, that was what's bin killin' the unicorns — never heard anythin' like it before.'

They walked on through the dense, dark trees. Harry kept looking nervously over his shoulder. He had the nasty feeling they were being watched. He was very glad they had Hagrid and his crossbow with them. They had just passed a bend in the path when Hermione grabbed Hagrid's arm.

'Hagrid! Look! Red sparks, the others are in trouble!'

'You two wait here!' Hagrid shouted. 'Stay on the path, I'll come back for yeh!'

They heard him crashing away through the undergrowth and stood looking at each other, very scared, until they couldn't hear anything but the rustling of leaves around them.

'You don't think they've been hurt, do you?' whispered Hermione.

'I don't care if Malfoy has, but if something's got Neville ... It's our fault he's here in the first place.'

The minutes dragged by. Their ears seemed sharper than usual. Harry's seemed to be picking up every sigh of the wind, every cracking twig. What was going on? Where were the others?

At last, a great crunching noise announced Hagrid's return. Malfoy, Neville and Fang were with him. Hagrid was fuming. Malfoy, it seemed, had sneaked up behind Neville and grabbed him for a joke. Neville had panicked and sent up the sparks.

'We'll be lucky ter catch anythin' now, with the racket you two were makin'. Right, we're changin' groups – Neville, you stay with me an' Hermione, Harry, you go with Fang an' this idiot. I'm sorry,' Hagrid added in a whisper to Harry, 'but he'll have a harder time frightenin' you, an' we've gotta get this done.'

So Harry set off into the heart of the Forest with Malfoy and Fang. They walked for nearly half an hour, deeper and deeper into the Forest, until the path became almost impossible to follow because the trees were so thick. Harry thought the blood seemed to be getting thicker. There were splashes on the roots of a tree, as though the poor creature had been thrashing around in pain close by. Harry could see a clearing ahead, through the tangled branches of an ancient oak.

第15章 禁　林

"你觉得那像是马蹄声吗？如果你问我的话，我认为不是，那就是杀死独角兽的家伙——那种声音我以前从来没有听见过。"

他们继续在茂密、漆黑的树林间穿行。哈利总是紧张地扭头张望。他有一种很不舒服的感觉，好像有人在监视他们。他很高兴有海格和他的弩陪伴着他们。可是，刚拐过小路上的一个弯道，赫敏突然一把抓住海格的胳膊。

"海格！快看！红色火花，其他人有麻烦了！"

"你们俩在这儿等着！"海格喊道，"待在小路上别动。我去去就来。"

他们听见海格噼里啪啦地穿过低矮的灌木丛。哈利和赫敏站在那里对望着，心里非常害怕。渐渐地，海格走远了，他们只能听见周围树叶在风中沙沙作响的声音。

"你说，他们不会受伤吧，嗯？"赫敏小声问道。

"马尔福受伤我倒不在乎，可是如果纳威出了什么意外……都是我们拖累了他，害他到这里来受罚的啊。"

时间一分一秒过得很慢。他们的耳朵似乎比平常敏锐得多。哈利简直能捕捉到风的每一声叹息以及每根树枝折断的声音。出了什么事？其他人在哪儿？

最后，随着一阵嘎吱嘎吱的巨大响动，他们知道是海格回来了，马尔福、纳威和牙牙也跟他在一起。海格怒气冲冲。情况似乎是这样的：马尔福搞了个恶作剧，他悄悄藏到纳威后面，然后一把抱住纳威。纳威吓坏了，就发射了红色火花。

"你们俩闹出了这么大动静，现在，我们要抓住那东西就全凭运气了。好吧，我们把队伍换一换——纳威，你跟我和赫敏在一起。哈利，你和牙牙，还有这个白痴一组。对不起，"海格又小声地对哈利说，"不过他要吓唬你可没那么容易，我们还是赶紧把事情办完吧。"

于是，哈利和马尔福、牙牙一起朝禁林中心走去。他们走了将近半个小时，越来越深入森林内部，后来树木变得极为茂密，小路几乎走不通了。哈利觉得地上的血迹也越来越密了。一棵树的根上溅了许多血，似乎那个可怜的动物曾在附近痛苦地扭动挣扎过。哈利透过一棵古老的栎树纠结缠绕的树枝，可以看见前面有一片空地。

CHAPTER FIFTEEN The Forbidden Forest

'Look –' he murmured, holding out his arm to stop Malfoy.

Something bright white was gleaming on the ground. They inched closer.

It was the unicorn all right, and it was dead. Harry had never seen anything so beautiful and sad. Its long slender legs were stuck out at odd angles where it had fallen and its mane was spread pearly white on the dark leaves.

Harry had taken one step towards it when a slithering sound made him freeze where he stood. A bush on the edge of the clearing quivered ... Then, out of the shadows, a hooded figure came crawling across the ground like some stalking beast. Harry, Malfoy and Fang stood transfixed. The cloaked figure reached the unicorn, it lowered its head over the wound in the animal's side, and began to drink its blood.

'AAAAAAAAAAARGH!'

Malfoy let out a terrible scream and bolted – so did Fang. The hooded figure raised its head and looked right at Harry – unicorn blood was dribbling down its front. It got to its feet and came swiftly towards him – he couldn't move for fear.

Then a pain pierced his head like he'd never felt before, it was as though his scar was on fire – half-blinded, he staggered backwards. He heard hooves behind him, galloping, and something jumped clean over him, charging at the figure.

The pain in Harry's head was so bad he fell to his knees. It took a minute or two to pass. When he looked up, the figure had gone. A centaur was standing over him, not Ronan or Bane; this one looked younger; he had white-blond hair and a palomino body.

'Are you all right?' said the centaur, pulling Harry to his feet.

'Yes – thank you – what *was* that?'

The centaur didn't answer. He had astonishingly blue eyes, like pale sapphires. He looked carefully at Harry, his eyes lingering on the scar which stood out, livid, on Harry's forehead.

'You are the Potter boy,' he said. 'You had better get back to Hagrid. The Forest is not safe at this time – especially for you. Can you ride? It will be quicker this way.

'My name is Firenze,' he added, as he lowered himself on to his front legs so that Harry could clamber on to his back.

There was suddenly a sound of more galloping from the other side of

第15章 禁　林

"看——"他低声说，举起胳膊拦住马尔福。

一个洁白的东西在地上闪闪发光。他们一点点地向它靠近。

没错，那正是独角兽，它已经死了。哈利从没见过这样美丽、这样凄惨的情景。独角兽修长的腿保持着摔倒时的姿势，很不自然地直伸着；它的鬃毛铺在漆黑的落叶上，白得像珍珠一样。

哈利刚朝它跨近一步，突然一阵簌簌滑动的声音使他停住了脚，呆呆地站在原地。空地边缘的一丛灌木在抖动……接着，从阴影里闪出一个戴兜帽的身影在地上缓缓爬行，像一头渐渐逼近的野兽。哈利、马尔福和牙牙都呆若木鸡地站在那里。那个穿斗篷的身影来到独角兽身边，低下头去，对准尸体一侧的伤口，开始喝它的血。

"啊啊啊啊——！"

马尔福发出一声可怕的尖叫，撒腿就跑——牙牙也没命地逃走了。那戴兜帽的身影抬起头，一眼就看见了哈利——独角兽的血滴落在它胸前。它站起身，飞快地向哈利走来——哈利吓得动弹不得。

就在这时，一阵剧痛穿透哈利的头部，这是他以前从没有过的感觉，就好像他的伤疤突然着了火一般——他视线模糊，跟跟跄跄地向后退去。他听见身后有马蹄小跑的声音，什么东西从他头顶越过，朝那个身影扑去。

哈利的头疼得太厉害了，他扑通跪倒在地上，过了一两分钟才缓过劲来。当他抬起头时，那个戴兜帽的身影已经不见了。一个马人站在他身边，不是罗南，也不是贝恩，这个马人显得更年轻些。他的头发是白金色的，长着一副银鬃马的身体。

"你没事吧？"马人把哈利拉起来，问道。

"没事——谢谢你——刚才那是什么东西？"

马人没有回答。他的眼睛蓝得惊人，像淡淡的蓝宝石。他仔细地打量着哈利，目光停留在哈利额前那道鲜明而涨红的伤疤上。

"你就是波特家的那个男孩，"他说，"最好回到海格身边去。森林里这个时候不太安全——特别是对你来说。你会骑马吗？这样可以快一些。我叫费伦泽。"他又补充了一句，一边弯下前腿，把身体放低，让哈利爬到他的背上。

突然，从空地另一边又传来了更多的马蹄声。罗南和贝恩从树丛中

CHAPTER FIFTEEN   The Forbidden Forest

the clearing. Ronan and Bane came bursting through the trees, their flanks heaving and sweaty.

'Firenze!' Bane thundered. 'What are you doing? You have a human on your back! Have you no shame? Are you a common mule?'

'Do you realise who this is?' said Firenze. 'This is the Potter boy. The quicker he leaves this Forest, the better.'

'What have you been telling him?' growled Bane. 'Remember, Firenze, we are sworn not to set ourselves against the heavens. Have we not read what is to come in the movements of the planets?'

Ronan pawed the ground nervously.

'I'm sure Firenze thought he was acting for the best,' he said, in his gloomy voice.

Bane kicked his back legs in anger.

'For the best! What is that to do with us? Centaurs are concerned with what has been foretold! It is not our business to run around like donkeys after stray humans in our Forest!'

Firenze suddenly reared on to his hind legs in anger, so that Harry had to grab his shoulders to stay on.

'Do you not see that unicorn?' Firenze bellowed at Bane. 'Do you not understand why it was killed? Or have the planets not let you in on that secret? I set myself against what is lurking in this Forest, Bane, yes, with humans alongside me if I must.'

And Firenze whisked around; with Harry clutching on as best he could, they plunged off into the trees, leaving Ronan and Bane behind them.

Harry didn't have a clue what was going on.

'Why's Bane so angry?' he asked. 'What was that thing you saved me from, anyway?'

Firenze slowed to a walk, warned Harry to keep his head bowed in case of low-hanging branches but did not answer Harry's question. They made their way through the trees in silence for so long that Harry thought Firenze didn't want to talk to him any more. They were passing through a particularly dense patch of trees, however, when Firenze suddenly stopped.

'Harry Potter, do you know what unicorn blood is used for?'

'No,' said Harry, startled by the odd question. 'We've only used the horn

第15章 禁 林

冲了出来，腹胁处剧烈地起伏着，汗水淋漓。

"费伦泽！"贝恩怒吼道，"你在做什么？你让一个人骑在你背上！你不觉得丢脸吗？难道你是一头普通的骡子？"

"你们有没有看清这是谁？"费伦泽说，"这是波特家的那个男孩。得让他赶紧离开这片森林，越快越好。"

"你都跟他说了些什么？"贝恩气冲冲地说，"记住，费伦泽，我们发过誓的，绝不能违抗天意。难道我们没看出行星运行显示的预兆吗？"

罗南不安地用蹄子刨着地上的土。

"我相信费伦泽认为他这么做完全是出于好意。"罗南用他那忧伤的声音说道。

贝恩生气地踢着后腿。

"出于好意！那件事和我们有什么关系？马人关心的是星象的预兆！我们没必要像驴子一样，追着在我们森林里迷路的人类乱跑！"

费伦泽气得突然用后腿直立起来，哈利只好紧紧抓住他的肩膀，才没有被摔下来。

"你们没有看见那只独角兽吗？"费伦泽咆哮着对贝恩说，"你们不明白它为什么被杀死了吗？还是行星没有向你们透露这个秘密？我一定要抵抗那个潜伏在我们森林里的家伙，贝恩。是的，如果必要的话，我要和人类站在一边。"

费伦泽说完，轻盈地转过身；哈利紧紧地贴在他身上，他们向树林深处冲去，把罗南和贝恩撇在了后面。

哈利完全不明白是怎么回事。

"贝恩为什么这样生气？"他问，"还有，刚才那是什么东西，你把我从它手里救了出来？"

费伦泽放慢脚步，提醒哈利把头低下，躲开那些低垂的树枝，但他对哈利的问题却避而不答。他们默默地在树林间穿行，许久没有说话，哈利还以为费伦泽不愿意再跟他说话了呢。然而，就在他们穿过一片特别茂密的树丛时，费伦泽突然停下了脚步。

"哈利·波特，你知道独角兽的血可以做什么用吗？"

"不知道，"哈利听到这个古怪的问题，不由得吃了一惊，说道，"我

and tail-hair in Potions.'

'That is because it is a monstrous thing, to slay a unicorn,' said Firenze. 'Only one who has nothing to lose, and everything to gain, would commit such a crime. The blood of a unicorn will keep you alive, even if you are an inch from death, but at a terrible price. You have slain something pure and defenceless to save yourself and you will have but a half life, a cursed life, from the moment the blood touches your lips.'

Harry stared at the back of Firenze's head, which was dappled silver in the moonlight.

'But who'd be that desperate?' he wondered aloud. 'If you're going to be cursed for ever, death's better, isn't it?'

'It is,' Firenze agreed, 'unless all you need is to stay alive long enough to drink something else – something that will bring you back to full strength and power – something that will mean you can never die. Mr Potter, do you know what is hidden in the school at this very moment?'

'The Philosopher's Stone! Of course – the Elixir of Life! But I don't understand who –'

'Can you think of nobody who has waited many years to return to power, who has clung to life, awaiting their chance?'

It was as though an iron fist had clenched suddenly around Harry's heart. Over the rustling of the trees, he seemed to hear once more what Hagrid had told him on the night they had met: 'Some say he died. Codswallop, in my opinion. Dunno if he had enough human left in him to die.'

'Do you mean,' Harry croaked, 'that was *Vol*–'

'Harry! Harry, are you all right?'

Hermione was running towards them down the path, Hagrid puffing along behind her.

'I'm fine,' said Harry, hardly knowing what he was saying. 'The unicorn's dead, Hagrid, it's in that clearing back there.'

'This is where I leave you,' Firenze murmured as Hagrid hurried off to examine the unicorn. 'You are safe now.'

Harry slid off his back.

'Good luck, Harry Potter,' said Firenze. 'The planets have been read wrongly before now, even by centaurs. I hope this is one of those times.'

He turned and cantered back into the depths of the Forest, leaving Harry

第15章 禁 林

们在魔药课上只用了它的角和尾毛。"

"那是因为杀死一只独角兽是一件极其残暴的事。"费伦泽说,"只有自己一无所有,又想得到一切的人,才会犯下这样的滔天大罪。独角兽的血可以延续你的生命,即使你已经奄奄一息,但是你必须为此付出惨重的代价。你为了挽救自己的生命,屠杀了一个纯洁的、柔弱无助的生命,所以从它的血碰到你嘴唇的那一刻起,你拥有的将是一个半死不活的生灵,一条被诅咒的生命。"

哈利望着费伦泽的后脑勺,它在月光下闪着银色的斑点。

"可是,谁会那么不择手段呢?"哈利大声说出了自己的疑问,"如果一辈子都要受到诅咒,那还不如死掉,是吗?"

"不错,"费伦泽表示赞同,"除非你只是用它拖延你的生命,好让你能够喝到另一种东西——能使你完全恢复精力和法力的东西——使你长生不老的东西。波特先生,你知道此刻是什么东西藏在学校里吗?"

"魔法石!当然啦——长生不老药!但我不明白是谁——"

"你难道想不到吗,有谁默默地等了这么多年,渴望卷土重来?有谁紧紧抓住生命不放,在等待时机?"

一时间,就好像一只铁爪突然攫住了哈利的心脏。在风吹树叶的沙沙声中,他仿佛又一次听见海格在他们初次见面的那天晚上所说的话:"有人说他死了。我认为纯粹是胡说八道。他身上恐怕已经没有多少人性,也就谈不上死不死了。"

"难道你是说,"哈利用低沉而沙哑的声音说,"是伏地——"

"哈利!哈利,你没事吧?"

赫敏沿着小路向他们跑来,海格气喘吁吁地跟在后面。

"我很好。"哈利说,他简直不知道自己在说什么,"独角兽死了,海格,就在那边的空地上。"

"我就把你留在这儿吧,"费伦泽在海格赶去查看独角兽尸体时低声说,"你现在没有危险了。"

哈利从他背上滑了下来。

"祝你好运,哈利·波特。"费伦泽说,"以前,命运星辰就曾被人误解过,即使马人也免不了失误,我希望这次也是这样。"

CHAPTER FIFTEEN   The Forbidden Forest

shivering behind him.

Ron had fallen asleep in the dark common room, waiting for them to return. He shouted something about Quidditch fouls when Harry roughly shook him awake. In a matter of seconds, though, he was wide-eyed as Harry began to tell him and Hermione what had happened in the Forest.

Harry couldn't sit down. He paced up and down in front of the fire. He was still shaking.

'Snape wants the stone for Voldemort ... and Voldemort's waiting in the Forest ... and all this time we thought Snape just wanted to get rich ...'

'Stop saying the name!' said Ron in a terrified whisper, as if he thought Voldemort could hear them.

Harry wasn't listening.

'Firenze saved me, but he shouldn't have done ... Bane was furious ... he was talking about interfering with what the planets say is going to happen ... They must show that Voldemort's coming back ... Bane thinks Firenze should have let Voldemort kill me ... I suppose that's written in the stars as well.'

'*Will you stop saying the name!*' Ron hissed.

'So all I've got to wait for now is Snape to steal the Stone,' Harry went on feverishly, 'then Voldemort will be able to come and finish me off ... Well, I suppose Bane'll be happy.'

Hermione looked very frightened, but she had a word of comfort.

'Harry, everyone says Dumbledore's the only one You-Know-Who was ever afraid of. With Dumbledore around, You-Know-Who won't touch you. Anyway, who says the centaurs are right? It sounds like fortune-telling to me, and Professor McGonagall says that's a very imprecise branch of magic.'

The sky had turned light before they stopped talking. They went to bed exhausted, their throats sore. But the night's surprises weren't over.

When Harry pulled back his sheets, he found his Invisibility Cloak folded neatly underneath them. There was a note pinned to it:

Just in case.

第15章 禁 林

他转过身,撇下浑身发抖的哈利,慢慢跑回了森林深处。

罗恩在黑暗的公共休息室里等他们回来,不知不觉睡着了。当哈利粗暴地摇醒他时,他嘴里正嚷嚷着一些魁地奇比赛犯规之类的话。不过,几秒钟后,他就完全清醒过来,睁大了眼睛,专心地听哈利对他和赫敏讲述禁林里发生的事情。

哈利激动得坐不下来。他在炉火前踱来踱去,身上仍然在发抖。

"斯内普要替伏地魔弄到魔法石……伏地魔在禁林里等着……我们还以为斯内普只是想靠魔法石发财……"

"别再说那个名字了!"罗恩惊恐地小声说,仿佛担心伏地魔会听见似的。

哈利不听他的。

"费伦泽救了我,他不应该这样做……贝恩非常恼火……说这样会扰乱命运星辰预示的事情……星象一定显示伏地魔要卷土重来……贝恩认为费伦泽应该让伏地魔杀死我……我猜那也在星象中显示着呢。"

"你能不能别再说那个名字!"罗恩压低了声音说。

"所以我现在只能等着斯内普去偷魔法石,"哈利极度兴奋地往下说,"然后伏地魔就上这儿来,把我干掉……好,我想这下贝恩该高兴了。"

赫敏显得非常害怕,但她仍然想出话来安慰哈利。

"哈利,大家都说,神秘人一直害怕的只有邓布利多。有邓布利多在这里,神秘人不会伤你一根毫毛的。而且,谁说马人的话就一定正确?我觉得那一套听上去像是算命,麦格教授说,那是一类很不精确的魔法。"

天色渐渐发亮了,他们才停止了谈话,嗓子又干又痛,精疲力竭地上床睡觉。然而,这晚上还有一个意外在等着哈利呢。

哈利拉开床单时,发现他的隐形衣叠得整整齐齐,放在床单下面。隐形衣上还别了一张纸条,写着:

以防万一。

CHAPTER SIXTEEN

Through the Trapdoor

In years to come, Harry would never quite remember how he had managed to get through his exams when he half expected Voldemort to come bursting through the door at any moment. Yet the days crept by and there could be no doubt that Fluffy was still alive and well behind the locked door.

It was swelteringly hot, especially in the large classroom where they did their written papers. They had been given special, new quills for the exams, which had been bewitched with an Anti-Cheating spell.

They had practical exams as well. Professor Flitwick called them one by one into his class to see if they could make a pineapple tap-dance across a desk. Professor McGonagall watched them turn a mouse into a snuff-box – points were given for how pretty the snuff-box was, but taken away if it had whiskers. Snape made them all nervous, breathing down their necks while they tried to remember how to make a Forgetfulness Potion.

Harry did the best he could, trying to ignore the stabbing pains in his forehead which had been bothering him ever since his trip into the Forest. Neville thought Harry had a bad case of exam nerves because Harry couldn't sleep, but the truth was that Harry kept being woken by his old nightmare, except that it was now worse than ever because there was a hooded figure dripping blood in it.

Maybe it was because they hadn't seen what Harry had seen in the Forest, or because they didn't have scars burning on their foreheads, but Ron and Hermione didn't seem as worried about the Stone as Harry. The idea of Voldemort certainly scared them, but he didn't keep visiting them in dreams, and they were so busy with their revision they didn't have much time to fret about what Snape or anyone else might be up to.

第 16 章

穿越活板门

哈利恐怕永远也记不清，他是怎样通过那些考试的，因为那些日子他整天提心吊胆，随时提防着伏地魔破门而入。不过随着时间一天天地过去，似乎路威仍然在那扇紧锁的门后面，安然无恙地活着。

天气十分闷热，他们答题的大教室里更是热得难受。老师发给他们专门用于考试的新羽毛笔，都是被念了防作弊咒的。

另外还有实际操作的考试。弗立维教授叫同学们挨个儿走进教室，看他们能不能使一只凤梨跳着踢踏舞走过一张书桌。麦格教授看着他们把一只老鼠变成一个鼻烟盒——盒子越精美，分数越高；如果盒子上还留着老鼠的胡须，就要扣分。考魔药学时，他们拼命回忆遗忘药水的调配程序。斯内普站在背后密切地注视着，同学们的脖子后面都能感觉到他的呼吸，这使他们心里非常紧张。

哈利全心全意地投入考试，尽量忘记前额上剧烈的刺痛。自从他上次从禁林里回来，这种疼痛的感觉就一直纠缠着他。纳威看到哈利整夜睡不好觉，以为他患了严重的考试恐惧症。实际上，哈利是不断被过去的那个噩梦惊醒，而且现在比过去更糟，因为噩梦里又多了一个戴着兜帽、嘴角滴着鲜血的身影。

罗恩和赫敏倒不像哈利这样整日为魔法石担心，这也许是因为他们没有看见哈利在禁林里遭遇的情景，也许是因为他们的前额上没有那道烧灼般疼痛的伤疤。伏地魔确实令他们害怕，但他只是一个抽象的概念，并没有来纠缠他们的梦境，而且他们整天忙着复习功课，也没有时间去操心斯内普或其他什么人可能会采取的行动。

CHAPTER SIXTEEN — Through the Trapdoor

Their very last exam was History of Magic. One hour of answering questions about batty old wizards who'd invented self-stirring cauldrons and they'd be free, free for a whole wonderful week until their exam results came out. When the ghost of Professor Binns told them to put down their quills and roll up their parchment, Harry couldn't help cheering with the rest.

'That was far easier than I thought it would be,' said Hermione, as they joined the crowds flocking out into the sunny grounds. 'I needn't have learnt about the 1637 Werewolf Code of Conduct or the uprising of Elfric the Eager.'

Hermione always liked to go through their exam papers afterwards, but Ron said this made him feel ill, so they wandered down to the lake and flopped under a tree. The Weasley twins and Lee Jordan were tickling the tentacles of a giant squid, which was basking in the warm shallows.

'No more revision,' Ron sighed happily, stretching out on the grass. 'You could look more cheerful, Harry, we've got a week before we find out how badly we've done, there's no need to worry yet.'

Harry was rubbing his forehead.

'I wish I knew what this *means*!' he burst out angrily. 'My scar keeps hurting – it's happened before, but never as often as this.'

'Go to Madam Pomfrey,' Hermione suggested.

'I'm not ill,' said Harry. 'I think it's a warning ... it means danger's coming ...'

Ron couldn't get worked up, it was too hot.

'Harry, relax, Hermione's right, the Stone's safe as long as Dumbledore's around. Anyway, we've never had any proof Snape found out how to get past Fluffy. He nearly had his leg ripped off once, he's not going to try it again in a hurry. And Neville will play Quidditch for England before Hagrid lets Dumbledore down.'

Harry nodded, but he couldn't shake off a lurking feeling that there was something he'd forgotten to do, something important. When he tried to explain this, Hermione said, 'That's just the exams. I woke up last night and was halfway through my Transfiguration notes before I remembered we'd done that one.'

Harry was quite sure the unsettled feeling didn't have anything to do with

第16章 穿越活板门

最后一门考的是魔法史。只要再坚持一个小时，回答出是哪几个古怪的老巫师发明了自动搅拌坩埚，他们就自由了，就可以轻轻松松地玩上整整一个星期，直到考试成绩公布。当宾斯教授的幽灵叫他们放下羽毛笔，把答题的羊皮纸卷起来时，哈利忍不住和其他同学一道欢呼起来。

"比我原先以为的容易多了，"当他们随着人群一起来到外面阳光灿烂的场地上时，赫敏说道，"我其实不需要去记'一六三七年的狼人行为准则'，以及小精灵叛乱的经过。"

赫敏总喜欢在考完之后再重温一遍考试内容，但罗恩说这使他感到恶心。于是他们慢悠悠地顺坡而下，来到湖边，一屁股坐在树下。那边，一只巨乌贼躺在温暖的浅水里晒太阳，韦斯莱孪生兄弟和李·乔丹正在轻轻拨弄它的触须。

"多好啊，再也不用复习了。"罗恩快活地吐了口气，伸展四肢躺在草地上，"哈利，高兴一点嘛，一个星期以后我们才会知道考得多么糟糕，没必要现在就为这个操心。"

哈利揉着他的前额。

"我真想知道这是什么意思！"他突然恼火地说，"我的伤疤一直在疼——以前曾经疼过，但从来不像现在这样频繁发作。"

"去找庞弗雷女士看看吧。"赫敏提议道。

"我没有生病，"哈利说，"我认为这是一个警告……意味着危险即将来临……"

罗恩打不起精神来，天气实在太热了。

"哈利，放松一点儿，赫敏说得对，只要有邓布利多在，魔法石就不会有危险。不管怎么说，我们没有发现任何证据，能够确定斯内普打听到了通过路威的办法。他上次差点被咬断了腿，不会匆匆忙忙再去冒险尝试的。假如连海格都背叛邓布利多，那么纳威就可以入选英格兰魁地奇球队了。"

哈利点了点头，却怎么也摆脱不了一种隐隐约约的感觉，似乎他忘了做一件事，一件非常重要的事。当他想对两个朋友解释这种感觉时，赫敏说："这都是考试在作怪。我昨天夜里醒来，忙着复习变形课的笔记，随后才突然想起那门课已经考过了。"

然而，哈利可以确定，那种不安的感觉与考试没有丝毫关系。他望

CHAPTER SIXTEEN   Through the Trapdoor

work, though. He watched an owl flutter towards the school across the bright blue sky, a note clamped in its mouth. Hagrid was the only one who ever sent him letters. Hagrid would never betray Dumbledore. Hagrid would never tell anyone how to get past Fluffy ... never ... but –

Harry suddenly jumped to his feet.

'Where're you going?' said Ron sleepily.

'I've just thought of something,' said Harry. He had gone white. 'We've got to go and see Hagrid, now.'

'Why?' panted Hermione, hurrying to keep up.

'Don't you think it's a bit odd,' said Harry, scrambling up the grassy slope, 'that what Hagrid wants more than anything else is a dragon, and a stranger turns up who just happens to have an egg in his pocket? How many people wander around with dragon eggs if it's against wizard law? Lucky they found Hagrid, don't you think? Why didn't I see it before?'

'What are you on about?' said Ron, but Harry, sprinting across the grounds towards the Forest, didn't answer.

Hagrid was sitting in an armchair outside his house; his trousers and sleeves were rolled up and he was shelling peas into a large bowl.

'Hullo,' he said, smiling. 'Finished yer exams? Got time fer a drink?'

'Yes, please,' said Ron, but Harry cut across him.

'No, we're in a hurry. Hagrid, I've got to ask you something. You know that night you won Norbert? What did the stranger you were playing cards with look like?'

'Dunno,' said Hagrid casually, 'he wouldn' take his cloak off.'

He saw the three of them look stunned and raised his eyebrows.

'It's not that unusual, yeh get a lot o' funny folk in the Hog's Head – that's one of the pubs down in the village. Mighta bin a dragon dealer, mightn' he? I never saw his face, he kept his hood up.'

Harry sank down next to the bowl of peas.

'What did you talk to him about, Hagrid? Did you mention Hogwarts at all?'

'Mighta come up,' said Hagrid, frowning as he tried to remember. 'Yeah ... he asked what I did, an' I told him I was gamekeeper here ... He asked a bit about the sorta creatures I look after ... so I told him ... an' I said what I'd

第16章 穿越活板门

着一只猫头鹰扑扇着翅膀掠过蔚蓝色的天空，往学校的方向飞去，嘴里叼着一张纸条。只有海格一个人给他写过信。海格是永远不会背叛邓布利多的。海格绝不会告诉任何人通过路威的办法……绝不会的……可是——

哈利突然一跃而起。

"你到哪儿去？"罗恩带着困意问。

"我突然想起一件事。"哈利脸色变得煞白，"我们必须马上去找海格。"

"为什么？"赫敏喘着气问，竭力赶上他。

"你们难道不觉得有些奇怪吗？"哈利一边匆匆跑上草坡，一边说道，"海格最希望得到的是一条火龙，而一个陌生人的口袋里偏巧就装着一只火龙蛋？有多少人整天带着火龙蛋走来走去？要知道那是违反巫师法律的呀！你们难道不觉得，他们能找到海格不是太幸运了吗？我怎么以前就没有想到这一点呢？"

"你到底想做什么？"罗恩问，但是哈利只顾飞跑着穿过场地，往禁林的方向奔去，没有回答他的问题。

海格坐在小屋外面的一把椅子上，裤管和袖子高高地挽起，对着一个大碗，忙着剥豌豆荚。

"你们好，"他笑着说，"考试结束了？有时间喝杯茶吗？"

"好的，谢谢。"罗恩说，可是哈利打断了他。

"不了，我们有急事。海格，我有一件事要问你。你还记得你玩牌赢得诺伯的那天晚上吗？和你一起玩牌的那个陌生人长得什么样儿？"

"不知道，"海格漫不经心地说，"他不肯脱掉他的斗篷。"

他看见三个孩子脸上立刻显出惊愕的神情，不由得扬起了眉毛。

"这有什么好奇怪的，猪头酒吧——就是村里的那个酒吧，总是有一些稀奇古怪的家伙光顾。那家伙兴许是个卖火龙的小贩吧。我一直没有看清他的脸，他戴着兜帽呢。"

哈利扑通跌坐在那一碗豌豆旁边。

"你当时跟他说了什么，海格？你提到霍格沃茨没有？"

"兴许提到了吧。"海格皱着眉头使劲回忆，"对了……他问我是做什么的，我就告诉他我是这里的猎场看守……他又稍微问了问我照看的是哪些动物……我就告诉他了……然后我说我一直特别想要一条

CHAPTER SIXTEEN   Through the Trapdoor

always really wanted was a dragon ... an' then ... I can' remember too well, 'cause he kept buyin' me drinks ... Let's see ... yeah, then he said he had the dragon egg an' we could play cards fer it if I wanted ... but he had ter be sure I could handle it, he didn' want it ter go ter any old home ... So I told him, after Fluffy, a dragon would be easy ...'

'And did he – did he seem interested in Fluffy?' Harry asked, trying to keep his voice calm.

'Well – yeah – how many three-headed dogs d'yeh meet, even around Hogwarts? So I told him, Fluffy's a piece o' cake if yeh know how to calm him down, jus' play him a bit o' music an' he'll go straight off ter sleep –'

Hagrid suddenly looked horrified.

'I shouldn'ta told yeh that!' he blurted out. 'Forget I said it! Hey – where're yeh goin'?'

Harry, Ron and Hermione didn't speak to each other at all until they came to a halt in the Entrance Hall, which seemed very cold and gloomy after the grounds.

'We've got to go to Dumbledore,' said Harry. 'Hagrid told that stranger how to get past Fluffy and it was either Snape or Voldemort under that cloak – it must've been easy, once he'd got Hagrid drunk. I just hope Dumbledore believes us. Firenze might back us up if Bane doesn't stop him. Where's Dumbledore's office?'

They looked around, as if hoping to see a sign pointing them in the right direction. They had never been told where Dumbledore lived, nor did they know anyone who had been sent to see him.

'We'll just have to –' Harry began, but a voice suddenly rang across the hall.

'What are you three doing inside?'

It was Professor McGonagall, carrying a large pile of books.

'We want to see Professor Dumbledore,' said Hermione, rather bravely, Harry and Ron thought.

'See Professor Dumbledore?' Professor McGonagall repeated, as though this was a very fishy thing to want to do. 'Why?'

Harry swallowed – now what?

'It's sort of secret,' he said, but he wished at once he hadn't, because

第16章 穿越活板门

火龙……后来……我记不太清了，他不停地买酒给我喝……让我再想想……对了，后来他说他手里有一个火龙蛋，如果我想要，我们可以玩牌赌一赌……但他必须弄清我有没有能力对付这条火龙，他可不希望火龙到时候跑出去惹是生非……于是我就对他说，我连路威都管得服服帖帖，一条火龙根本不算什么……"

"他是不是显得——显得对路威很感兴趣？"哈利问，竭力使自己的口吻保持平静。

"没错——挺感兴趣的——你能碰到几条三个脑袋的狗呢，即使在霍格沃茨附近？所以我就告诉他，路威其实很容易对付，你只要知道怎样使它安静下来，放点音乐给它听听，它就马上睡着了——"

海格脸上一下子露出惊恐的表情。

"我不应该把这个告诉你们的！"他脱口说道，"把我说的话忘掉吧！喂——你们上哪儿去？"

哈利、罗恩和赫敏一路上没有交换一句话，一直跑进门厅才停住脚步。刚从外面的场地上进来，门厅里显得格外阴冷、黑暗。

"我们必须去找邓布利多，"哈利说，"海格把通过路威的方法告诉了一个陌生人，那个穿斗篷的不是斯内普，就是伏地魔——他只要把海格灌醉，就很容易套出他的话来。我只希望邓布利多能相信我们。只要贝恩不出来阻拦，费伦泽是会为我们作证的。邓布利多的办公室在哪儿？"

他们环顾四周，似乎指望看到一个指示牌为他们指点方向。从来没有人告诉过他们邓布利多住在哪儿，也不知道有谁曾被带去见过校长。

"我们只好——"哈利的话没说完，门厅那头突然响起一个声音。

"你们三个待在屋里做什么？"

是麦格教授，怀里抱着一大摞书。

"我们想见邓布利多教授。"赫敏说。哈利和罗恩认为她表现得非常勇敢。

"想见邓布利多教授？"麦格教授重复了一句，似乎他们有这样的想法是非常可疑的，"为什么？"

哈利咽了一口唾沫——怎么说呢？

"这是一个秘密。"话一出口，他立刻就希望自己没有这么说，因为

CHAPTER SIXTEEN Through the Trapdoor

Professor McGonagall's nostrils flared.

'Professor Dumbledore left ten minutes ago,' she said coldly. 'He received an urgent owl from the Ministry of Magic and flew off for London at once.'

'He's *gone*?' said Harry frantically. '*Now*?'

'Professor Dumbledore is a very great wizard, Potter, he has many demands on his time –'

'But this is important.'

'Something you have to say is more important than the Ministry of Magic, Potter?'

'Look,' said Harry, throwing caution to the winds, 'Professor – it's about the Philosopher's Stone –'

Whatever Professor McGonagall had expected, it wasn't that. The books she was carrying tumbled out of her arms but she didn't pick them up.

'How do you know –?' she spluttered.

'Professor, I think – I *know* – that Sn– that someone's going to try and steal the Stone. I've got to talk to Professor Dumbledore.'

She eyed him with a mixture of shock and suspicion.

'Professor Dumbledore will be back tomorrow,' she said finally. 'I don't know how you found out about the Stone, but rest assured, no one can possibly steal it, it's too well protected.'

'But Professor –'

'Potter, I know what I'm talking about,' she said shortly. She bent down and gathered up the fallen books. 'I suggest you all go back outside and enjoy the sunshine.'

But they didn't.

'It's tonight,' said Harry, once he was sure Professor McGonagall was out of earshot. 'Snape's going through the trapdoor tonight. He's found out everything he needs and now he's got Dumbledore out of the way. He sent that note, I bet the Ministry of Magic will get a real shock when Dumbledore turns up.'

'But what can we –'

Hermione gasped. Harry and Ron wheeled round.

Snape was standing there.

'Good afternoon,' he said smoothly.

第16章 穿越活板门

麦格教授生气了,她的鼻孔翕动着。

"邓布利多教授十分钟前离开了。"她冷冰冰地说,"他收到猫头鹰从魔法部送来的紧急信件,立刻飞往伦敦去了。"

"他走了?"哈利万分焦急地说,"在这个时候?"

"邓布利多教授是一个非常了不起的巫师,日理万机,时间宝贵——"

"可是这件事非常重要。"

"你们要说的事比魔法部还重要吗,哈利?"

"是这样,"哈利说,他把谨慎抛到了九霄云外,"教授——是关于魔法石的——"

麦格教授无论如何也没有想到会是这件事。她怀里的书稀里哗啦地掉到地板上,她没有去捡。

"你们怎么知道——"她结结巴巴地问。

"教授,我认为——我知道——斯内——有人试图去偷魔法石。我必须和邓布利多教授谈谈。"

麦格教授用交织着惊愕和怀疑的目光看着他。

"邓布利多教授明天回来。"她最后说道,"我不知道你是怎么打听到魔法石的,不过请放心,没有人能够把它偷走,它受到严密的保护,万无一失。"

"可是教授——"

"波特,我知道自己在说什么。"她不耐烦地说,然后弯下腰,捡起掉在地上的书,"我建议你们到户外去晒晒太阳。"

但是他们没有这么做。

"就在今晚,"哈利确定麦格教授走远了听不见时,赶紧说道,"斯内普今晚就会穿过活板门了。他所需要的东西都弄到了,现在又把邓布利多骗离了学校。那封信准是他送来的,我敢说魔法部看到邓布利多突然出现,一定会大吃一惊。"

"可是我们能有什么——"

赫敏猛地吸了一口冷气。哈利和罗恩转过身来。

斯内普站在那里。

"下午好。"他用圆滑的口吻说。

CHAPTER SIXTEEN   Through the Trapdoor

They stared at him.

'You shouldn't be inside on a day like this,' he said, with an odd, twisted smile.

'We were –' Harry began, without any idea what he was going to say.

'You want to be more careful,' said Snape. 'Hanging around like this, people will think you're up to something. And Gryffindor really can't afford to lose any more points, can they?'

Harry flushed. They turned to go back outside, but Snape called them back.

'Be warned, Potter – any more night-time wanderings and I will personally make sure you are expelled. Good day to you.'

He strode off in the direction of the staff room.

Out on the stone steps, Harry turned to the others.

'Right, here's what we've got to do,' he whispered urgently. 'One of us has got to keep an eye on Snape – wait outside the staff room and follow him if he leaves it. Hermione, you'd better do that.'

'Why me?'

'It's obvious,' said Ron. 'You can pretend to be waiting for Professor Flitwick, you know.' He put on a high voice, 'Oh Professor Flitwick, I'm so worried, I think I got question fourteen b wrong ...'

'Oh, shut up,' said Hermione, but she agreed to go and watch out for Snape.

'And we'd better stay outside the third-floor corridor,' Harry told Ron. 'Come on.'

But that part of the plan didn't work. No sooner had they reached the door separating Fluffy from the rest of the school than Professor McGonagall turned up again, and this time, she lost her temper.

'I suppose you think you're harder to get past than a pack of enchantments!' she stormed. 'Enough of this nonsense! If I hear you've come anywhere near here again, I'll take another fifty points from Gryffindor! Yes, Weasley, from my own house!'

Harry and Ron went back to the common room. Harry had just said, 'At least Hermione's on Snape's tail,' when the portrait of the Fat Lady swung open and Hermione came in.

'I'm sorry, Harry!' she wailed. 'Snape came out and asked me what I was

第 16 章 穿越活板门

他们呆呆地盯着他。

"在这样的天气,你们不应该待在屋里。"他说,脸上肌肉扭曲,露出一个古怪的笑容。

"我们刚才在——"哈利说,其实他也不知道自己要说什么。

"你们需要小心一些。"斯内普说,"像这样到处乱逛,别人会以为你们想干什么坏事呢。格兰芬多可经不起再丢分了,是吗?"

哈利脸红了。他们转身朝外面走,可是斯内普又把他们叫了回去。

"提醒你一句,波特——如果你再在半夜三更到处乱逛,我要亲自把你开除。祝你愉快。"

他大步朝着教工休息室的方向走去。

三个人一来到外面的石阶上,哈利就转身看着罗恩和赫敏。

"好吧,我们现在必须这么做,"他急切地小声说,"一个人负责监视斯内普——等在教工休息室外面,如果他出来,就跟着他。赫敏,这件事最好由你来办。"

"为什么是我?"

"那还用说,"罗恩说,"你可以假装在等弗立维教授。"他装出一种尖细的女声,"哦,弗立维教授,我太担心了,我觉得我第十四题的第二问答错了……"

"呸,闭嘴。"赫敏说,但她还是同意去盯住斯内普。

"我们俩最好待在四楼的走廊外面。"哈利对罗恩说,"咱们走吧。"

但是这一部分计划没有执行成功。他们刚来到那道把路威与学校其他地方隔开的门口,麦格教授就突然出现了,这次她忍不住开始大发脾气。

"我想,你们大概以为自己比一大堆魔法咒语还厉害吧?"她咆哮着说,"够了,别胡闹了!如果下次我再听说你们又跑到这儿来,就给格兰芬多学院扣掉五十分!是的,韦斯莱,给我自己的学院扣掉五十分!"

哈利和罗恩灰溜溜地返回公共休息室。哈利刚说了一句"至少有赫敏盯着斯内普呢",就看见胖夫人的肖像猛地转开,赫敏钻了进来。

"对不起,哈利!"她呜咽着说,"斯内普出来了,他问我在那里做

CHAPTER SIXTEEN   Through the Trapdoor

doing, so I said I was waiting for Flitwick, and Snape went to get him, and I've only just got away. I don't know where Snape went.'

'Well, that's it then, isn't it?' Harry said.

The other two stared at him. He was pale and his eyes were glittering.

'I'm going out of here tonight and I'm going to try and get to the Stone first.'

'You're mad!' said Ron.

'You can't!' said Hermione. 'After what McGonagall and Snape have said? You'll be expelled!'

'SO WHAT?' Harry shouted. 'Don't you understand? If Snape gets hold of the Stone, Voldemort's coming back! Haven't you heard what it was like when he was trying to take over? There won't be any Hogwarts to get expelled from! He'll flatten it, or turn it into a school for the Dark Arts! Losing points doesn't matter any more, can't you see? D'you think he'll leave you and your families alone if Gryffindor win the House Cup? If I get caught before I can get to the Stone, well, I'll have to go back to the Dursleys and wait for Voldemort to find me there. It's only dying a bit later than I would have done, because I'm never going over to the Dark Side! I'm going through that trapdoor tonight and nothing you two say is going to stop me! Voldemort killed my parents, remember?'

He glared at them.

'You're right, Harry,' said Hermione in a small voice.

'I'll use the Invisibility Cloak,' said Harry. 'It's just lucky I got it back.'

'But will it cover all three of us?' said Ron.

'All – all three of us?'

'Oh, come off it, you don't think we'd let you go alone?'

'Of course not,' said Hermione briskly. 'How do you think you'd get to the Stone without us? I'd better go and look through my books, there might be something useful ...'

'But if we get caught, you two will be expelled, too.'

'Not if I can help it,' said Hermione grimly. 'Flitwick told me in secret that I got a hundred and twelve per cent on his exam. They're not throwing me out after that.'

第 16 章 穿越活板门

什么,我说在等弗立维。斯内普就去找他,我只好赶紧跑开了。我不知道斯内普现在去哪儿了。"

"好吧,看来只能这样了,是吧?"哈利说。

赫敏和罗恩都盯着他,只见他脸色苍白,眼睛炯炯发亮。

"我今晚偷偷从这里溜出去,我要争取先把魔法石弄到手。"

"你疯了!"罗恩说。

"你不能这样做!"赫敏说,"你没听见麦格和斯内普说的话吗?你会被开除的!"

"**那又怎么样**?"哈利大声说,"你们难道不明白吗?如果斯内普弄到了魔法石,伏地魔就会回来!你们难道没有听说,当年他想独霸天下时,这里是个什么情形吗?如果让他得手,霍格沃茨就没了,也就无所谓开除不开除了!他会把学校夷为平地,或者把它变成一所专门传授黑魔法的学校!你们难道看不出来,现在丢不丢分已经无关紧要了?你们难道以为,只要格兰芬多赢得了学院杯,他就会放过你们和你们全家吗?如果我没来得及拿到魔法石就被抓住,那么,我就只好回到德思礼家,等伏地魔到那儿去找我。那也只比现在晚死一点而已,因为我是绝不会去投靠黑魔势力的!我今晚一定要穿过那道活板门,你们俩说什么都拦不住我!伏地魔杀死了我的父母,记得吗?"

他气冲冲地瞪着他们。

"你是对的,哈利。"赫敏细声细气地说。

"我要用上我的隐形衣,"哈利说,"幸亏它失而复得。"

"但是它能把我们三个人都罩住吗?"

"我们——我们三个人?"

"哦,别傻了,你难道以为我们会让你单独行动吗?"

"当然不会。"赫敏泼辣地说,"你怎么会想撇下我们,独自一人去找魔法石呢?我最好去翻翻我的书,也许能找到一些有用的……"

"可是如果我们被抓住了,你们两个也会被开除的。"

"也许不会,"赫敏坚决地说,"弗立维偷偷告诉我说,我在他那门课的考试中得了一百一十二分。这么高的分数,他们是舍不得把我赶走的。"

CHAPTER SIXTEEN   Through the Trapdoor

After dinner the three of them sat nervously apart in the common room. Nobody bothered them; none of the Gryffindors had anything to say to Harry any more, after all. This was the first night he hadn't been upset by it. Hermione was skimming through all her notes, hoping to come across one of the enchantments they were about to try and break. Harry and Ron didn't talk much. Both of them were thinking about what they were about to do.

Slowly, the room emptied as people drifted off to bed.

'Better get the Cloak,' Ron muttered, as Lee Jordan finally left, stretching and yawning. Harry ran upstairs to their dark dormitory. He pulled out the Cloak and then his eyes fell on the flute Hagrid had given him for Christmas. He pocketed it to use on Fluffy – he didn't feel much like singing.

He ran back down to the common room.

'We'd better put the Cloak on here, and make sure it covers all three of us – if Filch spots one of our feet wandering along on its own –'

'What are you doing?' said a voice from the corner of the room. Neville appeared from behind an armchair, clutching Trevor the toad, who looked as though he'd been making another bid for freedom.

'Nothing, Neville, nothing,' said Harry, hurriedly putting the Cloak behind his back.

Neville stared at their guilty faces.

'You're going out again,' he said.

'No, no, no,' said Hermione. 'No, we're not. Why don't you go to bed, Neville?'

Harry looked at the grandfather clock by the door. They couldn't afford to waste any more time, Snape might even now be playing Fluffy to sleep.

'You can't go out,' said Neville, 'you'll be caught again. Gryffindor will be in even more trouble.'

'You don't understand,' said Harry, 'this is important.'

But Neville was clearly steeling himself to do something desperate.

'I won't let you do it,' he said, hurrying to stand in front of the portrait hole. 'I'll – I'll fight you!'

'*Neville*,' Ron exploded, 'get away from that hole and don't be an idiot –'

'Don't you call me an idiot!' said Neville. 'I don't think you should be

第 16 章 穿越活板门

吃过晚饭,他们三个紧张地避开别人,坐在公共休息室里。没有人来理会他们;实际上,格兰芬多的学生们现在都没有话要对哈利说了。很多天来,哈利第一次不为这件事感到难过。赫敏忙着翻阅她所有的笔记,希望能碰巧看到一道他们待会儿要去解除的魔咒。哈利和罗恩很少开口说话,心里都在想着即将要做的事情。

同学们一个个上床睡觉去了,公共休息室里的人渐渐减少。

"可以去拿隐形衣了。"罗恩说。这时,李·乔丹也终于伸着懒腰、打着哈欠离去了。哈利跑到楼上,冲进他们漆黑的宿舍,取出隐形衣。就在这时,他无意间看见了圣诞节时海格送给他的那支笛子。他把笛子装进口袋,准备用它去对付路威——他觉得自己没有心情唱歌给那条大狗听。

他快步跑回公共休息室。

"我们最好在这里就穿上隐形衣,看看它能不能把我们三个都遮住——如果费尔奇看见一双脚自己在地上走——"

"你们在做什么?"房间的角落里响起一个人的声音。纳威从一把扶手椅后面闪了出来,手里抓着他的那只蟾蜍莱福。看样子,刚才莱福又为获得自由而抗争了一番。

"没什么,纳威,没什么。"哈利说着,赶紧把隐形衣藏在背后。

纳威盯着他们做贼心虚的脸。

"你们又打算出去。"他说。

"没有,没有,"赫敏说,"我们不想出去。纳威,你为什么不去睡觉?"

哈利看了看门边的那台老爷钟。他们不能再耽搁时间了,斯内普大概已经在奏音乐,哄路威入睡了。

"你们不能出去,"纳威说,"还会被抓住的。那样的话,格兰芬多可就变得更倒霉了。"

"你不明白,"哈利说,"这件事非常重要。"

可是纳威这次像是铁了心,不顾一切地要阻拦他们。

"我不让你们这样做。"他说着,赶过去挡在肖像洞口前面,"我要——我要跟你们较量一下!"

"纳威,"罗恩勃然大怒,"快从那洞口闪开,别做一个白痴——"

"不许你叫我白痴!"纳威说,"我认为你们不应该再违反校规了!

CHAPTER SIXTEEN — Through the Trapdoor

breaking any more rules! And you were the one who told me to stand up to people!'

'Yes, but not to *us*,' said Ron in exasperation. 'Neville, you don't know what you're doing.'

He took a step forward and Neville dropped Trevor the toad, who leapt out of sight.

'Go on then, try and hit me!' said Neville, raising his fists. 'I'm ready!'

Harry turned to Hermione.

'*Do something*,' he said desperately.

Hermione stepped forward.

'Neville,' she said, 'I'm really, really sorry about this.'

She raised her wand.

'*Petrificus Totalus*!' she cried, pointing it at Neville.

Neville's arms snapped to his sides. His legs sprang together. His whole body rigid, he swayed where he stood and then fell flat on his face, stiff as a board.

Hermione ran to turn him over. Neville's jaws were jammed together so he couldn't speak. Only his eyes were moving, looking at them in horror.

'What've you done to him?' Harry whispered.

'It's the full Body-Bind,' said Hermione miserably. 'Oh, Neville, I'm so sorry.'

'We had to, Neville, no time to explain,' said Harry.

'You'll understand later, Neville,' said Ron, as they stepped over him and pulled on the Invisibility Cloak.

But leaving Neville lying motionless on the floor didn't feel like a very good omen. In their nervous state, every statue's shadow looked like Filch, every distant breath of wind sounded like Peeves swooping down on them.

At the foot of the first set of stairs, they spotted Mrs Norris skulking near the top.

'Oh, let's kick her, just this once,' Ron whispered in Harry's ear, but Harry shook his head. As they climbed carefully around her, Mrs Norris turned her lamp-like eyes on them, but didn't do anything.

They didn't meet anyone else until they reached the staircase up to the third floor. Peeves was bobbing halfway up, loosening the carpet so that

第16章 穿越活板门

而且当初是你们鼓励我勇敢地反抗别人的！"

"没错，但不是反抗我们呀。"罗恩气急败坏地说，"纳威，你根本不知道你在做什么。"

他向前跨了一步，纳威扔掉蟾蜍莱福，那小东西三跳两跳就不见了。

"来吧，过来打我呀！"纳威举起两只拳头，说道，"我准备好了！"

哈利转向赫敏。

"想想办法吧。"他焦急地说。

赫敏走上前去。

"纳威，"她说，"这么做我真是非常非常抱歉。"

她举起魔杖。

"统统石化！"她把魔杖对准纳威，大喊了一声。

纳威的手臂啪地贴在身体两侧，双腿立正，站得笔直。他的整个身体变得僵硬了，原地摇摆了几下，便扑通一声脸冲下倒在地上，看上去像木板一样硬邦邦的。

赫敏跑过去把他翻转过来。纳威的上下牙床锁在一起，说不出话来。只有他的眼珠在转动，惊恐地望着他们。

"你把他怎么了？"哈利小声问道。

"这是全身束缚咒。"赫敏难过地说，"哦，纳威，我真是太抱歉了。"

"我们必须这样，纳威，没时间解释了。"哈利说。

"你以后会明白的，纳威。"罗恩说，然后他们从纳威身上跨过去，穿上了隐形衣。

可是，撇下纳威躺在地板上动弹不得，他们总觉得这不是一个好兆头。在情绪高度紧张的情况下，每一座雕塑的影子都像是费尔奇的身影，而远处传来的每一丝风声，听上去都像是皮皮鬼在朝他们猛扑过来。

就在他们要登上第一道楼梯时，突然看见洛丽丝夫人躲在楼梯顶上。

"哦，我们踢它一脚吧，就踢这一次。"罗恩在哈利耳边悄悄地说，可是哈利摇了摇头。他们小心地绕过洛丽丝夫人，它用两只贼亮亮的眼睛朝他们望来，但是并没有进一步的动作。

他们一路没有碰到一个人，顺利来到通往四楼的楼梯口。只见皮皮鬼正蹦蹦跳跳地往楼上走，一边把楼梯上的地毯扯松，想害别人摔倒。

CHAPTER SIXTEEN   Through the Trapdoor

people would trip.

'Who's there?' he said suddenly as they climbed towards him. He narrowed his wicked black eyes. 'Know you're there, even if I can't see you. Are you ghoulie or ghostie or wee student beastie?'

He rose up in the air and floated there, squinting at them.

'Should call Filch, I should, if something's a-creeping around unseen.'

Harry had a sudden idea.

'Peeves,' he said, in a hoarse whisper, 'the Bloody Baron has his own reasons for being invisible.'

Peeves almost fell out of the air in shock. He caught himself in time and hovered about a foot off the stairs.

'So sorry, your bloodiness, Mr Baron, sir,' he said greasily. 'My mistake, my mistake – I didn't see you – of course I didn't, you're invisible – forgive old Peevsie his little joke, sir.'

'I have business here, Peeves,' croaked Harry. 'Stay away from this place tonight.'

'I will, sir, I most certainly will,' said Peeves, rising up in the air again. 'Hope your business goes well, Baron, I'll not bother you.'

And he scooted off.

'*Brilliant*, Harry!' whispered Ron.

A few seconds later, they were there, outside the third-floor corridor – and the door was already ajar.

'Well, there you are,' Harry said quietly. 'Snape's already got past Fluffy.'

Seeing the open door somehow seemed to impress upon all three of them what was facing them. Underneath the Cloak, Harry turned to the other two.

'If you want to go back, I won't blame you,' he said. 'You can take the Cloak, I won't need it now.'

'Don't be stupid,' said Ron.

'We're coming,' said Hermione.

Harry pushed the door open.

As the door creaked, low, rumbling growls met their ears. All three of the dog's noses sniffed madly in their direction, even though it couldn't see them.

'What's that at its feet?' Hermione whispered.

第16章 穿越活板门

"那是谁？"他们踏上楼梯，迎面向他走去时，皮皮鬼突然眯起那双总喜欢恶作剧的黑眼睛说道，"我知道你就在那儿，虽然我看不见。你是食尸鬼，还是幽灵，还是学生小鬼头？"

他升到半空中停住，眯起眼朝他们这边望着。

"有个看不见的东西在这里鬼鬼祟祟地乱窜，我应该去向费尔奇汇报。"

哈利灵机一动，有了个主意。

"皮皮鬼，"他用嘶哑的声音轻轻说，"血人巴罗不想被别人看见，自然是有他的道理。"

皮皮鬼大吃一惊，差点从空中摔下来。他及时稳住身子，在楼梯上方一英尺的地方盘旋着。

"对不起，血人大人，巴罗先生，爵爷，"他甜言蜜语地说，"都怪我，都怪我——我没有看见您——我当然看不见，您隐形了嘛——请原谅小皮皮鬼的这个小小玩笑吧，爵爷。"

"我在这里有事要办，皮皮鬼，"哈利低声吼道，"今晚不许再来。"

"遵命，爵爷，我一定遵命。"皮皮鬼说着，又重新升到空中，"希望您事情办得顺利，巴罗大人，我就不打扰您了。"

他说完便飞快地逃走了。

"真精彩，哈利！"罗恩小声说。

几秒钟后，他们就来到了四楼的走廊外面——那扇门已经开了一道缝。

"怎么样，看到了吧，"哈利悄声说道，"斯内普已经顺利通过了路威。"

看到那扇半开的门，他们似乎更明确地意识到了即将面临的一切。哈利在隐形衣下扭头看着罗恩和赫敏。

"如果你们现在想打退堂鼓，我不会怪你们。"他说，"你们可以把隐形衣带走，我已经不需要它了。"

"别说傻话。"罗恩说。

"我们一起去吧。"赫敏说。

哈利把门推开了。

随着吱吱嘎嘎的开门声，他们耳边立刻响起了低沉的狂吠。大狗虽然看不见他们，但它那三个鼻子全朝着他们这边疯狂地抽动、嗅吸着。

"它脚边是什么东西？"赫敏小声问道。

CHAPTER SIXTEEN   Through the Trapdoor

'Looks like a harp,' said Ron. 'Snape must have left it there.'

'It must wake up the moment you stop playing,' said Harry. 'Well, here goes ...'

He put Hagrid's flute to his lips and blew. It wasn't really a tune, but from the first note the beast's eyes began to droop. Harry hardly drew breath. Slowly, the dog's growls ceased – it tottered on its paws and fell to its knees, then it slumped to the ground, fast asleep.

'Keep playing,' Ron warned Harry as they slipped out of the Cloak and crept towards the trapdoor. They could feel the dog's hot, smelly breath as they approached the giant heads.

'I think we'll be able to pull the door open,' said Ron, peering over the dog's back. 'Want to go first, Hermione?'

'No, I don't!'

'All right.' Ron gritted his teeth and stepped carefully over the dog's legs. He bent and pulled the ring of the trapdoor, which swung up and open.

'What can you see?' Hermione said anxiously.

'Nothing – just black – there's no way of climbing down, we'll just have to drop.'

Harry, who was still playing the flute, waved at Ron to get his attention and pointed at himself.

'You want to go first? Are you sure?' said Ron. 'I don't know how deep this thing goes. Give the flute to Hermione so she can keep him asleep.'

Harry handed the flute over. In the few seconds' silence, the dog growled and twitched, but the moment Hermione began to play, it fell back into its deep sleep.

Harry climbed over it and looked down through the trapdoor. There was no sign of the bottom.

He lowered himself through the hole until he was hanging on by his fingertips. Then he looked up at Ron and said, 'If anything happens to me, don't follow. Go straight to the owlery and send Hedwig to Dumbledore, right?'

'Right,' said Ron.

'See you in a minute, I hope ...'

And Harry let go. Cold, damp air rushed past him as he fell down, down, down and –

第 16 章　穿越活板门

"看样子像一把竖琴，"罗恩说，"肯定是斯内普留下来的。"

"显然只要音乐一停，它就会醒来。"哈利说，"好吧，你听着……"

他把海格的笛子放到嘴边，吹了起来。他吹得不成调子，但刚吹出第一个音符，大狗的眼皮就开始往下耷拉。哈利几乎是不歇气地吹着。慢慢地，大狗的狂吠声停止了——它摇摇摆摆地晃了几晃，膝盖一软跪下，然后就扑通倒在地板上，沉沉睡去。

"接着吹，别停下。"罗恩提醒哈利，与此同时，他们脱去隐形衣，蹑手蹑脚地朝活板门走去。靠近那三颗巨大的脑袋时，可以感觉到大狗那热乎乎、臭烘烘的气息。

"我想我们可以把活板门拉开了。"罗恩一边说，一边望着大狗的身后，"赫敏，你愿意第一个下去吗？"

"不，我可不愿意！"

"好吧。"罗恩咬了咬牙，小心地从大狗的腿上跨了过去。他弯下腰，拉动活板门上的拉环，门一下子敞开了。

"你能看见什么？"赫敏着急地问道。

"什么也看不见——一片漆黑——也没有梯子，我们只好跳了。"

哈利一边仍在吹着笛子，一边朝罗恩挥了挥手，引起他的注意，又用手指了指自己。

"你想第一个下去？真的吗？"罗恩说，"我不知道这个洞有多深。把笛子给赫敏，让她继续哄大狗睡觉。"

哈利把笛子递了过去。在音乐停顿的这几秒钟里，大狗又咆哮起来，并开始扭动身子，可是赫敏刚把笛子吹响，它就又沉沉地睡去了。

哈利从大狗身上爬了过去，从那个洞口往下看。下面深不见底。

他慢慢顺着洞口滑下去，最后只靠十个手指攀住洞口边缘。他抬头看着罗恩说："如果我出了什么意外，你们别跟着下来。直接到猫头鹰棚屋，派海德薇给邓布利多送信，行吗？"

"好吧。"罗恩说。

"过会儿见，我希望……"

哈利松开了手，寒冷、潮湿的空气在他耳边呼呼掠过。他向下坠落，坠落，坠落，然后——

CHAPTER SIXTEEN   Through the Trapdoor

FLUMP. With a funny, muffled sort of thump he landed on something soft. He sat up and felt around, his eyes not used to the gloom. It felt as though he was sitting on some sort of plant.

'It's OK!' he called up to the light the size of a postage stamp which was the open trapdoor. 'It's a soft landing, you can jump!'

Ron followed straight away. He landed sprawled next to Harry.

'What's this stuff?' were his first words.

'Dunno, sort of plant thing. I suppose it's here to break the fall. Come on, Hermione!'

The distant music stopped. There was a loud bark from the dog, but Hermione had already jumped. She landed on Harry's other side.

'We must be miles under the school,' she said.

'Lucky this plant thing's here, really,' said Ron.

'*Lucky*!' shrieked Hermione. 'Look at you both!'

She leapt up and struggled towards a damp wall. She had to struggle because the moment she had landed, the plant had started to twist snake-like tendrils around her ankles. As for Harry and Ron, their legs had already been bound tightly in long creepers without their noticing.

Hermione had managed to free herself before the plant got a firm grip on her. Now she watched in horror as the two boys fought to pull the plant off them, but the more they strained against it, the tighter and faster the plant wound around them.

'Stop moving!' Hermione ordered them. 'I know what this is – it's Devil's Snare!'

'Oh, I'm so glad we know what it's called, that's a great help,' snarled Ron, leaning back, trying to stop the plant curling around his neck.

'Shut up, I'm trying to remember how to kill it!' said Hermione.

'Well, hurry up, I can't breathe!' Harry gasped, wrestling with it as it curled around his chest.

'Devil's Snare, Devil's Snare … What did Professor Sprout say? It likes the dark and the damp –'

'So light a fire!' Harry choked.

'Yes – of course – but there's no wood!' Hermione cried, wringing her hands.

第16章 穿越活板门

扑通。随着一声奇怪而沉闷的撞击声，哈利落到了一个柔软的东西上。他坐起来，朝四下里摸索着。他的眼睛还没有适应这里昏暗的光线。他觉得自己仿佛是坐在某种植物上面。

"没问题！"他冲着洞口喊道，现在洞口看上去只是邮票大小的一块光斑，"是软着陆，你们可以跳了！"

罗恩紧接着就跳了下来。他四肢着地，落在哈利身边。

"这是什么玩意儿？"他一开口就问。

"不知道，好像是一种植物。大概是铺在这里缓冲坠落的。来吧，赫敏！"

远处的笛声停止了。大狗又发出了响亮的狂吠，但是赫敏已经跳了下来。她落在哈利的另一边。

"我们一定离学校很远很远了。"她说。

"说实在的，幸好有这堆植物铺在这里。"罗恩说。

"幸好什么！"赫敏尖叫起来，"看看你们两个！"

她猛地跳起来，挣扎着朝一面潮湿的墙壁移动。她之所以这样挣扎，是因为她刚一落下，那植物就伸出蛇一般的卷须，缠住了她的脚脖子。而哈利和罗恩呢，他们在不知不觉中已经被长长的藤蔓缠住了双腿。

赫敏在藤蔓还没来得及把她牢牢抓住之前，总算挣脱出来。此刻她惊恐地看着两个男孩拼命撕扯那些藤蔓，但是他们越是挣扎，藤蔓就缠得越快、越紧。

"别动了！"赫敏对他们喝道，"我知道这是什么了——这是魔鬼网！"

"哦，我真高兴，总算知道它叫什么名字了，这对我们大有帮助。"罗恩气呼呼地说，向后躲闪着，不让藤蔓缠住他的脖子。

"你闭嘴，我正在想怎么把它杀死！"赫敏说。

"拜托你快点想，我透不过气来了！"哈利大喘着气说，拼命扯住一根要缠住他胸脯的藤蔓。

"魔鬼网，魔鬼网……斯普劳特教授是怎么说的？说它喜欢阴暗和潮湿——"

"那么就点火烧它！"哈利几乎要窒息了。

"是啊——当然可以——可是这里没有木柴啊！"赫敏大声说道，焦急地拧着双手。

CHAPTER SIXTEEN   Through the Trapdoor

'HAVE YOU GONE MAD?' Ron bellowed. 'ARE YOU A WITCH OR NOT?'

'Oh, right!' said Hermione, and she whipped out her wand, waved it, muttered something and sent a jet of the same bluebell flames she had used on Snape at the plant. In a matter of seconds, the two boys felt it loosening its grip as it cringed away from the light and warmth. Wriggling and flailing, it unravelled itself from their bodies and they were able to pull free.

'Lucky you pay attention in Herbology, Hermione,' said Harry as he joined her by the wall, wiping sweat off his face.

'Yeah,' said Ron, 'and lucky Harry doesn't lose his head in a crisis – "there's no wood", *honestly*.'

'This way,' said Harry, pointing down a stone passageway which was the only way on.

All they could hear apart from their footsteps was the gentle drip of water trickling down the walls. The passageway sloped downwards and Harry was reminded of Gringotts. With an unpleasant jolt of the heart, he remembered the dragons said to be guarding vaults in the wizards' bank. If they met a dragon, a fully grown dragon – Norbert had been bad enough ...

'Can you hear something?' Ron whispered.

Harry listened. A soft rustling and clinking seemed to be coming from up ahead.

'Do you think it's a ghost?'

'I don't know ... sounds like wings to me.'

'There's light ahead – I can see something moving.'

They reached the end of the passageway and saw before them a brilliantly lit chamber, its ceiling arching high above them. It was full of small, jewel-bright birds, fluttering and tumbling all around the room. On the opposite side of the chamber was a heavy, wooden door.

'Do you think they'll attack us if we cross the room?' said Ron.

'Probably,' said Harry. 'They don't look very vicious, but I suppose if they all swooped down at once ... Well, there's nothing for it ... I'll run.'

He took a deep breath, covered his face with his arms and sprinted across the room. He expected to feel sharp beaks and claws tearing at him any second, but nothing happened. He reached the door untouched. He pulled the handle, but it was locked.

The other two followed him. They tugged and heaved at the door, but it

第16章 穿越活板门

"你疯了吗？"罗恩吼道，"你到底是不是巫师？"

"哦，对了！"赫敏说着，一把抽出魔杖，挥动着，嘴里念念有词，然后就像那次对付斯内普一样，让魔杖头上射出一道蓝色风铃草般的火焰。在短短几秒钟内，两个男孩就觉得藤蔓在退缩着躲避光明和温暖，松开了对他们的纠缠。藤蔓扭曲着，抽动着，自动松开了缠绕在他们身上的卷须，哈利和罗恩终于完全挣脱了出来。

"幸亏你在草药课上听得很认真，赫敏。"哈利说道，他和赫敏一样退到墙边，擦着脸上的汗。

"是啊，"罗恩说，"也幸亏哈利在关键时刻没有像你一样慌了手脚——'可是这里没有木柴啊'，真是的！"

"这边走。"哈利指着一道石头走廊说道。这是唯一可走的路。

他们听见，除了他们自己的脚步声外，还有水顺着墙壁缓缓滴落的声音。这道走廊顺坡而下，这使哈利联想到了古灵阁。他的心猛地跳动了一下，想起了传说中看守巫师银行金库的那些火龙。如果他们碰到一条火龙，一条完全成年的大火龙——诺伯就已经够难对付的了……

"你能听见什么动静吗？"罗恩小声问。

哈利侧耳细听。前面似乎传来了轻轻的沙沙声和叮叮当当的声音。

"会不会是一个幽灵？"

"我不知道……好像是翅膀扇动声。"

"前面有亮光——我看见有什么东西在动。"

他们来到走廊尽头，面前是一间灯火通明的房间，上面是高高的拱顶形天花板。无数只像宝石一般光彩夺目的小鸟，扑扇着翅膀在房间里到处飞来飞去。房间对面有一扇厚重的木门。

"你说，如果我们穿过房间，它们会朝我们发动进攻吗？"罗恩问。

"有可能。"哈利说，"它们看样子倒不太凶恶，但如果一下子全部冲过来，恐怕……管它呢，反正也没有别的办法……我跑过去。"

他深深吸了口气，用手臂挡住面孔，飞快地冲到房间的另一头。他以为随时都会有尖利的嘴巴和爪子来撕扯他，结果却平安无事。他毫发无损地来到那扇门边，拉了拉把手，门是锁着的。

罗恩和赫敏也跟了过来。他们一起又拉又推，可是木门纹丝不动，

CHAPTER SIXTEEN   Through the Trapdoor

wouldn't budge, not even when Hermione tried her Alohomora Charm.

'Now what?' said Ron.

'These birds ... they can't be here just for decoration,' said Hermione.

They watched the birds soaring overhead, glittering – *glittering*?

'They're not birds!' Harry said suddenly, 'they're *keys*! Winged keys – look carefully. So that must mean ...' he looked around the chamber while the other two squinted up at the flock of keys. '... Yes – look! Broomsticks! We've got to catch the key to the door!'

'But there are *hundreds* of them!'

Ron examined the lock on the door.

'We're looking for a big, old-fashioned one – probably silver, like the handle.'

They seized a broomstick each and kicked off into the air, soaring into the midst of the cloud of keys. They grabbed and snatched but the bewitched keys darted and dived so quickly it was almost impossible to catch one.

Not for nothing, though, was Harry the youngest Seeker in a century. He had a knack for spotting things other people didn't. After a minute's weaving about through the whirl of rainbow feathers, he noticed a large silver key that had a bent wing, as if it had already been caught and stuffed roughly into the keyhole.

'That one!' he called to the others. 'That big one – there – no, there – with bright blue wings – the feathers are all crumpled on one side.'

Ron went speeding in the direction that Harry was pointing, crashed into the ceiling and nearly fell off his broom.

'We've got to close in on it!' Harry called, not taking his eyes off the key with the damaged wing. 'Ron, you come at it from above – Hermione, stay below and stop it going down – and I'll try and catch it. Right, NOW!'

Ron dived, Hermione rocketed upwards, the key dodged them both and Harry streaked after it; it sped towards the wall, Harry leant forward and with a nasty crunching noise, pinned it against the stone with one hand. Ron and Hermione's cheers echoed around the high chamber.

They landed quickly and Harry ran to the door, the key struggling in his hand. He rammed it into the lock and turned – it worked. The moment the

第16章 穿越活板门

赫敏又试了试她的阿拉霍洞开咒，也无济于事。

"怎么办？"罗恩问。

"这些鸟……它们不可能只是用来做装饰的。"赫敏说。

三个人注视着那些小鸟在头顶上飞来飞去，闪闪发亮——闪闪发亮？

"它们根本不是什么鸟！"哈利突然说道，"它们是钥匙！带翅膀的钥匙——你们仔细看看。显然这意味着……"哈利环顾着房间的每个角落，罗恩和赫敏仰头凝视着那一大群飞舞的钥匙。"……有了，你们瞧！飞天扫帚！我们必须上去逮住那扇门的钥匙！"

"可是上边有好几百把钥匙呢！"

罗恩仔细查看那扇门的锁。

"我们要寻找一把古色古香的大钥匙——可能是银色的，就和那个门把手一样。"

他们每人抓起一把扫帚，双脚一蹬升到半空，冲进了密集的钥匙阵。他们拼命抓捞，可是这些被施了魔法的钥匙躲闪得太快，简直不可能抓得住。

不过，哈利作为一个世纪以来最年轻的魁地奇找球手，并不是徒有虚名的。他在搜寻飞行目标方面有着过人的技巧。他在五彩缤纷的小翅膀的漩涡中穿行了一分钟后，就注意到一把大大的银钥匙的翅膀耷拉着，好像曾经被人抓住、粗暴地塞进了钥匙孔里。

"就是它！"他对罗恩和赫敏喊道，"那把大钥匙——在那儿——不，不是这儿，是那儿——带着天蓝色翅膀的那个——羽毛全都倒向了一边。"

罗恩飞快地朝哈利所指的方向冲去，结果一头撞在天花板上，差点从飞天扫帚上掉下来。

"我们得把它包围起来！"哈利喊道，眼睛一直盯着那把翅膀被折断的钥匙，"罗恩，你从上边堵住它——赫敏，你守在下边，别让它往下飞——我来把它抓住。好了，**现在开始**！"

罗恩向下俯冲，赫敏朝上一蹿，钥匙避开了他们俩，哈利紧紧跟在后面。钥匙迅疾往墙上飞去，哈利向前一扑，随着一阵刺耳的嘎吱声，他用一只手把钥匙按在了石墙上。罗恩和赫敏的欢呼声在高高的房间里回荡。

他们迅速降落，哈利向那扇门跑去，钥匙还在他的手里挣扎。他把它塞进锁眼，用力一拧——没错，就是它。咔嗒一声，门锁刚一弹开，

CHAPTER SIXTEEN   Through the Trapdoor

lock had clicked open, the key took flight again, looking very battered now that it had been caught twice.

'Ready?' Harry asked the other two, his hand on the door handle. They nodded. He pulled the door open.

The next chamber was so dark they couldn't see anything at all. But as they stepped into it, light suddenly flooded the room to reveal an astonishing sight.

They were standing on the edge of a huge chessboard, behind the black chessmen, which were all taller than they were and carved from what looked like black stone. Facing them, way across the chamber, were the white pieces. Harry, Ron and Hermione shivered slightly – the towering white chessmen had no faces.

'Now what do we do?' Harry whispered.

'It's obvious, isn't it?' said Ron. 'We've got to play our way across the room.'

Behind the white pieces they could see another door.

'How?' said Hermione nervously.

'I think,' said Ron, 'we're going to have to be chessmen.'

He walked up to a black knight and put his hand out to touch the knight's horse. At once, the stone sprang to life. The horse pawed the ground and the knight turned his helmeted head to look down at Ron.

'Do we – er – have to join you to get across?'

The black knight nodded. Ron turned to the other two.

'This wants thinking about ...' he said. 'I suppose we've got to take the place of three of the black pieces ...'

Harry and Hermione stayed quiet, watching Ron think. Finally he said, 'Now, don't be offended or anything, but neither of you are that good at chess –'

'We're not offended,' said Harry quickly. 'Just tell us what to do.'

'Well, Harry, you take the place of that bishop, and Hermione, you go there instead of that castle.'

'What about you?'

'I'm going to be a knight,' said Ron.

The chessmen seemed to have been listening, because at these words a knight, a bishop and a castle turned their backs on the white pieces and walked off the board leaving three empty squares which Harry, Ron and Hermione took.

'White always plays first in chess,' said Ron, peering across the board.

第16章 穿越活板门

钥匙就又飞走了。它一连被抓住了两次,样子显得疲惫不堪。

"准备好了吗?"哈利用手握住门把手,问罗恩和赫敏。他们俩点了点头。于是,他把门拉开了。

第二个房间里一片漆黑,什么也看不见。可是他们刚跨进去,房间里突然灯火通明,照亮了一幕令人震惊的景象。

他们站在一副巨大的棋盘边上,前面是黑色的棋子,那些棋子都比他们还要高,似乎是用黑石头之类的东西刻成的。在房间的那一头,与他们面对面的,是一些白色的棋子。哈利、罗恩和赫敏吓得浑身发抖——那些高耸的白棋子的脸上都没有五官。

"现在怎么办呢?"哈利小声问。

"这还不明显?"罗恩说,"我们必须下棋才能走到房间那头。"

他们看见白棋子后面有一扇门。

"怎么下法?"赫敏紧张地问。

"依我看,"罗恩说,"我们必须充当棋子。"

他走到一个黑骑士身旁,伸手摸了摸骑士的马。立刻,石头就活了过来,马用蹄子刨着地上的土,骑士转过戴着头盔的脑袋,望着罗恩。

"我们是不是——嗯——必须跟你们一起才能过去?"

黑骑士点了点头。罗恩转身望着哈利和赫敏。

"需要考虑一下……"他说,"恐怕我们必须取代三个黑棋子……"

哈利和赫敏没有说话,看着罗恩在那里思索。最后罗恩说:"是这样,你们可别怪我说话不客气,不过说实话,你们两个下棋都不怎么样——"

"我们没有生气,"哈利赶紧说道,"快告诉我们怎么做。"

"好吧,哈利,你代替那个主教;赫敏,你去那儿,代替那个城堡。"

"那么你呢?"

"我来做一个骑士。"罗恩说。

那些棋子似乎都在听他们说话,他话音刚落,一个骑士、一个主教和一个城堡就转了个身,背对着白棋子,走出了棋盘,留出三个空位子,让给了哈利、罗恩和赫敏。

"规矩是白棋先走。"罗恩说,朝对面望过去,"对了……你们看……"

一个白色的卒子向前移动了两格。

CHAPTER SIXTEEN   Through the Trapdoor

'Yes ... look ...'

A white pawn had moved forward two squares.

Ron started to direct the black pieces. They moved silently wherever he sent them. Harry's knees were trembling. What if they lost?

'Harry – move diagonally four squares to the right.'

Their first real shock came when their other knight was taken. The white queen smashed him to the floor and dragged him off the board, where he lay quite still, face down.

'Had to let that happen,' said Ron, looking shaken. 'Leaves you free to take that bishop, Hermione, go on.'

Every time one of their men was lost, the white pieces showed no mercy. Soon there was a huddle of limp black players slumped along the wall. Twice, Ron only just noticed in time that Harry and Hermione were in danger. He himself darted around the board taking almost as many white pieces as they had lost black ones.

'We're nearly there,' he muttered suddenly. 'Let me think – let me think ...'

The white queen turned her blank face towards him.

'Yes ...' said Ron softly, 'it's the only way ... I've got to be taken.'

'NO!' Harry and Hermione shouted.

'That's chess!' snapped Ron. 'You've got to make some sacrifices! I'll make my move and she'll take me – that leaves you free to checkmate the king, Harry!'

'But –'

'Do you want to stop Snape or not?'

'Ron –'

'Look, if you don't hurry up, he'll already have the Stone!'

There was nothing else for it.

'Ready?' Ron called, his face pale but determined. 'Here I go – now, don't hang around once you've won.'

He stepped forward and the white queen pounced. She struck Ron hard around the head with her stone arm and he crashed to the floor – Hermione screamed but stayed on her square – the white queen dragged Ron to one side. He looked as if he'd been knocked out.

Shaking, Harry moved three spaces to the left.

The white king took off his crown and threw it at Harry's feet. They had

第 16 章 穿越活板门

罗恩开始指挥黑棋作战。棋子们默默地听从他的调遣。哈利的膝盖在发抖。万一他们输了呢？

"哈利——往右前方移动四格。"

当他们的另一个骑士被吃掉时，他们才开始真正感到了恐惧。白王后凶狠地把那个骑士打翻在地板上，把他拖出了棋盘。骑士面朝下躺在那里，一动也不动。

"没办法，只好这样了，"罗恩说，他看上去很震惊，"这样你才能去吃掉那个主教。赫敏，去吧。"

每次他们的棋子被吃掉时，白棋子都表现得心狠手辣，毫不留情。很快，墙边就横七竖八地倒了一大堆毫无生气的黑棋子。有两次，多亏罗恩及时发现哈利和赫敏处境危险，想办法替他们解了围。罗恩自己在棋盘上冲锋陷阵，吃掉的白棋子差不多和他们失去的黑棋子一样多。

"快到了，"他突然低声说道，"让我想想——让我想想……"

白王后把她没有五官的脸转向了罗恩。

"是的……"罗恩低声说，"只有这个办法了……我必须被吃掉。"

"不行！"哈利和赫敏同时喊道。

"这是下棋！"罗恩厉声说，"总是需要做出一些牺牲的！我走一步，她就会把我吃掉——你就可以把国王将死了，哈利！"

"可是——"

"你到底想不想去阻止斯内普？"

"罗恩——"

"快点，如果再不抓紧时间，他就已经把魔法石拿到手了！"

没有别的办法了。

"准备好了吗？"罗恩喊道，脸色苍白，但神情十分坚决，"我去了——注意，赢了以后立即行动，别在这里耽搁。"

他向前跨了一步，白王后立刻扑了过来。她举起石头手臂，朝罗恩的脑袋上重重砸了下去，罗恩一下摔倒在地板上——赫敏失声尖叫，但没有离开她的格子——白王后把罗恩拖到一边。看样子罗恩好像被打昏了。

浑身颤抖的哈利向左边移动了三步。

白国王摘掉头上的王冠，扔在哈利脚下。他们赢了。白棋子纷纷鞠

CHAPTER SIXTEEN   Through the Trapdoor

won. The chessmen parted and bowed, leaving the door ahead clear. With one last desperate look back at Ron, Harry and Hermione charged through the door and up the next passageway.

'What if he's –?'

'He'll be all right,' said Harry, trying to convince himself. 'What do you reckon's next?'

'We've had Sprout's, that was the Devil's Snare – Flitwick must've put charms on the keys – McGonagall transfigured the chessmen to make them alive – that leaves Quirrell's spell, and Snape's ...'

They had reached another door.

'All right?' Harry whispered.

'Go on.'

Harry pushed it open.

A disgusting smell filled their nostrils, making both of them pull their robes up over their noses. Eyes watering, they saw, flat on the floor in front of them, a troll even larger than the one they had tackled, out cold with a bloody lump on its head.

'I'm glad we didn't have to fight that one,' Harry whispered, as they stepped carefully over one of its massive legs. 'Come on, I can't breathe.'

He pulled open the next door, both of them hardly daring to look at what came next – but there was nothing very frightening in here, just a table with seven differently shaped bottles standing on it in a line.

'Snape's,' said Harry. 'What do we have to do?'

They stepped over the threshold and immediately a fire sprang up behind them in the doorway. It wasn't ordinary fire either; it was purple. At the same instant, black flames shot up in the doorway leading onwards. They were trapped.

'Look!' Hermione seized a roll of paper lying next to the bottles. Harry looked over her shoulder to read it:

> Danger lies before you, while safety lies behind,
> Two of us will help you, whichever you would find.
> One among us seven will let you move ahead,
> Another will transport the drinker back instead,
> Two among our number

第16章 穿越活板门

躲后退,让出一条路,径直通向那扇门。哈利和赫敏悲哀地回头看了罗恩最后一眼,便冲过门,顺着下一道走廊往前走去。

"他会不会——"

"他不会有事的。"哈利说,同时也在努力使自己相信这一点,"你认为接下来会是什么呢?"

"我们已经通过了斯普劳特的机关,就是那道魔鬼网——给那些钥匙施魔法的肯定是弗立维——麦格教授把棋子变了形,使它们活了起来——下面就剩下奇洛的魔法,还有斯内普的……"

他们又来到一扇门前。

"行吗?"哈利小声问。

"进去吧。"

哈利把门推开了。

一股令人作呕的臭气扑鼻而来,他们只好撩起衣服挡住鼻子。两人的眼睛也被熏出了眼泪,他们透过模糊的泪眼,看见了一个巨怪。这个巨怪比他们上次较量过的那个还要大,一动不动地躺在前面的地板上,失去了知觉,脑袋上有一个血淋淋的大肿块。

"太好了,我们用不着同这个巨怪搏斗了。"哈利低声说。他们小心翼翼地跨过巨怪的一条粗腿。"快走吧,我气都喘不过来了。"

他拉开下一道门,一时间,两人简直不敢看接下来是什么在等待他们——然而这里并没有什么可怕的东西,只有一张桌子,上面排放着七个形状各异的瓶子。

"斯内普的魔法,"哈利说,"我们应该怎么做?"

两人刚跨过门槛,身后就腾起一股火焰,封住了门口。这火焰不同寻常,是紫色的。此时,通往前面的门口也蹿起黑色火苗。他们被困在了中间。

"看!"赫敏抓起放在瓶子旁边的一卷羊皮纸。哈利站在她背后,和她一起读道:

> 危险在眼前,安全在后方,我们中间有两个可以给你帮忙。
> 把它们喝下去,一个领你向前,另一个把你送回原来的地方。
> 两个里面装的是荨麻酒,三个是杀手,正排着队等候。

CHAPTER SIXTEEN   Through the Trapdoor

> hold only nettle wine. Three of us are killers, waiting hidden
> in line. Choose, unless you wish to stay here for evermore.
> To help you in your choice, we give you these clues four:
> First, however slyly the poison tries to hide
> You will always find some on nettle wine's left side;
> Second, different are those who stand at either end, But if
> you would move onwards, neither is your friend;
> Third, as you see clearly, all are different size,
> Neither dwarf nor giant holds death in their insides;
> Fourth, the second left and the second on the right
> Are twins once you taste them, though different at first sight.

Hermione let out a great sigh and Harry, amazed, saw that she was smiling, the very last thing he felt like doing.

'*Brilliant*,' said Hermione. 'This isn't magic – it's logic – a puzzle. A lot of the greatest wizards haven't got an ounce of logic, they'd be stuck in here for ever.'

'But so will we, won't we?'

'Of course not,' said Hermione. 'Everything we need is here on this paper. Seven bottles: three are poison; two are wine; one will get us safely through the black fire and one will get us back through the purple.'

'But how do we know which to drink?'

'Give me a minute.'

Hermione read the paper several times. Then she walked up and down the line of bottles, muttering to herself and pointing at them. At last, she clapped her hands.

'Got it,' she said. 'The smallest bottle will get us through the black fire – towards the Stone.'

Harry looked at the tiny bottle.

'There's only enough there for one of us,' he said. 'That's hardly one swallow.'

They looked at each other.

'Which one will get you back through the purple flames?'

Hermione pointed at a rounded bottle at the right end of the line.

第 16 章　穿越活板门

选择吧，除非你希望永远在此停留。
我们还提供四条线索帮你选择：
第一，不论毒药怎样狡猾躲藏，
其实它们都站在荨麻酒的左方；
第二，左右两端的瓶里内容不同，
如果你想前进，它们都不会对你有用；
第三，你会发现瓶子大小各不相等，
在巨人和侏儒里没有藏着死神；
第四，左边第二和右边第二，
虽然模样不同，味道却是一样。

赫敏长长地嘘了口气，哈利惊讶地看见她居然露出了笑容，他自己是无论如何笑不出来的。

"太妙了，"赫敏说，"这不是魔法——这是逻辑推理——是一个谜语。许多最伟大的巫师都没有丝毫逻辑推理的本领，只好永远被困在这里。"

"我们呢，我们也出不去了，是吗？"

"当然不会，"赫敏说，"我们所要知道的都写在这张纸上呢。七个瓶子：三个是毒药；两个是酒；一个能使我们安全穿过黑色火焰，另一个能送我们通过紫色火焰返回。"

"但我们怎么知道该喝哪一瓶呢？"

"给我一分钟时间。"

赫敏把那张纸又读了几遍。她在那排瓶子前走来走去，嘴里自言自语，一边还指点着这个或那个瓶子。终于，她高兴地拍起手来。

"知道了，"她说，"这个最小的瓶子能帮助我们穿过黑色火焰——拿到魔法石。"

哈利看着那个不起眼的小瓶子。

"里面只够一个人喝的了，"他说，"还不到一口呢。"

他们互相望着。

"哪个瓶子能使你穿过紫色火焰返回？"

赫敏指指最右边的一个圆溜溜的瓶子。

CHAPTER SIXTEEN   Through the Trapdoor

'You drink that,' said Harry. 'No, listen – get back and get Ron – grab brooms from the flying-key room, they'll get you out of the trapdoor and past Fluffy – go straight to the owlery and send Hedwig to Dumbledore, we need him. I might be able to hold Snape off for a while, but I'm no match for him really.'

'But Harry – what if You-Know-Who's with him?'

'Well – I was lucky once, wasn't I?' said Harry, pointing at his scar. 'I might get lucky again.'

Hermione's lip trembled and she suddenly dashed at Harry and threw her arms around him.

'*Hermione!*'

'Harry – you're a great wizard, you know.'

'I'm not as good as you,' said Harry, very embarrassed, as she let go of him.

'Me!' said Hermione. 'Books! And cleverness! There are more important things – friendship and bravery and – oh Harry – be *careful!*'

'You drink first,' said Harry. 'You are sure which is which, aren't you?'

'Positive,' said Hermione. She took a long drink from the round bottle at the end and shuddered.

'It's not poison?' said Harry anxiously.

'No – but it's like ice.'

'Quick, go, before it wears off.'

'Good luck – take care –'

'GO!'

Hermione turned and walked straight through the purple fire.

Harry took a deep breath and picked up the smallest bottle. He turned to face the black flames.

'Here I come,' he said and he drained the little bottle in one gulp.

It was indeed as though ice was flooding his body. He put the bottle down and walked forward; he braced himself, saw the black flames licking his body but couldn't feel them – for a moment he could see nothing but dark fire – then he was on the other side, in the last chamber.

There was already someone there – but it wasn't Snape. It wasn't even Voldemort.

第16章 穿越活板门

"你喝那一瓶。"哈利说,"你先别插嘴,听我说——你回去找到罗恩——从飞钥匙的房间里抓两把扫帚,它们会载着你们穿越活板门,从路威身边通过——直接去猫头鹰棚屋,派海德薇去给邓布利多送信,我们需要他来援救。我也许可以暂时牵制住斯内普,但我绝不是他的对手。"

"可是哈利——如果神秘人和他在一起怎么办?"

"嗯——我以前侥幸逃脱过一次,记得吗?"哈利指着额头上的伤疤说,"说不定还能逢凶化吉的。"

赫敏的嘴唇颤抖着,她突然冲向哈利,伸出双臂搂住了他。

"赫敏!"

"哈利——你知道吗,你是个了不起的巫师。"

"我不如你出色。"哈利非常难为情地说,赫敏松开了他。

"我!"赫敏说,"不过是死读书,再靠一点儿小聪明!除此之外,还有许多更重要的东西呢——友谊和勇气——哦,哈利——可要小心啊!"

"你先喝,"哈利说,"你能肯定是这两个瓶子吗,不会弄错吗?"

"绝对不会。"赫敏说。她从右边那个圆瓶子里喝了一大口,浑身打了个寒战。

"不是毒药吧?"哈利担心地问。

"不是——但是像冰一样,寒冷刺骨。"

"快点儿,走吧,过一会儿它就失效了。"

"祝你好运——千万小心——"

"快走!"

赫敏转过身,径直穿过了紫色火焰。

哈利深深吸了口气,抓起那只最小的瓶子。他转身面对着黑色的火苗。

"我来了。"他说完,一口喝光了小瓶子里的液体。

它确实像冰一样,一下子渗透到他的全身。他放下瓶子,向前走去。他鼓起勇气,看见黑色的火苗舔着他的身体,但是他毫无感觉——刹那间,他什么也看不见了,眼前只有黑色的火焰——接着,他就顺利地来到另一边,进入了最后一个房间。

那里面已经有一个人了——不是斯内普,甚至也不是伏地魔。

CHAPTER SEVENTEEN

The Man with Two Faces

It was Quirrell.

'*You!*' gasped Harry.

Quirrell smiled. His face wasn't twitching at all.

'Me,' he said calmly. 'I wondered whether I'd be meeting you here, Potter.'

'But I thought – Snape –'

'Severus?' Quirrell laughed and it wasn't his usual quivering treble, either, but cold and sharp. 'Yes, Severus does seem the type, doesn't he? So useful to have him swooping around like an overgrown bat. Next to him, who would suspect p-p-poor st-stuttering P-Professor Quirrell?'

Harry couldn't take it in. This couldn't be true, it couldn't.

'But Snape tried to kill me!'

'No, no, no. *I* tried to kill you. Your friend Miss Granger accidentally knocked me over as she rushed to set fire to Snape at that Quidditch match. She broke my eye contact with you. Another few seconds and I'd have got you off that broom. I'd have managed it before then if Snape hadn't been muttering a counter-curse, trying to save you.'

'Snape was trying to *save* me?'

'Of course,' said Quirrell coolly. 'Why do you think he wanted to referee your next match? He was trying to make sure I didn't do it again. Funny, really ... he needn't have bothered. I couldn't do anything with Dumbledore watching. All the other teachers thought Snape was trying to stop Gryffindor winning, he *did* make himself unpopular ... and what a waste of time, when after all that, I'm going to kill you tonight.'

Quirrell snapped his fingers. Ropes sprang out of thin air and wrapped

第17章

双 面 人

是奇洛。

"你！"哈利惊愕得喘不过气来。

奇洛笑了。现在他的脸一点也不抽搐了。

"是我，"他冷静地说，"我刚才还在想会不会在这儿遇见你，波特。"

"可是我以为——斯内普——"

"西弗勒斯？"奇洛大笑起来。这笑不是他平常那种尖厉刺耳的颤音，而是一种令人胆寒的冷笑。"是啊，西弗勒斯看上去确实不像个好人，是吗？他像一只巨型大蝙蝠到处乱飞，这对我们倒是很有帮助。有他在那里，谁会怀疑可—可—可怜的，结—结—结结巴巴的奇洛教—教授呢？"

哈利无法相信这一切。这不可能是真的，不可能。

"可是斯内普曾经想害死我！"

"不，不，不，想害死你的是我。那次魁地奇比赛的时候，你的朋友格兰杰小姐冲过来点火烧斯内普，无意中把我撞倒了。她破坏了我对你的凝视，其实只要再坚持几秒钟，我就把你从扫帚上摔下去了。要不是斯内普一直在旁边念破解咒，想保住你的性命，我早就把你摔死了。"

"斯内普想救我？"

"当然是这样，"奇洛冷冷地说，"你说他为什么要给你们的第二次比赛当裁判？他要确保我不再害你。真是可笑……其实他犯不着费这番心思。有邓布利多在场，我什么也做不成的。其他老师都以为斯内普想阻止格兰芬多队获胜，他确实弄得自己很不受人欢迎……不过，这一切都是浪费时间，不管怎么说，我今晚一定要把你干掉。"

奇洛啪地打了个响指。说时迟那时快，只见凭空蹿过来几条绳索，

CHAPTER SEVENTEEN — The Man with Two Faces

themselves tightly around Harry.

'You're too nosy to live, Potter. Scurrying around the school at Hallowe'en like that, for all I knew you'd seen me coming to look at what was guarding the Stone.'

'*You* let the troll in?'

'Certainly. I have a special gift with trolls – you must have seen what I did to the one in the chamber back there? Unfortunately, while everyone else was running around looking for it, Snape, who already suspected me, went straight to the third floor to head me off – and not only did my troll fail to beat you to death, that three-headed dog didn't even manage to bite Snape's leg off properly.

'Now, wait quietly, Potter. I need to examine this interesting mirror.'

It was only then that Harry realised what was standing behind Quirrell. It was the Mirror of Erised.

'This mirror is the key to finding the Stone,' Quirrell murmured, tapping his way around the frame. 'Trust Dumbledore to come up with something like this ... but he's in London ... I'll be far away by the time he gets back ...'

All Harry could think of doing was to keep Quirrell talking and stop him concentrating on the Mirror.

'I saw you and Snape in the Forest –' he blurted out.

'Yes,' said Quirrell idly, walking around the Mirror to look at the back. 'He was on to me by that time, trying to find out how far I'd got. He suspected me all along. Tried to frighten me – as though he could, when I had Lord Voldemort on my side ...'

Quirrell came back out from behind the Mirror and stared hungrily into it.

'I see the Stone ... I'm presenting it to my master ... but where is it?'

Harry struggled against the ropes binding him, but they didn't give. He *had* to keep Quirrell from giving his whole attention to the Mirror.

'But Snape always seemed to hate me so much.'

'Oh, he does,' said Quirrell casually, 'heavens, yes. He was at Hogwarts with your father, didn't you know? They loathed each other. But he never wanted you *dead*.'

第17章 双面人

把哈利捆了个结结实实。

"你太爱管闲事了,不能让你再活在世上,波特。万圣节前夕,你在学校里到处乱转,我当时就知道,你看见我去查看守护魔法石的机关了。"

"是你放那个巨怪进来的?"

"当然是这样。我对付巨怪有一套特别的办法——你肯定已经看见了我是怎么教训那边房间里的那个家伙的,是吧?倒霉的是,当大家都匆匆忙忙到处寻找巨怪时,早已对我起了疑心的斯内普直接赶到四楼,试图阻拦我——不仅我的巨怪没把你打死,甚至那条三个脑袋的大狗也没有把斯内普的腿咬断。

"好了,静静地等着吧,波特。我需要仔细看看这面有趣的镜子。"

直到这时,哈利才发现奇洛身后立着的东西,正是厄里斯魔镜。

"这面镜子是找到魔法石的钥匙,"奇洛喃喃地说,用手沿着四周的镜框敲了一遍,"只有邓布利多才拿得出这样的东西……不过他此刻在伦敦呢……等他回来的时候,我早就远走高飞了……"

哈利能想到的唯一办法就是让奇洛不停地说话,不让他把注意力集中到魔镜上。

"我看见你和斯内普在禁林里——"他冒冒失失地说。

"没错,"奇洛懒洋洋地说着,一边转到镜子后面去查看,"他那时候已经盯上我了,想知道我究竟进行到了什么地步。他一直在怀疑我。他想吓唬我——其实他哪里吓得住我,有伏地魔做我的靠山呢……"

奇洛从镜子后面转了回来,贪婪地盯着镜子里面。

"我看见魔法石了……我正在把它献给我的主人……可是它藏在哪儿呢?"

哈利拼命想挣脱束缚他的那些绳索,却被越缠越紧。他必须阻止奇洛把全部注意力都集中到魔镜上。

"可是斯内普总是显得那么恨我。"

"哦,他确实恨你,"奇洛漫不经心地说,"天哪,他当然恨你啦。当年他和你父亲一起在霍格沃茨念书,这你不知道吧?他们俩互相仇恨,不共戴天。不过他可从来不希望你死掉。"

CHAPTER SEVENTEEN   The Man with Two Faces

'But I heard you a few days ago, sobbing – I thought Snape was threatening you ...'

For the first time, a spasm of fear flitted across Quirrell's face.

'Sometimes,' he said, 'I find it hard to follow my master's instructions – he is a great wizard and I am weak –'

'You mean he was there in the classroom with you?' Harry gasped.

'He is with me wherever I go,' said Quirrell quietly. 'I met him when I travelled around the world. A foolish young man I was then, full of ridiculous ideas about good and evil. Lord Voldemort showed me how wrong I was. There is no good and evil, there is only power, and those too weak to seek it ... Since then, I have served him faithfully, although I have let him down many times. He has had to be very hard on me.' Quirrell shivered suddenly. 'He does not forgive mistakes easily. When I failed to steal the Stone from Gringotts, he was most displeased. He punished me ... decided he would have to keep a closer watch on me ...'

Quirrell's voice tailed away. Harry was remembering his trip to Diagon Alley – how could he have been so stupid? He'd *seen* Quirrell there that very day, shaken hands with him in the Leaky Cauldron.

Quirrell cursed under his breath.

'I don't understand ... is the Stone *inside* the Mirror? Should I break it?'

Harry's mind was racing.

'What I want more than anything else in the world at the moment,' he thought, 'is to find the Stone before Quirrell does. So if I look in the Mirror, I should see myself finding it – which means I'll see where it's hidden! But how can I look without Quirrell realising what I'm up to?'

He tried to edge to the left, to get in front of the glass without Quirrell noticing, but the ropes around his ankles were too tight: he tripped and fell over. Quirrell ignored him. He was still talking to himself.

'What does this mirror do? How does it work? Help me, Master!'

And to Harry's horror, a voice answered, and the voice seemed to come from Quirrell himself.

'Use the boy ... Use the boy ...'

Quirrell rounded on Harry.

第17章 双面人

"可是几天前我听见你在哭——我以为斯内普在威胁你……"

奇洛的脸上第一次闪过一丝恐惧的震颤。

"有的时候,"他说,"我觉得很难遵从我主人的指令——他是个伟大的巫师,而我的力量这样薄弱——"

"难道你是说,当时和你一起在教室里的是他?"哈利吃惊地问。

"不论我走到哪儿他都跟我在一起,"奇洛平静地说,"我是在环游世界时遇到他的。我当时还是一个傻乎乎的小伙子,对善恶是非有一套荒唐的想法。是伏地魔指出了我的错误。世上没有什么善恶是非,只有权力,还有无法获取权势的无能之辈……从那以后,我就忠心耿耿地为他效劳,不过我也有许多次令他失望。他对我一直非常严厉。"奇洛突然颤抖了一下,"他从不轻易原谅我的错误。我没能把魔法石从古灵阁偷出来,他非常不高兴。他惩罚了我……并决定从此更加密切地监视我……"

奇洛的声音渐渐低得听不见了。哈利想起了那次到对角巷去的情景——当时他怎么就没有想到呢?他那天明明看见了奇洛,还跟他在破釜酒吧里握过手呢。

奇洛压低了声音咒骂着。

"我不明白……难道魔法石藏在镜子里面?我是不是该把镜子打破?"哈利脑子里飞快地转动着。

此时此刻我心里最大的愿望,他想,就是赶在奇洛之前找到魔法石。所以,如果我对着魔镜照一照,就应该看见自己找到了那块石头——这就意味着我能看到石头藏在哪儿!可是,我怎样才能在不被奇洛发现的情况下,过去照一照魔镜呢?

他试着悄悄向左边移动,想趁奇洛不注意时挪到镜子前面。可是,缠住他脚脖子的绳索实在太紧了,他绊了一下,摔倒在地。奇洛没有理睬他,还在那里自言自语。

"这面镜子是怎么回事?它究竟有什么功能?帮帮我吧,主人!"

哈利惊恐地听见一个声音在回答,那声音好像是从奇洛本人身体里发出来的。

"利用那个男孩……利用那个男孩……"

奇洛转向哈利。

CHAPTER SEVENTEEN   The Man with Two Faces

'Yes – Potter – come here.'

He clapped his hands once and the ropes binding Harry fell off. Harry got slowly to his feet.

'Come here,' Quirrell repeated. 'Look in the Mirror and tell me what you see.'

Harry walked towards him.

'I must lie,' he thought desperately. 'I must look and lie about what I see, that's all.'

Quirrell moved close behind him. Harry breathed in the funny smell that seemed to come from Quirrell's turban. He closed his eyes, stepped in front of the Mirror and opened them again.

He saw his reflection, pale and scared-looking at first. But a moment later, the reflection smiled at him. It put its hand into its pocket and pulled out a blood-red stone. It winked and put the Stone back in its pocket – and as it did so, Harry felt something heavy drop into his real pocket. Somehow – incredibly – *he'd got the Stone*.

'Well?' said Quirrell impatiently. 'What do you see?'

Harry screwed up his courage.

'I see myself shaking hands with Dumbledore,' he invented. 'I – I've won the House Cup for Gryffindor.'

Quirrell cursed again.

'Get out of the way,' he said. As Harry moved aside he felt the Philosopher's Stone against his leg. Dare he make a break for it?

But he hadn't walked five paces before a high voice spoke, though Quirrell wasn't moving his lips.

'He lies ... He lies ...'

'Potter, come back here!' Quirrell shouted. 'Tell me the truth! What did you just see?'

The high voice spoke again.

'Let me speak to him ... face to face ...'

'Master, you are not strong enough!'

'I have strength enough ... for this ...'

Harry felt as if Devil's Snare was rooting him to the spot. He couldn't

第17章 双面人

"好吧——波特——上这儿来。"

他双手一拍，捆绑哈利的绳索就自动松开了。哈利慢慢地站起身来。

"过来，"奇洛又说了一遍，"照照镜子，把你看到的告诉我。"

哈利朝他走去。

"我必须对他撒谎，"他不顾一切地想，"我必须先照照镜子，然后编出一套谎话来骗他，就这么做。"

奇洛凑到他的身后。哈利闻到一股奇怪的气味，似乎是从奇洛头上的围巾里发出来的。他闭上眼睛，站到镜子前面，随即把眼睛睁开了。

他看见了镜子里的自己，一开始脸色苍白，神情惶恐，可是片刻之后便露出了笑容。镜子里的哈利把手伸进口袋，掏出一块鲜红的石头，然后眨眨眼睛又把石头放进了口袋——这时，哈利觉得有一件重重的东西真的落进了自己的口袋。真是不可思议——他就这样得到了魔法石。

"怎么样？"奇洛不耐烦地问，"你看到了什么？"

哈利鼓起勇气。

"我看见自己在跟邓布利多握手，"他胡乱编造地说，"我—我为格兰芬多赢得了学院杯冠军。"

奇洛又开始骂骂咧咧。

"你给我走开。"他说。

哈利退到一边时，感觉到魔法石就贴着他的大腿。他敢不敢现在就带着它逃走呢？

但他刚走了不到五步，就听见一个尖厉的声音说话了，而奇洛的嘴唇根本没有动。

"他在说谎……他在说谎……"

"波特，回到这儿来！"奇洛喊道，"把实话告诉我！你刚才看见了什么？"

那个尖厉的声音又说话了。

"让我来跟他谈……面对面地谈……"

"主人，你的体力还没有恢复啊！"

"这点力气……我还是有的……"

哈利觉得自己仿佛被魔鬼网缠住了，浑身上下动弹不得。他呆呆地

CHAPTER SEVENTEEN   The Man with Two Faces

move a muscle. Petrified, he watched as Quirrell reached up and began to unwrap his turban. What was going on? The turban fell away. Quirrell's head looked strangely small without it. Then he turned slowly on the spot.

Harry would have screamed, but he couldn't make a sound. Where there should have been a back to Quirrell's head, there was a face, the most terrible face Harry had ever seen. It was chalk white with glaring red eyes and slits for nostrils, like a snake.

'Harry Potter ...' it whispered.

Harry tried to take a step backwards but his legs wouldn't move.

'See what I have become?' the face said. 'Mere shadow and vapour ... I have form only when I can share another's body ... but there have always been those willing to let me into their hearts and minds ... Unicorn blood has strengthened me, these past weeks ... you saw faithful Quirrell drinking it for me in the Forest ... and once I have the Elixir of Life, I will be able to create a body of my own ... Now ... why don't you give me that Stone in your pocket?'

So he knew. The feeling suddenly surged back into Harry's legs. He stumbled backwards.

'Don't be a fool,' snarled the face. 'Better save your own life and join me ... or you'll meet the same end as your parents ... They died begging me for mercy ...'

'LIAR!' Harry shouted suddenly.

Quirrell was walking backwards at him, so that Voldemort could still see him. The evil face was now smiling.

'How touching ...' it hissed. 'I always value bravery ... Yes, boy, your parents were brave ... I killed your father first and he put up a courageous fight ... but your mother needn't have died ... she was trying to protect you ... Now give me the Stone, unless you want her to have died in vain.'

'NEVER!'

Harry sprang towards the flame door, but Voldemort screamed, 'SEIZE HIM!' and, next second, Harry felt Quirrell's hand close on his wrist. At once, a needle-sharp pain seared across Harry's scar; his head felt as though it was about to split in two; he yelled, struggling with all his might, and to his

第17章 双面人

站在那里，看着奇洛举手解下头上的围巾。这是怎么回事？大围巾落了下来，奇洛裸露的脑袋看上去小得出奇。然后，他慢慢地原地转过身去。

哈利想放声尖叫，但发不出一点儿声音。在原本该是奇洛后脑勺的地方，长着一张脸，哈利从来没有看见过这样狰狞恐怖的脸。那张脸的颜色白如粉笔，红通通的眼睛放出光来，下面是两道细长的鼻孔，看上去像一条蛇。

"哈利·波特……"他耳语般地说。

哈利想往后退，可是双腿不听使唤。

"你看看我变成了什么样子！"那张脸说，"只剩下了影子和蒸气……我只有和别人共用一具躯体时，才能拥有形体……不过总有一些人愿意让我进入他们的心灵和头脑……在过去的几个星期里，独角兽的血使我恢复了一些体力……那天你在禁林里看见奇洛为我饮血……一旦我弄到了长生不老药，我就能够重新创造一个我自己的身体……好了……你为什么不把你口袋里的魔法石交给我呢？"

原来他知道！哈利的腿突然又有了知觉。他踉跄着后退。

"别犯傻了，"那张脸恶狠狠地说，"最好保住你自己的小命，投靠我吧……不然你就会和你父母的下场一样……他们临死前苦苦地哀求我饶命……"

"撒谎！"哈利猛地喊道。

奇洛后退着朝他逼近，使伏地魔仍然能盯着哈利。现在那张邪恶的脸上露出了狞笑。

"多么感人啊……"他用嘶哑的声音说，"我一向都很敬佩勇气……是的，孩子，你父母当年都很勇敢……我先动手杀你的父亲，他倒是宁死不屈，勇敢地跟我搏斗……你母亲其实不用死的……她拼着命要保护你……好了，把魔法石给我吧，别让你母亲白白为你丧命。"

"休想！"

哈利猛地冲向那扇燃着黑色火焰的门，伏地魔尖叫起来："**抓住他！**"紧接着哈利就感到奇洛用手紧紧抓住了他的手腕。顿时，哈利额头上的伤疤钻心地疼痛起来；他觉得自己的脑袋仿佛要裂成两半；他大声喊叫，拼命挣扎；随后，他吃惊地发现奇洛松开了手，他额头的疼痛也减

CHAPTER SEVENTEEN The Man with Two Faces

surprise, Quirrell let go of him. The pain in his head lessened – he looked around wildly to see where Quirrell had gone and saw him hunched in pain, looking at his fingers – they were blistering before his eyes.

'Seize him! SEIZE HIM!' shrieked Voldemort again and Quirrell lunged, knocking Harry clean off his feet, landing on top of him, both hands around Harry's neck – Harry's scar was almost blinding him with pain, yet he could see Quirrell howling in agony.

'Master, I cannot hold him – my hands – my hands!'

And Quirrell, though pinning Harry to the ground with his knees, let go of his neck and stared, bewildered, at his own palms – Harry could see they looked burnt, raw, red and shiny.

'Then kill him, fool, and be done!' screeched Voldemort.

Quirrell raised his hand to perform a deadly curse, but Harry, by instinct, reached up and grabbed Quirrell's face –

'AAAARGH!'

Quirrell rolled off him, his face blistering too, and then Harry knew: Quirrell couldn't touch his bare skin, not without suffering terrible pain – his only chance was to keep hold of Quirrell, keep him in enough pain to stop him doing a curse.

Harry jumped to his feet, caught Quirrell by the arm and hung on as tight as he could. Quirrell screamed and tried to throw Harry off – the pain in Harry's head was building – he couldn't see – he could only hear Quirrell's terrible shrieks and Voldemort's yells of 'KILL HIM! KILL HIM!' and other voices, maybe in Harry's own head, crying, 'Harry! Harry!'

He felt Quirrell's arm wrenched from his grasp, knew all was lost, and fell into blackness, down ... down ... down ...

Something gold was glinting just above him. The Snitch! He tried to catch it, but his arms were too heavy.

He blinked. It wasn't the Snitch at all. It was a pair of glasses. How strange.

He blinked again. The smiling face of Albus Dumbledore swam into view above him.

'Good afternoon, Harry,' said Dumbledore.

第17章 双面人

轻了——哈利茫然四顾,寻找奇洛,只见他痛苦地弓着身子,看着自己的手指——他眼睁睁地看见一个个手指上冒起了水泡。

"抓住他!**抓住他!**"伏地魔又尖叫起来。奇洛向前一扑,把哈利撞翻在地,骑在他身上,用双手掐住哈利的脖子——哈利的伤疤又是一阵剧痛,他眼前发黑,但他还是看见奇洛在痛苦地号叫。

"主人,我抓不住他——我的手——我的手!"

奇洛虽然仍用膝盖把哈利压在地上,但他的手已经松开了哈利的脖子,此刻他正困惑地盯着自己的手掌——哈利可以看见它们像是被火烧伤了似的,红得发亮。

"那就把他干掉,傻瓜,快点行动!"伏地魔用刺耳的声音说。

奇洛举起手,准备念一个致命的咒语,可是哈利出于本能,猛地抬手抓向奇洛的脸——

"啊!啊!啊——!"

奇洛从哈利身上滚了下去,他的脸上也冒起了水泡。哈利突然明白了:只要奇洛一碰到自己裸露在外的皮肤,就会感到剧痛难忍——哈利要逃生,唯一的希望就是死死抓住奇洛,让奇洛痛得无法对自己施咒。

哈利跳了起来,一把抓住奇洛的手臂,死也不肯撒手。奇洛惨叫着,拼命想把哈利甩掉——哈利的头痛也越来越剧烈——他眼前发黑——只能听见奇洛可怖的尖叫和伏地魔恶狠狠的咆哮:"**杀死他!杀死他!**"另外还有一些声音在喊着:"哈利!哈利!"不过,这也许是他脑海里的幻觉。

他感到奇洛的手臂挣脱了他,他知道一切都完了,接着他就沉入了一片黑暗,向下坠落……坠落……坠落……

一个金色的东西在他头顶上闪烁。是飞贼!他想把它抓住,但胳膊沉重得抬不起来。

他眨了眨眼睛,原来那根本不是飞贼,而是一副眼镜。多么奇怪。

他又使劲眨了眨眼睛,面前渐渐浮现出阿不思·邓布利多那张笑眯眯的脸。

"下午好,哈利。"邓布利多说。

CHAPTER SEVENTEEN   The Man with Two Faces

Harry stared at him. Then he remembered. 'Sir! The Stone! It was Quirrell! He's got the Stone! Sir, quick –'

'Calm yourself, dear boy, you are a little behind the times,' said Dumbledore. 'Quirrell does not have the Stone.'

'Then who does? Sir, I –'

'Harry, please relax, or Madam Pomfrey will have me thrown out.'

Harry swallowed and looked around him. He realised he must be in the hospital wing. He was lying in a bed with white linen sheets and next to him was a table piled high with what looked like half the sweet-shop.

'Tokens from your friends and admirers,' said Dumbledore, beaming. 'What happened down in the dungeons between you and Professor Quirrell is a complete secret, so, naturally, the whole school knows. I believe your friends Misters Fred and George Weasley were responsible for trying to send you a lavatory seat. No doubt they thought it would amuse you. Madam Pomfrey, however, felt it might not be very hygienic, and confiscated it.'

'How long have I been in here?'

'Three days. Mr Ronald Weasley and Miss Granger will be most relieved you have come round, they have been extremely worried.'

'But sir, the Stone –'

'I see you are not to be distracted. Very well, the Stone. Professor Quirrell did not manage to take it from you. I arrived in time to prevent that, although you were doing very well on your own, I must say.'

'You got there? You got Hermione's owl?'

'We must have crossed in mid-air. No sooner had I reached London than it became clear to me that the place I should be was the one I had just left. I arrived just in time to pull Quirrell off you –'

'It was *you*.'

'I feared I might be too late.'

'You nearly were, I couldn't have kept him off the Stone much longer –'

'Not the Stone, boy, you – the effort involved nearly killed you. For one terrible moment there, I was afraid it had. As for the Stone, it has been destroyed.'

第17章 双面人

哈利先是呆呆地盯着他，然后突然想起来了："先生！魔法石！是奇洛！他得到了魔法石！先生，快——"

"不要激动，亲爱的孩子，你说的这些话已经有点过时了，"邓布利多说，"奇洛没有拿到魔法石。"

"那么谁拿到了？先生，我——"

"哈利，请你镇静一些，不然庞弗雷女士就要把我赶出去了。"

哈利咽了口唾沫，环顾四周。他意识到自己是在医院里。他躺在一张铺着洁白亚麻被单的病床上，旁边的桌子上堆得像座小山，似乎半个糖果店都被搬到这里来了。

"都是你的朋友和崇拜者送给你的礼物。"邓布利多笑吟吟地说，"你和奇洛教授在地下教室里发生的一切，是一个完完全全的秘密，而秘密总是不胫而走，所以，全校师生自然全都知道了。据我所知，你的朋友弗雷德和乔治·韦斯莱本来还想送给你一只马桶圈。他们无疑是想跟你逗个乐子，可是庞弗雷女士觉得不太卫生，就把它没收了。"

"我在这里住多久了？"

"三天。罗恩·韦斯莱先生和格兰杰小姐若是知道你醒过来了，一定会觉得松了口气。他们一直担心极了。"

"可是先生，魔法石——"

"看来没法子分散你的注意力。好吧，咱们就谈谈魔法石。奇洛教授没有能够把它从你手里夺走，我及时赶到阻止了他。不过我必须说一句，你其实一个人就对付得很好。"

"您赶到那儿了？您收到赫敏派猫头鹰送给您的信了？"

"我和它显然是在空中错过了。我一到伦敦，就发现我应该回到我刚刚离开的地方。我赶来得恰是时候，正好把奇洛从你身上拉开——"

"原来是您。"

"我还担心已经太晚了。"

"差一点儿就来不及了，我已经支撑不了多久，魔法石很快就要被他抢去了——"

"不是魔法石，孩子，我指的是你——你为了保护魔法石差一点儿丢了性命。在那可怕的一瞬间，我吓坏了，以为你真的死了。至于魔法石嘛，它已经被毁掉了。"

CHAPTER SEVENTEEN The Man with Two Faces

'Destroyed?' said Harry blankly. 'But your friend – Nicolas Flamel –'

'Oh, you know about Nicolas?' said Dumbledore, sounding quite delighted. 'You *did* do the thing properly, didn't you? Well, Nicolas and I have had a little chat and agreed it's all for the best.'

'But that means he and his wife will die, won't they?'

'They have enough Elixir stored to set their affairs in order and then, yes, they will die.'

Dumbledore smiled at the look of amazement on Harry's face.

'To one as young as you, I'm sure it seems incredible, but to Nicolas and Perenelle, it really is like going to bed after a very, *very* long day. After all, to the well-organised mind, death is but the next great adventure. You know, the Stone was really not such a wonderful thing. As much money and life as you could want! The two things most human beings would choose above all – the trouble is, humans do have a knack of choosing precisely those things which are worst for them.'

Harry lay there, lost for words. Dumbledore hummed a little and smiled at the ceiling.

'Sir?' said Harry. 'I've been thinking ... Sir – even if the Stone's gone, Vol– ... I mean, You-Know-Who –'

'Call him Voldemort, Harry. Always use the proper name for things. Fear of a name increases fear of the thing itself.'

'Yes, sir. Well, Voldemort's going to try other ways of coming back, isn't he? I mean, he hasn't gone, has he?'

'No, Harry, he has not. He is still out there somewhere, perhaps looking for another body to share ... not being truly alive, he cannot be killed. He left Quirrell to die; he shows just as little mercy to his followers as his enemies. Nevertheless, Harry, while you may only have delayed his return to power, it will merely take someone else who is prepared to fight what seems a losing battle next time – and if he is delayed again, and again, why, he may never return to power.'

Harry nodded, but stopped quickly, because it made his head hurt. Then he said, 'Sir, there are some other things I'd like to know, if you can tell me ...

第17章 双面人

"毁掉了？"哈利不解地问，"可是您的朋友——尼可·勒梅——"

"哦，你居然还知道尼可？"邓布利多问，语气显得很高兴，"你把这件事搞得很清楚，是吗？是这样的，尼可和我谈了谈，我们一致认为这是最好的办法。"

"可是，那样一来，他和他妻子就要死了，是吗？"

"他们存了一些长生不老药，足够让他们把事情料理妥当的。然后，是啊，他们会死的。"

看到哈利脸上惊愕的表情，邓布利多笑了。

"我知道，对你这样年纪轻轻的人来说，这似乎有些不可思议；但是对尼可和佩雷纳尔来说，死亡实际上就像是经过非常、非常漫长的一天之后，终于上床休息了。而且，在头脑清醒的人看来，死亡不过是另一场伟大的冒险。你知道，魔法石其实并不是多么美妙的东西。有了它，不论你想拥有多少财富、获得多长寿命，都可以如愿以偿！这两样东西是人类最想要的——问题是，人类偏偏就喜欢选择对他们最没有好处的东西。"

哈利躺在那里，一时间不知道说什么好。邓布利多愉快地哼着小曲，笑眯眯地看着天花板。

"先生，"哈利说，"我一直在想……先生——尽管魔法石不在了，伏地……我是说，神秘人——"

"就叫他伏地魔吧，哈利。对事物永远使用正确的称呼。对一个名称的恐惧，会强化对这个事物本身的恐惧。"

"是，先生。是这样，伏地魔还会企图用别的办法卷土重来，是吗？我的意思是，他并没有消失，对吗？"

"对，哈利，他没有消失。他仍然躲在什么地方，也许正在物色一个愿意让他分享的躯体……他不算是真正活着，所以也就不可能被杀死。他当时只顾自己溜走，完全不顾奇洛的死活；他对敌人心狠手辣，对自己的追随者也冷酷无情。不过，哈利，你也许只是耽搁了他，使他不能马上恢复力量，将来还需要另外一个人做好充分准备，和他决一死战——但如果他一而再再而三地被耽搁，也许就再也无法恢复力量了。"

哈利点了点头，但很快就停住了，因为这使他感到头痛。然后他说："先生，还有一些事情我不太明白，不知道您能不能告诉我……我想了

CHAPTER SEVENTEEN — The Man with Two Faces

things I want to know the truth about ...'

'The truth.' Dumbledore sighed. 'It is a beautiful and terrible thing, and should therefore be treated with great caution. However, I shall answer your questions unless I have a very good reason not to, in which case I beg you'll forgive me. I shall not, of course, lie.'

'Well ... Voldemort said that he only killed my mother because she tried to stop him killing me. But why would he want to kill me in the first place?'

Dumbledore sighed very deeply this time.

'Alas, the first thing you ask me, I cannot tell you. Not today. Not now. You will know, one day ... put it from your mind for now, Harry. When you are older ... I know you hate to hear this ... when you are ready, you will know.'

And Harry knew it would be no good to argue.

'But why couldn't Quirrell touch me?'

'Your mother died to save you. If there is one thing Voldemort cannot understand, it is love. He didn't realise that love as powerful as your mother's for you leaves its own mark. Not a scar, no visible sign ... to have been loved so deeply, even though the person who loved us is gone, will give us some protection for ever. It is in your very skin. Quirrell, full of hatred, greed and ambition, sharing his soul with Voldemort, could not touch you for this reason. It was agony to touch a person marked by something so good.'

Dumbledore now became very interested in a bird out on the window-sill, which gave Harry time to dry his eyes on the sheet. When he had found his voice again, Harry said, 'And the Invisibility Cloak – do you know who sent it to me?'

'Ah – your father happened to leave it in my possession and I thought you might like it.' Dumbledore's eyes twinkled. 'Useful things ... your father used it mainly for sneaking off to the kitchens to steal food when he was here.'

'And there's something else ...'

'Fire away.'

'Quirrell said Snape –'

'*Professor* Snape, Harry.'

'Yes, him – Quirrell said he hates me because he hated my father. Is that true?'

第17章 双面人

解这些事情的真相……"

"真相，"邓布利多叹息着说，"这是一种美丽而可怕的东西，需要格外谨慎地对待。不过，我会尽量回答你的问题，除非我有充分的理由守口如瓶，那样的话，我希望你能原谅我。我当然不能说谎话骗你。"

"是这样……伏地魔说他当年杀死我母亲，是因为我母亲拼命阻止他杀死我。可是，话又说回来，他为什么想要杀死我呢？"

邓布利多这次重重地叹了口气。

"哎呀，你问我的第一件事，我就不能告诉你。今天不能，现在不能。总有一天，你会知道的……暂时先别想这件事，哈利。等你再长大一些……我知道你不愿意听这样的话……等你做好了准备，你自然就知道了。"

哈利明白再多说也没有用。

"那么，为什么奇洛不能碰我？"

"你母亲是为了救你而死的。如果伏地魔有什么事情弄不明白，那就是爱。他没有意识到，像你母亲对你那样深深的爱，是会在你身上留下印记的。不是伤疤，不是看得见的痕迹……被一个人这样深深地爱过，就算那个人已经死了，也会留下一个永远的护身符。它就在你的皮肤里。正因如此，奇洛不能碰你。奇洛内心充满仇恨、贪婪和野心，把灵魂出卖给了伏地魔，他碰了身上标有这么美好印记的人，是会痛苦难忍的。"

说到这里，邓布利多假装对窗外的一只小鸟发生了浓厚的兴趣，哈利便趁这个时间用床单把眼泪擦干了。当声音重又恢复正常时，哈利说道："还有那件隐形衣——您知道是谁送给我的吗？"

"呵——你父亲碰巧把它留给了我，而我认为你大概会喜欢它。"邓布利多的眼睛里闪着狡黠的光芒，"很有用的东西……当年，你父亲在这里上学的时候，主要是靠它溜进厨房偷东西吃。"

"还有另外一件事……"

"尽管问吧。"

"奇洛说斯内普他——"

"是斯内普教授，哈利。"

"是的，是他——奇洛说，斯内普教授恨我是因为他当年恨我父亲。这是真的吗？"

CHAPTER SEVENTEEN   The Man with Two Faces

'Well, they did rather detest each other. Not unlike yourself and Mr Malfoy. And then, your father did something Snape could never forgive.'

'What?'

'He saved his life.'

'*What?*'

'Yes ...' said Dumbledore dreamily. 'Funny, the way people's minds work, isn't it? Professor Snape couldn't bear being in your father's debt ... I do believe he worked so hard to protect you this year because he felt that would make him and your father quits. Then he could go back to hating your father's memory in peace ...'

Harry tried to understand this but it made his head pound, so he stopped.

'And sir, there's one more thing ...'

'Just the one?'

'How did I get the Stone out of the Mirror?'

'Ah, now, I'm glad you asked me that. It was one of my more brilliant ideas, and between you and me, that's saying something. You see, only one who wanted to *find* the Stone – find it, but not use it – would be able to get it, otherwise they'd just see themselves making gold or drinking Elixir of Life. My brain surprises even me sometimes ... Now, enough questions. I suggest you make a start on these sweets. Ah! Bertie Bott's Every-Flavour Beans! I was unfortunate enough in my youth to come across a vomit-flavoured one, and since then I'm afraid I've rather lost my liking for them – but I think I'll be safe with a nice toffee, don't you?'

He smiled and popped the golden-brown bean into his mouth. Then he choked and said, 'Alas! Earwax!'

Madam Pomfrey, the matron, was a nice woman, but very strict.

'Just five minutes,' Harry pleaded.

'Absolutely not.'

'You let Professor Dumbledore in ...'

'Well, of course, that was the Headmaster, quite different. You need *rest*.'

'I am resting, look, lying down and everything. Oh, go on, Madam

第17章 双面人

"是这样，他们确实互相看着不顺眼，很像你和马尔福先生。后来，你父亲做了一件斯内普永远无法原谅他的事。"

"什么事？"

"他救了斯内普的命。"

"什么？"

"是的……"邓布利多幽幽地说，"人的思想确实非常奇妙，是吗？斯内普教授无法忍受这样欠着你父亲的人情……我相信，他这一年之所以想方设法地保护你，是因为他觉得这样就能使他和你父亲扯平，谁也不欠谁的。然后他就可以心安理得地重温对你父亲的仇恨……"

哈利努力思索着这段话，但这使他的头又剧烈地疼痛起来，他只好不往下想了。

"对了，先生，还有最后一个问题……"

"是最后一个吗？"

"我是怎么把魔法石从魔镜里拿出来的？"

"啊，我很高兴你终于问我这件事了。这是我的妙计之一，牵涉到你和我之间的默契，这是很了不起的。你知道吗，只有那个希望找到魔法石——找到它，但不利用它——的人，才能够得到它；其他的人就只能在镜子里看到他们在捞金子发财，或者喝长生不老药延长生命。我的脑瓜真是好使，有时候我自己也感到吃惊……好了，问题问得够多的了。我建议你开始享受这些糖果吧。啊！比比多味豆！我年轻的时候真倒霉，不小心吃到了一颗味道臭烘烘的豆子，恐怕从那以后，我就不怎么喜欢吃豆子了——不过我想，选太妃糖口味的总是万无一失的，你说呢？"

他笑着把那颗金棕色的豆子丢进嘴里。接着他呛得喘不过气来，说："呸，倒霉！是耳屎！"

校医庞弗雷女士是个善良的女人，但是非常严厉。

"只见五分钟。"哈利恳求道。

"绝对不行。"

"你让邓布利多教授进来了……"

"是啊，那当然，他是校长嘛，自然有所不同。你需要休息。"

"我不是正在休息嘛，您看，躺在床上，什么也不做。哦，求求您了，

CHAPTER SEVENTEEN   The Man with Two Faces

Pomfrey ...'

'Oh, very well,' she said. 'But five minutes *only*.'

And she let Ron and Hermione in.

'*Harry!*'

Hermione looked ready to fling her arms around him again, but Harry was glad she held herself in as his head was still very sore.

'Oh, Harry, we were sure you were going to – Dumbledore was so worried –'

'The whole school's talking about it,' said Ron. 'What *really* happened?'

It was one of those rare occasions when the true story is even more strange and exciting than the wild rumours. Harry told them everything: Quirrell; the Mirror; the Stone and Voldemort. Ron and Hermione were a very good audience; they gasped in all the right places and, when Harry told them what was under Quirrell's turban, Hermione screamed out loud.

'So the Stone's gone?' said Ron finally. 'Flamel's just going to *die*?'

'That's what I said, but Dumbledore thinks that – what was it? – "to the well-organised mind, death is but the next great adventure".'

'I always said he was off his rocker,' said Ron, looking quite impressed at how mad his hero was.

'So what happened to you two?' said Harry.

'*Well*, I got back all right,' said Hermione. 'I brought Ron round – that took a while – and we were dashing up to the owlery to contact Dumbledore when we met him in the Entrance Hall. He already knew – he just said, "Harry's gone after him, hasn't he?" and hurtled off to the third floor.'

'D'you think he meant you to do it?' said Ron. 'Sending you your father's Cloak and everything?'

'*Well*,' Hermione exploded, 'if he did – I mean to say – that's terrible – you could have been killed.'

'No, it isn't,' said Harry thoughtfully. 'He's a funny man, Dumbledore. I think he sort of wanted to give me a chance. I think he knows more or less everything that goes on here, you know. I reckon he had a pretty good idea we were going to try, and instead of stopping us, he just taught us enough to help. I don't think it was an accident he let me find out how the Mirror worked. It's almost like he thought I had the right to face Voldemort if I

第17章 双面人

庞弗雷女士……"

"哦，好吧，"她说，"可是只准五分钟。"

于是她让罗恩和赫敏进来了。

"哈利！"

赫敏看样子又要伸开双臂搂抱哈利，但她及时克制住了自己，这使哈利松了口气，因为他的头仍然很疼。

"哦，哈利，我们都以为你肯定要——邓布利多担心极了——"

"整个学校都在谈论这件事，"罗恩说，"当时到底是怎么个情况？"

真实的故事比没有根据的谣传更加离奇和惊心动魄，这种情况是非常罕见的，而现在就是这样。哈利把一切原原本本地讲给他们听：奇洛、魔镜、魔法石和伏地魔。罗恩和赫敏听得非常专心，每到惊险的地方，他们就紧张得倒抽冷气，当哈利讲到奇洛的缠头巾下面的那副面孔时，赫敏失声尖叫起来。

"这么说，魔法石没有了？"最后罗恩问道，"勒梅快要死了？"

"我也是这么说的，可是邓布利多认为——他说什么来着？'在头脑十分清醒的人看来，死亡不过是另一场伟大的冒险'。"

"我早就说过他有点神经兮兮的。"罗恩说。他心目中的英雄变得这样不可理喻，他感到非常震惊。

"后来你们俩的情况怎么样？"哈利问。

"噢，我很顺利地返回去了。"赫敏说，"我把罗恩唤醒——很是花了一些时间呢——然后我们飞快地冲向猫头鹰棚屋，想同邓布利多取得联系，不料却在门厅里碰上了他。他已经知道了——他只说了一句：'哈利去追他了，是吗？'然后就赶紧朝四楼奔去。"

"你说，邓布利多是不是有意要你这么做的？"罗恩说，"把你父亲的隐形衣送给你，还有一切的一切？"

"哎呀，"赫敏忍不住说道，"如果他真是这样——我的意思是——那就太可怕了——你很可能被杀死的。"

"不，不是这样，"哈利若有所思地说，"邓布利多是个很有意思的人。我认为他大概是想给我一个机会。他似乎对这里发生的事情多多少少都知道一些。我觉得他十分清楚我们打算做什么，他没有阻止我们，反而暗暗地教给我们许多有用的东西。我认为，他让我懂得魔镜的功能绝不

CHAPTER SEVENTEEN The Man with Two Faces

could …'

'Yeah, Dumbledore's barking, all right,' said Ron proudly. 'Listen, you've got to be up for the end-of-year feast tomorrow. The points are all in and Slytherin won, of course – you missed the last Quidditch match, we were steamrollered by Ravenclaw without you – but the food'll be good.'

At that moment, Madam Pomfrey bustled over.

'You've had nearly fifteen minutes, now OUT,' she said firmly.

After a good night's sleep, Harry felt nearly back to normal.

'I want to go to the feast,' he told Madam Pomfrey as she straightened his many sweet-boxes. 'I can, can't I?'

'Professor Dumbledore says you are to be allowed to go,' she said sniffily, as though in her opinion Professor Dumbledore didn't realise how risky feasts could be. 'And you have another visitor.'

'Oh good,' said Harry. 'Who is it?'

Hagrid sidled through the door as he spoke. As usual when he was indoors, Hagrid looked too big to be allowed. He sat down next to Harry, took one look at him and burst into tears.

'It's – all – my – ruddy – fault!' he sobbed, his face in his hands. 'I told the evil git how ter get past Fluffy! I told him! It was the only thing he didn't know an' I told him! Yeh could've died! All fer a dragon egg! I'll never drink again! I should be chucked out an' made ter live as a Muggle!'

'Hagrid!' said Harry, shocked to see Hagrid shaking with grief and remorse, great tears leaking down into his beard. 'Hagrid, he'd have found out somehow, this is Voldemort we're talking about, he'd have found out even if you hadn't told him.'

'Yeh could've died!' sobbed Hagrid. 'An' don' say the name!'

'VOLDEMORT!' Harry bellowed, and Hagrid was so shocked, he stopped crying. 'I've met him and I'm calling him by his name. Please cheer up, Hagrid, we saved the Stone, it's gone, he can't use it. Have a Chocolate Frog, I've got loads …'

Hagrid wiped his nose on the back of his hand and said, 'That reminds me. I've got yeh a present.'

第 17 章 双面人

是偶然的。他好像认为如果可能的话，我有权面对伏地魔……"

"是啊，这就是邓布利多不同凡响的地方。"罗恩骄傲地说，"听着，你明天一定要来参加年终宴会。分数都算出来了，当然了，斯莱特林得了第一名——你错过了最后一场魁地奇比赛，没有你，我们被拉文克劳队打得落花流水——不过宴会上的东西还是挺好吃的。"

就在这时，庞弗雷女士闯了进来。

"你们已经待了将近十五分钟了，快给我**出去**吧。"她坚决地说。

哈利踏踏实实地一觉睡到天亮，觉得元气差不多恢复了。

"我想去参加宴会，"当庞弗雷女士整理他的一大堆糖果盒时，哈利对她说，"可不可以啊？"

"邓布利多教授说允许你去。"她不以为然地说。似乎在她看来，邓布利多教授并没有认识到宴会具有潜在的危险。"又有人来看你了。"

"噢，太好了，"哈利说，"是谁？"

他话音未落，海格就侧着身子钻进门来。海格每次走进房门，都显得像个庞然大物。他在哈利身旁坐下，看了他一眼，就伤心地哭了起来。

"都——怪我——这个——笨蛋！"他用手捂着脸哭泣，"是我告诉那个恶棍怎样通过路威的！是我告诉他的！他什么都知道了，就是不知道这个，而我偏偏告诉了他！你差点就没命了！都是为了一只火龙蛋！我再也不喝酒了！我应该被赶出去，一辈子做个麻瓜！"

"海格！"哈利说。他十分震惊地看到海格因悲哀和悔恨而颤抖，大颗的眼泪渗进他的胡须。"海格，他总有办法打听到的，我们说的可是伏地魔啊，即使你不告诉他，他也总有办法知道的。"

"你差点就没命了！"海格抽抽噎噎地说，"哦，你别说那个名字！"

"我就要说，**伏地魔**！"哈利大声吼道。他看见海格吓得惊慌失措，才停止了喊叫。"我曾经面对面地和他相遇，我当面叫了他的名字。海格，求求你，快活一些吧，我们保住了魔法石，它现在不在了，伏地魔再也不能用它作恶了。吃一个巧克力蛙吧，我有一大堆呢……"

海格用手背擦了擦鼻子，说道："这倒提醒了我。我也给你带来了一件礼物呢。"

CHAPTER SEVENTEEN The Man with Two Faces

'It's not a stoat sandwich, is it?' said Harry anxiously and at last Hagrid gave a weak chuckle.

'Nah. Dumbledore gave me the day off yesterday ter fix it. 'Course, he shoulda sacked me instead – anyway, got yeh this ...'

It seemed to be a handsome, leather-covered book. Harry opened it curiously. It was full of wizard photographs. Smiling and waving at him from every page were his mother and father.

'Sent owls off ter all yer parents' old school friends, askin' fer photos ... Knew yeh didn' have any ... D'yeh like it?'

Harry couldn't speak, but Hagrid understood.

Harry made his way down to the end-of-year feast alone that night. He had been held up by Madam Pomfrey's fussing about, insisting on giving him one last check-up, so the Great Hall was already full. It was decked out in the Slytherin colours of green and silver to celebrate Slytherin's winning the House Cup for the seventh year in a row. A huge banner showing the Slytherin serpent covered the wall behind the High Table.

When Harry walked in there was a sudden hush and then everybody started talking loudly at once. He slipped into a seat between Ron and Hermione at the Gryffindor table and tried to ignore the fact that people were standing up to look at him.

Fortunately, Dumbledore arrived moments later. The babble died away.

'Another year gone!' Dumbledore said cheerfully. 'And I must trouble you with an old man's wheezing waffle before we sink our teeth into our delicious feast. What a year it has been! Hopefully your heads are all a little fuller than they were ... you have the whole summer ahead to get them nice and empty before next year starts ...

'Now, as I understand it, the House Cup here needs awarding and the points stand thus: in fourth place, Gryffindor, with three hundred and twelve points; in third, Hufflepuff, with three hundred and fifty-two; Ravenclaw have four hundred and twenty-six and Slytherin, four hundred and seventy-two.'

A storm of cheering and stamping broke out from the Slytherin table. Harry could see Draco Malfoy banging his goblet on the table. It was a

第17章 双面人

"不会是白鼬三明治吧?"哈利担心地问,海格终于勉强地笑出了声。

"不是。邓布利多昨天放了我一天假,让我把它整理出来。当然啦,他完全应该把我开除的——行了,这个给你……"

看上去像是一本精美的皮封面的书。哈利好奇地打开,里面贴满了巫师的照片。在每一页上朝他微笑、挥手的,都是他的父亲和母亲。

"我派猫头鹰给你父母的老同学送信,向他们要照片……知道你没有他们的照片……你喜欢吗?"

哈利说不出话来,但海格全明白了。

那天晚上,哈利独自下楼去参加年终宴会。刚才庞弗雷女士大惊小怪地拦住他,坚持要给他再检查一遍身体,所以,当他赶到礼堂时,里面已经坐满了人。礼堂里用代表斯莱特林的绿色和银色装饰一新,庆祝他们连续七年赢得学院杯冠军。主宾席后面的墙上,挂着一条绘着斯莱特林蛇的巨大横幅。

哈利一走进去,礼堂里顿时变得鸦雀无声,然后每个人突然又开始高声说话。他走到格兰芬多的桌子旁,坐在罗恩和赫敏中间,假装没有注意到人们都站起来盯着他看。

幸好,片刻之后,邓布利多也赶到了,礼堂里的嘈杂声渐渐平息下来。

"又是一年过去了!"邓布利多兴高采烈地说,"在尽情享受这些美味佳肴之前,我必须麻烦大家听听一个老头子的陈词滥调。这是多么精彩的一年啊!你们的小脑瓜里肯定都比过去丰富了一些……前面有整个暑假在等着你们,可以让你们在下学期开始之前,好好把那些东西消化消化,让脑子里腾出空来……

"现在,据我所知,我们首先必须进行学院杯的颁奖仪式,各学院的具体得分如下:第四名,格兰芬多,312分;第三名,赫奇帕奇,352分;拉文克劳426分,斯莱特林472分。"

斯莱特林的餐桌那儿爆发出一阵雷鸣般的欢呼声和跺脚声。哈利看见德拉科·马尔福用高脚酒杯使劲敲打着桌子,那副样子真让人恶心。

CHAPTER SEVENTEEN The Man with Two Faces

sickening sight.

'Yes, yes, well done, Slytherin,' said Dumbledore. 'However, recent events must be taken into account.'

The room went very still. The Slytherins' smiles faded a little.

'Ahem,' said Dumbledore. 'I have a few last-minute points to dish out. Let me see. Yes …

'First – to Mr Ronald Weasley …'

Ron went purple in the face; he looked like a radish with bad sunburn.

'… for the best-played game of chess Hogwarts has seen in many years, I award Gryffindor house fifty points.'

Gryffindor cheers nearly raised the bewitched ceiling; the stars overhead seemed to quiver. Percy could be heard telling the other Prefects, 'My brother, you know! My youngest brother! Got past McGonagall's giant chess set!'

At last there was silence again.

'Second – to Miss Hermione Granger … for the use of cool logic in the face of fire, I award Gryffindor house fifty points.'

Hermione buried her face in her arms; Harry strongly suspected she had burst into tears. Gryffindors up and down the table were beside themselves – they were a hundred points up.

'Third – to Mr Harry Potter …' said Dumbledore. The room went deadly quiet. '… for pure nerve and outstanding courage, I award Gryffindor house sixty points.'

The din was deafening. Those who could add up while yelling themselves hoarse knew that Gryffindor now had four hundred and seventy-two points – exactly the same as Slytherin. They had drawn for the House Cup – if only Dumbledore had given Harry just one more point.

Dumbledore raised his hand. The room gradually fell silent.

'There are all kinds of courage,' said Dumbledore, smiling. 'It takes a great deal of bravery to stand up to our enemies, but just as much to stand up to our friends. I therefore award ten points to Mr Neville Longbottom.'

Someone standing outside the Great Hall might well have thought some sort of explosion had taken place, so loud was the noise that erupted from

第 17 章　双面人

"是啊，是啊，表现不错，斯莱特林。"邓布利多说，"不过，最近发生的几件事也必须计算在内。"

礼堂里变得非常安静，斯莱特林们的笑容也收敛了一些。

"呃，呃，"邓布利多清了清嗓子，"我还有最后一些分数要分配。让我看看。对了……

"第一——罗恩·韦斯莱先生……"

罗恩的脸一下子涨得通红，活像一个被太阳晒干的红萝卜。

"……他下赢了霍格沃茨许多年来最精彩的一盘棋，我为此奖励格兰芬多学院五十分。"

格兰芬多们的欢呼声差点把施了魔法的天花板掀翻。他们头顶上的星星似乎也被震得微微颤抖。可以听见珀西在大声告诉其他级长："是我弟弟，你们知道的！我最小的弟弟！顺利通过了麦格教授的巨型棋盘阵！"

大家好不容易才平静下来。

"第二——赫敏·格兰杰小姐……她面对烈火，冷静地进行逻辑推理，我要奖励格兰芬多学院五十分。"

赫敏把脸埋在臂弯里；哈利怀疑她肯定是偷偷地哭了。长桌周围格兰芬多的同学们个个欣喜若狂——他们整整上升了一百分！

"第三——哈利·波特先生……"邓布利多说。礼堂里顿时变得格外寂静。"……他表现出了大无畏的胆量和过人的勇气，为此，我还要奖励格兰芬多学院六十分。"

喧闹声简直震耳欲聋。那些一边把嗓子喊得嘶哑，一边还能在心里计算分数的同学们知道，格兰芬多现在是四百七十二分——和斯莱特林的分数完全一样。他们已经打成了平手——如果邓布利多能多奖给哈利一分就好了。

邓布利多举起一只手。礼堂里渐渐又安静下来。

"勇气有许多种类，"邓布利多微笑着，"对付敌人我们需要超人的胆量，而要在朋友面前坚持自己的立场，同样也需要很大的勇气。因此，最后我要奖励纳威·隆巴顿先生十分。"

如果有人此刻站在礼堂外面，可能会以为这里发生了爆炸，格兰芬多餐桌上的欢呼声一浪高过一浪。哈利、罗恩和赫敏站起来高声喝彩，

CHAPTER SEVENTEEN The Man with Two Faces

the Gryffindor table. Harry, Ron and Hermione stood up to yell and cheer as Neville, white with shock, disappeared under a pile of people hugging him. He had never won so much as a point for Gryffindor before. Harry, still cheering, nudged Ron in the ribs and pointed at Malfoy, who couldn't have looked more stunned and horrified if he'd just had the Body-Bind curse put on him.

'Which means,' Dumbledore called over the storm of applause, for even Ravenclaw and Hufflepuff were celebrating the downfall of Slytherin, 'we needa little change of decoration.'

He clapped his hands. In an instant, the green hangings became scarlet and the silver became gold; the huge Slytherin serpent vanished and a towering Gryffindor lion took its place. Snape was shaking Professor McGonagall's hand, with a horrible forced smile. He caught Harry's eye and Harry knew at once that Snape's feelings towards him hadn't changed one jot. This didn't worry Harry. It seemed as though life would be back to normal next year, or as normal as it ever was at Hogwarts.

It was the best evening of Harry's life, better than winning at Quidditch or Christmas or knocking out mountain trolls ... he would never, ever forget tonight.

Harry had almost forgotten that the exam results were still to come, but come they did. To their great surprise, both he and Ron passed with good marks; Hermione, of course, came top of the year. Even Neville scraped through, his good Herbology mark making up for his abysmal Potions one. They had hoped that Goyle, who was almost as stupid as he was mean, might be thrown out, but he had passed, too. It was a shame, but as Ron said, you couldn't have everything in life.

And suddenly, their wardrobes were empty, their trunks were packed, Neville's toad was found lurking in a corner of the toilets; notes were handed out to all students, warning them not to use magic over the holidays ('I always hope they'll forget to give us these,' said Fred Weasley sadly); Hagrid was there to take them down to the fleet of boats that sailed across the lake; they were boarding the Hogwarts Express; talking and laughing as the countryside became greener and tidier; eating Bertie Bott's Every-Flavour Beans as they

第17章 双面人

只见纳威惊讶得脸色煞白,一下子就被挤上来拥抱他的人群淹没了。他从来没有给格兰芬多赢过一分啊!哈利一边欢呼,一边用胳膊肘捅了捅罗恩,然后指指马尔福。看马尔福的样子,即使他刚刚被人施了全身束缚咒,也不会显得比现在更吃惊、更恐慌。

"这就意味着,"邓布利多不得不大声吼叫,才能盖过雷鸣般的欢呼喝彩,因为就连拉文克劳和赫奇帕奇的学生们也在庆祝斯莱特林的突然惨败,"我们需要对这里的装饰做一些小小的改变。"

他拍了拍手,立刻,那些绿色的悬垂彩带变成了深红色,银色的变成了金色;巨大的斯莱特林蛇隐去了,取而代之的是一头威风凛凛的格兰芬多狮子。斯内普正在同麦格教授握手,脸上强挤出尴尬的笑容。他的目光和哈利相遇了,哈利顿时就明白了,斯内普对他的态度丝毫没有改变。哈利觉得这没有什么可担心的。似乎明年的生活又将恢复正常,至少恢复到霍格沃茨一贯的状态。

这是哈利一生中最美好的夜晚,比赢了魁地奇比赛、欢庆圣诞或打败巨怪的日子还要美好……他永远、永远也不会忘记这个夜晚。

哈利几乎忘了考试成绩还没有公布。那一天终于到来了,没想到,他和罗恩都以很高的分数通过了考试,这使他们感到十分意外。赫敏自然是获得了全年级第一名。就连纳威也侥幸过关了,他的草药学成绩不错,大大弥补了在魔药学上丢失的分数。他们本来以为,高尔笨得像头猪,为人又自私刻薄,这次大概会被开除,不料他竟然也通过了。这似乎有点美中不足,但是正如罗恩所说,生活是不可能样样顺心的。

好像是在突然之间,他们的衣柜空了,东西都装到了行李箱里,纳威的蟾蜍躲在盥洗室的角落里被人发现了。通知发到了每个学生手里,警告他们放假期间不许使用魔法("我一直希望他们忘记把这个发给我们。"弗雷德·韦斯莱遗憾地说)。海格负责带领他们登上渡过湖面的船队。现在,他们已经坐上了霍格沃茨特快列车,一路谈笑风生,看着窗外的乡村越来越青翠,越来越整洁。列车驶过一个个麻瓜的城镇,他们吃着比比多味豆,脱掉了身上的巫师长袍,换上夹克衫和大衣;终于,列车

CHAPTER SEVENTEEN The Man with Two Faces

sped past Muggle towns; pulling off their wizard robes and putting on jackets and coats; pulling into platform nine and three-quarters at King's Cross station.

It took quite a while for them all to get off the platform. A wizened old guard was up by the ticket barrier, letting them go through the gate in twos and threes so they didn't attract attention by all bursting out of a solid wall at once and alarming the Muggles.

'You must come and stay this summer,' said Ron, 'both of you – I'll send you an owl.'

'Thanks,' said Harry. 'I'll need something to look forward to.'

People jostled them as they moved forwards towards the gateway back to the Muggle world. Some of them called:

'Bye, Harry!'

'See you, Potter!'

'Still famous,' said Ron, grinning at him.

'Not where I'm going, I promise you,' said Harry.

He, Ron and Hermione passed through the gateway together.

'There he is, Mum, there he is, look!'

It was Ginny Weasley, Ron's younger sister, but she wasn't pointing at Ron.

'Harry Potter!' she squealed. 'Look, Mum! I can see –'

'Be quiet, Ginny, and it's rude to point.'

Mrs Weasley smiled down at them.

'Busy year?' she said.

'Very,' said Harry. 'Thanks for the fudge and the jumper, Mrs Weasley.'

'Oh, it was nothing, dear.'

'Ready, are you?'

It was Uncle Vernon, still purple-faced, still moustached, still looking furious at the nerve of Harry, carrying an owl in a cage in a station full of ordinary people. Behind him stood Aunt Petunia and Dudley, looking terrified at the very sight of Harry.

'You must be Harry's family!' said Mrs Weasley.

'In a manner of speaking,' said Uncle Vernon. 'Hurry up, boy, we haven't got all day.' He walked away.

第17章 双面人

停靠在了国王十字车站的 $9\frac{3}{4}$ 站台。

他们花了很长时间，才全部走出站台。一个干瘪的老警卫守在隔墙处，一次只允许两三个人通过，这样他们就不会一大堆人同时从坚固的墙壁里进出来，引起麻瓜们的注意。

"你今年暑假一定要来我们家里玩，"罗恩说，"你们俩都来——我会派猫头鹰去邀请你们的。"

"谢谢，"哈利说，"我确实需要有个盼头。"

他们走向返回麻瓜世界的出口，不断有人从他们身边挤过，其中有些人喊道：

"拜拜，哈利！"

"再见，波特！"

"还是这样出名。"罗恩说着，咧嘴朝他一笑。

"在我要去的地方就不是了，我向你保证。"哈利说。

他、罗恩和赫敏一起通过了出口。

"他在那儿，妈妈，他在那儿，快看哪！"

是金妮——罗恩的妹妹——但她指的并不是罗恩。

"哈利·波特！"她尖声尖气地叫道，"快看哪，妈妈！我看见了——"

"别大声嚷嚷，金妮，对别人指指点点是不礼貌的。"

韦斯莱夫人笑眯眯地低头看着他们。

"这一年很忙吧？"她问。

"忙极了。"哈利说，"谢谢您送给我的乳脂软糖和毛衣，韦斯莱夫人。"

"哦，那没什么，亲爱的。"

"我说，你准备好了吧？"

是弗农姨父，他还是那样一张红得发紫的脸膛，还是那样一大把胡子，还是用愤怒的目光瞪着哈利。在这个挤满普通人的车站上，哈利竟然明目张胆地提着一只装着猫头鹰的笼子，真是可恨。他身后站着佩妮姨妈和达力表哥，他们一看见哈利，就显出一副惊惶不安的表情。

"你们一定是哈利的家人吧！"韦斯莱夫人说。

"也可以这么说吧。"弗农姨父说，"快点，小子，我们可耽搁不起一整天。"他转身走开了。

CHAPTER SEVENTEEN   The Man with Two Faces

Harry hung back for a last word with Ron and Hermione.

'See you over the summer, then.'

'Hope you have – er – a good holiday,' said Hermione, looking uncertainly after Uncle Vernon, shocked that anyone could be so unpleasant.

'Oh, I will,' said Harry, and they were surprised at the grin that was spreading over his face. '*They* don't know we're not allowed to use magic at home. I'm going to have a lot of fun with Dudley this summer ...'

第 17 章 双面人

哈利还要留下来再跟罗恩和赫敏说几句话。

"那就过完暑假再见吧。"

"祝你假期——嗯——愉快。"赫敏说，她不敢相信地望着弗农姨父的背影，很吃惊世界上居然有这样令人讨厌的人。

"哦，我会愉快的。"哈利说。他脸上绽开了一个灿烂的笑容，使罗恩和赫敏都感到诧异。"他们不知道我们在家里不许使用魔法，这个暑假，我要好好地拿达力开开心……"

WIZARDING WORLD